The Age of Aquarius

By

Bobby Legend

LEGEND PUBLISHING COMPANY
Legend Publishing Company
P.O. Box 429
Garden City, MI 48136
legendpublishingcompany.com

The events, people, and places herein are depicted to the best recollection of the author, who assumes complete and sole responsibility for the accuracy of this narrative.

The opinions expressed herein are those of the author, who assumes complete and sole responsibility for them, and do not necessarily represent the views of the publisher or its agents.

This novel is based on a true story.

ISBN: 9780982168721

Printed in the United States of America
For information or to order additional books, please write:

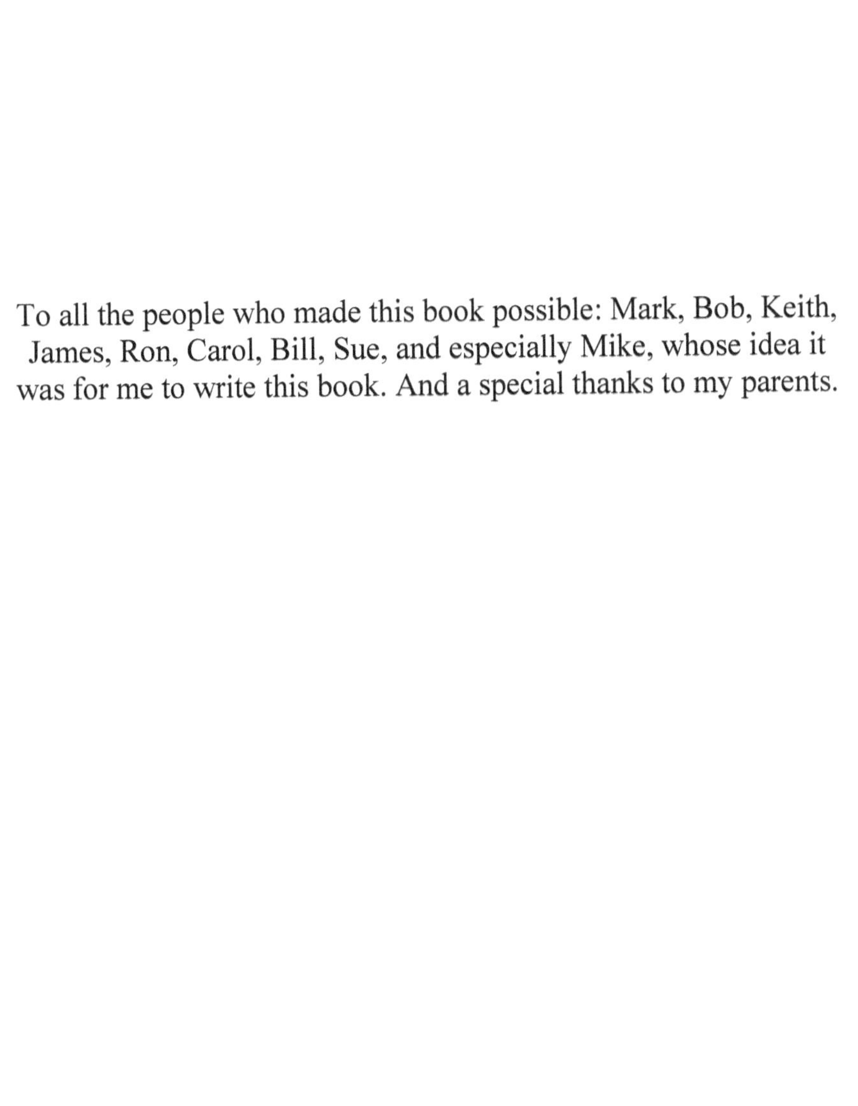

To all the people who made this book possible: Mark, Bob, Keith, James, Ron, Carol, Bill, Sue, and especially Mike, whose idea it was for me to write this book. And a special thanks to my parents.

INTRODUCTION

This is a true story about a bright young man on a magical adventure traveling from America to Asia. His knowledge is expanded while traveling and studying in Spain with World Academy of Foreign Exchange Students. That adventure turned an honor student's life upside down and changed it for good. This young man goes through many trials and tribulations during his adventurous travels. He had grown disillusioned about America's war in Vietnam and vowed to leave America and never return. So he traveled to the magical land of Afghanistan and began a new life in an old part of the world. That magical adventure turned into a hellish nightmare.

CHAPTER 1

TRIP TO SPAIN:
HE LEAVES A BOY, RETURNS A MAN

My name is Robert "Bobby Legend" Willingham, and this is my true story. It begins when I was a young, naive sixteen-year-old teenager who grew into manhood during a summer vacation in 1967—a vacation that would take me on a long journey halfway around the world and into the dark shadows of the underworld.

Just a few weeks before the school year ended, my beautiful Spanish teacher, Miss Gibleyou, gave me the surprise of my life.

"Roberto," said Miss Gibleyou, gleefully, "you have been selected by the World Academy of Foreign Exchange Students to represent Michigan to study Spanish at the universities of Madrid and Granada. Because you have excelled in this language, you and another student, Arlene Schwablen, have been chosen for this prestigious scholarship. *Muy Bueno.* And I have been chosen to be a chaperone for our group."

All right, I thought to myself. *I'm in love with Miss Gibleyou anyway, and I'll be close to her all summer.* Then I thought about all the good times we'd have and couldn't wait. She was my eleventh grade Spanish teacher and I had a super crush on her. She had just graduated from college and always wore tight and low-cut dresses to class. I sat right in front of her desk and was madly in love with her.

But my bubble was soon to burst. A few weeks later, she explained to the class that she couldn't go to Spain. She was getting married and declined to be the chaperone for the trip. Boy was I bummed when I heard that news. That ruined all of my plans and dreams. I was heartbroken and refused to go to Spain. But my parents had spent all their money on new clothes for my trip, so I decided to go after all.

I met part of the group at Metro Airport in Detroit. The rest would meet us in New York at Kennedy Airport. That's where I fell in love again, this time with someone my own age. Her name was Marilyn—an angel at first glance. She had light blonde, long, flowing hair covering her shoulders and very petite, cute, and beautiful long legs. It was love at first sight for both of us.

But soon all hell had broken loose. Here we were, a group of nearly thirty people, in the middle of Kennedy Airport and no one knew what to do. Instead of Miss Gibleyou as our chaperone, she had been replaced with a funny-looking man by the name of Webber. He was a counselor at a rival high school in our city.

There were also a few Spanish students from that school who had been selected to travel with us to Spain as exchange students. One girl in particular, Debby, was one of the most beautiful girls in the world. Her father owned a cement factory and a large construction company and was one of the richest men in our city.

Our group had just found out that we didn't have plane reservations for our trip to Spain. Now all the students were thinking that this was just a big rip-off. So our chaperone, Mr. Webber, began making frantic long-distance phone calls to the parent company of World Academy.

"Bob," said Mr. Webber, "give me all your change. I'll pay you back later." So I handed him a sock full of change.

"Mr. Webber, there's fifty-two dollars in change in that sock. I saved it from my lawn service," I told him.

"Thank you, Bob," he replied, as he rushed to the phone.

I should have had him sign an IOU for that money, because he never repaid me. However, he did locate a plane for the group. But there was just one problem—it wouldn't depart for another nine hours. So our group had a lot of time to kill. What does one naive chaperone do with a dozen or more kids with raging hormones?

"What are we going to do now?" asked Debby, to no one in particular.

"Do you kids have any suggestions?" asked Mr. Webber. "What would you like to do for the next nine hours?"

Arlene suddenly came up with an idea. She would call her father. He was presently divorced from her mother but was on call twenty-four hours a day as the doctor for Kennedy Airport. This would also be a treat for Arlene. She hadn't seen her father in over a year.

Mr. Webber agreed to the idea, so we waited for Arlene's father to meet with us. And within twenty minutes, we were being introduced to the man who reminded me of and looked very similar to the famous football coach Vince Lombardi.

After everyone had been introduced, Arlene's father took nine of us in his Cadillac to a high-class restaurant for an exquisite dinner of steak and lobster, and he paid for it all. The others in our small group had stayed behind to wait for the ones who hadn't yet arrived but had also been selected by World Academy and were coming in from all parts of the United States.

Mr. Schwablen was an excellent host and showed us a nice evening. We definitely enjoyed ourselves. Finally, near one in the morning, he returned us to our group. We said goodbye and thanked him for such a nice time.

Now there were twenty-two of us total. The youngest was sixteen and the oldest was our chaperone and leader, Mrs. Urfer. The oldest exchange student was nineteen and the son of a Chicago dentist. By this time, Marilyn and I had become very good friends. In fact, we had become boyfriend and girlfriend. It happened just that fast.

An hour after Mr. Schwablen had dropped us off we boarded our flight. But it wasn't to Spain. It was to Glasgow, Scotland. We didn't know what was happening, but to the kids in our group this diversion was an unexpected treat.

Arriving at Glasgow Airport, our next step was to find transportation to our next destination, London. While the chaperones were deciding what to do next, a few of us kids had decided to meet the Scottish people. So we sought out a taxi driver and asked him what it cost to rent his cab. But the man kept repeating the same phrase over and over, which we didn't understand.

"On cen a meel," said the taxi driver.

"What did you say?" asked Marilyn.

"On cen a meel," repeated the taxi driver.

None of us could understand this man. Marilyn thought he had asked for food, so she reached into her bag and handed the man a nice juicy apple. The taxi driver didn't say a word but just smiled. Then he looked at us inquisitively and bit into the apple. Again he said something, but we still couldn't understand him. We thought he must have been speaking in his native Gaelic tongue. Finally, Jimmy B, the Harvard student, figured it out.

"Hey, guys, I think he's saying, 'one cent a mile'," surmised Jimmy, as the taxi driver nodded in agreement.

However, by the time we figured out what the taxi driver had said, it was time to board the train for London, England, and Gatwick Airport, where we were to catch a plane to Spain.

None of us had ever been out of the U.S., and this was becoming quite an adventure. And trying to understand the different dialects and accents of the different countries was, at times, confusing to say the least. Especially standing behind some beautiful girls in the "queue" and listening to the way they talked with their heavy accents, was indeed very different, exciting to my ears, and I enjoyed it immensely.

We finally boarded the train near midnight. Many in the group were very weary. Marilyn and I tried to get a compartment to ourselves, but we soon learned that they were for everyone and had to share it with others from our group. Most of us slept in our cramped quarters as best we could.

After a long and uneventful train ride through Scotland and England, we had finally arrived at Victoria Station in London. Our group had over ten hours to wait before our plane departed for Spain, so our chaperones decided we would visit some of London's tourist attractions. We also had reservations for lunch at one of London's finer restaurants. Instead of riding a taxi or bus to our intended destination, our chaperones decided we needed exercise. So we walked.

The first landmark we saw was the famous London Bridge. Our group walked across it and all over it and it never fell down. Then we walked past the famous clock, Big Ben, as it boomed in the afternoon bustle and hustle of the city; and when we stopped outside of Buckingham Palace, a few of us tried in vain to make the palace guards smile and laugh. But we only seemed to make them angry. In fact, one of the palace guards scared the heck out of me when he suddenly jumped out and lunged toward me. Even Mr. Webber was flabbergasted.

"Bob, what have you done? The guards aren't supposed to move while on duty," remarked Mr. Webber.

As we began walking away from that situation, we noticed that the guard's superior came out and scolded the man for moving from his post. Mr. Webber gave me a dirty look, but I just remained silent as we walked toward our destination, an upper-class restaurant, to taste the cuisine of England. That was a big day I will never forget. After an hour of walking, we finally made it to the restaurant. As we entered this exquisite dining facility, the maitre d' seated us at a large table. While sitting around a table for twenty-two people, we became bored waiting for the waiters to serve us the first course. Our entire group noticed that the waiters were soused to the gills—very, very drunk. Someone had told them that we were rich, spoiled brats from America who didn't behave.

Our lunch began with soup—a cold, tasteless bowl of tomato soup. When most of us started to complain about the cold soup, the waiters swooped up each bowl with sarcastic remarks, telling us to go back to America.

Jim, the six-foot-four rich hippie kid from Washington, D.C., flicked at his left earring and began berating the waiters.

"Bob, don't you know that we are in England to see how the English snobs live," boasted Jim, as the waiters became more and more irritated. "We don't call you guys 'British Bulldogs' for nothing," he added, looking directly into the drunken eyes of a belligerent waiter.

The waiter Jim had been harassing and staring at suddenly came over to confront him. As he waited for an apology, Jim jumped up and knocked the serving tray out of his hand and to the floor. Everything on the tray went flying through the air and all over the room. Tomato soup went flying everywhere, soup on Jim, soup on the waiters, and tomato soup all over everyone in the room. It seemed like the American Revolution had begun all over again. It was the British servants against the outspoken Americans.

Throughout this commotion, Mr. Webber and Mrs. Urfer yelled and screamed at our group, but it did no good.

"Let's get the hell out of here!" yelled Mrs. Urfer, as cups and saucers were flying to and fro across the room.

Hippie Jim and one of the waiters were tightly locked in a holding pattern, the young beating the old, the sober defeating the drunk. The Americans had beaten the English once again. Mr. Webber tried breaking Jim and the waiter apart, but as he did, he was hit square in the nose.

"Let's get out of here!" shouted Mr. Webber, as blood streamed out of his nose.

One by one, we ran out the door and into the bright lights of the city; we hadn't even finished one course of our meal.

"Poor Mr. Webber. He doesn't know what he's gotten himself into," I said to Marilyn, as our group stood waiting for instructions from our fearless leaders.

While standing outside of the restaurant, Mr. Webber flagged down a bus to take us to Gatwick Airport instead of the train. He wanted to get out of London as fast as possible and didn't want anything else to happen. Our group quickly boarded the bus and headed for our destination.

Our plane would depart for Madrid, Spain, in just over two hours. By the time we had arrived at the airport, we had less than an hour to wait. Needless to say, the chaperones kept the group out of mischief while we waited for our departure.

Arriving on time at Madrid Airport, we were met by Mr. Sanchez, one of our college Spanish professors, a short, stout man who walked with a limp because his right leg was five inches shorter than his left. We had learned that Franco's Army had captured him during the Spanish Civil War and tortured him by pulling out his fingernails and toenails, one by one. Without any medical attention to mend his wounds, gangrene had set in and his foot had to be amputated. Mr. Sanchez mentioned that he held no bitterness, animosity, or malice toward Franco's regime and that life for him had proceeded to get better and better.

When he talked, he had so much enthusiasm that his face would turn a beet red. This little jovial man reminded me of Santa Claus without the beard. He was a delirious, funny man.

Our group couldn't get a dorm on the campus of Madrid University, so we had to stay in a new apartment building just a few miles off campus, which was similar to a small hotel. Hippie Jim and I shared a beautiful room on the third floor overlooking the soccer field. Our group used the convention room as our classroom.

Mr. Sanchez and Mrs. Temple were our foreign language professors.

Mrs. Temple was an exotic-looking woman with long, dark, straight, shoulder-length hair Her beautiful, brown sultry eyes gave you goose bumps every time she looked at you, while her petite, long-legged body slithered and swayed to a beat, all its own. She walked like an angel and talked the way she walked. She had a charming English accent and a sweet and soft, sultry, low voice. She was one of the most beautiful women I had ever seen.

Mr. Sanchez asked each of us in the group our names and the usual obvious questions, such as, how old were we? What state were we born in? What type of job did we want? And many other informal questions.

This was a very informal classroom. People walked in and out anytime they wanted. And servants served tea and cookies while we were in the classroom learning our lessons.

During the second day of class, one of the servant's dogs came into the classroom and, as usual, nobody noticed. It was a cute black and white spotted dog with an outline of a circle around one eye, just like the dog in *The Little Rascals.*

While Hippie Jim was answering the professor's question, the little dog walked up to him, sniffed, cocked his rear leg, and started pissing on his pant leg. When Jim noticed what was happening, he yelled at the dog and pushed it away with his foot, while the class erupted in laughter. To no one's surprise, because of that incident, the class ended.

After morning classes had ended, it was time for relaxation. Behind our dorm was a beautiful soccer field. During this time off, others from our group and I would play our Spanish friends in a nice friendly game of soccer. But after fifteen minutes of running up and down the field, I had to quit.

Being a diver on our high school swimming team, I thought I was in good physical shape. However, after playing just a few minutes of soccer, I knew I wasn't in the shape I had thought. I played football, baseball, basketball, and a few other sports, but soccer wasn't one of them. Hippie Jim, on the other hand, was an excellent soccer player.

I never figured that in 1967, a tall, longhaired male with an earring in his ear would be good at anything other than making trouble, but Jim was a natural at soccer. By the time the game had ended, Jim had scored three goals, including the game winner. I was tired out just watching him play.

After the game, Jim and I returned to our room and took a siesta. Then after sleeping for an hour or so, we got dressed and took the bus into the city of Madrid.

The city was very big and beautiful. During the day, especially the afternoon, the city of Madrid was dead. Everyone was taking a siesta. However, come seven o'clock at night, everything and everyone came alive. All the bright, neon lights advertising the city's thriving businesses and the people hustling and bustling reminded me of New York City or Las Vegas, Nevada.

Jim and I walked down the main drag of Madrid, a well-lit, 4-lane, extra-wide street. As we were talking and walking, many young streetwalkers accosted us. This was the first time anything like this had happened to me and having just turned seventeen, this really was an adventure.

As the female nightwalkers approached us, I wasn't too sure of myself. At first, I was very shy. But after some coaxing from my more experienced roommate, we started having some fun with them.

Even though these girls spoke and understood very little English we were able to communicate with them by speaking our dialect of Spanish and using hand signals.

Being a tall and lanky man, Jim used his hands to show one girl how big he was and waved them as though he was telling the joke about the fish that was "this big," stretching them out to three feet and then slowly moving them closer and closer together until they were about a foot apart. The girls smiled and looked at each other.

"*Ah chi wawa,*" said the black-haired nightwalker, as the two girls licked their red-painted lips and started laughing.

They told to us to follow them. So Jim and I happily obeyed their commands and followed them to their hotel room, a small, dark room with twin beds. I wasn't very happy about being in the same room right next to my roommate with everything out in the open. But I didn't complain and put my money on the dresser, about two-hundred *pesetas*—the equivalent of around twenty U.S. dollars.

Jim and I sat on one of the twin beds and watched as the girls began to undress. We couldn't control our emotions and acted like two little kids, punching each other on the arm, laughing and playing around, not noticing that the girls had taken off all of their clothes. When we turned and looked at the two naked nightwalkers, we thought we were at the zoo. We were staring at two hairy mammals. We knew they were females before they had undressed, but now we weren't so sure. Their two slender bodies were completely covered by a mass of thick, black, kinky hair from their shoulders to the toes on their feet. It looked utterly disgusting.

Within a minute, we had picked up our jaws off the floor, grabbed the money off the dresser, and then ran out of the room with the speed of Flash Gordon. Once we were far enough away from the zoo where those two female mammals hibernated and fornicated, we started laughing our heads off. I had almost lost my virginity to a female gorilla.

"Hey, Bob, let's go to the movies," said Jim.

"I hope the movie is better than the horror show we just left," I said, as we both laughed.

We walked to the movie theater a few blocks from the hotel we had just exited. *For a Few Dollars More,* starring Clint Eastwood, was playing, but only in Spanish. The English version wouldn't play for another week, but we decided to go anyway. Watching and listening to the movie in Spanish was more fun than I thought. I really hadn't noticed how much the movie had lost in the translation until I had seen the movie in America. However, I enjoyed it more in Spanish than in English anyway.

Once the movie had ended, we left the theater and rode the bus to our dorm. But Jim and I didn't return to our building; instead, we walked to a local bar just a few doors down from our dwelling. We had learned that the kids here started drinking alcohol at a very early age and drank wine with every meal because the wine was much cleaner than their water. So I wasn't worried about being kicked out of the bar for being underage.

It was a very small bar with just a dozen or so stools, two tables along the wall, and one pinball machine next to a jukebox. We stayed there for over three hours. A couple of those sexy female Madrid nightwalkers tried to take us back to their room, but after the surprise we had gotten only a few hours before, we decided against it.

Jim and I stayed at the bar drinking screwdrivers, playing pinball, and listening to the Beatles song "Strawberry Fields." We played it so much that the bartender kicked us out of the bar, screaming and yelling that he was tired of listening to that song after four hours and had a headache—and it wasn't from the music.

I couldn't even remember walking from the bar to the dorm. However, I did remember entering the dorm and being met by Mr. Webber and Mrs. Urfer. They were sitting in chairs and confronted us as we came in.

"Where were you tonight, Bob?" asked Mrs. Urfer, giving me a disgusted look.

"Well, Bob, we are waiting for an answer," asked Mr. Webber.

"Ah...we went to the city and saw a movie," I said, staring at the floor.

"You expect us to believe that?" snapped Mrs. Urfer, as I remained silent.

"Even I could have thought up a more original excuse," opined Mr. Webber, trying to hold back his anger as his round little "Howdy Doody" face and little lobe-less ears began turning different shades of red.

"You little people are in deep trouble," uttered Mrs. Urfer with her upper-class distinction about her.

Mrs. Urfer thought and acted as though she was better than everyone else was. She had that unfriendly, aristocratic, nose-up-in-the-air type of attitude. She should have been in the Marine Corps. Then, she probably was, I thought to myself.

"Bob, from now on you are to be in the dorm by ten o'clock every evening. Also, you are not allowed to visit the city on school nights, and you are not allowed to see the girls," said Mr. Webber.

I interrupted him. "What do you mean by 'the girls'?" I asked, as Jim looked at me and began laughing.

I couldn't figure out what Hippie Jim was laughing at until Mr. Webber continued his dialogue.

"The GIRLS downtown, Bob; that's what I mean," barked Mr. Webber, shaking his head in disgust. "Have you been drinking, Bob?" He gave me a very suspicious and disgusted look.

Mr. Webber always looked at me during this confrontation. *Why doesn't he look at Jim when he is yelling at us?* I thought. Maybe he was afraid of Jim. Hippie Jim didn't take any crap from anyone, including Mr. Webber.

"Well, Bob, we are waiting. Have you been drinking?" asked Mrs. Urfer, giving me a cold stare.

"No," I said, lying through my teeth. "We are not allowed to drink liquor." Jim and I looked at each other and nearly began laughing.

Mr. Webber and Mrs. Urfer were very angry with us. They then dismissed us and sent us upstairs to our room.

However, once I had entered the elevator I started getting an upset stomach and cried out in pain. As we reached the third floor, the doors on the elevator opened. Marilyn, Arlene, and a few other students came out of their rooms to see what caused all the commotion. So I began telling them about the confrontation Jim and I had had with Mr. Webber and Mrs. Urfer.

Mr. Webber, alias "the penguin," not only looked like a penguin but also waddled like one. With his penguin waddle, "Howdy Doody" face, and "Dumbo" floppy ears, he had become the butt of our jokes.

Halfway through my story, I began having the dry heaves and had to run to the bathroom to regurgitate. That situation put an end to the fun evening.

The next morning in class, Marilyn nursed my hangover and me. One thing led to another and we started petting and fondling each other, only to be interrupted by our female professor, Mrs. Temple.

"Bob! Bob, there will be no petting in my classroom. No kissing, touching, or fondling. Understand, Bob?" bellowed Mrs. Temple.

"Yes, I understand. I'm sorry. I won't do it again. I promise," I replied, crossing my fingers behind my back.

Mrs. Urfer stood up and told the class what extracurricular activities were on our agenda. We were to tour Toledo, the city of sword factories, which forges the best metals in the world for weapons, mainly swords. We were also going to visit the city of Barcelona, where we were to watch a bullfight; then on to Malaga to sit on their white, sandy beaches and swim in the Mediterranean; and finally to our final destination, the University of Granada.

The next morning, we were on our way to Toledo, a very old, small, clean, and beautiful city where the one-lane, cobblestone roads were used to the *clunk* of the horseshoe rather than the *roar* of an engine. It brought us back to the days of Don Quixote.

Our group climbed out of the Mercedes bus and walked into a small and very old sword factory that had forged swords as far back as the fourteenth century for many famous knights, kings, and people of the cloth—all within these same walls.

As we were led into the foundry, we watched as they forged all the swords by hand, as the blacksmiths had done in the fourteenth century. I suddenly caught myself in a daze, daydreaming about my fantasy. As I watched the blacksmith pounding the red-hot molten metal, I fantasized that they were making my special sword—a magic sword—to slay the fierce, fire breathing dragon and rescue the princess, marry her, and live happily ever after.

However, I was soon knocked back to my senses as the other members of our group were pushing me to the other side of the room. This was where the hand polishing and engraving occurred. In one of the rooms, you could only get in with a security clearance. This was where the precious jewels and gold were put into the swords. The leader of Spain gave these special swords to other dignitaries and leaders of the world.

As we were leaving the factory, the owner gave each one of us in the group a small, hand-engraved, hand-jeweled, twenty-two-inch sword. We later found out that these same swords were selling in tourist shops for well over fifty dollars. We were deeply pleased with our gifts and our new friends.

Another part of the factory contained a well-stocked jewelry store, and we were to go on a shopping spree. At least, that's what the owner was hoping. But I was out of money already and had been waiting more than a week for my parents to send me some. Then Hippie Jim walked by and told me to keep the two sales girls busy. He told me that he would give me half of whatever he got. I really didn't know what he had in mind, but I did as he asked. I wouldn't understand the ramifications of his words and actions until I had returned to the dorm.

While I was busy having the sales clerk show me some jewelry, Hippie Jim was stealing everything in sight. Without any security personnel or surveillance cameras, he was able to steal over two thousand dollars worth of gold and silver jewelry.

When we had returned to the dorm room, Jim dumped the stolen jewelry onto the bed and told me to pick out any twelve items. There was so much that it covered nearly half the mattress. There were gold rings, bracelets, necklaces, and pendants. Everything was at least eighteen to twenty-two carat gold. I picked out my prizes and thought no more about it.

The next week, we were on our way to the modern city of Barcelona, a much larger city than Toledo. Toledo was living a slow and delicate pace, as in the "Old World." Barcelona, however, was just the opposite, a bustling, hustling city with the same faults of any growing metropolis: smog, crime, traffic delays, and an overcrowded, overgrowing population.

However, everyone forgot their troubles on Saturdays and went to the bullfights. On that particular day, our group was elected to pick out the bulls for the day's events. We all hustled into a portion of the stadium where the bulls were being contained. All twenty-two of us were standing on a very narrow wooden bridge overlooking the corrals that held the ferocious, man-killing beasts. If there had been just one more person standing on that weak platform, it would have collapsed. As the bridge began to sag, I held on for dear life while one of the Spanish representatives walked along pointing at different bulls.

I was allowed to pick out one of seven that were chosen to entertain us. We had picked out seven of the nastiest-looking demons to fight in the ring that day. Once that chore was finished, we were ushered into the stadium to the bleacher seats. The smell of flowers and fresh dirt was in the air.

I was especially anxious to see a real bullfight, which I had never before experienced. After it was over, I never wanted to see another one. The Spanish people believed that bullfighting was a "macho" sport. I came away with the feeling that if the game were played fair, man against beast, then it would be a macho sport. But not how they played the game.

The event started like a circus. All the matadors, picadors, and everyone else involved circled the arena to the roar of the crowd. Then, as the arena cleared, the first bull was let out of its pen. The bull waited in the center of the ring, looking around at the crowd, staring, snorting, and kicking up the fresh dirt with its powerful front legs, as if to show that he was king and "come knock me off my throne."

I figured the matador would enter the ring now and fight the bull. Instead, two horses and their riders entered the ring. Their horses were covered with a thick protective mattress to keep them from being injured or gored by the bull's horns. The riders carried long, wooden lances to stab the bull in the shoulders.

As the bull charged the horse, the riders plunged their lances into the bull's shoulders repeatedly, trying to destroy the muscle tissue and ligaments so the bull couldn't lift up its head and ram its horns into the horse or matador. This also kept the head of the bull in one position. After ten or fifteen minutes of lance goring to the bull's shoulders and neck area, this brutality continued. With blood dripping from the large open wounds, the riders left and the picadors entered the arena.

The picadors surrounded the bull, holding three to six two-pronged forks in their hands. They looked like large carving forks. One by one, they charged the bull, plunging two big forks at a time into the same location that the lancers had just opened up.

The picadors tried to hit both sides of the bull's neck and shoulder area. They plunged the forks deep into the neck, deep enough so the bull couldn't throw them out. This kept the bull's head down so he couldn't gore his victim. Once that was done and the bull had ten or twelve long forks in its neck area, the brave and fearless "macho" matador came into the arena.

The big macho matador bowed to the crowd. If the matador is a crowd favorite or famous, the crowd applauds louder and louder. Then the famous matador throws his cap to the woman he loves and offers her the bull as a gift.

Then as graceful as a swan, the matador goes through his ritual. As the bull tries to gore his opponent, the matador smoothly moves to the side. The closer he comes to the bull's horns, the wilder the crowd reacts. This went on for over thirty minutes as he waved the red cape in front of the bull's eyes, while teasing him with a Spanish dance step.

When the time was right, the crowd decided if the bull would be saved or killed. If the bull had performed well, it was spared until the next bullfight. However, this particular bull was rejected by the crowd and ruled to die.

Now the matador went eye to eye with the bull. With one hand, the matador held his cape near his face and with the other, he held onto the sword. Then he took aim and plunged it deep into the victim's neck, clear through to the heart. However, the bull whipped its head and threw the sword high into the air. The matador had to walk thirty feet away to pick it up before he plunged it again and again, until the crowd started throwing bottles and anything else that was handy and close by. The matador was embarrassed and angry. Now, for a fifth time, he was poised perfectly. He aimed and lunged. This time, the sword stayed in.

Suddenly, the assistant matadors came running into the arena and circled the bull waving their beautiful white and red capes in the air, confusing it and making it spin in circles while it lost more and more of its blood. Then the bull finally collapsed on the ground, slowly dying. As the bull's lungs filled with blood and its life seeped out of its veins, the matador stood over the fallen beast and plunged a large butcher knife into its brain. The bull died instantly.

When that was done, the workers hooked the bull up to a pair of horses and dragged its carcass around the arena for all to see. The crowd went wild. They were ecstatic that the matador was victorious. After the fourth bull was executed in the same fashion, our leader, Mrs. Urfer, decided we had seen enough of this brutality and unjust sport.

We left the arena, loaded ourselves into the bus, and then headed for a special bar to meet the winning matador of that day's performance.

As we waited to be introduced to the matador, I was asked to dance with a beautiful female Spanish flamenco dancer. I never knew flamenco dancing could be so sexual and sensual. That was the night I learned how to flamenco dance. At the end of the dance, this beautiful dark-skinned woman gave me a kiss on the lips that melted the boots off my feet. I had suddenly lost all thought and memory. As the night wore on, the more sangria I drank, the better I danced, or so it seemed.

By the end of the enchanted evening, it felt as though I had drunk a gallon or more of their sangria. The room wouldn't stop spinning, and I had a very upset stomach.

However, I was able to sleep during our long bus ride to our new dorm in Granada. Needless to say, I woke up the following morning with an extreme headache.

Well, we arrived in Granada as hardcore exchange students. Due to a lack of college professors, our group was left without one—and without a classroom.

Therefore, to kill time, I went out and bought a few gifts for friends, relatives, and myself. Of course, a teenage boy needs a good, sharp knife, so I bought one: a stiletto. The blade ejected from the center of the handle when the button was pressed. I also bought a handmade twelve-string acoustic guitar.

I met a young Spanish teenager at the music store and after ten minutes of speaking half-English and half-Spanish with him, we walked over to his house—or should I say mansion?

His home was a giant, stucco-style, old mission-type with three massive floors of magnificent beauty.

When you entered the house through giant double doors, directly ahead was a huge double-sided staircase with two twelfth-century knights of shining armor standing guard, one on each side. Each side of the surrounding walls of the hallway was covered with rare and magnificent Goya paintings. Along the walls of the staircase to the second floor were many other famous paintings. The artists included Renrau, Van Gogh, Picasso, Monet, Da Vinci, Velasquez, and many others.

The main floor contained a large room that was used for the music room and was full of electric guitars and other musical instruments and equipment.

My new friend introduced me to his four band members and to a teenage female groupie. She was lying on the couch in her bra and panties and not quite as hairy as the two Madrid hookers were, but she ran a close second.

As we talked music, I looked around the room. These walls were also full of very old and rare paintings, whose signatures included more Goyas', a Velasquez, another Picasso, a Raphael, and a painting by Michelangelo.

My new friend also pointed to a few newer paintings of a surrealistic nature by an artist named Dali. But he thought all of Dali's paintings were subliminal and ugly. He didn't think of them as valuable art. He thought of them as junk. He liked the more contemporary art, the new "mod" art.

I could have traded him a Peter Max painting for one of his rare fourteenth or fifteenth century paintings if I had brought one with me.

After a brief conversation with my friend and his band members, we decided to play a few songs together. We played rock music for more than four hours. They really liked my singing and guitar playing, especially when I sang the words in English. Our best song was "Help" by the Beatles.

During and after our jam session, the young Spanish girl who had been lying on the couch tried to seduce me. We couldn't communicate very well in Spanish, so we communicated with our lips. She taught me how to "French" kiss. I eventually used this new experience on my new girlfriend, Marilyn.

It was getting late and I had to return to the dorm. I had spent nearly six hours with my new friend and now had to leave. I said goodbye and promised to return another day. He seemed like a very good and honest person. I later learned that he was the richest teenager in Granada. His father was a first cousin to General Franco.

I returned to the dorm and went directly to Marilyn's room. We had started seeing each other as the summer progressed. Her room was just down the hall from mine. The males were on the east wing and the females were on the west. Marilyn and I would learn about the facts of life together, lying on the bed, petting, kissing, and hugging. Later, near the end of the trip, I would make love to her.

One day while lying on her bed, I noticed these white objects flying past the window. When I walked over to get a better look, I could see that the objects were paper airplanes. I poked my head out of the window and looked to the right. I saw a hand throw a small piece of engineering artwork into the windy air currents. The paper airplanes picked up speed, flying faster and faster, then climbed higher and higher, before they landed gently onto the cobblestone street below.

I ran out of Marilyn's room to the room down the hall. I wanted to see who was making these beautiful gliders. To my surprise, it was Hippie Jim and Harvard Jim, two people I had never expected to see playing this childish game. They were making these paper airplanes using two sheets of paper. This extra weight made the gliders fly farther, faster, and longer.

They quickly showed me how to make them and a few minutes later, we were having a contest to see whose plane would fly the farthest. During the next three and a half hours, the three of us must have made and flown over two thousand paper airplanes out of our third floor window. When we looked out to the street below, it looked as if it had snowed. A beautiful white fluff covered the street fifty feet to the right and fifty feet to the left. The street was a solid white.

We hadn't noticed how much of a mess we had made until some of the storeowners came out screaming and shaking their fists at us. One owner kept ranting and raving that we, as young Americans, were the disgrace of the world. He told us to go back to our own country and destroy our own land.

I will admit, when our group first arrived, there wasn't one speck of dirt or piece of paper on their beautiful cobblestone street or sidewalks. It was spic and span. Now, however, was a different story.

The townspeople came from blocks away to see what all the commotion was about. We had only been in this town for two days and already they wanted to get rid of us. Mrs. Urfer came into the room screaming at us.

"You little people get to the street and clean up your mess!" she bellowed.

"Clean it up yourself!" screamed Hippie Jim. "I'm not your slave. They have street cleaners for that, and I'm not going to take their jobs away from them."

Mrs. Urfer, her face a beet red, looked as though she were going to explode. Her eyes nearly popped out of their sockets. Then she began to choke on her words. I'd never seen her upset before.

While Hippie Jim and Mrs. Urfer continued arguing, everyone else left the room and went outside to clean up the street. It took the three of us nearly four hours to mess it up, but only an hour to clean, so it wasn't so bad—except when Mrs. Urfer and Mr. Webber bawled us out. They treated us like little children. That's what we objected to the most. It was the same old song: treat us like kids and we'll act like kids; treat us like adults and we'll act like adults.

As the group was called together that night, we were told that Hippie Jim would be leaving for the United States in the morning for talking back to Mrs. Urfer.

Jim's father was called and told how he had misbehaved and that the World Academy wouldn't tolerate devious acts against other members of the group. Therefore, he would have to pay for Jim's return airfare to America. That was very ironic, because Jim had told me at the beginning of the trip that his father had paid him just to get rid of him for the summer. Now he was paying to get him back.

Mrs. Urfer had yet another surprise for us.

"Also, people, we will meet another group tomorrow night," she said. "We will walk over to the campus dorm and meet with a group from New York City. I hear they are all on the dean's list and some of the elite people of New York. So be on your good behavior." As she said those words, she looked directly at me.

Mrs. Urfer had a sixth sense. She knew when something unexpected was going to happen. You never second-guessed her and most definitely never talked back to her. She had a distinct crusty upper-class air about her. She was always winning the argument, even if she was wrong. She would grind you up and spit you out. But either way, she got rid of you if you crossed her.

Two nights later, our group, minus Hippie Jim, got all dressed up in our best clothes, ready to meet all the Rhodes scholars at Granada University. We were all a little tense and nervous, worrying that our group might not live up to their expectations. Mrs. Urfer was particularly worried. She wanted everything perfect.

Our group marched in two single-file lines through the city of Granada, all of us in our best suits and dresses trying to pretend that we were all little rich kids getting the best education that money could buy. We were only acting this way for Mrs. Urfer. She was at wit's end. She was doing her best, but when she was bumping heads with people like Hippie Jim, and me, by the end of the summer, Mrs. Urfer would be a nervous wreck.

Our group arrived at the dorm as perfect ladies and gentlemen. However, nobody from the other group greeted us. So Mrs. Urfer ushered us into a big living room and ordered us to sit down. We did as we were told. There were a number of couches and chairs on which to sit while we waited for our hosts.

Within a few minutes of our group's arrival a few young teenage girls, about eighteen years old, came into the room barefoot and dressed in cut-off short shorts and scruffy denim blue C.P.O. shirts. Then a couple more pretty teenage girls came slinking slowly into the room. Within five minutes, there were approximately twenty people in their group. Nearly all were female. There were eight girls to every guy in their group. However, there weren't any chaperones, only students. Many of the young females were flirting with many of us young men as we sat nervously in our seats and smiled in approval.

Mrs. Urfer and Mr. Webber were aghast at the dress of this New York City group. They were all sloppily dressed with long, dirty, scruffy hair. Even the boys had long, dirty, scraggily hair. The last female to enter the room came in smoking a cigarette. She sat right next to Mrs. Urfer, but not on the cushion.

When this young woman sat on the arm of the couch and put her cigarette out on the decorative wooden carving that covered it, Mrs. Urfer became irate. Her eyes nearly popped out of their sockets. She was aghast at this group's lack of responsibility and quickly stood up and began screaming to our group.

"Class, single file!" Her face turned a beet red. "Everybody back to the dorm! Nobody, and I mean nobody, is allowed to come back to this temple of evil, this den of iniquity!"

However, I didn't want to leave. My hormones were raging after seeing so many sexy and beautiful young women. I was the last in line. As I slowly walked out the door, one of the girls who had been flirting with me followed me and squeezed my butt. All the way to the street, she pleaded with me.

"Promise me you'll come back to visit?" asked the beautiful, blonde-haired goddess.

"Sure, I'll be back," I promised her. "I always keep my promises. By the way, what's your name?"

"I'm Jenny," she said, as she gave me a quick kiss on the lips and then ran back to her building.

While we walked back to our dorm, I memorized the cable car tracks and the names of the streets so I could find my way back to her dorm. I decided to visit there the next night. Even though Mrs. Urfer had banned our group from ever returning to their dorm, I couldn't wait to see Jenny and her girlfriends again.

The next night, I walked out of our dorm just after supper. I was glad to get out of that place. It had been another dinner of chicken cooked in a gallon of olive oil. I despised the way the Spanish people cooked their food, using huge amounts of olive oil.

I walked directly to the forbidden group's dorm. I remembered the way perfectly, and it took me only an hour to walk there.

When I knocked on the dorm door, I was surprised to see my fantasy dream. I was warmly greeted by a dozen or more well developed young women and not a chaperone in sight. I couldn't believe my luck. I was the only male among a dozen of lovely, horny, young women. This was my definition of heaven. They remembered me from the night before, especially Jenny. She came out of the crowd and gave me a luscious kiss on the lips to break the ice.

After I had introduced myself and we had exchanged pleasantries, we got down to serious lovemaking. Nineteen sixty-seven was sure the year of "free love." I learned that very quickly that night.

I also learned that one of the two New York group's chaperones had run away with a young female Spanish student, and they married. Their other chaperone was a female wino. She stayed in her room and drank and had been on a continuous drunken stupor since their group had first arrived in Granada. The only time she would come out of her room was to search her students' rooms to confiscate any liquor or drugs that they might have. When the chaperone found any contraband, she would confiscate it and return to her room to continue her drunken binge. However, she didn't confiscate all the contraband.

Sally, one of the girls I had made love to, pulled out a small prescription bottle filled with a green powdered substance and held it in front of my eyes.

"Do you know what this is?" asked Sally, an eighteen-year-old brunette.

"I don't know. Let me smell it," I said, as I grabbed the plastic vial out of her hand, popped the lid, and then smelled it.

"What do you think it is?" asked Jenny, as she sat on my lap on the bed.

"This stuff looks like and smells like oregano," I said, as all the girls laughed.

Sally grabbed the vial out of my hands and poured the powdered green substance into a rolling paper. She quickly rolled the stuff into a cigarette and lit it. As she inhaled deeply, she coughed a few times, then passed the cigarette to Jenny.

"You guys smoke oregano?" I asked, as they all busted out in laughter.

"Of course not," cooed Jenny, as she exhaled the smoke and passed it to me.

"Then what is it?" I said, as I grabbed it from her hand.

"It's pot. Reefer, Mary Jane," said Jenny.

I looked at her in confusion.

"What's that?" I asked, as I put the cigarette to my lips and inhaled deeply.

"It's marijuana," said Jenny, laughing as I exhaled the weird-tasting smoke and began coughing.

Up to that point, I hadn't even smoked cigarettes. I coughed and coughed and my eyes became red and teary. "Sally, where did you get this stuff" I asked.

"Why?" asked Sally.

"I would like to get some for myself," I lied, trying to act macho. "Sally, can you help me find some?"

Sally looked at me through the smoky haze and smiled.

"Go to the Olympic swimming pool and look for a short, stocky, tough guy with dark, shiny black hair with a long *Fu Manchu* mustache and goatee. You can't miss him," she said.

"What's his name?" I asked her.

"He goes by the name of Ramone. Oh, one more thing. He has a tattoo on his right forearm of a black and orange dragon."

"Bob, have you ever smoked pot as good as this?" asked Jenny, as she snuggled up to me and laid her head on my shoulder.

"Many times," I lied. "Mostly at parties. My friends and I chip in money and buy a few bags."

"Bags? How much pot is in a bag?" Sally asked me.

Holy shit, I thought. *How much is in a bag? What do I say?* I didn't know anything about this drug business, but I had to prove to these lovely young women that I was an old pro at it. I started thinking: pints, quarts, gallons, pounds, and ounces. Then it hit me—ounces. That sounded good.

"Ounces," I blurted out. "We always buy a few ounces for our parties," I said, acting very confident and cocky.

"Oh, a quarter of a pound at a time. Boy, you rich kids know how to throw a party," said Robin, another girl I had made love to that night.

The more these young women talked, the more confident I got.

Besides the pot that we were smoking, we were also passing around a few bottles of wine. After hours of partying, Robin went to a refrigerator and brought out a small baking sheet of sugar cubes. Then she handed a sugar cube to each one of us. There were twelve of us in the room—eleven girls and me.

"Have you ever taken acid?" asked Robin, returning to her seat on the dirty floor.

"What kind of acid?" I asked, as the girls giggled.

"LSD 25. You know, pure acid," said a stoned Robin, her eyes red and dilated.

"What do you want me to do with it?" I asked, holding it up to the light.

"Just put it in your mouth and let it melt," purred Jenny.

"I've never taken acid before," I said, trying to sound hip. "But I guess I'm going to try it now." I held the cube in my hand.

Jenny grabbed the cube out of my hand and placed it on my tongue. I sat back and waited as it melted in my mouth. I watched as all of the girls did the same.

"Shit, we need some more wine," said Robin.

"I'll get some for us," I replied.

"I'll go with you, then we can get back to some real partying," purred Jenny, as she grabbed my hand and pulled me to the door.

Jenny and I went down to the corner cafe, which had just opened up after siesta. I purchased four bottles of very strong red wine.

"Muy fuerte," I told the bartender. He then handed me four large bottles.

When we returned to the dorm, there was still no sign of their chaperone or any of the guys in their group.

I was the only male at the party, and the only guy among all of these gorgeous young women. I jumped from one girl to another, kissing, hugging, and fondling them, which all the girls seemed to enjoy.

Again, I had sex with Robin and Jenny. Then I began to feel the strange and weird affects of the LSD. The room started to wiggle, weird patterns started forming, and I felt very light-headed. I had a very anxious feeling come over my being. It was a very weird feeling. A few minutes later, I was tripping my brains out. Things seemed to go by my eyes at a very rapid speed. Everything seemed surrealistic, like looking through a fishbowl full of water. And I couldn't control my thoughts. I was too high to even think.

After many hours of tripping, smoking pot, and drinking wine, we were all getting pretty drunk and stoned. Three of the girls and I went to one of their rooms and were naked within minutes.

For a guy who had just lost his virginity, this was the way to lose it—not with some hairy Spanish hooker I would have to pay money to. Nevertheless, to lose it to these beautiful girls was a dream comes true, especially for a seventeen-year-old male with raging hormones.

All I seem to remember was Jenny on top of me, then Robin, and then Sally—and a swirl of black, brown, and blonde hair all over my naked body. I was showered with their kisses and love. The smell from their erotic perfumes and female odors put me in a hypnotic trance.

My head was swirling, whirling and felt swollen, like an overfilled helium balloon. When I looked at my feet, they seemed to be a mile away. All aspects of sight and sound were out of scale to normal activities. I had never experienced anything like this before, but I was enjoying it.

The smoking, the booze, the acid, and the girls were a new experience for me. I finally understood what "free love" had meant. However, the drinking I didn't like. But it went with the party. If the others were doing it, I would join in. I didn't want anything to upset this beautiful evening with these gorgeous young women.

When we were finished with our fun in one room, we wandered into another where I found myself with more naked women. This was truly heaven. By the end of the evening, I had slept with ten of the twelve girls. Besides being very exhausted, high as a kite, and floating on air, I was also blind drunk.

About one in the morning, while a few of the girls and I were making love in Jenny's room, their alcoholic chaperone suddenly barged in. We quickly covered ourselves as best we could under the circumstances, but the chaperone was very angry and confiscated the last full bottle of red wine before breaking up the party. She looked directly into my bloodshot eyes, gave me an evil stare, and yelled at me.

"Leave this dorm! Who are you anyway?" she shouted, as she stumbled around the room, ranting and raving.

Before I could answer her, she stumbled out of the room taking the bottle of wine she had just confiscated. Now it was my turn. I had to get dressed and stumble back to my dorm. The only problem was, I couldn't see very well. It was well past one in the morning, and I was still blind drunk and higher than a kite. I would have to follow the cable car tracks to get back to my dorm because I wouldn't be able to read the street signs.

The girls walked me out to the street and said good night. They each gave me a quick kiss on the lips and a pat on the behind. Robin and Jenny gave me a kiss I would never forget. I gave them one last hug and thanked them all for a wonderful and unforgettable evening. I just hoped I could remember it the following morning.

After we said goodbye, I was left to the dark and damp night. To this day, I don't know how I made it back to my dorm. But I do know that I made it in one piece, and I snuck into the dorm without my chaperones seeing me. However, I didn't go directly to my room, like I should have. Instead, I went to Marilyn's room and woke her up.

I was still very drunk, stoned, and smelled of alcohol as I started mumbling to her about my night's escapades. We didn't want to awaken her roommate, so we walked down the hall and stood next to a window while I continued telling her my story. Marilyn wasn't too happy when I mentioned the girls at the party. She was madder still when I refused to tell her what I had done at the party, although I did let it slip out that I had been smoking. But I didn't tell her what I had smoked. She had a pretty good idea I wasn't talking about cigarettes. She also knew I had drunk a little too much wine.

"Marilyn, this is a night I will never forget," I told her, stoned out of my mind.

She held onto me so I wouldn't fall down. But in a sudden moment of anger, she released her hold and my right shoulder fell into the large glass window, cutting a one-inch-long gash into my biceps. The noise from the breaking glass was very loud, and the commotion woke up everyone in our dorm. Marilyn quickly walked me to my room and then left. She didn't want to get into any trouble.

Within two minutes, nearly everyone from our group was peering into my room to find out what was going on. By this time, I was still very stoned and drunk. In fact, I was quite incoherent when Mr. Webber and Mrs. Urfer began asking me many questions. While they gave me the third degree, Mrs. Urfer's son, who was a medical doctor, stitched the gash in my shoulder.

"Where have you been, Bob?" asked Mr. Webber.

"Where did you go tonight, Bob?" asked Mrs. Urfer.

I remained silent. I really couldn't understand what they were jabbering about. When they got tired of asking me questions and not getting any answers, they aimed their questions at Marilyn. But she didn't know much either. So I blurted out the answer.

"I was visiting the students from New York," I snapped.

"I told you, Bob, never to visit those disgusting hippies again," said Mrs. Urfer. "What else did you do, Bob?"

Then Mr. Webber jumped in. "You're drunk, and I bet you have even been smoking cigarettes, haven't you, Bob?" he asked.

"You are a disgusting sort, Bob," snorted Mrs. Urfer. "Wait until your father hears about this."

"From now on, Bob, we'll watch you day and night. You will go where we will go," stated Mr. Webber.

"Did you do drugs tonight, Bob?" asked Mrs. Urfer.

"No," I lied, still tripping like crazy and completely out of it.

Never had I experienced anything like it before. I didn't know enough about it to be frightened. I just thought the high was similar to pot. I had not only been a virgin at sex, but at drugs, too. But I learned fast.

As Mrs. Urfer began peering into my eyes, I suddenly passed out on my bed and didn't awaken until morning.

Boy, what a night. My head was pounding a heavy beat. I had a horrendous headache and a very upset stomach. I had a hard time getting out of bed, but I had to.

Mrs. Urfer had called the group for breakfast. I was in no mood to eat, but if I didn't, Mrs. Urfer would reprimand me.

All my peers were staring at me and completely silent as I came into the room, walked to the breakfast table, and plopped myself into a chair. The room was spinning as I waited for my meal. A few minutes later, the waitress served us. The first thing I saw was a plate of two undercooked, nearly raw eggs swimming in a pint of olive oil. My stomach began turning over and over until I couldn't hold back any longer. I regurgitated all over Mr. Webber's shoes and his lower pant legs.

Arlene, President of our high school Spanish club, was also sitting at our table. As I regurgitated my stomach's contents, she watched in amazement and disbelief. But my sickness suddenly attacked her, too, and she regurgitated all over Mr. Webber's shoes and pants also. As sick as I was, I couldn't help laughing at this sick joke. Nevertheless, the chef should have known better than to give me olive oil with my eggs. They would certainly know better the next time.

I was still under the influence of the LSD and very light-headed and dizzy. Every time I stood up the room began to swirl and spin, so I had to return to my room to rest. The minute I entered my third-floor room, I went directly to the window and opened it for some fresh air. I quickly stuck my head through the open window and after inhaling a few deep breaths of fresh air, my stomach finally settled down. Then, as I looked down to the street below, I noticed an outside cafe adjacent to the hotel. I figured this was the place that made our group's food every day.

But thinking about food had made me weak in the knees, so I lay down on the bed to gather my energy and strength. After an hour or so, I had become bored and restless, so I returned to the only window in my little room and watched the customers at the cafe. I noticed two small boys sitting at a table waiting for their mother's return. And when they had become bored, they began throwing paper wads at each other.

A few minutes later, I was also throwing paper wads to the cafe below. At first, I tried hitting the little boys, wanting to join in on their fun. But once they saw me, the jig was up.

A waiter walked near the hotel's wall and looked up at me,

waved his fist in a menacing manner, and then yelled out, "Stop throwing garbage on our customers! You are chasing them away."

I quickly backed away from the window. I didn't want to get into any more trouble. So I returned to my bed, pouting and in a bad mood. That damn waiter stopped my fun, I thought to myself. But my mood suddenly changed when Marilyn and Joan came into my room to console me.

Joan was from New York and Marilyn was from Pennsylvania. Joan was a petite, beautiful redhead with rosy cheeks and a smile that could light up a dark room. She also had a jovial and trusting personality and was from a rich Jewish family in Great Neck, New York. She had been selected by World Academy just as Arlene and I had. Marilyn was from a small village called New Castle. She was a beautiful, tall, and lanky blonde-haired goddess, and I had fallen in love with her at first sight.

The girls and I were bored, so the three of us decided to go to a bar that night, one that I was familiar with. The rich kid from Granada had taken me there with some of his female groupies. It was called "The Cave."

This particular bar was built right into the side of a black granite mountain, and the walls, tables, and chairs were all carved out of the same black granite. This bar was an incredible sight. It was dimly lit with blue and red lights and soft music whispered throughout, which seemed to be coming out of the granite walls.

When we entered, I immediately took Marilyn to a dark corner and ordered two screwdrivers. Then, while waiting for our drinks, we began some heavy necking and petting. I had learned quite a lot from the ten females I had made love to the night before. My hormones raged as we necked in the corner. But before it could get out of hand, Joan came to the table with her new boyfriend, some Romanian guy with the name of Natasse. I had learned many years later that this guy had been one of the best professional tennis players in the world.

Joan and her boyfriend joined us at our table. Marilyn and I were only interested in necking, and Joan's new boyfriend was only concerned with tennis. That's all he talked about—tennis, tennis, tennis.

Marilyn and I were rather bored by the conversation, so we decided to leave and walk back to the dorm. We had to get up early the next morning because we wanted to swim at the Olympic swimming pool before it became too crowded.

It was called the Olympic Pool because it's an Olympic-size swimming pool and Spain's Olympic swimmers trained there every day. It also had a three-tier diving platform and three springboards—a ten-meter, a five meter, and three-meter. But there was a picnic table blocking the stairway to the ten-meter platform. Evidently, too many people had gotten hurt diving from more than thirty feet up because they had lacked the proper training and knowledge on the physics of diving.

So that morning when we arrived at the pool, I automatically walked to the blocked stairway. It didn't hinder me in the least. I just climbed over it and continued on my way to the top of the highest platform. I had never dived from that height before, but being a springboard diver on my high school swim team, I was confident I could do it. I also wanted to make a big impression on Marilyn and my other classmates.

I looked out into the open sky, trying not to look down and then took three deep breaths of fresh air. I shook my arms, legs, and my whole body, trying to ease my fears. I took another three deep breaths and walked slowly toward the end of the ten-meter platform.

My first dive was one I had been good at on the springboard. But now I was diving from a platform. I would have to take a running start four feet from the end of the platform then throw myself into the dive. I decided on a one and one-half forward somersault in the tuck position.

I straightened up my body and bounced off the end of the platform, throwing myself forward into a spin. My tuck was nice and tight. However, it was a little too tight. I began to spin too fast and out of control. I tried to compensate for my excessive speed by loosening my tuck, but I overcompensated. Instead of landing in the water head-first, I spun a little too much and landed smack-dab on my back. This completely knocked the wind out of my body. I couldn't breathe. I was doing everything I could just to stay afloat, trying not to look like I was hurt.

I finally got up enough strength to swim to the edge of the pool. By the time I had reached it, I was moaning, groaning and gagging from swallowing too much chlorinated water. I rested for a few minutes to gather enough strength to lift my battered and bruised body out of the pool and look confident doing it.

I shook off the cobwebs and climbed the stairs to the ten-meter platform once again. I stood at the edge of the platform and looked down at all the people. They looked so small and so far away I nearly decided against diving again, but I took three quick deep breaths and began to relax. Finally, I got the nerve to dive into the water. Again, I tried the forward one and one-half front somersault in the tuck position.

I jumped off the end of the platform and began my forward spin. It felt good for the first few seconds. Once again, I began spinning faster and faster. By the time I had come out of my tuck, I had hit the water with such force I thought I had broken every bone in my body. I had landed right on my back, *again—smack, crack,* ooh, ouch, *whish* went my body. I cried out in immense pain and agony. Not only did it knock the breath out of me, but I also lost consciousness for a few seconds. I tried not to look like an utter fool and drown in front of everyone and slowly swam to the edge of the pool again, then shook off the cobwebs in my head from the lack of oxygen to my brain. A few minutes later, I lifted myself out of the pool, walked slowly to the stairway, and climbed the steps to the top platform once again. And again, I tried a one and one-half forward somersault.

It didn't fail. Three consecutive dives and three times I had landed on my back. It felt like I had hit solid cement. Landing in the water on my back after falling from more than thirty feet up was equal to a spanking with a large wooden paddle from a three-hundred-pound coach. Believe me it hurts.

This last time I had landed on my back I tried to sink to the bottom of the pool and drown myself, but my conscience wouldn't let me. Once I was able to swim to the side of the pool, I came out to catch my breath and decided never to dive from that height again. But I refused to give up and dove from the three-meter platform.

Just as I hopped out of the pool, I saw the person with whom I had wanted to speak. He was speaking with another man as I walked over to him.

"*Que pasa,* Ramone?" I asked, hoping it was the right person.

"What do you want, gringo? Do I know you?" he asked in English, while looking at his friend standing next to him.

"Are you Ramone?" I asked, looking at the tattoo on his arm.

"Yes, I am Ramone. Now what is it that you want?"

"Sally, the girl from New York who lives on the campus at the university told me to talk with you about something I need."

"What do you need?"

"Sally told me you could get me anything that I wanted."

"Yeah, but it will cost you," replied Ramone, smiling.

"How much is it going to cost me? I don't have too much money on me right now. How much pot can I get for five American dollars?"

"Shut up, gringo," snapped Ramone.

I was low on funds. I had written more than once to my parents to send me more money, so five dollars was *mucho dinero* to me.

We walked inside to the men's locker room. As we entered the room, I handed Ramone a five-dollar bill. He stopped and said a few words to his buddy, who in turn reached into his shirt pocket and pulled out a small matchbox. Ramone grabbed it and opened it to show me the pot. Then he put it up to my nose to smell.

"This stuff is super good," said Ramone, smiling. "You can get high from just smelling it."

At that time, I believed him. As a teenager, I was very trusting and naive. But for five dollars, I expected more than a little matchbox full. I thought I should get at least three or four times that amount. I gave Ramone the impression that I wasn't happy with the deal and acted as though I was being ripped off.

"Ramone, this isn't worth five dollars. I want more pot. Where is the rest of it?" I asked him.

"Ah, caramba." he sighed.

As we argued, we continued to walk toward the opposite end of the locker room until he stopped at one of the lockers. Ramone kept talking under his breath in Spanish as he opened the locker door and reached for a large paper bag that was full of marijuana. Then he handed his friend a small empty paper sack, then reached into the big bag of pot and started filling the smaller sack with it. I wondered how he could keep that stuff in his locker without being busted. It smelled as though a dead skunk had died there.

While I watched the door, worried someone would come in and see what was going on, Ramone continued to fill the small sack with a strong, sweet, skunky-smelling pot until it was filled to the brim. The bag was so full he couldn't get another bud into it.

"Ramone, that's enough," I told him.

I thought he was going to ask for more money after he had given me all of that pot, but I didn't have any to give him. I was sure all the stuff Ramone had given me was worth far more than five dollars. Then another thought had crossed my mind: what would I do with all of it?

"Ramone, can I ask you a question?" I asked.

"Sure, go ahead."

"How come you gave me so much marijuana?"

Ramone looked shocked and confused and then said, "'Cause you gave me five dollars."

"Yeah, so?" I asked.

"This is five dollars worth of pot," he said, patting my small paper sack of marijuana.

I thought to myself, *Wow, what a deal. Boy, is this guy as stupid as he looks or what?* Ramone looked at me as though he had just read my mind.

"Senor, you may feel like a bull that has just bred with ten cows, but that stuff only cost me ten cents."

"You're kidding?" I asked, not believing him.

"I just bought a two hundred-pound bale for two dollars. In Spain, the farmers cut it down because it grows wild and makes the cows and bulls act crazy when they eat it. If I didn't buy it from them, they would just burn it. Then I sell it to crazy gringo tourists like yourself," he snickered.

"Well, Ramone, I appreciate that."

"Thank you, Senor. You can always see me here at the pool if you ever need my help again. *Adios, amigo,*" said Ramone, acting as though he had just pulled the wool over the eyes of another stupid gringo tourist.

I turned and walked in the opposite direction. *What am I going to do with all of this pot?* I thought to myself.

I didn't go back to Marilyn and the others in our group; instead, I went directly to my locker, dressed and then placed my bag of pot into a larger one. Then I quietly left the pool and walked back to the dorm to the sanctuary of my tiny bedroom, which contained one small window, a single bed on each side, and a sink and a shower to wash in, but no toilet. That was just down the hall from my room and had to be shared with the others on our floor. .

I made it back to my dorm without any problems or distractions. When I walked through the front entrance, the clerk saw me carrying the small paper sack and questioned its contents.

"What do you have in that sack, a live or dead skunk?" he asked. I remained silent. "Whew, whatever it is, it stinks," he said, holding his nose with one hand while fanning the air with his other.

"It's just my lunch," I said, as I quickly ran up the stairs to my room and locked the door.

I tried to think of something to do with all of this pot but didn't have any idea. If Hippie Jim were here he would know what to do, I thought to myself. But I was on my own on this one. Then there was a knock on my door.

"Just a minute," I shouted.

Oh my God, what do I do now? I thought to myself. *I need to hide it.* I quickly pulled out my chess set, placed the stuff into the empty cavity of the chessboard, and shut it. But there was too much pot, and it wouldn't close completely. So I stood on it and smashed the stuff down until it closed tight and locked.

I placed the chess pieces into a sock, then placed the sock and chessboard into a large plastic bag, sealed it, wrapped some clothes around it, sprinkled my strong cologne all over it, and then hid it in the bottom of my suitcase along with all my other gifts.

By the time I answered the door, the person who had knocked was gone.

I decided to go over to the other dorm and visit Sally, Jenny, and the rest of their female friends. I wanted to tell them what I had gotten at the pool and have another party. I was roaring to go all over again. If I was caught, at least it would be for a good reason. Oh, what energy I had as a young teenager.

Just as I was exiting my room, Mrs. Urfer stopped by and told me about our group's next activity.

"We are going to the Alhambra this afternoon to a piano recital and *everyone* is attending—that includes you, Bob," stated Mrs. Urfer. "The Spanish elite and the American Diplomatic Corps will also be in attendance, so be on your best behavior." Then she turned and walked away.

But I didn't want to go to some stuffy piano concerto and knew I had to do something to get out of it. With all those important people attending, I knew we would have to dress up, and I wasn't dressing up again for anyone.

Now I was a man of the world, a freewheeling kind of guy. Instead of wearing my suit, I dressed into my tight-fitting jeans, my knee-high deerskin moccasin boots, and my madras shirt. I looked into the small, dirty mirror to see how I looked and noticed that my hair was getting long and thick. Now I was ready for action, not some boring piano recital.

So I began to put my plan together and quickly sought out Mrs. Urfer to speak with her. I finally found her down the hall from my room and told her about my problem.

"Mrs. Urfer, I can't go to the Alhambra. I'm not feeling too well," I said.

"Now what's wrong, Bob?" she asked, giving me a suspicious look.

"I'm sick to my stomach, Mrs. Urfer. I think I've got food poisoning," I lied.

"What did you get food poisoning from, Bob?" she asked, acting unconcerned.

"I think I got it from eating all that olive oil." I began making regurgitating noises until Mrs. Urfer was utterly disgusted by my behavior and attitude.

"Okay. If you are sick, you can stay in your room and stay in bed. I do not want you to leave it for any reason. We will be gone for three hours, and you are to stay in your room the whole time, is that understood, Bob?" she asked, giving me the evil eye.

"Okay. I'm going to my room to lie down now," I replied, returning to my room as Mr. Webber followed me.

Just as I was about to lie down on my bed, Mr. Webber entered my room. "Bob, to make sure you stay in your room, I'm going to lock you in. It's for your own good," he said.

"What happens if there is a fire and I can't get out?" I retorted.

"Well, Bob, that's a chance you'll have to take. Just think, if there is a fire we can say that we had a 'Bob a que'. Get it?" he asked, laughing as he shut and locked my bedroom door.

Hell, I was three floors up, with no rope, ladder, or even a fire exit. There was absolutely no way to get out of that room unless I jumped out of the window to the streets thirty feet below. Once I was locked in, I was totally screwed.

There I was, all dressed up and ready to party and I was locked in a stuffy room with no way out. When I became bored, I could stick my head out the window and watch the people eating at the cafe. There were three or four tables sitting a few feet away from the hotel wall, and if the wind was blowing in the right direction, I could spit and hit one of the customers as they were eating their meal.

What if I have to go to the bathroom? I thought to myself. I couldn't leave the room because the door was locked and the toilet was outside in the hall. What was a poor boy supposed to do in a predicament like that?

For the next few hours, I tried to keep myself occupied so I wouldn't become bored. But it was useless. After an hour or so, I began yelling and screaming for someone to free me from my locked room. But nobody came to help me.

For nearly two hours, I thought up ways to get back at the adults who had put me in this situation, or should I say "predicament." But I couldn't think of anything. I guess my brain wasn't working that well, but my bladder sure was. After thinking so hard, my stomach had become upset, and I had to take a dump—but I had no bathroom to go in. I looked at the sink, then at the shower, then at the sink again, and then at the open window. That's when my idea hit me—if this didn't get their attention and attract someone to my door, nothing would, I thought to myself.

I quickly walked over to the open window, pulled down my tight-fitting blue jeans, and hung my butt over the windowsill for all to see, then proceeded to drop my heavy load to the ground below.

A minute or so later, I heard one person speak, then another, then more and more. I looked directly below and could see six or seven people gathered in a close circle as a waiter pointed a finger at me.

I quickly wiped my butt with the greatest of ease using a sheet of notebook paper and let it fall to the ground.

Just as I was pulling up my blue jeans, I heard a loud thumping sound. Some of the cafe patrons were pounding on my door. Then they began screaming at me.

"Open the door!" shouted the enraged cafe patrons.

"Let's kill the gringo!" shouted another.

"I'm sorry," I shouted. "The door is locked, and I don't have a key to unlock it. You will have to wait for Mrs. Urfer and Mr. Webber to open the door before you can kill this gringo."

The enraged people continued to pound and beat on my door until I thought they would break it down. I was very frightened, but I held my ground and refused to speak to them. After five or ten minutes of yelling and screaming, the angry patrons left. I didn't hear another word about this little episode until our group came back from the Alhambra. Then all hell broke loose.

The group had returned to the hotel about ten o'clock that evening after a delightful show. They had been gone about four hours. The chaperones had returned in a jovial and happy mood—until they found out what had transpired earlier that afternoon.

When I heard the sound of someone inserting a key into my door, I just gritted my teeth and expected the worst. Then, a few seconds later, as I was sitting on the bed as though nothing had happened, the door swung open and Mr. Webber stood in the open doorway for what seemed like hours before he finally spoke up.

"What the hell happened, Bob?" he asked, trying to hold back his anger.

"What do you mean, Mr. Webber?" I asked, acting very innocent.

"These people said that you...you—well...you went to the bathroom out the window and that your feces splashed on some patrons who were eating their meals at the restaurant. I know this can't be true, is it, Bob?" he asked, dumbfounded, while his face turned red with anger and steam began rising from his forehead and ears.

"No, it's not true," I lied. "I told you people that I was sick, but you still locked the door to my room. What was I supposed to do? I had nowhere to go to the bathroom when I became ill. Was I supposed to go on the floor...or in the sink or shower?"

When Mr. Webber tried to speak, I wouldn't let him. He didn't know how to react with such a crazy teenager. I just kept on and on, ranting and raving about being locked in. That's when Mrs. Urfer stepped into my room and gave her two cents.

"Bob, that's the last straw," she replied, trying to contain her anger. "We are going to call your father and make him pay to send you back home to America. We've had enough of your tomfoolery."

"You can't do that," I snapped. "It wasn't my fault that I went to the bathroom out my window. You locked me into my room. What else could I do?" I didn't know what else to say but tried my best to get myself out of the trouble that I had gotten myself into.

"Bob, we are going to send you back to the States, even if we have to send you back as baggage," retorted Mrs. Urfer.

"You do what you have to do, and I'll do what I have to do," I told her.

Early the next morning, Mr. Webber was on the phone talking to my father. I overheard him say that he had caught me smoking cigarettes and possibly an illegal substance, although he couldn't prove it. I also overheard him telling my father about my escapade in my bedroom. Then Mr. Webber handed me the telephone giving me that "now you're in trouble" look.

I proceeded to tell my father my side of the story. During the conversation, Mr. Webber overheard me talking about the Detroit riots. Our families lived in the same neighborhood, and he was very worried about his wife and family. The phone conversation suddenly went from talking about my problems to talking about the riots. Mr. Webber grabbed the phone out of my hand and began talking to my father about the trouble in Detroit.

After talking about the riots for more than ten minutes, the conversation suddenly shifted again to my problems. But within a few minutes, my father had straightened out the misunderstanding. He had told Mr. Webber that I was their problem for the rest of the summer, and if they wanted to send me back home, they would have to pay for the airfare. That's the way their conversation ended.

Mrs. Urfer was so upset when she didn't get her way with my father that she began lecturing me.

"That's what's wrong with these kids today. Their parents lack the responsibility and let their kids run rampant and do as they please," she said, speaking to nobody in particular but looking in my direction.

There were only a few weeks left before we headed back to America.

The summer was ending and I, more or less, had stayed out of trouble since the locked-room incident. The day had finally come when we had to leave the beautiful city of Granada.

I had learned many different things that unforgettable summer, even though my real love, Miss Gibleyou, never came along. But I had quickly forgotten about her once I met Marilyn. I grew up quite fast during those four months.

We had our bags packed and were ready for the long plane ride home.

Marilyn and I continued saying goodbye right up until our plane departed. We couldn't keep our hands off each other, so Mr. Webber stepped between us and broke us up. He even separated us during the flight home and wouldn't allow us to sit together. Marilyn sat at the rear of the plane and I, near the front, a few seats from the chaperones so they could keep an eye on me.

Needless to say, our group arrived at Kennedy Airport without any problems. That is, until I was searched by customs.

Mrs. Urfer, her son, and Mr. Webber all went through ahead of me.

I had completely forgotten about the stuff I had hidden away in my suitcase. Then, within a flash, I remembered. Just at that moment, my knees became weak and I started to sweat profusely because I hadn't taken the pot out of my suitcase and thrown it away. I had also been carrying a small, live lizard in an empty cigarette box and my stiletto knife. I had these objects in my front pants pocket. This stuff was illegal contraband and so was the pot that was hidden in my chess set. When the customs man opened my suitcase, a putrid, skunky smell filtered out and filled the surrounding area.

"What is that awful smell?" asked the inquisitive customs man. "Didn't you wash your dirty underwear?"

"My cologne must have spilled out all over my clothes," I lied, looking deeply into his eyes.

This young and inexperienced customs man just looked at me suspiciously and slammed my suitcase shut. I smiled and thought I was home free, but then he reached across the counter and felt my pants pockets. Now I was worried that the customs man would find the knife or lizard and bust me for that. Then he would have a good reason to search my suitcase more thoroughly and was sure to find the pot. I was beginning to worry, so I called out to Mrs. Urfer.

"Mrs. Urfer, this guy is hassling me," I whined, as she stood ten feet in front of me, having gone through customs already.

"I'm not responsible for you anymore, Bob. From now on, you are on your own," she replied, as a big grin came upon her face.

She didn't want anything to do with me. Any trouble I had gotten myself into I would have to get out of on my own.

"Take all the stuff out of your pants pockets," ordered the young customs man.

"I don't know why you are doing this to me."

I slowly reached into my right front pants pocket and pulled out my cigarette box, which contained my live and illegal lizard. I held it out in front of me and showed it to him.

"What's that?" asked the customs man.

"It's just a pack of cigarettes. We are allowed to smoke cigarettes, aren't we?" I asked him sarcastically.

The customs man again reached over the counter and felt the big bulge in my right front pants pocket.

"What is that?" he asked, impatiently tearing at my pants pocket, trying to find my contraband. "Take it out!"

I put my cigarette pack into my shirt pocket and slowly pulled out my stiletto knife, holding it out in front of me, so he could get a good look at it.

"Let me have it," ordered the customs man.

"No. It's mine," I replied, not letting him handle it.

"These types of knives are illegal. So I will have to break the blade and dispose of it. This is considered a weapon," he explained rather politely.

But I didn't want to hear his excuses. I'd bought it, and I didn't want to give it up for any reason.

"Give me the three dollars that I paid for it. I didn't know this type of knife was illegal in America, so I should be reimbursed for it."

However, the young, inexperienced customs man wasn't buying it.

"Give it to me right now!" he shouted, becoming very impatient with me.

"No, give me the money I paid for it," I retorted, being very obstinate.

"Give it to me right now or I'll let the police take you to jail, then they'll take it from you," snapped the customs man.

When I still refused to give it to him, he became even more upset and angry.

"I'm only going to tell you once more. Give me the knife right now or I'll send you to Queens County jail. They have a way with smart-ass teenagers who break the law. Well, what's it going to be, me or jail?" he said, his body shaking with anger as he waited for me to hand over the knife.

"Here, take it. I hope you cut your fingers off," I replied, angrily slapping the knife into his outstretched hand.

Whew, I thought to myself. Thank God, he didn't find the stash that I had hidden in my suitcase. That day I was very, very lucky.

When I finally arrived back home and had taken everything out of my suitcase, I remembered my chess set. I opened the chessboard and grabbed the contraband from within.

I weighed the stuff that Ramone had sold me for five dollars and was surprised to learn that the pot weighed over two pounds. I wasn't sure what to do with it, but then my friends told me how they had tried pot over the summer. One suggested I sell some of it to them. And that's exactly what I did.

My friend helped me break the big bag of pot into forty smaller bags. We had filled forty sandwich bags with nearly an ounce each. When I finished selling them, I had more than five hundred dollars in my pocket from that five-dollar purchase in Spain. That's when I decided to go into business for myself.

Ramone thought that he had gotten the last laugh. He was wrong—I did.

That was my summer with World Academy. It was a crazy time in my life that I will never forget. And I'll talk about it for years to come.

CHAPTER 2
MOROCCAN DELIGHT

Well, here we go again. It was nearing the end of 1969, and I was getting ready to hop on another Pan Am jet. This time it was heading for Rabat, Morocco, instead of Madrid, Spain.

Boy, things had really changed in my personality since the days of my World Academy expedition. My curly, fuzzy hair had grown down past my shoulders. I was now an anti-war activist and believed the Vietnam War to be a political and illegal war. I refused to have anything to do with the military regime.

My outlook on life since my World Academy days had changed, due to the different people with whom I had met and talked. If my parents had known in the summer of 1967 that I would return from Spain as a longhaired hippie radical, they would never have let me travel overseas in the first place.

Here I was, getting ready for my next adventure to Morocco.

I was very worried that customs at Rabat Airport might send me back to America. It was rumored that they weren't letting longhaired hippies into their country.

However, I had made a commitment to my beautiful mother that if I would get my hair cut short, she would purchase my round-trip plane ticket to any country in the world.

I had consulted with some of my new friends—whom I had met while selling them some of my Spanish pot—about this project, and after long conversations with them, I chose Morocco.

One of my main reasons for going there was to purchase illegal contraband. My new friends told me that it was possible to purchase large amounts and many different types of hashish from around the world. I was told that hashish was legal in Morocco and much of it was imported from other countries, such as Lebanon, Nepal, Afghanistan, India, Pakistan, and many others; Morocco also had their own brand of hashish.

I was told hashish and opium could be bought in government-controlled shops or in the bazaars. The way my friends talked, the stuff could be purchased from one of these small shops, and I would be able to pick out ten or twenty different types of hashish from all over the world.

I was hoping that I could send the stuff back to America, the same way I had done it two years before. I had thought about sending it through the mail system also. I was very naive in those days.

It was a cold January day in Michigan, and I wanted to be anywhere else but my hometown. The day had finally come when I was to depart for Morocco. First, I had to fly to New York to catch the flight to Rabat. Once I arrived at Kennedy Airport, I boarded a Pan Am jet for a ten-hour plane ride.

When I arrived at the Rabat Airport, it was nearly two o'clock in the morning. I was very nervous as I walked over to the customs counter with my luggage, waiting for the customs official to search it for any contraband or pornography that was illegal in their country.

I handed the customs officer my passport. He gave me a suspicious look as he looked at my passport photo. He had me turn around so he could check out the length of my hair. Before I had disembarked the plane, I had watered it down and combed it behind my ears to make it look shorter than it actually was. He eyed my long hair with disdain and suspicion.

"Why do you want to visit Morocco?" asked the customs man.

I just shrugged my shoulders and then blurted out my answer. "I'm just a tourist on a short vacation," I replied, as my body began to shake uncontrollably.

I thought for sure that he would send me back to America. Instead, he pointed toward the doors. "Welcome to Morocco. We are your servants," he said.

Boy, was I surprised and very happy. I quickly grabbed my suitcase and walked toward the doors into the warm, January night air. I wanted to rent a taxi, but at this time of night, there was only one taxi available and it already held seven passengers. The cab driver waved to me, so I crammed into the taxi also. Then we zoomed into the dark night.

Wow, this country was beautiful. There were millions of stars in the night sky, shining in the pale moonlight. I had to pinch myself to make sure I wasn't dreaming.

Nearly two hours later, we arrived at a very expensive hotel.

What I mean by expensive was five dollars per night, which also included a continental breakfast. I figured I would stay at this hotel for one night and then find a much cheaper hotel. I had very little spending money. I had saved what money I had for the purchase of the hashish.

This country, from what little I'd seen, seemed completely different from Spain. I had to stay in a group in Spain. Here, in Morocco, I was on my own. I knew very little about the country, other than what I had been told by my new friends and what I had read in books and magazines like *National Geographic.*

I would soon find out that my friends knew absolutely nothing about this beautiful country. I also had to learn their money system, the language, their customs, and how to budget my money— especially if I wanted to buy hashish. I had to pay for my room and board and any gifts for my parents and friends.

I only had thirty days left before my ticket expired. It would be obsolete after that period of time. My mother had bought me an excursion-type ticket. This meant I had to arrive and depart on a specific time and date. I had to stay at least twenty-nine days and no more than thirty. I had to depart on the exact time and date the ticket specified, or I would have to purchase a new ticket. I never really thought about that though.

As I was riding the elevator to my hotel room, I asked the operator a few simple questions.

"Do you know where I can buy some hashish?"

He didn't quite understand me, so I had to use sign language. With one hand I was pretending to smoke a pipe and with the other hand, I made circling motions, pointing to my head, while rolling my eyes, acting as if I were drunk and sleepy. That did it. Now he understood what I wanted.

"Hashish," said the elevator operator, as a big smile came upon his face.

"Yes!" I shouted with glee.

He followed me into my hotel room and placed my suitcase on the bed. He stood with his hand outstretched waiting for a tip, or so I thought. I gave him a one-dinar tip, to which he shook his head no. I put two more dinars in his hand, which added up to fifty cents in American money. But this time, he kept saying one word.

"Chars. Chars," he said, pointing to the money in his hand.

"That's when it hit me—he wanted money for the hashish. I didn't really want to give him the money, unless he gave me the hashish at the same time. But I wanted it so badly I was willing to trust him and take the chance—that is, if it didn't cost me an arm and a leg.

I quickly counted out thirty-dinars and held it in my outstretched hand. I let him pick out the amount of money he needed to buy the hashish. Even though we couldn't converse in one particular language, I was fairly certain he knew what I wanted to buy.

I was hoping I wouldn't get ripped off, so I let him take twenty dinars. That was equal to about two American dollars. Two dollars doesn't sound like much money, but by the time this excursion trip would be over, two dollars would be as hard to get as two million. My newfound friend took the money and left the room. I still worried about getting ripped off.

I had a little time to kill before my friend would return, so I decided to take a shower. Just as I had finished my shower, there was a loud knock on my hotel door. When I opened it, I was surprised to see the elevator man standing there. He had a very big grin on his face that showed every tooth in his mouth—all five of them.

As he walked into the room, speaking Arabic, all I could understand was, "Meester, Meester." But when he reached into his shirt pocket, he brought out a round, sweet-smelling, marble-sized black chunk of hashish. It weighed about four grams. I grabbed the piece of hashish to smell it and look at it more closely. I was very happy with my purchase. In fact, I was so happy that I immediately pulled out ten more dinars and handed the money to my new friend. I thanked him and told him that I would see him tomorrow to buy some more. I hoped he understood me. He just smiled that toothless grin and closed the door behind him, heading for the elevator.

The second he departed and exited my hotel room, I started jumping and dancing around the room with joy. I was ecstatic over my purchase. I never knew it could be so easy. Within an hour of arriving in Rabat, I had scored. I hoped this was an omen of good things to come in the days and weeks that lay ahead.

After a few minutes, I quieted down and began making a small pipe out of the paper tube of a coat hanger, and for the screen, I used a small piece of aluminum foil from my gum wrapper. When that was complete, I crumpled up a few pieces of hash and put it into the bowl of my homemade pipe. Then I lit the hashish and took a few deep puffs. After each toke, I coughed my brains out. But after two good tokes, I had to put the pipe down. That was enough. This hash was excellent. I was as high as I wanted to get. In fact, I was super stoned. I was so relaxed that I had fallen asleep within minutes on just two puffs, dreaming about the adventures that lay ahead.

The next morning I woke up very early. I thought I had only paid for one night at the hotel, so I set out to find a much cheaper hotel elsewhere. I wanted to save as much money as possible so I could buy the hashish.

I had less than two-hundred dollars to spend, so I had to be very conservative with it, because my excursion fare plane ticket couldn't be used for another four weeks.

So I packed my bags and hopped a taxi to the other side of town to find a much cheaper hotel. I found a small, dingy hotel that was ninety percent cheaper than my last hotel. It only cost me one dollar a day, instead of five.

However, a few days later, I met some of the people with whom I had ridden from the airport to the hotel, and they told me that I had paid for two days, not just one. I guess we had arrived so late that the manager had allowed us two days instead of one. But I was still satisfied with my new surroundings.

I had found a decent, clean hotel room. Besides having a big, soft mattress, the room was equipped with a bathtub that was as big and deep as a Jacuzzi. The tub was three feet deep and four feet square. When it was full of water, you could practically swim in it. The room was on the second floor with a balcony that overlooked the city.

I quickly cleaned up, unpacked my bag, and left the room to find my new Moroccan friend, the elevator man. I wanted to purchase some more of that potent black hash. I had hoped that he could help me toward this endeavor or know someone who could.

The city of Rabat was much bigger than I had expected.

My hotel was in the "new city." Directly north of my hotel, up in the foothills, was the "old city" of Rabat. Remaining intact for thousands of years, it had been completely and totally unchanged from western civilization. The people lived in small mud and straw huts. I had been warned by other Moroccans not to go into that village. Supposedly, it was filled with thieves and murderers who would sooner cut your throat than to look at you.

I finally reached the hotel I had stayed at the night before. I asked the receptionist if the elevator man was around. But as luck would have it, it was his day off.

That was my luck, always bad. I asked a few other hotel workers if they knew where I could buy some hashish. Most of them ignored me; others gave me dirty looks, and some even spit on me and told me to leave their country. However, that didn't stop me from accomplishing my goal. I wanted to find some more hashish, so I decided to ask my taxi driver where I could find some.

"Go to the old city, but be very careful," said the taxi driver.

"Why is that?" I asked.

"It isn't safe to go there alone. And you must leave before the sun goes down," he warned.

I laughed at his threats. Hell, I was nearly nineteen years old. Nobody was going to scare me away. I had come too far to leave empty handed. I would almost risk life and limb to buy a few pounds of hashish.

My friends back home had told me that I could go to the main bazaar and buy any kind of hash from around the world. I took this as the gospel truth. Young and naive, that was me. I soon found out it wasn't as easy as everyone back home had said it would be.

After asking several taxi drivers to take me to the old city, I finally hired one, but it had cost me three times the normal rate. I had to pay a total of six dollars. I was depleting my savings faster than I had expected. Reluctantly, I paid the fare. Within fifteen minutes, I was walking around the old city of Rabat. This was where the Moroccan government had kept its lower caste of people—the poor, the sickly, the discarded, and the homeless: the ones nobody wanted.

I saw open raw sewage running down the center of Main Street, and the public bathrooms drained into the open streets. The small children played not only near it but also in it.

As I walked along the road, a small crowd started gathering. They followed along behind me. The small children came up to me and asked for money. One kid even started to eat a handful of urine-soaked dirt he had just scooped up off the ground. He kept holding out his hand for money, like it was a trick he was doing for me. I immediately handed him a few Moroccan coins. That was a big mistake. Once I gave one kid money, all of the kids wanted some.

Luckily, one of the storeowners came out and chased most of the crowd away.

Before they could all run away, I asked if they knew where I could buy some hashish. They didn't understand right away, so I used my sign language technique again. Pointing my finger to the side of my head, I began rotating it in small circles, while trying to look and act drunk, and with my other hand I pretended to smoke a pipe. I hoped one of the kids would understand my primitive hand signals.

Somehow, I got through to one of the boys. He suddenly grabbed my hand and walked with me for about one block to a small, mud hut with a dirt floor. He sat me in one corner of this small, dark, and dirty, foul-smelling room. Then he walked out, leaving me alone.

Evil thoughts were running rampant through my mind. Thoughts of murder and robbery were just a few. I was just about to leave when two funny-looking men in tattered rags called clothing walked through the door. I nearly broke out laughing when they both smiled at me. Their toothless grins were too much to bear. Neither one had more than five or six teeth in their mouths. Somehow, I was able to control myself. They were still worthy of my respect. However, neither could understand nor speak English. I had to use my primitive sign language techniques once again. I explained to the two men exactly what I wanted. I thought I had finally gotten through to them.

Soon there were three and then four men in the room. Before long, the small, dark room was packed full. I had become their guest of honor. We spoke in English, Arabic, and sign language. Within a few minutes, a small boy walked into the room and pulled out a small bag of "kef" (pronounced "keef") from his shirt pocket. Kef was similar to marijuana, not at all like hashish. However, I didn't know too much about hashish at that time in my life. So I watched as one of the toothless Arabs started making me hashish, or so I thought. But when I saw him adding nuts, flour, and other ingredients, I was flabbergasted. I didn't know what they were making. One hour of baking and it was finished. It ended up as a cake.

They had me taste a morsel of it, and it tasted terrible. They seemed to enjoy it, but I hated it. This plan didn't work out too well for me.

Now it was getting late in the day and the sky had already turned dark. I started getting paranoid and frightened. I felt very uncomfortable.

When I started to leave, an argument ensued between the two toothless men. It seemed one of them didn't make any money on the deal, and he wanted to take it out on me. However, another man jumped up to hold his friend back, so I grabbed the cake and ran outside to a taxi.

Finally, back at my new hotel room, I still had a little of that black hash left. A few tokes of that, and I'd fall asleep right away.

As I puffed away on my homemade hash pipe, I remembered

that one of the men in the old city had mentioned the city of Marrakesh. He said that I could find lots of hashish there. That's also what my friends in America had told me.

But I had yet to see, as my American friends had told me, the bazaar that sold hashish from all over the world. That was a pure fantasy. I had also found out that hashish wasn't legal in Morocco either. Boy, did I have lots to learn.

I relaxed and continued to smoke my black, sweet-tasting hashish, using my homemade pipe. Within a few puffs, I was fast asleep, dreaming about the train ride to Marrakesh. The singing of the song "Marrakesh Express" by Crosby, Stills, and Nash rang through my head as I drifted off to sleep.

The January weather in Morocco was perfect. Every day was clear blue skies without a dark rain cloud in sight. At night, the sky was aglow with millions of twinkling diamonds—it astounded me. I wondered why it looked so different here than in America. The stars seemed much closer together on this side of the planet.

After the dismal results from my excursion trip to the old city, I decided to head for Marrakesh and try my luck there. So the next morning I packed my bags, including the kef cake, and hopped a cab to the train station.

I purchased my ticket and noticed I was already very short on funds. I thought two-hundred dollars would be plenty of money for my trip. But things cost more than I had expected. In many ways, it was just as expensive as America. I had read in a magazine that you could live in Morocco on less than a dollar a day. I guess that would have been true if I had lived in a tent and ate one meal of rice a day.

Now, I was riding the "Marrakesh Express." I forgot about my money troubles by watching the beautiful scenery from the train window. The sky was as blue as the ocean's waves that washed onto the sandy white beaches. We followed the ocean's coastline all the way to Marrakesh. A few times, we passed villages that were thousands of years old.

Sometimes, we would see kids who lived near the tracks trying to get our attention. They would hoot, holler, and wave at us. We thought the kids were cute and funny until we heard a loud "crash" and "thud." One of the train windows had shattered just a few feet from my seat, so I jumped up and stood in the aisle. That's when I noticed that an older lady, a tourist from Europe, had been struck in the side of the face by the flying rock that had been thrown by one of the kids standing near the tracks. These kids waited and hoped that the train would stop so they could beg for money. When the train didn't stop or even slow down, they threw more rocks.

The porter came by and apologized to everyone for the incident, including the woman who had been injured.

A doctor on board quickly bandaged the old woman's injury.

As I turned to return to my seat, I bumped into another tourist, a beautiful young woman. We exchanged names and began a long conversation. She told me her name was Pat and many interesting things about how she had been touring Morocco with two guys from California. Just at that moment, the two guys she had been traveling with sat in the seat across from us. We exchanged pleasantries, and then Pat introduced them to me. Their names were Jim and Pete. Pete was the taller of the two, but Jim seemed to be the one in charge of their small group. They were going to Marrakesh for the same reason that I was. They were in Morocco to do a big hash deal. All of us wanted to find the hash fields.

I still had a little of that black hashish left, so I offered to share it with them. When they accepted to smoke it with me, we went to the train's lavatory. As the train rocked back and forth, I began putting a few small chunks of hash into my handmade pipe.

As I filled the bowl, Pat reached out and her hand hit my crotch. She seemed to be holding onto me to catch her balance, or so I thought. I acted as if I hadn't noticed what she had done and proceeded to show Jim and Pete the type of hash I had. Within five minutes, the hash went up in smoke.

We returned to our seats and fell asleep for the last leg of our long journey. Finally, we had reached the Marrakesh train station. We agreed that I would tag along with my new friends. So we rented a taxi and headed for the center of town.

I was sitting in the front seat with the driver and Jim, Pete, and Pat were sitting in the rear seat. When I turned to speak with Jim, I noticed Pat was giving him a blowjob. I couldn't believe my eyes. I couldn't believe what I was seeing. Now I wondered if Pat had grabbed my crotch by accident or if she had been "sizing me up" when we were smoking the hash on the train. I was definitely keeping an eye on her.

Our taxi arrived at the hotel in the center of the city. This area was known for its hippie hangouts. We rented rooms at the "French" hotel. They got a room, and I had one all to myself.

As we walked up the stairs to our rooms, we passed a small, thin, curly haired hippie who looked very similar to Bob Dylan. Pat and I looked at each other in utter amazement.

"Nah," said all four of us in unison, as we shook our heads in disbelief and continued to our rooms.

After I put my baggage in my room, I started toward Jim, Pete, and Pat's room. However, out in the hallway, a pretty redheaded female suddenly distracted me. We said "hello" and she invited me to her room, which was on the roof of the hotel.

"What's your name?" I asked this beautiful, redheaded, European female.

"Rachael. I am from France," she said, as we walked to her room. "What's your name?"

"Bob. I'm from America," I said. "Rachael, do you know where I can buy some good hash?"

"I might," she replied.

When we entered her room, there was another girl sitting in a chair with a guy. I guess it was her boyfriend. The girl's name was Louisa. She spoke fairly decent English, much better than Rachael. So I could understand her, and she could understand me.

"What are you doing in Marrakesh?" asked Rachael.

"I'm looking to buy some good hash," I told her.

"How long have you been in Morocco?" asked Rachael.

"I stayed in Rabat for nearly a week before I traveled to Marrakesh, and I haven't had very good luck in finding my product."

"That's because the hash comes in at Tangier and Tetrahn, not Rabat or Marrakesh," explained Louisa.

They explained to me how they had just traveled all the way from Tangier and were low on funds. They needed money, badly, so they offered to sell me an ounce of their sweet-smelling blonde, Lebanese hash. Finally, I had found what I had come for. However, they wanted thirty dollars for the ounce. It was much more than I had expected to spend for the hash. I thought I could buy a kilo of hashish for the price that they were asking. But it was too good to turn down. I wanted it, so I bought it.

I had mentioned to Rachael about the stuff I had bought in the old city of Rabat. I told her how I thought I was buying hashish, but it turned out to be a big blob of crap.

I left the room to retrieve the stuff to show Rachael. I wanted to see if she knew what the stuff was. When I returned to the room, I showed Rachael and Louisa the stuff that had been made for me. Rachael looked at it and tasted it. She knew right away what it was. She called it "kef" cake. It was a marijuana cake that tasted like nutty, buttery dirt. I asked Rachael if she wanted it, and she gladly accepted. I was glad to get rid of it. I was anxious to show Pat, Pete, and Jim my score, so I politely excused myself from my new friend's presence.

"Rachael, will I see you tomorrow?" I asked, as I walked to the door.

"We are going back up north, now that we have some money," she said.

"Where are you going?" I asked.

"Well, thirty dollars should get us to Italy, if not all the way to France," said Rachael.

"Do you want to sell some more hash?" I asked.

"No, I'm sorry. We only have enough left for the trip," said Rachael.

We said goodbye, then I left their room and headed directly to Pat's room. I was very anxious to show them my find.

"Come in," said a female voice.

I opened the door, only to see a naked Pat straddling Jim's naked body. Pat was riding him like a wild nymphomaniac. Her large naked breasts and hips were bouncing wildly. They continued "balling" as I walked into the room and shut the door behind me. They didn't seem to mind my presence. Hell, they hadn't noticed me at all.

There were two double beds in their small, damp, and mildew-smelling bedroom. Jim and Pat were wildly making love in one, and Pete was enjoying a cigarette in the other. He was under the sheet. I figured he must have just finished balling Pat and now it was Jim's turn. I tried not to notice what they were doing. They sure didn't notice what I was doing.

"Do you guys want to get high?" I asked, as I held out my ounce of newly purchased hash. Pat and Jim reluctantly stopped their lovemaking and looked at my prize.

Jim left the room and headed for the bathroom. Pat lay naked on the bed, playing with herself.

"Do you want some head?" asked Pat, as she seductively fingered her snatch.

I was embarrassed by her actions, so I acted as though I hadn't heard her.

"She wants to know if you want a blowjob," interjected Pete.

Again, I acted as if I hadn't heard the question. But Pete wouldn't let up and asked again.

"Do you want your dick sucked? Pat sucks a really mean dick," he said, with a big grin on his face.

As he said this, Pat looked at me and began sucking on the finger that she just had in her snatch.

"Well, do you want me to suck you off?" purred Pat, as she continued to play with her snatch.

"Sure," I mumbled, as I walked over to her and sat on the bed.

She began unbuckling my pants while Jim was still in the bathroom and Pete was relaxing in the other bed. But just as she got my pants down and was about to suck me off, Jim came out of the bathroom and shouted to us, "Get dressed. We're going to celebrate our arrival in Marrakesh. Let's go out to the madina."

"What's the madina?" I asked.

"That's the center of town. We're going to the madina and party!" shouted Jim.

So with that, I zipped up my pants and waited while Pat and Pete dressed. Then we went out into the Moroccan night air.

We walked to the center of town where everything was going on and watched as the street vendors were selling and hawking their wares, from bread to carpets—but still no hashish, only kef.

So we visited a restaurant where long tables were packed with long-haired hippies, deep in a cloud of kef and opium smoke. Many were smoking thin, long opium pipes filled with the evil drug. However, most were smoking kef and passed chillums full of it or tobacco mixed with hash.

"Boom Shankar, chillum," chanted the hippies, before they smoked it.

They passed the chillum to me. As I curled my hands around the thin stem of the bull's horn, I wrapped a wet piece of cloth around the stem to cool the smoke as it passed into the lungs. This makes it easier on the throat, so the person smoking the drug doesn't cough too much and become sick. I inhaled deeply. With one big puff, I began to cough and cough as I disappeared behind the big cloud of kef smoke.

My head began spinning, and the room seemed to glow in all different colors. I coughed so much, I wanted to go into a corner and die. Boy, smoking out of a chillum was a totally new experience for me and my three new friends. This was how the people smoked their hashish in Asia and especially India. But it was more of a religious ceremony with the Hindu people.

We asked some of the hippies where we could find some hash to buy, but it wasn't to be. Many of them told us to go to the cities of

Tangier or Tetrahn. Supposedly, the imported hash from the Middle East and Asia came into those two ports, just as Rachael said. However, a few of the hippies told me to try the small villages in the surrounding mountains.

We were soon heading back to the hotel. As we were leaving the restaurant, a small, streetwise Arab boy approached us. He seemed to remind me of someone, but I couldn't put my finger on it at the time.

"Can I do anything for you?" asked the small boy.

"Get us some hashish," said Jim.

The little Arab boy directed us into a small teashop. We ordered tea while we sat down to relax. This kid couldn't have been more than twelve years old, but he had the street smarts of a twenty-year-old, and he spoke fairly good English.

"Where can we buy a large quantity of hashish?" asked Pete, as I looked around to see if there were any cops in the building.

"Go to a small village in the mountains, where they grow the crops," said the small but wise Arab boy.

As the kid began explaining which village to go to, I was startled to see him fondling Pat's breasts and snatch—and she let him do it. Then he asked us a funny question.

"Who do I look like?" He turned his face to one side and then the other to show off his profile.

He looked just like Sammy Davis Jr. But before I could say it, he shouted, "Sammy Davis Jr.!" We all laughed.

It was getting late, so we returned to the hotel. We wanted to get up early so we could rent a car and drive up into the mountains to see if we could find the treasure we so dearly hunted for.

As we climbed the staircase to our rooms, the guy who had passed us on the stairs earlier was going down the stairs once again. Each time he was surrounded by two or three beautiful blonde bombshells. Pat, Pete, Jim, and I stopped and stared, then shook our heads in disbelief. We were sure the guy was Bob Dylan.

I said goodnight to my new friends and went alone to my musty, damp room. I stuck a few small tabs of blonde Lebanese hashish into my homemade pipe and then lit it. After two good tokes, I drifted off into a deep, blissful sleep, yearning for the morning.

All four of us were up before dawn so we could get an early start to the mountains.

I was getting very low on funds. I checked my money and noticed I only had about forty-five dollars left out of nearly two-hundred.

I figured there would be four of us to split the car rental four ways. Boy was I mistaken. I let Pete handle the paperwork with the rental agent. When he asked me for my driver's license and twenty dollars, I handed him both items without asking any questions. I didn't want them to know that I was really broke. I found out later that I had paid half of the car rental instead of a quarter of it.

I wanted to drive the car because they had used my driver's license, and I was responsible for the vehicle. But the car was a French-built Renault with the gearshift on the dashboard. After ten minutes of stopping, stalling, and grinding the gears, I gave up. I had never driven a stick shift, let alone one with the gearshift on the dashboard. So I let Pete try his hand at it. He handled the car much better than I did.

After three times around the median fountain, we were ready for our mountainous excursion. We drove for almost four hours before we came to a small village. Men in military uniforms greeted us.

"Do you know where we can buy some hashish?" I asked the soldier.

By using sign language and broken English, we were able to communicate with the soldiers. But halfway through our conversation, we realized this wasn't a very good idea. Suddenly we thought about jail. The soldiers were giving us the evil eye, as though they wanted to lock us up and throwaway the key, so we decided to give up our search and head back to Marrakesh empty handed.

As Pete and I were watching the beautiful scenery, Jim and Pat were in the back seat, fondling each other. Squeals of ecstasy filled the car as we continued our long drive on this winding, narrow mountain road.

Finally, we were back in the city. What a long day of driving and nothing to show for it. We returned the car around dusk.

We decided to leave Marrakesh. I had to return to Rabat very soon or my plane ticket would expire. My money was almost depleted, and I had just enough left to purchase a train ticket for my return to Rabat with a few dollars left over for a cheap hotel room, food, and a few gifts. I had less than five days left on my excursion ticket before I had to return to America.

Jim, Pete, and Pat wanted to try their luck at the eastern city of Fez. One of the hippies had told us that was where the hash was and that it was practically legal there. But that's the same thing I had been told by my friends in America. Anyway, I didn't have the time or money to make both trips. I had to return to Rabat.

We returned to the hotel and decided to go up on the roof, where there was a small restaurant, to order our dinner before we retired for the evening. As we climbed the staircase to the roof, we could hear an acoustic guitar playing and a beautiful, deep voice singing. As we quietly walked to a table, we noticed that the guy singing and playing the guitar was the same guy who had passed by us before, always chaperoned by two gorgeous, blonde-haired goddesses.

We had asked another couple who were eating dinner if the man singing was who we thought it was. They confirmed our opinion that the man playing the acoustic guitar and singing in a rich, deep voice was none other than Bob Dylan. He had been in Morocco on a short vacation, relaxing after a motorcycle injury a few years before, and was there entertaining a few of his close friends. Here was Bob Dylan singing four songs without a microphone.

This had been the highlight of my trip so far. I wanted to ask him for his autograph, but I was too shy and embarrassed. My only wish right then was to have a camera to take his picture.

We finished our dinner and returned to our separate rooms. Once again, I filled my pipe with the only hashish I had been able to score in Marrakesh. I would surely run out within the next few days. But I was only concerned with tonight. After a few good tokes, I drifted off to sleep thinking how lucky I had been to see a great performer and my idol, Bob Dylan, singing for eight or ten people, halfway around the world.

Around 7a.m., I was suddenly awakened by a loud knock on my door. When I opened it, I was surprised to see Pat standing there. She strolled into my room and sat on the edge of my bed.

"I want to finish something I started a few days ago, but was interrupted," purred Pat, as she seductively pulled down my underwear and gave me a great blowjob.

What a way to start the day, I thought to myself. When she completed her task, she thanked me and I did likewise. Then we proceeded to Pat's room to awaken Pete and Jim.

Within ten minutes, we were heading for the train station, even though we were headed to two different cities. We wouldn't part company for another few hours until we reached the famous city of Casa Blanca.

The train ride went along smoothly. Within four hours, we were at the city Humphrey Bogart had made so famous, Casa Blanca. We still had about two hours to kill before we had to board our trains to our particular destinations.

As we were leaving the train station to walk around and take in the sights of the city, two seedy little Arab men approached us. They looked like brothers, but one was a foot shorter than the other. They reminded me of Abbott and Costello.

"You want to buy some hashish?" said the tall, dirty Arab.

He showed us a green, rectangular slab wrapped in cellophane. It looked to be about three ounces of green hashish, or so he said. We followed the seedy little men to a seedy little restaurant that seemed to have police officers seated everywhere. Immediately, I pointed this out to my companions. I began feeling paranoid, as did my three friends.

"This is very good hashish. How much you want to buy?" asked the short Arab.

"We're too worried about being set up for a bust," I replied, looking at the men very suspiciously.

"It's okay. Most of these people are my friends," he said.

We just shrugged our shoulders and proceeded to talk business. But I still had a paranoid feeling about the situation in which we had put ourselves. Especially with the number of police that were in the restaurant.

"Let me see the packet of hash," I said.

When he handed me the cellophane packet, I opened it and smelled its contents.

"This stuff isn't any good," I said, as I looked at Pete and Jim. "I don't even think this stuff is hashish." I held it up so they could smell the green stuff.

I gave the Arab his green hash, then showed him the small piece of blonde Lebanese hashish that I had.

"This is the kind of hashish we want," I said, as I handed the little chunk to the man.

He reached out and grabbed it from my outstretched hand, then held it under his nose and smelled it. Then he put it into his shirt pocket and acted as though I didn't notice what he had just done. When he turned to talk to Jim, I interrupted them.

"Can I have my piece of hashish back, please?" I asked the short Arab, staring him directly in his brown eyes.

The short and seedy Arab man played dumb. He acted as though he hadn't understood a word I had said. So I reached over the table into his shirt pocket and pulled out my little piece of hash. It was only a couple of grams, but that's all I had. I made sure I got it back.

The man started yelling at me, but Jim calmed him down by talking business again. Jim made a deal with him for twenty pounds of this so-called hashish. We walked to a small mud hut a few blocks away, where he weighed out the proper amount. Jim counted out five-thousand American dollars, and then handed it to that shady little character.

"I'm telling you, Jim, don't buy it," I pleaded.

"Why not?" asked Jim.

"It's no damn good. I'm telling you. I don't think it's even ha-shish," I opined, shaking my head in disgust.

But Jim wouldn't listen.

"I have lots of money, so I'm not worried. Plus, I don't want to go back home empty-handed," Jim retorted.

Here I was, nearly broke, and they had thousands of dollars. But yet, I had to pay for half of the rental car. So now, I was actually happy they were getting ripped off by purchasing this crap. Jim even gave me four packets because I refused to buy any. I knew it wasn't any good, but I took it anyway, thinking that maybe I was just too high from my hash and maybe this stuff was good after all.

Once the business was finished, we headed back to the train station. This was where we split up. Jim, Pete, and Pat were going to Fez to find their motherload, and I was heading back to Rabat, then to America to find my mother. We said goodbye and shook hands. Pat kissed me, then grabbed my crotch and gave it a yank.

"Keep it hard," she said, as we departed and boarded our separate trains.

I figured I had just enough money to live on for maybe four days. My return plane ticket to America would expire in nearly three days. Once I had paid my hotel bill, I hoped to have enough money left over to send the four packets of so-called hash that Jim had given me to America.

I relaxed back in my seat and listened to the sound of the moving train until I had fallen fast asleep. But before I knew it, I had arrived at the train station in Rabat.

I found a cheap hotel to stay at for the few days that remained on my excursion trip. I had just enough money to pay the hotel bill, buy a few gifts for family members, and send the stuff Jim had given me to America. I also needed to buy something to hide the green stuff in.

But I had to be careful. A couple of Canadian hippies told me that Moroccan customs would open any package sent to America.

I put my bags in my room and walked to a nearby bazaar. With very little money to spend, I had to be very thrifty.

I found the gifts I needed within an hour or so. I bought a beautiful sheepskin, a couple of handmade silver and copper vases, plus a couple of miniature rectangular leather trunks with a curved top. They were very small, approximately three inches wide by five inches long by three inches high. The boxes were exactly the right size to hide the green slabs of the so-called hashish that Jim had given me.

When I was completely finished with my shopping, I walked back to my hotel room. The minute I entered the room, I began fitting the green slabs into the bottom of the leather boxes. Then I packaged them into cardboard boxes. After sealing the boxes, I had a hotel clerk take my two packages to the post office and mail them to the addresses printed on the outside of the packages. I also gave him a few extra dinars for a tip, plus enough money to cover the postage costs.

He was happy to do me the favor. I shut the door and lay on the bed to relax and think about my future. Heck, I thought it would be difficult to send contraband through the mail system, but so far it had gone quite easily. I figured I had found a new way to smuggle hashish into America.

However, ten minutes later, my dream had turned into a nightmare. My daydreaming had been interrupted by a loud knock on my door. When I opened it, I was surprised to see the hotel clerk standing there, holding my packages.

"What's wrong?" I asked the clerk.

"The customs man said that you have to bring the parcels to the post office yourself."

He apologized, handed the packages to me, and then turned and walked away.

Now I'm in deep shit, I thought to myself. Just then, the two Canadian tourists I had talked with before stopped by my room.

"How are you guys doing today?" I asked.

"We overheard your conversation about sending parcels to America. That way is no good," said the Canadian hippie.

"Why not?" I asked.

"It's too easy to get busted. I told you before; Canada is the way to go. Canada has no customs check. The American government pays the Moroccan government, in hard American currency, to check and open any parcels that are being sent to America. They open the parcels right in front of you, so if they find any contraband you go directly to jail and nobody will be able to help you out of that situation," he replied.

"Thanks for telling me. I'll do as you suggest." We shook hands then the two Canadian hippies continued on their merry way.

So I changed the American address on the packages to a Canadian address. However, the only address in Canada I knew of was to the post office in Windsor. It was just a hop, skip, and a jump from Detroit, Michigan. But I had just enough money to send these packages and not much left over for anything else. Now that I had changed the addresses on the two parcels, I grabbed them and headed for the Rabat post office.

As I entered the post office, I noticed a big commotion in the far corner of the large room. Two longhaired hippies were being handcuffed. There were a couple of ripped-up packages on the floor near their feet with about twenty pounds of kef protruding from the ripped parcels.

I had overheard the customs officers asking the two hippies many questions. They were German citizens, trying to send their parcels to Frankfurt. However, it seemed the American government also paid the Moroccan government to search any parcels destined for Germany to help in their war on drugs. The American government didn't like the idea of the U.S. military personnel getting stoned on illegal drugs.

When the customs men found illegal contraband in any parcel that they searched, they kept it and then sold it back to the dope dealers. This way, they had an incentive to search the parcels. When I saw what had happened to these two German citizens, I became very nervous and felt like walking out of there. But it was too late. Now I couldn't turn back.

I slowly placed the two packages on the old beat-up table in front of the customs officer. He just kept staring at me, looking right through me. I couldn't move. It was as if I had been turned into stone. I just knew I was going to end up like those two German hippies who had just left handcuffed and crying. I was sure the customs man was thinking that he had another doper to haul off to jail.

He finally turned the parcels toward his face and read-the address. His ugly face turned a beet red. He gave me a hideous, dirty look as though I had spoiled his day. Then he asked for six dollars for postage. I only had a total of eight dollars left to my name. I wanted to get out of that post office as quickly as possible, so I counted out the correct amount of money and handed it to him. He picked up my parcels and tossed them onto a large pile of outgoing mail.

I turned and walked out of the building as fast as I could without drawing suspicion to myself. Finally, something had gone right for a change.

I nearly crapped my pants when I saw the two German hippies being arrested. I thought I was also going to end up handcuffed and jailed. So to say the least, I was very happy as I walked back to my hotel room. My only concern now was the little money that I had left. I had a total of two dollars to live on for nearly two days before my plane departed for America.

That night, I filled the bowl of my pipe with my blonde Lebanese hash and lit the sweet-tasting tads. After a few good tokes, I quickly fell asleep thinking about my future. Many good thoughts danced through my head. I slept like a log.

I awoke the next morning from a loud argument on the street below my outside balcony. I hopped out of bed to see what all the commotion was about. I strained to see, as the morning dew wasn't out of my eyes yet, so everything was still blurry, until my eyes finally focused on the problem.

It was a beggar, or should I say half a beggar. Here was a little Arab man with no legs, sitting on a little four-wheeled cart to get around on. Two police officers were trying to persuade him to move on and beg somewhere else. The storeowner was losing business. It was a very high-class antique store, mostly for the rich tourists, and the half-man was scaring away his customers. At least, that's what I thought they were arguing about.

After ten minutes of arguing with the two policemen, the little guy grabbed two small wooden blocks with his hands and used them as extra height so his tiny half-body wouldn't drag on the ground. He used them to walk to his three-wheeled tricycle. He grabbed the handlebars and lifted his half-body up into the seat. Then he bent down and picked up his little begging cart while cussing out the two police officers and storeowner who had chased him from the scene. Then he was off, peddling his tricycle with his hands.

I only had one day before I would arrive back in the good old U.S. of A.

The stuff that I had sent to Canada should arrive without any problem, if the two Canadian hippies were right. However, once the parcels had made it past Canadian customs, I would have to pick them up at the

Windsor post office and drive the illegal contraband through Canadian and American customs to get the stuff back into the United States. At least the Canadian had explained to me how to send the stuff back without getting busted. Now I had to figure out a way to get into America.

I intended to spend the last day of my vacation relaxing and smoking the last of my Lebanese hashish. I had hoped to have an easy day of it, but instead I had a miserable day. I didn't have enough money to eat or to rent a taxi to take me on the forty-mile drive to the airport. It would take an hour, by car, to get there and even longer if I had to walk.

I had packed all my clothes and gifts. Everything was ready to go. But I did have a few problems to contend with. First, I had to find out the way to the airport. Then I had a suitcase that weighed thirty pounds when empty. It was one of those that could be thrown out of an airplane at twenty-thousand feet, hit concrete, and not open up or break. It was a super heavy-duty suitcase. Once everything was packed, it weighed even more, and because of my lack of funds, I would probably have to hitchhike to the airport. That meant I would have to carry it along with me.

All day long I worried about my situation—and worrying on an empty stomach made me nauseous—so I smoked nearly all of my good hashish until I fell asleep.

I awoke the following morning with over four hours to get to the airport.

I had less than two dollars left. I rented a cab as far as the two dollars would take me, which got me halfway to my destination. Now I was completely broke.

The cab dropped me off on a crowded bridge. Traffic was snarled and backed up due to workers repairing the bridge, and I was in the middle of it. I stood to the side of the road, hitchhiking.

When the Moroccan motorcycle police saw me hitchhiking with my oversized suitcase, they pulled up alongside of me and got off their motorcycles. They motioned for me to open my suitcase and proceeded to search it for any illegal contraband. While one officer was busy searching my luggage, the other asked to see my passport. When they didn't find any illegal contraband and saw that my passport was in order, they immediately stopped traffic on the bridge and ordered a truck driver to drive me to the airport. I was very thankful for their help and cooperation.

Everything bad I had been told about the Moroccan police

wasn't true. I had expected to be hassled into paying a bribe, so they would leave me alone, but that wasn't the case. These policemen only wanted to help me. I was relieved when the truck started rumbling toward the airport. Within an hour, we had arrived there, with plenty of time to spare before my plane to America departed. I thanked my truck driver and waved goodbye as he sped away.

I lugged my heavy luggage up to the airport baggage counter and handed my excursion ticket to the female ticket agent. She looked at my ticket, and then asked for thirty dollars for an excursion tax. I was in total shock. Today was the last day before my ticket expired. I begged and pleaded with the female ticket agent and tried to explain my situation to her.

"I wasn't told about this excursion tax when I purchased the ticket," I whined.

"I'm sorry, but it's out of my hands," said the agent, as she handed me my ticket and walked away from the counter.

When my pleading didn't work, I tried the crying act. That didn't work with the ticket agent either. They refused to do anything about my situation. What was I to do? Now I was stuck in Rabat with a ticket that would expire within the next few hours, no money in my pocket, no place to stay, and I hadn't eaten in over thirty hours. I was shit out of luck.

I decided to return to the hotel where I had stayed for the last few days. I would have to wait until I could get some money wired to me from my parents in America.

But before leaving the airport, I grabbed my suitcase and asked a few tourists if I could borrow thirty dollars to pay the airport tax so I could fly back to America. But nobody was the least bit interested in helping me. All I got were dirty looks and spit on. So I left the airport and started hitchhiking back to the city of Rabat. Within three hours, I was back at the hotel that I had left nearly six hours before.

I spoke with the manager of the hotel about my predicament. He was nice enough to allow me to stay in a room and feed me until I could repay my debt. He kept my suitcase as collateral. Well, at least I wasn't out in the street. I went to my room to relax and think.

I decided I would have to visit the American Embassy for help. I was told if I was ever in trouble, I should go to the American Embassy. There was supposed to be a law that stated: "The U.S. State Department was there to help any American who needed it." I would soon learn that this statement was a big joke.

I didn't have any more hashish to smoke to help me relax. But I didn't really want to smoke any anyway. I just wanted to go back home to America. I finally closed my eyes and fell asleep after tossing and turning for three or four hours.

The next morning, I got directions to the American Embassy and began walking down the beautiful, tangerine-lined streets. Within fifteen minutes, I was standing in front of the embassy counter telling the heavy-set mustachioed male clerk my problems. However, he acted as though he hadn't heard a word I had said.

"I'm sorry, the embassy isn't here to help out destitute Americans," said the fat, mustachioed man standing behind the counter.

Here I was five-thousand miles away from home and broke, and he was telling me he couldn't help one of his countrymen.

"Why not?" I asked.

"Are you a dope dealer?" he asked.

"Why would you ask me that?"

"Many young Americans are in Moroccan jails for dope smuggling."

"I'm not a dope smuggler, only a dumb, naive, young tourist on vacation who ran out of money because Pan Am airlines refused to honor my plane ticket," I replied.

"I'm sorry, but we have no money to give to destitute tourists," he said repeatedly.

I was beginning to get angry. Just as I was about to explode, in walked an old, blonde-haired American female alcoholic. She began crying and sobbing to the fat clerk behind the counter about how she was completely broke and destitute.

"Would you help me?" cried the wrinkled-faced old woman.

Suddenly, I watched the fat man as he turned and reached into a metal box and pulled out an American ten-dollar bill. He reached over the counter and handed it to her, then patted her hand and gave her a reassuring smile.

"Come back if you need any more help," the clerk assured the old woman.

When I heard and saw what had just transpired and how he had discriminated against me, I wanted an answer. I listened to his excuse and reasoning as to why he would give her money and not me. He gave me some lame excuse about how she had been in Morocco for years and had an alcohol problem, and that he felt sorry for her.

I demanded to see his superior. I was introduced to the ambassador. The only thing he was able to do to help my situation was to send a telegram for me to my parents. When and if I had received any money, I would have to pay the embassy five dollars for sending the telegram.

"Mr. Ambassador, don't do me any favors," I said sarcastically.

I sent the telegram to my parents asking for money. Now all I could do was to wait and hope. I half-heartedly thanked the ambassador and strolled back to the hotel. Within five days, I had received one hundred dollars from Western Union. But I still had to get a new plane ticket.

I returned to the American Embassy and showed the ambassador my old, unused plane ticket. I told him my story again. He phoned the Pan Am headquarters in Casa Blanca and talked to the CEO of the company. After a short conversation, he hung up the phone and told me I was to take the bus to Pan Am headquarters to receive another ticket.

The next morning, I boarded a bus and headed for Casa Blanca. When I arrived, I was accosted by a hoard of beggars. I tried to chase them away, but a few of them walked along with me to the Pan Am building, all the while begging for money. I felt very sad because I didn't have any money to give them. But they wouldn't take "no" for an answer.

I finally reached the building, but not before throwing a few Moroccan coins into the street so the beggars would quit hanging on to me and begging for money.

As I entered the Pan Am building, the CEO met me as I walked up to the receptionist's desk. We walked into his office, where he handed me another plane ticket to New York and apologized for any inconvenience I may have experienced. I quickly thanked him and left his office.

I rode the bus back to Rabat feeling happy and relieved. However, those feelings soon dissipated when I learned that my plane wouldn't depart for another two days. I was already low on funds because I had repaid my back bills, and once I had finished paying off my most recent bills, I again would have barely enough money to hire a taxi to take me to the airport.

For the next two days, I stayed around the hotel room. I didn't have any money to spend to do anything else, but I did have just enough money to pay my taxi fare to the airport. So when the time came, I rented a taxi and made it safely to the airport without any problems. However, I had arrived there about two hours before my flight departed, so I mingled with the other tourists. Most of them were just like me, broke and looking for a big hash score.

All the people who were taking the same flight as me were hippies and heads, except for two American businessmen who had been on vacation. They were carrying antique Moroccan rifles and blunderbusses. As it was getting closer to departure time, some of the hippies who had tried to get their seating arrangements became frustrated and angry. Now, it seemed, there was a ten-dollar airport tax, per person, to be paid before we could board the plane. Oh, great. Here we go again, I thought to myself. I thought I was never going to leave Morocco.

I walked over to the other ten or so people who didn't have the money to pay this tax either. We all wondered aloud what the heck we were going to do. I tried explaining to one of the female passengers about the trouble I had gone through a week before over this very same problem, and she started crying. Each time I tried to console her, she just cried louder.

The two business executives walked over to our little group to find out what all the commotion was about. When we explained our situation, the two men looked at each other and asked how many of us needed the ten dollars. There were ten of us. They gave each one of us an American ten-dollar bill so we could get our butts out of Morocco and back to America. We couldn't thank them enough.

At last, I was on the plane heading for good old U.S. of A. The girl who had been crying sat in the seat next to me and offered me a hash cookie. We both shared it and told each other of our excursion in Morocco. We were both looking forward to getting back home. Each of us had lost nearly twenty pounds of body weight.

Within an hour, that cookie had kicked in. I fell asleep with the girl's head on my lap. We didn't wake up until we had landed at Kennedy Airport in New York City.

CHAPTER 3

ROBBED IN ENGLAND-BUSTED AT
NEW YORK CUSTOMS

Finally, after an eight-hour flight from Rabat to New York, I was back in America once again. Going through customs wasn't a problem this time.

I had put almost an ounce of the green stuff that Jim had given me into the sleeve of my jacket. I had no money, only this so-called hashish. I still had to figure out how I was going to get back to Michigan. I had relatives living in Albany, New York, so I decided to head in that direction. If I could somehow get to Albany, I could borrow the money to fly to Detroit.

Once my baggage had been searched by customs, I began looking for someone to buy some of this green stuff I had smuggled into the country. All I needed was a few dollars, just enough to buy a bus ticket to my Uncle John's house in Albany. While wandering through the Pan Am building at two o'clock in the morning, I looked around for some longhaired hippies. There weren't many people around except for two rich-looking male hippies waiting for their flight to depart to Asia.

I sat down next to the two hippies and started a conversation with them. I told them I had just arrived from Morocco. In turn, they talked about their future trip to Afghanistan. They were going there to see if the stories they had heard about the country were true. I wished them luck and discussed with them the anguish I had suffered in Morocco. I also talked about the fantasies my friends had told me about the country, ninety percent of which had been untrue. I had found that out firsthand.

The hippie with long blond hair was telling me about the hash fields in Afghanistan, where hash was legal and only cost two or three dollars a kilo. I just thought to myself, *Yeah, that's what I was told about Morocco.* I figured most of what he had been told was pure fantasy, too, not reality. I was sure he would find that out as soon as he arrived in Afghanistan.

As we talked, I showed these two guys the gifts I had bought in Morocco, hoping they would be interested in something to buy. I showed them the wall carpets, the beaded necklaces, and the sheepskin. But they weren't interested in any of it until I took off my jacket, reached down into the liner of the left sleeve, and pulled out a piece of the green stuff that Jim had given me.

I didn't tell them it was hashish because I would have been lying. But the blonde-haired guy grabbed the piece out of my hand, put it under his nose, and smelled it. He thought it was pressed kef, not hashish. He told me he had seen and smoked some of the same stuff back in California. Immediately he wanted to buy some from me. But when his buddy had checked it out, he told his friend that the "stuff wasn't any good" and not to buy it. So instead of buying the whole piece, which was about an ounce in weight, he bought half of it. I finally had enough money to purchase a bus ticket to Albany.

Within six hours, I was back in Michigan. However, my parents didn't want me at their house, so I moved into an apartment with two childhood friends, Keith and Greg. Actually, Keith let me stay while Greg was hitchhiking around California looking for drug connections.

I needed money to pay the rent and other bills, so I started selling the green stuff. I still had to wait for the stuff that I had sent to Canada. This stuff wasn't that good, but people still bought it. In fact, it sold so well that I was sold out in just a few days. I had the only stuff around, and my package to Canada had just arrived.

I drove over the bridge to Windsor, Canada, taking my college books to have an alibi at the border. I also had a friend tag along with me so we looked like two students going over to visit another student.

We picked up the package at the post office. When the postal worker looked at my driver's license, which showed I was a citizen of America, he became suspicious. He asked me why I hadn't sent the parcel to America. I told him that I was going to school in Windsor and I didn't have an address to send it to, except to this post office. Reluctantly he bought the story and handed me the parcel.

We drove to the river's edge and opened the package. Its contents had spilled all over. When I'd packed it in Morocco, I had crushed some of the green stuff into a powder and placed it into a copper vase, then stuffed a sock into the top so it wouldn't spill out, but it had. So I scooped the contents up and put it into the sock. Then I placed the sock into the trunk of my car under a tire and out of sight.

A few minutes later, we took off toward the bridge to Detroit. I told my friend Mike not to say a word and to let me do all the talking when we stopped at the customs check.

Within a few minutes, we had arrived at the U.S. customs station, where I was asked the usual questions. How long had I been visiting Canada? I told him that we had gone to my friend's house to study, but he wasn't at home so we came right back. The customs officer could see a stack of college books sitting between Mike and me. Then Mike opened up his big mouth and told the customs man that we had been in Canada just long enough to have a cup of coffee. That's when the officer became suspicious.

"I thought you said you didn't stop anywhere?" asked the customs man. "Pull the car over so we can search it."

I looked angrily into Mike's eyes. If my eyes had been a weapon, they would have killed him. *We are going to get busted now,* I thought to myself. Just as I put the car into gear, we heard a loud screech, bang, and crunch.

I turned and looked over my shoulder and saw that a big rig truck and trailer had smashed into the back end of the car in front of it. It was smashed like an accordion. Thank God it was in the lane to my right, or I would have been the accident victim. As we looked to see what had happened, the customs man who had just told us to move the car to the side to be searched now was motioning for me to move ahead so they could get the snarled traffic moving again.

I stomped my foot on the accelerator so I could get out of there in a hurry. Once we were in America, I scolded Mike for opening his big mouth and almost getting us busted. He quickly apologized for his idiotic mistake.

Once I had arrived home, I weighed the stuff. I had almost two pounds of this so-called hashish or pressed kef. But there was nothing else around, the town was dry, so the people loved the green stuff. I had made enough money to buy some real good hash, but there was none available, so I decided to make another trip overseas, this time to England to score some hashish. I decided I would send it back to Canada and start my business that way.

I bought a round-trip ticket to London on a student charter flight. I was on my way to England. During the plane ride, I met the owner of the charter company. We hit it off immediately and became close friends. Through our conversation, I came to believe that I could charter a plane to India for many of my friends and students from Ann Arbor. I was to meet him in a few days at his favorite pub. He was going to show me the town of London and just party.

I rented a room at the Grovsner House, right at the Victoria train station, which in its heyday was the best hotel in London. It was still one of the nicest hotels in London.

Once I had placed my luggage in my hotel room, I went out on the town to see if I could score some hashish to help me sleep. I no longer drank liquor or alcohol of any kind, so pot or hash was best for me. I started asking a few longhaired hippies if they knew where I could buy some good hashish.

I ran into one guy who had some nice black Affy hash for sale, but only one gram. I bought what he had, then continued on my merry way—that is, until a seedy-looking hippie character stopped me.

"Do you want to buy some Colombian pot?" asked the hippie.

"No thanks, I want to buy some hashish," I replied.

The hippie said that he could help and escorted me to a pub a block away. He asked me for ten English pounds, which was about fifty American dollars. He told me he would have to go around the comer to get the stuff. But I wasn't that naive to front him the money, so I told him to get the stuff first and then I'd give him the money. He didn't like that idea too much but he agreed anyway.

He turned and walked away. I thought I'd never see him again, but within ten minutes, he had returned to the pub. He brought with him an envelope of a red powder. It was so dark and smoky in the pub that I couldn't smell or really see the stuff that well, and was a little suspicious because it was all powder. But it looked like red Lebanese-type hashish. So I took out the correct amount of money that he had asked for and gave it to him. By the time I'd put the envelope in my jacket pocket, he was gone, like a puff of smoke.

I returned to my hotel room and looked at my purchases. The black Affy smelled and looked very good, but the red stuff didn't. Now that I could see it in the light, it looked like incense. I figured I had gotten ripped off.

Just as I started to fill my pipe, my telephone rang. It was the manager of the hotel, telling me there were two gentlemen wanting to see me about some business. I couldn't figure out who it could be. The only thing I could think of was that they must have gotten my name and hotel from the guy I had met at the pub. I had mentioned where I was staying, just in case he could help me score some hashish.

I told the manager that it was all right, and he could send them to my room. Just to be on the safe side, I put my money into the side of a chair, deep under the cushion, so I wouldn't have any money on me if they tried to rob me. I had figured to sit in that chair anyway.

A few minutes later, I heard a knock on the door and answered it. I saw these two weird-looking, dirty, longhaired, grubby hippies. One of the guys looked just like the flute player and singer of Jethro Tull. He had long, scruffy hair and beard that looked as though he hadn't washed it in over a year. As we talked, he kept falling in and out of consciousness.

I invited them into the room. But before I could sit in my chair, the Jethro Tull impersonator sat in it. I had to sit in one adjacent to it. They told me they had some hashish to sell, but didn't have any on them. I was beginning to get a little suspicious of them, and the Jethro Tull impersonator kept nodding off as we talked. His buddy mentioned that his friend was an opium addict and had a fix just a few minutes before they had arrived.

As I talked to the coherent hippie, the dirty one asked to go to the bathroom. The bathroom wasn't in my room but down the hall, so I directed the opium addict toward the bathroom while the other hippie and I continued the conversation. Then he interrupted me. He wanted to see if his friend was all right, so he left the room also. As I waited for them to return, I became very nervous. Nearly five-minutes had passed and they had not yet returned. Just then, I thought to check the chair for the money that I had hidden between the cushion. It was gone! I panicked and immediately phoned the front desk.

"Did you see those two men who came to my room?" I asked the clerk.

"They just left the hotel a few minutes ago."

"I was just tied up and robbed by those two guys! Call the police!" I shouted.

While waiting for the police, I ran down to speak with the hotel manager. I explained to him again what had happened.

He told me, "The Grovsner House has never had a robbery." This was a first for the hotel.

I returned to my room and waited for the police to arrive. I had to think up a story so I wouldn't be arrested. I decided I would tell them exactly what I had told the hotel manager. Within minutes, the Bobbies had arrived and were all over my room. There must have been twenty or more of them searching my small hotel room.

The cords from two of the lamps were cut and lying on the bed, the lamps broken and lying in a heap in a comer of the room. I showed the head Bobbie the umbrella that the robbers had left.

"Can you get the robber's fingerprints off of it?" I asked.

The Bobbies just laughed. Then their leader said, "This isn't America, you know. There isn't any way we can lift fingerprints off of an umbrella." Then he added, jokingly, "Put it in lost and found. Maybe they'll come back for it."

I gave them all the pertinent information concerning my case, including a complete description of the two hippies who had robbed me. After an hour of answering the policemen's questions, they proceeded to leave my room, leaving me little hope of ever catching the two dogs who had robbed me of my funds. Now I was nearly destitute once again, and overseas. All I had to my name was about eighty dollars.

I telephoned the charter airline company and explained to the owner what had happened. He was quite concerned, because we were to discuss business while I was in London. He had hoped that I would contract a charter flight from America to India and was very disappointed hearing about my robbery. But he understood, and I made arrangements to fly back to America that following morning.

By the time I had left the next morning, the hotel lobby was full of newspaper reporters. I guess this robbery at the Grovsner House was a big story. This was their first robbery in over sixty years. But I didn't want to confront the reporters and tell them the story I had told the Bobbies—that I wanted to buy sitars and the two gentlemen who had robbed me had told me they had just returned from India with a load of them and needed to sell them cheap because they had a cash flow problem. I just didn't think the reporters would believe my story.

I just wanted to sneak out of the hotel and run to the train just outside of the hotel's door. I couldn't be late to my train or I would be late for my plane, and they wouldn't have another charter going to America for another four days. So I had to make the train on time.

As I ran past the hoard of reporters, one of them finally noticed me and began chasing after me. The race was on. There were nearly thirty reporters chasing ten feet behind me. If the train didn't leave on time, I would be stuck answering these reporters' dumb questions. Luckily, just as I boarded, the train began to move.

"All aboard!" yelled the conductor.

Then the train began to pick up speed. I watched as the reporters walked away, dejected and angry for not getting a story. But I didn't care. I was heading for Gatwick Airport to catch my charter flight to America. Nine hours later, I was on the ground at Metro airport in Detroit, Michigan.

The minute I arrived, I telephoned my roommate Keith and told him to come and pick me up. Keith and his girlfriend, Kathy, whom I had asked to go to London with me, met me at the airport an hour after I had landed. I explained to them what had happened.

As I was speaking, Keith interrupted me to tell me that there was some good Affy hashish in town. It had just come in this morning. Just my luck—I could have spent my money buying this new hash instead of losing all of my money on that crazy one-day excursion trip to England. With the money I had spent on this trip, I could have bought a half a pound of this Affy hashish. Now I'd be lucky to buy one ounce. That was all the money I had left over from my trip.

Keith had mentioned about a new hash connection he had just met in one of his college classes. He promised to introduce me to him later that evening. My bad luck was about to change to good luck.

I had the distribution network set up in four different cities to unload as much hashish as I could get my hands on. Later on that night, I was to meet the person who could supply me with the goods I needed and the quality and quantity that I wanted. Plus, the price was good enough that I could make a decent profit. Now my dream was about to come true.

That night, Keith and I drove way out to a desolate country road to visit this new hash connection. Keith introduced me to his friend Jim. We hit it off right away, as though we had known each other all of our lives. We created a lasting friendship that endures to this day.

I ended up buying an ounce of some nice, pungent black Affy. He also had some spicy red Lebanese sack hash for sale. But I could make more money selling the black Affy because the red wasn't as potent. The red Lebanese sack hash was so named because the plant's pollen is placed into a white linen sack and then pressed in a hydraulic press. Affy pollen is pressed by hand, using water and fire.

When I purchased my hash, I told Jim that I would be back for more. Then Keith and I left the house and headed back home.

Within two hours I had sold all of the hash in grams, so I went back to Jim's place to buy some more. He had nearly sold out of the black Affy, so I bought everything he had left and used the rest of my money to buy the red Lebanese. This time I had bought over three-hundred dollars worth of hashish.

The only bad part about sack hash is that the linen bag is also included in the weight, which I paid for, but couldn't sell to my customers. That was the only drawback with sack hash. I kept the sacks as souvenirs and used them to make shirts.

Within two weeks, I had enough money saved to move out of Keith's place and into a big house with two other good friends, Bill and Sue. I rented a bedroom from them. I had known Bill since I was four years old. They weren't married, but they acted like it.

From the day I moved in with them, business began picking up. Living in a college town made selling hashish very easy. It didn't matter to me whether my customers were students or dopers. They were one and the same to me. This was strictly business.

Bill had introduced me to a number of new hash connections. I met another big hashish dealer named Chuck. He was selling pounds of hash, not ounces. Now I was selling more and more quantity, but not making as much money as I had when I had been selling grams. But the more money I made, the faster I spent it—on anything and everything.

One day Bill and I decided to visit the city pet shop. I wanted to buy an exotic pet. I didn't know exactly what type of pet I wanted, although I did know that I wanted something different. The second I entered the store, my eyes immediately spotted a tiny baby leopard. The pet storeowner told me it was called a "miniature leopard" from Asia. They lived near and in Afghanistan.

I was nineteen years old and had already traveled to many countries, including Spain, Scotland, England, and Morocco. I knew that one day I would travel to Afghanistan. That was where the best hashish was grown. So when the pet storeowner mentioned that the exquisite animal came from Afghanistan, I had to buy it.

"Can the animal be tamed?" I asked the owner.

"Yes, in three months. However, you should wear leather gloves when handling her," he replied.

So I handed over three-hundred dollars and went home with my first wild pet. Even though the storeowner had to use gloves to pick her up, she was as small as a six-week-old kitten. But she still had the sharp claws and teeth of a frightened, wild animal. When I would pick her up to hold her, she would never try to bite me; she would just try to claw me to get away, only because she was afraid of me.

The storeowner had told me the leopard was a female. But I would learn almost two years later that "she" was a "he"—a male leopard—and males were very rare. He was one of two known males in the U.S. Within a few days, the miniature leopard and I had become good friends, which I believed to be female. I kept her in an open dog cage where she could come and go as she pleased, and she loved to play on the windowsill next to the screen window.

When I played with her and petted her head, I knew she really loved and enjoyed it 'cause she would close her eyes and purr. But then she would realize it was a human petting her and would shy away for a minute or so, then return to play again. This would go on for an hour or more. Then she would return to her cage and relax when she became too tired. I called her "Kali Durga." In the Hindu language, "Kali" meant bloodthirsty and "Durga" meant more bloodthirsty.

When I left for Europe and Asia, I had to give Kali to my aunt, who had two female Siamese cats. Her two females kept trying to breed with Kali, but she wouldn't have anything to do with them. When my aunt took her to a vet for shots and her check up, that's when we found out Kali was a male leopard. To say the least, that was a big surprise.

However, I still had my cat when I moved from Bill and Sue's house and into a new house in Ann Arbor with my new friend and connection, Chuck.

Within six months of living with Bill and Sue, I had saved plenty of money and my business had grown very quickly. But now the house was getting too hot. I was getting paranoid about all the traffic that had passed through there in the last six months.

I decided it was time to move into a new house. That's when Chuck and I had agreed to become roommates. Things went well for the first few months, but then the hash business slowly came to a halt as hash became scarce. The stuff that did come through wasn't worth the money. I was spending more money than I was making and my luck was beginning to go bad. I had broken up with my one true love, Amy, over my drug situation. Now my money was running low with nothing to sell.

One night, while Chuck was at college and I was at a friend's house playing poker, our place was hit by a burglar. Our house was no longer safe. They came in looking for drugs and money and completely wrecked the house, turning over furniture, mattresses, dresser drawers, and anything else they thought might have hidden drugs.

Chuck and I decided right then and there that we would go our separate ways. At least they didn't hurt my leopard. I ended up taking Kali to my parent's house. I decided to stay there, too. However, that didn't work out too well because they didn't want the trouble that seemed to follow me wherever I went. So I talked another childhood friend, Bob C., into traveling to Europe with me. I had asked him to go before when I traveled to London, but at the time, he didn't want to travel. Now he was very excited about the trip and wanted to go.

We decided to travel to Germany, buy a van, drive it to Lebanon, fill it with hashish, drive it back to Europe, and then send the van loaded with hash back to America. Well, that was our plan, anyway.

Within a week of moving out of the house with Chuck, I was on my way to Frankfurt, Germany. Bob and I figured that would be the cheapest place to buy a VW van. We didn't know there would be drugs there, too.

We arrived at Frankfurt Airport and hopped a bus to the city. We ended up near the main railway station, which seemed to be the slummier part of the city, and were able to find only one hotel that had a vacancy. This hotel was for the down-and-out alcoholics, low-lifes, and tourists with very little money. We asked for the cheapest room in the hotel and we got it. It was a piss-smelling, smoke-filled room, but it did have clean feather beds, not like the mattresses in America. These were big and fluffy and fit perfectly snug to one's body. You kind of sunk into it. Actually, the room wasn't that bad once you got used to it. At least we had a roof over our heads.

Over the next few days, we searched the city for a van and also asked some German hippies where the heads stayed. Everyone we asked seemed to point in the same direction—to a park a few miles away. So we hopped onto the #25 tram, hopped off at the correct exit, and found the park with very little trouble. Once there, we asked the hippies where we could find some hashish to buy. Within an hour, we had found someone who could help us in our endeavor. We were to meet this person that night at a Frankfurt nightclub called "Club 4." He had promised that we could buy whatever we needed.

Our funds were running low and trying to buy a van at a good price was nearly impossible. Not only that, but we had run into another little obstacle. We had to have power of attorney papers from one of our parents to buy the van. Neither Bob nor I were old enough to purchase the van on our own. The legal age was twenty-one. So we came up with another plan of action.

We decided to buy a kilo of hash in Frankfurt, and I would carry it back to America. I would sell it, buy a gram of pure LSD, and sell that when I returned to Europe. Acid was a big seller there and was selling for ten to twenty dollars a hit. It was possible to make four thousand hits from a gram of acid.

While I was doing the drug end of the deal, Bob would buy the van and fix it up so two people could live in it. We figured by the time I returned to Frankfurt, the van would be ready to go and we could leave for Lebanon. That was the plan anyway.

Once we had decided on a course of action, we were ready to party. So we dressed in our best blue jeans and headed for Club 4 to meet our hash connection. As we entered the club, there were hash dealers on both sides of the hall, selling their wares. We picked out a guy who was selling some spicy red Lebanese at very cheap prices.

"Hey man, cut me a nice chunk for thirty marks," I told the hash dealer.

Thirty marks was less than ten American dollars. Using a sharp knife, he cut off a nice chunk, including part of the sack, and weighed it on a small, hand-held scale. It weighed out to nearly seven grams and at least half a gram of that was the sack.

Finally, after three days in Germany, we were able to buy some decent hashish. We walked into the darkened room looking for a table away from anyone who could see us smoking hash. But as we walked into the club, we noticed many people sitting at their tables, smoking hash. And none seemed to be worrying about the police busting them, so we decided to pick a table on the main floor close to the stage. The club had two floors: the main floor, and one four feet higher, which also had many table and chairs. The two floors were separated by a small, white, wooden picket fence.

I filled our hash pipe up with the red Lebanese hash that Bob and I had just purchased and fired it up. Not having smoked anything for three days, we were really buzzed after just a couple of tokes. My body had succumbed to the hash smoke, and I was finally relaxed.

Nearly thirty minutes later, my hash connection from the park was at the table, motioning for me to go with him. Bob stayed behind while I followed the guy outside to a waiting black Mercedes automobile. They placed me into the back seat alone, and off we went into the dreary, wet, rainy night. Faster and faster, we traveled the winding streets. I held on for dear life as the car swerved from one side of the road to the other. I yelled for them to slow down, but either they didn't understand me or they just didn't care. I figured they were trying to lose anyone who might have been following them.

I had absolutely no idea where they were taking me. I hoped and prayed that they were trustworthy. As naive as I was, I trusted everyone. But their crazy driving and my paranoia frightened me. I started thinking that they could drive out to a desolate spot, kill me, take my money, and leave. And who would know? Nobody, that's who. I didn't even know my connection's name. I just trusted them.

After fifteen minutes or so of driving recklessly, we stopped in what seemed to be the back of a schoolyard. Just as we stopped, another car pulled alongside of ours. A big, burly guy handed me a paper bag and asked for twenty-two hundred marks. That was about eight hundred American dollars.

I was supposed to get a kilo of blonde or red Lebanese hash, but instead he had given me a bag of black Affy spaghetti hash. This hash was rolled by hand in long, thin, round strips similar to a strand of spaghetti. Then they are added together to form one big strip, two inches in diameter and six inches long.

When they saw that I was satisfied, they drove me back to Club 4, but this time at a much slower speed. As we arrived at the club, I thanked them and promised to do business with them again very soon. They nodded in agreement and left the area.

I walked into the club carrying a big grocery sack full of black Affy hashish. No one at the club even bothered or questioned me about the bag and its contents.

I walked down the steps to the main floor, and then to my table. Bob was sitting there patiently waiting for my return and immediately began scolding me for being gone so long. But he shut up when I reached into the big grocery sack and pulled out a nice, five-gram chunk of the black Affy.

I filled the hash pipe and handed it to him so he could test our product. As he lit the bowl and inhaled deeply, he began to cough his head off, so he passed the pipe to me and I did the same. This hash was so potent and pungent that we coughed on each toke. In fact, we had to muffle our coughs so we wouldn't interrupt the band that was playing. This black Affy was much better than the red Lebanese that we had purchased earlier that evening. Just a couple of tokes and we were flying high.

As we smoked our hash and listened to the band, I thought I had heard someone call my name. But I wasn't sure. I thought I was just imagining it. So I sat back in my chair and took another long toke on the hash pipe. I was totally relaxed and in a very good mood. Then, just at that moment, I thought I had heard someone call out my name again. "Bob."

"Bob, did you hear someone call out my name?" I asked.

"No," he replied.

However, Bob C. was nearly asleep. The hashish had knocked him out. Once again, I thought I heard someone call my name. I turned and looked around the dark room to see if someone had been calling my name. Sure enough, there was a guy waving in my direction from across the room, sitting on the second floor.

As I focused my eyes in this darkened, smoke-filled room, I noticed that I had seen this guy before. Then it hit me—the guy was Jim, one of the Americans that I had met and toured with in Morocco. *What a small world,* I thought. Here was a guy I had met just six months before, five thousand miles away in a faraway country, and now I saw him in a club in Frankfurt, Germany.

I quickly leaped over the white picket fence that separated the two floors and introduced myself to the three people sitting at Jim's table. We talked about our time in Morocco.

"Jim, what happened to Pete and Pat, the other two travelers we trekked with in Morocco?" I asked.

"They went to Kabul, Afghanistan to cop some hash," replied Jim, then took a deep drag on his cigarette.

"So, what happened?" I asked, anxious to hear the story.

"Well, they met their connection and scored over one hundred and ninety kilos of some exquisite black Affy hash."

"Did they get out of the country with it?" I asked him.

"They left customs in Kabul without a problem. Then they were to change planes in Beirut, Lebanon, go through their customs connection, and head to Germany."

"Did they make it?" I asked.

"Well, they landed in Beirut and picked up their luggage, all six bags full of pungent Affy hashish. Then they went to catch their flight to Frankfurt. Going through Beirut customs to board their Frankfurt flight, they were busted."

Then he explained to me how they had made one stupid mistake. Instead of going through Beirut customs on Thursday, they should have departed for Frankfurt on Friday. They should have waited an extra day due to the international times zones. Their customs connection wasn't there on the day they went through customs. They had been told which numbered line to go through, but they screwed up on the time differences and both ended up in Beirut prison.

"Are they still rotting in prison?" I asked him.

"Pat, the nympho, screwed her way out. Pete spent nearly fifty-thousand dollars paying bribes, supposedly to the right people, which evidently wasn't enough. He's still there."

"When the prison guards know a person has money, the jailers make promises that they can't keep. So they try and get as much money out of you as fast as they can, until one day you've run out of money and you're still in prison," I opined.

Jim and I exchanged pleasantries and stories and before we knew it, they were closing the club. We said goodbye, and I promised to see him again at the club. However, we had forgotten to exchange addresses. I figured I would run into him again at the club, except that never happened. It turned out to be the last time I'd ever see him.

Bob and I walked back to our hotel room while I carried the grocery sack full of black Affy hashish. I was so high I hadn't even thought about getting busted. At last, we had arrived at our hotel room. That next day, I bought my return plane ticket to America. Now we put our plan into action.

Bob helped me tape the hashish under my arms and into the crack of my ass. It was mighty uncomfortable. When I had to turn, either to my right or left, the tape would dig into my skin, and I would have to bite my lip so I wouldn't scream out loud. That night, I had to sleep with the hash taped to my body so I would get used to it and be ready for the long airplane ride to America.

Once on the airplane, I thought about the week I had just spent in Frankfurt. I had the happy experience of visiting my first whorehouse. I'd never visited a country where the prostitutes would come up to you while waiting for the streetlight to change and grab your balls and manhood in their hand, then whisper vulgar language to entice the customer.

"Do you want fuck?" asked the prostitute in broken English, as she fondled my manhood.

Needless to say, I spent quite a bit of money and time at the whorehouse directly behind my hotel room. After my first experience there, I returned to my hotel room and told Bob about my experience. He had to leave the room to investigate while I went down the street to an adult nightclub where the barker would stand outside and entice the customers with beautiful, naked women.

As I walked into the darkened nightclub, very few people were in the place. In fact, I was the only customer in the club at the time besides the two women up on stage making love to each other, and I do mean *making love*. They were holding each other in a sixty-nine position, lip-locked to each other's female genitalia.

I was invited to sit down in a small booth by a large-breasted woman. When I accepted her invitation, she pulled the curtain to keep us hidden from the other patrons and then lowered her top, exposing her large, pink breasts. I bent down to suck one into my mouth, but she just laughed and shoved me away.

"Not so fast. Let's have a drink first," said the female tease.

She quickly ordered champagne. When it arrived at our table, I opened my wallet to pay for the drinks, but instead, she reached out and grabbed a twenty-dollar bill from it and paid the waitress. I had expected some change from the transaction, but I never received any.

The beautiful, large-breasted female kept up her tease. She flirted with me and fondled my genitals, all the while ordering more drinks at twenty dollars a pop. I had spent nearly one-hundred American dollars before I wised up. When I finally got up the nerve to ask her to bed, that's when she stood up and left my booth. She suddenly turned her attention to another customer.

Here I was, a young, naive teenager in a big city in a country where I didn't speak or understand their language, being hustled and ripped off by these Nazi club owners. When I refused to pay such an outrageous bill for my drinks, the club owner threatened to break my neck. After I was coerced into paying the bill, the female prick teaser motioned for one of the club's henchmen, who escorted me out the front door.

I left the premises to find a law enforcement official. However, when I told them my situation, they told me there was nothing they could do. It was my own fault. They told me that I should have asked the price of the drink before I purchased it. They were absolutely correct. I had learned a hard lesson that day. That's why the place was empty of customers when I had first entered the club. They were only for dumb, naive tourists and suckers, like me. All the locals knew about these nightclubs. With the money I had spent in that nightclub, I could have spent two days at the whorehouse.

Once I returned to my hotel room, I began thinking about my little suitcase. After my experience lugging my big, heavy suitcase all over Morocco, I now used a little and very light suitcase.

The night before my plane departed for America, I had been searching through the pockets of my clothing, when I noticed about half a gram of very small particles of the black Affy hash. They were just little specks and tads. I refused to throw them away and didn't think anyone at customs would find them. I figured I could smoke it later, after I had arrived home.

I suddenly awoke out of my daydream and realized I was aboard the Pan Am flight to America. We had been in the air for nearly two hours. I tried to relax and think positive thoughts, but each time I turned my body the tape would cut into my skin. The hash taped to my body constantly pinched my skin almost to the point that I wanted to cry out in agony. The pain would stay with me for the next six or seven hours, so I decided to alleviate it.

I tried to take a few tokes of hash without anyone noticing me. I filled up my little hash pipe, which I had carried onto the plane with a few small tads (pieces) of the red Lebanese that I had purchased at Club 4. The cabin lights were dim, and the man next to me was sleeping, so I figured this would be the best time. I bent down, close to the window, and inhaled my first toke. I inhaled too deeply and began to cough my head off. That one toke was one toke too many.

Hoping not to bring attention to myself, I held my breath to stop coughing. However, the hash smoke seemed to linger in the air above my head. I prayed that nobody had seen me. I was sure if they had seen me smoking my hash pipe, they would have made a big stink about it, but nobody said a word. I felt confident that nobody had seen a thing.

Within six hours, I'd be arriving in New York. I wanted to return to Michigan as fast as possible so I could sell the hash, buy the gram of LSD, and fly back to Frankfurt to meet Bob C. Then we would sell the acid as we traveled throughout Europe to the Middle East.

When I arrived in my hometown, I figured I could sell the hash for one or two-thousand dollars, even more if the town was dry. I would use half of that money to buy the acid and the return plane fare to Germany. I had hoped that the gram of acid would make us ten times the amount of money that the hash would bring in. That was the plan anyway.

Just as I snapped out of my hypnotic dream, I noticed the celebrity, Tony Bennett, making his way down the isle of the airplane, shaking hands and signing autographs as he went. He had been traveling with his new young wife and brand new baby. Twenty minutes later, the plane landed at Kennedy Airport.

I was the first to retrieve my luggage. I only had one small suitcase, which was so small I could have carried it with me and placed it in the luggage compartment above my seat. I had absolutely nothing to declare because I hadn't bought any tourist souvenirs or gifts. That was another mistake I had made, although I never considered that a problem. I had always slipped through customs unharmed.

I carried my luggage to the closest customs counter and placed my lone suitcase on it. The customs official searched its contents and waved me through the line. I was quite relieved at that point. Now I was on my way to catch a flight to Detroit. But just as I began walking toward the doors to freedom, a fat man wielding a large, strong-smelling cigar, dressed in a gray suit, showed me his gold detective's shield as he held my declaration papers in his hands.

"Follow me," said the fat man, chomping on his stale cigar.

I followed this law enforcement official, with suitcase in hand, to a small, dimly lit room that contained a small table and two chairs. He directed me into a chair and shut the door behind me. Then he sat in the other chair, directly in front of me. Suddenly, the fat man jumped up and grabbed my suitcase out of my hand. He set it, unopened, on top of the table. Just as he did that, another man walked into the room and shut the door behind him.

The fat man proceeded to ask me some questions as the skinny man opened my suitcase and began searching its contents. Like an idiot, I didn't object. I tried to remain cool and not give myself away.

"I see you traveled to Germany," said the fat detective.

"Yeah, so what?" I asked.

"You traveled all the way to Germany and you didn't bring back any souvenirs. Why is that?" asked the fat man, as the other man continued searching through the clothing in my suitcase.

"I was visiting a sick aunt and didn't have the money to buy any gifts," I lied, looking the detective directly in his eyes.

I don't think the fat detective believed me, while the other detective was making grunting sounds as he rummaged through my one piece of luggage and was becoming more and more frustrated by the lack of finding any illegal contraband—that is, until he came to the last article of clothing, my Levi jacket, the same jacket that had the half-gram of powdered black Affy hash in one of the pockets. I should have smoked it back in Germany. But no, I had to save it.

Now it was going to cost me—but how much?

When the skinny detective checked the last pocket of my Levi jacket, I watched as his eyes grew to twice their size, nearly coming out of their sockets, and a wide grin appeared on his crater-marked face. He had found the mother lode.

"I found it!" he yelled gleefully, as he set a white sheet of paper on the table and poured the contents out of my jacket pocket onto it.

As the tiny BB-sized black tads fell onto the white paper, a few of the tads landed near me, so I picked them up with my fingertips and started eating them—that is, until the fat man slapped me upside the head and had me spit them out. He acted as if I was eating cyanide pellets or all of his precious evidence. He ordered me to stand up and when I did, he began searching my body. He also felt my pants pockets to see if I had any more illegal contraband. I surmised he was looking for the stuff I had been smoking on the plane by the way he was searching me.

I started to hold up my arms over my head, but he ordered me to put my arms down. *Great,* I thought, *he's not going to search under my arms.*

As the fat detective was thinking, he suddenly noticed my shirt underneath my sweater. He lifted my sweater and started searching the shirt pocket. As he searched the pocket for any illegal contraband, he felt the bulge under my left arm.

"Are you packing heat?" he asked.

"What do you mean?" I asked.

"Are you carrying a gun?"

"No, it isn't a gun." I was hoping he wouldn't ask me any more questions.

I wasn't about to tell him what was really under my arm, so I waited for him to make the next move. He began ripping at my sweater and shirt to find out what was under my arm.

"Stop!" I barked. "I'll undress for you. You got me." I looked him directly in the eyes and gave him a cold, hard stare.

I began undressing until I was naked from the waist up. The detectives were very surprised at the quantity of hashish I had been concealing on my body. The fat detective reached out and ripped off the scotch tape that had been holding the hash to my body. He was so anxious to get at the illegal contraband that he had ripped off a four-inch-long piece of skin along with the scotch tape. When I screamed out in pain, the fat man slammed me against the wall so hard that my head pushed a three-inch indentation into the plaster.

No longer was the fat man being a nice guy. He picked me up by my pant legs and then ripped my pants from my body. More hashish fell onto the floor as I was being held upside down against my will. Finally, he let my nearly naked body fall to the floor. When I stood up and tried to take the rest of the hash from my taped body, which had been concealed by my underwear, again I was knocked down, punched, and beaten by the fat detective. His skinny partner stood to the side laughing all the while his partner had been beating me.

As the fat detective continued to beat and pummel me with his fists, I began screaming, as the pain had become unbearable. The noise and commotion coming from the small room got the attention of another law enforcement official. He barged into the room to see the fat man standing over me, while I lay on the dirty, cold floor, beating me unmercifully with his fists and feet. This officer, whether he knew it or not, had literally saved my life. I was sure that if he had not come into the room when he had, I would have been a dead man. He stopped the fat man and saved me from a horrendous beating.

Within ten minutes, I had received medical attention. Once the paramedics mended my wounds, I was arrested and driven to a precinct in Queens, New York, for booking.

"Welcome to America," said an officer, as I was being fingerprinted.

While being fingerprinted and booked, somehow someone had started a rumor that I was in the mob. I kept hearing the whispered word, "Mafia." But I didn't think much about it until the inmates and police officers began treating me with more respect.

At first, I thought they treated me this way because I was dressed better than everyone in the police station and looked as though I had money.

Then I learned that I had been sharing a cell with one of the head honchos in the Genovese family, who had been arrested and booked for a narcotics violation. He had been busted with two kilos of pure cocaine, and at that time, cocaine had been selling for nearly a hundred grand per kilo. The other inmates thought I had been busted with him, so I played along.

I was allowed one telephone call. However, I quickly found out that my parents had had their number changed while I had been out of the country. It was also an unlisted number, so the operator refused to help me. Here I was, locked up in jail six hundred miles away from my home, and I had no way of letting my parents know.

Once my booking was completed, I was handcuffed to other prisoners, put on a bus, and taken to Riker's Island. This place was the East Coast Alcatraz. As soon as I entered this ungodly den of iniquity, I mentioned to the guards that I hadn't received my phone call.

"Tough," barked a mean-looking guard. "We don't care if you got your phone call or not. Welcome to hell."

Evidently, they hadn't heard the rumor yet. They weren't treating me with respect. However, by the time we had been assigned to our dorm rooms, somehow the rumor had gotten started, again. At least the new cons were treating me with respect.

The dorm room was a big gymnasium-type room, where all the new cons were placed to detox from their narcotic addiction. There they were also assigned to a cell in a certain cellblock and a cellmate before they were transferred to the main building. I had been assigned to "D" block.

The dorm room must have held five hundred new inmates, and only two of them were white—my cellmate, John, and me. My cellmate was a high school senior who had been caught stealing his school's P.A. system. He explained to me that he had done the delinquent act on a dare from his high school buddies. It was just a prank—or so he said.

We each promised to help each other, whoever was released first. Neither one of us could contact our parents. I knew the reason I couldn't contact my parents and his parents refused to take his call. They were tired of his law breaking because he had broken the law just a few months before. So we made a pact to call each other's parents if and when we were released from this evil prison.

Three days later, we were escorted to our permanent cells. We had been the only white people in the dorm, and now we were the only white people in our cellblock.

I had been treated with respect by the cons from my dorm, so now I was hoping these cons in my cellblock had also heard the rumor about me and would treat me with that same respect. I kept my fingers crossed.

However, it seemed they hadn't heard the rumor about my mob affiliation. I was getting absolutely no respect from them at all. More and more inmates had been coming up to me, trying to start a fight. They would stand face to face with me and order me about, demanding different items from me, and if I didn't get them for them, they would threaten to kill me. I had become tired of all the threats, so I refused to come out of my cell. However, the guards didn't like that, so they would come to my cell and pull me out.

After five days in my new cellblock, I was finally allowed to use the telephone. I had asked the operator for the number, but they refused to help me. I had to telephone one of our neighbors and hope that they would answer the phone. Sure enough, Terry, who was a few years older than me, answered the phone.

I explained to him where I was and the situation I had gotten myself into. I told him to contact my parents and tell them about my predicament. I gave him the court date of my arraignment and told him to tell my parents to meet me at the Queens courthouse in New York City for my arraignment. Then I was cut off when the guard grabbed the phone from my hand and hung it up.

I just hoped and prayed that Terry would do what I had asked. I didn't want to stay a day longer than I had to. These guys in this prison were real, hardened criminals. They were murderers, rapists, and armed robbers—all violent offenders. Then there was John and me, two young, naive punk teenagers who were afraid for our lives.

On the seventh day at Riker's Island, all the cons from D block were lined up in single file to go to the cafeteria for breakfast.

As we began walking toward the cafeteria, a fight suddenly broke out at the front of the line. One of the hardened inmates had grabbed a sharpened pencil from one of the guard's shirt pockets and proceeded to poke out the guard's eyeball and kick it toward the cafeteria. Then the crazed con pummeled the injured guard as he lay bleeding on the floor until the guard lay unconscious.

Finally, six other guards surrounded him and began beating him with their wooden batons. You could hear his bones break. They whacked him upside the head, and you could actually see the lumps come up. But nothing seemed to stop this animal. The more the guards hit him, the more he fought back. This crazed con wouldn't stop. When you thought the guards had gotten the upper hand, suddenly you would see one of them flying through the air as the maniacal con tossed him as though he were a kid's rag doll. The inmate had grabbed one guard around the neck and nearly twisted his head off.

Then, more and more guards appeared, trying to subdue the crazed con while continuously beating and kicking him, until they all backed away for just a second. At that moment, the room became silent—we could have heard a pin drop. But then the silence was broken by a loud *pop, pop, pop, pop, pop.* It was the sound of gunshots. We watched as the crazed con staggered backwards, then heard one more "pop," and a stream of blood spurted about five feet in the air as the bullet struck an artery. Suddenly, the crazed con's body went limp and he fell down with a thud into a pool of blood.

The guards swarmed over the dead man's body, kicking it as they walked by just to make sure he was dead. Then one of the guards blew his whistle and had us march in single file back to our cellblock. As soon as we entered the cellblock, a big, mean black con who had been bugging me all week, ordering me to get him this and that, wanted a carton of cigarettes from me, and he wanted them now. This guy was a good six-foot-three or four inches tall, with the body of a weightlifter, and must have weighed a good 230 pounds.

While I was leaning against the wall, he came over to me and began poking me in my chest. He began ordering me to come up with the cigarettes or money. If I didn't, he threatened to cut out my heart and cook it for supper. As he poked me in the chest, a big crowd gathered around us. As more and more people watched, the black guy got braver and braver and kept poking me in my chest harder and harder. Each time he did this, he turned to his friends with a big smirk on his face and asked them if there was anything they wanted from me. Just as he turned his head to the right, I just reared back, made a fist, and let it fly with all my might. The punch clearly surprised my black aggressor and his buddies, which caught him under the chin and lifted him two inches off the floor. He landed hard on his butt, dazed and confused. Before he could move, I kicked him under his chin with the power of a big Mack truck, completely knocking him out. Then I looked to the crowd of cons.

"That's the way the Genovese family handles low-life scum," I snapped, as I walked away and watched as the black man's friends helped him up off the floor.

"I'm going to kick your ass, then kill you," screamed the black thug, as his friends struggled to help him to his feet.

His friends just looked at him as though he was crazy to threaten a member of the Mafia. Then one of them spoke up. "I ain't fucking with no Mafia, man," said one of the black man's friends.

After that incident, nothing similar ever happened again for the rest of my stay at Riker's Island.

A few days later, I was finally taken to arraignment. I just prayed that my parents would be there. However, I still didn't know if they even knew I had been thrown in jail. But when I walked into the courtroom, to my surprise and amazement, my prayers had been answered. My parents were sitting in the front row.

Once the arraignment started, the prosecutor wanted me on a one-hundred thousand dollar bond. He told the judge that he had heard a rumor that I was involved with the Genovese mob. When the judge heard that, he looked down at his court docket and asked the prosecutor why he thought the defendant had anything to do with the Genovese family. The prosecutor replied that he had heard this from one of his snitches at Riker's Island. *Great,* I thought to myself. I started the rumor so it would help me in jail, and now it was hindering me in the courtroom. But in the long run, it did help me.

The judge looked at my parents and then told the court that due to the defendant's young age and no previous criminal record, he was releasing me into my parent's custody. I was allowed to leave the state, but I had to return a few months later for sentencing.

But once I returned to my old stomping grounds, nothing really changed. I had two months to party before I had to return to New York for sentencing. At the time, I didn't know whether I would get jail time or not.

However, that didn't stop me from partying. In fact, I had just come from a weekend at the Goose Lake concert. It was a miniature Woodstock, where the top rock bands played for three long days and where people were selling red Lebanese and black Affy hash in large quantities. So I bought a few pounds of each.

Then a few weeks after Goose Lake, my attorney called and told my parents that I wouldn't be going to jail and that I would get probation and wouldn't have to return for sentencing.

Luckily, the attorney we had hired was my judge's grandson. So once the case had gone through all the motions, I ended up with one year of probation that would be expunged from my record if I didn't get into any more trouble. To say the least, I was totally relieved. That was the news for which I had hoped.

Now that I wasn't going to jail, I could get my business started again, better than ever. Especially after all the hashish I had purchased at the Goose Lake concert. I had stashed it, thinking I would get some jail time, but I had lucked out for a change.

I had been staying at my parents' house since I had gotten out of Riker's Island, and with business booming and making more money than ever before, I still had to be very discreet and cautious. It was nice not having to pay rent and having a home-cooked meal every day. But I had also been working fourteen hours a day at a tool and die shop. Now that my business was doing so well, I decided to quit my job. I was making more money selling hash.

Then things began going bad. There was too much traffic with people visiting and phoning at all hours of the day and night, and my parents started hassling me about it. Then Mark, a friend of mine, stopped by the house and told me I was going to get busted. When I heard that, I decided to phone another friend of mine who worked at the local police department to see if the rumor was true. Sure enough, Mark had been correct. The bust was coming down within forty-eight hours.

I knew Bob C. was traveling in Europe somewhere in his VW van. So I decided to return to Frankfurt to the same hotel we had stayed at before. I figured I would tell his mother and when Bob contacted her, she could relay my message and we could meet in Frankfurt and travel Europe together. I packed what little clothes I had and had Mark drive me to the airport.

While waiting for my flight to depart, I had eaten a tab of synthetic mescaline. A few minutes before boarding, I told Mark to get his money together for plane fare and traveling expenses and he could join me in Frankfurt, Germany, at the Stat Zurich Hotel. I told him we would hitchhike across Europe to Asia, unless we ran into Bob C., and then we could ride in his van.

Mark was all for the idea. He only needed a few hundred dollars for the plane fare and another hundred or more dollars for traveling expenses. And once we had reached Turkey, I had been told it was possible to live on one dollar a day.

I had nearly seven hundred dollars, and whatever Mark could dig up should be more than enough for traveling expenses. Whether he came or not, I was on my way to Afghanistan via Frankfurt, and all points thereafter.

However, my trip had started on a very bad note. As I was standing in line to board my flight to Frankfurt, I had forgotten that I had my hash pipe in the pocket of my Levi jacket. It was the same jacket in which the detective had found the hash tads that had gotten me busted in New York.

As we boarded the plane, the flight attendants and security guard were searching the passengers with metal detectors. I was the last person to be searched, by a rookie security guard. The metal detector went off when it hit my metal hash pipe. The guard looked at my long hair and dilated eyes and then his adrenaline took over. He began hassling me about illegal contraband and then found the hash pipe. He had me empty my pockets. He also wanted to body search my person in the hopes of finding illegal drugs.

I started getting off on the mescaline I had eaten earlier, so I didn't feel like arguing with this jerk and yelled at him so everyone near us could hear.

"Let's go in the bathroom and you can check up my asshole," I bellowed. "Better yet, give me back my airline ticket. I'm going to tell the airlines why I'm not flying on their plane."

The startled rookie guard looked at me with disdain as I held out my hand for my ticket. That did it. He just motioned me onto the plane, but refused to relinquish the hash pipe.

Within ten minutes, I was off to the wild blue yonder. I would be in Frankfurt, Germany in seven or eight hours.

CHAPTER 4

BACK TO EUROPE-HEADING FOR AFGHANISTAN

Well, here I was again, in good old Frankfurt, Germany. Frankfurt Airport is the weirdest one I've been to. It has a black, rubberized floor that makes the whole airport soundproof and noiseless. You can't hear your own footsteps or the clop-clop of the wooden shoes that so many German women wear.

Once I had passed through customs, I hopped a bus from the airport to the Stat Zurich Hotel, hoping that Bob C. would be there or maybe a letter explaining where he was. But no luck—he wasn't there, and he hadn't left any messages or a letter for me either.

And there weren't any hotel rooms available. That meant if Stat Zurich didn't have rooms available, neither did the other hotels in Frankfurt. So now I had to find a place to crash. I didn't have a youth hostel card, so I couldn't stay there. Anyway, it would have cost me at least twenty-five dollars just for their membership card, then another eight or ten dollars for the room. So that was out of the question. I wasn't going to spend that kind of money on just a room for one night.

I figured that Mark would be in Frankfort within twenty-four to thirty-six hours. He told me that he was coming for sure. He wanted to travel to Afghanistan as badly as I did, or at least I thought he did.

I let him use my car to drive me to the airport and to pick up any other stuff he needed for the trip. Then he would return it to my parents' house and head for the airport. I hoped and prayed he would do as he promised, so instead of wasting money on a room, I decided to save the money and spend the night on a park bench.

At the time I decided on that course of action, it was only ten in the morning and quite warm outside.

A few weeks before my trip to Frankfurt, I had purchased a beautiful, handmade leather jacket with a built-in backpack for traveling in the cold mountains of Europe. The liner of the coat worked similar to a sleeping bag, and the backpack had enough room for three days of food. I could wear the coat with or without the backpack filled.

I figured that if it didn't get too cold, I would sleep in the park. And by morning, Mark should have arrived in Frankfurt. Then we could begin our trip to Asia.

As I waited for nightfall, I bided my time looking for my hash connection—the one from whom I had bought the kilo of black Affy six months earlier. By the afternoon, I had found him, but he wasn't the same person. He looked very sick, and his face had turned yellow, as if he had jaundice.

"You look sick, man. What are you into now?" I asked.

"I'm into heroin. I can get you some if you want," replied the hash connection, looking as if he were going to regurgitate.

"Thanks, but no thanks. Can you get me some hash?"

"I think so. Follow me," he said, as we left the park.

For nearly five hours, we had visited many of this guy's drug connections with no luck. It seemed everyone was selling heroin. However, after the sixth or seventh house we visited, we were able to score some brown Affy hash. It came in one-eighth-inch-thick, three-inch-square slabs, sealed in cellophane. It looked as though it might have been sent in an envelope or letter from a country in Asia. It smelled and tasted like Affy. It exploded in my lungs and got me stoned in two tokes, like Affy. I was satisfied, so much so that I bought two slabs for about thirty dollars each. Now, at least, I had something to smoke while waiting for Mark to arrive.

I broke the slabs into tiny pieces and put the hash into a prescription vial so it would be easier to carry.

By the time I had returned to the park, the sun had just begun going down. So I parked my butt on a park bench near the duck pond. While sitting there, an American hippie approached me and tried to sell me some acid. But I wasn't interested in that, so we continued talking about different things, such as the Vietnam War and how we were able to get out of the draft. Then suddenly, in a flash, there were German cops everywhere.

Right in the middle of our conversation, the hippie I had been talking with suddenly yelled out, "Cops!", then turned, and ran through the bushes. But I was too stoned to move or understand what the heck was happening. Not really hearing what the guy had yelled, I continued to sit on the park bench minding my own business, as though nothing had happened. I just sat with my hands in my pockets, holding onto the vial of hash, debating whether or not to throw it, but instead sat very still. Luckily that was the smartest thing I could have done.

A German policeman came over to me but only looked in my direction. He didn't ask me one question. But the American hippie I had been talking with hadn't been so lucky. The police caught and searched him and found a very large amount of LSD in his shoulder bag, then carted him off to jail while I sat on that cold, steel park bench with my hands in my coat pockets, waiting for the warm morning sun.

An hour after the cops had left the park, the cold night air began to numb my body. It was getting colder and colder by the minute. I covered my head and ears with the hood that attached to the jacket, but that didn't help too much. The jacket wasn't living up to my expectations, and I was beginning to freeze my butt off. I tried to shut my eyes to sleep, but my shivering kept me awake. So I smoked a bowl of my exquisite hashish and slowly, as my head started whirling and spinning, was able to fall asleep.

However, I awakened four hours later, almost frozen like a Popsicle. I decided to get up and walk around the city until I could find an all-night spot or just somewhere warm where I could sleep for another four or five hours. I finally ended up at the underground tram station. There were quite a few people there looking for a warm place to lay their heads until morning.

As I walked down a long corridor, searching for an empty space, I walked around one unconscious fellow who was wallowing in his own puke. He was sprawled out on the cold concrete floor and the right side of his face, up to his nose, was lying in it.

A few minutes later, I had found my spot and lay down in an empty comer of the station away from everyone. I fell asleep as soon as I closed my eyes. But it seemed just as I had fallen asleep, a subway attendant swept through the place and kicked everyone out so they could lock up the station. It was now two in the morning, and we were tossed back into the miserable, freezing, cold night air. I was so tired I wanted to find any place that was warm.

Within a few blocks of the subway, I came across an empty phone booth. It was a little cramped, but at least it got me out of the cold. At least it was bearable, and I knew I wouldn't freeze to death. If I hadn't been so stoned and so slow to react, I could have been spending the night in a warm jail along with that American hippie.

As soon as I laid my head on my knees I fell asleep, dreaming about the adventures that lay ahead.

As soon as the sun came up, so was I. It must have been about five in the morning, but I didn't care. Mark would be here soon, and we would be on our way to Asia.

I found a public bath where I could take a hot shower and warm my cold, aching bones. When that chore was finished, I walked across town to the "hotbonhoff" or main train station so I could buy something to eat and telephone Mark. I was hoping that he had already departed for Germany. However, to my disbelief, Mark answered the phone.

"Mark, when are you going to leave for Frankfurt?" I asked.

He acted as though he had forgotten everything we had talked about the day before at Metro airport.

"I can only come up with about three hundred dollars," he said.

"That's just fine. We will use your cash money for emergencies only and use my traveler's checks for buying the necessities."

"I'll call the airlines and make my reservation later today. I should be in Frankfurt within twenty-four hours," he promised.

"Don't let me down. I'm counting on you. I'll be at the Stat Zurich Hotel waiting for you. I'm not going to sleep another night outside in the freezing cold."

That's where our conversation ended because my time was up. So we said goodbye and then I hung up the phone.

Not knowing if Mark would show up or not, I decided to spend the money and rent a room for the night at the Stat Zurich Hotel. I hoped it would have at least one vacancy. But just my luck, the hotel was booked solid and there were no rooms available. I left a message for Mark with the hotel clerk just in case, telling him where I would be if I wasn't at the hotel.

I tried finding other accommodations for the night but after searching for many hours, I came away empty-handed. I finally ended up at the same park bench I had stayed on the night before. This time, I only stayed until nightfall. Then I walked to the underground subway station and slept there until they kicked everyone out. I ended up sleeping in the same phone booth that I had slept in the night before. Before falling asleep, I promised myself that this would never happen again and that within twenty-four hours I would buy a sleeping bag before I froze to death.

When morning came, I woke up and headed for the public bath to take another hot shower to warm up my cold bones. Once I had accomplished that chore, I walked directly to the Stat Zurich Hotel to rent a room before they were all booked up. However, just as I was walking into the hotel, Mark was walking out. Boy was I surprised. I never thought he would get here that fast, but I was glad he did.

After hugging each other and shaking hands, we congratulated each other for being at the right place at the right time. Then we walked back inside the hotel to rent a room for the night. We were lucky. They had one room available; however, it only had one single bed. But we had to make do. We would be leaving for Asia in a day or so, anyway.

We rented the room, and then decided on a course of action. Before we could hitchhike anywhere, we needed to buy durable sleeping bags for the trip. They were the most important necessity. We asked a few people for the best place to buy them and were directed to the U.S. Army P.X. Once there, the clerk told us that all the sleeping bags had been sold but two. So we bought them thinking that they were both the adult size. But a few days later, when I used it, I found out that I had purchased a kid's bag. Mark had bought the adult size, and I had gotten stuck with the junior size. The flannel bag only came up to my chin. My face and head were exposed to the elements. However, if I slept with my knees bent, I could cover my head.

That evening, we were all packed and ready to travel. We didn't have a map or a clue how to get to our destination, Afghanistan. I figured we would ask hippies along the way. That's how I learned the route to Turkey—from the "heads" at the park. And many of them told me not to travel through Greece, that the Greek government didn't like long-haired hippies. In fact, before they were allowed to enter the country, they had to cut their hair or had to turn around and travel an alternate route. But I had also heard the same thing about Morocco, which turned out to be a fallacy.

Mark and I decided to stay away from Greece and travel through the communist countries of Yugoslavia and Bulgaria. We would actually be playing it by ear, taking it one day at a time.

It was time for bed. We wanted to get up as early as possible and hit the Autobahn. We had to share that little single bed, but we somehow managed all right.

We toked some of the Affy I had purchased the day before and that put us in dreamland. We had slept peacefully throughout the night until a loud pounding on the door awakened us very early the following morning. I awakened in a daze and forgot the vial of hash

I had left sitting on the nightstand next to the bed. I hadn't even thought about it as I walked to open the door. The second I opened it, the brute force of two big, heavy-set men pushed me back as they barged through the open door and into the room. The two evil-looking men didn't say a word, they just pushed their badges into my face, then a few seconds later, yelled something in German, which I didn't understand.

"I don't understand what you are saying," I told the two men, shaking like a leaf.

One of the men motioned for my passport. When I turned toward the bed to retrieve it, I noticed that Mark was still sleeping. I couldn't believe that he could sleep through all of this noise and commotion. Mark was still snoring loudly as I handed the policeman my passport. Then he muttered for Mark's passport. I turned and walked back toward the bed, calling out Mark's name, trying to wake him up out of his blissful snooze.

"Mark, wake up. We have company!" I yelled, as I discreetly grabbed the vial of hash from the nightstand and hid it under the pillow, trying not to draw attention to myself. "They want your passport." But Mark didn't move.

After calling his name a few more times, he finally awoke out of his deep slumber. Once he put on his glasses and focused his eyes, he handed me his passport, and I handed it to the policeman. The policeman looked at each of us and then to our passport photos. Once he was satisfied we weren't the people he was after, he handed the passports to me.

"What did you want?" I asked one of the policemen.

"We had a report that Red Army terrorists were holed up in this hotel. We thought you were the terrorists," replied the fat policeman in broken English.

At least they hadn't hassled us about the vial of hash I had hid under the pillow.

Finally, the two cops left the room and shut the door. With all of the morning's excitement, we couldn't get back to sleep. So we got an early start to the Autobahn.

We paid our hotel bill and then headed out the door into the cool, damp air. After a twenty-minute walk, we were standing at the entrance of the Autobahn with many other travelers heading toward Munich. We didn't carry much luggage. All I carried was my sleeping bag and my coat, which I could turn into a backpack when needed. I had left what little belongings I had in a locker at the main train station.

I wished I had taken my clothes with me. I had learned later that Levi jeans were selling for as much as fifty American dollars in other parts of Europe and Asia. Oh, well. I hoped to retrieve them one day. However, I figured that if I made it to Afghanistan, I would live there for the rest of my life. I had no plans of returning to America or Europe.

Within ten minutes, we had gotten a ride from an electrical engineer named Gunther. He was going home to Munich to visit his family. He worked in Frankfurt and drove home on the weekends. Lucky for us, he spoke perfect English. He was in his early thirties and liked Americans, especially draft dodgers.

However, we explained to him that we had gotten out for disabilities. Mark had been denied a military career because of his bad eyesight. He was blind in his right eye and damn near blind in the left. I got out of the draft for a number of different ailments, including a back injury. In addition, I had told the army that I was crazy. We talked about many different subjects during our three-hour ride to Munich.

"I like you two guys. You make me laugh. I am going to buy you a real German dinner," promised Gunther.

"Gunther, why are you going over one-hundred miles per hour?" I asked.

"There is no speed limit on the Autobahn. These roads were built during World War II for the tanks. They are over three feet thick," he said.

"They are good roads. I haven't seen a pothole yet," opined Mark.

"Have you guys ever tried LSD?" asked Gunther, as a big smile crossed his face.

"We both have. Why?" I asked.

"My girlfriend has been bugging me to try it with her and her friends."

We explained to Gunther about the effects of LSD on the human body and when would be the best time to try it. We also explained about having a bad trip and how not to have one.

Our ride to Munich went by quickly. As fast as Gunther had been driving, we had arrived at the north end of Munich in less than three hours. We had driven over two hundred and fifty miles in less than three hours.

However, before he dropped us off, we stopped at a nice German pub. Gunther kept his promise and bought each of us an exquisite meal of sauerkraut and wienerschnitzal and beer. The meal looked excellent, but it was everything I hated. Mark, however, loved this type of food. I had to force myself to eat it and pray that I wouldn't regurgitate. It stayed down for awhile, until Gunther began toasting us.

We toasted our new friendship with German beer. I hated any kind of alcohol, but out of respect for Gunther, I drank nearly all of the beer he had bought for me. But before I could finish it, I had to excuse myself and walk behind the restaurant to regurgitate. Mark and I loved the meal; it was my stomach that hated it.

We thanked Gunther and said goodbye. Gunther continued his drive to his family while Mark and I walked through the town. But before leaving, he had explained to us that it was illegal to hitchhike inside city limits. So we had to walk and walk and walk. During this little exercise, the sun had come out and the weather had turned very warm.

We noticed a large fountain in the middle of the street, so we decided to wash our faces in it. But before we had even started, a large, heavy-set man stopped by and began screaming at us, except we didn't understand what he was saying and continued washing. When the fat man continued screaming at us, we figured he didn't want us using his fountain as a washroom and walked away.

It took us all day to reach the southern end of the city. It was over a six-mile walk. It was beginning to get dark, so we stopped at a big park called "English Park" and decided to camp there for the night. However, we had camped near a river. That was a major mistake, because we both woke up in the middle of the night, freezing. I tried to start a fire in a foggy, wet mist, but being so close to the river had gotten everything wet. Nothing would catch on fire. Mark was able to fall back to sleep, but I wasn't. My sleeping bag was so small I shivered all through the night from the cold, damp night air. I was finally able to thaw out in the early morning sun.

I hadn't slept at all. But I didn't care. It was the day before the Easter holiday, and we were only a few hours from the Italian border, heading for Venice.

The day before, we had walked over six miles through the city of Munich and today we were walking again, but this time on the Autobahn and hitchhiking.

After an hour or so of walking and hitchhiking along the Autobahn, we had absolutely no luck finding a ride. All we got were mean and weird looks from the passengers and drivers of the cars that had passed us. We couldn't figure out why we weren't getting any rides—that is, until two motorcycle policemen pulled up alongside of us. They explained to us in their best broken English that it was illegal to hitchhike on the Autobahn, and we had to return to the nearest entrance. To legally hitchhike, all hitchhikers had to stand on the entrance of the Autobahn. Anything else was forbidden. We were quite happy with the officers for not giving us tickets.

We turned around and walked back to where we had started. By the time we had reached the entrance, there must have been over fifty people hitchhiking. We had to walk to the end of the line, which practically put us on the Autobahn again. Mark thought it would take us four or five hours to get a ride with all the hitchhikers ahead of us. Even though the cars that came by were few and far between, I wouldn't give up.

"Mark, I'm going to get us a ride, right now," I said, feeling very confident as I put my thumb out.

However, we would have to wait until all the people ahead of us had gotten a ride and then it would be our turn: That's how hitchhiking worked in Europe. Except five minutes after I had told Mark I was going to get us a ride, a VW Bug pulled off the Autobahn and stopped alongside of us. The passenger, a young male college student, asked us if we wanted a ride to Italy. We didn't think twice about it. We gladly accepted.

As we stepped into their vehicle, we noticed that many of the hitchhikers who had been waiting for a ride started running after us, cursing, screaming, and shaking their fists, wanting to pull us out of the car and beat our brains in for taking the ride out of order.

Just as the angry mob approached the car, our new friends put their car into gear and roared back onto the Autobahn, leaving the others in a puff of smelly exhaust smoke.

Our two friends told us they were college students studying in Germany. Now they were going home for Easter vacation. They picked us up because we looked like Americans and they wanted to speak English with us. However, we found out later, when we had arrived at the Italian border that they had picked us up for a different reason.

As we drove through the Austrian Alps, the scenery was spectacular. The steep, Rocky Mountains, covered in a clean, crisp, white sheet of freshly fallen snow, careening along the narrow road of the small, two-lane highway, seemed to go on forever. We went higher and higher, until we were deep in a foggy mist amongst the clouds. I thought we were in heaven. But my awe suddenly turned into terror as we raced down the long and winding mountainous road, so fast that my ears popped. We had rounded so many curves that I became dizzy. Finally, we were stopped at the Italian border.

The Italian customs officer came to the driver's window and asked for our passports. He also asked the driver some other pertinent questions, to which he pointed to us. Then the customs officer carried all of our passports into his office while we waited in the car. All of a sudden, there were at least ten customs officials who had surrounded our vehicle and literally pulled the two Italian boys out of the car, right through the side windows. They didn't even bother to open the car doors and just grabbed each one of them by the shirt and jerked them out in one swift motion. Mark was so frightened by this surprise attack that he pissed his pants. We thought we would be next on the customs officials' agenda to be manhandled for some ungodly reason, but we didn't know for what.

Mark and I started to get out of the car, but one of the customs officers motioned for us to stay where we were. So we sat, nervously biting our fingernails, wondering what the hell was going on. As the customs officers were hauling our two Italian friends into the customs office, two other officers began searching the car. While Mark and I were sitting in the back seat, they took away the two Italians' luggage but didn't touch our bags or search our persons.

I was scared stiff. I was carrying a prescription vial containing nearly an ounce of hash, plus an oversized hash pipe that I had stuffed into my pants. I knew if they searched me, they would surely find my illegal contraband and throw me in jail. I started getting very nervous, thinking the worst, when finally, an hour later, the two Italians finally came out of the customs office carrying their luggage. They secured their luggage and then jumped into the vehicle. We then headed for the next city in Italy. When we asked them about their problems at the border, they just said that customs had to release them and that it was a case of mistaken identity and left it at that.

Our trip had finally started. We had gotten to Italy without spending any money, other than the few dollars we had spent at the army base for our sleeping bags. However, I was still curious about the customs stop at the Italian border.

"What happened back at the border?" I asked the driver.

"The real reason we picked you up was to fool the customs officials and not be hassled, but it didn't work," he replied.

"Why did you want to fool the border patrol?" I asked.

"We are radicals and are taking our political manifestos and literature back to our followers in Italy, which is against the law there," replied the driver.

"You're political protesters, protesting against your government, and that's against the law?" I asked.

He nodded yes and explained the situation. It seemed the customs men could have put them in jail, but instead they took all of their illegal literature and destroyed it, letting them off with a warning.

Two hours after we had left the Italian border, we were saying goodbye to our two Italian friends. They dropped us off just around dusk at a little town called Trento.

Mark and I walked through the small Italian town peering through the shop's windows as we went along. We decided to visit a small cafe. It seemed to be the hangout for the in crowd, because it was crowded with young adults. Soon all the people in the room were staring at us with their evil, piercing eyes. We just nodded our heads in recognition of their unfriendly stares.

Slowly the crowd of young wishers surrounded us. At first, they just seemed nosy and inquisitive. They seemed to be joking around with us, or so we thought, because they were laughing and touching us. But soon the touching turned into shoving. Mark and I slowly walked backwards out the door with the angry crowd of young adults following us.

We tried to explain to them that we were American tourists on vacation. But it seemed our hippie appearance, with our long, scraggly hair and dirty clothes, offended their vanity.

Soon we were walking faster and faster, but the crowd of fifty or so followed, still yelling and swearing at us. Luckily, we noticed a sign that said POLICIA. So we quickly walked toward the building, thinking the crowd would stop following us. They didn't.

Mark and I tried going into the building, but the front door wouldn't open. We yelled for anyone inside to help us and open the door.

"We need help!" I screamed at the top of my voice.

The police still hadn't come to our rescue. Mark and I turned to confront the angry crowd and, using sign language motions with our hands, we tried to relay the message that we were friends and didn't want any trouble. But the crowd didn't understand us. As they edged closer on this bright, moonlit night, I noticed a flash of light in the hand of a teenage male. When I was able to focus my eyes on the shiny object, it appeared to be a switchblade knife.

"Mark, do you see what I see?" I asked, fearful of what might happen next.

Mark responded with a positive nod, so I began pleading with the crowd, once again telling them that we didn't want any trouble. But this macho, knife-wielding Italian teenager still walked toward us. He kept waving it around, all the while screaming and yelling at us in his native tongue. I surmised that the young punk was telling us that he was going to carve us up into small pieces and feed our bodies to the dogs.

Slowly, he began climbing the steps to the front door of the police station. Mark and I had backed up as far as we could, until we were backed against the station door. Just as this Italian punk reached out to stab me, the door suddenly opened and a policeman appeared. The punk with the knife quickly hid it behind his back and retreated into the crowd. But the cop had seen what he had done and made him turn the knife over to him, which he did. Then the policeman broke up the crowd. He was our lifesaver. Mark and I thanked him and shook his hand.

"You should leave here as soon as possible," suggested the officer, in his best-broken English.

"We have no place to sleep," I replied.

"Sleep near the police station tonight in case something happens between now and morning."

We did as he suggested. We picked out a big pine tree on the police property to sleep under. The fallen pine needles made a nice and comfortable mattress to sleep on. The tree seemed to hug and caress us and kept us warm all through the night. Even though the temperature had fallen below thirty degrees, it felt as though it was seventy. We slept peacefully, even after everything that had happened. By morning, we were all rested up and continued our trek to Venice.

We were no longer on the Autobahn, so we hitchhiked as we walked along the road. Suddenly, a VW Bug screeched to a halt right alongside of us. Within ten minutes, we had ourselves a ride. Amazingly, it was our two Italian friends who had picked us up outside of Munich. They promised to take us within fifty miles of Venice.

We put our gear into their car and they put their car into gear and headed toward Venice. As we began telling our story about the night before, after they had dropped us off in the little town of Trento, the car suddenly screeched to a halt as Italian police cars came from every direction and surrounded our car. Suddenly, armed cops jumped from their vehicles with guns drawn; some were holding machine guns.

"Get out of the car with your hands over your heads!" barked a police commander, as he leveled his machine gun at us.

As our two friends in the front seat were slowly climbing out of the car, the passenger suddenly pulled a hand grenade out of his jacket pocket and held it out in front of him. He held the grenade with one hand while holding the pin in the other.

"I'm going to kill us all," yelled the crazed Italian, as he threatened the police with his grenade.

Man, what a vacation, I thought to myself. It had been going pretty well until we had gotten involved with these two Italians. Now I thought we were all going to die. All of this happened within a matter of a few seconds. Mark and I were so shocked, we couldn't speak or move, and the guy with the grenade wouldn't back down and neither would the police. This went on for only a matter of minutes, but it seemed like hours. Then, when the grenade wielding Italian yelled something to the police and nearly tripped over his own feet, they converged on him, grabbed the grenade out of his hands, slammed him to the ground, and handcuffed him.

At the same time all this was happening, the other Italian and driver of the car was being jumped on, wrestled to the ground, and handcuffed by a number of policemen. Then they threw him into the police van. But his friend with the grenade didn't fare as well. When they wrestled him to the ground, they not only handcuffed him but also cracked his head wide open against the cement road. Then they let him lay in a pool of his own blood while they waited for the ambulance to arrive to mend the injured terrorist's head.

Mark and I were still sitting, frozen, inside the car. Finally, the police ordered us out of the vehicle and proceeded to handcuff us. Not only was I scared stiff, but I also had my stash of hash in the crotch of my pants. They placed us into the police van along with the one Italian and took us to the same police station that Mark and I had gone to for help the night before, except this time we were inside the jail, not outside of it. We tried explaining to them why we were with those two radical students and that we were just American tourists on vacation. But they didn't want to hear it.

"Just sit and shut up. You are not in America anymore," bellowed the jailer.

"We want to see our ambassador," I whined. "We are innocent. We just stepped into that car not more than ten minutes before you surrounded it."

The police didn't care what we had to say. They threw us into a cell without telling us why. After more than four hours of sitting in that little jail cell, the jailer finally opened the cell door, then gave us back our passports and told us that we had gotten a ride with some crazy revolutionaries. Then he let us go. Luckily, they never searched me, or I would still be in that jail cell. But before we left the police station, I had a few questions of my own to ask.

"Why didn't you arrest those guys when we arrived at the border yesterday?" I asked the policeman.

"We needed to follow them to find out where they hid their weapons and heavy artillery," he replied. "We found their hideout last night, but not the suspects. We were waiting for the right time to pick them up so there wouldn't be a shoot-out and nobody would get hurt. Before we could stop them, they picked up you two guys."

"I guess we were at the wrong place at the wrong time," I said.

"Actually, we thought you were part of their gang until we had gotten things sorted out," said the policeman.

When I had been satisfied with their answers, we headed out the door for Venice. This time we decided to spend the money and travel in style by train. Within an hour, we had walked to the train station, purchased the tickets, and boarded the train to Venice. I used my traveler's checks to purchase our tickets. I had heard that American dollars were worth more in Asia, so we saved Mark's fifty cash dollars to spend later.

A few hours later, we were in beautiful Venice. We hoped to have a better time here than we had in our last town. We walked from the train station through the city of canals and narrow passageways and noticed that the quaint little houses that had been built centuries ago were now being eroded due to the water swishing and lapping against them.

The sights were beautiful, but the smell was terrible, which came from industrial waste, garbage, and raw sewage that flowed freely through the canal's water and into the open seas. Even with a good breeze, the putrid smells still lingered in the air. In some spots near the canal, as we walked toward San Marco Square, the air wasn't breathable. You literally had to hold your breath when you passed a certain area. The city sure didn't look as pretty as the movies had showed it. To me, Venice was one big garbage pit.

As we walked along the canals, we looked for hippies who had just returned from Asia so we could ask them for directions to Afghanistan. It seemed that hippies were either coming from or going to Asia. That's why we didn't need a map to find our way. We could always ask the people who had just returned from there.

When we reached San Marco Square, everyone was waiting for the pope to appear to give thanks to the people and pray for their salvation. I had forgotten—today was Easter Sunday.

Realizing it was Easter, I had suddenly forgotten about the incidents from the day before, as though it had all been a dream. And I quickly thought about the future and the days that lay ahead of us. Now we were actually in Venice, Italy. We had made it there in three days and had spent only thirty dollars.

We asked some hippies where there was a youth hostel or place we could sleep for the night, and they pointed to a small island across from the square. Mark and I climbed aboard a water taxi and headed for the hostel. As we approached the island, the hostel's outside cafe was full of longhaired hippies playing guitars and singing songs in English. As the taxi pulled into a slip, Mark and I quickly disembarked and headed straight for them. When we reached the café, we pulled up a chair and listened to the music.

We talked to a young couple who had just returned from India and were staying at the youth hostel. I asked them questions concerning the youth hostel and other things. I wanted to know how much it cost each night for a room and how many days travel to Asia. They explained that the best and cheapest way to travel to Afghanistan was by train through Yugoslavia, Bulgaria, and then to Istanbul, Turkey. From that point, we could travel by bus or train, whichever we preferred, to Erzurum, Turkey.

Erzurum was the city from which my grandparents had come. They had lived just outside the city in a little village along Lake Von called Gadding. The Turkish Army slaughtered their families in 1913. From there we would have to travel by bus to Tehran, Iran.

We thanked the couple for the information and decided to catch a train for Istanbul instead of spending the money for a hotel room. We could sleep on the train. That is, if it wasn't too expensive. If need be we would hitchhike.

So we returned to the Venice train station. Once there, we purchased the train tickets to Turkey, using my traveler's checks. We wanted to save Mark's cash for special occasions. But the train wasn't leaving for five hours, so we decided to head back to San

Marco Square to wait for the pope to arrive.

The square began to fill up with thousands of people waiting for a glimpse of him. Nearly four hours of waiting finally paid off. The pope finally arrived and stood outside on the church's balcony overlooking the square, where he blessed the masses. A warm feeling of bliss and calm suddenly filled my spirit. Then for no reason, I started to cry and then started praying.

Afterwards, I asked Mark to look at his watch and tell me the time. We only had an hour before our train would depart, so we headed for the train station once again. The pope was still giving Mass to the masses, but we had to leave. From that day forward, I felt as though nothing bad would happen to us. But I was too optimistic.

Well, we boarded the train for Istanbul and got a compartment to ourselves. I still had the hashish and pipe with me. Even with all that had happened to us, I still had it on me. But I had completely forgotten about it until now.

"Mark, what should I do with the hash? I don't want to get busted with it in a communist country."

I thought the communist police or soldiers would kill us if they caught us with illegal contraband. So Mark and I decided to eat and smoke the rest of my stash before we entered Yugoslavia and then throw the hash pipe out of the window as the train roared down the tracks. Within a few hours, it would be nightfall, and we would be in Yugoslavia.

CHAPTER 5

TRIPPING IN ERZERUM

Well, here we were, on our way to Istanbul, Turkey. We were now going through a communist country, and even though we weren't carrying any illegal contraband, we were still worried and fearful of what was to come.

We were on the famous train, the Orient Express. It was now in a frightful, dilapidated state and not the exquisite, classy, grand train that it had once been. This old and slow train still had a sense of nobility, class, and grandeur, but the compartments were damp and mildew stained. Even so, it was still the most well known train in existence.

In Morocco, I had traveled on the Marrakesh Express, and now I was traveling on the Orient Express. This train was definitely an exquisite piece of artwork, with all the intricate, hand-carved woodwork of mahogany and oak and mosaic tile, which was nearly one hundred years old. It was an incredible icon and masterpiece that was taking Mark and me on our overland adventure. This would be just one more tale to add to the thousands that it had already endured. Imagine the stories this train could tell.

Mark and I were still worried about the stories we had heard about the way the communist soldiers and customs officials treated non-communist tourists. We had heard that they would bring drug-sniffing dogs on board the train to search for any illegal contraband and that the customs officials would threaten tourists with imprisonment until you paid them their price. But I guess we were lucky. We didn't have any trouble of that kind at all, at least not from the big, bad communist customs officials.

Early the next morning, the train had stopped in the city of Zagreb, Yugoslavia. Mark and I were very hungry, so I decided to step off the train to get us something to eat. However, there was only one store open at this early morning hour. There wasn't any place to buy

104

food, only vodka. The Yugoslavian people had no idea what a supermarket was.

Traveling from Italy to Yugoslavia was like night and day. Italy was similar to America in material goods, especially good food—not so in Yugoslavia. That country was bare to the bone.

While looking into the storefront windows, all food stores were bare. Alcohol was their only commodity. Therefore, I gave up the food hunt and began walking back to the train. That's when I noticed the communist soldiers carrying their Kalashnikov machine-guns, goose-stepping in unison, and their commander, at the head of the pack, looking for someone to shoot.

The second I had seen those machine-gun-toting, goose-stepping soldiers, I completely forgot how hungry I had been and ran to the train. They seemed to be looking for trouble, and I refused to give them a reason to start some—they could shoot me. Within a few short minutes, the train was rolling along the winding tracks, rocking back and forth and side to side. We had finally escaped the evil-looking soldiers' clutches.

The beautiful, green rolling hills and mountainous scenery passed quickly as dusk settled upon us. After watching hour upon hour of green rolling hills and meadows, not once did I see any sheep or beef herds, or even any cows. In fact, I didn't see anyone farming the land at all: All this beautiful, luscious, fertile land and no farms. No wonder their food stores were bare.

We didn't stop again until we had reached the Bulgarian border. We had ridden this train for nearly two days and still hadn't eaten any food. We had nothing in our bellies, and Mark and I were completely famished. It had been more than forty hours since our last meal, and that had been in Venice.

As the train slowed down for a customs stop at the Yugoslavian-Bulgarian border, I quickly jumped off to search for some needed food. Not knowing how long the stop was for, I hurriedly glanced into a few open shops. One was a bar that sold beer and vodka. All of their workers were so drunk they staggered as they walked. The next store was a small meat market, except the counters were empty of meat. I looked in one small shop after another. The last store that I had visited had one edible item for sale—well two, if you count the raw pig's feet that were hanging about and the chocolate marshmallow pies. I would never have purchased them or for that matter, eaten them in America. But after forty hours of starvation, I would learn to love them. It was either the chocolate marshmallow pies, pig's feet, or a few shots of vodka. So I chose the pies. I only purchased four of them due to a cash-flow problem. I used all the American money I had on hand when they refused to accept my traveler's checks. They offered to swap an additional four marshmallow pies for my fourteen-caret gold high school class ring. I turned them down. I paid them ninety American cents for four pies and returned to the train.

All of these stores had refrigerated glass meat counters, but they were completely void of meat and Freon. This place was a joke. I wondered how these people lived without any decent food, unless they thought chocolate marshmallow pies were a delicacy.

I entered my compartment and handed Mark two of the pies. He ripped open the cellophane as though he was a starving animal using his claws to rip open his prey. I tried to eat one, but they must have been ten years old. They were hard as a rock and smelled as if they had been dipped into urine brine, and they were poisonous. Thirty minutes after eating them, Mark and I had stomach cramps and diarrhea, which lasted until we reached Istanbul, Turkey, a day and a half later.

That was our first taste of communism, and a pitiful taste it was. We hoped Bulgaria would be a little better—food wise, that is. We were still very sick and needed to eat a solid, nutritious meal. We hadn't seen any fruits or vegetables in any stores in Yugoslavia. We hoped that they had exported it all to Bulgaria and were about to find out as the train pulled into Sofia station.

The city of Sofia looked as though it had been built during the sixteenth century. It seemed to bustle and hustle like any other big city. But like in Yugoslavia, we hadn't seen any food vendors hawking their wares, and the meat markets and grocery stores were completely bare of the essentials. I didn't even see any pig's feet hanging about. However, I continued my journey, searching for a needle in a haystack, hoping one shop would have some decent food to fill our bellies.

A few minutes later, I noticed scores of people waiting in long lines in front of another shop a block away. I wondered what all the commotion was about, so I walked up near the front of the line to peer into the store's window.

I thought and hoped that it was a soup line where hungry, destitute citizens could get a free, hot meal. But I was wrong. These hundreds of townsfolk were standing in line waiting to purchase vodka and cigarettes. That was it. No food—only liquor and cigarettes. What a diet to live on. I concluded that the reason there were so many alcoholics in their country was that they drink to forget how hungry they are. That would curb anyone's appetite.

I turned and walked back toward the train. But then I turned down another street to check a few other stores for food. The first store I entered was a meat market. Again, this store was completely empty. I asked the clerk where I could purchase food, but she couldn't understand me. So I tried using my hands and sign language, pointing to my mouth and patting my stomach. Then I showed her my money. Finally, she just smiled and then mumbled something, which I thought was her word for food.

When she saw my confused look, her old, red, wrinkled, and weathered face smiled a toothless grin and she yelled out, "Istanbul!" At the time, I didn't understand what she had been trying to convey to me—that is, until we reached Turkey.

Just as I was leaving her shop empty-handed to return to the train, a big guy flew past me, nearly knocking me down. A second later, a small band of communist soldiers followed after him, shouting warnings for him to stop. The guy suddenly whirled around and pointed a Luger pistol at them, then yelled some words and fired the weapon. As I heard the *pop, pop, pop, pop* of gunfire, I turned and dove back into the store and hugged the floor. As I dove for safety, I heard the crackle and *rat-a-tat-tat* of machine-guns firing from four or five of the soldiers' weapons.

When the shooting had stopped, I slowly lifted myself off of the dirty floor and nervously walked outside to inspect the carnage that had occurred. None of the soldiers had been injured. However, I can't say the same for the other guy they had been shooting at. He had been shot so many times that his body had literally been cut in half, and his head—decapitated—was sitting a foot or two away from his body. *They don't mess around over here,* I thought to myself. When the soldiers noticed I was watching them, they shouted at me in their Bulgarian language.

But I didn't understand them and shouted, "I am an American and don't understand your language!" trying hard not to show my nervousness.

To my surprise, one of the soldiers spoke to me in English and asked for my passport.

"What are you doing here?" he asked.

"I was on my way to Istanbul, and I just stopped to get something to eat," I replied.

He looked at me as though I was a spy or something evil, then pushed my passport back into my hands and gestured for me to leave the scene. Immediately, I ran back to the train and into the four-foot-by-four-foot cubicle Mark and I shared as we journeyed across communist countries to the Middle East and then to our final destination, Afghanistan, the land of milk and honey—or better yet, the land of potent hash. That was the rumor, anyway.

"Mark, did you see what happened to that guy?" I asked, as I shut the compartment door.

"No. By the time I ran to the window to see what all the commotion was about, it was over. They were dragging the body away and keeping inquisitive people at a distance," Mark explained.

Ten minutes after the shooting, the train had departed from Sofia station and headed toward Istanbul. We were on our way once again.

The Orient Express was living up to its reputation for surprising and mysterious happenings. These last couple of days had been more adventurous than all my years in America.

After traveling more than three days, we were nearly to Istanbul. Another day and a half and we would be there. Then we would have to ask the hippies coming from Asia the way to Afghanistan.

We still didn't have a map or visas, for that matter, and had to find out what visas, if any, were required for our long journey. We hoped to be in Afghanistan within another week or so. We wanted to visit the country that Genghis Khan had invaded and defeated. But our number one priority was to find the best hash available and get as high as we could.

I eased back into my seat, stretched out my legs, shut my eyes to relax, and reflected on what I had just witnessed. At least four soldiers, if not more, had fired their automatic weapons at their live target. So many bullets hit the guy's body that the force of those bullets spun him round and round, and the bursts were so powerful that they tore the body in two, the head landing a few feet from where the body had fallen, as if the victim had been hit by cannon fire.

Once the shooting had stopped, the soldiers patted each other on the back and congratulated themselves for doing such an outstanding job. Then they passed a pack of cigarettes around while they laughed and shouted with glee.

I watched as one of the soldiers walked over to the decapitated head and spit on it. Instead of retrieving it and placing it alongside its body or even covering it up with a blanket or tarp until the ambulance arrived, he just let it lay while another soldier walked by and kicked it, soccer style, over to the body. Thinking how sick this scene had been, I suddenly awoke in a deep sweat. My daydream had turned into a nightmare. I felt nauseous.

Later that night, we learned from one of the train conductors that the soldiers had killed a Bulgarian serial killer and rapist. When he tried to escape from the manhunt, they shot him.

"That is what the Bulgarian government does when they know the person accused is one hundred percent guilty," said the communist train conductor as he punched our tickets. "They don't waste the people's time or money on a trial. This way is fast and cheap. And it is good training for the soldiers."

"Well, that's a quick justice system. That's what America needs," I opined, as the conductor exited our compartment.

However, another tourist traveling on the train had explained to Mark and me that the victim had been running away from a death sentence. He had been an outlawed opponent of the government and had been sentenced to death for speaking out against communism. He had shot his weapon in self-defense against the oppressors of his country. I guess he died for his cause.

Gee, this trip was getting dangerous. First, we were confronted by a radical Italian with a hand grenade, and then we had been witness to a shooting that resulted in a brutal killing. I wondered what we would experience next. Lately, we had experienced starvation. We had visited Sofia and couldn't find anything to eat, except for two chocolate marshmallow pies, which I couldn't eat completely. In fact, everything I had eaten came up nearly as fast as it went down.

Our next stop was Istanbul, Turkey. We had traveled through Germany, Austria, Italy, Yugoslavia, and Bulgaria in less than four days. Another day or so and we would be arriving in Istanbul. I was really excited. My whole body was on a constant high just from this magical adventure. But this was also the country where my grandparents had been born and lived into their teen years. Then they were forced to flee or die.

Well, it was getting late, and I lay back down on the padded seat. It wasn't too uncomfortable, just a little short, about the same length as my sleeping bag, so I had to keep my knees bent. Other than that, it was perfect.

But I was still starving. I wondered how the people who lived in these communist countries put up with not having a substantial food supply.

Now I knew—if the people did speak out, they would be hauled away to some desolate area to be shot and murdered, never to be heard from again. In America, we were always told that this is the way it is in communist countries, and now I had seen it firsthand. It wasn't just propaganda. It seemed to be the truth.

Nothing more exciting happened during our train ride on the Orient Express. We finally reached Istanbul by the following afternoon. As soon as we jumped off the train, we met a group of hippies with long, dyed, red hair.

"Which way to Afghanistan?" I asked a dazed and confused young adult female from the group.

"All you have to do is ride the ferry across the bay to the train station on the eastern side," she said, as she stroked her long red hair.

The Turkish government hadn't built a bridge so the train could travel across the bay to the other side. Now we would have to ride on a different train. The Orient Express stopped on the west side of Istanbul and could go no further.

Mark and I would start this part of our expedition from the eastern side of Istanbul and continue to the end of the line. The train stopped approximately two hundred miles from the Turkish-Iranian border. From there, we would have to ride buses. We thanked the hippies for their help and left to look for some good food to eat.

Istanbul had a completely different economy than the two communist countries through which we had just traveled. There were restaurants everywhere, small diners with food similar to America's. We stopped and bought a couple of kabob sandwiches with pita bread and washed them down with a few cold bottles of Pepsi. Boy was that tasty. After not eating for a few days, this food sure hit the spot.

Istanbul was a very westernized city. I was very happy about that, and it had only cost us about fifty American dollars for travel expenses—and that included the cost of our sleeping bags. And we still had over seven-hundred dollars between us. We debated whether to sleep in Istanbul or on the train to Erzurum.

As we walked toward the ferry, I noticed all the people. The streets were packed with thousands of people. Packed in like a can of sardines. We walked with the crowd, and then boarded the ferry for the train station on the eastern side of the city.

But one thing we had forgotten before we left Istanbul was a visa for Iran. Up to this point, visas weren't required for the countries we had visited. We hadn't even thought about visas—that is, until we arrived at the Turkish-Iranian border.

Thirty minutes after boarding the ferry, we had reached the station, bought our tickets to Erzurum, and boarded the train. We had an open train this time with fifty or more people sitting in separate seats. We were sitting across from a young English couple who were also traveling to Afghanistan. They were, it seemed to me, just two average tourists with no interest in hashish or drugs at all. They were going to look at the tourist attractions, which was the farthest thing from my mind.

Sitting behind the English couple was a big, black army officer and his European girlfriend. He was a captain stationed in Erzurum and returning to his base. He had been on leave for more than a month.

A young Danish hippie couple occupied the two seats directly behind us and in the seats across the aisle from them was an Austrian couple who were very educated.

Within a few hours, we had all become good friends and were telling our most recent adventures and mishaps. Mark and I had lots to tell our little group. We were like one big happy family.

A few hours into our trip, the army captain took out a fifth of whiskey and passed it around to all our newly acquired friends, with each taking a few swigs from the bottle except me. I hated the taste of any type of alcohol, especially hard liquor. Everyone in our little group soon became very drunk and opened up, telling their innermost secrets.

The English couple told us that they had taken a boat from London to Greece and had lots of fun, until they arrived at their destination. The Greek customs officers were very vulgar and mean and made the young couple strip completely naked, then searched them for illegal contraband. When no drugs were found, customs still refused them entry into their country unless they gave up all of their medicines, such as antibiotics, quinine for bad drinking water, and prescriptions for different allergies. The English couple was abused, blackmailed, and very upset with the Greek government and told anyone who would listen.

"Never go to Greece unless you want to be humiliated and treated with evil hatred," stated the couple, with the utmost disdain for the Greek government.

That was the reason why Mark and I refused to travel through that country and instead, traveled through the communist countries. I also had heard that they wouldn't allow hippies to enter their country unless they were rich, clean, and had short hair.

The Austrian couple sitting behind us were very quiet. During our conversations, I had learned that the guy was a professor from the University of Austria. He was filming different tourist attractions and wanted to see for himself what it was that attracted all the young adults to India and Asia.

I thought they were just like me and Mark, looking for the best hashish in the world. That basically was my goal in a nutshell. Then I hoped to send it to my friends in America. I wanted to sell them the same stuff that I was smoking in Asia. I guess that was pretty much my reason for traveling halfway around the world to Afghanistan. However, I didn't tell our new friends the real reason why we were going to Asia. We explained to them that we were just students taking a break from our studies.

Within a few hours, after everyone had told their stories and adventures, we all lay back to sleep the night away. Within another twenty or thirty hours, we would arrive in Erzurum. When we did finally reach the city, it was nearly dark.

Our small group of new friends left the train station together, except the army captain. We said goodbye to him and his girlfriend as they headed for the army base. The rest of our group headed for a decent hotel.

As we walked down the dirt road, past the mud and straw huts and buildings, an eerie feeling came over my body. Not only was this the city where my grandparents had been born, but just a few kilometers away, their families had been massacred by Turkish Army troops in a little village near Lake Von called Kelli.

The massacres took place in 1913 during the Ottoman Empire when the Turkish soldiers overran peaceful Armenian villages and slaughtered everyone in sight. It was their way of ethnic cleansing.

My grandmother was made to watch as her pregnant sister had her belly ripped open by a soldier's bayonet. Then he stabbed at the opened stomach and penetrated the seven-month embryo. He picked the baby up with the end of his bayonet and waved it in the air.

"This is the Armenian flag," bellowed the Turkish soldier, as my grandmother looked on.

This was always in the back of my mind as we walked around the city looking for a hotel. After checking all the decent hotels for a vacancy, we ended up in one that was run-down and dilapidated but had one vacant room with just enough beds for all six of us. Our group included Mark and me, and the Austrian and English couples, while the Danish couple went on their own.

Our group was leaving for the Turkish-Iranian border in the morning, so the hotel manager knew he had us over a barrel. He had the only hotel room available and took advantage of the situation. He charged each of us five American dollars. We argued with him for more than five minutes but couldn't change his mind.

Mark and I paid our money, unloaded what little baggage we had, and then told the others that we were going to get something to eat and check out the town. As we walked down the darkened alleys, we asked the storeowners if they knew where we could buy some hash. But after getting dirty looks and spat upon, we got very paranoid. We didn't want to get busted and end up in a dirty Turkish jail, so we headed back to our hotel room.

Nearly halfway there, a beautiful, blonde-haired Danish girl stopped us. She wanted to know if we wanted to buy any LSD.

"What kind?" I asked.

"It's orange sunshine and real smooth. It isn't cut with speed. It's really good acid," she replied.

We bought two tabs, one for each of us, and immediately popped them into our mouths and let them melt under our tongues.

As we walked back to our hotel room, I started feeling the effects of the drug, feeling light-headed and anxious. I looked at Mark and him at me, and we both laughed out loud. We were getting higher and higher as each minute passed.

Within a few more minutes, we were back in our hotel room. By this time, Mark and I were flying high. We looked at the two couples as they were relaxing on their beds and acknowledged their presence. When they asked us about the city and what time the bus was leaving in the morning, we tried answering their questions, but the words wouldn't come out right. The English couple looked at me as if I was crazy, so I had to tell them why Mark and I were acting so strangely.

"We're tripping on acid," I told them.

The two couples didn't know what to do or think. I felt as though they didn't trust us anymore. They suddenly wanted to shut off the light and get some sleep.

"We can't sleep," I exclaimed, as Mark and I got out of bed and walked out into the hallway.

Twenty feet outside our door was a warm kerosene heater and the ghostly outline of a longhaired hippie. But I wasn't sure if there was a body there, or if I was just hallucinating. It seemed like it took forever to reach the heater. But when I did, I learned that I hadn't been hallucinating. There, next to the heater, was a skinny, scruffy hippie with straight, dark, waist-length hair. He told us that he was from Belgium and returning home after visiting India for eight months. He had left when his money ran out. We tried talking to him, but he could tell that we were high on something.

"What are you guys stoned on?" he asked.

"We're tripping on orange sunshine acid," I mumbled.

I also explained to him that we were higher than a kite and would be leaving early in the morning for the Iranian border. He spoke and understood English perfectly, even though we weren't making much sense. He mentioned that he had also tripped many times before.

"What time in the morning do you leave for Iran? You should get some sleep," he said.

"We need to get some sleep, but this acid is too speedy. We tried to buy some hash, but didn't have any luck," I told our new friend.

"In Turkey, you must be very careful," whispered the hippie. "There are many more secret police and undercover narcotic agents than tourists. They will sell you the hash or opium and then tell the police to get you busted. The narcs get a reward . . . plus the police return the hash to them so they can use it again to catch the next dopers."

"I'll keep that in mind from now on," I replied.

Those words made a deep impression in my mind, and I would remember them forever. After chatting for about ten minutes, I mentioned again that I was very hyper and couldn't sleep.

"I might have something that might help you sleep," said the Belgian hippie. He returned to his room and retrieved a small pipe and what looked like a small chunk of black glass. "I bought this opium in Iran, near the Afghan border. I have just enough for my trip home."

As he talked, he filled the pipe with the strong-smelling, pungent narcotic. I had never tried it before that night, so I didn't know how I would react to it. I watched as the Belgian hippie lit the bowl, took a long, slow drag on the pipe, and then let the smoke slowly escape through his nostrils. The opium bubbled up and grew into a hollow ball as the flame of the match came in contact with it. He passed the pipe to me, so I put it to my lips while he lit the opium for me. I took a long drag. The second the smoke filled my lungs, I could feel a very warm rush pass throughout my body. Within a nano-second, I had come completely down from the LSD. I couldn't believe it: coming down so fast from the acid was incredible.

After my toke, I passed the pipe to Mark. He took a long, deep drag and nearly passed out. Once kneeling, now he was falling to the floor. I grabbed the pipe out of his hand and gave it back to our Belgian friend.

"Do you want another toke of opium?" asked the Belgian.

"Sure," I replied, as I waited in anticipation and excitement.

He quickly cleaned the bowl of the pipe, filled it with the pungent drug, and then passed it to me. Then he reached over and lit it for me, while I proceeded to take a long, deep toke. I inhaled with all my might, wanting to empty my body of the acid. I held my breath and must have passed out. The next thing I knew, I woke up looking at the ceiling. So many wild and bright colors raced past my eyes as I continued to hallucinate from the drugs I had consumed. I was in a deep fog and had completely forgotten about taking the acid. I was on a new high, a narcotic high. The edgy feeling was almost gone. The opium had taken the speed out of the acid. Now I was completely calm, and my head was in a cloud of colors. After Mark had taken his turn on the pipe, we began another conversation.

"Can we buy some of your opium?" I asked the Belgian.

"No, I'm sorry, but I don't have that much. But if you give me one American dollar, you can each have a good night toke."

We kindly obliged, and Mark handed him a dollar. So our friend filled the bowl once more and we took our good night tokes. Once that task was completed, it was time to return to our rooms. We said goodbye to our Belgian friend as we were heading in the opposite directions—he, going west to Europe, and Mark and I, heading east for Asia. We quietly returned to our rooms, where everyone was already sound asleep.

Mark and I had to share a single bed, but within ten minutes, I was fast asleep, only to awaken a few hours later to catch the bus to the Turkish-Iranian border.

When we purchased our tickets that morning, we found that we needed visas to enter Iran. The only problem with that was the Iranian Embassy was back in Ankara. We could either turn around or go back two thousand miles, or, for a few dollars, the bus driver promised to get us entrance visas at the border so we could travel through Iran legally. We decided to pay him the money and take the chance because we had traveled too far to turn back now. So we boarded the bus and headed to the Iranian border.

CHAPTER 6
IRANIAN MADNESS

Well, we were on our way to the Turkish-Iranian border, which was only two hundred miles away. I said goodbye to Turkey but promised myself that I would return one day to claim the property and home that my grandfather's parents had owned and in which they had died.

We had spent less than seventy dollars so far traveling halfway around the world, nearly five thousand miles in just seven days. So I didn't want to travel all the way back to Ankara just to get a three-day transit visa.

If we had to spend twenty dollars for two visas, it would be well worth it. We were just four or five days from the Afghan border and I was too anxious and excited to turn back now. But I was also getting very nervous, wondering if the bus driver would keep his promise concerning our transit visas.

After just an hour of traveling on these snowy, winding, mountain roads, on this old and rickety bus with very bald tires, I was beginning to worry. Every few minutes the bus driver would curse and honk his horn at the other crazy drivers, and there weren't any guardrails to stop us from hurtling down a five thousand foot ravine.

Here we were in the Ararat Mountains where Noah had landed his ark—where it had supposedly split into two parts and was covered by hundreds of tons of dirt. But the Turkish government wouldn't allow anyone in that area to investigate. If you were caught near there, the soldiers shot you—no trials, no judges, just the executioner. So no one dared to go near Mr. Ararat without government permission.

The scenery in this area was so green and beautiful—I couldn't help but daydream about the land of my ancestry. This country was filled with history, ancient Armenian history.

As we got closer to the border, my forehead and hands began to sweat because I worried about our transit visas and thought about all the secret and undercover police that our Belgian friend had told us about. If we did try to bribe the customs official, would they bust us for it?

Then my mind shifted to another thought when I noticed that one of two Muslim men sitting across from us had pulled out a white handkerchief from his vest pocket. I watched as he unfolded it and noticed that it was filled with a mysterious herb—the herb was actually hashish. So I suddenly got brave and asked him if the stuff was hashish. He didn't say a word but had a smile on his face that stretched from ear to ear. I must have guessed correctly.

I looked deep into the old Muslim's scarred, weather-beaten face. He had a six-inch-long scar on the left side of his cheek that went from the corner of his eye to within a quarter inch of his mouth. When he noticed me staring at the scar, he motioned to it with his finger and explained by using sign language that it had come from a dogfight. I figured it must have happened over a bet.

Then I asked him if I could see the hashish and he replied, "Chars." I wasn't sure what that word meant, but I knew that it had something to do with the hashish. He then folded up the handkerchief and passed it over to me. Before I even opened it, I could smell the sweet, pungent smell of the hash. After checking it more closely, I handed it back to him, wishing if only I could smoke it.

"Can I buy some from you?" I asked him.

He shook his head no and opened the handkerchief, dividing its contents between him and his friend, and then they ate it and chewed the hash as if it were candy. If I had tried that I would have thrown up, which I nearly did anyway, just watching them munch on the stuff. I looked over to them and just smiled.

"Do you have any more hashish?"

The two Afghan men knew exactly what I was talking about, but just smiled and shook their heads no. So I started a conversation with them.

"My friend and I are going to Afghanistan," I told him.

"We are also traveling to Afghanistan . . . Kabul, Afghanistan. . . . That is our homeland," explained the old Afghan man sitting closest to me.

He could speak very little English, but he seemed to understand me. So we continued our conversation.

"We are traveling to Kabul, too. When we arrive there we will visit you," I promised him.

The old Afghan man wrote his name and address on a piece of paper and handed it to me. But it was written in Farsi, and I couldn't read it.

"Show this paper to any Afghan and he will give you directions to our hotel. Please come and visit with us," he begged.

"How much money does it cost for a kilo of hashish in Kabul?"

"Two dollars," he said, as he held up two fingers.

"Did you understand my question?"

"Yes. One kilo of powder costs two dollars."

But I still wasn't sure if he had understood my question, so I held up two American dollar bills. When he nodded his head yes, I knew that he had understood.

"What is powder?" I asked.

"That is what 'chars' is made from," he replied.

Then it dawned on me. "Chars" was the Farsi word for hashish. I had heard this word in Morocco, but I never knew what the word meant. And I didn't understand what he meant about the "powder," but it wasn't important. We continued our conversation, becoming good friends.

If someone were watching us, they would have thought I was a deaf mute the way I talked with my hands. But the old Afghan man and I understood each other quite well.

Finally, we had arrived at the Turkish-Iranian border. First, we had to go through Turkish customs. Then, once they had inspected our belongings, we would have them inspected again by the Iranian customs officials.

It only took a few minutes for Turkish customs to inspect our baggage. After that, we waited in line for Iranian customs to inspect it. I wanted the bus driver to be near Mark and I so he could help us just in case the Iranian inspector gave us any trouble, but he was nowhere in sight.

A few minutes later when I had reached the front of the line, the Iranian customs official asked for my passport and luggage. After he checked my passport for a visa, he gave me a very dirty, disgusting look, and his face became distorted and red from anger. I thought he was going to explode. He told me I had to return to Ankara to apply for an Iranian visa. He would not let me pass without one.

As I was about to plead and argue my case, the bus driver came over and told Mark and me to stand to one side and just wait.

Nearly everyone else had passed through Iranian customs. I thought Mark and I were the only ones left but to my surprise, the two old Afghan men with whom I had spoken on the bus also needed transit visas. Now all four of us were in the same predicament.

I walked over to my Afghan friend and asked him about his visa. He kept mumbling something about ten dollars and pointed to his eyes, so I thought he wanted to see ten dollars. I walked over to Mark and asked him to give me an American ten-dollar bill.

After Mark retrieved the money from his hidden money belt, I walked over to my Afghan friend and held out my hand, showing him the money. Suddenly, he grabbed the bill, walked to the other side of the room, and stood by his friend. His actions took me by surprise, and I didn't quite know what to do. I walked over to Mark and explained to him what had just transpired. We debated on a course of action—ten dollars was a lot of money to us.

I decided to get the money back, so I put my plan into motion. I returned to the other side of the room and stood next to my Afghan friend who had taken the money. I began talking to him using sign language and broken English. After much prodding, I finally got him to show me the ten-dollar bill. As soon as I saw it, I snatched it from his hands, walked very quickly to the other side of the room, and stood near Mark.

I looked over to the Afghans and they had dazed and puzzled looks on their faces. Mark and I broke out in laughter. But our laughter dissipated when the bus driver came to us and explained that we had to pay five dollars each for a seven-day transit visa through Iran. And there was another problem: I had to pay for two additional visas.

It seemed the two Afghans didn't have the money to purchase the visas they needed, so it was either buy all four visas or all four of us would have to return to Ankara and get them there. But I wanted to continue our adventurous journey to Afghanistan. I wanted to push forward, not backward. So I agreed to pay the extortion.

"I will give the customs official ten dollars now and ten dollars when we receive the visas," I explained to the bus driver.

The bus driver walked to the Iranian customs official to see if he would agree to my offer. I watched as the two men argued and after a lengthy conversation, the official finally gave in. He agreed to give all four of us seven-day transit visas. Mark and the Afghans had received their visas first and were waiting on the bus, while I was the last one to leave the customs office.

All the other passengers were waiting for me so we could continue our journey east. We were all very anxious, including the Iranian customs official. He was following twenty feet behind me, yelling for his money. I still owed him ten dollars, but we already had our visas, so I decided not to pay him. As he continued his outburst, I walked faster and faster toward the bus. Then just as I reached it, I yelled to the customs official that my money was in my friend's bag and promised to get it for him.

When I boarded the bus, the customs official was still ten feet away waiting for his money. But a few seconds later the bus raced away. I opened a window and yelled to the customs man that I was sorry and waved goodbye. He just shook his fist in the air and yelled something in Farsi. He slowly disappeared as the bus traveled toward the Iranian city of Tabriz.

This bus wasn't the best, but it wasn't the worst, either. Within four to five hours, we would be near Tabriz, a city high up in the Ararat Mountains. There was very little snow on the mountaintops, so the grass was a luscious green, as spring was in the air. You could smell it.

Just as I was about to close my eyes to take a little nap, I was quickly awakened by a loud banging noise. Then suddenly the bus veered to the right and stopped. The bus driver motioned for us to sit in our seats and stay calm while he checked out the problem. He returned with a disgusted look on his face and told everyone to get off the bus while he fixed the flat tire. The bus's right rear tire was flat, so we weren't going anywhere for a few hours.

There were still four or five hours of sunlight left in the day, so I was sure we wouldn't freeze to death here in the mountains. I wasn't so sure, however, what time we would arrive in Tabriz, even though the bus driver had a schedule to keep. We were anxious to get to Kabul as quickly as possible, but there was nothing we could do about this situation.

Mark and I walked over to the Afghans and stood next to them. I hoped they weren't angry with me for taking back the money, but I had still paid for their visas so I didn't know how they would react. We nodded in recognition of each other. Then the old man with the scar introduced himself. His name was Serab. His friend's name was Nabul. We, in turn, introduced ourselves.

"I don't like to be in this area without some type of protection," said a worried Serab. "In Afghanistan, we are allowed to carry weapons, rifles, or guns anywhere in the country. Here, we have no protection against bandits and thieves. If we don't get the bus fixed and leave soon, it will get cold—cold enough to freeze."

Boy, he didn't sound very optimistic. So I changed the subject.

"Serab, how can you eat that hashish like it was candy?" I asked.

"After years of ingesting chars, it doesn't bother me at all. We wanted to eat it before we arrived in Iran because they have too many bad policemen and very bad jails," he said.

I guess they didn't want to take any chances. Mark and I felt the same.

Just then, the bus driver came over to us. "Stay near the bus 'cause it will only take a few minutes to change the tire," he exclaimed.

But I knew that wouldn't be the case. Not the way these people worked. Even if they knew what they were doing and had all the right tools, it would still take them half a day to fix the flat tire.

So Mark and I decided to take a little walk and take in the sights. We thought we might get lucky and find some hash plants or maybe some opium poppies. Iran was the type of country that could grow some nice pot. We even thought about asking the locals if they had any good hashish or opium for sale. At the very least, we could find a good spot to take a pee.

I had heard from some Germans that Iran had been one of the biggest exporters of opium until America and the shah decided to destroy all the poppy fields and either executed the addicts or put them in jail. This turned into a war against the poverty-stricken population. These were the people who had worked the poppy fields. When they were arrested, their owners would pay their fines, then let them work the fields to pay back the loans. But the farmer could never repay his debt in full, so the landowner kept the farmer in his control. They became slaves and indentured servants. But what could they do? This was a way of life in this part of the world.

Then my thoughts turned to other matters. It was time to return to the bus. We had only been gone for about twenty minutes but were anxious to get back on the road.

We were approximately fifty feet away from the rear of the bus, hidden by some bushes and trees, when Mark and I noticed all the passengers were standing near the rear of the bus, with their hands held high above their heads. They were being robbed of their jewelry and valuables at gunpoint by a bunch of mountain bandits, just like the Afghans had predicted.

Mark and I stayed behind the bushes and watched as the four

robbers confronted the passengers. Three of the bandits pointed rifles at them, while the fourth held out an empty pillowcase and had them fill it with their valuables.

Throughout this whole ordeal, the bus driver and his helper continued to work on the flat tire. They were never hassled by the bandits. I wondered if it had been set up.

Then, as the bandit finished collecting the valuables, he started yelling to his buddies. All I could understand was the word: "Americans, Americans."

Mark and I were the only Americans on the bus, so that bandit must have been yelling for us. We stayed hidden until they ran to their old beat-up dump truck and left the area. If this was a set-up job, they must have thought Mark and I were loaded with dollars, as if we were millionaires. We must have been the targets, but we got lucky this time.

We waited at least ten minutes after the bandits had left before we returned to the bus. Everyone began talking to us at the same time. I couldn't quite understand their questions. But I sure knew what they were saying just by the dirty looks and evil stares we were getting. From the shunned response of the passengers, they acted as though the robbery was our fault.

They believed the bandits picked this particular bus because it carried American tourists with lots of money. They seemed to think if Mark and I hadn't been on the bus, the bandits wouldn't have robbed us. Now it was a job for the Iranian police. They would hunt down the bandits once we had made out our report to the authorities.

Within an hour, after the departure of the bandits, the tire had been changed and we were on our way once again toward Tabriz, not as happy as when we had left that morning, but just as tired. So I tried to relax in my seat and take a nap. I leaned against the window, shut my eyes, and dreamed of my adventures that lay ahead. I just hoped we wouldn't run into those bandits again. The next thing I knew, the lights inside the bus had come on, and the bus driver started yelling at us.

"Go into the hotel, get a room, and then meet me in the lobby. Once you get your room, you can come back to the lobby and tell the authorities what happened. We'll be leaving at six in the morning for Tehran," he yelled.

Everyone filed out of the bus and entered the hotel.

Mark and I rented a room and paid forty cents for it. This time Mark and I got a room all to ourselves. Plus, it had two single beds with clean sheets and blankets and a kerosene stove. The room was nice, clean, and warm.

Mark and I walked down to the lobby once we had put our gear away. Some of the passengers were already telling their stories to the police authorities about what had transpired back on the highway. When Mark and I entered the room, everyone stopped what they were doing and stared straight at us. You could hear a pin drop. We again got the dirty looks and cold, inquisitive stares. Even the police acted as if it was our fault. I couldn't understand these people. Just because we were Americans, they blamed us. Even the police blamed us.

"The bandits robbed the bus because they thought or maybe even heard rich Americans were on it," explained the police captain, looking directly at Mark and me.

They think all Americans are very rich with money coming out of our sphincter muscles. They think just because we travel so far that we must be rich. Boy, if they only knew. They see the American magazines that show how Americans live, in big brick houses, each with a garage, pool, two or three cars, and satellite dishes. They read and look at all this propaganda and they think that we have lots of money, lots of dollars.

We explained to them that we weren't rich and that we were truly sorry for what had happened, but it wasn't our fault. They didn't want to hear it. The police told us we could go back to our room, that they had enough information. So off we went.

I couldn't wait until morning. I was excited because another few days and we would be arriving in Afghanistan.

As soon as I entered our hotel room, I immediately went to bed. The minute my head hit the pillow, I closed my eyes and began dreaming about the days ahead. I didn't awaken until the manager of the hotel pounded on our door, telling us that the bus would be leaving for Tehran in thirty minutes. At least I'd had a peaceful night. So far, it had been one crazy, adventurous trip. I wasn't sure what to expect next.

While waiting for the bus to be loaded and fueled, we had just enough time to eat a continental breakfast. We had some coffee and rolls with fresh butter. That hit the spot. We all loaded into the bus and headed for our next stop, Tehran. I sat back in my seat, shut my eyes, and prayed that we wouldn't see the bandits or have another flat tire.

We were about ten to twelve hours away from Iran's largest and most westernized city. We sat across from our Afghan friends, Serab and Nabul. Within a few minutes, Serab and I had started a conversation.

"The people are disgusted and fed up with the shah because he is just a puppet for the American government," exclaimed Serab.

The shah was also allowing the Iranian women to expose themselves in public, like American women. Iran was becoming too westernized too fast.

The people were also fed up with the shah's secret police. They brutalized and tortured their own people. I believed everything he told me. Serab seemed to think there would soon be a revolution in Iran. Evidently, he seemed to know what he was talking about. Everything he had told me came to be true years later.

We were halfway to Tehran, and the weather was getting warmer and the scenery more spectacular. The most beautiful and colorful mountains surrounded us. They were actually made of bright purples, reds, greens, and light blues, and shiny, white, glimmering snow peaks topped them off. The view was awesome. The colors were so bright, it was as if I was tripping on acid or having flashbacks.

The scenery was too beautiful to believe, and the air smelled so clean and fresh. This was definitely God's country. The clouds in the blue sky were like big, fluffy white pillows, and they seemed to change into all different types of figures. Each cloud would morph into something different—one would look like an angel and then morph into the face of Jesus, then morph again into a horse. As I watched the clouds change into different images, more and more objects appeared. Mark even mentioned to me about the clouds changing into images of people.

"Mark, I'm seeing different things, too," I said, as we looked at each other in amazement.

We were only a few hours outside of Tehran, and I was still worried about the bandits. They could still be following us, I thought to myself. But the police in Tabriz told us that they had taken everything from everyone already, so they probably wouldn't strike the same bus twice.   Then I remembered about needing a visa for Afghanistan.

"Mark, we forgot to get our visa for Afghanistan," I exclaimed.

"We still have time for that," he replied.

I figured we could get the visa in Tehran, the biggest city in Iran, if the Afghan Embassy was there. We would have to find out before we traveled any further. We couldn't afford to take another chance without first obtaining the proper travel permits. I didn't want to be turned away at the border for not having a visa. The Afghan customs officials might not be as friendly as the Iranian officials had been. This time I wanted to get the visa legally, even if we had to pay to get them. I would tell the hotel manager in Tehran about our visa problem. He would know what we would have to do and tell us where to go.

So far, we had spent about eighty dollars, and that included the visas for the two Afghans. We had budgeted our money fairly well, spending very modestly.

We pulled into Tehran at eight o'clock in the evening and were dropped off right in front of a nice, cheap hotel.

"The bus will be leaving at six in the morning for the city of Meshad," bellowed the bus driver as he sped away.

That was our next step toward our goal. I was that much closer to realizing my dream. By this time tomorrow night or a little later, we would be in Afghanistan. I couldn't wait. I was truly excited.

We rented another nice cheap room with clean twin beds and a warm kerosene heater for a mere fifty cents apiece. I was getting to like Asia more and more. A dollar went a long way in this part of the world.

Just as we were going to bed, there was a knock on our door. When I answered it, there was a longhaired hippie standing there.

"Can I help you?" I asked the hippie.

"Do you want to buy some LSD?" he asked.

"No. We are getting up early for our trip to Afghanistan, and we just tripped on some orange sunshine two days ago in Erzurum. Come inside for a minute; I don't want anyone else to hear my business," I replied, as he entered the room and closed the door. "Where can we buy some hash?"

"I know a place near Tehran University, but you have to be very careful because the police shoot dopers and dope dealers on sight in Iran. They shoot first and answer questions later," exclaimed the hippie.

"I'm sorry, I didn't get your name. I'm Robert and this is Mark. We are Americans."

"My name is Hans, and I'm from Switzerland. I'm glad to meet you," he replied, as we shook hands. "We can go to the university tomorrow and buy some hash."

"We don't have the time, Hans," I said. "We have to get our visas for Afghanistan tomorrow, then we have to purchase our bus tickets to Meshad."

"The Afghan embassy is in Meshad, not Tehran," remarked Hans.

"Boy, we thought it was here in Tehran. I'm glad you told us. But we still need to buy bus tickets," I told Hans.

"Why take the bus? For a few dollars more, you can ride the train to Meshad. It's much better than riding the hot bus. The trip to Meshad is all desert terrain. It will be very, very hot on the bus. The train is air conditioned and it is brand new," he said. "I've traveled this route many times before, so I know the best way to travel."

"Hans, are you traveling in our direction?" asked Mark.

"Yes, I am."

"Why not travel with us? You can show us the way," pleaded Mark.

"Not only that, but we can travel in a group and look out for each other," I remarked.

"That sounds like a good plan to me," added Mark.

"Me, too," replied Hans.

Hans was also traveling to Kabul, Afghanistan to find drugs, but his were of a different variety. He wasn't interested in hashish. He was interested in buying certain chemicals for producing LSD that couldn't be purchased in Europe but could be procured easily in Afghanistan.

"Well, we better get some sleep so we can get an early start to Meshad. We'll see you in the morning, Hans," I said.

"Okay, but the train doesn't leave until ten in the morning," replied Hans, as he walked out the door. "We should be there at least an hour early. I'll come by and pick you up for breakfast." Then he left our room and shut the door behind him.

Ten minutes later, we were fast asleep.

We woke up bright and early and ate a delicious breakfast of Kellogg's Rice Krispies with ice-cold milk and a large glass of fresh-squeezed orange juice—and paid a total of forty cents for it. While we were dining, our Swiss friend, Hans, sat down at our table.

After breakfast, we headed to the train station. We followed our new friend as he walked through alley after dirty alley. Within fifteen minutes, we had arrived at the train station.

Actually, it looked more like the Taj Mahal. It was a huge monolith, built of beautiful pure white Italian marble. Inside this gigantic castle were hundreds of exquisite oil paintings and statues of the world's most famous artists. These paintings could have hung in any world famous museum. This station must have cost more than one billion dollars to build. I figured the trains must be made out of solid gold. I just couldn't believe this place. The Iranian government had built a train station similar to a palace.

We purchased our tickets to Meshad. That was the end of the line, like Erzurum was the end of the line in Turkey. However, there were still many hundreds of miles to travel to the border of Afghanistan. We would have to travel this portion of the trip by bus. It didn't really matter to me. I was that much closer to my goal.

Once we had reached Meshad, we would set out to get visas for Afghanistan. Hans figured this would only take an hour or two at the most. Then we could buy our bus tickets for the Afghan border and be on our way.

I kept thinking to myself, *just one more day,* and we'd be at our destination, Afghanistan, the land of hashish and opium, where the Hindu Kush and Pamir mountains reach high into the sky—and where Genghis Khan destroyed city after Afghan city with his legions of soldiers. This was my dream come true, or just about to come true. I was very excited and anxious to get to Afghanistan.

We had a few hours to kill before the train departed, so we decided to check out the artwork of the train station. We walked for fifteen minutes and saw famous painting after famous painting, but not a chair in sight. There wasn't any place to sit in this train station. So we gathered in a small semicircle in a corner on the floor.

Within a few minutes a policeman came near, then another, then a third, telling us we could not sit on the floor. If we wanted to sit down, we had to go to the station's restaurant and order some food. But you weren't allowed to sit in there without ordering something. I explained to the officers that we had already eaten breakfast and were just waiting for our train to arrive so we could travel to our destination of Meshad.

As we were speaking with the policemen, a crowd of nosy Iranians started forming around us. They looked at us as though we were creatures from outer space. It was as if they had never seen longhaired hippies before. More than twenty people had gathered around us.

One by one, the policemen disappeared, but the crowd of Iranians stayed. They watched us as if we were animals in a zoo.

That gave me an idea. I whispered in Mark's ear that I was going to walk on my hands and wanted him to ask for money from those staring at us, like the monkey does for the organ grinder.

When we agreed on what we would do, I began walking on my hands, and Mark started begging for money. The crowd was rather amused at our clowning around. They smiled and laughed. They knew we were only joking around.

Everyone got a laugh out of it except the policemen. They came over and broke up the crowd, then gave me a stern warning and lecture about standing on my hands and begging for money—that was against the law in Iran, and we could go to jail for it. I tried explaining to them that it was all a joke, but they didn't think so.

"Go to the other side of the room until the train comes in. You put your lives in jeopardy when you joke around like that. It could start a riot," said an angry policeman.

Boy, this trip would get us into trouble yet. We moved over to the other side of the big hall and away from the crowd. But we couldn't get away from the policemen's shadows. They not only watched us but also escorted us to our train and waited until it had departed. Finally, we were on our way to the city of Meshad and points east.

Our whole ten-hour trip was desert scenery. Watching from our window, we saw giant desert turtles and lizards, some at least four feet long, and one being chased by a desert fox. I also saw a lot of dead animal bones, such as donkey, horse, cow, and camel. There wasn't much plant life either, including cactus.

The desert temperature during the day was one hundred and thirty degrees in the shade, but the train was air conditioned, which made our living conditions very comfortable. And we bought our two first-class tickets for only a total of three dollars. Like I said before, the dollar went a long way in this part of the world.

By the time we had arrived in Meshad, there was very little daylight left, so we decided to get our visas right away. Hans knew the way to the Afghan Embassy, and we arrived there within ten minutes. Luckily, it was still open. But we were told to leave our passports and pick them up in two hours. We had no choice and left them with the consulate worker.

Then we headed for the bus station to purchase our tickets for the last leg of our journey to Afghanistan. But we had arrived too late. There was only one bus available, and it was completely full and leaving for the Afghan border in five minutes. We would have to wait until morning and leave on the first available bus. All three of us were completely disappointed. We would have to wait another day to reach our magical destination.

After purchasing our bus tickets, we walked around the small village looking for a cheap, clean hotel. There were only two hotels in this little village, and one was the Intercontinental, which housed the rich people. That place was completely out of our budget because their rooms went for two-hundred dollars per night. The only other hotel was reasonable, but there was one problem: it had been booked solid. There wasn't a room available anywhere. I asked the hotel manager if he knew of any other place where we could rent a room for the night. He just smiled a silly grin and told us that we could sleep in the barn behind the hotel for ten cents each. It was our decision to make.

We didn't have a choice. We figured there must be some type of bedroom in the barn, so we paid the hotel manager the money he had asked for without first looking at the room. To our amazement, there wasn't any bedroom. In fact, there wasn't any room, just a barn full of animals, including us. It was a stable, nothing more. We had to bed amongst the animals—two donkeys, two goats, and three one-humped camels. Now I knew how Noah felt.

At least there was enough straw to make a decent, soft, comfortable bed. The smell was a little hard to take, though.

We stored our luggage in the stable while we went to retrieve our passports at the Afghan Embassy. Just as we arrived, they were closing the doors, but we managed to talk our way into the place. The Afghan ambassador personally showed us our one-month visas that he had issued.

"How much money do you have?" asked the ambassador.

"We have over seven-hundred dollars between us, and we want to spend it all in your country," I exclaimed.

He was very happy to hear that.

"How can you acquire such vast amounts of wealth? I only make twenty dollars a month as a diplomat. Your families must be very rich in your country," the ambassador retorted.

"We are just poor Americans on a vacation," I told him.

He would not believe me. "How can you travel all this distance? You must have millions of dollars," he said.

To him, our seven-hundred dollars seemed like seven million. He wished us good luck and returned to his office. We took our passports and headed back to the hotel—or should I say stable.

It was dark by the time we returned to our digs, so we lit a candle for light and spread our sleeping bags over the straw. We were only two stalls away from the donkeys, and the smell of the animals was in close proximity, but it was still nice, warm, and comfortable. At least we had a roof over our heads.

We relaxed on the straw and talked about our future bus trip. Hans wanted to take the bus directly to Kabul, purchase his chemicals, and return to Europe. On the other hand, Mark and I wanted to take our time traveling to Kabul. We wanted to see and visit all of Afghanistan and weren't in any hurry.

Within an hour, we had talked ourselves to sleep, only to be awakened by an Iranian pointing a gun and flashlight in our faces. There were three of them, speaking broken English and making demands. The man pointing the gun wanted our valuables. I was still half-asleep and sitting up, wrapped in my sleeping bag. All of us were terrified—the Iranians of us and we of them. We were worried that once they robbed us, they would kill us.

"Take whatever you want. We only want to make our pilgrimage to Afghanistan!" I screamed.

Mark had taken off his pants before he climbed into his sleeping bag, so the robber took them, his watch, and his money—almost forty American dollars. Lucky for me, I had on a money belt around my waist, which they overlooked, but they did take my cowboy boots. Hans lost his money, passport, ring, and watch. But the thieves still weren't satisfied and wanted our American passports.

"They are at the Afghan Embassy, processing our visas!" I shouted.

Luckily, the armed robbers believed me and quietly left without physically hurting us. All of this happened within five minutes.

Once they had left, we ran to the hotel and woke up the manager to tell him what had happened. He, in turn, called the police. They arrived at the hotel within five minutes. We explained the situation to them and why we had been sleeping in the barn.

"Who knew that the tourists were sleeping in the stable?" the policeman asked the hotel manager.

That seemed to be the right question because the hotel manager gave the policeman a few names. Then they began to investigate the crime in earnest. We were worried that we wouldn't be able to leave in the morning for Afghanistan.

When the policemen left, we returned to the stable. However, within a few hours, at about five in the morning, the police arrived at the hotel with the three men who had robbed us.

This was the quickest police work I had ever experienced. Two of the robbers had been beaten to a bloody pulp, but the third must have given the correct answers because he didn't have a bruise or cut on him.

The police handed over all our possessions that had been stolen, including our passports, jewelry, and watches. They even returned Mark's pants and my cowboy boots. Everything that had been stolen was returned to us, including our money.

Everyone from the hotel manager to the police and even some villagers apologized to us for their friends' actions. We were very happy, but tired. We had just enough time to catch our bus to the border. It was nearly six o'clock in the morning. Four buses had already departed for the border, which meant that there were only two available for the trip to Afghanistan. In fact, one was already filled with passengers and just pulling away from the station.

So we boarded the last bus. We had purchased our tickets the night before and handed them to the bus driver, then sat in the only seats available. Luckily, there were three vacant seats, just for us. I wanted to keep our baggage close at hand, but there wasn't much room inside the bus so we decided to put our luggage and sleeping bags on top of the bus with the other luggage. This bus was an old, rickety shell and only had enough room for the passengers.

Finally, we were off and heading for the border of Afghanistan. So far, Mark and I had spent about eighty-five dollars for this adventure. And once we arrived in Afghanistan, we thought we would be able to live on less than one dollar a day for room and board. If that were true, we could live there for a few years on the money that we had—and that was exactly what I intended to do. I hadn't planned on returning to America any time soon. I actually believed I would die in Afghanistan.

I leaned back into my seat and nodded off to sleep. I was so tired. Nearly every other day we had experienced an adventure of some kind or another. I was sleeping peacefully until my dream suddenly turned into a nightmare when I thought about the robbery the night before and how the police had told us that the suspects would be shot in the morning: that they had already been judged and found guilty. They should have been executed by now, I thought. Just as I heard the shot, smelled the gunpowder, and saw the smoke slowly seep from the rifle's barrels, I awoke in a deep sweat.

A few minutes later, we arrived at the border. We passed through Iranian customs without any trouble. However, we ran into a little trouble at the Afghan border—it was closed.

CHAPTER 7
DYSENTERY AND OPIUM IN KANDAHAR

We had arrived at the Afghan border about an hour too late. It had just closed a few minutes before, so the Afghan customs officials refused to check out our luggage. We were told that we would have to stay overnight and then go through customs in the morning. We had no choice but to do what we were told. But that wasn't our only problem.

When we tried to retrieve our sleeping bags from the top of the bus, the soldiers wouldn't allow it and were furious with us. They were afraid that we might smuggle illegal contraband into their country.

We were furious that they wouldn't allow us to retrieve our sleeping bags so we could stay warm during the cold desert night. After our little misunderstanding, Mark and I were ushered, by the soldiers, toward a small hotel. Hell, there were only three buildings in our immediate area—the hotel, the customs office, and a small house about ten yards away from the hotel.

As we walked, I looked up into the clear, starry night and yelled to the gods, "We made it!"

And just then, an eerie feeling came over me. I couldn't believe that we were looking at the stars from the other side of the planet. It looked completely different from this side of the globe. But a few seconds later, I was brought back to reality when I began shivering. It was now about eleven o'clock at night and very cold and damp. Boy, we really needed those sleeping bags.

Mark and I were the first to reach the hotel and rent a room. I asked for a room for two and was escorted to a small ten-foot-by-ten-foot room with no beds, only a clean cement floor, and no blankets or sleeping bags. So we asked the manager for blankets, but he had none—we would have to make do without them. At least we were out of the cold and had a roof over our heads.

Within a few minutes, the manager had returned to the room with two more passengers from the bus and explained to us that we would have to share the room.

Mark and I looked at each other and just shrugged our shoulders and sighed. We gave in, thinking that there was enough room for two more people. However, that was naive thinking. To my surprise, we had to share the room with nearly all the passengers from our bus. This was the only available room in the hotel, so we all had to share it.

Some of the tourists were lucky—they had carried their sleeping bags with them on the bus and were allowed to use them. Now the room was completely packed with at least twenty-five people of all ages and nationalities.

Mark and I ended up in the center of the room. I only had enough room to sit up—everyone else had staked their territory and lay down to rest. So I decided to take a walk outside and get some fresh air. I also wanted to see if I could buy some hash from the locals. If I had to sleep with all these people in this confined space, I needed something to knock me out.

Off I went, following the narrow trail that led from the hotel to a small mud house. A few minutes later, I had reached the place and saw an old Afghan man sitting outside with his feet flat against the ground and his butt hanging an inch or so off it. These people could sit in that position all day and night. I nodded to him and greeted him with a big smile. He returned my smile with a big, toothless grin and greeted me.

"A Salaam Ali cume," he said.

I used sign language and broken English to explain to the old man that I wanted some hashish. When his eyes lit up, I knew that he had understood.

"Ah, chars," replied the old man, smiling.

Then he reached into his shirt pocket and pulled out a one-inch square of some exquisite, hard, brown Afghani hashish. When he handed it to me, I placed it under my nose and smelled it. It had a very pungent, sweet smell and was excellent hashish. I asked him if he had any more. I knew he had understood me when he again reached into his shirt pocket and handed me four additional one-inch square pieces of the same hash.

"How much money do you want for this?" I asked the man.

"Two Tomans," he replied.

That was about thirty cents in American money. I gave him five

Tomans and he was so happy that he gave me another two pieces of hash, which now totaled seven. Together, they must have weighed more than a half-ounce. I was very happy with my purchase. I said goodbye to the old man and walked back to the hotel room smiling.

Boy, would Mark be surprised, I thought. He didn't want me to do anything stupid and get busted, especially being at the border with all the guards, soldiers, customs officials, and policemen. In this part of the world, they put you in prison and throw away the key for having dope.

When I returned to the room, there was barely enough room for me to sit down. Everyone else was lying down—that is, until I brought out the hash. When I showed Mark what I had found, everyone else in the room became inquisitive and were anxious to try it.

"Mark, find me a pipe so I can load a bowl," I insisted.

Within seconds, one of the tourists gave Mark a small brass hash pipe, so I began to fill the bowl with small chunks of this primo hash. I was nervous and excited because it had been well over a week since we had smoked anything except for the opium that we'd had in Erzurum more than four days before.

When I finished loading the bowl, it was time to party. It was my hash, so I took the first toke. I inhaled deeply, coughed my head off, and passed out. I woke up about thirty seconds later with spit hanging from my mouth.

Mark had taken the pipe out of my hands, put it to his lips, and inhaled deeply, then passed it to another. Nearly everyone in the small, crowded room took their turn on the pipe. In fact, not one person turned it down—not even the older tourists. I refilled the bowl more than four times to quench the thirst of my roommates.

After everyone was pretty well stoned from the hashish, the old man who had sold it to me came into the room and sat down in the typical "Afghan stoop," facing us. At first, we couldn't figure out what he wanted. He didn't say anything. He just sat and smiled a big, toothless smile. Everyone, being so stoned, started laughing. The whole room was filled with laughter. The more the old toothless man smiled, the more we laughed. He was absolutely hilarious. I laughed so hard that I damn near pissed my pants. Then it dawned on me what the old man wanted—to collect the rent from everyone in the room.

"How much money do you want?" I asked the old man.

He pointed to each one of us and said, "One Toman."

He was asking about ten cents from each one of us for the use of the room. I couldn't believe how cheap things were in this part of the world. I handed my money to the Afghan gentleman and watched as he collected the money from the rest of the boarders.

Again, the room exploded in laughter. This old man was quite a character. He would have been a big hit on a TV program like Johnny Carson's *Tonight Show*. He was very funny, and being so stoned made him seem even funnier.

Once the old Afghan man had collected his money, he left the room.

One by one, my roommates began drifting off to sleep while Mark and I continued smoking the hashish and talking about our trip. Before I knew it, everyone around me was lying down and fast asleep. The room was so crowded that there wasn't any place for me to lie down. I tried, but nobody would move over to make room for me. I began feeling claustrophobic, so I decided to get some fresh air.

I left the room and walked into the cold and damp night air. I decided to sleep on the bus, even though I had been the first person to rent the room. I was angry over the fact that I had scored the hash and turned everyone on to it but yet they couldn't make room for me so I could stretch out and lie down.

I went inside the bus and tried to stretch out over the seats, but it was just too cold to fall asleep. I tossed and turned, my teeth chattered, and my whole body was shivering as I tried to sleep. This went on all during the night and brought back memories of the few sleepless winter nights I had spent on the streets of Germany while waiting for Mark to arrive from America.

I thought I would freeze to death while sleeping on the bus, but I knew I was still alive the next morning when I was awakened by the noise from the Afghan soldiers and customs officials going to work. Finally, we were able to retrieve our luggage from the top of the bus, which we took directly into the Afghan customs office to be inspected.

It took approximately an hour for the Afghan customs officials to inspect the entire contents of our bus and its occupants. Once that task had been completed, we boarded the rickety bus and headed toward our first stop—the city of Herat, nearly four hours away.

As the bus raced away from the Afghan border, it left huge black clouds of diesel smoke floating in the air. I thought of it as a remembrance of the dark night that I spent freezing in the bus.

Once we reached Herat, we could rest up and get ready for the trip to Kandahar. I wanted to leave as soon as possible. I was also anxious to get to Kabul to buy a kilo of hashish for two dollars from our Afghan friends we had met on the bus and to find the best hash Afghanistan had to offer.

By noon, we had arrived in the city of Herat, a city that went back thousands of years where buildings were still being made using mud and straw. The bus driver had dropped us off in front of an inexpensive hotel where we rented a room with two beds for a total of forty-Afghani—about forty cents in American money.

After we had stored our luggage in our room and smoked a bowl of hash, we went out for lunch. We each had a kabob sandwich with pita bread, and washed it down with a cold Pepsi that cost us twenty cents each. It was true: a person could live here and live well on a dollar per day.

This was great for us, but this was a very poor country. The average yearly income for a family of four was fifty dollars.

When we returned to the hotel, I decided to ask one of the hotel workers, a young man, maybe in his mid-twenties, if he knew where I could buy some hash. His eyes lit up and a big grin appeared across his face, then he reached into his vest pocket and pulled out a nice big chunk of green hash. It looked to be about an ounce in weight.

"How much money do you want for that hash?" I asked the hotel worker.

But he didn't understand me and asked a small, ten year old Afghani boy to translate for him. Again, I asked the question, and after a short conversation between the boy and the hotel worker, the boy explained to me that his friend wanted ten Afghani for the chunk of hash. I was happy to give him the money. This was the type of hashish I had been looking for; it smelled similar to the Lebanese hash I had purchased in Morocco, but much stonier.

I returned to my room and showed Mark what I had just scored. We loaded up the pipe and smoked a few bowls, and coughed our heads off. After three or four healthy tokes, we nodded off until we were awakened a few hours later by a loud knock on our door. When I answered it, I was surprised to see the hotel worker standing there holding a ten-Afghani bill in his hand. Then, using sign language, he asked for the hash that he had sold me.

I was puzzled. I didn't understand why he wanted it. When I showed him the chunk of green hash, he grabbed it from my outstretched hand and threw the money at me, then turned and left the room.

Mark and I looked at each other in utter confusion. We didn't understand why this had happened, so I followed the hotel worker down the hall to find out why he had changed his mind. I found him with the small boy who had been our interpreter, so I walked over and confronted them.

"Why did he take the hash from me?" I asked the boy.

"In Afghanistan, we don't smoke hashish pure—like the tourists do. It is against our religion to smoke the powder. It must be made into hashish first," he replied.

"How do they do that?" I asked.

"They take the green powder and mix it with hot water and then fire it to make it into hashish."

"What is the green powder?"

"The green stuff that you bought is the powder the hash is made from. We believe that if people smoke it in powder form, like you were doing, they will go mad and live by themselves in the mountains," the boy replied.

He explained the situation thoroughly. The Afghan people didn't smoke hashish in its pure form, and they couldn't let others smoke it like that for fear of angering God and bringing harm to themselves and the ignorant.

"Can you find us some green powder to buy so we can have it made into hash?" I asked the boy.

"I can take you to a hashish maker where you can watch and see how hash is made, and then you can buy some from him . . . if you want."

"How much money will it cost me for one kilo of your number one hash?" I asked.

"I think thirty dollars, but I'm not sure," he replied.

I decided to buy a kilo of hash, even though Mark thought it was too expensive. He wanted to wait until we arrived in Kabul so we could buy it from our Afghan friends for two dollars. But I wasn't sure if they could get it for us at that price. Mark tried to talk me out of it, but I refused to listen to his reasoning. This was one of the main reasons I had come to Afghanistan—to see just how hashish was made.

Within an hour, Mark, the boy, and I had traveled to the other side of the city to see the hash maker. This was the dirtier and seedier side of town. We walked down winding and narrow, filthy alleys as streams of urine and waste ran down the middle of them. I became paranoid and worried about being robbed, beaten, and even killed.

Finally we arrived at a small mud and straw hut. We walked up to a flight of dirt stairs and into a large barren room with mud walls and a dirt floor. There was a large water pipe and a small charcoal stove sitting in the center of it. Two old Afghan men with long white beards and turbans, wearing the typical Afghan garb—the long shirt, baggy pants, vests, and thick black rubber shoes—sat in the Afghan stoop position and greeted us in their native tongue.

"*A Salaam Ali cume,*" said the old men.

"May God be with you," the boy replied.

The boy spoke to the old men in Farsi, telling them that Mark and I wanted to buy a kilo of hash and wanted to watch as they made it. Everything seemed to be all right. They wanted thirty-five dollars per kilo—twenty-five for the pollen or powder, as they call it, and ten dollars to press it into hashish. I agreed to their conditions, and they proceeded to start the show.

Within a few minutes, another old man came into the room carrying a small metal pan, two sheets of clear six-mil plastic (one big and one much smaller), and a bag filled with one kilo of green pollen. They laid out the large plastic sheet, which was about four feet square, onto the dirt floor near the charcoal stove and placed the smaller sheet, which was about two feet square, on top of it but to one side. Then they poured the sack of green pollen onto the large piece of plastic.

They took a metal teapot of boiling water, poured about two cups of it into the empty pan, and added about four big handfuls of pollen. They continued to add pollen until it had a very thick consistency to it—so thick, in fact, that when they tipped the pan upside down, the pollen wouldn't fall out until the pan was hit with a hard object. Then the hot, wet pollen was dumped onto the large plastic sheet near the large mound of dry pollen.

The wet clump of pollen was very, very hot, but that didn't stop one of the old men from kneading it, as if it were dough. Then he began adding dry pollen to the wet. However, before he began his little chore, he added a small amount of "ghee" or animal fat to the palm of his hands so they wouldn't blister from the heat of the hot pollen.

He then took a handful of wet, hot pollen in each hand and dipped it into the dry pollen, kneading it until he had the texture and consistency he wanted and then flattening it into a one-inch-thick, six-inch-round disc. When that part of the operation was completed, he laid the disc on top of the red hot charcoals and fired both sides until it began to burn. Then he took the patty off the hot coals and again kneaded it between his hands, adding dry pollen until he had the consistency he wanted. He repeated this operation twenty-six times until the kilo of pollen had disappeared. Then he wrapped each of the patties, one at a time, into the small plastic sheet and walked on them with his bare feet.

He actually kneaded the hash with his feet. After a few minutes of this, he unwrapped the sheet and repeated the firing process four or five more times before his task was complete. They had made a total of twenty-six, one-inch-thick, six-inch round patties. Each patty was dark black on the outside and light green on the inside. It was very excellent hashish, but I wanted to find better.

I wasn't quite satisfied with the quality of the hash. I had expected better. But now, at least, I had something to send to my friends in America—that is, if I could find a safe way to send it. I really hadn't thought too much about that yet. We would have to wait until we reached Kabul to decide on a course of action.

Mark and I had waited nearly three hours while we watched the two old men turn powder into hashish. It had been quite an adventure to see how it was made. Now I knew the difference between the powder and the hash. It didn't make a difference to me if it was pressed or not, but it was a big deal with the Afghans.

Now it was time to head back to the hotel. I happily paid the two old men the thirty-five dollars that they had asked for and then placed the kilo of hash patties into Mark's small backpack, but I carried it with me. Mark was too paranoid to carry the illegal contraband. He was afraid we were going to get busted. He didn't mind smoking it, he just didn't want to take a chance and risk his freedom in a foreign land. So when we returned to the hotel room, I placed the kilo of hash into my luggage and carried it wherever we went.

The next morning, we were on our way to Kandahar. It was a long, twelve-hour trip and well over six hundred kilometers from Herat. It would be a long, hot ride. That didn't matter to us. By now, we were used to it.

We were told that the Russian government had built the road from Herat to Kandahar and the American government built it from Kandahar to Kabul. The two superpowers competed against each other for Afghanistan's friendship.

The road we were currently traveling on was built similar to the German Autobahn. It was built extra sturdy and extra tough so the Afghan military could have easy access for their tanks and other heavy armaments to defend against the "Mujahedeen" or freedom fighters.

The freedom fighters openly carried automatic weapons and used them against the Afghan government when it interfered in their smuggling runs. These people had smuggled weapons, drugs, and other illegal contraband between Pakistan and Afghanistan for the past two thousand years. If the Afghan government wouldn't bother the freedom fighters, they in turn wouldn't bother the Afghan government troops. Sometimes confrontations happened, though.

The ride from Herat to Kandahar was a pleasant one. The lush scenery and odd-looking mud houses and villages kept my interest. It seemed the closer we got to Kandahar, the hotter and drier the weather became.

I soon learned that Kandahar was in the middle of the desert and very close to the Pakistan border. The only people who lived in that area were the nomads, Mujahedeen, and smugglers, and during the summer months, it would get as hot as one hundred and forty degrees in the shade.

Within an hour of the city, we made a pit stop. We were allowed to get off the bus to stretch our legs and take a bathroom break. We had stopped near a small river where local people were washing up and some were even drinking the water, so I figured it would be all right to drink a little of it. But as Mark and I put the water to our lips, one of the Afghans from the bus yelled out, "Bad water!" and tried desperately to stop us from drinking it. We spit the water out as fast as we could and walked back to the bus not thinking any more about this incident.

We arrived in Kandahar just before dusk, found a decent hotel, and rented a room on the second floor with two comfortable beds and a large double door with a balcony that overlooked the city.

Once we had placed our luggage in the room, we walked down to the restaurant below to eat a good, hot meal. I asked the waiter for some tea, and he asked me in Farsi if I wanted *teriot* with it. But I didn't understand the word bond didn't answer him, so he spoke in broken English.

"Opium," said the waiter.

Oh, now I understood him. "Yes," I said gleefully, as Mark ordered the same.

The waiter came back with the tea, but no opium. "Where is the opium?" asked Mark.

The waiter smiled and pointed to the cup. He had already put the opium in the tea, and it had dissolved. At that moment, I didn't believe him. However, my opinion changed once I had tasted the tea—it had a very bitter taste. By the time I had finished it, the potent opium had kicked in. We paid the bill and walked back to our room, and then had a good night's sleep for a change. I slept like a newborn baby.

The following morning, we walked around the city and visited many of the small clothing shops for their leather goods. I wanted something in which to conceal the hash so I could send it back to America without it being detected. But then I had another idea, so I walked into a shoe store and conversed with the Afghan salesman.

"Can you put hash into shoes?" I asked.

"We can," replied the salesman.

"Can you put hash into my cowboy boots?" I asked, pulling up my pant leg so they could see my boots.

"We can," he beamed.

So I bought a nice pair of leather sandals to wear while they put hash into the soles of my boots. But I decided not to use the pressed hash that we had just bought in Herat and used green pollen instead. I thought the pollen tasted and smoked much better than the pressed stuff. The shoe salesman refused to use the pollen and wanted me to use the pressed hash, but I was adamant. It took a lot of begging, pleading, and bribing with lots of money to have them made my way. In the end, they did it my way.

I returned to the shoe store the following day and picked up my cowboy boots. The salesman handed me the finished product to try on, and they fit perfectly. However, they had much thicker soles now, so I would only wear them going through customs. I didn't want to take the chance with the boots falling apart, so I packed them away and continued wearing the sandals.

Forty-eight hours after reaching Kandahar, Mark and I suddenly came down with dysentery. We figured we had caught the bug from the polluted river water we drank when we stopped outside of Kandahar. We had made a big mistake and were in utter misery for more than five days. We couldn't eat or sleep and were constantly bedridden.

During the day and night, we were always running to the bathroom. Many of these trips were for naught. I would lie in bed and suddenly my stomach would fill up with air, as if I were pregnant. Then I would have to run to the bathroom, and nine out of ten times, I never made it in time. Before I could unlock the door, the diarrhea had filled my pants and was running down my legs, while at the same time, I regurgitated. Stuff came out of me at the same time from both ends. I had to clean myself up and wipe the crap off my legs and pants and the puke off my chin. This went on for five days. I had absolutely no energy, whatsoever.

On the third day, whimpering in pain and agony, Mark and I were so sick that we forgot to shut the big double doors. While we were lying in bed, unconscious, the city was accosted by a big sandstorm. When we awoke, we were covered with an inch of sand, as was the floor.

I felt miserable. After five long days, Mark was feeling much better, but I was still very ill.

So to pick up our spirits we decided to visit a park we had heard about. It was supposed to be one of the Seven Wonders of the World.

We decided upon a buggy ride rather than a taxi—a buggy was much cheaper but the ride was much longer, two hours compared to only twenty minutes by taxi. But by the time we had arrived at this magnificent park, I was sicker than a rabid dog. Mark was feeling fine, so he went off exploring by himself while he left me to suffer alone.

This park was similar to the Mojave Desert and Yosemite National Park, all rolled into one. But I was in no mood to explore it. I ate a little of the opium I had purchased from the waiter at the restaurant and hoped it would make me feel better. But it only made me sleepy and also moved my bladder.

My diarrhea had returned and created a big problem. This park had no bathrooms or toilets and very little cover to hide myself from prying eyes. However, I did find one tree that would help me in my conquest, so I climbed it. I figured no one could see me if I was up in a tree hidden by leaves, but I was wrong.

Just as I began doing my business, two Afghani men walked directly underneath me. When they heard a gurgling sound, they looked up into the tree, right at me. They started yelling and pointing their fingers at me. So I quickly grabbed a handful of leaves from the tree and proceeded to wipe myself, then pulled up my pants and jumped down to the ground as fast as I could, running in the opposite direction of the two yelling men. Then I started looking for

Mark. Within ten minutes, I had found him and explained what had just occurred. I talked him into returning to the hotel.

We found the driver who had driven us to the park, so we hired him to drive us back into town. However, halfway into the trip, one of the buggy's wheels fell off. When the driver couldn't fix it, all three of us got a ride in another buggy that was passing by. We finally made it back to our hotel after an exhausting four-hour buggy ride, and I was still very sick. However, by morning, I was feeling a bit stronger.

We decided to visit a few shirt and coat shops. We walked past shop after little shop. These shops, on both sides of the street, were just small, eight-or ten-foot-square wooden boxes, nailed and connected together to make one long row of wooden buildings. Nearly all the stores and gift shops were built like this.

As we passed each store, the owners would greet us in a warm fashion.

"Hey, mister, you want to buy hashish, opium? What do you want?" chanted the storeowners.

"No, thanks," I replied, as we passed by.

But after an hour or two of window shopping, we broke down and visited one of these small wooden shops. As we entered, I noticed three tourists sitting in the back, smoking a big water pipe of hashish. The owner asked Mark and me if we wanted to share the *hookah* with the Americans. We gladly obliged him and walked into the back of his tiny shop.

Mark and I introduced ourselves to the three longhaired American male hippies. Their names were Larry, Eric, and Billy. They reminded me of the famous trio, Larry, Moe, and Curly of the Three Stooges. We asked them where they were from and where they were going. I was surprised to learn that they had grown up in a city very near my own called Oak Park and were traveling in the same direction as Mark and I—Kabul. We mentioned to them that we were headed there also.

All of us were talking, smoking, and laughing, when all of a sudden the small store became pitch black. Someone outside the store had shut the front door, locking us in this small eight-foot-by-eight-foot wooden box. The store was full of hash smoke so we couldn't breathe very well.

Eric cried out that he was claustrophobic and started screaming at the top of his voice, "Let me out of here!"

Nobody answered. All of us began to worry about a lack of oxygen.

Suddenly the storeowner yelled that he would free us if we paid him one thousand Afghani and if we didn't, he would contact the police. Then we would go to jail for smoking hashish. Now we were very scared, especially Mark. He was nearly in tears and didn't want to end up in jail. Just then, Mark started banging on the wooden door with his fists as hard as he could.

"Let us out of here!" yelled Mark.

After nearly ten minutes of pounding and screaming as loud as we could, we heard someone talking with the storeowner. We over-heard this man telling the storeowner that he was a guest of the Afghan government and to release us immediately or he would bring the police and have him arrested for kidnapping and bribery.

Suddenly the door swung open and light once again entered the premises. Eric jumped out first and went directly after the storeown-er. I was surprised to see that the person who had helped win our release had ridden with us on the train from Istanbul to Erzurum. He was traveling with his wife and was a professional filmmaker.

He explained to us that he was doing research on Afghanistan for the University of Austria and had been given permission to film by the king of Afghanistan, which meant that he had lots of power in this country. We thanked him for his help and said goodbye to him and the three Americans. Then Mark and I returned to our hotel room. We would be leaving for Kabul in the morning. After the epi-sode with the crazy storeowner, I couldn't get out of Kandahar fast enough.

We purchased our tickets for the trip to Kabul and boarded the bus. After nearly a week of feeling miserable, we were finally head-ed toward our final destination.

I still hadn't found a good way to send the hash, except for the boots. I began asking different hippies we had met on the trip if they had found a way to smuggle hash out of the country, but nobody wanted to give away their trade secrets. So far, the boots seemed the best idea—either that or carry it on my person over land. But I would have to find a way to send the hash once I had reached Kabul. We had to send our mail from that city anyway. The post office in the cities of Herat and Kandahar refused to send it, explaining that we had to send it from Kabul from the main post office.

We finally arrived in Kabul in the afternoon. We left the bus sta-tion and walked through a rather large and crowded bazaar. It was packed, like sardines, with thousands of Afghans. As we walked and looked, Mark felt someone reach into his back pocket, where he kept his passport. I kept mine inside my boot just for this reason and told Mark to do the same, but he wouldn't listen. We continued our walk through the crowded bazaar when Mark came over to me again, saying that someone was trying to steal his passport. He said if he did it again, he would catch the thief, red-handed.

A few minutes later, Mark felt the man's hand reach into his back pocket and grabbed it before he could escape. Everyone around us noticed what had just transpired. Mark retrieved his passport from the Afghan's hand and didn't think too much about the incident. However, the Afghans thought it was a very big deal and wanted Mark to get his revenge.

Mark tried not to pay any attention to the crowd and tried to leave, but they wouldn't allow it. They wanted Mark to beat the guy up and told Mark that if he didn't do something, the police would cut off the thief's hand. So Mark started beating on him with his fists. The thief didn't resist or defend himself. The crowd loved it and kept urging Mark on. When Mark wanted to stop, the crowd refused to let him leave, so he had to continue his onslaught for another ten minutes before they were finally satisfied.

After Mark and I had walked out of the bazaar, we began looking for a good, cheap hotel. Hans, our Swiss friend who had traveled with us from Tehran to Herat, had mentioned a place called the Najib Hotel. It was a good, cheap hotel that catered to hippies from all over the world. So we rented a cab to take us there and arrived in a joyful mood. We couldn't get over the fact that we were in Kabul, Afghanistan, and were on the other side of the globe.

The hotel had plenty of rooms available, with or without beds. Mark and I decided to stay in the cheaper room—the one without beds—and it only cost each of us ten Afghani, about ten cents. We would have to sleep on the floor and share it with four other hippie tourists, so we rented a space on the second floor in which to throw our sleeping bags.

When we entered the room, one of our roommates was filling a four foot-high water pipe with some Afghani pot and invited us to smoke it with him. So we obliged him. When it was my turn, I pressed the pipe to my lips and inhaled deeply. Within seconds, I began to cough, gag, and spit up. Even smoking from a water pipe, the *cannabis Indica* was very harsh and tough on the lungs, but oh so heavenly. Just one toke and the room began to spin.

Mark and I asked the hippies about the hot spots in Kabul. One told us about a restaurant-hotel on Chicken Street called Ziggy's where many hippies stayed and which was well known for their ice cream milk shakes. We were also told that we could buy any type of pharmaceuticals from the drug store—cocaine, morphine, and even heroin—all manufactured by well known pharmaceutical companies. The heroin was made in Germany during World War II and was one hundred percent pure. But I'm getting ahead of myself.

When we heard about the pharmacy, our eyes lit up. But I had second thoughts. The only reason I had asked Mark along on this adventurous trip was to get him away from the hard core drugs in America, especially heroin. Now we could buy it from our local pharmacy, but at least not for another day or so. We wanted to relax and rest up.

We relaxed by smoking hash and pot all day long in our dormitory room and slept that night on the uncomfortable, hard wooden floor. It was too darn hard for me, and I refused to sleep on it another night. The very next morning, I paid an extra ten Afghani and rented a single room with a bed. Mark didn't want that comfort and got angry with me for spending the extra money. But I didn't care—it was my money. I offered to pay for his bed, too, but he refused.

Directly across the street from our hotel was a small juice stand. One man stood outside and sold fresh carrot, grape, orange, strawberry, melon, and many other types of juice. You name the fruit, and he had it. He would make a tasty drink out of one fruit or a combination of them all. It was really delicious and cheap. A sixteen-ounce glass of juice cost a nickel. You couldn't beat the price.

After we drank our juice, we walked to a restaurant and ate breakfast, usually hot oatmeal with milk. We ate the same foods as in America, except bacon. That was a no-no. For lunch, if we wanted to eat cheaply, we would buy one or two nice big cucumbers from a cucumber vendor at a cost of five-Afghani each, and that included three different spices for additional flavor. The vendor would even peel them for us. They were quite delicious and very inexpensive.

If we wanted to splurge for lunch, we would have a kabob sandwich and Pepsi. However, that was a bit more money—about twenty cents. So it was true. You could actually live well in Afghanistan for less than a dollar a day.

Afghanistan was incredible and the local people were quite friendly, not like the belligerent people of Turkey and Iran. The Afghan people were different. If you respected them, they respected you.

Within a few days, we had met the same three guys—Larry, Eric, and Billy. They were also staying at the Najib Hotel but would be leaving for Pakistan within the next few days.

When they asked us if we wanted to travel with them, I refused their invitation, but Mark said yes. I was finally at my dream destination and didn't want to leave the country. I wanted to stay in Afghanistan the rest of my life, so I wasn't interested in traveling at all. I was more interested in visiting the pharmacy.

Before Mark left for parts unknown, we decided to visit the pharmacy. Mark wanted to buy some cocaine and inject it, but I was always vehemently against cocaine and frightened of needles. But now, for some ungodly reason, my fear had disappeared. I told myself that it was all right because we were buying legitimate pharmaceuticals from a legitimate pharmacy, and I gave in to the needles, deciding it was just another way to get high. That was the insane reasoning—or excuse—I used, anyway.

When we arrived at the pharmacy, I was like a little kid in a candy store. However, the man behind the counter looked just like the devil. He had pitch-black hair with a Van Dyke goatee and mustache and evil, beady-looking eyes. I was waiting for him to turn around so I could see his forked tail. When he looked at me, his cold stare went right through my being. He made one's body shiver in fear. Mark and I called him "the Devil."

We proceeded to buy a gram of pure Peruvian pharmaceutical cocaine and two syringes. I had never put a needle in my arm and wasn't too anxious to do it now, but Mark said he would inject me. He had the experience and had injected narcotics many times in America. I thought by Mark traveling with me, I would get him away from narcotics and needles, but now it was all around us and legal.

When we returned to the hotel, we decided to use my room to inject the pure pharmaceutical cocaine. Once there, Mark put a very small amount of the powdered cocaine into a spoon about the size of a tiny baby aspirin. Then he added ten drops of water to the gold powder and heated the bottom of the spoon to purify the water. I watched as it turned into a clear liquid. Then he added a small cotton ball into the liquid, placed the needle into the cotton ball, and sucked the stuff into the syringe. He injected me first, and I immediately felt a warm buzz rush through my whole body. Then my body went completely numb and I passed out. When I awoke, Mark was standing over me ready to resuscitate me, but I had regained consciousness within a minute or so.

Boy, what a rush, I thought to myself. But I knew I would never try that stuff again. Mark enjoyed the high, but I didn't. In fact, I'd hated it.

"Mark, get that stuff out of my room. I don't want to see it again," I barked.

"Rob, this stuff is very pure and very potent. You shouldn't have injected so much," he replied.

"I'll never do cocaine again as long as I live," I snapped.

A few days later, Mark decided to leave for Pakistan with the three hippie Americans from Oak Park. I refused to travel with them.

"Rob, our visas are up," said Mark. "We have to leave and renew them in Pakistan. Then we can return to Afghanistan and stay legally."

"I'm never going to leave Afghanistan. If I do, it will be in a pine box," I promised, as Mark and I parted and went our separate ways.

While Mark was away, I decided to sell some of the hashish that we had made in Herat to some of the new tourists who arrived daily. Within a few days, I had tripled my money and still had a few hash patties left over for smoking. I had sold most of the hash to three Italians. Actually, I sold it to two Italian men, Antonio and Phillip, and one American female, Kathy, who had married Phillip. After we had introduced ourselves, we talked about our adventurous excursions.

We had become good friends over the next few days. However, one day when I entered their room I was stunned to see them injecting themselves with opium. This was a new experience for me. When they offered me some of the narcotic, I should have rejected their offer, especially after the bad experience I'd had injecting cocaine, but strangely, I accepted.

I remembered that I still had the syringe I had bought at the pharmacy, so I returned to my room and retrieved it. When I returned to the Italians' room, Antonio used my syringe to inject the evil drug into my naive and virgin veins. I had never ever injected anything into my body until I had tried cocaine with Mark. This was the second time I had injected a narcotic.

They had purchased the opium from a teashop in Kandahar—that city was a big opium producer, which was one of the money crops the freedom fighters smuggled across the border to and from Pakistan. The Italians also told me what shop to visit in Kandahar if I ever needed to buy a large quantity of opium. They sold three types—for eating, smoking, or shooting.

Injecting opium was a completely different buzz from the cocaine. This was a warm, mellow "I don't care about anything" type feeling. I really liked this high. I didn't like the needles, but I wanted to fit in with my new friends and would return to their room most every night for my fix. However, within a few days, their opium supply had disappeared into their veins, and now my body was suddenly calling for it. They didn't have any, nor did they know where to purchase any in Kabul. They knew I was in a tight fix, so they talked me into going to the pharmacy with them to purchase some morphine. They explained to me that a morphine high was similar to the opium buzz, but much, much better.

Strangely enough, we went to the same pharmacy to which Mark and I had gone to buy the cocaine. I gave them three dollars and waited outside while they went inside to buy a bottle of twenty half-grain morphine tablets, which were produced by a giant German pharmaceutical company.

When I heard Phillip call the pharmacist "the Devil," I felt a cold shiver go through my body. That was the same name that Mark and I had given him. When I asked the Italians about it, they explained that everyone called him "the Devil." So I had been right all along. This pharmacist was "the Devil."

When we returned to the hotel, we went directly to the Italians' room to get high. Antonio fixed me first because I had paid for the morphine. Putting half a tablet or a quarter grain into the syringe, he then added boiling water to the narcotic. As he shook the ingredients in the syringe, the morphine dissolved into a clear liquid. After letting the syringe cool down for a minute or so, Antonio injected me with the morphine.

The second the drug entered my blood stream, I felt a super-hot rush reach every part of my body. The rush was so strong that I had to lie back on the bed to feel the total effect of the narcotic. I felt as though my body was suddenly floating. The heavenly rush was incredible, even better than the opium. My whole body felt as though my insides were on fire. I had never felt this good in my entire life— all the pain and aches in my body had suddenly disappeared.

But I didn't want to be this way. I hated narcotics and needles. I couldn't figure out what had come over me to put a needle into my veins and inject a heavy narcotic. However, I decided that heroin was bad and the pharmaceutical morphine was all right. So from that day on, I had Antonio or Phillip inject me with the drug.

Within a few days, Antonio had moved into my room. Every morning, a few minutes after I had opened my eyes, I would have him inject me with morphine. In return, I paid for his room and drugs. Antonio and I had become close friends, almost like brothers.

I had learned from our conversations that Antonio had been a high school chemistry teacher when he lived in Italy. Phillip was also a teacher. However, they were both considered revolutionaries so the Italian government always harassed them. They decided to take a leave of absence from work and visit Afghanistan for a while until things cooled down. Then they hoped that they could return without too much harassment from their government.

They explained to me that they had headed a political organization that the establishment regarded as a threat to Italy's national security and were worried about being assassinated. When they told me this, I wondered if the Italians who had picked us up hitchhiking in Germany and Italy belonged to their radical organization.

Nearly a month after I had met them, Phillip and Antonio decided that they wanted to visit northern Afghanistan to buy some good hash and get it as cheap as possible. They wanted to buy one or two kilos of primo hash to smuggle back to Italy so they could sell it to their friends. They believed they could buy hash at five dollars per kilo in the Balkh province. At one time, some Afghans had told me that I could buy hash for two dollars a kilo, but I never went to visit them to see if it was true. However, Balkh was known for its excellent hash crop.

So Phillip, Antonio, and Kathy let me tag along with them. Afghanistan didn't have any trains, so the next best way to travel was by bus. We purchased our bus tickets to the Balkh province and the religious city of Mazare Sarif, seven hundred kilometers north. The Muslims who couldn't make the pilgrimage to Mecca would travel to Mazare Sarif to pray at the holy mosque.

We would be going through some beautiful, lush land and pass the famous cities of Bamyan and Bandimere, two very historical cities. But we would have to stop there on the return trip. The Italians wanted to get the hash as quickly as possible, and then once that chore was completed they could take the time to visit those cities.

But it would be a long ride on an old and rickety bus and the seats were extremely hard and uncomfortable. In fact, some of the tourists sat on top of the bus with the luggage—that was third class. Not only would this trip be a tiring one but I also decided not to bring any morphine. I didn't think I needed it. I had been injecting it every morning and nearly every night for nearly two weeks straight, so I wanted to quit for a while. I didn't want to become addicted. I really thought that I could go without it. Boy was I wrong.

By the time we had arrived in Mazare Sarif and rented our hotel rooms, everyone was dead tired. I shared my room with Antonio. However, this night I didn't have any morphine to relieve my body of its aches and pains. Luckily, I fell asleep without feeling too bad, but the next morning was another story. I needed a fix as soon as I woke up but didn't have anything to take. My body had never before felt this type of sickness. I felt very weak and lightheaded, absolutely no energy at all. But I persevered and pushed forward. Antonio and I walked a few doors over to pick up Phillip and Kathy.

After a small breakfast of coffee and bread, we boarded a taxi to take us to a few hash farms. Just as we pulled into traffic, an Afghan policeman hopped into the front passenger seat with the driver and me. That caught everyone off guard. We didn't know what to think or what to expect. We looked at each other wondering what the hell was going on. We really thought he had come along to bust us once we had purchased the hash. The next thought we had was that he was just riding to another destination. However, he was still with us when we arrived at the first hash farm.

As we drove onto the property, about a dozen armed men pointed their automatic weapons directly at us and surrounded our vehicle. We stepped out of the taxi very slowly and cautiously. The taxi driver explained to the leader why we had traveled to his farm. When he understood that we wanted to buy some hash, the armed men became very friendly and showed us their acres of hash plants, even though planting season had just started one month before. The plants were just beginning to grow, but some were already a half-foot in diameter and twenty feet tall. Others were much shorter, which looked more like stubby bushes or small trees.

The leader of the armed camp explained that many of the plants were grown inside for a few months and then replanted outside in the fertile mountainous soil. Ninety percent of the plants were approximately five feet tall, and the foliage was one to twenty feet in diameter.

The hash farmer tried selling us his whole fall harvest, which he figured would gross more than two thousand kilos of hash pollen.

However, when they learned that we only wanted to buy one to two kilos, their friendly attitude disappeared, and they became very angry.

They explained to us that the least amount of hash pollen they would sell was one hundred kilos at five dollars per kilo. Then we would have to pay another five dollars per kilo to have the pollen pressed into hash. That quantity was beyond our means and we had to turn them down; however, before we could leave, we had to give the leader of the armed gang some money for showing us the farm. So I gave the hash farmer an American five-dollar bill. That seemed to please him because a big smile appeared on his face. That also seemed like a good time to leave his farm. We quickly climbed into the taxi, including the Afghan policeman, and continued our journey to the next Afghani hash farm a few miles up the mountain.

All of us were very paranoid of the policeman. The taxi driver told us he was riding along to ensure our safety, but we didn't believe him. We still believed he was there to bust us. After hearing how the government of Turkey and Iran treated drug smugglers, we figured Afghanistan wasn't any different. We had to be very discreet, but with an Afghani cop riding along to watch our every move, how could we be discreet? We figured he would either throw us in jail or ask for "baksheesh," which means "bribe" in Farsi.

We drove another five-thousand feet above sea level toward the top of the Hindu Kush Mountains. We were now approximately eight thousand feet above sea level. The narrow, winding mountain road was littered with fallen rocks—so many, in fact, that we had to stop and remove some of the bigger ones to proceed to the hash farm.

When we finally arrived, a large, angry crowd of armed Afghan men with automatic rifles greeted us once again. As we climbed out of the taxi, we noticed three American jeeps with large caliber machine guns sitting to one side. They explained to us that they used them to chase away any government troops or anyone else who wanted to destroy their hash crop. This was practically the only way these people living in the mountains could make a living.

With an annual income of fifty dollars, thousands of people died from starvation every winter. Usually in the fall, one member of each family would travel to Kabul to sell their valuables to get enough money to feed and clothe their family during the winter months.

We followed the leader of the group and his band of rebels a quarter of a mile up the mountain through a heavy growth of trees and brush. After walking up a steep and rocky mountain for nearly an hour, we finally came to a large, twenty-hectare plot of hash plants. Most of the plants were small, green, bushy plants. However, to one side of the garden was one hectare full of plants that were twenty to thirty feet tall, with trunk diameters of ten inches and bigger, and they still had four or five months of growing before harvest.

When we finally left the field, our clothes smelled as if ten skunks had just sprayed us all at the same time. We stunk, and it was from brushing up against the *Indica* plants. The leader told us that we could take some nice buds if it had been harvest time. However, if we wanted to buy any hash, we would have to buy last fall's crop, which he had stored in his warehouse. He thought we were interested in buying a large quantity.

When we explained to him that all we wanted was one or two kilos he became very angry and was disgusted with us for wasting his time. So, without the taxi driver mentioning it, I pulled out a five-dollar bill and handed it to the leader, which quickly soothed his anger.

The leader began firing his weapon into the air, yelling epithets. This scared the shit out of us, so we quickly jumped into the taxi and drove out of there as fast as we could. We were relieved to get out of there alive.

The taxi driver asked us if we wanted to visit another hash farm. We decided to visit one more farm in the hopes of purchasing some hash. We hadn't even seen any hash yet, only young plants. We would have to settle on last year's crop, but we didn't care as long as it was excellent hash and at a good price.

Within an hour, we were at our third hash farm. To everyone's surprise and relief, we were greeted by only one armed Afghan man and not by a large group. Once we had explained our situation to him, his face brightened, then he turned and walked away, so we followed behind. But instead of showing us his hash plants, the farmer took us to a small mud shed, a small ten foot-square room with a seven-foot-high ceiling. When he opened the door, the smell was overwhelming.

The room was completely full of pollen and a four-foot-high sheet of plywood was placed against the doorway so the pollen wouldn't fall out when the door opened. He wanted the same exact price for his pollen as the last farmer—five dollars per kilo and another five dollars to press it into hash.

The Italians decided to buy the hash, while I stood to the side, just in case the cop busted them, then I could bail them out of jail. We were still very paranoid and puzzled about the cop. Had he really come along to protect us, or had he come along to bust us? We were just about to find out.

The Italians bought two kilos of reddish-brown pollen, not the green that I had bought in Herat and Kandahar. They decided to press it into hash themselves when they returned to Kabul. The farmer was happy for the business, and we were happy to finally find a good quality of pollen. I was looking for something even better than the green or brown. I wanted to see a bright red or light blonde or jet-black hash, like I had purchased ten months before in Germany. I wasn't leaving Afghanistan anytime soon, so I would have lots of time to find my treasure.

I wondered where the opium plants were and asked one of the farmers. He explained that in this part of the country they grew very few poppy fields, but two provinces in Afghanistan did—one a few hundred miles east of Mazare Sarif, called "Badakhsan," and the other in the southern part of the country, called Kandahar, which included the city of Kandahar.

The Badakhsan province had the highest percentage of morphine base in their opium, nearly fifteen percent. That's the same percentage of morphine base that the poppy plants have in the golden triangle of Thailand, Burma, and Laos. I wanted to mix opium and hash pollen together to make a more potent form of hash.

Well, after we had dropped the cop off and gave him twenty-Afghani baksheesh for not busting us, and paid off the taxi driver, we returned to the hotel near dinnertime. I was sick to my stomach. I suddenly realized that I had become addicted to morphine. That's the reason I didn't bring it with me. I didn't want to become addicted. I figured if I didn't have any, I couldn't do it. But before I could fall asleep, I had to have a fix and asked Phillip to sell me one of his morphine tablets. So Phillip injected me with a half-grain of morphine. I must say, I slept peacefully that night.

We had to wake up early the next morning to catch the bus to Bamyan. We also wanted to visit the famous city of Bandimere.

As we rode the bus south, I began feeling guilty about being addicted to morphine. Never in my life did I think I would get involved with needles and narcotics. The excuse I used was peer pressure. The morphine clouded my thinking, and the high felt so good and the rush so intense and overwhelming, the addiction became secondary to the euphoric high. The high was more important, and the morphine gave me a feeling of euphoria and energy but most of all, confidence. And the extra burst of energy was very helpful in this high altitude—Kabul was two miles above sea level.

Well, we were finally on our way to the beautiful and historical city of Bamyan. This was supposed to be one of the Seven Wonders of the World, and a city that Genghis Kahn and his followers had looted and reeked havoc upon, killing all of the Buddhist priests and religious followers.

The city contained two giant statues of Buddha that were carved out of the Hindu Kush Mountains. One of the rock statues stood nearly two hundred feet tall and one hundred feet in diameter in the standing position. The entrance started at the big toe, with stairs going up more than thirty floors, and the head contained a large conference room where the Buddhists priests studied, and many smaller rooms for sleeping, praying, and meditating.

The smaller Buddha statue was an exact replica of the larger one. However, it was only half the size and carved out of the side of the mountain approximately one hundred yards from the larger one. This Buddha also contained rooms for studying for priesthood, and when they graduated as priests, they were allowed to move into the larger Buddha.

When Genghis Khan and his soldiers ravaged and plundered the city, they tried to destroy both Buddha's. They literally hacked at the mountainous rock with their swords, tearing large chunks from the arms and legs of these stoic statues, but the rock was too much for them. They gave up without completely destroying them, and the evidence is still visible today.

The statues looked as if they had been destroyed by cannon fire, but they were still an awesome sight that took your breath away. These had been built more than a thousand years before Genghis Khan came to destroy them and were truly full of history. They were surrounded by lush, green valleys and magnificent, brilliant waterfalls just like Brazil's Amazon rainforest.

The city of Bandimier was farming country, with very fertile land and the smell of spices in the air, like the Garden of Eden. And there were grapevines that were over three thousand years old.

But we had to return to Kabul. The Italians were in a hurry to return to Italy, and I was anxious to get back to buy some morphine from "the Devil." But we still had many hours left to travel and many roadblocks and checkpoints to pass. At each checkpoint, the police and soldiers boarded the bus to look for criminals or anyone who looked suspicious. They even gave us the evil eye, wanting to bust us so they could take us out behind their barracks and execute us. I had heard that they executed drug dealers and even foreigners without giving them a trial. This was not a country in which to get busted. But luckily, nothing happened.

We arrived in Kabul late at night and went directly to the Najib Hotel. Before I went to bed, I bought another morphine tablet from Phillip and had him inject it into my vein so I could get a good night's sleep. I was now injecting one grain per day, one tablet in the morning, just after I awoke, and one just before I went to bed. I really didn't understand what I had gotten myself into. I wondered who would inject me once my Italian friends had left. But that very next day, I answered my own question and began injecting the morphine myself twice a day. Soon, I became an old pro at it.

A few days later, my Italian friends had left me and were headed back to Italy. They were going to carry the hash on their bodies when they crossed the borders. Within a week I, too, would be heading back to Europe. I hadn't planned to leave Afghanistan this soon, but my money had run out faster than anticipated. I had just enough to buy one or two pair of shoes, have the soles filled with hash, and send them back to America. But first, I had to buy the hashish.

I walked around town all day looking at different grades of pollen at different tea and clothing shops. Finally, three hours later and too tired to walk, I met an Afghan hash maker named Moktar (pronounced Moke-tar). He was living with his younger brother Sabul on the roof of an old, run-down apartment in a small, one-room mud hut. While I followed him to the roof through dark, dirty hallways and up dirt stairs, wondering if I was going to get robbed or killed, Moktar told me that he was a freedom fighter from Kandahar living in Kabul to make money for his family.

It seemed to take forever to reach the roof. But after a long and harrowing climb, I finally entered a dimly lit room with a bamboo mat covering most of the dirt floor. Moktar reached into a small wooden barrel, pulled out a plastic bag of hash pollen, and showed it to me—the best I'd seen since I had arrived in Kabul. It was green pollen but with a purple tint, and the aroma was quite skunky. When he opened the sack, the room soon reeked of a pungent, skunky smell. I offered to give him ten dollars for a half kilo of the pollen and five more to press it for me. I didn't have much money left, so I could only afford this small amount and not the whole kilo. Reluctantly, Moktar agreed.

I sat in the dark room waiting and watching as Moktar's brother, Sabul, fanned the charcoal fire in the small stove. Once the coals were red hot, Moktar placed a small pan of water on them and then, as the water began to boil, he added the pollen to it, using nearly half of what I had just purchased. As Moktar did that, Sabul laid out all of the utensils used in the making of the hashish.

I sat and watched in amazement as Moktar's magical hands began to turn the powder into some exquisite hashish. He went through the same procedures as the hash man in Herat. He kneaded it with his hands and feet repeatedly until he had the desired consistency. When he began to make them into round discs, I stopped him and explained that I wanted the hash made into rectangular slabs so it could be put into the soles of shoes. Moktar understood perfectly and folded the plastic sheet to the size I wanted, then placed approximately one hundred grams into it and rolled it into long, rectangular slabs. Now it could be cut to the design of the shoe.

Moktar also told me about a shoemaker who could help me—for a price—and would take me to him the following day. I nodded in agreement and promised to give him an extra five dollars for helping me.

Finally, after more than two hours, the hash had been pressed. I had nine long, thin, rectangular slabs, which was more than enough for my plan. If anything was left over, I would smoke that on the return trip to America. I paid Moktar and promised, once again, to give him an extra five dollars when he introduced me to the shoemaker. He agreed and promised to meet me at my hotel room in the morning.

I placed the hash into my shoulder bag, said goodbye to my new Afghan friends, and headed out the door. I walked across the roof and into the dirty, dark hallways of the mud and straw apartment house. When I passed a couple of Afghan policeman who were praying in their little rooms, I thought they were going to bust me for the hash, but nothing happened. One even smiled at me as if he knew what I had been up to. By the time I had reached the street, I was a nervous wreck. I thought for sure I was going to get busted. Thank goodness I made it back to my hotel room without an incident. And to relieve my anxiety, I quickly fixed my nightly dose of morphine.

Now I could relax and think about what lay ahead. The next chore on my list was to have my shoes made. That's what I was thinking about as I fell asleep. Early the next morning, I was awakened by a loud knock at my door and opened it to find Moktar standing alone in the hallway. I left him there and quickly fixed a tablet of morphine. Then we left for the shoe store, which was just around the corner from my hotel.

As we walked, Moktar explained to me that the owner wasn't at the store but that his brothers could make the shoes for me. Within ten minutes, we had arrived there. It was a very small store with six workers. They each worked with their legs crossed, in a small cubicle three feet off the floor. In front of them was a small table that held their tools. They had to work this way all day long.

Moktar introduced me to one of the workers and explained the situation. He told them I needed one or two pair of shoes made with hash in the soles. When we had reached an agreement, I took the hash out of my shoulder bag and handed it to Moktar and he, in turn, handed it to the worker. He moved the worktable out of his way and jumped down from his small cubicle to the floor.

The worker took the hash into a back room and returned within a few seconds. He then started tracing my feet onto a sheet of white paper. Once he had completed that task, he took a few measurements of different areas of my foot. I had Moktar explain to the shoemaker to keep the shoes on the light side. I wanted them to look and feel like regular shoes.

I purchased two pairs of sandals for a total of twenty dollars and gave the shoemaker a ten-dollar bill. The rest was to be paid when the job was completed. I was to return in two days to pick them up. Moktar's work was done, so I thanked him for his help and handed him his five dollars. As he thanked me, we hugged each other and headed toward the door.

"Moktar, I'll return to Kabul in six months if everything works out. If not, I'll be in jail," I said with a smile.

"Good luck," he retorted, as we walked out the door and into the crowded city in opposite directions.

I had to send these sandals through the customs office, not the post office. Any parcel being sent from Afghanistan had to go through the customs office. The post office only dealt with envelopes and letters. I figured I would be taking a chance and risking my life, but if they weighed like any other pair of shoes, I shouldn't have any problem. I had visited the customs office before, checking it out and being nosy, and befriended one of the customs officials. He seemed pretty friendly, so I wasn't worried about sending the sandals.

I returned to my hotel room and waited patiently for the next two days. Finally, it was time for me to pick up the shoes. So I returned to the shoe store and looked for my shoemaker. The worker recognized me immediately and jumped down from his little cubicle to wait on me. He walked to a rear table, retrieved two pairs of beautiful, black leather Roman-type sandals, and handed them to me to try on. They were exquisite—not too heavy—and fit perfectly. They were much better made than my cowboy boots.

I was totally satisfied with my purchase. If I had the money, I would have had another pair made to wear back to Europe. But for now, that was out of the question. My money was slowly disappearing. I was damn near broke and still needed to pay for postage on any parcels that I sent. I would barely have enough money for bus fare to Europe. It brought back memories of Morocco.

Before I left the shoe store, the shoemaker gave me all the unused hash. I had quite at bit left. What I didn't smoke, I figured I could sell to new arriving tourists and make a few extra dollars this way. Now I had to buy a few more tourists gifts to send with the shoes. So I walked to a bazaar and purchased a few Afghan velour gold-trimmed vests and a few bright-colored Afghan shirts, which were made of a light, sheer, silk-like material and very comfortable. I spent another ten dollars, nearly depleting my funds.

I decided to send one pair of sandals to America and one pair to Canada. Just in case one parcel didn't make it through customs, the other would. I just couldn't believe how inexpensive these handmade sandals were—a mere ten dollars for each pair of open-toed leather sandals, which buckled at the ankle. It would have cost more than one hundred and fifty dollars a pair to have them handmade in America, minus the hash, of course.

Now I was ready to make the parcels. I found a couple of small cardboard boxes and placed each pair of sandals into a plastic bag, then into each box. I did the same to the shirts and vests. Then I sealed the boxes and hopped a taxi to the customs office, a small building behind the main post office. I had one package addressed to America and the other to the post office in Windsor, Ontario, Canada, just as I had done from Morocco.

As I walked into the customs office carrying a parcel under each arm, one of the customs officials explained to me that I couldn't send packages through their office in boxes, they had to be sent in a cloth bag, which I could purchase a few steps away at the bazaar. Just as I was about to leave, my friend came out of the back room. When he saw me, he smiled, walked over, and shook my hand.

"What do you need, Bob?" asked Mr. Ramazie.

"Mr. Ramazie, I need to send these two parcels to America."

"I am sorry, but you will have to send the gifts in the white cloths bags that are approved by our government," he explained.

"That was explained to me already," I told him.

"What do you have in the packages?" he asked.

Instead of telling him, I showed him. I opened the parcels so they could check the items and tried not to be nervous as I showed them the gifts.

"Why do you want to send shoes to America?" asked Mr. Ramazie.

"They are a birthday gift for my father, and handmade shoes cost hundreds of dollars in America," I explained.

When one customs official began inspecting the shoes more closely, I began to sweat and worry.

"What do you have inside of them?" asked the customs officer, inspecting the shoes.

"Please be careful and try not to destroy my sandals. They are gifts for my father," I snapped.

That got their attention. They stopped inspecting and placed the shoes back into the boxes.

"Bob, leave the parcels in our office, go to the bazaar, and buy the correct packing material," said Mr. Ramazie.

I thanked them and headed for the bazaar. Within minutes, I had purchased two white cloth sacks, which were the size of a regular grocery bag and *very* cheap, only a few cents each. I walked back to the customs office and handed the bags to my Afghan friend. But before we repackaged the bags, I had written the addresses on them in big, bold letters. I just hoped the customs officials wouldn't notice the two different addresses. They might get suspicious.

I was *very* lucky. They hadn't noticed because they couldn't read English. A few minutes later, the bags had been packed and sealed. Then a thin metal wire was looped through the top lip of the material. Once the top of the bag was pulled tight, a lead weight was slipped over the two ends of the wire and then smashed with a special government seal.

Now that the parcels had been inspected and sealed, they wouldn't be inspected again. Now I had to carry them over to the post office to pay the postage for shipping. I just hoped Saraj, my friend who worked at the post office, wouldn't see me. He might become suspicious. He would wonder where I had gotten the money to buy these gifts because I had told him that I didn't have any. Now I wasn't sure what to tell him.

As I walked into the post office I looked for Saraj, but he was nowhere in sight. So I took the bags over to another clerk. The cost for postage for both parcels was only two dollars. That was it. I even wrote my own name of the bags, even though I had addressed one to America and one to Canada. They had gone through Afghan customs without any trouble, so I was sure that they would make it to their destination. I paid the postage and returned to my hotel room. I would stop by the post office at another time and say goodbye to Saraj.

Every day, I had stopped by the post office to send letters. I always handed them to the same clerk—Saraj.

During the time I had spent in Kabul, he and I had become very close friends. He spoke and understood English very well. He explained to me that his uncle was a customs inspector and if I gave him enough money, I could send as much hashish to America as I wanted. Even though it sounded like a great deal, I turned him down. I told him that I just wanted to be his friend, not his customer.

Over a period of four months, I constantly turned down Saraj's offer.

Every time I had visited the post office, he asked me that same question. But now I was returning to America and wanted to take him up on his offer.

As I entered the post office, I noticed Saraj standing behind the counter waiting on a customer. When he saw me a few seconds later, he smiled. As I stepped over to shake his hand, he asked the same question.

"Bob, do you want to send hash to America?" he asked.

"Saraj, if I do decide to send some hash I can't give you any extra money, but I can pay for postage. I'm going to America to get more money so I can return to Afghanistan in a few months. Then I will give you and your uncle the money for this deal."

"I will help you send the hash," he promised.

Saraj even gave me the hash for the envelopes. He had busted a German tourist earlier that day when he tried to send it without paying *baksheesh*. When Saraj opened the German's eight-by-twelve-inch envelope, he found the hash hidden among a stack of photos. Then the German was arrested and taken to jail, all because he had tried to send the package without paying the proper people.

At this post office they didn't have dogs to sniff out the drugs, they had a blind psychic—a small, hunchback man that used his nose to sniff out illegal contraband. The clerks would hand him a small package or envelope and he would hold it to his nose, take a whiff, and know if it contained drugs or not. That was his only job, and he was right every time. So I was very happy to have befriended Saraj.

I returned to my hotel room and made the envelopes, as Saraj had explained to me. The hash he had given me was excellent and was the kind I had been looking for since I had arrived in Afghanistan. I placed less than thirty grams on the wooden floor and flattened the hash as thin as possible, to about an eighth of an inch, using a Coke bottle as a rolling pin. When that task was completed, I wrapped the flattened hash in cellophane, placed the rectangular slab between two post cards, taped up the edges so the hash couldn't be seen, and placed one hash-filled post card into each envelope. I had a total of five envelopes for Saraj. I wrote on the outside of each envelope, in bold letters, **Negatives and Photos—Do Not X-ray**. The next day I took all five envelopes to the post office and handed them to Saraj, along with the money for postage.

"Saraj, are you sure the envelopes will get to America safely, without any problems?" I asked.

"They will, so don't worry, Bob."

"If everything goes all right and God is with me, I will be back within six months. Maybe sooner," I promised him.

I thanked Saraj and said goodbye as I left the Kabul post office. Now I had sent hash to myself and to a close friend and wanted to be in America by the time it arrived. That meant I would have to arrive there within seven days. So I looked up into the beautiful blue sky, closed my eyes, and made a wish to be in America at this very moment. Just my luck—it didn't come true.

By the following day, I had packed my bag and was ready to leave Afghanistan the same way I had come, overland. First, I had to get an exit visa. Mine was a few months overdue. I was hoping I could pay a fine, but I had also heard that they gave jail time for letting one's visa expire. So I went to the minister of interior and after a lengthy conversation with an official, I was ordered to pay a fifteen-dollar fine or spend eight months in jail. I happily paid the fine and was relieved that I had gotten off so easy. And once I had my Afghan and Iranian visas, I was ready to start my trip back to Europe, but not before I shot up my last tablet of morphine. I decided to quit cold turkey and really believed that I could do it. I couldn't afford the stuff anyway. But then, ten minutes before I boarded the bus to Kandahar, I had sold ten dollars worth of my hash to a couple of tourists. And then, as I boarded the bus, a guy grabbed me from behind.

"Can I talk to you for a minute," asked an English hippie.

"Sure," I said, as we walked a few feet away from the bus.

"Do you have any more hash for sale?" he asked.

I still had about four ounces left. "Do you have any dollars?"

"I'm from England, but I have American dollars," he replied.

"How much hash do you need?"

"About ten dollars worth—that is, if you have that much."

He explained how he had traveled to Kabul from Kandahar with the people who had just purchased the hash from me and now was headed to India.

While he talked, I reached into my shoulder bag and pulled out my stash of hash. I had two slabs left, so I gave him one. I needed the money more than I needed the hash.

Once he saw how good it was, he asked for another five dollars worth. So I ripped my last slab in two and gave him the biggest half. He handed me a total of fifteen American dollars and walked away happy. After that transaction, I boarded the bus to Kandahar.

CHAPTER 8
WITHDRAWAL FROM MORPHINE

Well, I was doing something I never thought I would be doing—returning to America. I was on my first leg on my return trip to Europe and heading for Kandahar. I hadn't taken any morphine for the last two days and felt very light-headed; I had stomach cramps and no energy. So I decided to buy some opium as soon as I arrived in Kandahar and visit the teashop that my Italian friends had told me about.

Finally, after a long, ten-hour bus ride, I reached Kandahar. We only had a one-hour layover before we headed for heart, so I had to take care of business rather quickly. I left the bus and walked to the teashop to purchase some opium. As soon as I entered, the clerk knew exactly what I wanted.

"What type of opium do you want—to inject, smoke, or eat?" asked the clerk.

"I want to smoke it," I told him.

I remembered Phillip telling me to eat the opium, but I also remembered when Mark and I had smoked it in Erzurum. The clerk turned and walked into a curtain-covered back room and after a few minutes returned with a big plastic bag full of more than ten pounds of a rock-hard, dark brown substance.

"How much do you want?" asked the clerk.

"How much money do you want for an ounce?"

"Ten dollars."

"Hell, that's more than a kilo of primo hash costs," I snapped.

I didn't have that much money left, so I had to spend it wisely. But I also didn't want to get sick on my return to Europe. Reluctantly, I handed him the money, and he gave me an ounce of the hard, reddish-brown, glass-like substance. I shoved it into my pants pocket and then walked back to the bus with less than thirty dollars to my name and the hash in my boots. I couldn't even afford to ride the train and would have to ride the bus all the way to Germany—or hitchhike if my money ran out. I wasn't really worried, though. There was always someone, usually another tourist, willing to help a poor, destitute hippie. I figured I might even have to beg for money. It seemed every time I traveled to a far-off land, I always ran out of funds.

Every time I worried about my troubles that lay ahead, I ate a small chunk of opium. I also sat in the very back of the bus so I wouldn't bother anyone when I smoked my hash. But there were times when a few of the passengers sitting close by inhaled the potent secondhand smoke and became upset. When that happened, I put the pipe away until we stopped for prayer. Then, after the passengers had gotten off the bus to pray and it was completely empty, I would light my pipe and smoke my hash. And this happened five times each day so the Muslim passengers could roll out their prayer rugs toward the city of Mecca and pray to God. Then, after ten minutes of prayer, we were on our way once again. So between smoking my hash and eating my opium, I stayed high all day long while riding on this old, dilapidated bus.

I was very anxious to return to America, so I traveled day and night. I wanted to get to Europe within seven days or less, but that depended on my funds. If I had the money, I'd have flown back to America instead of riding buses.

We arrived in Herat late at night and too late to catch another bus to the border. So I rented a hotel room for the night, which meant more money out of my pocket. But I needed a hot shower and a good night's sleep, anyway. I threw my luggage into my room, borrowed a clean towel from the hotel manager, and walked to the bathroom to take a shower. But I had forgotten my soap, so I quickly ran back to my room to get some. Just as I opened the door, I noticed the hotel manager rummaging through my belongings. I caught the bastard red-handed. He knew that if I called the police, they would cut off his hand for stealing. His face turned a bright red and he started apologizing right away. However, I noticed he had found my bag of opium and had placed it on the bed for all to see.

He pointed to the baggie and said, "You should be careful with that."

"Get out of my room before I call the police," I shouted.

"I won't charge you for the room," he added, and quickly left the room.

That was agreeable with me. Any money saved was money

earned as far as I was concerned.

The next morning I was off to the Afghan-Iranian border. I figured to be in Tehran within twenty-four hours even though I'd have to ride the bus non-stop. We had already passed through Afghanistan customs without any trouble. A few minutes later, the bus stopped in front of the Iranian border hospital for a health check. A western-dressed Iranian official came onto the bus and asked to see everyone's World Health booklet. He was looking for expired inoculations. I didn't think too much about it until he ordered me off the bus. I didn't understand what the heck was going on and quickly but discreetly hid my bag of opium under my seat. I didn't want to take a chance and get busted, especially in Iran. Then I stepped off the bus and walked over to the official to question him.

"Why was I the only person taken off the bus?" I whined.

"I can't let you enter my country until you have your cholera shot," he exclaimed.

It seemed my cholera shot was overdue, but I continued to argue with him.

"Please, I must get back to America as soon as possible," I pleaded.

"Go back to Kabul and get your shot or stay at our hospital for thirty-six hours," he bellowed, as he walked toward the hospital and I followed.

"You could let me in your country without a cholera shot," I whined.

"You could start an epidemic," he shouted.

However, I didn't want to hear that. I had to get to America as soon as possible. Then I noticed one of the male passengers on my bus filming my antagonistic actions as I pleaded with the health official. But I didn't care and quickly followed the official into the hospital still ranting and raving. Then I followed him into a back room where he had been boiling water in a metal teapot. While he was in front of the hot plate pouring hot water from the teapot into a cup, I slammed my passport wallet against the wall. It made such a loud smack that it surprised him, and he spilled boiling water all over his hands and arm. Then, in a fit of rage, he grabbed a large eighteen-inch pipe wrench and began swinging it over his head threatening to kill me with me.

"Please stop. I'm sorry and I apologize for my actions," I whined, as I backed away from his swinging pipe wrench. "Please, don't hurt me. I'm SORRY."

But my pleas had no effect on this huge, six-foot-tall, three-hundred pound madman. He kept up his swinging ways, and I continued backing away toward the front door. His face was completely distorted and red with anger, and his eyes bulged out of their sockets. If he had hit me with that pipe wrench, he would have killed me. Heck, just using his hands he could have put me out like a cigarette. The only thing that saved me was an English couple who had walked through the front door of the hospital and saw this demented man swinging the pipe wrench at me. They yelled at him to stop what he was doing, and he finally put the wrench down. When he calmed down, he ordered me to walk up the street to the Iranian customs office.

"I want you to walk to the customs shack just two-hundred feet straight ahead and have your bags checked," snapped the health official, completely out of breath from swinging that large pipe wrench.

I did as he ordered. When I entered the customs office, a guard stopped me.

"What do you want?" he asked.

"I'm sick and I have to stay at the hospital because my cholera shot is overdue, so you need to check my baggage," I explained.

He just gave me a strange look and began talking to himself. Without checking my luggage, he told me to go. I thanked him, exited the building, and returned to the hospital. But before I went in, I noticed that my bus was still parked there, so I boarded it and retrieved the valuable narcotic that I had hidden under my seat. I shoved the bag of opium into my pants pocket and proceeded to the hospital. As I checked in at the front desk, a doctor came into the room and introduced himself.

"Hello, I'm Dr. Asam. I just need to give you a cholera shot and take a stool sample."

At first I thought he was going to body search me and discover my opium, but he didn't. He only wanted to give me a check-up and a cholera shot.

"Doc, how long will I have to stay here?" I asked.

"After thirty-six hours, if you don't show any signs of cholera, you will be free to leave," he said, giving me the shot.

A few minutes later, I was taken to my room. It was a big, clean, dormitory-type room with twenty or so empty beds and big electric fans that kept the room cool during the hot afternoons. I decided to eat a gram of opium and relax on a nice, clean, comfortable bed. I thought I was the only patient until a tall, thin, light-skinned black Englishman with a huge Afro (nearly two feet in diameter) walked into the room carrying a flute around his neck. When he noticed me, he stopped and introduced himself.

"How are you doing? My name is Josh. I just came into the hotel an hour before you arrived. Man, it must be God's work that we have met at this particular place. There must be a reason," he philosophized.

I agreed with him. And as we relaxed on our beds, we continued our conversation. Within a few hours, Josh and I had become good friends. And while waiting for our time to expire, we would sometimes walk behind the hospital and sit near a big oil derrick to smoke the little bit of hashish I had carried along with me. I had about a quarter of an ounce of hash and three quarters of an ounce of opium left. I shared the hash with my new friend but saved the opium for myself, gradually taking less and less each day, using it to withdraw from my morphine habit. I explained my problem to Josh, so he understood when I didn't offer him any opium.

There wasn't much to do at the hospital, no music to listen to or books or magazines to read. Boredom set in very quickly. Sometimes I would go through a hole in the fence that surrounded the hospital and walk out into the desert. I found the old bones of dead animals, mostly camel and donkey. There wasn't much else to look at, except for the giant cacti.

The desert was beautiful in its own way. The desert flowers in bloom hid the bones behind their beauty. The weather was hot during the day and cool at night. I tried to think of this stay as a small vacation within a vacation. As much as I wanted, I couldn't do anything about my situation. As the Englishman said, "it was fate."

Besides finding a new friend, I had also found a new way to smuggle hash into Iran. Just make sure your cholera shot was overdue. That way you bypass the main Iranian customs office and the guards are so frightened that they might catch the disease that they just wave you on your way. I could have brought a vanload of hash into the country using this method, but I remembered that in Iran, they shot anyone who was caught with illegal narcotics—no judge, jury, or trial. They just stand you up against a wall and bang, you're dead. In fact, Josh talked about a German couple who had been caught here at the Iranian border trying to smuggle twenty pounds of opium in their van. The Iranian soldiers impounded the van and then took him and his girlfriend behind the customs building and shot them both.

The German embassy was outraged over the deaths of two of their citizens, but there was nothing that they could do about the situation. They were dependent on Iranian oil, and if they gave Iran an argument over their political differences, Iran would stop the oil shipments. So Germany had its hands tied.

And so did I. But I would be out of the hospital very shortly and on my way to America. If I'd had to stay longer than two days, I would have starved. They only fed us rice and milk—hot rice with cold goat's milk for breakfast and cooked rice and a small glass of cold milk for dinner. We only had two meals per day, and the rice tasted as though it had been cooked in kerosene. I gagged every time I put it near my mouth. So by the second day of my hospital stay, I was starving.

When I couldn't stand it any longer, I gave a hospital orderly a few Afghan coins to buy some food at the local grocery store. But it was a Muslim holiday and many of the stores were closed. Although he did bring back something for us to eat besides rice—chocolate-covered marshmallow cookies, similar to the ones I had bought in Yugoslavia, which I hated. I was nauseated just looking at them. Josh, however, liked the cookies.

The morning of the third day, we were allowed to leave the hospital and enter Iran. We walked slowly into the little village and past the customs office. They had stamped our transit visas as we left the hospital. That's why it would be easy to smuggle illegal contraband into Iran. Just let your cholera shot expire, then vacation at a nice, clean hospital for a few days and drive your van loaded with hash into Iran without going through or being searched by customs officials.

When we walked into the main part of the village, I went directly to a restaurant and ordered a 7-Up ice cream float. It was delicious. While I drank my float, the clerk and I started a friendly conversation.

"I just stayed a couple of days at your hospital and I liked it. The workers were very helpful and friendly," I said.

The clerk seemed to be very nice and cordial, and my long hair didn't seem to bother him. That is, until he asked me what country I was from. I had made the mistake of telling him that I was from America and just at that exact moment, Josh walked into the store. The clerk who had been friendly just a few seconds before suddenly become outraged at the sight of my friend's gigantic Afro and the color of his skin and ordered us out of his establishment.

We left the restaurant, calling the clerk a racist. As we walked down the street toward the bus station, a few angry Iranian males followed us, yelling filthy, dirty names at us in English and Farsi. Within minutes there were more than fifty angry Iranians following us. Then someone in the crowd threw a rock at us. Soon others followed, and rocks were being hurled at us from all directions. We ran toward the bus station a few hundred yards ahead of us. Luckily, we dodged the rocks being thrown at us and finally reached the bus depot.

Standing outside the station were a couple of policemen. They watched intently as the crowd got closer and closer. Finally, the policemen demanded the crowd to stop.

"Don't come any further!" yelled one of the policemen. "If you don't put down your rocks and disperse you'll be arrested and thrown in jail!"

When the mob hesitated, the policemen brandished their weapons. They pulled out their side-arm revolvers and fired into the air. The crowd dispersed in a flash. The cops didn't mess around. They meant business.

Josh and I purchased our bus tickets to Tehran via Meshad. It was basically the same way I had come, except this time I wouldn't be riding a train. As long as I continued taking my daily dose of opium, I could have ridden a donkey to Europe and I wouldn't have cared.

We seemed to get hassled everywhere we went. The Iranians didn't like my friend's giant Afro. His light black skin didn't help him much, either. As long as the Iranians didn't harm us, I didn't let their belligerent actions bother me. Josh and I shared everything. We didn't have much nor did we have much money. However, we did have one problem. Josh wanted to stay in Istanbul for a few days or longer, and I wanted to leave right away. I *had* to leave right away. I wanted to travel non-stop to Europe. I was already two days behind schedule, so I didn't want to waste any more time. We decided to talk about it at a later time. We only had about twenty dollars between us and a little hash and opium.

I was still using the opium to withdraw from the morphine I had been injecting twice a day for a period of four months. I had never been in this predicament before and didn't know what to expect. However, I was doing fairly well. I had been taking less and less opium each day. I had already used over half of the ounce, so I had to use it very sparingly.

The bus ride from the Afghan-Iranian border to Tehran was long and hot. Going through the desert in 120-degree weather without air conditioning was so excruciating and painful that I had to eat a lot of opium to knock myself out during that time of the day. In fact, one side of my face had become very sunburned and blistered from using the window as a pillow. The sun had shined directly on my face as I was sleeping. But I didn't let it bother me. I continued thinking about the five envelopes and two parcels of hash I had sent to America and Canada. That kept my mind off my problems.

We had arrived in Tehran without incident two days later around nine o'clock in the evening. Josh and I located a bus that was leaving for the Iranian-Turkish border via Tabriz within the hour and decided to take it and sleep on it instead of wasting what little money we had on a cheap hotel room. We expected to arrive in Tabriz within twelve hours. Once there, we would get our Turkish transit visas and head directly to the Turkish border before it closed. We didn't have the money to spend for a hotel room. We had less than ten dollars left. That was it. We had just enough money to get us to Istanbul, but after that, it was uncertain. Josh and I still disagreed on when to leave Istanbul. I wouldn't change my mind, nor would he, so I planned on leaving Istanbul without him. But it was really up to Josh.

We arrived in Tabriz nearly ten hours later, early in the morning. After getting our transit visas for Turkey, we immediately walked to the bus station and purchased our bus tickets to Erzurum. I decided that if I had enough money I would take the train to Istanbul. Then, depending on how much I had left, I would either take the train or bus to Germany. And by the time I had arrived there, I was sure to be out of money. I figured if I had to, I would wire my parents for money. And I still had the hash in my boots that I had planned to sell there, so I wasn't too worried. I would worry about that problem when the time came.

We arrived at the Iranian-Turkish border just before nightfall. I threw my luggage on the table for the Iranian customs official to search. I looked him directly in the eyes as he began asking me questions concerning my stay in his country and noticed that I was speaking to the same customs official who had given me, Mark, and two Afghans our transit visas for Iran. When he asked if I was taking any gold, jewelry, or antiques out of the country, he looked at me as though he knew me, but he couldn't put a finger on it. So when he motioned for me to go, I picked up my baggage and walked away from his counter as fast as my nervous legs would carry me. Just as I was exiting the door for the Turkish border, I turned around to look at the Iranian customs official and noticed that he was also staring at me.

Suddenly, he raised his arm and yelled, "Ten dollars! Ten dollars!"

I quickly ran out the door to the Turkish side. But the customs officer followed me, shaking his fist.

"Ten dollars! Ten dollars!" yelled the Iranian customs officer, as he stopped well inside the Iranian border.

When he finally remembered who I was, it was too late. I was now in Turkey. A few minutes later, Josh and I went through Turkish customs without any problems. Then we boarded our bus and within thirty minutes were heading toward Erzurum, a city that had a special place in my heart.

I was feeling sickly and restless, so I ate a piece of opium and slept through the horrid bus ride. I didn't awaken until we had reached the bus station in Erzurum. Josh and I decided that we would ride the train to Istanbul. We could purchase third class tickets for the train and still have a few dollars left. Although neither one of us had changed our minds about leaving Istanbul, I was determined to go on even if I had to beg or panhandle for money. I just hoped that I had enough money to get me to Germany. Then I would be all right.

It would take over three days to travel from Erzurum to Istanbul, and I was completely out of hash, which had disappeared the night before, and nearly out of opium. I had only enough for one or two more days. I had been taking only a small piece each day, and traveling third class on this slow train was taking its toll on my body. In fact, we didn't get a seat for the first two days and had to sit and sleep on the floor of the train next to the bathroom. I slept right in front of the door where the passengers walked from one car to another.

Every time someone came through the door, I had to help open it 'cause it had a habit of sticking at the bottom. So I would have to kick the bottom of the door with my foot and slide it over to one side as the person on the other side pulled at the exact same time. That's what I did for two days of the three-day trip. On the second day, I ran out of opium. Having to lie on the floor of the train in the aisle and next to the bathroom, I couldn't dwell on being sick. Even though my body shivered and twitched uncontrollably and my stomach was cramped up, I still had to help the people open the door.

During the three-day trip, I didn't sleep a wink. I either had stomach cramps or was constantly opening the door. By the time I had arrived in Istanbul, I was sicker than a dog and hadn't regained my strength or stamina. But I continued on as we crossed the peninsula on the ferry. When we arrived on the western side of Istanbul, a large crowd of people was boarding the ferry as we were getting off. Suddenly, Josh and I had become separated. I looked all around but I couldn't see my English friend anywhere. I returned to the ferry to look for him, but he was nowhere to be found.

When I returned to the street, there were thousands of people wandering about. I continued walking toward the bus station, hoping my friend would be there. But when he wasn't, I figured that he must have gone with the other hippies we had met on the train.

Now I was traveling alone. I didn't need to get any more visas or shots and was ready for the ride to Europe. I didn't have enough money to ride the train, but I had just enough for the bus. So I spent the last of my money on the bus ticket to Munich, Germany. That's as far as my money would take me. I figured I would visit an army buddy of mine who lived in the city Wertheim, 100 kilometers north of Munich. But I would have to hitch a ride to his place.

As I walked to the back of the bus, I soon found out that they had sold more tickets than they had seats, and I didn't have a seat to sit on. All the other seats had been taken. The bus driver quickly alleviated the problem by spreading out the only seat that would open up to sit three people. That corrected my problem, but there were now two more Americans that needed to be seated. The bus driver solved this problem by placing two square five-gallon tin cans in the middle of the aisle, near three other Americans and me. But his effort was in vain.

Within a few minutes, the two Americans sitting in the aisle exploded in anger for not having proper seats. The driver quickly soothed their anger by telling them that a few of the passengers would reach their destination within an hour or so, then seats would be available, and that he was very sorry for the inconvenience. He explained to them that there was nothing else he could do unless they wanted to wait for the next bus, which wouldn't be leaving Istanbul until the next morning. So the two Americans had no other choice but to wait until seats were available. They seemed to be in as much of a hurry as I was to get back home. I wondered if they, too, had sent hash back home and wanted to get back before it arrived.

Well, an hour had passed and the two Americans were still sitting in the aisle, debating what to do, while I thought about selling my hash to my army friend in Germany. And as I looked in my address book for his address, I came across something unexpected—two Bulgarian dollar bills. I figured they were worth maybe one American dollar at the most. So I decided to exchange them for American money when I arrived at the Turkish-Bulgarian border.

An hour later, the two Americans became angry and restless, so one of them walked up front and asked the bus driver how much longer it would be before they could sit in a padded seat. The bus driver just yelled at them to sit down when the bus was in motion. He told them that passengers would be disembarking at the next stop. Well, three hours had passed and nothing had changed, so the Americans started another revolution. This time they both went up to the front of the bus to confront the bus driver. They wanted their seats and they wanted them now. The bus driver pulled the bus to the side of the road and stopped.

"Go back and sit down or get off the bus!" yelled the bus driver.

He promised the two Americans that they would have seats very soon.

Then one of the other passengers sitting behind the bus driver interjected his two cents.

"It is unfair, and they should get their money back or some type of reimbursement or compensation," opined a Pakistani man.

"Keep your mouth shut!" shouted the bus driver. "It is none of your business. This is between me and the two Americans."

"We are losing time and that involves me," responded the Pakistani man.

The bus driver nearly exploded, but his assistant calmed him down. After nearly a ten-minute bus stop, we were on our way once again. By the time we had reached the Turkish-Bulgarian border it was about four in the afternoon. Every one of the passengers was ready to explode. The two Americans were still sitting in the middle of the aisle on the tin cans.

But now that we had arrived at the border, we had a chance to stretch our legs for a few minutes. The bus driver had to take his paperwork and travel documentation into the customs office. However, a few minutes turned into hours. It seemed the bus driver had brought the wrong papers to enter Bulgaria. The customs official wanted two thousand dollars from him or the correct papers. But there was one problem: The owner of the bus company had to bring the paperwork, but nobody knew where to find him. So we sat and waited at the Turkish-Bulgarian border with no hope of going anywhere. In fact, we waited all night and into the morning.

At least I was able to sleep on the bus. I had run out of opium more than two days before and was feeling quite ill when, for some unknown reason, one of the Americans, a big, six-foot-six-inch giant named Dan, handed out sleeping pills to a few of his fellow passengers, including me. It really helped. I was still feeling the symptoms of withdrawing from the opium and morphine and this let me sleep like a baby. I slept all night long, sitting up in my seat, and didn't wake up once. The others slept outside in their sleeping bags.

Finally, by ten o'clock that morning, we were on our way to Bulgaria. The owner of the bus company had brought the correct papers to satisfy the Turkish customs officials, and we were allowed to continue on our journey. When the bus stopped ten minutes later at the Bulgarian customs office to turn in some more paperwork, I got out and walked to a small bank to change the two Bulgarian dollars into German marks or American dollars. I thought they would give me one or two American dollars, even though I had absolutely no idea how much the Bulgarian dollars were worth and was very surprised to learn that they were worth four times my best estimate. I received a total of eight American dollars. I was elated. At least I wasn't broke now.

A few minutes later, I was back on the bus and on my way to Yugoslavia. Within an hour, the two Americans sitting in the aisle started complaining to anyone who would listen that they would probably have to sit on the cans all the way to Germany. They were becoming so angry you could almost see the steam rising from their bodies. Then they began arguing about what actions they should take concerning their terrible situation, while the bus driver and the Pakistani passenger were arguing up front.

An hour out of Sophia, all hell broke loose. The bus suddenly swerved to the side of the road and stopped with a loud screech. The lights inside the bus came on and the bus driver and his assistant began fighting with the scrawny little Pakistani man and his wife. Seconds later, the bus driver pulled out a ten-inch knife and began slashing and stabbing the Pakistani man. When Dan saw what was happening, he jumped up from his seat, ran up front, punched the bully bus driver in the mouth, and then took the knife away from him and stopped the beating.

As things died down and everything seemed peaceful once again, the bus driver got behind the wheel and started the engine. But seconds later, one of the disgruntled Americans who had been sitting on the tin cans suddenly ran up front and took the keys out of the ignition. When the bus driver tried to get them back another fight broke out, this time between the two Americans who had been sitting in the aisle and the two Turks. The fight started up front and ended near the back of the bus. Finally, Dan intervened and broke it up. Then he returned the keys to the bus driver so we could continue our trip.

I discussed the situation amongst the other American passengers, and we decided to tell the authorities when we reached the Bulgarian-Yugoslavian border. We wanted the bus driver and his assistant arrested. Ten minutes after the eruption had subsided, the Pakistani man and his wife wanted to get off the bus. But we were in a desolate area and not a soul was around. He didn't care. He wanted off the bus and we couldn't talk him out of it. He was so frustrated and upset over being abused and beaten that he began crying.

The bus driver was a good three hundred pounds heavier and a good three inches taller than the scrawny little Pakistani man. The bus driver also had slashed and stabbed him with a knife and had his assistant join in on the melee. The two Turkish assailants had no right to fight with this man, and we were going to do whatever was necessary to get them arrested. But the Pakistani and his wife still felt humiliated and angry and refused to stay on the bus another minute. So the bus driver opened the door and let the Pakistani couple disembark on a pitch-black road with not a house or building in sight. As soon as they were off the bus, the two Americans who had been sitting in the aisle for the last few days finally had padded seats to sit on. Now they were up front sitting behind the bus driver. Everything went smoothly from that point on until we got to the Yugoslavian border.

We had a ten-minute layover, so a few of the Americans got off the bus and explained to the customs officials everything that had happened during our long journey. They told them that they wanted the bus driver and his assistant arrested and also wanted a new bus driver. However, there was nothing the customs official could do for us. He confronted the bus driver and warned him to behave himself or they would contact his boss in Turkey and explain the problems that the passengers were having and get him fired.

With that done, we were once again on our way westward, heading toward Europe. We didn't have any more trouble the rest of the trip. We drove non-stop all the way to Germany. Once we had reached the Yugoslavian-Italian border, we were in Munich within two days. This is where I had to get off—Dan, too. I had mentioned to him that I had hash in my cowboy boots, so a few minutes after the bus departed, I took out my knife and cut the soles off my boots and then placed the hash into a dirty sock.

"Can I have a piece of hash?" asked Dan.

"Sure. I owe you for helping me." I took out a small two-gram chunk of the green pollen and handed it to him.

Dan was very happy. I had expected more hash than I had, but made the mistake of using the pollen instead of the pressed hash. The pollen was just too bulky. I only had approximately thirty to forty grams at the most. The pressed hash was much, much denser. I could have placed two or three hundred grams in the soles, if I had used the pressed hash. But I didn't, and that was a big mistake. I would only get two to three dollars a gram, but right now, I needed the money.

Dan and I split up and went our separate ways. Now I had to find a way to get to the army base in Wertheim and only had a few dollars in my pocket. I figured once I got to my buddy's place, I could sell my hash and get enough money to buy a train ticket to England and, I hoped, a student fare plane ticket from London to New York.

Not having the money for public transportation, I hitched a ride to my buddy's small village and quickly found out that the villagers spoke only German. But luckily, the American soldiers spoke English and gave me directions to my buddy's apartment on the American army base. I couldn't stay very long because I looked too conspicuous. I was the only person with long hair. A hippie on an army base just doesn't look right.

My friend was surprised to see me standing at his door. After I explained my situation to him, he took me over to the barracks to sell my hash. He helped me immensely. I sold all but a few grams to one person, a black soldier. The base was dry, so I was able to sell my hash for four dollars a gram for a total of one hundred and twenty dollars. Now I had enough money to ride the train to Frankfurt and then to London, England. Most likely I would have to send a telegram to my parents asking them to wire money to me so I could purchase a plane ticket to America.

I only stayed one night at my friend's apartment, and the next morning I rode the train to Frankfurt. I arrived there that afternoon and decided to visit Club 4, the same club that I had visited nearly a year before. My train to England didn't leave until one in the morning, so I had a few hours to kill.

While kicking it at the club, I listened to a great band called Status Quo and met another American traveling to England that night on the same train, so we decided to travel together. I still had a gram or so of hash and my friend had a couple of tabs of acid so when he asked me if I wanted to trip, I quickly accepted. It had been a few months since I had dropped acid. So just as we walked out of the club, we each ate a tab of orange sunshine and then headed to the train station. By the time we had arrived, we were flying high. An hour later, we boarded the train and luckily, were able to get a compartment to ourselves, which is unusual in Europe, but it was also a blessing. We were much too high to speak with anyone.

An hour or two into our trip, as we were lying down across the seats, a rowdy group of soccer players came barging into our cabin. We had to sit up and share the room with a bunch of drunk, rude, loud, obnoxious teenage kids from Scotland. They had just played in a big tournament and placed second out of ten countries that had competed in the Junior World Cup Soccer tournament. Afterwards, they had celebrated by drinking beer and alcohol.

I explained to the drunken soccer players that my friend and I were tripping on acid and wanted them to quiet down. However, that didn't seem to matter to them. They continued to laugh, sing, and shout until we had arrived in Ostand, Belgium, nearly three hours later. From that point on, I traveled by myself and boarded the ferry that would take me to Dover, England. However, this ferry was a new type of transportation called a hydroplane. It floated over water and land, was also much faster, and rode much smoother than the regular ferry. This type of ferry rode over the waves, not into them.

I tried to get something to eat aboard the hydroplane but couldn't stand the smell of the alcohol and cigarette smoke that filled the room. It seemed all the people standing in line were all drunks or alcoholics waiting to buy more booze. Every person I looked at could barely stand and had bloodshot eyes and cigarettes hanging from their mouths, while they carried their liquor bottles back to their seats. I thought to myself, how lucky I was not being an alcoholic. That was one vice I didn't have.

It took less than five hours to cross the English Channel and reach Dover. Now we had to board the train. However, before boarding the train to London, we proceeded through customs.

The customs official examined my passport and asked me a few questions.

"Are you related to the queen?" he asked.

"Why do you ask that?"

"You do know your last name is related to the queen? They are cousins to the queen's family," he remarked.

"Is that right? I didn't know that, and I'm not related to the queen."

"How long are you going to stay in England and whom are you going to visit?" he asked.

"As soon as I receive my money from American Express, I will be leaving for America. Once I arrive in London, my money should be waiting for me," I retorted.

But I had made a big mistake by telling him I didn't have any money. He didn't want me in his country without any money to live on. Instead of begging and pleading with him to let me enter the country, I decided to make up a story.

"My relatives living in London will give me money if I need it," I lied.

"I knew you were related to the monarchy," beamed the customs officer.

"I have to be very discreet because of kidnappings and such," I whispered.

The customs officer smiled and handed me my passport.

"Welcome to England," he exclaimed.

I quickly grabbed my baggage, walked over to the train, and then found an empty cabin. I slept all the way to Victoria Station in London. I didn't bother to stop at the Grovsner Hotel. I couldn't afford it this time around. So I decided to walk to the tourist office to find a cheap place to stay, like maybe a youth hostel. I had just enough money to buy my meals and rent a cheap hotel room for a few days. I was no longer in a country where I could live on a dollar a day. It would now cost me at least five dollars a day for food and a bed.

I had to ride the tube to the outskirts of London to find the youth hostel. It was a co-ed dormitory-type situation in a five-story building that was being renovated. It was very cold and damp throughout the entire building, which contained large rooms with one hundred beds in each, where the boys and girls slept right next to each other.

I was directed to a room on the fourth floor and picked out an empty bed. Then I lay down because I had come down with a cold and was running a slight fever. I figured it was from my withdrawal from the morphine and opium, which I hadn't used in more than a week. As a mater of fact, I hadn't used any drugs since I had taken the acid in Frankfurt.

Without drugs, time seemed to stand still. Besides being ill, I was also very bored. All I could do was wait for the money that was already supposed to have been wired. It should have been waiting for me, but it hadn't yet arrived. But I found out later that it had been wired to Frankfurt the morning I had left from there. Now I had to wait until it was sent back to America and then rewired to London. It was four days before I received my funds to buy a plane ticket to New York. I was able to get a student rate on the ticket and had just enough money to purchase it. Even though it was a charter flight, I didn't mind at all. And two days later, I was back in New York.

CHAPTER 9
BACK IN THE U.S.A.

I arrived at Kennedy Airport in the afternoon on a bright and sunny day and passed through customs without a hitch. I spent all the money I had left to buy a bus ticket to Albany to see my relatives. I could borrow money from them to fly back to Detroit.

When I arrived at the bus station in Albany, I had to borrow a dime from a policeman so I could make a phone call to my uncle John. He picked me up in his new pickup truck, and I was very happy to see a face I recognized. He was one of my favorite uncles.

I hugged him and thanked him, then told him about my trip. I gave him some little trinkets I had purchased in Afghanistan for his family's hospitality.

Within a few hours, I was back in the city of my youth. Once thinking that I would never return to America or Michigan again, I was very happy to be home, but I had only planned to be around for a few months—just until I could save enough money to travel back to Afghanistan. That was my main goal, especially if the hash got through.

The day I arrived home, I asked my mom if any parcels had arrived for me. None had come yet. So I went over to my friend's house to see if he had received any of the hash envelopes.

"All five envelopes arrived on the same day," said Al.

He was very paranoid. He thought the cops were going to bust him.

"Don't worry, Al. Because I used your address, you can keep half of the hash from the five envelopes," I told him.

He agreed, and we divided up what he had left. I guess he had smoked some of it. The hash had arrived four days before I returned to America, so he had spent four days smoking. If he and his friends smoked two or three grams a day, he could have smoked well over ten grams. However, we each got forty grams out of the deal. I was just relieved it got through without any problems. I was more than satisfied.

Within two days, one of the parcels arrived. I waited three days before opening it, just in case the cops were waiting to bust me. They couldn't do anything to me if I hadn't opened the parcel. I was jumping for joy. I figured if this parcel had arrived, then the other should have arrived in Canada.

I drove across the bridge to Canada. I parked the car and walked to the Windsor post office. Once inside, I walked up to the counter and asked the clerk for a package addressed to me. I hoped he wouldn't get suspicious, but the man asked me the same question I had been asked when picking up the package I had sent from Morocco.

"Why did you send the parcel to this post office and not to your house?" asked the clerk.

"I'm a student at the university and at the time the parcel was sent, I didn't have a stable address, so I sent it here to the post office," I replied.

He seemed satisfied with my answer and handed me the package. I walked to my car as fast as my legs would carry me. I was overwhelmed with joy and happiness. Both of my parcels had arrived without any problems. Now I had to smuggle the sandals into the States.

Once in my car, I opened the bag and retrieved the sandals. I took off my old shoes, tossed them and the white cloth bag into a garbage container, and placed the sandals onto my feet. I placed the other items from the package into the back seat. Now I was ready to cross the bridge to Detroit.

The bridge was very busy, and it took a few minutes to arrive at the customs booth.

"Sir, how long have you been visiting Canada?" asked the customs official, peering into my vehicle and eyeing the items in the back seat.

"Not long. I went to see a friend of mine. He wasn't home so I came right back," I replied.

He motioned for me to move forward and to pull over to have the vehicle searched. I remained calm as I pulled the car over to the side in front of the customs office. Two other customs officials began searching my car very intently. I stood to one side as I watched them search. After ten minutes of an intense search of my vehicle, the officers gave up and let me continue on my journey. I thanked them, placed the car in gear, and happily drove away and into Detroit. Now I was home free.

The second I arrived home, I grabbed a sharp knife and began cutting the thread between the two soles to take out the hash. I wasn't quite sure how much hash was in each sandal, but they weren't that heavy. Once I had cut the thread holding the soles together, I ripped them apart and the hash fell out. I had approximately two ounces of pressed hash in each sandal. I had expected more, but it was enough to put a smile on my face. Now I had a total of ten ounces, including the ounce and a half that I had received from the envelopes I had sent to my friend Al.

I began to put my plan into motion—returning to Afghanistan. The first task on my list was to sell all of my hash, then buy an additional amount from one of my hash connections and sell that. I wanted to save as much money as possible within the next few months so I could live in Afghanistan for the rest of my life. This would be my main goal. I wanted to be ready to travel to Europe by June. That was just three months away.

I wanted to have enough money to buy a one-way plane ticket to Europe and at least six or seven-hundred dollars for spending money. I decided to speak with a few friends of mine—Jim, Ron, and John—to see if they were interested in traveling with me. They were college students and dealt drugs to make money to pay their tuition. All three were interested in traveling to Asia, especially when I mentioned that I had Afghan friends in the customs department and post office who would send hash for me.

I also explained how I sent the hash envelopes and the packages and wanted to find enough people I could trust to send hash to. If I planned to live in Afghanistan forever, I needed a way to make money. If I could send people a quantity of hash each month, we would split it fifty-fifty. I wanted them to sell my half for seven dollars a gram. That was the deal.

I gave the same deal to anyone who wanted to help me. I would even pay for the hash, postcards, postage, and any baksheesh that I had to pay to the customs officials. I was really making less than half, but I didn't care. I just wanted to make enough money to live on. I didn't expect to get rich. If I intended to live out my life in Afghanistan, I would need a job and this was the only paying job that was available in Kabul. I didn't want to become a millionaire; I just wanted to live comfortably.

Over the next few months, I talked to quite a few different people about my plans. Many were interested and many were not.

Most were too paranoid, regardless of whether I had connections in Afghanistan or not. Some friends who weren't interested in my deal wanted to know who I was sending it to so they could buy it from them. Here they had a chance of a lifetime—a chance to smoke the best hashish in the world delivered right to their door. They could have free hash instead of buying it for outrageous prices. Some just didn't want the responsibility of selling it. Others wanted me to use their address, but they would give the hash to another one of my friends to sell. That was all right, as long as I received my seven dollars a gram for my half. However, the ones selling the hash would have to sell it for more than seven dollars a gram if they wanted to make any money on the deal.

So I decided to only send hash to the people who would sell it themselves. Some of my friends even fronted me money—not much, but a few hundred dollars. They would be the first ones to whom I would send the hash envelopes. Once they had smoked some of the hash that I had sent from Afghanistan, they usually jumped at the opportunity for free hash, especially Afghani hash. Some of my friends weren't around for one reason or another. But I did see most of them. I even received addresses from friends of friends.

I returned to Jim's house to speak with him and his roommates about traveling to Afghanistan. Two months before, they were all for it. Now John wasn't too interested. He was doing his own deal in South America. He was going to Columbia to do a cocaine or pot deal. He wouldn't say too much about it. He tried talking Jim and Ron into his scam, but they were more interested in mine. Jim and Ron seemed even more enthused about traveling to Afghanistan than they had been two months before, as they asked more and more questions about it.

"We would really love to go to Afghanistan but we don't know for sure because we want to finish college. I'll think about it," said Jim.

Soon, after smoking some of my Afghani hash with them, Jim and Ron decided to go to Afghanistan with me. So I explained my travel arrangements. We would fly to New York City and then fly from there to either Germany or Italy. Then we would take the train and bus to Kabul.

"Jim, once we get to Afghanistan, my customs man will help me send hash to America," I promised.

Jim was so eager to implement my plan that he wanted me to move into his house until we left on our magical adventure. But I had to stay at my parents' house to meet with my other friends who wanted to try out the new partnership. I had gathered eight friends and high school acquaintances. Once I smoked some of my exquisite Afghani hash with them and explained how my system would work, they wanted me to leave for Afghanistan right away. However, I still needed to sell the rest of my hash, purchase my plane ticket to Europe, and save up over seven hundred dollars before I could even think about traveling.

The only person I couldn't talk into my proposition was my uncle Bud. At the time, he had never even tried illegal drugs. He didn't even drink alcohol. But then one day, he stopped at my parents' house to visit me. We were sitting in my messy room and I asked him if he wanted to smoke some hash. He started making up excuses for not wanting to try it. After I filled up the hash pipe with my powerful, explosive hash, I handed it to him.

"Take a big toke and hold it as long as you can," I told him.

He put the pipe up to his lips and I lit the bowl for him. He took a long drag and began coughing and choking. His eyes were watery and teary and his face was beet red, so he waited a few minutes before he took his second toke. Once again, he took a long, deep drag and tried to hold the smoke in, but it was too much for him. He began coughing his head off once again. I grabbed the pipe out of his hands and also inhaled the potent hash smoke.

"Bud, do you feel anything yet?" I asked.

"Nope, I don't feel a thing," he said, slurring his words.

I couldn't believe it. So I handed him the pipe again. I lit the bowl with a match and watched as he inhaled the exotic, harsh smoke. He took another long, deep drag and held it in for a few seconds and then began coughing as he exhaled the wicked smoke.

"Do you feel it yet?"

"No, not yet."

I couldn't believe it. Heck, after three or four good tokes of this stuff, he should have been laid out on the floor, especially with this being his first time getting high. He still didn't feel anything different. So after more than ten good tokes, he stopped without much luck.

"You must be immune," I told him, shaking my head in disbelief.

He just smiled and agreed with me. We talked a few more minutes and then decided to leave. I had to take him back to his house, about thirty miles away. It was also one of the hottest days of the year. It was nearly one hundred and four degrees and very humid. I was driving a big Pontiac Bonneville that had overheating problems, especially in this incredible heat.

As we got up to leave, Bud suddenly fell backwards onto my bed. Once he stood up, that hash finally hit him. He was smashed. He could barely walk to the car. I had to hold him up as we walked. I opened up the passenger door for him 'cause he forgot how. That's how stoned he was.

As I got behind the wheel of my car, my mother had just pulled up in the driveway and walked over to ask Bud some questions. But he didn't want to speak with her.

"Get going," mumbled Bud, or words to that effect.

He could barely walk, let alone talk, so I ignored my mother and sped away, heading toward Bud's house. However, within ten or fifteen minutes, my car began overheating. Bud was an excellent mechanic, so I wasn't too worried.

"What should I do?" I asked him, looking into his bloodshot eyes.

"Be calm. Just pull over and act natural," he replied. "Make sure you hide your dope."

"What the hell are you talking about?"

He looked around nervously, and then looked at me.

"Aren't the cops behind us?" he asked, turning his head to look out the rear window. "Damn, I could have sworn I heard police sirens. I thought the cops had pulled us over."

"No, there aren't any cops behind us. My car is overheating, and I wanted to know what I should do about it."

"Wait ten minutes and let the engine cool down."

So I pulled into a gas station parking lot and waited. I filled the radiator with water and started once again for Bud's house. As we drove along, he kept rambling on about how smashed he was.

"Does this stuff make you hallucinate?" he asked, slurring his words.

I just laughed and nodded my head. "Yes. You just smoked some of the best hashish in the world. To get something that good for the first time getting high, you're lucky you can still walk and talk." And right now, he had a hard time doing both.

After driving twenty miles, my car began overheating once again. That big 440 horsepower engine was just too big for the radiator. We had to stop at Edward Hines Park for thirty minutes to let the engine cool down. Bud was still high as a kite. By the time he had arrived at his house, his wife, Chris, was pissed off because he was so late. Then she noticed that her husband was acting strangely.

"Robert, what the hell is wrong with my husband?" asked Aunt Chris. "Why is he acting so differently and why is he struggling with his speech? What the hell is going on?"

Bud and I looked at each other and just shrugged our shoulders.

"Bud tried some of the hash I sent back from Afghanistan," I explained.

Immediately, Chris wanted to try it. She had never gotten high on hash or pot before, either. But she smoked cigarettes, as Bud did, so I started filling the pipe with the potent hashish. Chris reached across the table and grabbed the piece of hash that I had sitting in front of me.

"It looks like a piece of dog shit," she said, as she held it up close to her nose and smelled it.

"You're right. That's exactly what the Europeans call it—shit," I replied, as I filled the bowl with hash while Chris and I talked about my leopard, Kali Durga.

"Would you like to take care of my leopard?" I asked her.

"Sure," she replied.

She had two female Siamese cats, and I thought this would be the perfect place for my cat to stay while I was away. Chris really loved cats and was in a cat club.

"Chris, I will leave Kali Durga with you when I leave for Afghanistan," I said, as I handed her the hash pipe. "Hold the smoke in as long as possible."

As she put the pipe to her lips, I lit the bowl for her and she began inhaling the potent smoke. She was puffing so hard that the hash in the bowl suddenly caught on fire. I quickly blew out the small flame and a big cloud of hash smoke filled the room. When Chris exhaled, she coughed and spit all over the room. She couldn't stop coughing. She coughed and coughed and coughed. Bud and I couldn't stop laughing. Chris acted as if she was dying. Bud and I laughed even harder until our laughter became uncontrollable.

Chris quickly ran to the bathroom and started regurgitating into the toilet bowl. I couldn't believe it. She had only taken one toke—but oh such a big toke. Suddenly the room became quiet. She didn't come out of the bathroom for twenty minutes. When she finally came out, she was pale as a ghost. She looked like death warmed over. The potent hashish had overpowered her.

"What the hell is that shit?" she shouted, her eyes teary and red.

"I feel like I'm dying."

"Chris, do you want another toke," I asked.

"Hell no!"

After that, she never smoked hash again. But she did take care of my leopard.

Before I left Bud's house, we talked about using his address for sending hash. I offered him the same deal that I had offered my friends. I knew he was trustworthy, but Bud declined my offer. He didn't want to take the chance and end up in jail. I explained that he wouldn't have to sell it and that I could have someone else sell it for him or they could buy it directly. He still didn't want to risk it. So I didn't push it anymore. After an hour or so, I returned to my parents' house.

The next day I went over to visit another good friend of mine, Joe D. He lived a mile or so from my parents' house. I hadn't seen him yet since I had returned from Afghanistan, so I was anxious to show him what I had brought to America. When I arrived at his house, there were two other friends of mine visiting, Ray and Russ. They each had bought brand new Harley Davidson motorcycles. They were beautiful. One of the hogs was a Super Glide and the other was a regular Harley. They were both the same color, metallic blue.

We walked into Joe's garage to talk about the past six months and my trip to Afghanistan. We talked about my plan to live abroad and my need to find trustworthy people to whom I could send the hashish. I filled up my pipe with my potent Affy hash and we smoked, talked, and laughed. Then we started to talk about the motorcycles my two young friends had just purchased.

"You should let Robert and me take the bikes for a ride," said Joe.

"Robert, have you ever ridden a motorcycle before?" asked Ray.

"Yeah. In fact, I'm a pro," I lied, as I had never before ridden a motorcycle.

After a few minutes of silence, they broke down and relinquished their bikes—but only if they could ride along with us. So we quickly agreed. But I was only joking around about riding the motorcycle. The truth was, I hated motorcycles.

Two years before, I had ridden a small Honda moped that I had rented with a group of guys when we had vacationed in Florida for Easter break. I couldn't handle that little bike; now I was going to try to ride a big hog, the Harley Super Glide. Actually, I was quite frightened just by the thought of riding it. But I couldn't show my fear in front of my peers.

While Joe jumped on the regular Harley, I jumped onto the Super Glide. Ray sat behind me and Russ rode the back seat of his bike. I grabbed the key from Ray's hand, quickly crossed myself, said a small prayer, and then started the bike. *Well, at least I did that right,* I thought to myself.

"Ray, what is the gear selection?" I asked.

Once he explained it to me, we started out very slowly. I was doing all right going straight, but as soon as I tried to turn the corner, the bike wouldn't respond. Joe and his friend were two hundred feet ahead of us and couldn't hear Ray yelling at me, "Turn the bike! Turn the bike!"

That's the phrase that kept ringing in my ears as I rode the bike across the street, up a curb, across a newly sodded lawn, and into a newly built cement porch directly across from Joe's house. The engine was still racing as Ray reached over my shoulder and turned the key, shutting it down. We didn't hit the porch hard enough to do any damage to the motorcycle, but Ray wouldn't let me drive it again. So I returned to Joe's house and waited outside for the others to return. Within a few minutes, Joe and Russ came back.

"Robert, what the heck happened?" asked Joe.

"The bike wouldn't respond to my actions."

"Why not?" asked Joe.

"My leg got a charley horse, and I was trying to get the cramp out and the bike went out of control," I lied.

I acted as though I still had a slight cramp in my leg and rubbed it. When I was asked if I wanted to ride the bike again, I refused, giving them the excuse that I had to leave for important business. However, I didn't leave empty-handed. I had many more addresses for my livelihood.

The next few days I was traveling to and from my parents' house to Jim's house, thirty miles away. Jim and Ron were still interested in traveling to Afghanistan with me, so they began getting things together for the trip. Jim and I had talked about taking a large quantity of his American-made dress shirts and pants with him to give to my friends in the customs office. We also sent many of the items by airmail to Kabul so my customs official would receive them by the time we had arrived there. The Afghans liked American made goods, especially nice clothes. Also, this would show them that we were good friends.

Well, part of my plan wasn't going as scheduled. I wanted to purchase more hash once I had sold mine, but there wasn't any around. The state was completely dry. I had the only hash for sale, but was nearly out. I didn't even have much for my stash. I figured I would be able to buy other hash, but right now, that was not the case.

I lived at my parents' house waiting for something to break, except I started getting bored sitting at home with nothing to do. So I went out and purchased an expensive stereo system so I could play my nearly one thousand albums. I used almost all the profits I had made from the sale of my hash, so now I was nearly broke and out of hash.

I hoped and prayed something would come into town so I could make some money to buy my plane ticket to Europe. Now it was already August and still nothing had come in. Then Joe D. stopped by the house. He wanted to trade me three mini-bricks for my stereo. I really didn't want to trade because the pot wasn't that good. Plus, I didn't know too many people who wanted to buy pot. My customers only wanted to buy hash. And good hash was always easy to sell. But I wanted to return to Afghanistan, and Jim and Ron were nearly ready to leave. So I took the deal. Then Joe looked at my collection of albums and asked if he could have them. I figured I would never return from Afghanistan, so I wouldn't need them. Like a fool, I gave them to him. He took my albums and brand new stereo for three crummy mini bricks. But I had become desperate.

I telephoned Jim and explained the deal. He thought I was nuts, but he said he would help me sell the pot. He also talked me into bringing over my amplifier and electric guitar so we could jam. A black friend of his named Larry was also coming over to play the bass guitar. I had met him once or twice before. I agreed to Jim's demands and loaded my car with my pot, musical instruments, and amplifiers, then headed for his house.

After an hour's drive, I had arrived at Jim's house safely and unloaded the pot and musical equipment. We set the big amp up in the living room next to Jim's drum set. Once I had finished setting up my musical equipment, I showed Jim the three mini-bricks of pot. We opened one of the red cellophane mini bricks and broke up the pot into ounces. This was the weekend, and the town was very dry. This was the first stuff that had been around in three months, and Jim figured he could sell one or two pounds over the weekend.

Within a few hours, people—mostly college students—came to buy the pot. Things were going good, and one of Jim's roommates had talked me into dropping some acid. I had forgotten we were going to jam that night. But it was such a warm and beautiful night I took it without thinking. Within an hour, I was flying high. So Jim's roommate—whose name was also Jim, but we called him James—went out onto the roof of the house to watch the falling stars. This was the first time I had tried white microdot acid. I had tried many varieties of LSD, but never white microdot. It wasn't LSD 25, like the stuff I had tried in Spain, but it was fairly smooth and not too speedy. Within two hours, we were tripping our brains out. Suddenly, I heard another voice call me from inside the house.

"Rob, get ready to jam 'cause Larry, the bass player, is here, setting up his equipment," yelled Jim.

I walked into the house while James was still staring at the stars. Jim mentioned he had sold over twenty ounces already. That was a good start, I thought to myself. Now I had enough money to buy my plane ticket. But right now, I wasn't in any shape to think about anything. My mind was just too scattered.

As Larry walked outside to his car to retrieve some more of his musical equipment, Jim began to play his drums.

"Rob, get your guitar," yelled Jim once again.

Just as I walked across the room to pick up my guitar, the doorbell rang, so I walked over to answer it. As I opened the door, I noticed a tall, lanky, black, melting figure. For some reason, I just burst out laughing uncontrollably. I just couldn't stop laughing. It was Larry. He seemed to float right past me with the most quizzical look on his face.

"Larry, don't mind him, he's tripping on acid," explained Jim.

"Is there any more?" asked Larry.

"Sorry, but I'm out," retorted James, as he walked into the living room.

Larry began hooking up his equipment once again. I didn't want to play, but everyone in the room began chanting and clapping.

"Play!" shouted the small crowd. "We want to hear some music."

Just then, the doorbell rang again. Now it was Jim's younger brother Al.

He was on his way to a Rod Stewart concert in Chicago. Al and his entourage of four beautiful girls were traveling to their sixth consecutive Rod Steward concert, following his summer tour. Tonight, they had been invited to Stewart's hotel room to party before and after the concert. They had partied with him two nights before in New York. AI even looked like Rod Stewart. His group had just stopped by to pick up some pot to take along for the ride to Chicago.

Within a ten-minute period, they had come and gone. They would rather listen to the music of Rod Stewart and his group than our group, but that was all right with me. But just as they left, other people in the room began chanting again.

"Let's play. Let's play," the crowd shouted.

Jim and Larry wanted me to play the guitar, so I grabbed it and began to play the song "Purple Haze," except Larry didn't know it. He explained how he had just purchased the bass guitar and was still learning how to play. I quickly showed him some riffs, and we started playing again. However, halfway through the song, I had to stop playing.

"I'm too high and too stoned to play guitar anymore," I mumbled, as I set the guitar down and walked outside.

I went back onto the roof and looked at the stars, but within a few minutes, I had fallen asleep and didn't wake until morning. Jim was already awake and sitting at the kitchen table as I walked into the house. He had sold over four hundred dollars worth of pot for me. I was elated, but I still had over a pound left. If I could sell it all, I would only make seven hundred dollars. Joe really screwed me, but I guess I let him. This would still give me enough money to purchase my plane ticket to Europe and, I hoped, with enough money left over, send a few hash envelopes from Kabul, Afghanistan to my friends in America, thereby making enough money to support myself in a poor country.

Jim, Ron, and I had decided to leave for New York within a week. We would drive to New York and stay with Jim's girlfriend, Tina, until our plane departed for Europe. We decided to purchase student fare tickets to Milan, Italy. However, I still had a few chores to do before I could leave. I had to return my musical equipment to my parents' house and take my leopard to Aunt Chris's house.

When I took Kali Durga to my aunt's house, I explained to Chris what type of foods to feed my cat and what type of kitty litter to use. I also mentioned that I believed her to be a female and that she wouldn't cause any trouble with her other female cats.

Before I left their house, I tried talking Uncle Bud into using his address for sending hash envelopes, but he still resisted my offer.

Then Chris put in her two cents. "It's devil's smoke, and I don't want that stuff in my house," she said angrily.

"Well, goodbye. I'll write to you once in awhile," I told them as I walked out of their house.

I returned to my parents' house and wrote them a note, mentioning that I was off to Afghanistan again and that I would write them when I arrived at my destination. I left it on the kitchen table and finished packing my clothes. I only carried my backpack coat. Jim, on the other hand, took damn near everything he owned. It was mostly clothes for the customs man, so I didn't tell him what kind of hassle it would be carrying a big canvas navy duffel bag. It must have weighed over one hundred pounds, but he was carrying it so I didn't care. And we had sent a closet full of clothes to Kabul already.

Ron, on the other hand, was taking along playing cards and games. He didn't want to become bored, so I joked with him to take along a Frisbee. He actually liked the idea, so he brought one in his luggage. And we all brought sleeping bags. This time I had bought a good one that was made for an adult. Ron bought one that was made of goose down that zipped up to his chin and only weighed three pounds. His cost over two hundred dollars. Mine cost twenty dollars and was made out of cotton; Jim's was made out of flannel. They would all keep us warm.

Within a few days, we were on our way to New York. It only took us eight hours to drive to Tina's house. She was a young divorcee, currently divorced from a mobster. She received the house in the divorce and worried that her husband would kill her to get his house back. She was allowing us to spend the night; then using Jim's car, she would drive us to the airport the following morning. Jim told her she could keep his car until he returned from Afghanistan. This was the first I had heard that he wanted to return to America.

"Jim, I don't plan on returning to America. I'm going to live and die there," I told him.

At the time, I was very serious. I wanted to live there forever.

That night while relaxing at Tina's house, we talked about the trip to Afghanistan. Tina seemed very interested.

"I wish I could go," she said.

"Tina, do you want me to send you some hash? I'll give you the same deal I gave my other friends," I said, explaining my plan.

She agreed to try it for a while. She had some Mafia friend who loved to smoke hash. We talked into the early hours of the morning. We figured we could sleep on the plane, but the morning couldn't come fast enough as far as I was concerned.

Finally the time had come to leave for the airport. We were flying Air Italia. We were on time and boarded without incident. However, Jim was showing signs of airsickness and we weren't off the ground yet.

"What's wrong, Jim?" I asked.

"I get a slight case of claustrophobia and freak out sometimes in close quarters."

Oh boy, that's all I needed, I thought. But just then, I noticed a sign on the wall in front of the cockpit. I showed Jim the sign, which stated: THE POPE FLIES THIS PLANE. So we didn't have to worry about anything. This plane was in the hands of God. Jim seemed to relax a little bit. To keep his mind from worrying, I sat next to him, making conversation, and Ron sat behind us next to a monk. Our seats were larger than usual. It was like being in first class. Suddenly, the plane began taxiing down the runway to await its turn for departure for Milan, Italy.

CHAPTER 10

ITALY: UFO SIGHTING AND MORE

Finally, after months of planning, I was on my way to Europe, heading for Afghanistan. Within eight hours, we would be landing in the Roman Empire. We would land at Milan and take the train or bus to Venice. Jim and Ron didn't want to hitchhike. They had the money to travel in style, but I only had one hundred dollars, so I had to budget my funds.

The plane ride was smooth and the plane itself was exquisite. The steward came around and handed each passenger slippers and headphones for the movie. All these extras and they were free. On all the other planes in which I had flown, they'd charged for everything and never handed out slippers. The plane also had its own delicious smell, the smell of Italy—garlic and spaghetti sauce. The heavenly aroma was powerful and overwhelming. I loved it.

Within two hours, we were eating lunch. I had a nice cod in lemon sauce.

Jim had chicken and pasta. The meal was excellent. This was, by far, turning out to be my best plane ride. But why wouldn't it be? The plaque stated that this was the "Pope Mobile."

I reclined in my seat to relax. I put on my headphones and turned on the radio. I listened to pop music until I fell fast asleep. I dreamt about the adventures that were ahead of us and awoke just in time to watch the movie *Dillinger*. An hour after the in-flight movie, we ate dinner—what else but spaghetti and meatballs with garlic bread. We only had an hour or two to go before we landed at Milan airport.

I looked out my right side window into the pitch-black night sky. Looking across the aisle through the left side window it was still daylight. However, within five minutes, total darkness had surrounded the plane.

I was just settling back into my seat when someone sitting near the tail section started yelling incoherently. The stewardess walked over to the person and tried to calm her down. The woman pointed to the window on my side of the plane. The stewardess leaned over and looked out the window. One by one, everyone turned to look out the windows. Damn, if we were on a boat, we would have capsized from everyone rushing to one side. When I turned to look out the window, Jim's head was right next to mine.

"Jim, are you seeing what I'm seeing?" I asked.

There along the side of our plane was a UFO. A real UFO. It looked to be about one hundred feet in diameter and seemed to float right alongside of our plane. First, it was a bright round ball of white light. Then, within a flash, the bright light went out and there were three or four different colored lights that seemed to rotate around the craft. First, the light was blue, then green, then orange, and then purple, all rotating around the large, strange craft. The colored lights seemed to be above and below the windows of the huge craft.

After two or three minutes of watching the strange craft, the colored lights suddenly went out. Then a bright, white spotlight seemed to come from the bottom of the craft, shining on a smaller craft about fifty feet below the larger one that was following alongside of our plane, the "Pope Mobile."

"Where is God when you need him?" I joked.

I just couldn't believe my eyes. I had never seen an American aircraft that looked anything like what I was seeing now. The smaller craft came out of nowhere. We were looking right at the larger one when all of a sudden, the colored lights went out, the white light came on from the bottom of the large craft, and the smaller UFO showed up. It was like a magician's trick. Then, just as quickly as it had appeared, the smaller craft lit up like the North Star and within a flash of an eye, it was gone. The larger craft that was following alongside of our plane shut off the bright light from the bottom of the craft and the colored lights came on once again.

The UFO had been flying next to us for over five minutes. I wish I had brought a camera with me, but none of us had. In fact, I don't think anyone thought about taking a picture. We were too mesmerized by what we were seeing. I was getting dizzy watching these lights flash from the strange craft. But within a blink of an eye, the colored lights quit flashing, and then the bright white light covered the entire craft and disappeared up into the stars. Within a nano-second, the bright white light went up thousands of miles into the stars. I watched as it stopped high into the night sky. I looked at it until the plane turned away from it and began descending toward Milan.

I noticed everyone on the plane crossing themselves and thanking God. However, I didn't know whether they were doing that because we had landed safely or because they were thankful we hadn't been attacked by those strange crafts. We decided not to tell anyone about it, or they might think we were nuts. So we didn't speak about it again.

While we waited for our luggage to arrive, I noticed we were the only longhaired hippies at the airport. After waiting nearly thirty minutes, our luggage finally arrived. All I had to pick up was my sleeping bag. That was it. I carried my coat and sleeping bag. Jim, on the other hand, had way too much luggage. His navy duffel bag weighed at least one hundred pounds, plus he also had to carry his sleeping bag—that was another ten pounds. Ron carried a big backpack. I turned my coat into a backpack and tied my sleeping bag to it. We carried our luggage to the bus that was waiting to take us to the train station.

Within an hour, we had arrived at the Milan train station. We grabbed our luggage and made our way into the station. Jim struggled with his duffel bag. He was already cussing and bitching about the weight and size of his bag. Ron and I had to laugh. We had reminded Jim back in Michigan to buy a backpack, but he had refused, wanting to save money. So now he was paying for it. However, to help him out I elected to carry his sleeping bag for him. Actually, he was quite thankful for the help. Hell, we had just started our trip and already Jim was bitching.

As we walked through the train station, we noticed the brilliant artwork. This station was magnificent. It reminded me of an art museum. The walls were covered with beautiful sixteenth-century paintings of many famous artists. Right alongside of the paintings were large billboards with beautiful advertisements. Actually, the advertisements were in good taste and considered art themselves, especially the beautiful naked women who also adjoined the walls to advertise their wares.

We decided to buy tickets to Istanbul, Turkey. I wanted to ride the Orient Express again, if at all possible. I had talked so much about this famous train, and Jim and Ron had also heard and read about it, so we were all anxious to ride the train of all trains. We talked about buying first class tickets but decided against it to save money. I only had one hundred dollars to my name. I had less money this trip than I had the last time I had visited Afghanistan nearly a year before.

The train station was deserted, with only a handful of people milling around. We did notice, however, a few nice-looking girls standing by a snack bar and near the ticket counter. When we stepped into line to buy our tickets, a man came up to us and asked a question in Italian.

"We don't understand. Do you speak English?" I asked.

"Yes. Where are you going?" he asked me.

"We want to buy tickets to Istanbul. Has the Orient Express arrived yet?"

The man turned and stepped up to the ticket counter and asked the agent some questions in Italian that we couldn't understand. He then turned and looked over to us and started laughing. We also started laughing, not knowing what the hell we were laughing at. But we thought he was asking these questions for us. The man gave the ticket agent some money and the agent handed him a ticket. The man then turned to us and spoke Italian again.

"Chow," he said, as he walked away.

I guess the joke was on us. He just wanted to cut into the line. Finally, it was our turn.

"Is the Orient Express still running?" I asked the ticket agent. "We need to buy tickets to Istanbul."

"There are two trains to choose from," said the ticket agent. "We have a train that travels non-stop from Milano to Istanbul that leaves in about five minutes…or the Orient Express that departs in less than two hours."

We had just enough time to catch the first train if we ran, or we could wait an hour and a half for the Orient Express that stopped for a three-hour layover in Venice. Then it continued through Yugoslavia and Bulgaria. The trip took a day longer than the faster and newer train. But the tickets for the Orient Express were much cheaper than the faster train.

We grabbed our luggage and headed toward the gate for the train. But first, we stopped at the snack bar where the four girls were standing. They were just standing around, smoking and talking to each other. We sat down in a booth at the snack bar. While we were waiting, we bought something to drink. We were still quite full from the meals we had eaten on the plane, so we only ordered vanilla milk shakes and then relaxed and talked about the days ahead. We wondered if our trip would be as exciting as it had begun. But soon our conversation turned toward the girls.

Ron started to flirt with them. He was a good-looking guy. He was only five-foot-six, but he had a decent physique from lifting weights and working out at the gym. He had long, straight, dark brown hair with a Van Dyke mustache and goatee. He was a very intelligent artist. Jim looked just like Jim Morrison of the Doors, with the same weight, height, and physique and his hair and beard were identical. They both attracted women. I didn't. My hair was long and frizzy and my face was clean-shaven. I couldn't grow a beard if I tried. Don't get me wrong, I did have a girlfriend, but I just wasn't a lady-killer like Jim and Ron.

A few minutes later, the girls started looking toward our table and our eyes exchanged glances. Jim and I dared Ron to go over and introduce himself. That was all the urging he needed. He rose from our table and strode over with all the confidence of a Don Juan. He quickly introduced himself to the girls.

"Do you girls understand English?" asked Ron.

"I understand and speak very little," said the tallest girl in a deep, scruffy voice.

Ron offered them each an American cigarette. They each accepted and took one from the pack. Ron lit the cigarettes for them and asked them where they were going. One of the girls explained how they had skipped school and come to the train station to hang out. Jim and I couldn't believe how fast Ron could pick up women.

"I wish I had that type of persuasive power over women," I said, as Jim nodded in agreement.

"Ron does that all the time. For him, it's as easy as tying his shoes," replied Jim.

Just minutes later, Jim was over there talking with them, and I was sitting by myself, checking out a map of Europe and Asia that I carried in my shirt pocket. I was highlighting the route to Afghanistan from Milan. We should be in Istanbul in about three days. Once there, we would have to get Jim and Ron student identification because it's much cheaper to buy train and bus tickets using it, and you also get discounts on rooms at the youth hostels and hotels.

We still had well over six thousand miles to travel. Within twenty minutes, we would be on the train heading to Venice. I looked over at Ron and Jim, and they were all over the women. I noticed Ron had one of the girls against the wall, pressing his body into hers and feeling her butt while she gave him small, hen-pecking kisses. Jim had his arms around two of the girls. The girls motioned for me to come over, but I declined.

"I'm too busy with the map," I said. "Hey, you guys, we only have about twenty minutes before our train leaves. We should be heading toward the gate or the train will leave us behind."

"Don't worry, there are other trains," stated Ron.

"I want to ride on the Orient Express!" I shouted.

They still didn't listen and continued to talk and flirt with the girls. As I looked at the map, the waiter stopped at my table.

"Do you need anything else?" asked the waiter.

"No, but do you know if the train to Istanbul is usually on time?" I asked.

"Yes, the train is always on time."

"Where did you learn the English language?" I asked.

"I studied at the university. One day I hope to visit America. That is my dream."

"Well, good luck with your dream."

"Are those two guys your friends?" he asked, pointing to Jim and Ron.

"Yes. They are very good friends and we are headed for Asia."

"Do you know what kind of girls they are?" he asked, pointing to the girls Jim and Ron were flirting with.

"Students, I guess."

He snickered. "You don't know what kind of women they are?" he asked.

"Why? Are they prostitutes?" I whispered, not wanting my two friends to hear me.

The waiter just laughed again. "No, not prostitutes, but you know—not women," he replied.

"You mean transvestites?"

"Yes. They are not women, but men."

"Are you sure?" I asked.

"Yes," said the waiter.

"Jim, come here for a minute," I said, raising my voice.

At first, he refused and ignored me. But I was adamant. Finally, after much prodding, he came over to the table.

"What do you want?" he asked.

"Go get Ron and let's go catch our train," I replied, not wanting to tell him what I had just learned.

"Wait a minute. I want to get these girls' addresses and phone numbers," Jim retorted.

"Forget it—they're transvestites," I told him.

"You're crazy."

"Jim, if you don't believe me, go ask the waiter."

Jim turned to the waiter. Without Jim saying a word, the waiter confirmed my statements. Jim gave me a disgusted look and grabbed his bag. I grabbed mine.

"Ron, follow us," yelled Jim.

Jim and I continued toward the gate to our train as Ron ran to catch up to us. He wanted to know why we didn't say goodbye to the girls. Jim and I looked at each other and laughed.

"Let me in on the joke," Ron exclaimed.

"Those so-called girls are actually men in dresses," Jim told him.

"Are you guys kidding?" asked Ron.

"No. The waiter told us that those guys would skip school, dress up as women, and then pick up tourists," I explained.

Ron still wouldn't believe it, but you could tell that he was embarrassed so we agreed that we wouldn't talk about it anymore.

"I wasn't the one kissing and talking to those transvestites," I told him.

"Don't remind me," replied Ron.

"All right, I won't bring it up again," I said.

So far, all I could tell anybody was that we were Americans and we rode the "Pope Mobile." But soon we wouldn't tell anyone where we came from unless they asked. Then we would tell them that we were Canadian. Once we had left Italy, we wouldn't tell anyone we were Americans because Americans weren't popular in this part of the world.

After a short walk, we had finally reached our train. Among all the new and beautiful trains, one stood alone. It looked like it should have been scrapped and melted down years ago. This was the train we were riding to Istanbul. It was still an exotic piece of history. But Jim and Ron began hassling me about its poor condition.

"It will get us to Istanbul without any problems," I told them.

We boarded the Orient Express on time and picked out a clean, empty compartment. Then the conductor entered to check our tickets.

"Mr. Conductor, how long is the ride to Venice?" I asked.

"Without problems, four to five hours. If problems arise, then it's anybody's guess."

"Is this train in good condition?" I asked.

But he didn't answer my question. He just smiled, turned, and laughed as he walked out of our compartment. We just looked at each other and assured ourselves that everything would work out fine.

"At least it will be an adventure. Look what we have seen so far, and the trip is just beginning," I said.

It was now about eight o'clock in the evening. We would be arriving in Venice around one or two in the morning. Then we would have a four- or five-hour layover before we could continue our trip to Istanbul. Right now, all we wanted to do was relax and sleep. The seats were large enough that we could stretch out completely. Jim and Ron shared one seat, and I had the other all to myself. I didn't wake up again until the conductor stopped by to tell us that we had arrived in Venice and there would be a good four-or five-hour layover.

The train had to be cleaned and fueled, so we had plenty of time to kill. It was almost two in the morning and we were hungry. We left the train and headed toward San Marco Square. I actually remembered the way. The canals hadn't changed and the putrid, nauseous smell still hung in the air. Jim and Ron were shocked and couldn't believe how dirty the city of Venice was. Walking past a few of the canals, we had to hold our noses because the smell was so raunchy. Although I was used to the smell, Jim and Ron weren't. They had pictured Venice to be a clean and beautiful city. They were wrong.

Within ten minutes, we had reached San Marco Square. This early in the morning, there were very few people milling around. Not many stores were open either. We had hoped to find a cheap restaurant, but there was no such thing as cheap anywhere in Venice. We ended up buying some hot croissants and coffee. We buttered the croissants and dipped them into our coffee. That hit the spot.

After we ate our snack, just to kill some time, we rode the water taxi across the bay to the little island a quarter of a mile away. I wanted to show Jim and Ron the church and other tourist attractions on this tiny island. Actually, Jim and Ron weren't too impressed with the island until they saw the old chapel with its exquisite handmade woodcarvings and workmanship. After that, we window-shopped and walked around before we boarded the water taxi for the return trip to San Marco Square.

We only had an hour before our train departed for Istanbul, so we decided it was time to return to the train station. By the time we returned to the mainland, it was nearly six in the morning and the place was a madhouse. Tourists were everywhere. We couldn't get back to the station fast enough. This time we didn't stop to talk to any women, but Jim was still complaining about carrying his heavy baggage.

We walked to the station and boarded the train for Istanbul. We were leaving Venice and heading for Yugoslavia. Again we had a compartment to ourselves. It was a bright, sun-shiny day, and the weather was warm and beautiful. The scenery was very green and awesome. The green rolling hills with their beautifully built castles filled the landscape. We sat and relaxed for a few hours, staring out the compartment window at the surrounding beauty.

But then we started getting bored, so we decided to take a walk within the train. We stepped out into a small corridor with exit doors on each side to smoke a cigarette while we talked about our trip and watched as the scenery rolled by.

Standing next to us was an old monk dressed in sandals and an old, worn-out, dirty habit. He had the hood pulled over his head, showing only his gray beard and wrinkled, weathered face. He played with his rosary in one hand while he carried his Bible in the other.

The corridor was only a four-foot-by-four-foot area, so we were a little cramped in this small room. Within a short while, it had filled with smoke and laughter. But the laughter quickly dissipated because of the dirty stares and evil glare we were getting from the Lord's messenger. I guess we weren't appreciated in his presence.

Then the monk began screaming and yelling at us in Italian. We didn't understand what he was screaming about, and we didn't know what the heck was wrong. That is, until the conductor came into the corridor carrying a fire extinguisher. He thought there had been a fire because of all the smoke and yelling. However, when he saw that we weren't doing anything wrong, he calmed the monk and explained that we were only dumb American hippies on vacation.

The monk had told the conductor that he thought we were bandits and were going to rob or kill him and then throw his body off the train. He was very frightened. Well, the conductor settled everyone down and opened a window to get rid of the smoke and then left.

A few minutes later, we returned to our compartment and had just sat down when an Italian man came by and invited us to his compartment to share wine and bread with two of his friends—all Italian, blue-collar workers. We agreed and followed him to his compartment, which was right next to ours. Once everyone had been introduced, we all sat down and began a conversation. They didn't speak much English and we couldn't speak Italian, but we managed. As we talked and laughed with our new friends, we were each given a piece of tasty, freshly baked, homemade Italian bread and glasses filled with a strong red wine. Even though I didn't drink alcohol, I didn't want to seem rude and turn down their hospitality, so I drank the small glass of wine. But as soon as I had finished it, I felt super buzzed and was getting drunk quite fast. In fact, my head was spinning. I couldn't believe how strong it was, and it didn't taste bad, either. We really enjoyed their company. They told us that they were going back to their two-thousand-year-old village to see their families.

As the train rocked back and forth, we passed castle after castle. One of the Italians told us in broken English that Roman senators owned the castles during Caesar's reign. We also passed an abandoned, desolate city in ruins that I thought had been ransacked and destroyed during Jesus' time by the Roman soldiers. I learned that I wasn't too far off. Our new friends said the city had been destroyed by Alexander the Great and was now a tourist attraction. We were traveling right through history.

As I looked out the window, I swore I saw the ghosts of many Roman soldiers fighting the Greeks in a bloody battle. It seemed so real I had to turn my head away. When I looked again, they had disappeared. Watching this beautiful scenery made the long hours go by rather quickly. And before we knew it, our friends had arrived at their destination and their wives and children were waiting for them at the station. We waved goodbye and walked back to our compartment.

We would be in Yugoslavia within five or six more hours. I was happy with the progress we had made so far and couldn't wait to reach our final destination. But right at that moment, my head was still spinning so I lay down to rest. The wine had made all of us sleepy.

Ron was bored and asked me to play cards. I reluctantly agreed and we decided to play a few hands of Gin Rummy. Jim wanted to sleep, so he lay down while we continued playing cards. We had just played a few hands and were discussing what beautiful visions we had seen so far when suddenly we were interrupted by Jim's loud snoring—so loud that it shook the whole room. We yelled at him, threw dirty socks and shoes at him, but nothing could awaken him.

Then an idea hit us—we were going to get even and pull an old high school prank on him.

We filled a cup with warm water and placed Jim's hand in it. Within thirty seconds, a stain appeared on the front of his trousers. Ron and I had to control our laughter so we wouldn't awaken him. And just for a split second, Jim seemed to open his eyes. I thought he was going to get up and kill us. Instead, he just moved his head to one side and went right back to sleep.

Ron and I continued playing cards, but after a while, all of us had fallen asleep. I lay back on the seat, shut my eyes, and dreamed about the days to come.

We awoke the next day to a big "bang." They were adding cars to the train. They had added a diner car and another coal car. So we immediately headed for the diner. We needed a good, healthy breakfast.

In another hour, we would be leaving Yugoslavia and entering Bulgaria. Everything had been working out well so far, except for a few minor mishaps. We were better than halfway to Istanbul.

As we entered the diner, Jim began asking Ron and me questions about his wet pants. He couldn't remember how he had gotten them wet. Ron and I just burst out laughing.

"Jim, you must have pissed your pants from drinking too much red wine the day before," I opined. But he didn't believe us and ignored our reasoning.

Our thoughts quickly turned to food. We sat at a nearby table and then tried to order breakfast. There were people working in the diner, but they ignored us. There was a bartender standing behind the bar, a janitor who was busy sweeping up the dirt off the floor, and a young boy filling empty glasses with a liquid that I thought was water. But when he filled our glasses, I noticed little brown specks and little sperm-like animals swimming around in the dirty liquid. We passed on the so-called water and called for the waiter. The guy sweeping put down his broom and came over to our table.

"What you want?" asked the waiter in his best, broken English.

"A menu, please," Jim retorted.

We weren't sure if the waiter understood us or not, and we definitely couldn't understand him very well. But then he walked behind the bar and pulled out a few dirty menus. After he had cleaned each one with a rag, he handed them to us. They looked as though they hadn't been used in the last five years and were written in a foreign text. So we couldn't read or understand them.

So I asked the waiter in English, "Do you have eggs?" But he just stood in silence and acted as if he hadn't understood my question. So I repeated it. "Do you have eggs?"

He continued to look at me with a blank stare, then said something in his native language to the bartender. The bartender just shrugged his shoulders. So I stood up, put my hands under my armpits, flapped my arms, and cackled like a chicken, pecking my head back and forth. Everyone in the room broke out in laughter. We were the only customers in the diner car, so I wasn't embarrassed, just hungry. I think the waiter figured out what I was describing and shook his head no.

"Coffee?" I asked the waiter.

"Ah," said the waiter.

"Cafe ole?" I asked. The waiter gave me a big smile.

"Make that three coffees," said Jim, holding up three fingers.

Evidently, the waiter had understood and yelled the order to the bartender. But then, I remembered that the coffee was made with the same water that the young boy had poured for us. I just hoped and prayed that they boiled it for twelve minutes or longer. We also asked for some croissants, and the waiter brought over a bowl of week-old stale bread. Before we could eat it, we had to rip off the moldy parts. They also gave us what we believed to be butter, but it was actually animal fat—and it tasted terrible. We were so hungry that we ate it anyway and dunked our moldy, stale bread into the hot, oily coffee. We would have eaten just about anything.

Now I knew why no one else was eating in the diner car—there was nothing decent to eat. They did have a decent bar, though, so we ended up buying a bottle of Bulgarian wine to take back to our compartment to drink. The bread and coffee seemed to fill our empty bellies for the time being, but we didn't want to repeat the episode again. At least with the wine, we could drink ourselves into a drunken stupor and not think about eating. We only had another day of traveling before we reached Istanbul, so we could hang on until then. Now Jim and Ron understood why all the people were drunks in this country—they had no food to eat.

A few minutes later, we were back in our compartment. We sat back and relaxed while we looked out the window to watch the dreary scenery of this poor communist country. It was completely different from what we had seen in Italy.

At nine o'clock that evening, the train stopped and the Bulgarian customs officials hopped aboard. They came directly to our compartment and asked to see our passports. Within a few minutes, we had handed them over and tried to stay calm. Customs officials always made me nervous. But once they had looked them over and checked them out, they quickly returned them to us without incident. That was a big relief to me. In fact, I even had one of the customs officers stamp my passport so I would have something to remind myself that I had really traveled in Bulgaria. He happily obliged and stamped one of the pages with the Bulgarian insignia.

"You speak very good English," I told the customs officer. "How did you learn to speak our language so well?"

"All Bulgarian customs officials speak four or more different languages," he explained.

"Some speak up to eight." Then he bowed his head, clicked his heels together, and left the room. He and his partner departed the train.

The customs officials didn't go to any other compartment. They only came on the train to check us. So we must have been the only Americans on the train. Heck, I thought with such a famous train that it would be full of adventurous tourists. This train had a history all its own and only had transported the wealthy and famous. But that wasn't the case anymore. The travelers who had money to burn always rode the newer and faster train.

Night had come upon us. All of us seemed to be depressed. All day long we saw slum after slum of run-down shacks littered among rusted-out metal objects in this destitute country. It reminded me of the slums and poor sections of Detroit after a riot. This country was also very poor.

We were full of gloom, so we decided to open the bottle of Bulgarian wine, get drunk, and forget about our hungry stomachs. After eating such a disgusting breakfast, we didn't return to the diner for dinner. They didn't have any good food available.

We would arrive in Istanbul within another eighteen hours. Once we reached that city, we would be halfway to Kabul. We passed the bottle of wine and played our favorite card game, Gin Rummy. Jim and Ron refused to play for money. I was winning nearly every game, so they started making excuses for not wanting to bet. So instead of money we played for an extra swig of wine for each winning hand. I was drinking twice as much as they were, and not being a drinking man, I was getting very drunk, very fast. After my tenth winning hand, I passed out.

Guess what they did to me while I was out cold? You guessed it.

They placed my hand in a bowl of warm water and I pissed my pants. The next morning, I awoke in a puddle of urine. I had only one change of clothes, and I changed into them. And when that chore was finished, I had to sit down and gather my strength. I was still feeling the effects of my drinking. In fact, all of us were. So we decided not to eat breakfast. We would wait until we had arrived in Istanbul. We would reach the city about four in the afternoon.

We were very excited, even though we all had hangovers. I felt as though someone had walked in my mouth and on my head all night. My head was pounding like two sledgehammers hitting me at the same time, sending waves of nausea into my stomach. Now I knew why I didn't want to eat. I couldn't even if I had wanted to. Jim and Ron didn't feel much better.

The day was again beautiful, bright and sunny. About two in the afternoon, the train stopped in a small town to add and subtract some railroad cars. But the streets were nearly empty. The only people around were a small group of Bulgarian soldiers. We also noticed a few small stores nearby. We were getting hungry, so Ron decided to stretch his legs and check out one of the stores to see if they had anything to eat or drink. Jim and I stayed on the train trying to ease our aching bodies. Ten minutes later, Jim and I jumped up and looked out the window to see Ron screaming.

"Help! Help me! Help me!" he yelled.

We thought he was dying. We ran toward the front of the train— toward the sound of his screams. We disembarked and saw that a small group of soldiers had surrounded Ron with their automatic weapons. You'd think he had robbed a bank or killed someone. We didn't have any idea of what the hell was happening. Ron turned toward us as we called out his name. As we approached, half of the soldiers pointed their machine guns at us. I damn near pissed my pants again.

"Ron, what the hell happened?" I asked.

"I don't know what the hell happened. All I did was go into one of the stores to see if they had any food for sale, but it was empty, so I left to check out the next store. That's when the store owner came running after me, yelling and screaming, and that's when the soldiers surrounded me and drew their weapons," he replied, shaking.

"Do you speak English?" I asked the soldiers.

Before they could answer, the female storeowner spoke up.

"I speak very little English, but I don't think the soldiers do," she said.

She began speaking to the soldiers in Bulgarian. They just shook their heads no. So I spoke with the woman storeowner.

"What did my friend do?" I asked.

She pointed to Ron's face.

"What about his face?" I asked.

She stepped between the soldiers, grabbed the toothpick out of Ron's mouth, and held it up for all to see.

"He took this from my shop and ran away without paying for it," she said.

Damn, to get shot over a toothpick. I had heard it all now. Oh, I forgot. They had to cut down a five hundred-foot-tall, three hundred-year-old tree to make that toothpick. I guess Bulgarians take great pride in their toothpicks.

"In the country we come from, toothpicks are free," I told her.

"You must be Americans where the streets are lined with gold. You must be rich," replied the storeowner.

"Jim, give her a dollar and let's get back on the train," I snapped. Knowing our luck, the train would leave without us while we haggled over a toothpick.

"A dollar is too much money for a toothpick," argued Jim.

"Jim, do you want Ron to get shot, and maybe us, too, over one measly toothpick?" I asked.

So Jim reluctantly handed the woman a nice, crisp one-dollar bill.

"Is that enough?" asked Jim.

She just smiled, grabbed the dollar bill, and walked back to her non-grocery store. The soldiers released Ron from his brief arrest with only a dollar fine.

"Do you guys want to mention this again?" I joked.

"Let's not bring it up in any conversation," exclaimed Ron.

We all agreed, as we boarded the train. We suddenly realized we had just gotten screwed for a dollar. The woman took Ron's toothpick and never gave it back to him after we had paid her for it. Now she'd probably resell it. We had a little chuckle over that.

Another two hours and we'd be in Istanbul. We were really getting excited. We played a few more games of cards, but Ron was still too upset from that little incident. He still couldn't get over the fact that he'd had to pay for a toothpick. He thought she'd conned three dumb Americans, but I figured we had gotten lucky to get away for a dollar, even if she did sucker us. A dollar to her was like a thousand to us and would last them a week. Of course, all they had to buy with it was alcohol and cigarettes.

By the time I lay down, we were pulling into Istanbul train station. It was almost five o'clock in the afternoon. We grabbed our baggage and walked into the dirty streets of the city. The first thing we needed to do was to find a decent restaurant. Then we needed to buy student identification and Iranian visas. The stores were full of groceries and meats, similar to America. But the country to the west of them had nothing. We stopped at a small open cafe and ordered lamb kabob sandwiches and ice cold Pepsi.

CHAPTER 11

TURKEY: TRAIN RIDE FROM HELL

Man those lamb kabob sandwiches and Pepsi's were great. We each had three kabob sandwiches and two cold bottles of Pepsi. They sure hit the spot. Our stomachs were no longer crying out for food. This was the best we had eaten since our flight to Italy. In fact, the meal on Air Italia was better than some famous expensive restaurant food. But when the pope is the critic, it better be good.

Well, now we had to find a decent hotel. Walking in the city we noticed we were no longer the only tourists or longhaired hippies. It seemed everywhere we looked there were hippies around. Of course, this was the hippie trail to Afghanistan. There were longhairs from just about every country of the world. We even talked to one guy who was from Russia. He was a rich ambassador's son, so we stopped and asked a few of them if they knew of a good but cheap hotel that was close to the ferry.

The Turks still hadn't built a bridge across the bay, so we would have to ride the ferry to the eastern side of Istanbul to continue our journey. We followed a Dutch couple who was returning to their hotel, which was only a dollar a night. That was very reasonable and in our price range. When we arrived at the hotel, there were many longhaired hippies milling about, and I mentioned it.

"Ron, maybe we can buy some hash from one of them," I suggested. "But be careful. There are more narcs in this city than dopers. They will sell you the hash, and then call the police to bust you. The police give him his hash back, a reward, and a pat on the back. We have to be very careful or we could end up in a Turkish jail." So we decided against my idea.

We rented a room with three clean beds for two dollars. We tried to barter with the clerk and get the room for a dollar, but he refused.

"We change sheets daily," growled the clerk.

Two dollars for the room was the best price he could give us. We had no other choice but to pay him the money. We followed the clerk to the room and placed our baggage on the beds. Ron gave the clerk a quarter for a tip, but the guy threw it back to him. We didn't know his reason for returning the money. We wondered if he had thrown it back because it wasn't enough or if we had insulted him. Whatever the reason, the clerk left the room. We rested on our beds and talked about the things that needed to be done.

Jim and I were tired and wanted to stay in the room to relax, but Ron was much more energetic. He wanted to check out the city.

"Go for it, Ron," I said, as he left the room.

Jim and I stayed in the room while we talked and played cards. Within an hour or so, Ron returned to the room with the clerk—the same guy who had shown us the room. Ron explained that the clerk could get us some hash. However, he didn't want just money. He literally wanted the clothes off our backs. He wanted my Afghani vest, my Afghani shirt, Ron's pants, and Jim's belt, plus two dollars. He wanted all that for just two or three grams of hash, and it wasn't that special either, but we were hungry for it.

We hadn't gotten high on any hash since we had left New York. Even then, we'd only had a few tokes each. So we decided to give up our clothes. I figured we were headed to Afghanistan anyway and could buy more. So I peeled out of my vest and shirt. That left me with just a tee shirt. Ron gave the clerk the pants he had been wearing. The two were the same size, so they fit him perfectly.

The vest and shirt I had given him would have cost at least thirty dollars in America. However, in Kabul they cost me a total of six dollars. Ron's denim Levi's cost fifteen dollars in America and in Turkey, they were worth much, much more. Jim's belt probably cost five or ten dollars, so in all, we gave that clerk approximately seventy-five dollars worth of clothes plus the two American dollar bills for twenty dollars of hash. We would have paid ten dollars if we had bought it in America. The clerk probably paid less than a quarter. So we had gotten ripped off once again. We were definitely suckers, but we didn't really care. We just wanted to get high again.

The clerk gave us the hash and left the room with his new wardrobe. I was nervously waiting for the cops to bust down the door and haul us off to jail. Luckily, that never happened. Ron started looking for something out of which he could make a hash pipe. He found a small, round, elbow-shaped pipe and used a small piece of aluminum foil from a gum wrapper for the screen. He used a needle to poke numerous holes into it and then began loading the bowl with our newly purchased Turkish hash.

Ron took the first toke and then passed the pipe to me. I took a good, healthy toke and passed it to Jim. As soon as I inhaled that smoke, my head felt like it had just exploded. Suddenly, I was dizzy and my head was spinning. Boy that hash didn't look or smell that good, but it sure had a nice kick to it. Maybe it hit me so hard because I hadn't smoked any hash in such a long time. I didn't know the reason. I just knew that it was *good.* I had become stoned from just one toke. We each had a couple more tokes before we finally put the pipe down and decided to crash. We had many things to do on the following morning and should be able to leave Istanbul within two days, if not sooner. I thought about this as I laid my head on the soft and clean pillow and shut my eyes to dream about the adventures that lay ahead.

Soon, we would be leaving for Iran, and then Afghanistan. This was the last thing I remembered before waking up the next morning. I had slept so well that I hadn't even heard Jim snore. Once we were all dressed and ready for the day's chores, we smoked the rest of the hash before we left the room. It gave us a good appetite for breakfast.

We stopped at the front desk hoping to see the clerk who had sold us the hash, but it was his day off. Yeah, he was probably out selling the clothes we had traded him. He would be able to buy a business with the money he'd made.

We left the hotel and walked down the street to a little out-of-the-way restaurant. We ordered scrambled eggs, toast, and orange juice. This only cost each of us ten-Turkish Lira, which was worth about fifteen cents. The bank rate changed daily, but we were getting around seventy Liras to the dollar. It was just too good to be true. Things would get even cheaper the farther east we traveled.

It was about eleven in the morning, and we were looking to buy student identification. We stopped and asked a small group of long-haired hippie tourists if they knew where to buy some. After asking the fourth person, we learned of a place. The hippie directed us to a side street and a small cafe that also had a few tables outside. Sitting at one of the outside tables was a shrewd-looking character with squinty eyes and a long, jagged scar that went from the right side of his forehead all the way down to his chin. He looked like he belonged in a gangster movie. We slowly walked up to his table and spoke with him.

"Do you know where we can buy some student I.D.?" I asked the scary looking man.

"Yes. I can help you for a price," he mentioned in a French accent.

Oh, no. Here we go again. I hoped he didn't want our clothes. I didn't have any more to sell.

"How much?" asked Ron.

"What college do you want to use for the identification?" he asked, as he showed us the names of three or four European universities and one in Lebanon.

They all looked genuine. I picked Madrid University. Ron picked Frankfurt University, and Jim used Notre Dame University. First, we had to have pictures taken—the guy had his own Polaroid camera.

"Anyone could start their own business if they owned one of these babies," said the scar-faced man, stroking his camera. Yeah, right—just not in America.

Once he had snapped our pictures, he cut them to fit the page, glued them in place, and then stamped them with a special university stamp. When they were completed, the student I.D.s looked genuine.

There were many advantages to having them. Turkey and many of the European countries gave students a special discount for travel, rooms, food, and clothing. It only cost us each three American dollars and could save us over twenty dollars just in the purchase of train tickets to Erzurum. We thanked the guy for making them and were about to leave, but he continued with his sales pitch.

"I can get you anything you need," he said. "Even a brand new Mercedes Benz."

"Can you get us some hashish?" I asked.

He looked at me with utter disdain and snapped, "Hashish is bad, and the police will put you in jail for a long time. Get away and go now."

"I'm sorry I asked."

We quickly walked away happy but dismayed. *We better play it cool about the hash,* I thought to myself.

"Jim, maybe we'll ask a few hippies if they know where we can score some good hash," I suggested.

We started walking back toward our hotel. We stopped off to eat a lunch of kabob sandwiches washed down with Pepsi. That was the best food for the least amount of money. Three people could eat well and fill their bellies for less than a dollar. However, my money was being depleted very fast. I only had sixty dollars to my name.

When we finally reached the hotel, we asked a clerk to direct us to the Iranian Embassy so we could get our transit visas.

"The Iranian Embassy is not in Istanbul," he told us. "It is in Ankara. Nearly all of the embassies are there, including the Afghan embassy."

We would have to travel to Ankara for our visas. I didn't mind, though. We had to travel that way, anyway. It was on the way to Erzurum. But I didn't believe the hotel clerk, so I asked a few hippies who were also staying at our hotel about the whereabouts of the Afghan Embassy. Sure enough, the Afghan and Iranian embassies were indeed in Ankara. With that question answered, we went to our room to relax, but instead decided to take a nap for a few hours until dinner.

We visited the same restaurant as we had many times before and ordered our regular kabob sandwiches and Pepsi, plus a side order of vegetables. And it still only cost us less than a dollar. Jim and Ron couldn't believe how cheap it was to live here. They had never been out of America before and thought all of this was just a dream. I had traveled this road before, so I expected these unbelievable prices. But this was a whole new experience to Jim and Ron.

The city came alive at night. The restaurant patrons were going wild as belly dancers shook their boobs and bellies in front of the faces of the male customers. They kicked us out when Jim snuggled his nose into the bosom of one of the beautiful dancers. She didn't seem to mind, but the manager did. He came over to our table and expressed his anger.

"You must leave," he snapped. "Fondling isn't allowed."

We were escorted out of the restaurant, so we headed back to our hotel room. We had to get up early anyway. In the morning, we had to ride the ferry across the bay to the train station so we could continue our adventurous journey.

Once we had returned to our hotel room, we talked over what needed to be done for the following day. We had to leave the hotel by 6:00 A.M. to catch the ferry. We were all packed and ready to go. We were too excited to go to sleep, too tired to play cards, and too bored to stay in the room, so we decided to take the Frisbee outside and throw it around. We ran out of the hotel to the deserted street like a bunch of little kids, stood in a triangle thirty feet away from each other, and then tossed the Frisbee back and forth. Jim threw it to Ron, Ron threw it to me, and I threw it to Jim. We kept this up for five or ten minutes until we noticed more and more people watching us, mostly all Turks.

One of the guys in the crowd wanted to know what country we had come from. I blurted out "Canada" before Jim or Ron could say anything. They understood immediately why. I could only wonder what would have happened had I told them we were Americans. As much as the Turks hate Americans, with their mob mentality, they might have hung us. Hell, that would have given them a good excuse to take our Frisbee. But we were safe. Minutes later, a young man from the crowd asked if he could throw it. Then another yelled the same question. One by one, with all of them shouting and wanting to throw it, we finally gave in.

"Everyone who wants to throw the Frisbee, stand in a single line!" I yelled to the crowd, and they quickly formed one long line.

They had the whole street blocked off. Cars could no longer get through. The mob stopped them and turned them away so they wouldn't lose their place in line and their chance to throw that damn Frisbee. Suddenly fights broke out amongst the crowd when someone tried to cut into the line. But things settled down minutes later when the troublemaker was thrown to the back of the line.

It was totally dark, and there were at least a hundred or more people waiting to throw the Frisbee. After each person had taken their turn, they quickly ran to the end of the line, wanting another. We would be here till morning if this kept up, I thought to myself. We had already spent over an hour with these people, letting them play while we kept the tempers and tantrums to a minimum. After everyone had received one turn throwing the Frisbee we wanted to quit, but they wouldn't let us. They refused to let us leave and return to our hotel. So we allowed them to continue throwing the Frisbee, until one guy threw it on the roof of a nearby four-story building and we had no way to retrieve it. We were trying to think of a way when all hell broke loose. Suddenly a fight broke out between five or six people in the crowd. Actually, it was five people beating up on the one who had lost the Frisbee, then more and more joined in on the melee. All of them were attacking the same guy. Nobody came to his rescue, not even us.

We finally got the chance to return to our hotel room. After that little social event, we were very tired. Once we entered our room, we glanced out the window and noticed the fight in the street was still going on. Just then, the Turkish police came to the rescue of the battered Frisbee tosser and broke up the angry mob. Now we could finally get some sleep.

We didn't have any hash to smoke to help us sleep but we were worn out, so I thought it wouldn't be that hard to fall asleep. I was right. Once my head hit the pillow I fell fast asleep in minutes. I had heard that you could buy many different types of sleeping pills, but not narcotics, at nearly any pharmacy in Turkey. Although I never tried to buy any, it would have helped on sleepless nights.

We were up by five that morning. We had to get to the ferry and train station before the train left for Ankara. We had to stop there to get our Iranian and Afghan visas. The closer we got to the ferry, the more crowded the streets became. When we reached it, there were thousands of people everywhere. It was overwhelming trying to walk through this big mob of unruly people. But somehow we managed and paid out three Liras for our passage across the bay to the eastern side of the city.

The boat ride only took a total of five minutes to reach the isthmus. The steps leading to the train station reminded me of the scene in the movie *Rocky,* where he runs up the steps of the Philadelphia courthouse. The two buildings looked identical. The British built it in the late eighteen hundreds.

We climbed over four hundred stairs. Jim was struggling so much with his duffel bag that he wanted to leave it behind. So Ron and I took turns helping him lug it up the stairs. It was a heck of a climb, but we made it and purchased our tickets to Ankara. However, we had arrived too late for the newer and faster train and would have to take the slower one. It stopped at a few more cities and villages than the other train, but it was much cheaper. Although I wanted to reach Afghanistan as soon as possible, I had no other choice, and my money was dwindling fast.

When we arrived at the gate, the train was waiting for us. We were able to get a compartment all to ourselves. We were very happy about that. The train wasn't a passenger train, as the others had been, but a freight train with only one passenger car and a diner car among the hundred or so cars hooked together. It was as if they had put these cars on just for us. The train was well over a mile long. Our car was at the end, so I couldn't see the engine.

When the conductor came to get the tickets, I asked him about the train.

"Are we the only passengers on this train?"

"Yes," he replied.

I must have said something funny because he started laughing as he walked out of our compartment. So I was right after all. We were the only passengers on the train. I kidded Jim and Ron that we had the train to ourselves. We thought we were the lucky ones. Boy was I wrong. Within an hour, I knew we had made a big mistake. That was when we stopped at the first town.

We stopped for nearly ten minutes before the train started up again. It accelerated to about twenty miles an hour and then started slowing down again until it completely stopped. We watched as they unhooked and took away one freight car, and then connected the cars together again. This same ritual happened every time we stopped at a town. The whistle blew, the engine smoked and sputtered, and then continued toward the next town.

As we rounded a long, winding curve, I could finally see the engine. There were at least two-hundred freight cars. Boy, did we take the wrong train. We stopped at every city or town that the train passed through. We didn't pass one up, and after a few hours of this, we had become very irritated and restless. At this rate, it would take us a week to reach Ankara, let alone Afghanistan.

The train might have moved along at a snail's pace, but the scenery was immaculate. The first day we followed the sea. The blue sky and blue sea was a picture you couldn't forget. I wanted the train to stop long enough so I could put my feet into the clear blue seawater.

We passed a small marina and saw three longhaired hippies sitting in an old wooden rowboat docked at the pier just kicking back and sunning themselves. I wished we could have stopped there for just a few hours or even days. But we were in too much of a hurry to get to Kabul. Not only that, but my money wasn't lasting as long as I had anticipated. I only had about fifty dollars left, and we still had a long journey ahead of us. I really had to conserve and budget my money better than I had been.

Riding on this slow train was very boring, so we played cards most of the time. We were going bananas after the first day. We stopped at every damn town. We had definitely taken the wrong train. The ticket agent never mentioned anything about the train stopping at every town or that we would be the only passengers. All we could do was eat, sleep, and play cards.

The second day passed without any excitement. The only people we could talk to were the workers in the diner car. During some stops, the road vendors would come aboard to hawk their wares.

They tried selling us perfume, cigarettes, and anything else that they carried with them. We had to save our money so we never bought anything. Finally, on the third day of traveling on this horrendous train, we arrived in Ankara. It felt like we had been traveling on it for a month. I was getting bedsores from sitting so long.

By the time we had arrived at a decent hotel, it was evening. We got a room similar to the one we had rented in Istanbul with three beds in one room. Before we went to sleep, we talked about what we were going to do in the days to come. Jim and I wanted to reach Kabul as soon as possible. After that hellish long train ride, we decided to fly to Kabul. That is, if it wasn't too expensive. However, Ron refused to fly. He wanted to travel by train and bus and didn't want to spend the extra money for flying. We went to sleep disagreeing and undecided on what we were going to do the following day. We still needed to get our transit visas.

We awoke bright and early the next morning. We ate a fulfilling breakfast of eggs, toast, coffee, and orange juice for only twelve cents each. It only cost five Turkish Liras and that day's bank rate was eighty-Liras to one American dollar. During breakfast, we talked about our plans. Jim and I were still adamant about flying to Kabul. Ron hadn't changed his mind either. He decided that he was going to travel on his own and that he would meet us in Kabul.

All three of us returned to the hotel. We asked Ron if he wanted to go to the Afghan Embassy with us, but he declined. He had to get his Iranian visa first. He could get his Afghan visa when he arrived in Meshad. Jim and I no longer needed to get an Iranian transit visa. We were flying over that country. We also wanted a three-to six-month visa for Afghanistan if we could get it. Usually, they only gave out a twenty-one day travel visa, and then you had to get an extension before the visa ran out.

Before Ron left us, we hugged him and said we would meet him at the Najib Hotel in Kabul in about a week. That's how long it should take him to travel overland. Jim and I should arrive in Kabul within two days. When Ron departed, Jim and I also left the hotel and headed for the Afghan Embassy. When we arrived there, we spoke directly to the ambassador concerning the length of our visas.

"Do you have enough money to live and travel on?" asked the ambassador.

"Of course we do. We have thousands of dollars to spend in your country," I lied.

"Your visas will be ready by tomorrow morning," he answered.

A few minutes after we had left the embassy we noticed two teens playing basketball on a nice new asphalt court. It reminded me of the courts we had in the schoolyards of America. This court was also the parking lot of an apartment building. As we walked by, we asked if they wanted to play a game or two of hoops. To our surprise, they answered in English.

"Yes," said one of the teens.

"Where did you learn to speak English so well?" I asked, as we entered the courtyard.

"America," said the teens in unison.

They explained that their fathers were pilots for the U.S. Army stationed in Ankara. They had been in Turkey for three years. They both went to an American school on the military base. They were each sixteen years of age and both much taller than we were. We were also more than three thousand feet above sea level, so the air was much thinner here than we were used to. But we still challenged these young teens to a game.

We spent the better half of the day playing basketball. The first team to reach ten baskets was the winner. Jim and I won the first two games out of five. However, they won the next three games. We couldn't catch our breath and couldn't adjust to the high elevation. The air was just too thin and we tired too fast. Other than that, they beat us fair and square. We exchanged handshakes and high praises. We told them that they had played a great game and the next time we visited Ankara we would play them again. Then we headed toward our hotel.

After leaving the basketball court, we stopped by a Pan Am airline office to find out when the next available flight was departing for Kabul and to purchase the plane tickets. The earliest flight was departing the following night with a layover in Tehran, where we would change planes for the flight to Kabul. So we would be arriving at our final destination within three days at a cost of one-hundred dollars each.

Although I didn't have enough funds to cover the cost of the plane ticket, Jim offered to loan me the money. I could pay him back when I received money from my friends in America. The plane departed from Ankara airport at 5:00 P.M. the following evening. We would arrive at Tehran airport two hours later, but we would cross over into a different time zone, which added an extra hour and a half onto the time. If the planes ran on schedule, we would arrive in Tehran around 8 or 9 P.M. the following evening.

Right next to the Pan Am office was the Ankara Hotel. This was one of the finest hotels in the world. It seemed nearly every famous dignitary had stayed there and had eaten at its restaurant, from kings and queens to European and American presidents to celebrities. Jim wanted to eat at the restaurant and when he offered to pay for dinner, I accepted. However, we weren't dressed up in suits, so I didn't think we would be allowed to enter the restaurant. Jim thought otherwise.

We entered the hotel's restaurant and were stopped at the door. At first, they refused to service us due to their conservative dress code. Then the maitre d' came over when he heard me call Jim's name. He thought Jim was the famous Jim Morrison of the Doors and waived the dress code. I winked at Jim and he winked back, so Jim decided to play the part.

"Mr. Morrison, what are you doing in Ankara?" asked the maitre d'.

"We're just on a short vacation until our next tour," replied Jim, not wanting to tell the truth.

The maitre d' asked for Jim's autograph and Jim happily obliged him. As word spread throughout the restaurant, more and more people were asking for Jim's autograph. Some tourists took our picture and some even asked to have their picture taken with him. So I snapped the pictures for the tourists. We didn't care. We were having fun and getting excellent service.

When we asked for a bottle of good red wine to drink with our dinner, the waiter returned with an excellent 1923 Burgundy. We had learned later that this year and type was one of the rarest wines of our time. It was a two hundred-dollar bottle of wine that had been given to us free of charge to drink with our dinner. We were very grateful. Along with the wine, we had filet mignon, baked potatoes, a salad, and garlic bread. It was an excellent meal and the best we had eaten since we had left America, even better than the Air Italia food.

However, once I began drinking that wine my head began spinning. This was very strong wine. I only had two small glasses and began feeling dizzy after the first one. As soon as we had finished one bottle of wine, the waiter brought us another bottle of red wine, a 1928 variety. One of the older women who had asked for Jim's autograph had sent the bottle over with her compliments. We glanced over at her table and toasted her, the Ankara Hotel, and the city. Everyone in the restaurant clapped.

When we had finished our dinner, the waiter brought us two big

Turkish cigars. Before he handed them to us, he cut off the ends and lit them for us. This was a classy place. By the time we had finished our wine and cigars, our heads were spinning. Trying to stand up was harder than I thought it would be. After two or three tries, I finally made it. Jim tried to pay the check but the maitre d' refused his money. Jim left it as a tip instead. It was well worth it.

The lady who had sent over the bottle of wine had paid for our meal. Jim walked over to the lady's table and thanked her. She, in turn, gave him her business card and hotel room number. She was hot to trot. She wanted Jim, but Jim didn't want her. He gave her the excuse that we were flying to Iran in an hour and didn't have the time. With that, we walked back to our hotel room—or should I say we staggered and stumbled back to our hotel room. Then I stumbled over to my bed and quickly passed out. I didn't awake until the morning.

We awoke early because we had to pick up our passports at the Afghan Embassy. We also wanted to kill some time and play those two teenage kids again in a game of hoops. As we walked and talked, I began to get light-headed and dizzy. The air was just too thin. I had forgotten that we were high up in the Ararat Mountains and the embassy was nearly at the top of it. We continued to walk up and up and up. I never noticed before how tired this lack of oxygen made me. Another reason I was so tired could have been due to my hangover.

We finally made it to the Afghan Embassy and retrieved our passports. They gave us each a three-month visa. We had wanted six months, but we didn't object. We walked back down the mountain and past the basketball court, but it was empty. Those two teenage kids were nowhere to be seen. I guess we had been too much for them the day before. We did have fun, though.

We returned to our hotel room and got our things together for the plane trip to Iran. The clerk would have a taxi waiting for us to take us to the airport at the appropriate time. A few hours later, we were on our way. We arrived one hour earlier than our scheduled departure time but the plane hadn't yet arrived. We learned that there had been a bomb threat and the plane had to return to the country of origin. The airport clerk didn't know the exact time of arrival or if the plane had even left the airport.

Jim and I had plenty of time to kill, so we decided to check out Ankara Airport and its stores. The shops were full of Meerschaum pipes and hand carvings. This beautiful, soft, white stone is shaped and carved into different faces and objects. Jim and I each purchased three of them. One large Meerschaum pipe cost ten dollars here in Ankara. In the tobacco shops in America, I've seen them for as much as two hundred dollars or more. We also purchased two smaller ones. After much use, these pipes turned different shades of brown and looked antique. They were exquisite. We were quite happy with our purchases.

Our plane finally arrived at Ankara Airport four hours late. We boarded an already full plane at 9:30 P.M. We sat on the airport tarmac for another hour so the maintenance personnel could refuel and inspect the plane. It would be one or two o'clock in the morning before we would arrive in Tehran. Then it would depart for Kabul three hours later. I guess we wouldn't get much sleep in Tehran.

As we waited, we talked about Ron, wondering how far he had traveled so far. Was he in Iran yet? Would he arrive in Kabul before us? He already had a two-day head start. Although we would be in Kabul within two days, I was so excited about traveling to that country that I just couldn't wait. Once I reached Afghanistan again, I would never leave. I promised myself that I would stay there until death.

Finally, after sitting on the tarmac for more than an hour, the plane started its approach to depart. I noticed that some of the passengers were pointing their fingers at Jim and me and talking aloud. All I could hear was them saying, "The Doors, the Doors." I also heard one girl say, "They must be on vacation." Suddenly the plane bolted upwards into the sky. We were finally on our way to Afghanistan via Tehran.

We were in the air for more than two hours. We weren't served any sandwiches or beverages of any kind, only a small bag of peanuts to munch on. After a long and boring ride, we finally landed in Iran. Tehran Airport was completely deserted and desolate. Everything was closed. In fact, customs didn't even search our luggage.

We boarded a bus and headed to the Intercontinental Hotel. Pan Am paid for our room and promised to buy us dinner. It was very late when we arrived there, but the hotel promised to make us a special meal. The clerk also told Jim that it was a pleasure to serve him and that he was a big Doors fan. Jim and I didn't say a word and just smiled at each other. Then we were escorted to our room and were surprised to learn that it was the presidential suite. The clerk explained that this room was only used for visiting dignitaries, such as kings, presidents, and other people of distinguished backgrounds.

And I guess even rock and roll stars.

As we entered this magnificent suite, the clerk mentioned that our dinner would be ready in fifteen minutes and the waiter would bring it to the room and serve it to us. We thanked the clerk and tried to tip him, but he refused. This suite was like a palace. There was gold everywhere. Gold faucets, his-and-her gold bathtubs, gold vases, and many other objects made of pure gold.

There were many oil paintings of world-renowned artists such as Van Gogh, Ruben, Picasso, Dali, Da Vinci, and many others with whom I wasn't familiar. There was also a plaque on the wall of many famous people who had stayed in this *very* room. Some of them I recognized, such as King Faisal of Egypt, Mahatma Gandhi of India, and General Franco of Spain, but the one name that stood out from all the other famous names was that of Adolf Hitler. When I saw that name, it made me *very* angry and *very* ill. I wondered how they could put Adolf Hitler's name among all the other decent, noble aristocracy. I wondered if they were going to put Jim's name on the plaque. To put a rock and roll star's name with all of these other famous people—I don't think so. At least it was something to talk about.

Jim and I each showered while waiting for our dinner. I had just finished my shower and was drying my hair when I heard a loud knock on the door. It was the waiter with our food. We hadn't ordered our food. It was made special, just for us. They had decided what we would eat.

We sat at the dining room table. Above us, a big chandelier, glittering like thousands of diamonds, lit up the room. The waiter served our meal. The first course was escargot. I had never eaten snails before, but I didn't want to embarrass myself. This was supposed to be a delicacy. Actually, the snails were quite good and had been marinated in butter and garlic and tasted similar to abalone. I had never expected something that looked so ugly to taste so good. I guess royalty ate this stuff daily. So we had to play the part and act like rich, spoiled, rock and roll stars that ate this stuff all the time.

"Give our compliments to the chef," Jim told the waiter.

"I will," he replied.

Our next course was lobster in a buttered sauce that had been flown in from the Arabian Sea. The red wine that was served with our meal was a 1932 vintage. It was delicious, but a bit fruitier than the wine we had drunk in the restaurant at Ankara Hotel. And this meal was as good, if not better, than the one we'd had there. We had no complaints. The dessert consisted of a large hot fudge sundae with two scoops of homemade vanilla ice cream. It was great. They also gave us after dinner cigars and a small glass of brandy.

I couldn't get over the fact that this Muslim country was serving alcoholic beverages. We had found out later that only tourists were allowed to drink it or buy it and that the Iranians could be hung for drinking even a small glass of it. When we had finished our dinner, we tried to tip the waiter but he refused our offer.

"It is my pleasure to serve you," he said.

When the waiter left the room, we were ready for bed. We had to get up in less than three hours. It seemed like I had just shut my eyes when we awoke to a loud banging on the door.

"Mister, mister, wake up!" screamed the hotel clerk. "You must leave immediately for the airport. The taxi will be leaving in ten minutes."

We quickly jumped out of bed, dressed, and walked with the clerk to the taxi. The clerk asked Jim to sign his autograph book. Jim just winked and smiled at me as he signed the guy's book. He wrote, "You have a nice hotel." And signed it: Jim Morrison and the Doors.

Then we jumped into the taxi and headed for the airport. We had to fly Arianna, which was the Afghan airlines, because the Afghan government would not allow Pan Am or any other major airlines to land at their airport. I prayed that they had decent pilots.

I didn't travel all this way to die in an airplane crash in the Hindu Kush Mountains. They'd never find us. I tried not to think about that as we boarded the plane without any acknowledgment from the other passengers that we were rock and roll stars. The plane was full of religious Muslims. They were returning from their annual pilgrimage to Mecca. All of the women were dressed in black chaderies (Burkas in Arab countries), so their bodies were completely hidden from view. The men seemed to be clergy of the Muslim faith. We were the only European or American tourists on the plane and definitely felt out of place.

Within two hours, we were landing at Kabul Airport. As the plane descended toward the city of Kabul, I noticed that the surrounding landscape was all mountainous terrain and desert. We landed at Kabul Airport safely, then walked to the customs counter and paid a three-dollar airport tax. We had our passports stamped and then cleared customs. Finally, we were in a taxi heading for the Najib Hotel. It wasn't a dream. I was actually in Kabul again.

CHAPTER 12
KABUL: DEAL WITH THE DEVIL

I had finally landed in Kabul and was very excited to see my Afghan friends. As the taxi headed toward the Najib Hotel, I decided to make one quick stop.

"Jim, I want to stop at the pharmacy first to see 'the Devil,'" I told him.

I wanted to buy a vial of morphine and a couple of syringes for Jim and me. I was sure the Devil would remember me. I had bought morphine from him six months before with my Italian friends, so I was sure I wouldn't have any problems. I gave the taxi driver directions to the pharmacy. He stopped right in front of the store, so Jim and I hopped out and went in. We had the taxi wait for us while we purchased our merchandise.

"Jim, buy yourself a syringe, while I pay for the vial of morphine and my syringe." He did as I suggested.

The vial of morphine was very cheap—only three dollars for twenty half-grain tablets. We paid for the items and returned to the taxi. Now we were ready to go to the Najib Hotel to relax and party.

"Take us to the Najib Hotel," I told the taxi driver.

I was happy to see that the hotel was still there and nothing had changed, although the grounds were somewhat muddy due to the heavy rainfall over the past few days. However, the weather was beginning to change from summer to fall. We rented a nice room with three beds, just in case Ron showed up. There were quite a few hippies staying at the hotel, including Billy and Larry, the guys from Oak Park. They were sitting in the hotel's outside cafe, drinking hot tea. They hadn't noticed me yet, so I walked over to their table and surprised them.

"Hey, how are you guys doing?" I asked. "Where are Mark and Eric?"

"Eric and Mark are still in Pakistan getting strung out on morphine," replied Larry.

"Speaking of morphine, I just bought some," I interjected. "We were headed to the room to do some now. Do you and Billy want to join us?"

They declined the morphine, but a friend of theirs named Tom wanted to join us.

"Can I buy a morphine tablet from you?" Tom asked.

"Do you have your own syringe?" I asked.

"I don't want to inject it, I want to smoke it," he replied.

"Sure, come on along. The more the merrier," I said.

All five of us walked to my hotel room and introduced ourselves.

"Jim and I flew in from Iran," I told them. "We just arrived in the city thirty minutes ago."

As I got my instruments ready for my injection of morphine, I continued my conversation with Larry and Billy. I wanted to know as much information concerning Mark as possible.

As I put my tablet of morphine into my spoon and added boiling water, Larry interrupted me, saying, "Eric wants to stay in Pakistan. He likes the easy access to morphine. There aren't any controls or regulations concerning morphine, plus it's much, much cheaper there than in Kabul."

The Devil smuggled the morphine illegally into Afghanistan from Pakistan. A large pharmaceutical company in Germany made it. But I was more interested in injecting it, not where it was made. I placed a tablet in one spoon for me and a half-tablet in another spoon for Jim. I also gave Larry's friend, Tom, one tablet. He crushed it up and smoked it on a piece of aluminum foil. He used a straw to chase the narcotic smoke into his lungs. I had finally cooked the morphine and sucked it up into both syringes. We had to be very careful. We didn't want to catch hepatitis or any other disease from dirty water or needles.

While I was getting ready to inject Jim, Larry was filling a hash pipe with some potent Afghani hash. When I noticed what Larry was doing, I thought to myself: *Isn't it ironic that I came all this way for the hash, but now I was so interested in the morphine that I forgot all about the hash.* As soon as Larry lit the hash pipe, the smoke filled the room. It had an excellent aroma of its own. That smell was Afghanistan.

Soon, that smell was interrupted by the smell of cooked morphine. When I injected Jim with the potent narcotic, he seemed to melt. He let out a little whimper and lay back on his bed. I then injected myself and felt a hot rush fill my entire body from the top of my head to the tip of my toes. All of my aches and pains completely disappeared. The feeling was something like I had never experienced. It seemed even better this time than it had six months before.

After a few minutes, Jim and I ruined the party. After about an hour of smoking hash and talking with our guests, Jim and I were extremely exhausted from our trip and not sleeping the night before. Our guests noticed this and excused themselves so we could take a nap.

This wasn't the presidential suite but it was a nice, clean room. It didn't have box spring mattresses but handmade hemp beds. Hemp rope was strung across its wooden frame from side to side. The mattresses were made of two-inch thick cotton. It served its purpose and was quite comfortable. The room cost forty-Afghani per day for both of us: about forty cents.

The bank rate was nearly one- hundred Afghani to the dollar. With a few thousand dollars, a person could live like a king here. That's exactly what I had in mind. I wanted to stay here forever. That is what I had dreamed about from the beginning of this excursion. Afghanistan wasn't as rich as other countries in the area, like Iran or Turkey. Those countries had television and trains. Afghanistan had neither, only radio and buses.

We awoke around dinnertime and went out to a local restaurant where we ate shish kabob and rice and then washed it down with Coca-Cola. However, this Coke was made in Kabul and wasn't as tasty as the stuff made in America. But being high on hash and morphine, nothing tasted normal.

Tomorrow, I would introduce Jim to my Afghan friends at customs and the post office. I had to set up my business right away. I only had twenty dollars left. Jim was buying the food and just about everything else. Hopefully, Ron would be arriving within the next few days. I still couldn't believe that we had finally made this long journey to Kabul. It felt as though I was still inside a dream. The dark night sky looked completely different from this side of the globe.

Kabul was high up, thousands of feet above sea level, in the Hindu Kush Mountains. The weather was very hot during the day and very cold at night. It was September and winter was just around the corner.

After we ate our dinner, we returned to our hotel room and smoked some of the hash that Larry had given us. After five or six tokes, we were off to dreamland. In fact, I was so smashed I couldn't remember if I had a dream or not. We awoke to the crowing of a rooster. I couldn't wait to get up to get high again. We got out our syringes that we had used the day before and I fixed us each a tab of morphine. The morphine seemed to speed us, to give us energy, high up in the Hindu Kush Mountains.

Jim hadn't done anything like this before, that is, before coming to Afghanistan. Come to think of it, neither had I. He had never injected anything before. He had never gone to a pharmacy and bought morphine before either. This was a totally new experience for Jim. This was the perfect country for our drug culture. The city of Kabul was full of drug-addicted hippies. It was so cheap to live here that I never wanted to leave.

Larry and Billy stopped by to see if we wanted to go to breakfast with them. We agreed and followed them to the Mustafa Hotel restaurant a few blocks away. It was a decent, clean restaurant. Jim and I ordered soft-boiled eggs, toast, fresh squeezed orange juice, and coffee for a total cost of forty-Afghani for both of us.

After Jim and I ate our breakfast, we rented a taxi to the post office. I wanted to introduce Jim to Mr. Ramazie, the customs man to whom we had sent the clothes. He was the customs official who searched parcels, and my other friend, Saraj, worked in the post office, mailing envelopes.

The parcels were checked in another part of the building and then brought to the main post office all packed and sealed. Then they were shipped to their destination. I would have to pay Mr. Ramazie for any parcels I wanted to send to America, and I still had to pay Saraj for the envelopes I had sent six months before.

First, we went to visit Mr. Ramazie. We walked into his office and he noticed me right away. He was very surprised and happy to see me, as I was to see him. We shook hands as I introduced him to Jim.

"Jim is the one who sent the clothes," I told him.

"Bob, why did you send used clothing and not new clothes?" asked Mr. Ramazie.

"They were new clothes, Mr. Ramazie, but we washed them before we sent them or they might make you itch. We carried more clothes for you all the way from America."

"Bob, can I get them now?" he asked.

"We will bring them by tomorrow. I need to send something to America right away so my friends will send me money," I replied.

"Have shoes made with hash in them," he retorted.

That was a good idea. He told me of a shoe store that he would send me to. All I had to do was buy the hash and the cobblers would do the rest. So Jim and I would have to look around town to see about purchasing a kilo or two of hash.

We said goodbye to Mr. Ramazie and walked over to the post office, which was on the other side of the building. I wanted to introduce Jim to Saraj. His uncle was one of the customs officials who checked and searched the packages and envelopes for illegal contraband. He was the person who had sent the five envelopes of hash to America for me. I had promised Saraj that if they made it through American customs I would return to Kabul and pay him within six months. I kept my word.

As we walked through the doors of the post office, I noticed Saraj right away as he worked behind the counter. He was helping a tourist. Actually, the tourist was begging Saraj not to open his film canister because it would ruin the film. How dumb did he think Saraj was? I thought.

"There is hash in this film canister and I'm going to open it to check," snapped Saraj.

"Forget it. Just give me my film back," begged the German tourist.

Saraj did as he was asked. The angry tourist grabbed the film canister and waddled out the door.

Now it was my turn. As I walked up to the counter, Saraj had his back to me. As he turned around to help me, he suddenly realized who I was.

"Bob!" he shouted.

"Hello, Saraj, my brother. I told you I would return within six months," I said, as we shook hands and hugged one another.

"Did the envelopes that I sent for you get to America?" he asked.

"They sure did."

Saraj was very happy to see me and I, him. I introduced Jim to Saraj.

"This is Jim, my good friend from America. He traveled with me to Kabul."

"I am very happy to meet you," he said, as they shook hands.

"Saraj, we are staying at the Najib Hotel," I told him. "So please come by when you have the time. I need to speak with you about sending some more hash envelopes to America."

"Yes, but please don't speak about it here," he whispered. "I will stop by your hotel room in a day or so; then we'll talk about it."

"I'll see you tomorrow, then. We have lots to talk about."

As I waved goodbye, Jim and I turned and walked out the post office door and back to the hotel to figure out what we needed to do. The first thing we decided on was to buy the hash that we needed for the shoes and the envelopes. But even more important at the moment was to get to our room, do some morphine, smoke some hash, and kick back. Then we would be able to think much more clearly.

The minute we entered our hotel room, I quickly cooked up a morphine tablet for each of us. This was to celebrate our good fortune. I had not one, but two customs officials who would send hash for me. I hoped to turn my last twenty dollars into twenty thousand. I didn't want to get greedy. I just wanted to make enough money to live in Kabul forever. I didn't want fancy cars or big mansions. I just wanted to live a long and peaceful life. If I had gone to Vietnam, most likely I would have been shipped back in a body bag by now. Here in Afghanistan I was only killing myself, not anyone else.

After doing the morphine, we smoked a couple of bowls of hash. This was decent Afghani hash, but not the best. Not like the hash I had sent to America. I wanted to find the best hash that Afghanistan had to offer, even if I had to mix a little opium with it. I wanted to send my friends in America the most potent hash possible. That was what I had been thinking as I passed out on my bed.

Tomorrow we would have to buy the pollen and then have it pressed into hash without getting busted. Immediately, I thought about Moktar. I also had to write a dozen or so letters to tell my friends in America where to wire the money and when to be expecting their first hash envelopes.

Jim and I awoke to the crow of the rooster once again. I didn't care what time I awoke—the earlier the better.

Every morning I was filled with excitement and anticipation at the thought of fixing my morphine. The hot rush raging through my body, inch by inch, was total ecstasy from the top of my head to the tips of my toes. That euphoric hot rush jump-started me in the mornings, especially on the cold mornings. It gave me an abundance of energy. However, it began taking over my soul. I never really gave a thought about addiction. I just liked the feeling of getting high.

I helped Jim with his injection, just as Antonio had helped me when I first began injecting the evil narcotic. Within twenty minutes of waking up, we were very eager and anxious to eat breakfast. So we walked to our local restaurant at the Mustafa Hotel and stuffed ourselves with Kellogg's Cornflakes and milk, buttered toast, and then washed it all down with a large, cold glass of fresh-squeezed orange juice. It sure hit the spot.

After we had finished eating our breakfast, Jim and I strolled the back streets of Kabul looking to buy some good hashish. The first place we visited was Moktar's rooftop apartment. When we finally reached the roof and knocked on Moktar's apartment door, someone I didn't recognize answered the door.

"Is Moktar or Sabul here?" I asked a big, heavy-set man.

"Moktar and his brother went back to Kandahar to visit their ailing mother," replied the male Afghan in broken English.

"Do you know when he'll return from Kandahar?"

"No, I don't. It shouldn't be too long."

"Tell Moktar that Bob stopped by to say hello."

I thanked the man, and then Jim and I went on our way and continued to walk the side streets and out-of-the-way places, trying to buy some decent hash without getting busted. Nearly every teashop we walked past had a barker trying to sell either hash or opium. They weren't too hard to find. All of them must have gone to the same business school of hash. They barked out the same phrase to potential buyers.

"Mister, mister, you want to buy hashish or opium?"

Every shop had the same green pollen for sale. I wanted to buy red or brown, or even gold pollen. But all we saw was green and we had to be very careful. It would be very easy for these dope sellers to take us into a back room, slit our throats, and rob us.

The first store we entered was a small teashop. The owner showed us his wares, but it was the typical green pollen. He wanted twenty dollars per kilo, plus another twenty dollars to press it into hash. But I quickly declined. I wanted to see if I could find a better, more potent pollen at a much cheaper price. Jim and I had decided to buy five or six kilos, so we wanted to get a better deal than twenty dollars a kilo.

We exited the store without buying anything. We walked down a few more side streets and checked out a few more shops without any luck, until we met a nice Afghani man named Tiar (pronounced Tie-are) sitting in a teashop. He wanted us to follow him to his house so he could show us some excellent pollen.

"I have the best hashish in Afghanistan," exclaimed Tiar.

"I hope so," I replied, filled with excitement.

We followed him through a dirty, smelly alley that had open sewage running down the center of the narrow corridor. We were gagging, choking, and coughing as we walked to his mud and straw-walled fortress. Finally, after a ten-minute stroll through that germ-infested alley, we had arrived at his castle. His beautiful wife and three of his twelve children met us at the door. A ten-foot-high mud wall surrounded his house. It had a small dirt courtyard. His house was a large, three-story building. He must have sold lots of hash to own such a large house.

Tiar introduced us to his family. His children were adorable. He had four sets of identical twins. Afterwards, Tiar directed Jim and me upstairs to his bedroom. There were no chairs to sit on, so we sat on the thin cotton mattress that was used for sleeping. Tiar would sit like all other Afghan people. I called it "the Afghan stoop." They would keep their feet flat on the ground, while their butt hung within an inch of it. They could sit like this all day long. Afghan people didn't like to use chairs. They were a luxury item, and with an average yearly income of fifty dollars, they couldn't afford that luxury.

Tiar placed a large, four-foot-square plastic sheet over the throw rug that covered the dirt floor. He then proceeded to pour kilos of reddish-brown pollen onto the plastic sheet. Then he cleared a large area of the room so he could work his magic. I had seen this ritual twice before, but I wanted Jim to see how hash was made.

Tiar was the typical Afghan male. His worn, weathered, wrinkled face, covered with a six-inch-long, thick, scraggly, black-and-gray beard, helped hide a look of hopelessness about him. But Tiar was a very religious and devout man. He seemed to be very honest and trustworthy. He also wore the typical Afghan garb, the baggy pajama-type pants, extra long shirt, cotton vest, and white turban. His life was so hard that he looked twice as old as his true age of thirty-eight. His wife, Mary, also looked older than her thirty years of age.

"Tiar, we want to buy six kilos of hash," I told him.

"I want twenty-five dollars per kilo but that also includes the pressing," he replied.

"We can't afford that. Please, give us a better price and we'll be back for more," I promised.

We bartered to a price of twenty dollars per kilo, which included the pressing. It would cost us one-hundred and twenty dollars for six kilos of pressed Affy hash. I was very excited. Jim was overly excited. He had never seen how hashish was made, but he would today. And he had never seen this much pollen in one pile before, either.

Tiar's wife entertained us with cookies and tea while we waited for the hash to be made. One of his sons brought in a small hibachi stove full of red-hot charcoals and placed it near the pile of pollen. Then Tiar placed a small sheet of plastic, covered with a light coat of ghee, over the larger one—just as the man had done months before in Herat, when I traveled with Mark. I figured these guys must have gone to the same hash making school when they were younger.

"The ghee will keep the hot pollen from sticking to the plastic," I told Jim.

Tiar reached for the large plastic bag of skunky, sticky, reddish-brown pollen and proceeded to pour the rest of its contents onto the other pile he had poured earlier. Our eyes widened, as we looked at the big pile of pollen—six kilos worth. Then Tiar began to make the hash. Jim was very anxious to see how it was made. Actually, so was I. I had seen it made a few times before but never in this quantity. Every time was a new experience for me.

Tiar placed a large pan of water onto the hot coals until it began to boil. Then he added nearly three kilos of the pollen into the boiling water until he had the consistency he wanted. When that step was completed, he took the pan off the hot coals and dumped it onto the small plastic sheet. Then he rubbed a small amount of ghee onto his hands so they wouldn't blister from the searing heat of the pollen, which I told Jim, and began kneading it while adding some of the dry pollen to it. He then would grab a handful of hot, wet pollen in each hand and place them into the dry pollen, kneading it until he had the consistency he wanted. He did this until he had a large, two-foot-round, two-inch thick slab. Once that step was completed, he placed the slab onto the hot charcoals until it began to smoke and burn. Then he flipped it over and waited until that side began to smoke. Then, at that exact moment, he grabbed it from the hot coals and placed it on the plastic sheet. He wrapped the plastic around the big slab and began kneading it with his feet—stepping on it and smashing it, making it dense and denser. He continued this ritual four or five times until all of the dry pollen was mixed with the wet. It took about three hours to get this far, and we were only half-finished. Now we had to press the big slab into one-hundred-gram post-card-sized slabs.

Tiar began tearing off small chunks of hash from the larger one. Then he folded the small plastic sheet around a small chunk of it so it couldn't escape and rolled it into a rectangular slab using a Coke bottle. Nearly five hours after we entered Tiar's house, we had finally finished our task. However, we still had to wait another hour until the hash slabs had cooled down.

When we had finished tallying the amount of post-card-sized slabs, we had counted seventy. Some would be used for the boots, and whatever was left over would be used for the envelopes and other parcels.

The slabs had finally cooled down and were stiff and hard but still soft enough to cut with scissors. Now they could be stacked without sticking together or falling apart. While I filled my bag with the hash, Jim gave Tiar six American twenty-dollar bills. We were happy to give him the money and the work. He had made quite a bit of money for his family. Tiar smiled and thanked us very graciously and then walked us to his front door.

"We'll come back again and soon," I promised, as we left his home and headed for our hotel.

We hailed a taxi instead of walking around with six kilos of hash under our coats. We were still very paranoid and weren't sure if Tiar would turn us into the police or not. In fact, Jim made me carry the hash so I would be the one to get busted. However, all our worries were for nothing. We arrived at the hotel safely.

When we entered our room, we were ready to celebrate. So I proceeded to cook some morphine, a tablet for each of us. We were each using two or three tablets daily. We didn't bother to think about getting addicted. At least I didn't. We just wanted to get high and feel good. The morphine and hash sure helped us do that.

Once we had injected our morphine, we lay down on our beds and talked about what needed to be done in the days to come. First, we would have to take the hash to the shoe man to have three pairs of boots made. I had less than twenty dollars, so Jim would have to loan me the money to pay for them. I planned to pay him back as soon as I had received the money from my friends back in America. I figured it would take me a month or two before my money would start arriving, so I would have to make my twenty dollars last until then.

We quickly fell asleep discussing our business opportunities and wondering what magical adventures lay ahead. The next morning, after we'd had our morphine fix, we left our hotel room to have breakfast before we walked to the shoe store just a block away from our hotel. I decided to use the same shoe store that Moktar had taken me to six months earlier. I carried the hash in a brown paper grocery bag, looking as if I was just carrying groceries. Once we entered the shoe store, I talked with the worker who had helped me in my quest six months earlier.

"Moktar sent me here."

The minute I said that, an old Afghan man stepped out of the small back room and directed me into it. He made Jim stay out in the front, I guess for security reasons, while I bartered with him.

"I need three pairs of boots made with hash in the soles," I whispered.

I quickly opened the grocery bag of hash to show him. Even though he didn't speak English and I didn't understand or speak his language, he knew exactly what I wanted done.

I had him divide the three kilos of hash evenly among the three pairs of boots. I had only brought half of our stash so I could use the other half for other things. The old man began showing me a variety of handmade shoes and boots that could be used in my endeavor. I settled on some simple six-inch high, round-toed, brown-leather boots that zipped along the side. The hash would be sewn into the soles with about four-hundred grams in each boot. That would be nearly one kilo for each pair. They would be very heavy, but with my customs connections it didn't matter.

After bartering with the shoemaker, we finally agreed on a price of 500-Afghani for each pair of boots plus another 300-Afghani for adding the hash to them, for a total of 800-Afghani or 2,400-Afghani for all three pairs. That added up to less than twenty-five dollars. Jim once again loaned me the money.

I gave the shoemaker half of the money before I departed his store, and the rest was to be paid when I picked up the boots in five days. The shoemaker was very happy for the business. To him twenty-five dollars was a lot of money. To Jim and me it was very little.

I thanked the old man as we shook hands, and then Jim and I walked back to the hotel to celebrate. We had already injected our morning dose of morphine before we set out for the shoe store, but now we would do an extra tablet just for the hell of it. We were on vacation and wanted to get high. By the time we had reached our hotel room, we were excited with anticipation of the coming events.

After injecting the morphine, we kicked back and smoked some hash, then talked about the days ahead. Our conversation quickly turned to Ron, wondering when he would arrive in Kabul.

"It should be any day now," Jim mumbled.

As we were talking, we heard a loud knock on the door, so I got up to open it. Thinking that it was Larry or Billy, we were very surprised and happy to see Ron standing at the door: speak of the devil. What a coincidence. It was like magic. Finally, eight days after we had left him in Ankara, he was here. We were quite excited by his presence. We all started talking at once, telling each other about our adventures. It seemed Ron had met some people in Kandahar who would help him smuggle hash.

"We have good connections right here in Kabul," I told him.

But Ron wanted to do his own thing. So I remained silent and filled the hash pipe so Ron could get high and relax.

"Ron, you want to try some morphine?" asked Jim, as I passed Ron the pipe.

"Hell no, why do I want to try that shit? I hate needles," snapped Ron.

"That's the way I felt, too, until I tried it," I retorted.

"Thanks, but no thanks," said Ron, as he lit the pipe and took a long, healthy toke.

We told Ron everything about our travels since he had left Ankara, and Ron told us about his travels to Kabul. He wanted to head to India as soon as possible. I tried to talk him out of it, but he was adamant. Jim was also interested in his ideas. They no longer wanted to use my connections because Ron supposedly had his own now. I tried to make him see things differently.

"Ron, if you don't know who you are dealing with, you are gonna get busted," I told him matter-of-factly. "You have to be very careful in Afghanistan. It's too easy to get busted and end up in a hellhole, namely an Afghani prison."

However, Ron didn't seem to care. He thought he had a sure thing. I tried reasoning with him but he was certain that he had the best way to smuggle hash back to America. So I stopped arguing with him. If they wanted to leave Afghanistan for India that was their choice. No matter what, I was going to stay in Kabul. I knew I had good connections. They were tried and true. I had already proved it six months earlier. I still had plans to live and die in Afghanistan.

Ron shared the room with us, using the third bed in our room. Now we would be a group of three. When we awoke the next morning, I began cooking the morphine for Jim and me. After I injected

Jim, I injected myself with the Devil's liquid. I felt a red-hot rush of energy race through my body and fell back onto the bed. All my aches and pains were completely gone. I had completely succumbed to the heavy narcotic. Once the rush was over the morphine speeded me and gave me super energy. Ron, however, wanted nothing to do with morphine.

"You can buy almost any drug or narcotic from the Devil's pharmacy," I reminded him. "There isn't much government control on pharmaceutical drugs. They can be bought right over the counter."

Ron liked that idea. He wanted to buy some pills for sleeping. So Jim and Ron walked to the pharmacy while I headed to the post office to mail some letters to my friends in the States and to say hello to my Afghan customs friends. I wanted them to stay my good friends and didn't want to use them just for my drug operation.

I hopped a taxi to the post office. When I entered the building through the large double doors, I immediately noticed Saraj standing behind the counter. There weren't many people there at the time.

"Saraj, how are you doing, my brother?" I asked from across the room.

Saraj reacted happily and smiled as I walked up to his counter.

"How are you, my friend?" he asked, reaching out to shake my hand.

"Good," I replied.

"What do you need, Bob?" he asked.

After some small talk, I got down to serious business.

"Saraj, I need to send some hash envelopes to my friends in America," I whispered.

"Good . Make them like you did before."

"I will be back tomorrow with some hash envelopes."

"No. Tonight, I will stop by your hotel room and pick them up," he said.

I nodded in agreement, then turned, waved goodbye, and walked out of the door. Then I quickly walked to the other side of the building to say hello to Mr. Ramazie at the customs office. When I entered through his office door, I noticed him sitting at his desk.

"Hello, Mr. Ramazie. How are you today?" I asked.

"Hello, Bob. I am fine."

"I will have the packages ready within six or seven days," I told him.

"Remember, you can't use boxes," he reminded me. "You must

use a white linen sack to send the boots and gifts and they must be left open so I can inspect and search them. Then I'll seal the bags with my special stamp."

"That sounds good to me, Mr. Ramazie."

"Put a few cheap gifts in with the boots so the package will look legitimate," he said, winking.

He wanted fifty American dollars for each bag sent. I would owe Jim quite a bit of money by the time my endeavor paid off. If everything worked out as I expected, it wouldn't be too long before I paid Jim back, with interest.

I said goodbye to Mr. Ramazie and hailed a taxi back to the hotel.

Larry and Billy were sitting in the hotel's restaurant drinking hot tea, so I stopped to say hello.

"Larry, have you guys seen Jim?" I asked them.

They both shook their heads no.

"What are you up to?" asked Billy.

"Our friend we had been waiting for finally arrived."

I invited them to my room but they declined. So I walked back to my room alone. Jim and Ron hadn't yet returned.

I fixed up one and a half tablets of morphine and injected it into my vein. The rush was really potent this time. It knocked me right down to the bed. The super hot rush filled my body. This was true ecstasy. My body felt as though it was floating on air. I had never felt a high like that before. I wanted more and more of this warm, loving feeling. I quickly fell into a deep, hypnotic sleep. I awoke to the sounds of loud laughing noises. Jim and Ron had finally returned to the hotel room around 10 P.M.

"Where have you guys been?" I asked.

"We met some heads and partied with them at their hotel room," replied Jim.

"I hope you had a good time," I said sarcastically.

Then out of the blue Jim said something that shocked me.

"We are leaving for Kandahar, Pakistan, and India in a day or two," he said.

Jim wouldn't look at me as he spoke. I was in total shock. I couldn't believe what he had just told me. I tried in vain to talk them out of it. But they used the excuse that their visas were expiring. I knew that wasn't completely true. Ron only had a seven-day transit visa, but Jim still had more than two months left on his. I even explained to Ron that all he had to do was pay a small fine for the days

he stayed past the visa's expiration date. That was what I had done
the first time I'd come here. But Jim and Ron were adamant. Nothing could change their minds, especially Ron's. He still refused to
tell me how he had planned to smuggle hash out of Afghanistan to
America. He did say, however, that his plan was foolproof.

"Ron, do you have a customs official in your pocket as your
connection?" I asked.

"No."

"Be careful. I told you before, it's very easy to land in jail."

"We're not going to land in jail," Ron retorted.

"Why do you guys want to leave now when we are just getting
our shit together?" I asked. "The boots will be ready in two or three
days, plus I'm going to send some hash envelopes in a day or so.
Within a week or two, the money should be arriving at the bank.
We should be on easy street within a month."

They didn't want to talk about it. Their minds were made up.
They would not listen to me. It had taken me six months to get a
good friendship with Saraj and Mr. Ramazie before I could send
hash to America without worrying about getting busted.

Ron and Jim didn't have this luxury. They thought they could do
it themselves without anyone's help.

"Well I wish you guys the best in whatever you do, but be *very*
careful. Remember, if you don't have the right connections you will
get busted."

I looked into Jim's eyes, and he just nodded his head in agreement. Not another word was said about that situation.

"Jim, I need to borrow another two hundred dollars before you
leave Kabul, and I will give you five hundred dollars when you return," I promised.

They planned to return to Afghanistan from India as soon as
their secret deal was completed. I really prayed that they wouldn't
end up in jail somewhere in Asia. You don't take any unnecessary
risks in these countries.

Well, I didn't expect it, but Jim and Ron left for Kandahar that
very next morning. Jim woke me up to inject him with morphine one
last time. I fixed each one of us a half-grain tablet.

"Jim, buy some opium in Kandahar if you start feeling sick from
morphine withdrawal," I said.

He had been injecting the pure, evil narcotic for almost two
weeks, at least once and sometimes twice a day. But like me, he
didn't think about getting addicted because we had never run out of

it. We could always buy it from the Devil, so I never worried about running out.

After Jim was re-energized from the morphine rush, he placed two one-hundred-dollar bills on the edge of the table for me.

"Thanks, Jim. I'll pay you back as soon as you return," I promised him, shoving the bills into my money belt.

With that, Jim and Ron were out the door heading for the bus station.

That was the last I saw of them as they left for Kandahar. Minutes later, I went to breakfast and saw Larry and Billy sitting at a table at the restaurant.

"How are you guys doing?"

"Good. Where are your friends?" asked Larry.

"Jim and Ron left for Kandahar, Pakistan, and India. I'm staying all alone now. Come by my room and we'll get high and rap."

"Yeah, maybe we will come over a little later," said Billy.

They had just moved from the Najib Hotel to the Mustafa Hotel a short block away. It was a little better than the Najib and a little more expensive. The Najib was both a hotel and a motel. The Mustafa was only a hotel, but with an excellent restaurant. That's where we ate nearly *every* morning.

"I will be at my hotel room in a few hours, but first I have to visit the bank and the post office," I said. "So stop by and we'll smoke some hash and do some morphine." Then I turned and walked out of the restaurant.

After eating a small breakfast at the Mustafa restaurant, I walked to the shoe store to see if the boots were ready. To my surprise, they were.

While I waited to take possession of them, I watched as these shoemakers worked. They each sat in a small, cramped cubicle with a small table in front of them. They had to sit with their legs crossed all day 'cause they didn't have any room to put their feet down. They must have been yoga masters to stay in that position for so long.

I paid the old man the rest of the money he was owed and checked out the boots. You couldn't tell by looking that they had hash in them. They looked perfect, but they weighed too much. They had used almost all of the hash I had given them. I had enough left over to make three or four envelopes, so there was well over four hundred grams in each boot. I thanked the man and then left the store.

These boots would be great to wear back to America, I thought to myself. You would only have to wear them for a few minutes at a time, just long enough to cross the borders. But they would probably fall apart if they were worn for long periods of time. The bottoms of the soles were just too thin. I just hoped they would make it through American customs.

Before I returned to my hotel room, I went to the bazaar to buy three large white linen sacks into which I would put the boots. I also bought some nice Afghan vests. I put one pair of boots and two nice vests into each sack. I made up two packages, but I hadn't decided to whom I would send them. I wanted to save the third pair of boots for another time.

I also made up six envelopes and addressed them to my friends in America. I addressed them to three different friends. Neither person knew each other. That way I would know if they were ripping me off or not. I figured that if one of my friends had received his envelopes then the others should receive theirs also. If one of them told me that they hadn't received the envelopes that I had sent them, and I knew my other friends had, then I would cross that person off of my list of partners and he'd never receive anything from me again.

I mean, I was doing all the work, using my own money to buy and send the illegal contraband, and taking all the risks. All I asked from them was to sell my half of the hash for seven dollars a gram, and with this hash, they could sell it the minute it was in their possession.

I had everything ready for the next morning. I took a taxi to the customs office and showed Mr. Ramazie the packages. He quickly searched the parcels, tied each of the bags with a metal wire, and then sealed them with a special lead stamp. From there, I took the parcels to the post office and handed them to Saraj. He looked surprised and then became suspicious.

"Do they have hash in them?" he asked, looking directly into my eyes.

"No," I lied. "Saraj, if they had hash in them I would have told you, then paid you baksheesh. I just brought them from the customs office and they checked and searched them before the packages were sealed."

"What's in them?"

"They're just gifts for some close friends. It's a pair of handmade boots and a couple of beautiful handmade velour Afghan vests."

Saraj still looked at me suspiciously.

"Is there hash in the boots?" he asked again.

"Saraj, I would have told you if there was. The customs man would have busted me if there were any hash in the packages. They even had a blind psychic check them by smelling and feeling them."

"Yes, I know," he said, still suspicious with my answers.

I knew Saraj had finally succumbed to the idea that there wasn't any hash in the packages when he handed me papers to fill out. I had to write my name and passport number and the names and addresses of the people the packages were being shipped to. This would be evidence in America if these packages were to get busted. They would know who sent them. I had gone too far to ask to have them returned, so I continued to fill out the necessary information. However, I did make a few slight changes. I misspelled my name and wrote down an incorrect passport number. I just hoped and prayed these post office officials wouldn't check the paperwork that closely.

I handed Saraj the papers and the correct amount of money for postage. Then I watched and waited for a post office official or police officer to arrest me for smuggling. I was relieved when Saraj returned and handed me a receipt for the packages.

"Your parcels will take a week to reach America. Tell me, Bob, is there hash in those packages?"

"Saraj, if there was hash in the packages I would have told you and paid you baksheesh. But I do have six envelopes to send. Come to my hotel room tonight and pick them up, along with the money."

"Yes, Bob, I will come over tonight after work."

"Goodbye, Saraj. I'll see you later this evening," I said, as we shook hands.

Walking back toward my hotel, just a few blocks from the post office, I noticed an acoustic guitar in a shop window. I walked in and asked the clerk if the guitar was for sale.

"It is, for twenty dollars," he replied.

I tried to barter with him for a better price, but he wouldn't budge. I didn't have a whole lot of money left, but I wanted to jam with Larry. And if I bought the guitar it would keep me occupied and out of mischief because I was lonesome staying by myself. Suddenly, while staring at the guitar, wondering if I should buy it or not, I fell into a trance.

I began thinking about Jim and Ron, wondering how far they had traveled by now. In Michigan, we had talked about living in Afghanistan forever. We were never going back to America. But now that Jim and Ron had gone, I'd probably never see them again. I had told Jim before he left that if he returned to Kabul, he would only stay a few weeks and then return to America to marry his girlfriend, Martha. I figured Ron would run back to his girlfriend, too. But I knew I wasn't going anywhere. I was sure to die here. Suddenly, I was snapped out of my trance when I felt the clerk tapping my shoulder.

"Mister, do you like the guitar?" he asked.

I grabbed the guitar and played a few chords. The neck was straight and it sounded pretty good, so I gave him a twenty-dollar bill.

With my guitar in hand, I hopped a taxi to the hotel. Once in my room, I had just started to relax when the hotel manager knocked on my door. Now that Jim and Ron were gone, he wanted me to move to a smaller room unless I wanted to pay the extra money. But he really wanted the room for new arrivals and showed me a room upstairs. It was all right. It was small, but decent. It had just enough room for one bed and a chair or two. It also had some beautifully colored paintings on the walls. It seemed that when these travelers became bored, they decorated the walls with their beautiful and magical artwork. Some were really incredibly exquisite. I wondered how these artists' minds worked.

I agreed to move into the smaller room upstairs and within an hour, I had moved in. I decided to celebrate for moving into my colorful room and purchasing a new acoustic guitar.

I put two tabs of morphine into the spoon. I wanted that red-hot rush. I just couldn't get enough of that special feeling, and within two minutes, I had it. A few minutes later, I sat up and started playing my new guitar, writing my own songs. I noticed I was quite creative, and the drugs seemed to help my creativity. The morphine gave me a boost in energy and the hash high gave me a deeper inspiration. I honestly felt that I had much more creativity here in Afghanistan than I had in America due to the heavy drug use.

I continued to write and play, play and write. Within a few hours, I had written two or three good songs. They came out of my mind like pouring candy out of the box into my hand. They were just spewing out of my head like the water pouring out of a garden hose.

I had just started filling my chillum with hash when I was interrupted by a knock on the door. It was Larry and Billy. Larry also had a guitar with him. Then he noticed my guitar.

"Where did you get the beautiful guitar?" asked Larry.

"I just bought it so we could jam together," I said, holding the guitar in front of me so Larry could check it out.

"That's a nice guitar," he said.

"How did you guys know I was in this room?"

"The manager told us when we went to your old room," replied Larry.

"Oh."

I started playing the songs I had just written a few hours before. As Larry joined in, Billy began walking around the room, checking out the artwork on the walls. He noticed one of the paintings was signed by a name I had recognized—Pablo Picasso. We wondered if it really was his signature. But what would he be doing in a cheap hotel like this one?

Billy was an artist and mentioned that the signature looked exactly like the ones on his paintings. I didn't argue with him. He might have been correct.

I decided that if I remembered, I would ask the hotel manager about Picasso's signature. He should know if he had ever visited this hotel.

We continued our jam session until it was time to sleep. They left for their hotel and asked me if I wanted to move in with them. But I declined their offer, at least for now. I told them that I would see them in the morning for breakfast.

Once they left the room, I quickly cooked up a tablet of morphine. Now I was injecting it two or three times a day—once in the morning, right after I woke up; once in the afternoon; and then once before I went to bed. I had also increased my dosage by fifty percent, and I still didn't think about getting addicted.

I had completely forgotten about Saraj. It was getting late, and he hadn't come over to pick up the envelopes. I was worried. I hoped nothing had gone wrong. I would have to see him tomorrow. I wondered if I should take the envelopes to the post office. That was the last thing I remembered as I fell fast asleep.

I awoke the next morning to the crowing of the rooster. This was the first time that I'd heard the rooster crow since Jim and Ron had departed. And the first thing I did was to inject my morphine. That gave me the extra boost of energy I needed to get up and out of the bed. The morning "do" kept my body warm in a cool room in the early morning.

Winter was in the air. I dressed quickly and then walked over to the Mustafa Restaurant where I met Larry and Billy.

"Larry, do you and Billy want to come over to my room and jam later?" I asked.

"Sure. I feel like jamming," replied Larry.

"I have to go to the post office first, so I'll see you there in two hours," I said.

They nodded in agreement.

I finished my breakfast and rented a taxi to the post office. I saw Saraj standing behind the counter with his back toward me. When he turned around, he was very surprised to see me.

"Saraj, why didn't you pick up the envelopes?"

"I'm sorry. I had to work late and didn't have time to stop by your hotel room. I would have missed my bus to my village," he replied.

Saraj seemed genuinely sorry. I believed him.

"That's all right. I brought the envelopes with me anyway," I whispered, opening my shoulder bag so he could see them.

He motioned for me to give them to him. So I quickly and very discreetly handed Saraj all six envelopes.

"I will come to your hotel room tonight to pick up the money," he said, as he looked around the room to see if we were being watched.

"Saraj, I moved into another room on the second floor in the same building. It's directly at the top of the stairs. You can't miss it," I explained.

"Don't worry, I'll find it," he said, as we shook hands.

I left the post office and headed back to my hotel in a taxi. I waited for Larry and Billy. Within an hour, they had arrived. We began jamming right away.

As we were playing, we were interrupted by a loud knock on the door. Surprisingly, it was the Austrian University professor, Mr. Schmidt, who had saved us from the wicked shop owner in Kandahar.

The big fellow was standing in the open doorway, smiling and holding his movie camera on his shoulder. I asked him what he had been doing for the last seven months since we had seen him last. He told us that he was filming all the paintings on the walls and ceilings of the different hotel rooms. It was a tree of knowledge. He was following the hippie trail to India. He wanted to tell the story of these unusually beautiful paintings and colorful drawings. As we talked, the professor noticed my chillum and pile of hash sitting on the bedside table.

"Would you make up a chillum of hash and smoke it in front of the camera?" asked Professor Schmidt.

"Will the film be shown in America?" I asked, concerned about being busted by the FBI.

"I promise you, it will never be shown in America. It is strictly for the Austrian University."

So I agreed and started breaking up the hash in small, BB-sized pieces and began filling up the Indian hash pipe. I used a wet rag for the filter. It cools the harsh smoke, which in turn soothes the throat. Then I held the chillum high above my head and toasted to the gods.

As I did this, I chanted the magical words: "Boom Shankar, chillum. Boom Shankar, chillum." And then proceeded to smoke it as Larry lit the bowl.

I took a long, heavy drag and had the hash burning good, and then took another three or four long puffs that completely filled the small room with Affy hash smoke. Then I passed the chillum to Larry and he did the same. We did this for the next thirty minutes while the professor filmed this wild experience. Finally, he had enough film.

"Thank you for helping me with my film. You will be its stars," he promised.

We just laughed, not believing him. However, he did film the incident in Kandahar more than seven months before when the shop owner locked us into his small clothing store, then demanded a bribe before he would let us out.

Now the professor had filmed us playing our guitars and smoking a chillum. It was quite an experience and all in good fun.

Professor Schmidt left us as we played our guitars. We worked on the songs that I had written. They were sounding pretty good. We played until my fingers developed blisters. Before Larry and Billy left my room, I reminded them that I would meet them at their hotel in the morning.

"Why don't you just move in with us?" asked Larry. "Then we could jam all the time."

"I'll think about it," I said, as they walked out the door.

I declined their offer for now. I lay down on the bed to take a nap. But I kept thinking about Jim and Ron, wondering how far they had traveled since leaving Kabul. I figured if they weren't in jail, they should be in West Pakistan by now. Then I thought about Mark and Eric. They were also traveling in West Pakistan. Thinking about my friend's travels put me in a sleepy trance, until my thoughts were again interrupted by a loud knock on my door.

I opened it to find Saraj standing in the hallway. I invited him into the room and greeted him with a big smile and a hug. He was a tall, handsome fellow who stood over six feet tall and weighed about one hundred and eighty pounds. He had short brown hair and a beautiful, bright smile with perfect teeth—a rarity in Afghanistan.

Saraj didn't wear the normal Afghan garb, at least not at work. He wore expensive, hand-tailored, European business suits. His family was quite rich in Afghan terms and closely related to King Zahir Shah-Kahn. That's the reason Saraj and his uncle had better government jobs than most.

Saraj was my best Afghan friend, and I didn't want him to feel that I was using him or taking advantage of him.

"Saraj, please sit down," I said.

"I can't stay too long. I have to catch the last bus to my village."

It would take him almost two hours to get home. He lived over eighty miles north of Kabul.

"Saraj, did you send the envelopes?"

"Yes. I gave them personally to my uncle. I watched as he placed them into the mail bag for America. I sent all six of them. So I need three hundred-Afghani for each envelope."

That was about twenty American dollars. If all six of the envelopes made it to their destinations, I should make about two thousand dollars, minus my costs. I thanked Saraj and paid him the money.

"Saraj, I'm never going to leave Afghanistan. I'm going to die here. This is my home now, and with your help my dream will come true," I said, with tears in my eyes.

"I will do everything in my power to make your dream come true. But now it is late and I must be leaving or I will miss my bus."

I thanked him again and promised to see him the following day at the post office.

As Saraj left my room, I lay down to sleep. I was very happy. Everything seemed to be turning out great. I had all the hash sent. And now all I had to do was wait for the money to roll in. I figured within a week it should start arriving at the bank. That was the last thing I remembered before waking up the next morning.

I was so excited and hyper that I forgot to fix my morphine and went directly to the Mustafa Restaurant. Larry and Billy were already sitting at a table. I sat down with them and began a conversation.

"Larry, have you heard from Eric and Mark?" I asked.

"I received a letter from Eric a week ago," he replied. "He is in a bind and complaining that he is out of money. His mother wants him to return to America. She's worried that he'll overdose on drugs."

"Why does she think he'll overdose?" I asked.

"Eric is really strung out on morphine. He's doing twice as much as you."

"What have you heard about Mark?"

"He's still with Eric, and just as strung out," Larry replied.

"Rob, you're pretty addicted to morphine yourself," said Billy.

"No way, I'll never get addicted to it. I know when to quit. I'm too smart to let that happen."

"Have you taken any morphine this morning?" asked Larry.

"I haven't yet. I'm going to fix after breakfast."

"We'll bet you that you can't go one day without doing your morphine," said Larry.

Larry and Billy believed I couldn't go a whole day without injecting my morphine and that I had become addicted to it.

"I'll take that bet. I can control my body using willpower," I told them emphatically.

Throughout breakfast, I kept thinking about the bet. The more I thought about it, the more my willpower evaporated. I just couldn't get addiction out of my mind. Finally, breakfast was over.

"Stop by my room later and we'll jam and get high," I said.

They agreed, but before I left, they reminded me of the bet.

"Remember our bet," said Billy.

"Don't worry, I won't forget."

I turned and walked out of the restaurant, heading toward my hotel. I couldn't get there fast enough. The walk, which takes about five minutes, seemed like eternity. I had absolutely no energy. It seemed as if I had walked five miles uphill instead of five-hundred feet. By the time I reached my room, my clothes were sopping wet from perspiration. I knew then that I was addicted to morphine.

As soon as I entered my room, I went for my dope kit and took out the syringe and bottle of morphine. I needed to inject some instant energy into my weak body. I needed that morphine rush and I needed it now. I had no control over my mind and body. I no longer had the willpower to overcome this evil narcotic—morphine.

As I injected the powerful narcotic, it quickly took control of my body. That hot, tingly, prickly feeling made my body come to life once again. I lay back as the hot rush burst through my veins from my head to my toes. My strength and energy finally returned. Actually, I felt human again—or did I feel super human? It seemed all my problems had floated away.

As I was putting my dope kit away, Larry and Billy stopped by. As usual, Larry brought his guitar along. I had written five more good songs, so we practiced every chance we could.

"You should move in with us so we can play every day," said Larry. "Your songs are good enough to record."

That's what I had hoped for. We were really enjoying ourselves as we played and sang our new songs. That is, until we were interrupted by a loud knock on the door. It wasn't really a knock but a loud pounding.

When I opened it, I saw a young teenage Afghani boy standing there. He must have been sixteen years old, but you could never tell an Afghani's actual age. They usually looked ten years older. These people lived a very hard life. For some reason, this young man was very angry. He suddenly barged into my room and began yelling and screaming inches from my face. I didn't have any idea what he was upset about. I didn't know if it was our hash smoking or our guitar playing and singing that upset him.

While this crazy young man kept ranting and raving, he suddenly slapped me across the right side of my face. It was a very hard slap. Larry and Billy were flabbergasted. They didn't have any idea what was going on and neither did I. I couldn't believe this was happening.

"Rob, what is this kid pissed off about?" asked Larry.

"Hell if know," I said, dumbfounded.

I had literally showed the Afghan out of my room and into the hallway when he suddenly reached out and slapped my face again. This time I fought back. The morphine gave me speed and energy like never before. I was like Mohammed Ali, moving like a butterfly and stinging like a bee. I would fake with my left hand and hit him with my right. Larry and Billy were cheering me on. Larry couldn't believe how fast I was. I had never taken a boxing lesson in my life, but now my reflexes were super sharp. This guy couldn't touch me. I was so fast that I would only slap him because I didn't want to hurt him. I wanted to show him that he couldn't win this fight. And as we were fighting, I could hear Larry and Billy complimenting my fighting ability.

"Man, is he good. I can't believe how fast his punches are," opined Larry.

"Rob is so fast, he's unbelievable," said Billy. "Look how he fakes with a right and hits him with his left."

As I took my eyes off my opponent to wink at my two friends, the young man suddenly raised his leg and kicked me square in the gut. I flew across the hall into closed double doors and made such a loud noise that other people came out of their rooms to see what all the commotion was about. This stunned and shocked me, that he was able to hit me. Although he hadn't hurt me, he *had* surprised me.

I quickly jumped back up, then started dancing and weaving toward my opponent. I made sure he wouldn't kick me again. I was now aware of that move. I continued to fake with my right hand and slap him with my left and visa versa. Finally, after fifteen minutes of nonstop action and slaps to the face, he suddenly turned and ran down the stairs screaming, yelling, and crying. I didn't want to fight the guy, let alone hurt him. I still had no idea why he was upset with me in the first place.

Actually, I really felt bad about what had just transpired. Larry and Billy were patting me on the back, raising my arm in victory and congratulating me for a job well done. They both praised my fighting ability. They told me that they had never seen anything like it. I was fast as lightning. They refused to believe me when I told them that I had never boxed before in my life.

After ten minutes, we were back playing our guitars and singing. We stopped to smoke and share a chillum of hash and relax for a while. They again asked if I wanted to room with them. I told them that I'd think about it and give them an answer in a few days, even though it would be cheaper to live with all three of us sharing the expenses. My funds were nearly depleted again. I only had thirty dollars left from the two hundred that Jim had loaned me. If money didn't come soon, I would be broke. But I didn't tell them that.

After our little talk, we began playing our guitars again. However, an hour later, we were abruptly interrupted once again. The door burst open and the young Afghan man, my boxing opponent, burst into my room. But this time, he brought two older and bigger Afghan men with him. These guys were well over two-hundred and fifty pounds and stood well over six feet tall.

The Afghan kid began yelling and screaming at me, but I couldn't understand him. Then I looked at the two burly men and just shrugged my shoulders and shook my head, as if to tell them that I was confused by this kid's actions. Larry, Billy, and I stayed seated and in utter shock as this kid started jumping up and down on my bed. Then he began kicking at my guitar as I held it in my lap. Then he lashed out and kicked Larry's guitar. I looked at the two burly men and motioned for them to stop this kid's rampage. They also watched in disbelief and were completely dumbfounded by his actions.

This kid was so upset that he was crying as he screamed and yelled in a language I couldn't understand. I motioned with my hands that if this kid wouldn't stop his craziness, I would stop him. I could tell from their facial expressions that the two Afghans also thought this kid was out of control.

Evidently, the kid brought these two Afghan men as his body-guards. He must have told them lies, because they didn't lift a hand against me. I spoke to them in broken English, telling them to stop this kid before he got hurt. They said something to him, but the kid refused to listen and continued his crazy antics.

When I stood up and started pushing the kid out of my room, he slapped me in the face. I didn't return fire but continued pushing him toward the open door. Suddenly, to my amazement, the two burly Afghan men, each one grabbing the kid under the armpit, picked him up and carried him out of the room. I quickly thanked them and shut the door. We could still hear the kid yelling and screaming as they carried him away.

Well, after that little incident, we didn't feel like playing the guitars anymore, so Larry and Billy went back to their hotel.

I still had to visit the post office to say hello to Saraj. I also had to stop by the pharmacy to buy two or three bottles of morphine.

I hopped a taxi to the post office, but Saraj wasn't there. He didn't come into work. I just prayed that he wasn't hurt or injured. With all that money I had given him the night before, I figured he had either gotten robbed or was at home celebrating his good fortune. Thirty dollars was a lot of money for an Afghan, especially for one day's work.

I checked the mailbox to see if I had any letters from home. I did. I had ten from friends in America. I didn't read them there. I waited until I returned to my hotel room.

Now I had to visit the pharmacy to buy my morphine. I only had a few tablets left and didn't want to run out. Within minutes, I had arrived there. But I had to wait because there were a few tourists ahead of me. Most of them were buying pure Bolivian or Peruvian cocaine.

My turn finally came, and I asked the Devil for four bottles of morphine tablets. As he handed me the bottles, I still couldn't get over the fact that his facial features, straight black hair, and evil, beady, piercing eyes reminded me of Satan. I wasn't surprised when I heard the other customers call him the Devil. The pharmacist was proud of the name.

I thought I was purchasing these drugs legally. I found out later that it was illegal to purchase narcotics without a prescription, but the Devil sold them anyway. However, we had to be discreet. If he were ever caught, the Afghan government would execute him by firing squad—and anyone else who was involved.

I purchased my four bottles of the evil narcotic for approximately thirteen dollars. I thought this should last me nearly a month. Lately I had been doing one or two tablets two or three times a day. Once in the morning, once in the afternoon, and once before I went to bed. My tolerance to the morphine was building up. I was injecting more and more to get the same high, since only a week before I had injected half a tablet. I didn't really care about addiction as long as I didn't run out.

As soon as I arrived in my hotel room, I went directly to my dope kit and cooked up the last two morphine tablets from my first bottle, which Jim and I had purchased when we first arrived in Kabul. As I injected the heavy, evil narcotic into my bloodstream, I felt a hot and tingly sensation rush through my body an inch at a time. I lay back onto the bed to enjoy the rush and fell right to sleep.

For the next week or so, nothing exciting happened. I was becoming very nervous and depressed waiting for the money to arrive at the bank. I was very nearly broke and had less than ten dollars in my pocket. I thought the money from America would arrive any day now. In fact, I began checking the Kabul bank every day, and then I would visit the post office to see Saraj and Mr. Ramazie.

Larry and I were still playing guitars, and I was still writing songs. I had written enough to fill an album. Although we didn't have anything to record with, we still had lots of fun.

One day, as Larry and I were playing our guitars, the manager of the hotel came into my room.

"You must leave the hotel because we are going to remodel. You will have two days to find another hotel," said the manager.

"Do you want to move into our hotel room now?" asked Larry.

"Okay, you finally talked me into it."

I had finally agreed to become their roommate. I left a message with the hotel manager just in case Jim and Ron returned to Kabul, letting them know that I had moved to the Mustafa Hotel to Larry and Billy's room.

I packed what few possessions I had into my bag, including my guitar, slung it over my shoulder, and walked over to the hotel. Larry and Billy had a very large room that had three beds, plus a table and chairs. My new room was on the second floor, overlooking one of Kabul's main roads, Chicken Street.

During the first week at this hotel, I met many other tourists from all parts of the world. Most of them were returning from India and talked of the atrocities that the Muslims were doing to the Hindus and Buddhists in East Pakistan. The Pakistani people called it "ethnic cleansing."

In my eyes, these Pakistani butchers were killing innocent civilians and were nothing but thugs and murderers. It was also rumored that India would soon intercede to help the innocent victims. This could start a war between the two countries and that could lead to a World War. 1971 was nearly over and it seemed the whole world was going "mad."

I wondered about Jim and Ron and hoped that they were safe and out of harm's way.

Right now, my only worry was about money, or lack of it. I had five dollars left and would be out of funds within a week. It had been over two weeks since I had sent the envelopes and packages. I hoped and prayed that the money had been wired to the bank. The following morning I would find out. Then I'd visit the post office.

Larry and I spent most of our days playing guitar just to pass the time. When it was time for bed, I always invited him and Billy to share my morphine. Usually they declined my invitation, but on this night, I was surprised that they wanted to split a tab between them. So I gave them a morphine tablet and I fixed myself two, while Larry and Billy smoked theirs, using aluminum foil and a straw. I lay back on the bed and let the hot, tingly, euphoric rush creep through my body. I was asleep within a few minutes.

The next morning after breakfast, I headed for the bank. I had a strong feeling that money was there for me.

I walked into the bank with an optimistic outlook and asked the teller for the book that listed the out-of-country money transfers. As I looked at the list of names, my excitement heightened when I saw my name listed in three places. Finally, my money had arrived from three different friends. However, nothing yet from the people I had sent the packages to. I just figured it would take a little longer for the parcels to arrive, so I wasn't really worried. Right now, I was about to collect over two thousand dollars. I was finally on my way to my dream. Saraj had come through for me once again.

I left the bank with two-thousand and fifty-two American dollars. I also exchanged a hundred of that for an equal amount of Afghani dollars. Although the current exchange rate was lower than a week ago, I still received ninety-eight-Afghani to the dollar. A week before, it was one-hundred and three to the dollar.

I placed my newly acquired funds into my hidden money belt and walked over to the post office to see Saraj. I needed to tell him that I had moved into another hotel. Saraj greeted me with a big smile. I was only able to speak with him for a few minutes due to his heavy workload.

"Saraj, I will have more envelopes to send," I whispered.

"Bring no more than six a day," he replied.

"Don't forget to stop by my new hotel room, and I will give you the money I owe you."

"Very good," he said. A big grin crossed his face.

"I have to leave now, but I'll see you later."

I left the post office and went to find my new hash maker, Tiar. I needed at least one more kilo of hash. I walked down that filthy, stinky alleyway to Tiar's mud fortress. He greeted me with a big smile and open arms.

"How are you, Tiar? I need another kilo of hash," I told him enthusiastically.

He invited me into his house and to the bedroom where I explained to him that I wanted another kilo of hash made into one hundred-gram postcard-size slabs like he had made before. He was happy to oblige. He pulled out a big bag of reddish-green pollen similar to the stuff we had used before. He also showed me a twenty-five pound bag of raw Badakhsan opium that he had purchased near the Russian-Chinese border. It was the largest quantity and freshest opium I had ever seen. Tiar said it was the best in the world with about fifteen percent morphine base. Although it was excellent opium, I wasn't interested at this time. I needed hashish. Tiar mentioned how he had just returned from an excursion trip to the provinces of Badakhsan and Balkh. He had purchased his hash from the city of Mazare Sarif.

As we talked, Tiar's wife entered the room offering tea and cookies. One of his sons brought in the hot charcoal stove as Tiar placed the large plastic sheet on the floor, as he had done many times before. Then he dumped a kilo of pollen onto it and began his hash making ritual. He went through the same steps as he had done before. Nearly two hours after I had arrived, the process was complete and I had eleven one hundred-gram slabs. I paid Tiar, thanked him, and headed for the rat-infested alley.

Once I reached the street, I hailed a taxi to take me to my hotel room. I showed Larry and Billy the hash I had just purchased. I told them not to let anyone into the room until I had finished making up the envelopes. Each slab fit perfectly between two post cards. I always wrapped them in cellophane to keep the skunky smell down. When I was finished, I had eleven one hundred-gram envelopes ready to be sent to America.

When I finished my work, we decided to celebrate. While we were singing and playing our guitars, a couple of nice-looking girls with French accents visited our room.

"Do you guys have any cocaine?" asked the tall and slinky redhead.

"No, all we have is hash and morphine," I told her.

As we introduced ourselves, the tall redhead, named Uby, walked over and sat next to me on my bed and asked me for a favor.

"Rob, can you loan me five-hundred Afghani? My lover will pay you back this evening."

After explaining who her lover was, I became more relaxed. I had seen him at the hotel at different times, so I believed her story. I thought I could trust her, and it was only five dollars, so I loaned her the money. The girls left, but not before Uby also borrowed a tablet of morphine from me.

There were more and more tourists in town. They were all coming from India, as had Uby and her companions. War had broken out between India and West Pakistan over atrocities in East Pakistan. All the hippies were filling up the hotels and the Afghan people were getting angry with all the trashy tourists.

A few hours after the two girls had left our room, Uby's lover stopped by.

"Have you seen my two French girlfriends?" he asked.

"They were here two hours ago and borrowed five-hundred Afghani from me, and you're supposed to pay me back," I told him.

He looked bewildered, confused, and surprised. "They tricked you. They are nothing but cocaine junkies and whores," he replied.

"You're kidding?"

"No, I'm not," he said. "Uby's the worst. She's strung out on cocaine and gets her money for food and dope by selling her body or conning other tourists. She's even visited different embassies, like the American Embassy, and asked them for money."

"Are you kidding? The American Embassy wouldn't give money to a junkie."

"The American Embassy always gave her ten or twenty dollars each time she went there," he said.

Hell, every time I needed help from the American Embassy they refused to help me. They would let me starve or die first before they would help me. That's America for you. They will help anyone else, but not their own people.

That French girl might have ripped me off for now, but I would see her again. She would either return the money or I'd take it out in trade. Not for myself, but for my customs connections, Saraj and Mr. Ramazie. That was something to think about anyway. Uby's lover left the room while Larry, Billy, and I continued to party throughout the night. I met many different people that night.

Over the next couple of days, I sent many hash envelopes to my friends in America. My friends who had received the envelopes told me in their letters that everything went perfect. So the envelopes I had just sent them should make it, also. But I still hadn't heard anything about the two parcels that I had sent. Other than that, everything was going as planned.

A few weeks after I had purchased my guitar, we were awakened by a loud knock on our hotel room door. Surprise, surprise— it was Jim and Ron returning from India. We hugged each other and shook hands. I was really happy to see them.

"Jim, did you have any trouble finding my new hotel room?" I asked him.

"No. The manager at the Najib Hotel told us where you were staying."

We had a lot to talk about. They told me about their trip to India. I guess the deal Ron put together didn't turn out too well. He evidently didn't have it together like he said he had, and they ran into a little trouble at the Afghan-Pakistan border.

Their story began when Ron met a man in a Kandahar shoe store who told him how to smuggle hash into Pakistan and then to India, where they could send it to America. They had purchased twenty different pairs of boots and shoes made with hash between the soles—similar to the ones that I had made, except not all of them were made correctly. Some were made very poorly. When Jim and

Ron had reached the Afghan customs office, the officials checked and searched their baggage very closely. The minute they located the many pairs of boots and shoes, they took a pen knife and began scraping and peeling away pieces of hash from the soles onto the table.

Jim said he nearly shit his pants when he saw that the customs official had found eight pairs of shoes with hash in them. Even though all twenty pair of shoes and boots had hash in them, they were allowed to keep twelve pair. However, after the customs officer and his partners had discussed the situation, they decided to throw Jim and Ron into jail. When Jim heard that, he began begging and pleading with them for leniency. He asked them if there was another way they could handle the situation, like paying a fine instead of going to jail. Again, the customs officials discussed the situation and told Jim that he must pay a one- thousand dollar fine or go to jail. Luckily, Jim had just enough money to get them out of their bind.

Once Jim had paid the fine, they only had twenty dollars between them. They even had to sell some of their hash to tourists and traded some with a Pakistani fisherman for fresh lobster because they couldn't afford to buy food.

After waiting a week or so, they received a wire transfer from America and finally had enough money to travel to Bombay, India, where they had to sell one pair of their boots to a tourist just to get enough money to send their other ten pair by ship to America. And then they were ordered to leave the country due to the conflict between India and East and West Pakistan.

Jim and Ron finally arrived in Kabul broke and hungry. Now the tables were turned. I had money and they didn't. After breakfast, I paid Jim the money that I owed him, giving him five-hundred dollars. He was very surprised and elated and asked me to go shopping with him. He was returning to America in a few days because he was homesick. He also wanted to get home before his packages arrived from India. He did promise, though, to return to Kabul within six months. But I didn't believe it. I told him again that he would go back home, marry his girlfriend Martha, finish college, and never return to Kabul.

"We'll see," Jim replied.

Ron, however, decided to stay in Kabul for a while. But for the time being, Jim and Ron moved in with Larry, Billy, and me. So we had to have the hotel manager add two more beds to the room. Now the room was a little crowded.

The next morning I went out and rented a brand-new four-wheel-drive Toyota Land Rover, then returned to the hotel and picked up Jim so he and I could go shopping at the better clothing stores. After visiting a few of the high-class shops we finally got the deal we wanted and purchased fur coats for each of us. Jim purchased a full-length, white rabbit fur coat and I bought a half-length snow fox. They would cost over a thousand dollars in America. Here, they cost about a hundred dollars.

I also purchased a couple of Afghan carpets and two antique, handmade Afghan flintlock rifles. One was a long-barreled rifle and the other was a smaller, horn-shaped barreled rifle called a "blunderbuss." Their stocks were all carved in ivory inlay. However, before they could be taken out of the country, I would have to get them stamped at the Kabul museum, and I did the very next day.

When Jim and I arrived there, we walked directly to the antiquities office. As the antiquities expert inspected the rifles, I asked him if they were real or reproductions. He told me that they were not fakes, but real antiques. I was very happy to hear that.

After the official stamped them, I thanked him and then browsed around the beautiful museum. It was filled with exquisite treasures. I was surprised to see that the jewels and its riches were left unguarded. With so many low-life junkies in town, they should have had the museum full of guards. Although we were there for only an hour, I didn't see anyone else visiting the museum.

When we returned to our hotel room, I asked Jim for a favor.

"Jim, would you take some of my gifts to my parents?"

"Sure, I don't mind."

He would take whatever I wanted. It wouldn't be too much, just a couple of handmade Afghani carpets, two antique flintlock pistols, and two antique flintlock rifles. The fur coat I would send at a later date.

The day before Jim departed Kabul, I rented a large two-bedroom apartment only walking distance to the center of town. One of the bedrooms even had a small fireplace in it. It also included a big living room, a big kitchen, a bathroom with two toilets—one for the male and one for the female—and a bathtub with a shower. Plus an electric hot water heater, a rarity in Kabul. The apartment also had a balcony that overlooked a garage and a side road that led to the airport. It was only a hundred and twenty-five dollars a month. At least now Jim would have a place to stay if and when he returned.

Now we could move into the apartment. Larry and Billy decided to stay at the hotel. They were getting ready to travel back to Europe and were waiting for Eric and Mark to return from West Pakistan. They would be arriving within a few days, due to the war.

I thought about Mark more and more, wondering how he was doing. He only had fifty dollars when he left Kabul nearly ten months before to travel to West Pakistan.

When Jim, Ron, and I arrived at my new apartment, we were amazed with the size of the rooms, especially the bedrooms. So I chose the one with the fireplace and Jim and Ron shared the other. Each room contained two double beds made of wood and hemp rope.

That night we celebrated Jim's departure from Afghanistan. He wanted to inject morphine one last time, so I obliged him. But when I asked him if he wanted to carry hash with him back to the States, he refused. He was too paranoid. He was flying from Kabul to Beirut to Paris, then to New York. So instead, I gave him gifts to take to my parents because Christmas was only forty days away.

Well, Jim was leaving, but I wasn't going anywhere. Even though my visa had expired, I decided to stay put. My business was just getting started and beginning to pay dividends.

I gave Jim a ride to the airport in my rental car. I had to return it that day anyway. I had rented it for five days. And during that time, I had spent a lot of money. So I would have to check the bank to see if any more money had arrived. I was sure it had because most of my hash envelopes should have arrived by now. And I was still waiting for money transfers from my friends concerning the two parcels containing the boots. Then, once I had checked the bank, I wanted to stop by the post office and invite Saraj and Mr. Ramazie over to my new apartment.

Before returning to the apartment, I stopped at an electronics store to buy a small portable cassette player and recorder. I needed to hear music other than my own. Plus I could use it to record my own songs. So I bought a decent Panasonic recorder for thirty dollars. It was worth every penny. Now I could have my friends in America send me the latest rock and roll cassette tapes of my favorite groups.

When I finally returned to the apartment, Ron was waiting for me. I showed him my new cassette recorder as we talked about the future.

"Rob, I've decided to return to Kandahar for a week or so to see my Afghan friend who helped me get the hash shoes made," he exclaimed. "I'll return to Kabul within a week or so."

"Ron, I'll be here when you return, so you know where to find me."

Ron kept his word and was gone the next morning. I was alone once again, but this time in my own apartment.

During the next few days, I visited Larry and Billy at their hotel room and they visited me at my apartment to play our guitars and talk.

"Larry, do you guys want to stay with me at my apartment?" I asked them. But they refused my invitation again.

"No, we will be leaving for Europe in the next couple of days," Larry replied. "That is, as soon as Eric returns from West Pakistan."

"When is that going to be?" I asked.

"The last letter Eric sent to me was three days ago," replied Larry. "It states that he would be in Kabul within a week."

"Did he mention anything about Mark?" I asked.

"He did. He said Mark was coming with him."

That was good news. I wanted to see how Mark was doing. Now that I had money, I was hoping he would be my business partner again.

Larry and Billy were worried about Eric's morphine habit.

"I wonder if Mark is still doing morphine?" I asked, to no one in particular.

"Eric stated in his letter that he was doing four morphine tablets in each injection, four or five times a day. He didn't mention anything about Mark's morphine habit," replied Larry.

Boy, he is addicted, I thought. Mark was probably just as strung out.

"Larry, if Mark comes to your hotel room, show him where I live and tell him that he can stay with me at my apartment. Would you do that for me?"

"Sure, why not."

That was the last time I would see Larry and Billy.

Two days later, someone was knocking at my apartment door. I got up to answer it. To my surprise, Mark was standing in the second floor corridor. I was in shock. He had much longer hair and a thick, long beard. I was very happy to see him. We didn't say a word; we just hugged each other. After a minute or so, the silence was broken.

"Mark, you can stay here with me," I told him.

"Great. I need a place to stay."

I invited him into my apartment and we walked into my bed-room.

"Are you still doing morphine?" I asked him.

"Yeah, I am."

"Do you want to celebrate this happy occasion with me and do some now?"

Mark just smiled and nodded his head. Just as I was about to ask him if he had a syringe, he pulled his dope kit from a small bag hidden in his boot. I didn't even bother to ask how many tablets he wanted. I just gave each of us four tabs. Hell, this was a day to celebrate. I hadn't seen him in over ten months. We had many tales and adventures to tell each other. This would be the first day of many that we would get high together.

I explained to him about the business I had started with a customs official.

"Mark, you can work for me. And you can stay here with me."

He agreed to work for me, if you call it work.

Business was going so good that I began selling hash packages to tourists. I would even send the packages to the destination of their choice, for a price. Through these people, I had met others who had their own secret ways of smuggling hash out of Afghanistan to Europe and America. One was an American hippie named Morgan, whom I had met while visiting a moneychanger in the bazaar. And at the time, he was under police guard. He explained to me that he had been arrested when the house at which he had been staying was searched for drugs and all the people there were taken to jail.

"Morgan, if you ever get out of jail, look me up," I told him.

"Where can I meet you?" he asked.

"Check out the restaurants on Chicken Street. I will probably be at Ziggy's. It's a restaurant-hotel for hippies."

"I have some good connections for smuggling hash."

I didn't know if he was truthful or not. He was in police custody, so how good could his connections be? They sure hadn't kept him out of jail.

After I exchanged American dollars for Afghan dollars, getting only ninety-Afghani to the dollar, I returned to my apartment.

Mark and I began experimenting with different ways of concealing hash. We even started using plaster casts, trying to mold the hash into different shapes and sizes, mostly of animals, such as elephants and camels.

First, I would wrap the hash completely in cellophane. Then I would tightly wrap electrical tape around it. This kept it waterproof. As I poured the plaster of paris into the mold, I would drop pieces of wrapped hash into it. Once the mold was completely full, we had to wait twenty-four hours for the plaster to harden. Then I had an Afghan paint them. Even though we had good results, I never sent any of the plaster castings. They broke too easily. They just weren't durable enough. We tried many different ideas.

One guy I helped to smuggle hash was from Australia. His father was a big, important scientist on the nuclear power commission.

I placed four one hundred-gram hash slabs that were sealed in cellophane into the walls of a cardboard box, placing one slab into each side. After peeling away the inside top layer of paper from the corrugated cardboard, I would then cut out the corrugated section in the middle of each side to the exact size of the slab, then glue the paper back to its original position, thus hiding the hash. Then I would put that box inside of a larger box, and put that one into an even larger one until I had four boxes within each other, hiding the hash. Then I filled the box with cheap tourist gifts.

I sent two of these hash boxes to the president of the nuclear commission in Australia. Two weeks after sending them, my friend wrote me thanking me for helping him. Both boxes had arrived safely to their destination.

I had sent nearly one kilo of hash for him and made nearly two thousand dollars on that deal. He was only one of many I had helped smuggle hash out of Afghanistan.

Business was so good that I began buying handmade Afghan carpets, sheepskin coats, and many other kinds of Afghan merchandise, such as lapis lazuli and other exotic items. I had bought so much stuff that the floor of my twenty-by-twenty-foot living room was wall to wall in thick, plush, handmade carpets. I had purchased carpets from every province of Afghanistan. However, the most colorful carpets I had were made in Armenia, Russia.

Another tourist I had met was a longhaired hippie from Colorado. He had just traveled from Japan and Thailand. He had purchased a beautiful Yamaha F.G. #300 acoustic guitar with a plush-lined case while he had visited Japan. I fell in love with his guitar and pleaded with him to trade or sell it to me. I offered to trade him my guitar, some carpets, and anything else he wanted. I even offered to send him hash when he returned to America. That caught his attention. We had finally agreed on a price. Actually, he wanted more than the guitar was worth, but I wanted that guitar. It was beautiful, and the tone was immaculate. I gave him his pick of any three carpets, my guitar, one hundred American dollars, and promised to send hash to his address in Colorado. We were both happy with our transaction. He gathered his newly acquired merchandise and walked out the door. I never saw him again.

One day, while I was out shopping for carpets, I ran into Morgan. However, this time, he was alone and free. He said he had paid a fine and they let him go. After rapping for a few minutes, he invited me to the house at which he was staying. He was living with some Californian hippies who called themselves the "Motherhood of Eternal Love." They smuggled hash and something new called "hash oil" into America.

So we hopped into a taxi and went to his place. Once there, he introduced me to his roommates. One who caught my eye was a girl from Japan. Her father was the Japanese ambassador to Afghanistan. We started talking and she told me that she traveled from Kabul to Hong Kong three times a year with kilos of Affy hash that she smuggled into the country, using the diplomatic pouch, and sold it to some big Kung Fu star named Bruce Lee. At the time, I didn't recognize the name. I was more interested in buying rock and roll cassette tapes, which she was selling. Many were of my favorite rock groups, like the Rolling Stones, the Beatles, the Kinks, and many other great bands. She wanted five American dollars per cassette. So I bought ten of them.

Before I departed, I gave Morgan a map to my apartment and invited him to stop by anytime.

"Morgan, you are always welcome at my place."

As I was saying goodbye to everyone, one of the Californian hippies named John took me aside and asked me a few questions.

"Rob, would you be interested in smuggling hash in false-bottom suitcases to Denmark?" he asked.

"I don't think so, John."

"Our plan is foolproof," he bragged. "Nothing can possibly go wrong. We haven't lost one suitcase in two years."

"Sorry, but I'm not interested. I am never going to leave Kabul, and I have my own connections that help me smuggle hash to America."

With that, I shut the door behind me and flagged down a taxi to return to my apartment. The next couple of days, I continued to check out the bank and post office. The money was coming in regularly and steadily, and the hash was going out steadily and regularly.

One early morning, Morgan knocked on my apartment door. He was with someone I didn't know. The way this person was dressed, I didn't know if he was a tourist or a true Afghani. He wore the typical Afghan clothing, including a white turban on his head. I was surprised to hear that he was a Canadian living north of Kabul in a small town called Paghman. His name was Ted. His hobby—raising and breeding fighting Koochie dogs.

"Rob, are you interested in working for me?" asked Ted.

"Doing what?"

"Making false-bottom suitcases that I sell to tourists. I will supply everything. Money to purchase the suitcases, plus the ten kilos of hash," he replied.

I was very interested, especially in learning how to make the suitcases. Because one day I might want to make my own false-bottom suitcases, so I agreed.

He returned in the morning with the money and instructions. The first task was to find as many bricks as possible. We would use these for weight when we glued the hash to the bottom of the suitcases. That was my first instruction.

I asked Mark if he would help me. When he agreed, I had him find the bricks. He didn't have far to look. Luckily, someone had built a small brick barbecue stove outside on the balcony and there were loose ones sitting to the side.

The next day, Ted stopped by again. He owned a nice VW van that he used for his transportation. I had dreamed about owning one some day. He gave me one hundred U.S. dollars and told me the brand of suitcase to buy. I needed to purchase two of them. He would bring the hash over as soon as it was pressed. He was having it made in Paghman. He also told me the brand of glue to purchase along with brushes and rubber gloves.

Ted had one bad habit: He never seemed to ask us, he TOLD us. He was always trying to boss us around, like we were just his slaves. I didn't like this guy's attitude, but I kept my mouth shut.

I had Mark go out and purchase suitcases made of a hard plastic. When that was done, we had to pull out the cloth fabric that lined each one. Once that task had been completed, the next step was to glue the hashish to the bottom of each case. But Ted hadn't brought the hash over yet. He was to bring it the following morning.

Mark and I just passed the time away by getting high and playing our music. Now that we had a cassette player and tape recorder to listen to all the new rock and roll tapes, we were having a great time. We never had it so good. We ate good food. We had the best and purest pharmaceutical drugs available, and we listened to great music. The only thing that was missing was women. I started thinking more and more about them.

I decided to write to a beautiful girl I had known in Michigan named Carol. I wanted to ask her if she wanted to visit Kabul and live with me. That's exactly what I did. Over the next few days, I wrote to her a number of times asking her if she would come and live with me. I waited patiently for her reply.

In the meantime, Ted had finally brought over the ten kilos of hash. It had all been pressed in a hydraulic press. The rectangular slabs were all the same exact size and weight. But the hash was just average. Ted said he'd paid two dollars a kilo. I didn't believe him. That was super cheap. I didn't mind paying a little more for my hash. I was happy to help out the Afghan people.

Ted looked over the suitcases and the work that Mark and I had done. He started yelling and screaming at me. He ranted and raved about not pulling out the fabric correctly. He was like a madman, a lunatic. I became angry.

"Ted, I don't need your money that bad to take your abuse. Get the hell out of my apartment, and you can take your suitcases and hash and shove them up your ass!" I yelled, as I threw the suitcases toward his feet.

Now it was my turn to rant and rave. I grabbed his suitcases and threw them out my front door.

"Get your ass out of my house and never come back!" I bellowed.

Within ten minutes, a young couple in their early twenties came to my apartment to apologize for Ted's idiotic behavior. They wanted me to complete the suitcases. They were being made for him and his girlfriend.

"Please reconsider and finish our suitcases," said the young man.

"Forget it. I don't want any part of it," I bellowed.

"Won't you reconsider?" asked the young man's girlfriend.

"No. I'm not going to change my mind, so please leave my house." I pointed to my front door.

With that, they turned and left.

Mark agreed with my actions. He didn't like Ted's attitude, either.

"Ted acted like a Nazi," Mark opined. "He treated us like we were his slaves."

"Not any more. I took care of that."

I sure didn't need Ted's money now. I was sending more and more hash envelopes to America each week. My packages, though, never paid off. One of them made it to its destination. But when my friend opened the parcel, he noticed that one of the boot's soles had been ripped open. The seam on one side of the boot had split open, showing the hash.

Within five minutes of opening the package, the FBI and the local police entered his house and searched it. They found the package immediately. They also found many letters that I had written to him, explaining my plans. Luckily, I never signed my name to them. I signed them with an alias.

The FBI confiscated the boots, package, and letters. My friend also lucked out. They never prosecuted him. He told them he was about to telephone the police to turn in the illegal contraband, but before he had the chance to do anything and before he was over the shock and surprise from the contents of the package, the police were breaking down his door. The prosecuting attorney believed him and let him off scot-free.

The other package I sent supposedly never arrived at its destination. I never sent either person another gram of hash. They were off my address list for good, and I would never write to them again.

However, I did receive letters from Jim and my dream girl, Carol. Jim had taken my gifts to my parent's house. He wrote that they were happy to hear from him and that my parents liked the gifts. He also stated in his letter that he and Martha were going to get married and that he was back in school for a semester and might return to Kabul for a short vacation during his semester break.

Carol wrote that she would love to come and live with me in Kabul and that she couldn't wait to see me. She also stated that there wasn't anything around except for my Affy hash, which people were selling for twenty dollars a gram. Carol promised that we would have a ball when she arrived, so I started making plans to get her here as soon as possible. I was hoping to have her in Kabul by Christmas. I would try, anyway. It was only three weeks away, so I had to work like crazy to get her there in such a short time.

I had to tell Saraj about Carol as soon as possible. I wanted to send Carol six hash envelopes to sell so she could buy her plane ticket to Afghanistan. And I wanted to make sure all of the envelopes would arrive at their destination safely, without any problems.

After explaining the situation to Saraj, he was very happy to help me and very anxious to meet my girlfriend.

"Saraj, I will bring the envelopes in a day or two. And don't forget our Christmas Eve party," I reminded him.

"Can I bring my cousin along?" he asked.

"Of course, bring him along. The more the merrier."

A week later, Ron returned from his trip to Kandahar completely out of money and with no place to stay. He told me about his trip, and his friend in Kandahar named Mammed. When Ron returned to Kabul, so did his friend. He came to open up a clothing store—but there was just one catch. He didn't have the money to open it. So Ron suggested I loan him the five-hundred dollars to help get it started.

"Ron, I don't want to talk business right now. I'm not in the mood. I *am* glad to see you, though. You can use one of the beds in Mark's bedroom."

Now there were three of us living at my apartment. At least it was better than living alone. Ron, Mark, and I talked the night away, catching up on the past week's news. I let Ron read the letter that Jim had sent.

"Jim says he's getting married to Martha," stated Ron.

"Yep, he's also going to return to Kabul," I replied. "You guys do know that I'm trying to bring Carol to Kabul, don't you?"

"Rob, can you help me bring my girlfriend to Kabul?" Ron pleaded.

"I guess I can help you. It'll be nice to have a couple of women around here.

I started making up envelopes to send to his girlfriend in Michigan. She would have to do the same as Carol and sell its contents. And she wouldn't have any problem because Jim could sell it for her. Carol had her own friends to whom she could sell the hash.

Now I had made plans to bring both girls to Kabul. I just hoped that Carol would arrive first. She should have received her envelopes by now.

Over the next few days, I was busy having hash made. I wanted to send as many envelopes to America as possible. It was Christmastime, and every post office in the world was very busy. I figured everything I sent should get through during this time.

One day near Christmas, Ron brought over his Afghan friend, Mammed. Ron introduced me to him and went directly into a sales pitch about opening up a store. I had always been interested in opening a legitimate enterprise, but I was a foreigner. I wasn't allowed to own a business, but Mammed could. I figured if I loaned him the money, I would have an Afghan working for me and be part owner in a clothing store. So this was my chance. Ron and I stepped into the back bedroom to talk.

"Rob, all you have to do is loan me five hundred dollars, and I promise to pay you back with interest. I will pay the loan off within a few months. Plus, you'll get a percentage of the profits and business," Ron promised.

"Ron, I'll bet you this guy will rip us off. It's just a scam to get money from us," I told him.

But Ron kept nagging me for the loan. So to get him to shut up, I agreed to his business proposal even though I had a funny feeling that I would never get my money back.

"Thanks, Rob," he replied happily, then shook my hand.

"Ron, I'm telling you, once this guy receives this money, he'll disappear. He'll return to Kandahar or go to another city in Afghanistan," I predicted. "The guy would be rich with five-hundred dollars in his pocket. But I will loan *you* the money, so you're responsible for it."

We returned to my bedroom where Mammed was waiting.

Ron and his friend were very happy when I reached into my pocket and pulled out a wad of hundred dollar bills. I counted out five one- hundred American dollar bills and handed them to Ron. Just as I did that, a premonition came over me.

"Ron, within a few months' time, your friend will leave the city and never return. And we will never see him again," I predicted once again.

But he refused to listen to my predictions. He trusted this guy with his life. But Ron was naive. Ron also told me that I could sell my merchandise at the store when he opened it. So now they would have to rent a building.

A few minutes later, the room was quiet again. The minute they received the money, they disappeared. I went into my bedroom and began writing letters to friends in America.

It was a few days before Christmas, and I was getting nervous, wondering if and when Carol would arrive in Kabul. I was very anxious for her arrival. I had never been to bed with Carol or kissed her, for that matter. She was just a very close friend. She had been the girlfriend of another friend of mine, but they had broken up nearly a year before. I was hoping that if she liked me enough, she would stay and live with me. She was very beautiful, with long, flowing, straight, black hair, and a very petite body at only five feet tall. But she was definitely all female. I had always fantasized about her and wondered how good she would be in bed. I would soon find out.

I finished writing my letters, and they were ready for mailing. So I headed for the post office to see Saraj. Ten minutes later, I was there and had given him all of my letters to send. I told him my girlfriend should be in Kabul very soon. We were both excited about her arrival. I also reminded Saraj about the party on Christmas Eve, which was just two days away.

I left the post office and headed for the pharmacy. I needed to buy a few more bottles of morphine. Mark and I had been going through a bottle every two days. Sometimes we were fixing three to four tablets each, two and three times a day.

Even though the exchange rate wasn't as strong as it had been, I was still receiving a decent rate of eighty-three Afghani to the dollar, down from one hundred.

At least the morphine was still cheap enough. It was now costing me approximately four dollars per bottle, up from three just a few weeks before. I still had two bottles left over from my last purchase, so I purchased five more from the Devil. I shoved the bottles into my shoulder bag, similar to a small leather pouch that many tourists carried, and headed toward Chicken Street.

That was all the major chores I had to do. I still had a few little things to do, though. I still needed to buy the liquor for the Christmas Eve party. I also wanted to stop at a carpentry shop near my apartment and have a case made to hold my cassette tapes. But this case would be a little different in design. I wanted a false bottom built into it so I could hide hash in it.

I decided to let Ron pick up the liquor. It was his recipe we were using to make the punch, and he was the person who would make it, so I decided to let him pick out the different liquors that were needed.

On my way to the carpenter shop, I ran into the French girl, Uby.

"I want the money that I loaned you," I snapped.

At first, she tried to deny that I had given her five-hundred Afghani. But after a few minutes of arguing, she backed down.

"I'm sorry. I am broke and don't have any money," she cried.

"Uby, do you want to work off your debt and even make some money?" I asked her.

She knew what I had in mind, but my question still surprised her.

"What did you have in mind?"

"It's not for me, but for some Afghan friends of mine."

I invited her to my apartment to talk over my plans. I decided to visit the carpenter shop at another time. As we talked about my idea, I showed Uby the apartment.

"You have a nice apartment," she remarked.

"Thank you. But I want to know, will you screw my Afghan friends? I want to give them a nice Christmas present."

I didn't tell her they were my customs connections, just good friends, and that I wanted to give them a Christmas surprise.

As we were sitting and talking, Uby became nervous and irritable.

"Can I shoot up some cocaine?" she asked.

"I don't care, Uby."

She began laying her dope kit out on my table.

"Do you have any morphine I could have?" she asked me.

"Yeah, I have a few tabs left."

"Can I have a tablet to mix with my cocaine?"

She called this mixture a speedball and explained how the morphine took the speedy cocaine high away. I really didn't know and didn't care. I had never tried that mixture before, so I took her word for it. I also fixed a few morphine tablets for myself.

Neither Ron nor Mark was around, so it was fairly quiet in the room. I tried to converse with her, but she told me to keep quiet as she injected her mixture of narcotics. Every time I tried to utter one word, she would tell me to shut up. I was getting very agitated and pissed off. This was my house, and I couldn't even speak.

Ten minutes later, she still had the needle in her vein. This is ridiculous, I thought to myself. She kept booting and rebooting into her vein. I just stared at her until I couldn't stand it any longer.

"Hurry up," I snapped.

Finally, after twenty minutes of silence and watching her shoot up, I wanted her to leave. She was ready to leave anyway.

"Can I borrow some money so I can go to the Devil's pharmacy and buy some cocaine?" she asked. "I am completely out, and I need to get some today or I'll be very sick. The Devil will give me four or five grams of pure Bolivian or Peruvian cocaine for five hundred Afghani."

She wanted me to give her money just to supply her habit. If that was the only way I could get rid of her, I decided to give it to her. As I handed her the money, I made her promise to return the following night to repay her debt with my Afghan friends.

"If you're really good with my Afghan friends, I will pay you extra. The better they like you, the better the tip. Plus, I will give you fifty dollars for each person," I promised her. "So be here around five tomorrow afternoon."

Uby agreed, then headed for the pharmacy.

Ron returned a few hours later. He had been at his friend's new store—the one in which I had invested.

"Ron, how is the new store doing?" I asked.

"Well, there is still more to do. Can we take some of your sheepskin coats and carpets to sell at the store? The store is too barren, and we need to stock it with more quality merchandise."

"I'll think about it, Ron. But right now, let's think about the party. You are going to be the bartender, so why don't you go out and buy the liquor and other ingredients that are needed."

I handed him thirty dollars, and he nodded in agreement, then walked out the front door to purchase the needed items.

Five minutes later, I was walking over to the carpenter shop. I spoke to the shop owner and explained what I wanted made. He didn't understand my language, so he called to his young twelve-year-old son to interpret for him. His son spoke very good English. So I explained to him the type of cassette case I wanted made.

We agreed on a price of ten dollars. The case would hold nearly one-hundred cassette tapes and two kilos of hash and would be finished in about ten days. They had a few other jobs to finish before they could start on my project. I gave them one-hundred Afghani as a down payment, then left the carpenter shop and headed for Chicken Street to buy a small Christmas tree.

This would be my first Christmas in Kabul and my first Christmas away from home and family. I got a kick out of decorating the Christmas tree. I was feeling great and on top of the world. Things couldn't be going any better.

I had picked out a nice tabletop spruce tree. It was only two feet tall, but it had a personality of its own. I also bought a few nice ornaments and a string of flashing Christmas lights. By the time Ron and Mark had returned, I had the tree decorated. And on the top of it, I had placed the Star of David. It was beautiful. It even brought a tear to my eye. And Ron and Mark were happily surprised. They loved the little tree. We toasted a bowl of hash to our Christmas tree.

It was also Mark and Ron's first Christmas in Afghanistan. Now I had to buy presents for each of them. I bought Mark three bottles of morphine and wrapped them in two one-hundred dollar bills. I was sure he would like his present. The last Christmas present I had given him was a half ounce of Affy hash when I lived with Bill and Sue about three years before. I couldn't decide what to get Ron. I had already sent the envelopes of hash to his girlfriend. That should have been enough, but I still had a day to think about it.

Finally, I ended up buying Ron, Saraj, and Saraj's cousin each a wool scarf and a pair of black leather gloves lined with rabbit fur. I thought they would enjoy that. Now I was ready for Christmas. The following night was Christmas Eve. We would have a great party.

The next day couldn't come fast enough for me. I was up early and began cleaning the house for the party.

Ron went out to buy a few more bottles of liquor and a few other essentials, which he had forgotten the day before. Mark was helping me sweep and clean. By mid-afternoon, the apartment was spotless. We sat down and relaxed and listened to rock music while staring at the flashing lights on the Christmas tree.

Within a few hours, Uby would be over to service my Afghan friends. This was going to be a great surprise to them. I just hoped they wouldn't turn my Christmas gifts away. I was sure they wouldn't.

Ron had the punch mixed so well that you couldn't taste any alcohol at all. It was against the Muslim religion to drink alcohol, so it couldn't smell or taste of it. And Ron had mixed it perfectly. It tasted like lemonade. He set the bowl of punch outside on the balcony to chill.

Within a few hours would be Christmas Eve, and then Christmas. It gave me goose bumps just thinking about it. Here we were celebrating Christmas halfway around the world, a place from which the three wise men had come to bestow gifts to the newborn child called Jesus. Even though I was agnostic at the time, I felt closer to the Supreme Being than ever before.

Around seven that evening, someone was knocking at my front door. I answered it. I was happy to see Uby standing there. I invited her into my apartment and introduced her to Ron and Mark. As we talked, there was another knock at the door. This time it was Saraj and his cousin, Abdul. He was very short, maybe five feet tall. Standing next to Saraj he looked like a midget. I greeted them in the Afghan tradition, kissing their cheeks on each side and then placing my right hand over my heart. I invited them into the bedroom that we had set up for the party and then introduced them to everyone.

Uby was the only female in the room. Saraj couldn't keep his eyes off her. He stared at her and seemed to be mesmerized by her presence. Ron handed everyone an empty glass and proceeded to fill them with his exotic mixture of potions. Everyone liked his punch.

We raised our glasses in the air and toasted Afghanistan, Christmas, and good friends. Within a few minutes, Saraj and Abdul were feeling very happy. They weren't as quiet and shy as they had been when they'd first arrived, and now they began to flirt with Uby. After serving them another drink or two, they were ready to receive their gifts.

"Saraj, I have a Christmas present for you and Abdul. Do you want some French love from Uby?" I asked, as I watched both their faces turn beet red.

Their faces lit up like the Christmas tree lights. Once they picked up their jaws from the floor and overcame the shock and surprise of my question, they couldn't say the word fast enough.

"Yes," roared Saraj, while Abdul just grinned.

"Do your stuff, Uby," I told her.

"Can I use one of your beds?" she asked.

"No, use the carpet on the bathroom floor."

She didn't seem to like the idea of lying on the bathroom floor, but there was more than enough room. I even handed her an extra carpet. Saraj and Abdul couldn't decide who was going to be first, so I flipped a coin. Abdul won and anxiously followed Uby into the bathroom. Saraj followed them to watch, but Abdul shut the bathroom door in his face.

I told Saraj to sit and wait in the bedroom with us. But he wanted to watch Uby and his cousin through the keyhole of the bathroom door, and I wouldn't let him. So he sat nervously waiting for his turn. But then, when we weren't looking, he would sneak to the bathroom and peer into the room through the crack in the door. I caught him more than once doing it. Saraj was a voyeur. After forty minutes, Abdul walked into the bedroom with a very wide grin on his face. His smile was so big and bright he could have lit up the room if the lights had been turned off.

Abdul told Saraj that Uby wanted him to go into the bathroom for his Christmas present. Saraj couldn't get there fast enough. However, within ten minutes, I was pounding on the bathroom door telling them to be quiet. Saraj was groaning so loud that you could hear him two blocks away. I had to pound on the door more than once. Finally, after thirty minutes, Saraj strolled into the bedroom walking on air, smiling and looking satisfied. Uby followed behind him. I handed them drinks and toasted the night. As we listened to music, talked, and continued to drink the punch, Mark and Uby excused themselves and left the apartment.

I handed Ron, Saraj, and Abdul their Christmas gifts. They thanked me as they opened them. We were all getting pretty drunk and the night was still early.

I asked them if they wanted to go bowling. There was a small four-lane bowling alley just a few blocks away from the apartment. It didn't have automatic pinsetters but pin boys. These young Afghan boys would sit above the pins, take away any fallen ones, and then reset each frame.

This was the only bowling alley in Kabul. Hell, it was the only bowling alley in Afghanistan. We agreed to go bowling even though Saraj and Abdul had never bowled before. I explained the strategy to them as we walked to the lanes. I told them that you roll a ball down the middle of the lane and try to knock all the pins down. If you don't get them all down on the first ball, you get another chance. I told them not to worry, that it was an easy and simple game.

When we arrived, there was only one young Afghan couple bowling. All the other lanes were empty—all three of them. I rented a lane and helped Saraj and Abdul pick out their balls so they would fit them correctly and wouldn't hurt their thumb or fingers. I wanted them to have fun. Saraj was throwing the ball every place else but the middle of the lane, mostly behind him. It was constantly slipping out of his hand, but he didn't care. He was having a ball. So was Abdul. They even threw the ball at the pin boy as he was clearing the fallen pins. They were outrageously funny. We were laughing hysterically.

We were so drunk and out of control that the young Afghan couple three lanes over were very angry with us for being so loud and boisterous. They didn't know what to think of us.

"Boy, Saraj, I would like to marry a beautiful Afghan woman like her," I said, pointing at the young lady who was staring at us.

She was one of the most beautiful Afghan women I had ever laid my eyes on. She was a ten plus. She was a modern, westernized Muslim woman who wore American-type clothes. Saraj said she was too expensive for me and that it would cost more than ten million Afghani to marry her. She was from a very wealthy family. She was in the league of kings and queens. Well, at least I could dream.

We bowled five games. We played until they closed the bowling alley.

Saraj and Abdul rented a taxi, taking them to Abdul's house. Ron and I walked back to the house. What a great night, I thought. Tomorrow was Christmas. I still had one present to give, and that was to Mark. He was waiting for us when we returned from the bowling alley. We toasted each other with one last glass of punch. Then we went to sleep to await the arrival of Christmas—our first Christmas away from home, halfway around the world. I still couldn't get over that thought.

I was the first to awake on Christmas morning. So I awakened Ron and Mark.

"Merry Christmas!" I shouted.

Before we did anything else, Mark and I did a large dose of morphine. I was so hung over from the night before that the morphine made me feel normal again. It made my cold body warm up instantly. After the hot rush subsided, I handed Mark his Christmas present.

"Merry Christmas, Mark," I exclaimed and then looked at Ron.

"Ron, I gave you your present last night and when I sent the envelopes to your girlfriend, Cindy."

"Rob, I didn't have the money to buy you a gift, and I want to thank you for letting me stay at your apartment and for helping me in my time of need," said a thankful Ron.

Mark thanked me, too. That's what Christmas is all about—not what you get, but what you give to others. It's better to give than to receive. At least that's the motto I live by.

Within a few hours, we would eat our Christmas dinner. I had cooked a nice turkey dinner. I made mashed potatoes and gravy, corn on the cob, and a nice salad with lemonade to drink. Mark and Ron helped set the table. It was an excellent meal and a great day. During our dinner, Mark mentioned that his Afghan visa expired in two days.

"Rob, I'm going to Pakistan for a while so I can renew my visa for Afghanistan," said Mark.

"I'll be here when you return to Kabul," I told him. "The door is always open."

Mark was like a brother to me. He was gone the next day.

Six more days and it would be New Year's—and my first New Year in Afghanistan. Each day seemed like a new experience for me. This was truly a magical adventure. I was a little unhappy and sad that Mark wasn't around. Ron was never around either. He was always visiting his friend's store. At least he could keep an eye on my merchandise and investment while he was there. The apartment was quiet, except when I played the cassette player. It gave me plenty of time to think.

Soon, Carol and Cindy should be arriving. I had expected Carol by Christmas, but she never made it. Now I was hoping by New Year's Day. The last letter I had received from her more than two weeks before stated that she had received all six hash envelopes and was in the process of selling it. She was still planning to visit but didn't give me an exact date of arrival. I still hadn't heard whether Cindy had received her envelopes yet. But I was too anxious for Carol's arrival to worry about Cindy. I would let Ron do that. I figured Carol would be my Christmas present—or should I say, my belated Christmas present. I could wait, but not much longer.

New Year's Day finally arrived and Ron had a big surprise for me. He had received two hits of windowpane acid from John, his roommate from Michigan, and wanted me to trip with him to celebrate the New Year. So when he offered me a hit of windowpane, I gladly accepted. It had been well over six months since I had tripped on acid. In fact, the last time had been at Ron's house just before we left for Afghanistan.

Ron placed his tab on his tongue and I did the same. It dissolved immediately. Within a few minutes an anxious feeling came over me, so I decided to walk to the carpenter shop to see how the cassette case was coming along.

As I walked into the shop, I noticed the young boy was working on it. When he saw me, he told me to sit down. But just as I did, a funny feeling came over me. I felt very light-headed, as everything seemed to bend out of shape and time seemed to speed up. Everything around me seemed to be exaggerated.

As I watched the boy, his actions and movements were followed by trails of colors. I was really getting off on this acid. I think the boy also noticed that I was high on something. As he smiled at me, his face seemed to distort and melt in an array of colors. I decided it was time to leave the shop. I told the boy I would be back the following morning and walked out the door.

When I returned to my apartment, Ron was still at home and just as stoned as I was. So I turned on the Christmas tree lights and cassette tape player. I played a Beatles tape, *Sgt. Pepper.* The music seemed to settle us down a bit. At least it relaxed me, but Ron couldn't sit still. He would pace back and forth in the room and constantly look out the big picture window, and then he would look at me in a funny way and say the same words repeatedly.

"They're coming for me."

"Ron, who's coming for you?" I asked.

But he never answered me. He just continued to pace back and forth in front of the window, and every few minutes he'd repeat the same words.

"They're coming to get me."

That's all he would say. He went on like this for two hours. I couldn't take his ranting and raving any longer.

"Ron, shut up and sit down. Nobody's coming for you. You're just a little bit too high," I told him.

That seemed to calm him down for a while, but it didn't last. He kept it up all night long. He would stand and stare out the window and then yell, "They're coming for me!"

When he really became paranoid, he would run from the bedroom, then hide in the bathroom for ten or fifteen minutes, and then return to the bedroom. The last time he said that phrase, "They're coming to get me," he ran into his bedroom and pulled the covers over his head trying to hide from whoever was coming after him. I didn't see or hear from him again until the next morning. I stayed up until the early morning hours tripping my brains out. This was sure some excellent acid.

For the next week or so, I passed the time buying hash, having it pressed, and making envelopes for Saraj to send. Then I would go to the bank to pick up the money that my friends had sent.

Finally, after waiting ten days, I picked up my cassette case from the carpenter shop. It turned out beautifully. It looked commercially built, but I still had to cover the outside with vinyl cloth. My cassette tapes fit perfectly.

Everything was going good for me. Now all that was missing was a woman. I expected Carol any day now. I had finally received a letter from her stating the day and time of arrival of her flight into Kabul. She would be arriving in less than a week.

But while I waited for her, I still had a few more envelopes to send out. Besides hash envelopes, I even sent a couple of morphine envelopes to a few friends in America. I crushed up the tablets and put them into the hash envelopes. I explained to them that it was pure pharmaceutical morphine and to only do a small match head of powder. It seemed they didn't believe the purity and did more than a match head. They did too much at one time because they wrote back saying it was the Devil's powder, that it was a death rush. They must have done five or six tablets worth of powder to get a rush that heavy. They just weren't used to pure narcotics. That was the problem. From that point on, I decided to only send the hash. I didn't want anyone dying on me.

I received another letter from Carol stating she would be in Kabul in two days. Now I was really getting excited. She couldn't get here fast enough as far as I was concerned. She had always been a fantasy to me, and my fantasy was about to come true.

While I was daydreaming about her arrival, I was interrupted by a loud knock on the door. As I opened it, rubbing my weary eyes, I got the shock of my life. To my surprise there was a gorgeous lady standing at my front door with a suitcase in her hand.

CHAPTER 13

THE GIRLS ARRIVE IN KABUL

This beautiful, blonde-haired girl standing at my apartment door wasn't Carol but another beautiful girl.

"Excuse me, is this Ron's apartment?" asked this beautiful blonde goddess.

"No, Ron is staying with me at my apartment. I'm Robert. You must be Cindy. Come on in, please."

"Yes, I'm Cindy. I'm glad to meet you. I have heard a lot about you," she said enthusiastically.

"Go wake Ron up," pointing to his bedroom.

For the next twenty or so minutes, all I heard was a bunch of muffled moans and smacking sounds. Finally, our house had a female presence. It had the smell of femininity and perfume. What heavenly odors. Cindy, a student at the University of Michigan, was a beautiful, twenty-year-old, blonde-haired, blue-eyed goddess with a soft, sexy, velvety, sultry voice. She was five feet six inches tall with long, flowing, straight, blonde hair and a 36-22-34 figure. Ron definitely had good taste. But mine was better—in my eyes, anyway. Carol was my dream girl.

A few days later, I was at Kabul airport awaiting Carol's arrival. The first time I went to meet her, she wasn't on the plane. So I immediately went to the post office to check for any letters that might explain her situation and why she had missed her first flight. Luckily, I found one. She didn't say why, but she had had to catch a later flight. I hoped she would be there by morning.

I was at the airport at the precise time her letter had stated. Again, she wasn't on the plane. I was confused and depressed. I thought for sure that she had flown on this flight. But now I didn't know what to think. Then I figured she must have missed her flight from Europe. Again, I went to the post office to check for any letters from her. This time, there wasn't one. So I decided to check the airport the following morning.

The next morning I was outside on the second level of the arrival deck, awaiting Carol's flight from England. As the people descended from the plane, I looked over every person until there wasn't anyone else to look at. I thought all of the passengers had disembarked, but after a one or two minute lull a few more passengers trickled out of the aircraft. Then I saw her. She was the last one off the plane. I was relieved.

Carol, my dream fantasy, had finally arrived. It was a great day for a celebration. I walked down to the lobby and waited as she went through customs. As she walked toward me, I walked up to her and gave her a big kiss and hug.

"Carol, I'm glad you're here," I said, with joy in my heart.

"I'm happy, too. We are going to have a ball when we get to your apartment," she promised, as she played with my crotch.

I was ready for it. I gathered her luggage and walked her to the taxi. As the taxi driver placed the luggage into the trunk, I put my arms around her, pulled her close to my body, and gave her a long, deep kiss. Our body heat was building to a feverish fire and our passion and desire was burning between our loins. Then the taxi driver interrupted our lovemaking. But Carol promised me a surprise when we reached the apartment.

"I can't wait," I told her, as we hopped into the taxi.

As I directed the taxi driver to my apartment, Carol and I held each other tight and fondled one another during our short ride. When we reached our destination, we couldn't get out of the cab fast enough. I grabbed Carol's baggage and then gave the taxi driver a big one-dollar tip. He was very happy and grateful as he drove away.

Then I escorted Carol to the apartment. I quickly unlocked the door and invited her in. As we walked from the hallway into the bedroom, I held her close to my side. Ron and Cindy came into the room, so I introduced them to her. We had all come from the same area in Michigan. My plans had worked out pretty well. The girls were finally here. It was no longer a dream or fantasy.

I helped Carol put her luggage away in my bedroom. Then, while putting her clothes away, Carol tried to strip me to give me my surprise. We began kissing and fondling each other but were soon interrupted with questions from Cindy about Carol's plane trip.

"Damn, Robert, I wanted to give you your surprise," said Carol, frustrated.

"We'll continue our sexcapade the first chance we get," I promised her.

She agreed, and then gave me a long "French" kiss before we walked into the other bedroom.

Cindy showed Carol around the apartment, most importantly the kitchen and bathroom. Then they started cooking dinner. This was great. This is what the apartment had been lacking: a woman's touch. This was really heaven. Money was coming in regularly and the hashish was going out regularly. Now my second wish had come true. Carol was really here with me.

After an hour or so, the girls had dinner ready. All of us gathered around the kitchen table to eat. They had made mashed potatoes and gravy, roast turkey, a green salad, and fruit cocktail for dessert. It turned out to be a fantastic day. After dinner, we were all worn out, so we went to our bedrooms to rest and relax. Finally, Carol and I could make love. My dream fantasy was about to come true.

After relaxing and letting our food digest, Carol and I started fooling around. We were fondling each other and making out like high school kids. I was searching to find her innermost desires. We had just surpassed foreplay, and I was about to mount her when Ron pounded on my bedroom door.

"Robert, answer the front door. One of your friends is waiting for you," he shouted.

"Who is it?"

"It's Mark. He wants to see you."

I looked at Carol as if someone had stabbed me in the heart. Carol saw that I was frustrated and gave me a big kiss.

"Don't worry, I'll make your wait worthwhile," she promised.

I just groaned in disgust and dressed my tortured body. I walked out into the hallway and talked with Mark.

"Rob, is it all right if I stay here for a while?" he asked.

"Mark, you're always welcome here. My house is your house."

"Thanks Rob," he said, as he entered the apartment.

"The house is a little fuller since you left," I told him.

"Why, what's up?" he asked.

"Mark, someone you know from Michigan has just arrived in Kabul so you will have to sleep in the living room. There are three or four beds in there, anyway."

"I don't mind staying in that room. So who's here? Did Jim return to Kabul?" he asked.

"No, it isn't Jim. Take another guess."

"It isn't Carol, is it?"

"Why do you say that?" I smiled.

Mark just smiled and shrugged his shoulders. He had never taken me seriously when I told him that I was going to bring Carol to Kabul to live with me. He thought I was joking around. Actually, he thought I was wishing and hoping for the impossible. Was he going to be surprised.

"Carol, come here for a minute. I want you to meet a friend of mine," I said in a loud voice.

Once she had dressed, she came into the hallway and was surprised to see Mark standing there.

"What a small world it is," said Carol.

"Boy, you can say that again," I replied.

Now there would be five of us staying at the apartment. We talked late into the night. Carol and I never got the chance to make love that night. We just lay together and held each other close.

A few days later, another friend stopped by my apartment.

"Morgan, what are you doing here?" I asked.

"Rob, can I stay at your apartment for a few days?" he pleaded.

"Well, I guess you can stay. But you will have to sleep in the living room and share it with Mark. You will also have to leave the apartment when I leave. But you are always welcome when I am here."

"One more thing," he added. "Can I leave my trunk full of clothes here until I return from India? I have to renew my Afghan visa, so I will be gone for a month or so."

"Yeah, I guess so."

Now we had six people staying at my apartment. But Morgan was gone within two days.

Mark and I continued to make hash envelopes and play our music. Then one day Mark and I got into a heated argument. Mark refused to take the hash envelopes to Saraj. He didn't want to take the chance of getting busted.

"Mark, there won't be a problem. All you have to do is hand the envelopes to Saraj. That's it," I told him.

But for some reason, he wouldn't budge. "Rob, I don't mind making the envelopes, but I don't want to get involved in the smuggling end of it."

He wanted to make the money but didn't want to take the risk. I was pissed off over that. He wanted me to take all the risk, but there was no risk involved. Saraj saw to that.

Not only were Mark and I having problems, but Carol and Cindy's attitudes had changed for the worse. They were always arguing about one thing or another. And Ron was having a problem with his Afghan partner and the store. It seemed Ron's friend went back to Kandahar and left one of his Afghan friends in charge of the store and he kicked Ron out. He told Ron not to return to the store. Ron told him he wanted his money back and his merchandise returned. The guy refused to give him anything.

"Ron, do whatever it takes, but get my money and merchandise back. I remember telling you even before I loaned you the money that your friend was going to rip us off. It looks like my premonition has come true," I told him with anger in my voice.

Ron still didn't believe his friend was ripping him off.

"When my friend Mammed comes back, everything will be straightened out," he promised.

"What happens if Mammed never comes back? He probably sold the store to the guy who is running it now. Mammed probably took the money and ran."

Ron would hear none of that. He kept standing up for his dear Afghan friend, Mammed. The minute I saw that guy, I knew what kind of person he was. I could read him like a comic book. Ron would have to learn the hard way. So now, everyone at the apartment was on pins and needles. The fun times were over.

Then one morning, shit hit the fan. Every morning for a week or two, Cindy kept hogging the bathroom. She would stay in the bathtub for hours, using up the hot water. By the time Carol and I wanted to use it to shower or bathe, the water was freezing cold. Some mornings, I nearly pissed in my underwear waiting for Cindy to get out of the bathroom.

After pounding on the door and yelling at her for over five minutes, I just barged in and pissed in the toilet. I didn't care anymore. This was my house, not theirs. I paid all the bills, not them. I figured if they didn't have respect for us, I wouldn't have respect for them. Then one morning, I came face to face with Cindy and tried to compromise with her.

"Cindy, we all have to share the bathroom so we'll make up a time schedule. One morning you will use the bathroom first and the next morning we will use it first," I told her.

I thought that had straightened out the problem, but I was wrong. Cindy disregarded the time schedule. So on that day, as soon as Cindy had filled the tub with hot water, I became irate and confronted her about it.

"Cindy, get out of the bathroom!" I snapped. "It's Carol's turn to use it."

"Cindy was very upset and stormed out of the room.

"Do something, Ron," she pleaded.

But Ron could do nothing. It was my apartment. I paid the rent.

Finally, Carol and I took a shower together.

Soon Ron and Cindy were talking about moving out and getting their own apartment.

"Ron, do what you think is best," I said, not caring what he did.

After that day, Ron and I tried to stay out of each other's way.

A few days later, Ron returned to Mammed's store to straighten out their differences. He was surprised to find the store closed and completely empty with a "To Rent" sign in the window. Ron just stood and stared for a few minutes, not believing what was happening to him. He slowly walked back to the apartment and came home looking like he had just lost a fight. He seemed to look to me for an answer.

"Well, Robert," he said, "I guess your premonition has come true. It looks like Mammed ripped me off. I'm sorry for not listening to you in the first place. If I had listened to you I wouldn't be in this predicament and none of this would have happened."

"You still owe me over a thousand dollars," I told him. "You're still responsible for the money and merchandise I loaned you for the store."

"You loaned the money to Mammed," he replied.

"Ron, don't give me that shit. I loaned that money to you, and you loaned the money to Mammed," I told him, angrily.

"Don't worry, I will pay you back everything I owe you. I don't know how long it will take, but I promise to pay you back every cent you loaned me."

Well, that never happened either. He never paid back one cent.

The next morning, Ron and Cindy were gone—they had completely vanished. They had moved out in the middle of the night without saying anything. This was the thanks I got for helping people, especially Americans. Actually, I was glad they were gone. Now Carol and I could relax. We practically had the apartment to ourselves. Only Mark was staying with us now. He wasn't around too much during the day, just at night to sleep.

Finally, Carol and I had the bedroom to ourselves without anyone listening in on our conversations. We could finally make love all night long, and it was wonderful. She was everything I had fanta-sized about. She was an angel and the answer to my prayers. I wouldn't mind marrying this girl, I thought to myself. She was my dream come true, and we were having a great time. I even went out and bought her a new Akai stereo system, which included a cassette player-recorder with two big speakers.

The cassette player would flip over the cassette automatically. I had never seen anything like it before. I thought it was magic. And each speaker cabinet had a twelve-inch speaker with a two-inch tweeter and woofer. They were very good speakers. Heck, this was an excellent stereo system. I had never seen that brand name in America, but Carol was very happy with it. The stereo could shake the whole apartment building if we turned up the volume too much. That's how good it was.

The days were getting better and better, even though Mark and I weren't getting along as well as I had hoped. He just didn't want to work anymore. He expected the money, as if I owed it to him, but he didn't want to do anything for it. I was getting fed up with his lousy attitude. But he still needed a place to stay and food in his belly. I couldn't just throw him out into the street. Carol didn't like Mark's bad attitude either.

"Robert, you don't owe him anything," remarked Carol, trying to comfort me.

"But Mark is a good friend of mine. We grew up together and went to the same schools. I will help him whenever he needs my help. Anyway, Mark is my problem, so don't worry about it. I can take care of the situation myself," I told her matter-of-factly.

Nothing else was said about this situation. We continued our new life together as if we were newlyweds.

I wanted to introduce Carol to Saraj and Mr. Ramazie, so we visited the post office. Saraj and his co-workers were very impressed with my girlfriend. I loved showing her off to my Afghan friends. Her 35-23-34 figure was an instant turn on. Saraj couldn't keep his eyes off of her.

"Saraj, due to the cold and snowy weather, I won't be stopping by the post office as often," I told him. "Carol and I are going to stay at home and renew our friendship. So stop by my apartment. Now that Ron and Cindy have moved out, we get a little lonely without any company. You are always welcome, Saraj."

We waved goodbye to everyone at the post office, then walked out the door into the freezing snow. We tried to hail a taxi but due to the bad weather there were none available, so we had to walk nearly all the way home. That made me angry.

"Carol, I'm going to buy us a vehicle so we won't have to walk in this bad weather again," I promised her, as we walked in the cold, deep snow.

I decided right then and there that the next thing I spent money on would be for a car or van. I figured I could always use a van. I could use it to smuggle hash if nothing else. Carol was also in agreement. We cuddled with our arms around each other as we walked home.

We were only a few blocks away from the apartment when we finally flagged down a taxi. This weather was terrible. It was well below zero, and there were a good three to four inches of snow on the ground.

But once we got to the apartment, we warmed up immediately. The logs burning in the fireplace were still very hot and warmed the room. We took off our coats and snuggled close to each other near the fireplace. We were in each other's arms, touching and kissing, probing for her tongue and she for mine. We had just torn each other's clothes off when Mark walked through the door. He didn't knock. He just barged in. When he saw us, he became embarrassed and turned his head.

"I'm sorry for the intrusion. I didn't hear any noise, so I didn't think anyone was here."

But I didn't believe him.

"Well, now you know. Now will you please leave the room?" I roared.

Mark just shrugged his shoulders, not saying a word, then turned and quickly left the room. I had decided that Mark had better straighten up his act or he could fine other digs to sleep at.

Once again, Carol and I snuggled near the fire and fell asleep. We awoke in each other's arms. Boy, it was nice to have someone to love.

That afternoon I got a big surprise. Ron and Cindy stopped by. It was the first time I had seen them since they'd snuck out without saying goodbye. I was very surprised to see them again, so I invited them into the apartment.

"Well, come on in, strangers. Long time, no see," I said happily.

"Thanks," retorted Ron.

"How have you guys been? Is everything going all right?" I asked.

"I'm homesick for America," replied Cindy.

"I would like to travel to India, but not until the war is over," said Ron.

I was very puzzled. I wondered why they had come to visit now. But I kept silent. However, Ron soon answered my puzzled frame of mind.

"What's new, Ron?" I asked.

"Rob, don't get mad, but I want to ask you a very important question," he said, while looking at the floor.

"Ask away, Ron," I told him, expecting that he needed money. He surprised me when he asked his question.

"Can I ask Saraj to send envelopes for me? I wouldn't ask, but we are nearly broke," he pleaded.

I could see he was in a real bind. He wanted to send some hash envelopes to some of his friends in America. I really felt sorry for him and Cindy.

"Ron, if Saraj will send the envelopes for you, I have no problem with that. Just be careful. Saraj will take your envelopes and money but won't send them."

"That's all right, I trust Saraj," he replied.

"Like you trusted your other Afghan friend, Mammed," I told him sarcastically.

Ron didn't mention anything about the money that he owed me, and I didn't mention it either. I never really expected to be paid back. Hell, when I gave him the money I knew then that I would never see it again. Ron quickly changed the subject.

"Rob, will you and Carol come and visit us at our hotel room?" he asked.

"Sure. We'll stop by every now and then to say hello. Don't forget, you guys can visit us, too," I said. A few minutes later, they were gone.

There still seemed to be tension in the air. I never really trusted them after they snuck out of the apartment, but we were still friends.

Mark and I were good friends, too, but our friendship was still strained. Mark still seemed to have an attitude problem. He just didn't want to work anymore and we argued more than ever over this situation. Finally, after more than a week of this, I couldn't take it anymore. I got fed up with his shenanigans and confronted him about it.

"Mark, what is the problem?"

"You don't pay me enough money for the work I do."

"Are you kidding? I give you one-hundred dollars a week plus room and board. Some weeks I don't make anything, but you still get paid," I reminded him, getting angrier by the minute.

Mark just shrugged his shoulders and left the room. I just couldn't believe his rotten attitude. What did he want from me? As good as I had been to him, I couldn't believe he was acting like this. Finally, I couldn't take it any longer and walked into his bedroom to speak my mind.

"Mark, find another place to stay. I'll still pay your bill for your hotel room until you decide what you want to do. You can come back and work for me or you can try and find work elsewhere," I told him.

He didn't say a word. He still had a very bad morphine habit, and I had been paying for his supply of morphine, too. But no more; he was on his own. Mark was so angry he stormed out of the apartment. I didn't see him for the next few days.

Now Carol and I were finally alone. We could run naked in the apartment without anyone watching, listening, or invading our privacy. We stayed in the apartment most of the time because of the cold weather.

The winter in Kabul was very wet, snowy, and cold. This city was two miles above sea level and there were over six inches of snow on the ground. During the day, the weather was warm enough to melt the snow just enough to make the ground muddy and wet, then at night, everything would freeze. But Carol and I loved it. We stayed near the fireplace and cuddled under the blankets. Sometimes, we would make love ten times a day—sometimes more. I was truly in heaven. We would get high and make love. Carol had just started injecting morphine. I was against it at first, but I couldn't refuse her if she asked.

"Carol, I don't want you addicted like me," I told her.

"I won't do it that often to get addicted," she promised.

"That's exactly what I said until it took over my willpower . . . and it will do the same thing to you."

"But I'm strong enough to take it or leave it," she retorted, not realizing the power of the drug.

I quit arguing with her and didn't say another word about it. I began sharing my morphine with her. Carol was only doing a half a tablet at a time, but that's how I'd started, and then you do one, then two, then more and more. But I felt she was old enough to decide for herself.

Everything was going fine until the day of the blizzard. I was nearly out of morphine, so I had planned to go to the Devil's pharmacy to buy ten or more bottles. But on this morning, I looked out the window and saw many feet of freshly fallen snow that had come during the night. There was at least four feet of snow on the ground. It took me hours to reach the pharmacy. And to my horror, it was closed. All the shops were closed. Most owners were outside of their stores shoveling snow away from their doorways.

I prayed that the pharmacy would be open the following day because I would be out of morphine within a day or so. I was beginning to worry. I told Carol about the problem, but she wasn't too worried about herself. She hadn't been using morphine long enough to become addicted. But I had become very addicted. I wasn't looking forward to withdrawal pains. I hadn't thought about eating opium to reduce my withdrawal symptoms, as I had done a year and a half earlier. I only thought about the morphine.

Two days later, I was completely out of it, so I hopped a taxi to the Devil's pharmacy. It was finally open. I went inside and had to stand in line behind a number of hippies and junkies waiting to buy narcotics. By the time it was my turn, he had run out of morphine. He didn't have anymore. It would be two or three days before he could replenish his supply. So I hopped back into the taxi and visited other pharmacies to purchase my evil narcotic. However, these shops either refused to sell it to me or they didn't have any. So now, I was in a bind. I returned to the Devil's pharmacy and pleaded with him for something to keep me from getting sick. He looked in a few small drawers behind the counter and handed me a two-hundred-milligram ampoule of opium hydrochloride.

"Will this help me from going through withdrawal symptoms?" I asked.

"Yes, it should help you until you can restock your morphine supply," he replied, with a devilish look.

I paid him less than a dollar for the ampoule and returned to the apartment. Mark was standing alongside Carol talking and waiting for me. He had learned from her that I had run out of morphine and offered us some. He had just enough to share with us. He said it was the last he had. I had no reason not to believe him and thanked him for helping me out. I could save the opium for a later time, if I needed it. Now I felt sorry that I had kicked him out. He had stopped by to tell me he wanted to work for me again.

"Sure, no problem," I told him. "Why don't you stay for dinner?

Carol made some real good food."

He quickly accepted.

After we fixed our morphine, we sat around the fireplace and conversed. We only injected half of our normal daily dose, so the high quickly dissipated.

That evening, my body craved more. Mark didn't have any morphine but a friend at his hotel had some—except there was only one catch: His friend was away and wouldn't return for a couple of days. So I decided to use the ampoule of opium. I didn't know what to expect.

I broke the top of the glass ampoule and sucked the evil narcotic into my syringe. I had injected about sixty percent of it when the rush overwhelmed me. I lay back on the bed with the needle still in my arm too stoned to take it out. Suddenly, I passed out and came to a few seconds later. After Mark had taken the needle out of my vein, he stood me up on my feet and walked me around the room.

"Mark, I'm fine!" I yelled. "The rush was just too heavy, so I just shut my eyes."

Mark and Carol tried telling me that I had overdosed, but that just wasn't true. I had just shut my eyes to enjoy the heavy rush, but they thought I was dying.

"You looked like you were dead," opined Mark.

"If I ever do die here, I want you to fill my casket with hash. Have the casket made with a false bottom and you can hide it there. Then send it to America. But that will never happen. I know my limitations."

Two-hundred milligrams of opium was just a little too much. The next morning, I returned to the pharmacy. Luckily, for me, the Devil had bottles of morphine for sale. Again, there were many junkies waiting in line to buy their drugs and narcotics. Finally, it was my turn. I bought twenty bottles. I wanted to buy more, but he had raised his price two dollars per bottle. When I'd first arrived in Kabul, I'd paid less than three dollars a bottle. Now the price was up to seven dollars. But I didn't argue. I was happy to pay it. In fact, I was glad that he had it at all.

During my visit there, I met a young American couple who had also purchased morphine. They, too, had run out during the blizzard and invited me to their hotel room to do our dope. It was only a block away, so I agreed. I needed a fix so badly that it was faster to get to their room than to mine. I would have fixed at the pharmacy if the Devil had let me. So we ran all the way to their hotel room. We ran through the snow, mud, and big wet puddles. We couldn't run fast enough. The second we entered their small hotel room, we got down to business.

"Did you bring a syringe?" asked my new friends.

"Yep, I have my dope kit in my shoulder bag." I quickly pulled it out and set it down on a small table.

Then I cooked up my morphine and sucked it up into my syringe. They were doing the same. As I injected the heavy narcotic into my vein, I noticed they were injecting it into the muscle of their arm.

"Why don't you inject into your vein?" I asked.

"The morphine is too strong that way," said the young female.

"That's what morphine is all about. The rush is the high," I exclaimed.

"It is also very addicting," she replied.

"No matter which way you inject morphine, it's still very addicting," I told them.

Once we were feeling alive and normal again, we chatted about America. They had come from New York City and were headed for India, but they had traveled as far as Kabul and ran out of money.

"I noticed you bought quite a few bottles of morphine, so I thought we could borrow some money from you," she said.

"Hell, I just spent the last of my money on the morphine," I lied. "I won't have any money for another week or so. I'm still waiting for a money transfer from America."

"Will you give us a bottle of morphine?" she pleaded.

That was probably the only reason they had asked me over to their hotel room. They just wanted to use me and try to get whatever they could. I should have left the room right then. But I still felt sorry for them. I remembered when I was out of money and dope. So I reached into my shoulder bag, pulled out two bottles of morphine, and handed them to the girl. Then I walked out of the room. I didn't say a word. I left without even knowing their names. I was a little pissed. I felt these low-life junkies had used me. Then I realized hell, this could be me one day. I would never think about people like that again. I respected people for their individualism and not their politics.

Carol was waiting for me in our bedroom when I returned to the apartment.

"I'll be your slave for the day," she purred, naked as a jaybird.

Just then, someone pounded on the door. I walked into the hallway and opened it. Mark had stopped by.

"I can't invite you in right now because Carol and I are busy. I can't talk to you right now so please forgive me but I have to go," I said, with a wink.

I just shut the door in his face. I felt bad for doing that, but he would understand.

That day, Carol was my sex slave. She did anything I asked of her. I was in total ecstasy. I was very happy that Carol had come to live with me. Whenever we were alone, we would never wear clothes. She walked around the apartment nude all the time. She tried to talk me into going nude, but I refused. It was just too cold in the room even though we had the fire in the fireplace going all the time. But I just didn't feel right, walking around nude. Not only that, but she would keep me excited and want sex all day long. Soon I was making excuses so I wouldn't have to make love all the time. She was my little nymph.

We acted like newlyweds for the first six months. Then, like any other normal couple, we slowed down. At least I did, anyway. Carol still wanted sex all the time. She was like a female bitch in heat. But I didn't give in. Well, sometimes I did and sometimes I didn't. Our sex life was still great.

One day, while sitting at the hippie restaurant, Ziggy's, I noticed an ad on the wall advertising a VW van for sale. I went to the room to find the owners to ask them about it. An American couple had it for sale. They wanted to return to America because of the war between Pakistan and India. They couldn't finish their travels as they had planned and needed money for their airfare.

Carol and I invited them over to the apartment to haggle over the purchase of their van. They wanted one-thousand dollars for it. But it was two different vans in one. From the sliding door to the rear of the vehicle was from a 1968 VW—the rest of it was from a 1964 VW. Both halves were welded together. It looked like a brand new van. You couldn't tell that it had been repaired. If they hadn't told me, I would never have known. There was only one problem with it—the engine needed to be rebuilt. They showed me on a map of the city where the VW garage was. It was only a few miles away. I offered them five- hundred dollars.

"That's all I can afford, so think about it and get back with me."

I really didn't expect them to take my offer. I figured they would sell it to someone else.

I also found out that I couldn't get insurance on it, so I would have to resell it here if I ever decided to leave Afghanistan.

But then, the very next day, I was told that I could get insurance through an American insurance company. I would have to have someone in America send me the correct forms to fill out, so my only concern was the blown engine. Other than getting the engine rebuilt, there weren't any other problems. A few days later, the couple agreed to sell it to me at the price I'd quoted them.

We drove to the Ministry of Interior to get the car registered and approved. I had to register the van in Carol's name. She had a valid visa. Mine had expired. I was afraid that the Afghan government would have fined me, thrown me in jail, or kicked me out of their country—possibly all three. So, to be on the safe side, we used Carol's passport. Once I handed the American couple the money for the van, the agreement was stamped notarized. We were now proud owners of a nice van. Now I had to take it to the garage to get the engine repaired.

The next day, Mark, Carol, and I drove the van to the garage. Mark was a decent mechanic and very mechanically inclined. He had worked on car engines before and was knowledgeable enough so the mechanic at the garage couldn't rip me off.

As we were talking to one of the garage mechanics, I noticed a well-dressed Afghan man in his fifties staring at Carol. He seemed mesmerized by her beauty. He came over and introduced himself as Mr. Kazamie. He was president of the Ministry of Finance. He explained that he was a relative of the king and his family. As he talked with us, he continued to stare at Carol.

"Do a good job for them," Mr. Kazamie told the mechanic. "They are my friends, very good friends. So give them a discount."

"It will cost one-hundred dollars to fix the engine," said the mechanic.

"That's fine," I replied. "When will the repairs be completed and when can I pick it up?"

"You can pick it up tomorrow."

It would have cost me three or four times that amount to have the engine rebuilt in America. So I was happy that my new friend, Mr. Kazamie, had intervened. I figured he must be an important man in Kabul the way everyone respected him and jumped at his every word.

As we were leaving the garage, Mr. Kazamie was outside standing near his car. He waved to us to get our attention. So we walked over to see what he wanted.

"Can I give you a ride to your hotel?" he asked.

"We don't stay at a hotel, we have our own apartment," I told him. "We will be happy to ride with you."

We hopped into his big Mercedes Benz. Within ten minutes, Mr. Kazamie had dropped us off in front of my apartment building.

"Mr. Kazamie, thank you once again for the ride. Please come by any time and visit," I told him.

"Very good. You and Carol must also come to my office at the Ministry of Finance and visit me."

I nodded in agreement, and then he was gone. I felt Mr. Kazamie was more interested in Carol than in me. But I didn't mind. I figured he might be a good person to know. I intended to stay in touch with this man. He may come in handy one day. I thought he just wanted to be good friends, but I soon learned that Mr. Kazamie had his own hidden agenda.

Over the next few weeks, Mr. Kazamie introduced Carol and me to his friends and co-workers at the Ministry of Finance. He also introduced us to his Harvard-taught son, Mahmed. He was just a three years older than I was—twenty-four.

Mahmed invited Carol and me to a lively nightclub. It was only open to the very rich and famous of Afghanistan. It was a modern, European-style nightclub. It had a well-built hardwood dance floor surrounded by strobe and flashing colored lights. The music they played and listened to was their own type of Afghan rock and roll. However, many of the songs were American or English. But at times, they also listened to their own cultural Afghan music. We were the only westerners allowed into the nightclub. They didn't allow any others. All the male Afghans flirted with Carol. I didn't mind though; it was all harmless and all in good fun. Not only that, but I went home with her.

Through Mahmed, I was introduced to some of the king's siblings. The one I knew best was the king's third son, whom they called Mohammed. Soon, Carol and I were meeting more and more of the king's relatives, such as his daughter and her seven-or eight-year-old son.

I learned many different things from these people. They constantly talked politics. And when they did, I acted like I didn't hear them. They were always talking about their relatives, especially the ones the king had jailed or interrogated, and about the dollar and German mark devaluation.

From these talks, I learned when the American dollar would be devalued. Then I would go to the moneychangers and buy thousands of dollars worth of Afghani before it devalued even further. They seemed to know what they were talking about, because the dollar devalued the exact day they said it would. They would also talk about the Russians invading their government, trying to bribe the king and his subjects. They would talk so much that I would get frustrated.

"Please, Mahmed, talk about something else besides politics. It's boring," I told him.

I learned many secrets listening to their long conversations. I also learned that the king never left the country because he was fearful of his powerful friends and relatives. They wanted to overthrow his government, even the king's own brother-in-law, who was also his cousin. These were the types of conversations to which I listened. They could talk about anything in front of Carol and me. We weren't a threat to them. They knew I had left my own country due to a crooked government that was involved in an illegal and unlawful war in a country that only wanted peace.

Because of all the warmongers in the military and American government, the war meant billions of dollars to the president's friends and close associates. It was all about money, not communism. So my Afghan friends didn't have to worry about me telling their secrets.

We would visit the club once or twice, about two months out of the year. That was our night on the town. Carol really enjoyed the nightclub environment. We did this for a year or so, even though my friendship with Mr. Kazamie didn't last. However, I continued my friendship with his son and the king's relatives.

One night, Mr. Kazamie dropped by the apartment and took Carol and me for a long ride in his fancy car. As we carried on a conversation, Mr. Kazamie interrupted me and asked if he could have sex with Carol. I was dumbfounded. I was very surprised and angry that he would ask a friend such a rude question. I wondered why he thought Carol was a prostitute, so I asked him:

"Mr. Kazamie, who told you Carol was a prostitute?" I asked.

"Your landlord told me. He said he had sex with her."

"Well, he's a liar," I snapped. "The only person Carol screws is ME. Now will you please return us to our apartment!"

After that night, Mr. Kazamie and I were no longer friends.

A few weeks earlier, Carol, Mark, and I returned to the garage to pick up my new van. But it wasn't quite finished. While we waited for the van to be cleaned up, we walked around outside, just being nosy. A small mud shack behind the garage housed a small machine shop, similar to the one my father owned where Mark and I had worked during our teen years.

I entered the room and introduced myself to the owner and his two helpers. They worked in their normal Afghan clothing. They looked like they were ready for bed, not for work. The owner smiled as he tried to understand my broken English and handed me his micrometer and motioned for me to check his lathe work. I just shrugged my shoulders and shook my head. I was shy and embarrassed, so I just turned away to let him continue working.

Seeing his shop, smelling the distinct shop odor of dirty oil fumes, and burning metal chips brought back good memories. It made Mark and me homesick. So we walked back to the garage, paid the bill, and drove my new van to the apartment.

As soon as we entered my abode, I went directly to my morphine to celebrate. We each celebrated by doing an extra tablet.

Now we could travel anywhere in Afghanistan and not have to pay for taxis to drive us around the city. We relaxed and talked about our future plans.

A few hours later, Mark left for his hotel room so Carol and I could lie down to relax. She was lying down in one bedroom and I, in the other.

I was engrossed in a German tabloid magazine I was reading. It was approximately eight or nine in the evening and everything was very quiet outside. Only the soft music playing on the tape player could be heard throughout the house. I had a small lamp on to illuminate the room while I read the story about witchcraft, cults, and witches. I was so engrossed in this story that it felt as though I had left my body and was watching myself reading.

The story was about a cult of satanic witches and warlocks. They were in a cemetery holding hands in a big circle, chanting for the devil. As they continued their séance, the cops came to arrest them. But suddenly a green mist covered the circle of devil worshipers, making them invisible. As I lay in a deep trance, it felt like my astral body was floating above, watching them. Then, within a wink of an eye, they seemed to disappear.

Just at the height of my trance, the lamp in my room suddenly exploded. Sparks shot out from it as though the bulb had exploded, then the lamp shorted out. Or so I thought. I immediately jumped out of bed and pulled the burning and smoldering plug out of the wall. Carol ran into the room to see what all the commotion was about. I tried to explain the situation, but at that moment, I was too shocked to speak. It was frightening.

I turned on the overhead light to see what damage had been done to the lamp. As I looked it over, I noticed that nothing was damaged. The bulb was still in one piece. I couldn't find anything else wrong with it, so I plugged it into the wall socket. To my surprise, it worked. I immediately got down on my knees and prayed to the Lord. I told God that from this day forward I believed in a Supreme Being. I was no longer agnostic. I believed. I told Carol about what had happened.

"Carol, God did that to the lamp. I was in such a deep trance, thinking about that cult and the devil, that God snapped me out of it," I told her, shaking.

If anything, that lamp should have shorted out, but it hadn't. Not even a burn mark on it, and the damn thing caught on fire. I was so upset and nervous that I had to fix another four morphine tablets to calm my nerves. Even Carol used that excuse. We talked about this experience for the next week or so. It was miraculous.

One morning, while working on the rear door latch on the van, I pinched the top of my thumb, which created a blister. As I was working, the blister burst. I didn't notice that grease had gotten into it. Within a few days, it had gotten badly infected. Within a week, my thumb had swollen up to three times its size. The infection was as big as a marble and full of pus. It looked hideous and hurt like hell.

Luckily across the hall from my apartment was a female Afghan doctor who had been schooled in France. I had never used her before because I'd never had a reason to. Now I did. I stepped into her office. But she didn't speak English, only French. I didn't speak or understand French, so I just held up my injured and swollen thumb and showed her the infection. She looked at it and felt it. She explained that the infection had not come to a head. It was still too hard. I was to make a return visit to her office in a few days, when the infection softened up. Then she would cut the swollen thumb and drain the infection.

Once I finally understood her, I tried to pay her but she refused my money. I still put a one hundred Afghani bill on her table and thanked her. She was very happy. I never did go back to her office.

Within a few days, the sore was soft enough that I took a sterilized needle and poked a hole into my pus-filled thumb. The pus began to seep out. Then I pressed down on the bloated, pus-filled blister and the pus squirted across the room. The marble-sized blister soon flattened out. I cut the dead skin away and cleaned the area with peroxide. It was finally healing. I had gone through hell for over three days from this infection. Sometimes the pain was so bad that I couldn't fall asleep. Even the morphine didn't take all the pain away. Some days the thumb felt like it was on fire.

But now, things were finally getting back to normal. Mark and I were still making hash envelopes for Saraj to send, and money was still coming in regularly.

One morning, Mark and I were playing our instruments, singing, and making up new songs when a knock on the front door interrupted us. So I answered it. It was Morgan.

"How ya doing?" I asked, as I invited him into the apartment.

"All right, but things didn't go as I planned. The war is over but the feud isn't," he remarked.

"Come on in. We were just jamming," I told him.

We walked into the living room. Mark and Morgan nodded to each other.

During our conversation, I mentioned to Morgan about my new van. But he was more interested in explaining to me how he wasn't able to visit India. He got as far as Pakistan and stayed just long enough to renew his Afghan visa. Then he asked me to give him a ride to his friend's house. He had an idea for making some quick money. So I agreed to drive him there. Morgan was surprised that I had bought a VW van. During our ride, he mentioned that he might be able to help me make money using the van. He told me he would explain more about it later.

When we arrived at the house, he introduced me to some of the people who lived there: a Danish couple named Hans and Elsa, and two guys, John and Tim, whom I had met before and who were in the Brotherhood of Eternal Love. Morgan mentioned to them that I had a smuggling scam, and they wanted to know how I did it. I refused to tell them. I wasn't giving away any of my trade secrets. Then the beautiful, blonde-headed Danish girl came into the room.

"Robert, are you interested in smuggling a couple of false-bottom suitcases to Europe," asked Elsa.

"No, I'm not interested," I told her, looking directly into her blue eyes.

"Does Carol want to do it?" asked Morgan.

"When I get back to the apartment, I'll ask her."

"We will give you five-thousand dollars when the suitcases are delivered to their destination," Elsa added.

"Well, I'll think about it."

"Do you know where we can buy about a thousand pounds of pollen?" John asked, interrupting my conversation with the beautiful blonde.

"Are you serious, John? What do you use all that for?" I asked.

"We use the pollen to make hash oil. Then we hire women to transport it to America."

"Do they smuggle it in false-bottom suitcases?" I asked.

"No. They hide it on their bodies."

I just shook my head in amazement. They had been in the hash business for years. So why would they need my help? I was curious about that, so I questioned them.

"Why do you need my help buying pollen? Don't you have your own connections?" I asked.

"The man we used to buy the dope from suddenly just got busted in a big drug raid and was hung just a few days ago," said John, looking at the floor.

"I'll think about your proposition. And I'll give you Carol's answer in a few days."

Just as I was about to leave the house, the Japanese girl from whom I had purchased the cassette tapes came into the room.

"Do you have any more rock and roll tapes for sale?" I asked her.

"I sure do."

I looked through her tapes, picked out four new releases, and gave her an American twenty-dollar bill. I placed them into my shoulder bag and left the house for my apartment.

I arrived just in time for dinner. Carol was a great cook. Nearly every night she cooked a four-course meal. But the morphine suppressed my appetite, so I didn't eat dinner that often, although I did try for Carol's sake.

I explained to Carol about the proposition that was offered to us, saying it would be like a European vacation. She was very curious and very interested in the amount of money that we could make off the deal. We talked about this for the rest of the evening.

The next morning, I visited the University of Kabul. I had heard from my Afghan friends at the nightclub about the police cracking down and jailing the tourists with invalid visas, so I figured I would sign up for classes. That way I hoped to get a student visa legally. I walked into the university and noticed a male clerk working behind a large, square counter.

"Salaam Ali cume. I would like to sign up for school classes," I told him.

"What classes would you like to sign up for?" asked the clerk in perfect English.

"I would like to take a language class."

"We teach many different languages, such as Russian, French, English, Spanish, and German. There are many. What are you interested in?"

"I want to learn an Afghan language."

"We teach Farsi, Pashtu, Dari, and a few others," he said.

"I will sign up for the Farsi language," I told him. "Also, would you write me a letter stating that I'm studying at the university, so if I get hassled by the police they can see that I'm here legally?"

"Of course; it will be my pleasure."

He wrote a letter and notarized it for me, stating that I was a university student studying Farsi. Now I had proof that I was in Kabul legally.

"Koda office," I said, as I thanked the clerk in Pashtu, then folded the letter and put it in my money belt for safekeeping.

I left the university, hopped into my van, and then headed back to the apartment to pick up Carol. I wanted to visit the Ministry of Interior to get my student visa.

Twenty minutes later, Carol and I walked into the main office. I handed my passport and the notarized letter from the university to one of the clerks behind the counter.

"I need to get a student visa because I'm studying at the University of Kabul," I pleaded, praying that things would work out.

I left the building thinking that I was going to get my student visa. Carol and I returned to the apartment to celebrate.

But first, we had to stop by the pharmacy. I needed to buy a few more bottles of morphine. Carol and I were going through a bottle every two days. When Mark was around, I went through one bottle each day. Carol was doing four tabs a day. I was doing ten to twelve. Mark was doing about the same amount.

And the price for a bottle of morphine was still going up. In fact, the last few times I had purchased the drug I'd had to pay more and more money. Now it was up to ten dollars a bottle. This was due to the devalued American dollar and the Devil's greed. But with the money I was making, ten dollars for a bottle of pure pharmaceutical morphine was still very cheap. I didn't care about the price, as long as I had the money to spend. And I wasn't about to go through withdrawal again. Besides, the rush from the morphine was incredible.

Over the next few days, Carol and I discussed the offers that had been made by Morgan's friends. Now Carol wanted to smuggle the suitcases to Denmark. This was supposed to be the perfect crime. They had the cases delivered to a person in Pakistan, where Carol would pick them up. Then she would fly from Pakistan to Zurich, Switzerland. She would disembark there and catch another flight to Copenhagen, Denmark. She was to look as though she had traveled through Europe in transit, not as if she had just traveled from Afghanistan. They said she couldn't take any gifts with her because that would make her look like a tourist, not a businesswoman.

I argued with the guys over the fact that customs would become suspicious if she got on a plane in Pakistan without any gifts. That was a good reason to get busted. But the Danish guy, Hans, got very angry. He explained how they had done the scam many times and had never had a problem. I argued with them to let her carry a carpet or something onto the plane even if she had to give it away to one of the other passengers. But they refused to listen. So I left the choice up to Carol. It was her butt that would sit in jail. She had the right to make up her own mind. She still wanted to go, so all of us agreed that Carol would carry two large, false-bottom suitcases with ten kilos of hash in them, five kilos in each.

Once in Denmark, she was to call a certain telephone number and give the cases to a certain person. He was to give Carol the money that was agreed upon. When she returned to Kabul, we would get paid five thousand dollars. Carol would leave for Pakistan in two days.

I wanted her to bring back a few important items that we couldn't get in Kabul. The two items I needed desperately were an electric hacksaw and an electric drill. I also wanted her to bring back a good dependable scale—a small, hand-held scale that would weigh from one gram to one-hundred kilos. As Carol and I were talking over our plans, a bad feeling came over me.

"Carol, if I thought anything could go wrong I wouldn't let you do this. You are much more important to me than a suitcase full of hash. If anything goes wrong, I'll do whatever is necessary to get you out of jail. But nothing is going to happen," I told her, hoping my words would come true.

"I hope not," she replied.

"Send me a telegram every day to the Kabul post office. Then I'll know how things turned out, and when you'll arrive in Kabul. Then I will meet you at the airport when you return."

"Will do."

Finally, the day had arrived. It was time for Carol to leave for the airport. She was getting last-minute instructions from the head honcho of this great smuggling plan. He was telling her who to meet and when and where to go once she had arrived in Pakistan. The cases were already there. He handed Carol her plane ticket and motioned that it was time to leave. All of us jumped into my van and headed for the airport. Just as we arrived, the passengers were already boarding the plane for Peshawar, Pakistan. I gave Carol a quick kiss on the lips.

"Take care of yourself, Carol. Don't forget to wire me as soon as you arrive in Denmark," I reminded her.

As she walked away, we watched as she boarded the plane—and then waited in the van until her flight departed. The plane vanished within five minutes.

As we rode back to my apartment, nobody said a word. You could hear a pin drop. *Now I'm alone again,* I thought to myself. So I asked Mark to stay with me until Carol returned. He agreed. Over the next couple of days, we became good friends again.

During the week that Carol was away, Mark and I were like brothers. The first couple of days I was a nervous wreck. I was worried that Carol would get busted. I didn't want anything to happen to that girl. For the first time I knew I had fallen in love with her. She was the only thing that I worried about. It seemed my life had become intertwined and wrapped around her. I needed her near me. I needed her presence around me. Hell, I just needed her.

I checked the post office daily to see if Carol had sent me a telegram. On the third day, my prayers were answered. She had arrived in Denmark safely. She wrote in her wire that the customs official in Pakistan became very suspicious of her because she had no gifts. But somehow, she'd talked her way out of it. She would explain more when she returned to Kabul in a few days. She gave me her telephone number in Copenhagen, so I went to the government telephone office and placed a call to her. It took over four hours before they could get the call through. By the time I talked to her, I was tired and in a bad mood. But as soon as I heard her angelic voice, my spirits picked up.

"Hello," said Carol, as she answered the telephone.

"Carol, I miss you, so hurry up and come back home," I begged.

"I will, but I ran into a little problem. The guy I gave the suitcases to said the hash weighed less than the ten kilos he expected. It was over one kilo light, supposedly."

"Carol, the hash was pressed in a hydraulic press. There was no way that it could lose weight. Either they made a mistake weighing it or the guy in Denmark is ripping us off."

As I was speaking, I quickly realized that I was saying this over an open line. I thought some type of law enforcement might be listening in on our conversation.

"What should I do?" she asked.

"Don't worry about anything. The missing weight is their problem. But don't forget to return with the items I asked for. Come home as soon as possible. I'll see you in a couple of days."

"I will."

"Well, I better go. Send me a wire with the arrival time of your flight. Then I will meet you at the airport."

"When I get home, we will have a ball," she said enthusiastically.

"Goodbye. I love you," I exclaimed.

I think those words surprised her. The phone went silent for more than ten seconds.

"Rob, did I hear you right?" she asked.

"You did."

"That makes me feel good."

"When you get back, I'll make you feel good. See you soon." With that said, I hung up the phone.

I was very happy hearing her voice and that she would be returning in a couple of days.

Sure enough, two days after our phone conversation I received a telegram from Carol stating the arrival time of her flight to Kabul. She would be here the following afternoon. I was very excited. I couldn't wait. Mark and I cleaned the house for her return.

When that chore was completed, I left the apartment and drove to the Interior Ministry to pick up my passport and student visa. As I walked into the building, the office was silent. Not one person seemed to be working. I waited until someone noticed me. Finally, a clerk stepped from behind the counter. When he didn't speak up, I did.

"May I see the gentleman who helped me last week?" I asked. "I am here to pick up my American passport. I left it here to acquire a student visa."

The clerk gave me a very quizzical look and quickly left the room. He returned with the man to whom I had given my passport. He greeted me with a smile and handshake.

"Hello," said the ministry official, as he handed my passport to me. "I am sorry but I couldn't, in good conscience, give you a student visa. You must return to your own country and apply to a college there."

"But I prefer to live in this country and go to school here in Kabul. Many of your countrymen are allowed to apply at our universities and get an education in America. So why can't I go to school in this country?" I asked.

"I'm sorry. But I can't, under any circumstance, issue you a student visa."

I tried everything. I even tried to bribe him with money. Nothing would change his mind. I even mentioned the names of my Afghan friends who were related to the king and his family, but it still didn't help.

"Can't you do anything for me?" I pleaded.

"I have been ordered by the king not to give any American or European a student visa."

Well, I got tired of arguing. I shoved my passport into my shoulder bag and then turned to leave.

"Thanks, but no thanks," I said to the ministry official.

I quickly left the building. I didn't care that he had turned me down. I planned on living in Kabul forever. If I did have to leave, I would either smuggle myself out of the country or pay a huge fine. That is, if they allowed it and didn't throw me into jail. I planned on dying here. I never wanted to leave.

I returned to my apartment and thought about Carol's return. She would be home the following day. Mark and I would meet her at the airport. I was so excited I hardly slept at all that night.

Finally, the time had come, so Mark and I jumped into my van and departed for the airport. We had arrived on time, but Carol wasn't on her scheduled flight. We rode home in silence. I didn't have any idea what the problem was. I went to the post office to see if there was a telegram from her, but there wasn't—just letters from my friends in America. I would check the post office again the following day. That night, I prayed for Carol's safe return.

That morning, as I was about to leave the apartment, I got the surprise of my life. Carol had arrived at the apartment. She had let herself in with an extra key. I was totally surprised. Even Mark came out to say hello. Now that Carol was home, things could get back to normal. She pulled me into the bedroom so she could talk to me in private.

"Mark, will you please leave the room so Carol and I can talk?"

Mark quickly turned and left the room as I hugged Carol as she explained her story to me.

"Rob, the Afghan customs official wouldn't allow the tools into the country without knowing who they were for. I tried to explain to him that they were only gifts, but he still wanted to see the person I was giving them to."

The customs official thought she was going to sell them, and that was illegal in Afghanistan. So I had to return to the airport with her to pick up the gifts. Carol also explained her situation in Denmark. It seemed the guy she had given the suitcases to now said that it was two kilos light. Not just one, but two. That meant there was only eight kilos of hash, not ten, and the guy only gave her money for eight.

"Carol, don't worry about it. That's their fault, not yours. They're gonna take the loss, not us. We're gonna get the money that was agreed upon—nothing more, nothing less. In fact, give me the money and I will give it to them."

I took out the agreed-upon five-thousand dollars and put the rest of the money into an envelope. So, if and when they stopped by, I would hand them the envelope. Hell, I could tell them that Carol had never returned. That she had ripped us all off, taking all the money with her. What could they do? Nothing. They would have to take my word for it. But I didn't do business that way. I was honest. I never screwed people and always kept up my end of the agreement. So they didn't have to worry about me. I had integrity. I waited for them to come to me.

A day after Carol had arrived in Kabul, we drove back to the airport and retrieved my gifts. After a few minutes of searching, we located the customs official Carol had dealt with.

"*Salaam Ali cume,*" I said to him.

"Yes, may I help you," he replied.

"I am here to pick up the tools my girlfriend had brought for me," I said, noticing that he had a badly deformed right hand.

"What are you using these tools for?" he asked.

"They are to help my Afghan friend's carpentry business," I told him.

As we talked, I nonchalantly and very discreetly slipped him a fifty-Afghani bill. He was surprised at what I had done, but he smiled and handed over the tools. We thanked him and then headed back to the apartment.

A week after Carol returned to Kabul, the Danish couple, Elsa and Hans, stopped by. Carol was sleeping and the apartment was quiet, but I still invited them in.

"Has Carol returned yet?" asked Elsa.

"Yes, she's in the bedroom sleeping. Have you talked to your friend in Denmark?"

"No, not yet," she replied.

"Well, your friend in Denmark told Carol the suitcases were two kilos light," I said, and then handed Hans the envelope of money. "Hans, I took out the agreed-upon sum."

After he counted the money, he screamed, "It's two-thousand dollars short!"

"I told you, talk to your friend in Denmark," I snapped. "We did our part. If you want to yell at someone, yell at your friend in Denmark!"

They continued to scream and yell as Carol walked into the room.

"What's all the commotion about?" she asked.

"Nothing, Carol. Go back to bed. I'll take care of it," I told her.

"I want more money," screamed Hans.

"Go talk to your buddy in Denmark," I told him, slowly walking them to the front door. "You're lucky to get any money. We took all the risk. Furthermore, Carol nearly got busted in Pakistan. Now get out of my house before I throw you out!"

They finally stormed out of my apartment. I didn't think I would ever see them again, but they had the gall to come back a week later. I didn't know what to expect as they entered my apartment.

"Do you want to do the scam again?" asked Hans, as if nothing had happened between us.

"Get lost," I snapped. "If I want Carol to smuggle false-bottom suitcases I will make them myself without your help. I have my own way of smuggling hash, and there's no risk whatsoever. Now, will you please leave my apartment and never come back. We don't need any of your aggravation."

They quickly departed.

We met a few other people with smuggling ideas or techniques—an interracial couple who had driven their Ford step van from Europe. The black guy, Gerome, was from New York City and the girl, Flower, was from Australia. He wanted to fill their van with hash and drive it to India. Then they would ship it by boat to America. Flower wanted to fly false-bottom suitcases to America, and she wanted Carol to travel with her and carry two suitcases of hash. I told Carol she didn't need to do it again. Once was enough. I wanted her with me. I didn't want to lose her.

But they didn't give up. Over the next few days, the couple visited us a number of times at our apartment and tried talking us into their smuggling schemes. I absolutely refused. But they continued to badger me about their plans.

"Flower, don't ask me anymore," I snapped. "If you need help buying the hash, I will help you with that. But that's it. Carol isn't risking her life for a few thousand dollars. My business is going too good. We're making a thousand dollars a week, sometimes more. So we aren't lacking for anything. We have everything we need to keep us comfortable."

"Well, we just thought we would ask," said Gerome. "Well, it's getting late so we'd better be heading back to our hotel room."

As the couple left our apartment, I wished them success in their endeavors. That was the last time we would see them, or so I thought.

Since my business was going so well, I decided to buy more carpets and Afghan merchandise to send back to America as gifts. I had hoped that my sister, Vicky Lynn, or one of my friends would open up an import-export business and then I could send them items from Afghanistan legally. We bought a couple hundred velvet vests and many different carpets, coats, and other valuable merchandise.

We loaded it all into the van and took it to the airport to send to America. I had three big trunks of Afghan vests and clothes. I also had fifteen carpets rolled up to send. As I brought the merchandise to the customs area, I noticed the same customs official who had helped me with the tools, so I thought he could help me again.

"Can you help me?" I asked the customs official. "I have a number of items to send to America. They are all gifts."

I didn't expect any trouble from this customs man, but I was wrong. The obese, bald, deformed inspector became very suspicious. He thought I was smuggling hashish. He had me open every trunk and take out every piece of clothing. He began to check every pocket in every vest, coat, and jacket. He even unrolled the carpets to see if I had stashed any drugs there. I wasn't that stupid. I wouldn't take a chance sending any type of contraband without knowing the customs official. Saraj was like a brother to me. I didn't know this guy, and these items were much too expensive to take the risk.

The inspector used his deformed hand to search the pockets of nearly one hundred vests, which took nearly two hours. Carol was getting very impatient. One thing I had learned in Afghanistan was to be patient, but I was becoming irritated. There were no drugs among my merchandise and I told him that. But he paid no attention to me. I sure wasn't going to give him any baksheesh this time. He wasn't helping me. He was being rude and obnoxious. I think he was angry because he didn't find any drugs. Finally, after four long hours, he completed his search of the merchandise.

"You may put the items back into the trunks," he said. "And you must roll up the carpets if you want to send them to America."

Carol refolded all the clothes and repacked everything. I rolled up the carpets and then paid for shipping; then we headed for home. I was glad to get out of there. This was one customs man who couldn't be bought. He was not the friendly type of person, like Saraj. After nearly four hours of torment, I just wanted to get to the apartment and relax. Carol felt the same way.

When we arrived home, Mark was in his room making up hash envelopes and called out that one of Morgan's friends had come by. He mentioned something about the Australian girl, Flower, getting a couple of suitcases of hash through American customs into New York. She had just returned to Kabul.

"The black and white couple wanted to talk to you," said Mark. That's all he would say.

"They know where I live if they want to talk to me," I told him.

I thought they wanted to ask us to smuggle suitcases to New York now that Flower had gotten through American customs so easily. I really didn't know what they wanted.

A few days later, I answered a knock at the door. It was Morgan. He wanted to retrieve his trunk. He was going to return to Europe. I showed him that his trunk was right where he had left it. However, I forgot that Carol had taken all the clothes out of it and washed and ironed them. She hadn't put them back so the trunk was empty. Morgan wanted his clothes.

"Carol, get the clothes that were in Morgan's trunk!" I yelled.

She stacked them in a pile and handed them to me. I handed them to Morgan.

"Morgan, we didn't know if you were ever coming back," I remarked, because he had been gone about two months longer than anticipated.

We also didn't think his stuff was that important, but Morgan thought otherwise.

"Where is my jewelry? It's not here," he snapped.

"Morgan, I don't know where your jewelry is," I replied, as I shrugged my shoulders. "Carol, did you see any jewelry when you cleaned out the trunk?"

"No. I only saw clothes, nothing else."

Carol knew nothing about it.

"Morgan, the only thing we found in your trunk was clothes. That was it, which Carol washed and ironed for you," I told him, getting a little angry.

We did him the favor and allowed him to leave his trunk here. If it had been important to him, he would have taken it with him or would have claimed it before now. He had supposedly been in Kabul for over two weeks and never mentioned the trunk until now.

"Mark, did you take any jewelry out of the trunk?" I asked him.

Mark just shook his head no. "I never even noticed the trunk."

Morgan wouldn't believe any of us. He picked up his trunk and stormed out of my apartment. I couldn't believe he was that angry over something so irrelevant. He didn't even say goodbye. I thought we were good friends. I guess I was wrong. I still considered him my friend even if he didn't. But it didn't matter. I would probably never see him again anyway. And I didn't.

A few days later, though, I did see the interracial couple. They stopped by the apartment one evening. They bragged about how they were able to smuggle two suitcases filled with ten kilos of hash into America.

I explained to them that it's much easier for an Australian tourist to get through customs than it was for an American citizen. Americans have a much tougher time going through customs. Usually the customs official had the American's drug or intelligence record in front of them. Tourists from other countries had a much easier time. They were never searched, usually due to a lack of customs information. But I congratulated them anyway, and asked, jokingly, if they wanted Carol to smuggle suitcases to America. To my surprise they didn't. They needed to buy a large quantity of hash. They had lost their drug connection due to a hanging—his own.

"Rob, can you get us two-hundred kilos of hash at a decent price?" asked Gerome.

"What's a decent price?"

"We don't want to pay more than ten dollars a kilo."

"At that price you can only buy the pollen," I told him. "You will have to pay extra if you want it pressed. But I will have an answer for you in a day or two. I will have to talk to a few of my Afghan friends. If it can be done, I will probably have to buy it up north. I can't get it that cheap in Kabul."

After Gerome and Flower left, I talked with Carol about this proposition.

"Are you going to buy the hash for them?" she asked me.

"If I do, you will have to stay here while I drive to Mazare Sarif to buy the hash."

"I want to go with you," she whined.

But I didn't want to take a chance of Carol getting busted. The soldiers or police could rape her, beat her, do anything to her, and I wouldn't be able to stop it. We finally agreed when I promised to return within two days. I really didn't know if it could be done that quickly. But I promised her anyway. The next day, I talked with Tiar about the proposition.

"Tiar, we have a chance to make some quick cash. How much will two hundred kilos of decent pollen cost us?" I asked him.

"I can buy hash in Mazare Sarif for two dollars per kilo," he replied. "But we will have to pay bribes to the police at the various checkpoints. If we don't, and they find the hash, they will probably shoot both of us. But I know exactly what to do to pass the road checks without any problems."

We finally agreed on a price. I would give him four dollars per kilo and one hundred dollars when we returned to Kabul. And I had to pay any baksheesh that was needed. Everything was agreed upon. If my friends agreed and gave me the money, we would leave in the morning.

I left Tiar's house and drove to my friend's house. Within a few minutes, I had arrived there. When I knocked on the door, Gerome answered. The house was full of people so we walked into his bedroom to talk.

"Gerome, I can get you what you want for a price of twelve dollars per kilo. I want ten dollars per kilo up front and two dollars per kilo when I return with the goods."

I would make about five dollars to seven dollars per kilo. I figured there wasn't much risk, so it was decent money. I could make well over a thousand dollars for two days' work. We agreed on the sum, and he handed me one-thousand dollars. I was to get another fourteen-hundred when I returned.

Carol packed me a small bag of clothes and food. We didn't talk much that evening; we just held each other close.

I picked up Tiar the next morning. Then I filled up the gas tank with fuel at a cost of one dollar. It was ten cents per gallon. At least gas wouldn't be much of an expense. I drove as Tiar checked the map. It would take us over ten hours of nonstop driving. That is, if everything went one hundred percent perfect. But this was Afghanistan, where nothing worked out perfectly. I was still hoping to get back within two days.

The first few hours of travel went unnoticed, even though it was picturesque scenery. But then, nearly four hours into our trip, we stopped for our first customs check. Now we had to buy travel vouchers to our destination. It was like paying a road tax. That only took about ten minutes. We would have to pay another road toll when we neared a small city called Dosi about halfway to our destination. Then it would be clear sailing to Mazare Sarif. We still had another six to eight hours of driving to go when Tiar took a few grams of hash out of his pocket and handed me some to eat. He chewed on his and told me to do the same. I slowly ingested the potent hashish. I damn near threw up as I chewed it. Time seemed to fly by after that.

The only time we slowed down was at a sheep crossing just outside a small village and the road checks. We passed beautiful, green, luscious jungle forests and then went through hot and dusty desert, then finally into the steep and high Hindu Kush Mountains near Mazare Sarif.

The hash that I had eaten seemed to put me into a deep trance. My mind was a blank. The ten-hour ride seemed to take only two. And I had even forgotten to do my morphine. I was still in a stupor when we reached our destination, Mazare Sarif.

Tiar directed me to his friend's hotel. We would visit a hash farm in the morning after a good night's rest and a good breakfast. It was dark by the time we reached the hotel. Tiar introduced me to his friend, Abdul, the owner of the hotel. He also owned the farm that we were going to visit in the morning.

There were only two hotels in the city. I had stayed at the other hotel the last time I had visited this city. This one was also a decent hotel. At least the room was clean with two big beds. I had to excuse myself and go to the bathroom to inject my morphine. I felt much better and relaxed after I took my medicine. I kept that a secret from Tiar, even though he had eaten a small portion of opium with his tea. He offered me some but I refused, telling him I didn't need it. I slept like a log.

We were up early the next morning. Tiar and Abdul had tea and biscuits for breakfast. I had morphine and the lunch Carol had packed for me. I ate peanut butter and jelly sandwiches with a little goat's milk to wash it down. Then all three of us boarded my van and headed for the hash farm using Abdul's directions. There were only four roads. One went north, one south, one east, and one west. We were traveling west, near the Russian border. I tried to remember if this was one of the farms I had visited before. But I couldn't remember.

After traveling nearly fifty miles through mountain terrain, we finally arrived at Abdul's hash farm. There were two small mud huts, one bigger than the other. One hut was used to live in and the other to store hash pollen. We were introduced to a few of the workers who plowed the fields and took care of the crops. They had finished farming this year's field and had harvested the crops more than three months before. Soon they would be planting the fields with hash and poppy. There were over ten hectares of fertile soil. Abdul was very wealthy by Afghan standards.

"You are lucky to be here," said Abdul. "A month before all the roads were snowed in. The weather just broke a few weeks ago."

Heck, it was almost sixty degrees outside. It was cold at night but warm during the day. The weather was worse in Kabul than in Mazare Sarif.

After showing us the fields, we walked to the storage hut. It was a single twelve-by-twelve-foot room. The walls were covered with stacks of big and little burlap sacks. There must have been over five-hundred sacks of hash pollen ranging from ten to one hundred kilos. Abdul told us he had four different grades, priced from fifteen dollars to two dollars a kilo.

I wanted the cheap stuff for my customers and a few kilos of the top grade pollen for myself. The owner showed us the different grades. The first grade was made from the biggest and tallest female plants. These plants grew to be twenty-five feet tall. They only used the female buds. The second grade was also from all female plants. This was made from the smaller plants. The third and fourth grades were made from female and hermaphrodite plants. Most of these plants had seeded. The THC content was not as potent as the top two grades. The average tourist or hash smoker couldn't tell the difference, but I could.

"Abdul, I want to buy two one-hundred-kilo sacks of the number four hash pollen for two dollars per and one ten-kilo sack of the number one pollen for myself," I told him.

Tiar was to make two dollars on each kilo I bought. I paid Abdul in dollars, and then we loaded the sacks into the van. I was quite elated with the deal. It was a real bargain. It had been worth the time and effort to travel this distance to purchase the hash pollen. It saved me thousands of dollars. Now, we had to reach Kabul with the load of illegal contraband without getting busted, which worried me because we would get checked more often going back.

The next morning, we left the hotel for Kabul. We used a blanket to cover and hide the sacks. We were on our way home. Tiar explained that we would be stopped at our first border check within an hour. The police at these checkpoints looked for smugglers.

"Don't worry, I have done this many times before," said Tiar, trying to ease my nervousness. "I am sure that we can pay baksheesh if they find the hash. But they can also shoot us on the spot."

And he told me not to worry! Then he handed me a piece of hash to chew on, which would relax me. But its taste still repulsed me and made me gag. I finally got it all down, and by the time we had reached our first check point I was pretty smashed. The hash had kicked in. I wasn't worried at all now.

As the Afghan police and soldiers walked up to the van, Tiar spoke with them. I knew he must have said the right thing when they started to laugh. He handed them a twenty-Afghani bill for road tax and they let us proceed. We traveled for another two hours before we came upon another checkpoint. This time the police checked the inside of the van and found the sacks. One of the officers wanted to know what was in them.

"It's only food, just rice," stuttered Tiar.

They didn't seem too startled by Tiar's revelation. They just looked into my eyes and asked for twenty-Afghani for road tax. Once I had paid it, the officers let us continue on our way.

That was a close call. If they had looked into the sacks, we could have been placed in jail or killed. I was sure the officers could smell the odor of the hash, although the bags did conceal the smell quite well. Tiar again told me not to worry.

We only had three-hundred miles and two checkpoints to go before we reached Kabul. We went through the next checkpoint without incident. They asked no questions. They only wanted the twenty-Afghani for the road tax.

The last checkpoint was about fifty miles north of Kabul and very close to home. I was getting anxious. Everything had worked out well so far. And I was certain that we would make it home in one piece and alive.

A few hours later, as we approached the last checkpoint, we noticed a long line of cars. The authorities were searching the vehicles.

"Tiar, what should I do?" I asked him.

"Don't worry. Just be quiet, and I'll take care of it."

Two officers walked up to the van.

"Where have you been?" asked the burly officer.

Before I could answer, Tiar answered for me. I couldn't understand what he was telling them, but they didn't seem to like it. One of the officers opened the passenger door and yanked Tiar to the ground. Tiar raised his arms to protect his face as the officer raised his rifle butt in the air as if he was going to smash Tiar's head in. He stopped just short of Tiar's face as Tiar pleaded with the officer.

Then I intervened. "What the heck is going on?" I yelled to the officers. "Why are you acting like this?"

No one would answer me. They just grabbed Tiar by the arms and dragged him to their small building. I tried to follow but another officer told me to stay in the van. So I sat and waited.

Finally, after twenty minutes, Tiar returned to the van. But he didn't get in. Instead, he walked up to my side window and snapped, "Give me two one hundred-Afghani bills. And hurry!"

I handed them to him without knowing what was happening. He walked back to the building. Within ten minutes, he had returned to the van once again.

"Tiar, what's going on?" I asked, as he got into the van.

"Leave now. Quickly," he said, shaking.

I did as asked. He wanted to get out of there and so did I. We were so frightened we didn't speak. But after ten minutes, I broke the silence.

"What happened back there?"

"The police thought I was the criminal they were looking for. But it was a case of mistaken identity. The two-hundred Afghani was baksheesh for the officers. They found a small amount of hash on me. If they had searched the van and found any more hash they would have taken us to jail or shot us."

"But why did they want the money?"

"They wanted two-hundred Afghani not to search the van. I told them there wasn't any hash in the van but the guards didn't care. They have a job to do. That's why I gave them the money, so they wouldn't harass us," he said, still trembling.

"It was worth the money to get out of there," I said, while chewing on my fingernails.

The last fifty miles went quickly. We were home within an hour. I stopped near Tiar's home and paid him the money he was owed.

"Thank you, Baba," said Tiar, calling me by my nickname.

"Thank you, for doing this deal. I'll see you in the next few days."

I drove home as fast as I could. I couldn't wait to see Carol.

As I walked into the apartment, Carol greeted me at the door. Mark came out from the living room to greet me. He had stayed with Carol while I was gone.

"I'm glad you're home," said Carol, after giving me a kiss.

"Mark, now that I'm back, you can go back to your hotel if you want. Carol and I want to be alone," I told him.

"No problem," he said, then walked back into the living room.

I had only been gone for two days, but it seemed like a month. I was glad to see friendly faces. I was even happy to see Mark. The next morning, I took the pollen to my friend's house. They were anxious to get the hash. They would still have to press it.

Gerome and Flower greeted me at the door and were very happy to see me. They helped me carry the sacks of hash pollen into the house and into the living room where we sat it on the floor. Now I wanted to get my money and leave. I was very paranoid and didn't want to get busted, and this house had been busted once before. I didn't want to be there if it happened again.

"Gerome, do you need someone to press the pollen?" I asked him.

"I don't think so. I know a Canadian guy who lives in Paghman. He has a hydraulic press," he replied.

When he told me this, I knew he was talking about Ted. I didn't tell them that I knew the guy. I'd let them find out for themselves what a big jerk he was.

When Gerome tore open the sack and pulled out a handful of pollen, the living room filled with people. Damn, I didn't know there were that many people living there. There must have been ten people in the room. I slowly pushed Gerome into an empty corner of the living room.

"Gerome, give me the rest of the money you owe me and I will leave."

"You know the deal that Carol did in Denmark? We were short-ed money, so what I owe you will make up for the other money."

"Gerome, if you don't want big trouble, you will pay me the money you owe me, NOW! And I don't want to hear any shit about it. The guy in Denmark should pay the money that is owed to you. He was the one who shorted you, not me."

I wanted my money, and he tried giving me excuses, but I refused to budge.

"We're even," he remarked.

"Gerome, I will ask you one more time, and then I won't be responsible for my actions," I snapped.

Gerome gave me a dirty look and then went into another room with two of the other guys while I waited in front of all his friends. I was really pissed off. He had embarrassed me in front of all these people. I would never forgive him. A few minutes later, he and his pals returned to the room and stood in front of me in a confrontational manner. I thought they were going to jump me and beat me, but instead, Gerome pulled out a wad of American bills from his pocket and handed me the money. It was exactly fourteen-hundred dollars.

"Rob, you're lucky I'm giving you the money, and you're lucky you're getting out of here alive," he said, threatening me.

I looked directly into his eyes and said, "Wise up, Gerome. I can have this place busted within ten minutes."

They followed me outside to the van. As I drove away, I yelled to them that I was going to the police station. Then I just drove off as fast as I could.

After the crap they'd put me through, let them worry. They didn't know whether I would bust them or not. But I never did. I went back to the apartment. Carol was waiting for me. She tried to get me into a sexy mood, but I didn't want sex at that moment. I was still too upset. I explained to Carol about the argument I'd had with Gerome.

"Robert, you do them a favor and they shit all over you," she said, as she rubbed the back of my neck.

"I will never do it again unless the money is too good to turn down."

Now I just wanted to relax. Carol and I decided to do some

morphine. I added an extra tab to each spoon to rush the anger out of me. It worked. After the rush subsided, I was still too high to worry about anything. That is, until the next morning.

That morning our landlord awakened us. He wanted us out of the apartment. He wanted to rent it to the Iranian embassy. I argued with him because I didn't want to leave the apartment. My rent was always paid on time and there was still a week until rent was due.

"We're not moving," I snapped. "We haven't done anything wrong. You don't have a good reason to kick us out of our house."

I was pissed, so I slammed the door in his face, swearing I'd never move out of this apartment without a fight. I was so angry, I spilled the morphine tablets all over the bedroom floor as I was trying to make my morning fix. Carol calmed me down, talking in her soothing voice.

The next morning, the landlord was knocking at my front door. As I peered through the door's tiny peephole, I noticed, standing next to the landlord, a seven-foot-tall giant of a policeman. As I opened the door, the landlord started yelling at me that I must leave the apartment or suffer the consequences, and that the policeman would throw me out if I didn't leave.

I took out the letter from my money belt that the school clerk had given me and handed it to the landlord. As he and the policeman were reading the letter, I got paranoid thinking that they might rip it apart, so I grabbed it out of my landlord's hands and slammed the door in their faces. But before I could lock it, they pushed it open.

"Carol, help me shut the door!" I yelled. She threw herself against it.

We tried with all our might to close the door. Finally, with one big burst of our morphine-induced bodies, we were able to shut the door on the landlord and his friendly giant. Carol and I had the strength of ten men, or so it seemed. I couldn't believe what we had done.

I peeked through the peephole and the two Afghans were talking amongst themselves. It seemed they couldn't believe how strong we were either. They just scratched their heads and left.

An hour after they had departed, I decided to hop in the van and go to the rental office. I wanted to rent a new apartment. I didn't want the landlord to return with any more police. My business was going too good to get thrown out of the country now. That's what could happen if they returned.

I talked with the salesman who had rented me the first apartment. He had a new apartment on the other side of town, about two miles from my old one. It had just been built. It had never been occupied and was a big, beautiful, third-story apartment with five rooms—two small bedrooms, a small kitchen with shower and bath, and a nice-sized living room. I could use all the rooms, including the living room.

The apartment complex had only four apartment units. There was a hairdresser and a tailor on the main floor and both second floor units were occupied. The top two weren't. Outside, was also a long walkway that ran along the entire unit. There were big windows in the master bedroom and the living room looking out onto Chicken Street.

Across the street stood a huge, rocky mountain where there were no houses. It stood alone. Looking out the kitchen window was an army fort hidden behind another large mountain. You could see the soldiers doing their morning exercises near the many stationary machine guns and cannons that protected it. I liked the apartment. It was only one-hundred and twenty-five dollars a month, and I had to pay the electric bill.

My business was well established and doing well, so I could afford this apartment. It was near a dead-end street, out of the eye of the police, and in a very quiet neighborhood. The only noise that could be heard was from the bus station a block away.

I returned to the rental office and gave the salesman the first and last months' rent. I could start moving in immediately.

I returned home and told Carol about the new apartment. She was angry with me for not taking her along to look at it. So instead of arguing with her, I drove her to our new apartment. I soothed her feelings by telling her that I'd wanted to surprise her and that this was her place.

"Carol, I will buy the necessities to make your life easier. I will buy you an electric stove and electric hot water heater like the one at our other apartment. And I will buy you whatever you want or need. I am here to please you," I promised her, rubbing her shoulders.

Once she had seen the apartment and the beautiful surrounding scenery and lovely views, she loved it. She had a few ideas of her own. She wanted to get material to make curtains for the windows and linoleum for the cement floors. I promised her anything to make her happy. I was really in love with this girl. I wanted to make her as comfortable as possible.

"We will stay here until I can afford to buy you a hash farm," I promised her.

She showed her approval by making love to me on the cold cement living room floor. After our little sexcapade, we drove back to our old apartment to start packing. Even though we had nearly a week before our lease expired, we wanted to get a jump on things.

We had accumulated quite a bit of furniture and miscellaneous items. Mark even helped us pack and move. And after two full days of moving, I still had six to ten loads of stuff to move, plus I needed to buy some things for the new apartment. So Mark and I went to the bazaar to buy some wood-burning stoves for the kitchen, living room, and bedrooms, while Carol stayed at the new apartment and unpacked everything.

A new department store had just opened in the center of town. It was a westernized department store like Sears or Montgomery Wards. It even had an escalator. The Afghans used it as an amusement ride. I bought a Carom board game so Saraj could teach me how to play the Afghan way, not the American way. We could buy practically anything here that we could buy in America. It was great, as long as I had money. By the time we left that store, I had bought a van full of merchandise. We took it back to Carol so she could put it in its proper place in our new apartment.

Over the next few days, we moved nearly everything into our new apartment. On the last night of our rental agreement, we still had a few more pieces of furniture to move. The following morning, the new tenants would be moving in, so we had to get everything out that night. We had no time left.

By ten o'clock that evening, we were loading the last few items into the van when that seven-foot-tall policeman came by to see what we were doing. This was the same policeman the landlord had brought over to kick us out of the apartment. He was a giant. As I was putting a wicker chair into the van, he came near me and said a few words in Pashtu, which I didn't understand.

When I tried placing the chair into the van, the officer knocked it out of my hands. Again, he said something in Pashtu that I didn't understand. He continued to talk in a loud voice, until he was yelling. I still had no idea what he was saying or what he wanted, just that he was a pain in the ass and was stopping me from moving. As I reached for the chair to place it into the van, the giant policeman again knocked it out of my hands. Then he slapped me in the face. I was very surprised and confused by his actions. I didn't know why he wouldn't allow Carol or me to put anything else into the van.

I ran to the servant's quarters at the apartment building but no-body was home. As I ran back to the van, a small crowd of Afghans had amassed to see what all the commotion was about. I asked the crowd for help, but they didn't understand me and I didn't under-stand them. So once again, I picked up the wicker chair and tried to place it into the van. Again, the giant policeman slapped my face, so hard that it knocked me six feet into the street.

When I stood up and brushed myself off, I resumed my position near the van. Carol went into the van and found a big, round stick, which was half the size of a baseball bat. I had used it as a rolling pin. She gave it to me to protect myself. As soon as the officer saw it, he thought I was going to use it as a weapon and began fighting me for control of it. I knew that if he took it away from me he would use it on me and probably kill me. So I hung on with all my might. Finally, as Carol jumped onto his back to help me, he let go of the stick and I threw it into the van yelling, "Bas! Bas! Enough! Enough!"

The crowd had swelled to over a dozen by now. Finally, some-one stepped out of the crowd and told me that it was against the law to move furniture at night. That was what the officer was trying to tell me. When the Afghan explained to the cop that I hadn't unders-tood what he had been saying, the cop then apologized to me and I to him. We shook hands, and then I grabbed the chair and put it back into the apartment. I would pick up the last few remaining pieces of furniture in the morning.

When I returned to the street, Carol and I got into the van and headed to our new apartment. On the way home, we argued about the fight with the giant policeman.

"Carol, what were you thinking when you handed me that club? If that guy had taken it away from me, he would have killed us both," I told her.

She didn't say a word. In fact, we didn't say too much the rest of the night.

The next morning, Carol stayed at the new apartment redecorat-ing while I went to the old apartment to gather the last few remaining items. Then I picked up Mark and headed to the bazaar to pick up the three stoves that I had ordered. They were being made special and by hand. They were complete and finished when we ar-rived. I paid for them, loaded them into the van, and then went to buy some linoleum for the five rooms of our new apartment.

When we returned to our new digs, Mark and I installed the new stoves. The first one was put in the kitchen to be used as the oven. The one for the living room and my bedroom was used for heat. But to make heat, I had to buy firewood, and that was a rare commodity and very expensive. I decided to buy two electric heaters.

Not only were these used for heat, but I also used one of them to fire the hash with. By now, I was pressing my own hashish. I was still going to Tiar and Moktar to buy pollen, but I saved money by pressing it myself.

Once the stoves were installed, Mark and I cut and laid the linoleum in all five rooms. Its color was light yellow, with red and orange flowers, like a Van Gogh painting. It was very beautiful and shiny, especially after it had been waxed. I then laid some of my Afghan carpets and glims (made for hallways—3ft. by 12 ft) on the living room and bedroom floors, while Carol made curtains for the windows.

"Carol, we will be here for the next five years, so we might as well be as comfortable as we can," I told her in a joyous manner.

My business was doing excellent and money was plentiful, so I began spending more of it. I purchased two more speakers for our stereo system. I bought them at the music store. Each speaker cabinet had two twelve-inch speakers with two three-inch tweeters. They were nearly three feet tall and cost over three-hundred dollars each. I also bought a 250-watt amplifier. I could blow the roof off this building with this stereo system. I also was having cassette tapes recorded and dubbed from English albums of all the famous rock groups at that store.

Now I had to buy some firewood for all the new furnaces I had bought. So I drove the van down the block to pick up a cord of firewood. Once there, I watched as the salesman weighed the wood on a balance scale. They weighed wood like they weighed gold. And it was damn near as expensive. I paid nearly a hundred dollars for a cord of wood. They helped me load it into the van, and I had Carol help me carry it into our apartment.

I kept the wood in the spare bedroom to keep it out of the cold and damp weather. I also cut it up there. But each time I split the wood with the ax it made a loud thud. The noise didn't bother me, but it apparently annoyed my neighbor directly below me. The first few times I cut the wood, I could hear the man telling his wife that the noise was driving him crazy. I tried to cut the wood as fast as I could, which only lasted a mere five or ten minutes because I didn't want to annoy anyone. I wanted to get along with everyone even though I rarely saw my neighbors, and when I did, they never complained about anything.

Never, that is, until early one morning when the guy in the apartment below mine tried to break down my front door with an ax of his own. As this crazy lunatic was breaking into our apartment, I was screaming for Aslam, the manager of the apartment complex. But before he arrived, this crazy man had broken the hinges off the door and was wielding the ax at my head trying to kill me. Just as he swung the ax at my head, I ducked and it hit the wall and got stuck. He had trouble getting it out of the wall, so I hit him with all my strength with a right cross that dropped him to his knees. As he was falling, I grabbed for his ax and got it away from him.

By this time, all hell had broken loose. This guy's wife was in the hallway screaming her lungs out. Finally, Aslam and a few of his friends had arrived. This guy was still trying to fight me and take the ax away from me, but I kept the madman at bay by threatening him with it.

As Aslam looked over the destruction and situation, I explained to him how this idiot broke down the door with the ax and tried to kill me. I had Aslam forcefully remove the nut from the premises. It took Aslam and three big friends to wrestle this guy out of my apartment.

"Aslam, either that guy goes or we are," I told him, while trying to catch my breath.

The apartment owner was there within the hour. He had the police escort the guy out of the apartment building. We wouldn't have any trouble from him anymore. The apartment owner told me, after the man's wife had told him, that the man had a nervous breakdown in Italy and was in Afghanistan for rest and relaxation. He had become obsessed with the notion that I was trying to drive him crazy. She said that he wasn't playing with a full deck.

Within a few days, an English couple and their twin girls had moved into the apartment below.

Our apartment was becoming a castle. I bought posters of Janis Joplin and Jimi Hendrix and had them framed, and then hung them on the walls in the living room. We also bought all new wicker furniture. Carol had made new curtains for all the windows and the stereo supplied all the magic. The floors were now completely covered with handmade Afghan carpets and glims, wall to wall.

My cassette collection would grow to over three hundred. The only thing of comfort we lacked was a telephone and a television.

We didn't need a telephone, and there was no television station in Afghanistan anyway. Afghanistan was decades behind other industrialized nations. We liked this apartment much more than the other one.

CHAPTER 14
THE CARNIVAL

Springtime was just around the corner. The snow was beginning to melt, and many of Kabul's roads were knee-deep in mud. We were very lucky to have the van. That is, until one morning while we were driving to the post office, my luck quickly changed. Just as we were crossing the first intersection from our apartment, an Afghan traffic cop waved his hands wanting me to pull over. Instead, I just waved to him and continued on my journey.

I wasn't about to stop, not with an expired visa. They could throw me out of the country or jail me, so I decided to keep going. As I looked into my side view mirror, I noticed that the traffic cop had flagged down a taxi and was chasing after my van.

"Carol, the cop is after me. I will stop in front of Najib Hotel and you jump out and wait for me there until I return."

To be on the safe side, she took the hash envelopes with her. And as she walked away from the van, the taxi pulled up behind me and then the cop jumped out and ran over to my side of the van. I opened the door to ask him what he wanted, but just as I did, he grabbed the door and slapped my face with the back of his hand, then yelled at me to "stay in the van."

He jumped into the passenger side and ordered me to drive. I really couldn't understand his language. He was speaking Pashtu. But I could still understand his hand language as he directed me to the police station.

Once I parked the van, I followed him into an old and dirty jail. He placed me into a chair and gestured for to me to sit and wait. Within five minutes, I was directed into a captain's office. Sitting in chairs were six or seven well-dressed men and women, including the captain. I stood in front of his desk as he questioned me in perfect English.

"These are my relatives," said the captain, pointing to the people in the chairs. "What country are you from?"

"I am from America," I said nervously.

"What would American police do if you refused to stop your car for them?" the captain asked me.

"They would probably shoot at me with their guns," I replied.

The captain proceeded to explain to his relatives what I had told him. I was becoming an adventure for them.

"Why didn't you stop and pull over when the officer gestured for you to stop?"

"Sir, I thought the officer was waving to me. That's why I waved back to him," I explained.

I was lying through my teeth. I didn't really expect him to believe me, but I said it anyway. Then I opened my money belt, pulled out the letter from the university, and showed it to him. Whatever the clerk wrote in that letter, it seemed to help immensely. He showed the letter to his visitors.

"You must pay a fifty-Afghani fine," said the captain. "Then you may leave."

I quickly paid him the fifty-Afghani and then shook his hand and everyone else's in that room. I folded the letter back into my money belt and left the police station.

I jumped into the van with a smile on my face and then quickly drove back to the Najib Hotel to pick up Carol. When I arrived, she was talking to some hippie Americans at their hotel room. They had a female puppy that they couldn't keep.

"Rob, can I keep the puppy?" asked Carol.

It was so small and cute with its fluffy red and white fur.

"Carol, it looks like a little fox. Of course you can keep it," I told her.

Carol hugged and kissed me. As we were driving to the post office, Carol became affectionate with the dog and me.

"The puppy does look like a little fox after all. I think I'll call her Foxy," she said happily.

Once we had finished our chores, we headed back to the apartment—this time with a new family member, a fluffy little puppy.

The minute we entered our abode, Carol and I went directly to our bedroom and fixed our morphine. A few hours later, we headed over to Ron and Cindy's hotel room, along with Foxy. We hadn't seen them in awhile, so we wanted to say hello and talk over old times. We weren't sure if they would be home or not.

I knocked on the door of their rooftop hotel room and to my surprise, Ron answered the door. He seemed happy to see us and invited us in. Carol and Cindy started gossiping immediately while Ron and I began a conversation. But then something else quickly drew my attention when I noticed a small, furry type of rat running around their small hotel room.

"Ron, what the heck is running around the room—or am I hallucinating?" I asked him.

Cindy interrupted us and said it was their pet mongoose. She called it by its name and it peeked out from under the bed covers and eyed me suspiciously. Cindy grabbed the furry little creature while our little puppy walked over to smell it and check it out. Little Foxy didn't know what to make of their little bundle of fur. As Cindy held onto it, Foxy began licking it and cuddling up to it. Within seconds, they had become close friends. Cindy released it and let it roam the room once again, and Foxy followed close behind.

It was a real treat watching these two amazing animals play with each other. I guess from our conversation with Ron and Cindy the animals were getting along better than they were. Cindy was getting ready to return to America and Ron was heading to India. They were always arguing and fighting amongst themselves.

"It's time for me to return to the University of Michigan. I've had enough of Afghanistan," remarked Cindy.

"Cindy, be sure to keep in touch and write me," I said. "Ron, if you want me to send you hash, I will. I will give you the same deal as I give my other friends. We will miss you."

After visiting for a couple of hours, we had to leave. Carol and I had to finish our chores. We all hugged each other and said goodbye. After that day, we would never see Ron and Cindy again. I wondered if I would ever hear from them again.

Two and sometimes three days a week I had four main chores to do. First, I had to take the hash envelopes to Saraj at the post office and check the incoming mail for letters from my friends and relatives. Next, I would go to the bank, check the book for wired money transactions, and pick up any money that had been sent to me. Then I'd go to the pharmacy and buy ten or so bottles of morphine. And my last stop was either to Tiar's house or Moktar's house to buy a few kilos of pollen. Then I would return to the apartment and fix Carol and me a big "do" of morphine. Once the rush had subsided, I would take the pollen that I had just purchased and make hash while Carol cooked dinner. I repeated this routine weekly.

Life was going great and business was going very smoothly. I had ten friends to whom I sent hash regularly, and money was coming in regularly. So we spent it many different ways. We went to a theater a few times each week that showed classic English-speaking American films, such as *Hello, Dolly; Caravans; Pinocchio,* and many others.

We bought all our food at a new supermarket built just for European diplomats. And when Carol wasn't cooking, we'd visit the best restaurants in Kabul. But most of the money was spent on Carol—fur coats, jewelry, and tailored clothes. We had it made in the shade with lemonade. I never wanted to leave this beautiful country.

In fact, business was so good that I expanded our market. Mark and I were not only making hash envelopes but also shoes and sandals. I used a wooden sandal that had rubber soles. We would peel back the sole, dig out pockets of wood, and replace it with hash. Then we would glue the sole back to the wooden sandal and sand the edge of the sole. It looked like new. We were always looking and finding inventive ways of sending hash. I found out we weren't the only ones trying to send hash out of the country. I was very suspicious of the people who lived directly below us.

The English couple who had just moved into the apartment below us also shared it with a young French couple. Both couples were in their early twenties, like Carol and me. But we had become aggravated by their presence. They would make loud pounding noises at night just when we were trying to sleep. We put up with this noise for over a week.

Finally, one night I got fed up. I pounded on our bedroom floor and yelled out, "Do whatever you are doing during day time hours! This time of night people are trying to sleep!"

We could hear them talking but couldn't understand what they were saying. However, they did stop the pounding and we could finally get some sleep. The next day, Carol and I watched as the French couple was getting out of a taxi. They were each carrying two big wooden statues.

I looked at Carol. "Carol, if that's what they were working on they are going to get busted. If they try to send those statues through customs without having a connection, they *will* get busted," I predicted.

"Why do you say that?"

Once I saw the statues, I knew what they were up to. Now I knew what all the pounding and loud noise was about. I figured they were hollowing out the statues and filling them with hash.

"The customs official will just throw them on the ground and break them," I told her. "Many tourists think the Afghan people are stupid. They soon find out how mistaken they are."

Within a few days, I found out I had been right. The French guy took six two-foot-high wooden statues filled with hash and tried to send them to France. The customs man looked at them, turned them upside down, and then scraped the bottom of one with his thumbnail, tearing away a piece of hash. That was it. Stupidity was the Frenchman's downfall. When the guy made them, he just sanded the hash flush with the wood and then painted over it. How stupid can you be? He deserved to get busted.

Once the customs man saw the small piece of hash, he took the other five statues and proceeded to smash them on the floor, spewing hash everywhere. The police were summoned and he was taken to jail.

My new neighbor, the Englishman, Keith, had told me this. And just a few months before another friend of his had smuggled hash the same way, but he took it in a car, overland. But to do it through the post office you had to know the customs man.

"Keith, what happened to the guy's wife?" I asked him.

"The French girl is staying with us until she can make enough money to return to France."

"And why are you in Kabul?" I asked.

"I work at the British Embassy as an English teacher,"

"I work at the university," I lied.

Keith and I were becoming good friends.

As the days grew longer, the weather was becoming warmer. It was spring.

One morning, when I fired up the hot water heater to take a shower something happened. Within a few minutes, the house was full of thick, black, sooty smoke. I opened the bathroom window and yelled for Aslam to help me. He came running into the apartment. I showed him what the problem was and he fixed it immediately. The flue had become stuck and wouldn't let the smoke out of the chimney. Instead, it all backed up into the apartment. We had to open up all the windows and doors to let the smoke escape. Luckily, the smoke didn't cause any damage to the furniture or carpets. And I made sure it would never happen again.

That very same day I went out and purchased a new seven-gallon electric hot water heater similar to the one we had at our other apartment and had the landlord hire a plumber to install it. Within two days, we were using it. No longer did I have to make a fire to take a shower. No longer did I have to wait an hour before the hot water heater was hot enough to use. We were back in the twentieth century.

I was honestly thinking of getting rid of all of our wood-burning stoves. At first, they were a good idea, but the wood was very expensive and when I brought the wood inside, it also brought with it bugs. So within a few weeks, I had bought a used electric stove and oven and a brand new Phillips refrigerator. I got rid of all the wood stoves except for the one in the living room. I used that as our fireplace. It created a romantic atmosphere.

Spring was over and summer was just around the corner. It was the month of April, and four young male Peace Corp volunteers had just rented the apartment across from ours. I told Carol to be extra paranoid and discreet and watch what she said until we knew more about these four Americans. I didn't want to get busted, so we tried to stay invisible.

I had been in Kabul for well over a year and had become good friends with the street merchants around the city of Kabul. Every day I would walk around the city and talk with the sidewalk vendors and bazaar merchants. When I first met them, I would just say hello and move on. Now I was helping them when they were ill. I would give them items such as Band-Aids or antibiotics. Soon all the street vendors were calling me over, telling me their ailments, and asking for a solution to their sickness. I was their street doctor. I must say I did help them overcome their ailments.

One of these vendors was a young kid called "Baba." He was a real sharp street hustler. He would do almost anything to make a buck. Nothing illegal, of course, but he knew an awful lot of information on the city's news.

Whenever I would hear rumors from the king's relatives, I would ask Baba if they were true, and nine times out of ten they were—even the one about the Russians invading the city.

I had first heard the rumor from my Afghan friends at the disco that the Russians were buying the king. So I asked Baba to confirm the story. He did. He was an encyclopedia of information.

Another Afghan I had met and become friends with was one who would come to Kabul two or three times a year. The first time I saw him he was traveling with a full-grown female Rhesus monkey. It was unreal and nearly human. I made friends with this monkey immediately. The monkey even made friends with me.

The Afghan even let me watch her when he went into a store to buy some food. I felt honored that he would trust me with his prized possession. Then some young Afghan kids came up to it and began to tease her and she went right after them. They turned and ran, but as she lunged for them, I pulled the rope to stop her from hurting them. When she stood on her feet she was over five feet tall and weighed two hundred pounds. When I pulled on the leash and told her to stop, she did what I said. She came back over to me and I petted her and talked to her to soothe her feelings. Her master saw the commotion and thanked me for watching her. I told him that if she ever had any babies that I would like to buy one. He told me she was pregnant and within a month would give birth. As I handed him the leash, I asked him to look me up when he returned to Kabul. He agreed.

A few days later, a Muslim holiday (Independence Day) was upon us and Saraj stopped by my apartment.

"Bob, do you want to go to the big carnival?" he asked.

"What carnival are you talking about?"

"During this time of year, a long celebration occurs. The Muslims who can't make the pilgrimage to Mecca try to go to the famous holy mosque in Mazare Sarif. This was where the great prophet Mohammed prayed and worshiped for a time. If for some reason they can't make the pilgrimage to either Mecca or Mazare Sarif, they come to the outskirts of Kabul and celebrate at the Kabul carnival. It lasts for over a week," he explained.

There were nearly as many Muslims who prayed at Mazare Sarif as in Mecca. So going to and from Mazare Sarif the people stopped off and partied at this yearly carnival. It was very similar to the Mardi Gras in New Orleans. At least that's the picture I had gotten from Saraj.

On Saraj's day off, Carol, Mark, Saraj, and I jumped into my van and headed three miles away to the outskirts of Kabul, heading north. It was a beautiful day. It started out overcast but the clouds burned off within thirty minutes.

When we arrived, there were cars and people everywhere. Nothing seemed organized. Thousands of cars were parked haphazardly along the side of the road. I had seen this same pandemonium when I drove to Woodstock. The cars stretched for miles. I never knew there were that many cars in Afghanistan, let alone Kabul. Finally, after traveling a good mile, we were able to find a parking spot.

Once we left the van, we walked for more than twenty minutes before we finally reached the carnival. This was supposed to be a peaceful holiday, but everywhere I turned and looked I saw and heard people yelling and screaming at each other. I couldn't believe this was a religious holiday.

Saraj estimated that there were nearly one-hundred thousand people. I thought there was more than that. It looked just like Woodstock. There was even a big stage for the musicians and dancers. As we walked through the crowds, we saw jugglers, fire-breathing sword swallowers, and magicians doing their tricks.

The carnival rides were a joke. They looked like they were made back in the early sixteen hundreds. The carnival reminded me of an old Errol Flynn movie, *Robin Hood.* They had the same type of carnival. Many of the rides were powered by either human or horse. There was a small Ferris wheel for children that were turned by hand. The children's boat rides were turned in a circle by a horse. One ride seemed to come out of a *Little Rascals* movie. A donkey walked in circles and turned the ride as it chased after a carrot that was held by a string from above and dangled in front of its mouth.

This whole carnival seemed to come out of a *Mad* magazine. One minute the crowd would be laughing, smiling, and clapping at the festivities and then, within a second, an argument would break out between two adults and then more people would join in. When they began taking sides, all hell broke loose. The arguments turned into a fistfight, first between two people, then three, then four, and then we would get the hell out of there and move to another part of the carnival.

The carnival and crowd was on about four thousand acres of desolate, dirty, rocky, rolling desert hills. Even though there were tense times, we were still having a great time. We ate great shish kabob sandwiches, washed down with half-cold Cokes. We stayed almost ten hours, until nightfall.

We listened and watched the different ethnic musicians and dancers from different parts of the country. Their dances told where they were from. This was something new for me. I learned a great deal of their history from the music and their dances.

Saraj was right—there were at least one-hundred thousand people watching and listening to the people on stage. Most of them were locals but many were foreign tourists also.

This is what many of the arguments seemed to be about. Half the people accepted the foreigners and the other half didn't. Then the arguing would stop and a fistfight would begin, usually between two locals. But one of the fights that broke out was between two European tourists.

As the music was playing and everyone was concentrating on the dancers on stage, a commotion started up a few yards away from us.

It seemed one guy tried to steal something from the other but got caught. Both men were very big. Each was at least six-feet tall and well over two hundred pounds. They both had long hair and the one who was caught stealing had a thick beard, almost ten inches long.

They were also junkies. I could tell right away because they had dyed their hair a bright orange—that was their calling card. They did this for recognition. When they arrived in a new city, they could go up to one of their orange-haired colleagues and find out where to cop a fix.

I knew that these guys meant business and played for keeps. Sure enough, when the victim confronted the thief, the thief pulled out a switchblade knife from under his Afghan shirt and flashed it up to the victim's eyes, then threatened him with it. When he jabbed the knife toward the victim's chest, the victim quickly jumped to one side and just as quickly pulled out his own knife.

Knives were plentiful in Afghanistan. This country was known for its manufacture of some of the best-made knives in the world, especially the switchblade knife.

Now I was watching two crazy guys circling, trying to get the edge on the other, trying to get the upper hand and the advantage to kill his prey. All the Afghans were standing around in a big circle mesmerized by the foreigners' actions. This was déjà vu all over again. This scene came right out of *West Side Story*.

As the two men circled one another, swinging and lunging with their knives, no one was trying to stop the fight, not even the policemen who were watching. The only ones who weren't watching the fight were the musicians and dancers. Well, they might have been watching while they played and danced, but I was too engrossed in the fight to care about what was going on, on stage. Carol was squeezing my hand so tight she cut off my circulation. And Mark stood silently until he couldn't stand it any longer and shouted out in frustration.

"Quit fighting before someone gets hurt!" he yelled to the two fighters.

I didn't know if they could hear Mark over all the other noise or if they understood him at all. But within another few minutes, it was all over. The thief got the worst of it. When he lunged at the victim for the last time, he missed. That left him wide open and within a foot of the other guy's knife. All I could see was the victim's hand disappear into the thief's gut. At first, I thought the guy just hit him with his fist and knocked the wind out of him. But then the thief let out a loud gasp. Just at that moment, everything became silent. You could hear a pin drop. Even the music and dancing had stopped. As the man's fist came out of the thief's stomach, the thief let out a muffled groan and also much of his blood and guts. The thief's opponent had grabbed a handful of intestines and stomach and tried to rip it out of the guy's insides. As the thief fell to his knees, he kept trying to put his guts back into his stomach. The other guy was covered in the thief's blood. His arm was bloody up to the elbow. It was one of the most hideous sights I had ever witnessed. Carol even regurgitated her food watching that horrendous episode.

Within a few minutes, it was all over. The thief was lying dead on the ground covered in his own blood. The killer was yelling at his wife or girlfriend.

"It's your fault this happened! I didn't want to be here in the first place!" he yelled.

I thought the policemen who had watched the fight would have arrested the guy for killing the thief, but instead everyone was patting him on the back and congratulating him for killing a low-down dirty thief. Neither Mark nor Carol nor I could believe they would let this guy get away with murder. Only Saraj could justify the homicide.

"In my country," explained Saraj, "a thief is like a murderer. They have no respect for themselves or anyone else. The first time someone is caught stealing, they get their hand cut off—their left hand, because that's the hand they eat with. The right hand they use to wipe their butts. They usually die from starvation because it's against their religious views to eat with their right hand. Most would rather die."

"Saraj, what happens to them if they get caught a second time?" I asked.

"The second time they get caught they are publicly executed at the town square where the executioner cuts off their head. That is the Afghan way of treating criminals. In the Afghan's eyes, the man who kills the thief is a hero, not a murderer," he said nonchalantly.

By this time we were all tired and disgusted, but overall we'd still had a good time. This carnival was quite different from any I had been to in America or Europe for that matter.

We walked back to the van, loaded our weary bodies into it, and then drove back to the city. Most of the people were still at the carnival, so it wasn't too difficult to turn the van around and weave in and out of the congested traffic. Fifteen minutes later, I had dropped Saraj off at his hotel room and then drove directly to my apartment.

"Mark, you can stay over if you want. You can sleep in the spare bedroom," I told him.

"I appreciate that, Rob. I didn't want to be alone tonight after witnessing a murder."

I couldn't blame him. Mark was always welcome at my apartment. He would occasionally stay at my place, but most of the time he stayed at one of the cheaper hotels. He liked to be where the action was. He liked to be around the hippies and women tourists. I was just the opposite. I liked to keep a low profile. I had to be very discreet, especially with an expired visa. I had to be very careful.

On the other hand, when Mark's visa ran out he went to Pakistan, where the morphine was very prevalent and cheap. He stayed there until he could get another entrance visa for Afghanistan. Then he would come back to Kabul and work with me making hashish, envelopes, and sandals. He was a big help to me but still refused to take chances with the customs people. He would work for me a couple days out of the week and earn enough money to keep him in food, clothes, morphine, and a roof over his head. He also knew that I would help him whenever he needed it. He was my very best friend. We grew up together from the age of seven. He was the brother I never had. We played in the same rock band, did the same drugs, and had the same philosophy about life. I would do anything for that guy. That's how close we were. In fact, Carol would become jealous at times because I would spend more time with him than with her. I didn't think so, but she did. Mark's visa was up and again he was off to Pakistan for a time.

Time was going by fast. It was damn near summer already. Foxy had grown into a beautiful, well-tamed collie. She was not only beautiful but also smart.

One late night, while reading in the bedroom, Foxy kept whining. She would walk to the bedroom door, sit facing the street, and whine. I got up to see what was going on. I looked out the window to the street below. The bright street light illuminated the dark night.

I noticed a large pack of dogs. I opened the bedroom door and went outside onto the patio. I watched as the wild dogs formed a small circle. Two of the large dogs seemed to be fighting one another while the others were sitting, watching, and waiting for the outcome. It looked as if each dog had the other by the mouth. But as the two large dogs backed away from each other, I noticed that in each of their mouths was a smaller dog. These two big dogs were trying to rip the little dog in two, probably to eat it.

When I saw what was actually happening I looked for something to throw at them to break up the fight. I picked up a couple of big rocks that I had on the porch and threw the first one as hard as I could from three floors up and fifty feet away. Smack! Bull's-eye. I hit one of the big dogs right in the side. It yelped and dropped the little dog from its mouth. Then I took aim and threw a second rock at the other monster dog still holding its prey. Thud! I hit it square in the side of the head. *What an arm,* I thought to myself. I *should have been a pitcher in the big leagues.* The big dog dropped his hold on the helpless little mutt. The small, disabled dog fell to the street. The big dogs just stood there and looked a little dazed.

The other wild dogs still sat in a circle calmly waiting to see what was going to happen. Just as one of the big dogs was about to lunge at the small hurt dog, I threw another rock at my target and hit it again, dead center. I threw a couple more rocks at the other big dog and that finally chased all the wild dogs away. I watched as two of the smaller dogs stayed with the hurt one to protect it. It was amazing how human these wild dogs seemed to be.

After a few minutes, the injured dog got up and limped over to my apartment building. It lay under a street lamp on the sidewalk and rested as the two other dogs stood guard to protect him from harm.

I watched for the next couple of hours so no harm would come to it. When I noticed the other dogs had returned and started to form in a pack to attack the little dog again, I gathered up some rocks and pelted the attacking animals. As the rocks hit their targets, the killer dogs scattered far away to lick their wounds.

The injured dog and its two companions stayed under the streetlight undisturbed. I even threw some of Foxy's food down to the dogs, which they ate in a matter of seconds. Foxy didn't seem to mind. It went for a good cause, and Foxy knew it.

The pack of wild dogs never did come back to maul that little dog. That was the first time I had actually seen wild dogs with my own eyes. I had heard about them but had never seen them. Now I had.

The Age of Aquarius

Something different and exciting was happening nearly every day here in this beautiful city of Kabul.

CHAPTER 15
SARAJ'S VILLAGE AND GENGHIS KHAN

The last time I delivered the hash envelopes to Saraj, he invited Carol and me to his village to have dinner and meet his family.

"Saraj, can I bring along my friend, Mark?" I asked.

Saraj knew Mark so he didn't mind. "Yes, you may bring your friend," he replied.

"Great. My birthday is coming up in a few weeks, and Mark should be back from Pakistan by then. We'll drive out to your village around that time. I'm looking forward to it."

Saraj was very happy. Just as we were about to leave the post office, he introduced us to his supervisor and the director of the post office, Mr. Bareck. He was my age, in his mid-twenties, with dark hair, my size, and quite handsome. As the months passed, Mr. Bareck and I became very good friends.

A day or two after my birthday, I visited the American Embassy to renew my passport. It had finally expired after five years. The consulate general noticed that my Afghan visa had expired but couldn't help me renew it. That was my responsibility. Little did he know, I didn't care about a visa. I never intended to leave Afghanistan.

I waited there nervously for nearly an hour before I received my new passport. I was worried that they would expose me to the Afghan government for my expired visa and get me kicked out of the country. But I got lucky.

The only trouble I had with the embassy was from a marine guard when he checked my shoulder bag for weapons. That was the biggest hassle they gave me. Needless to say, I left there very happy with a big smile on my face. Now I was ready to go to Saraj's village.

We picked up Saraj at lunchtime. He only had to work a half a day. It was a holiday for the Afghan people. Mark had returned to

Kabul a few days before, so he, Carol, Saraj, and I loaded into my van and headed to Saraj's village.

We would only stay for a few hours and eat dinner and then we would return home. During our ride, Saraj mentioned something about a wedding that was coming up in a few weeks.

"Bob, would you and Carol like to go to my cousin's wedding?" asked Saraj.

"Whose wedding is it, Saraj?" I asked him.

"It's one of my close relatives, a first cousin. It will take place in the old city of Kabul."

"Carol, do you want to go to the wedding?" I asked her.

"Sure, I would love to go."

"Mark, do you want to go to a wedding?" I asked.

However, Mark didn't seem too interested in the idea. "No. I don't think so."

"Saraj, Carol and I would be happy to attend your cousin's wedding. Should we bring a gift?"

"It isn't necessary. All that's required is your presence."

"Saraj, do me a favor and please remind me a day or two before the wedding just to be on the safe side or I might forget," I said.

"I will."

As we headed out of the city, we passed a golf course and a big lake.

"Saraj, what is the name of the lake?" I asked.

But as we passed by, I noticed that the lake was actually a dam.

"That isn't a lake, that is Cargar Dam," he said. "That's the reservoir that holds Kabul's drinking water. You are allowed to swim in it in the summertime."

It was a beautiful sight; Cargar Dam would become a special place for Carol and me.

The scenery was very beautiful and spectacular heading to Saraj's village. I had been this way before, but I had never seen it as green, bright, and colorful as it was today. We traveled about three hours and stopped at two police checkpoints to pay a road tax.

After almost driving sixty miles, Saraj told me to turn right. This took us off the main highway onto a bumpy dirt road. We drove another three miles before we entered his village. As the van slowly crept along, all of the village's children came out to satisfy their curiosity, coming to see what was going on. Many of the villagers had never seen an American. To them we were like animals in a zoo to gawk at. We didn't mind. We understood their curiosity.

A high mud wall surrounded this village. This wall, I was told, had kept out Genghis Khan.

This village was over one thousand years old. Mountains surrounded it on three sides and a clear blue stream ran through the center of it. The water was ice cold, clear, and running fast.

"Carol, Bob, please stand in the stream while I snap your picture," asked Saraj.

I pulled up alongside of it, and then Carol and I hopped out of the van. We took our shoes and socks off and stood in the middle of the ten-foot-wide stream. The water was freezing cold, as cold as ice. That's exactly what it was a week before it flowed between my feet. It came from the melting snow high atop the surrounding mountains.

"Hurry up, Saraj, and shoot the picture!" I yelled, as my teeth chattered. "This water is too cold to stand in for more than a few minutes."

Saraj quickly snapped about twenty pictures as he hung out of the driver's window.

Finally, I grabbed Carol, and we both jumped out of the stream. We put our socks and shoes on, jumped into the van, and headed for Saraj's home. Once there, he introduced us to his relatives and family. His grandfather was a tribal leader of the village and a close relative to the king. From what I gathered from our conversation, he and the king were first cousins. One thing was for certain—in Afghanistan, they were considered a very rich family. Their heritage began nearly a thousand years ago.

We were invited into the living room to sit and talk while we waited for dinner. Saraj's grandfather, who was well over ninety years old but looked sixty, talked non-stop. As Saraj translated for his grandfather, we listened intently. He started by talking about the walls that were now surrounding his village, which once upon a time had held Genghis Khan and his army at bay.

Khan's army had destroyed everything in its path and was heading for Saraj's village. But the villagers had heard about the havoc it had wreaked upon its enemies and how they had destroyed nearby villages and massacred its occupants, so they evacuated their homes and ran and hid behind the great walls for safety and sanctuary. Most of them abandoned all their riches, including clothes, food, and anything of value. Some even left behind carts filled with wooden and clay vats containing a mixture of opium and fermenting grapes, which were used as wine and a medicinal remedy. They were abandoned just as they were being driven to a larger village to be sold.

Khan and his army had set up camp near the village and planned to destroy and conquer it, as he had all the others. He sent scouts out to acquire information on it and its occupants. However, before they could gather any intelligence, they came across the long row of carts containing the vats of fermenting grapes. Instead of scouting the village and gaining an edge, they returned to the camp with the carts of contraband. Khan was enraged at his scouts for not obeying his orders and killed them. However, after quenching his thirst with the opiated wine, his opinion changed. He tried it and enjoyed it immensely. He sent out his couriers the next day to speak to the village elders about the ingredients in the vats.

The head elder, I was told, was Saraj's ancestor, a great-great-grandfather, times ten, that went back more than eight hundred years. He, along with other family members, was invited back to Khan's camp. Thinking that they would be killed, they ordered the remaining villagers to stand their ground. If attacked, they were to send the women and children to the mountains and the men were to stay and fight to the death. Instead, Genghis Khan became a friend to Saraj's ancestor and the rest of the elders. He listened intently as the old man talked of the secrets of their magic potion. The mighty Khan made an agreement to bypass their village and its inhabitants if the elders would teach his medicine men the secrets of their brew.

The elders were ecstatic. Not only did they agree but also they gave Khan many more carts filled with vats of their secret brew. They also gave him a prized gift, their very best grapevine, so he could plant it at his choosing. That spot was still marked today.

This village was one of the few that the mighty Khan had left standing. Over the centuries, men and women of Khan's clan married the opposite sex of Saraj's family. This meant that Saraj and his family were related to Genghis Khan's family. They were related to the Khans of Asia from Mongolia to India. This really was an amazing story. All of us were held spellbound.

Dinner finally arrived. It was the typical Afghan dinner of rice, lamb, greens, stuffed grape leaves, and hot tea. Saraj's grandfather said a prayer before we ate the meal. I wasn't that hungry for food; I was hungry for morphine. But Carol and Mark more than made up for me. They ate as if they hadn't eaten for days. In fact, they embarrassed me. They ate like pigs in a trough. They didn't lift their heads until their meals were finished. I couldn't finish my meal. The rice had a kerosene taste to it and didn't agree with my taste buds. However, I ate everything else. I didn't say anything about the rice, but

Mark and Carol hadn't noticed a difference in taste. They had seconds. They even finished my plate for me so I wouldn't embarrass or insult our hosts.

More than one-hundred thousand people died each winter in Afghanistan of starvation. That is why everyone finishes their plate. Saraj's family gave me funny looks all throughout dinner, so I explained to them my lack of hunger.

"I'm sorry," I told them. "I woke up early this morning and my stomach is very queasy. It has been a long day, and I am a little tired."

"My family understands, Bob," said Saraj.

Once dinner was over, we relaxed and drank our tea. As we drank, we talked.

"Bob, you and Carol are coming to my cousin's wedding, aren't you?" asked Saraj.

"Yes. We are, but I don't think Mark wants to go," I replied.

"I may have to go to Pakistan to renew my visa," replied Mark. "It's about to expire."

"Saraj, we would be honored to go to the wedding," I said. "But remember to remind me a day or two before, in case it slips my mind. That way we will definitely be ready."

"Good," said Saraj.

"Well, it's getting late and we have to get back to Kabul," I said, apologizing for not staying longer.

We said goodbye and thanked them for a splendid time. They invited us to visit their village again anytime we wanted. We had an open invitation.

We loaded ourselves into the van, but I didn't want to drive. I had driven there, but now I was just too tired to drive back to Kabul.

"Mark, will you drive?" I asked.

"I'm too tired to drive," he whined.

"Carol, will you drive us back to Kabul?" I pleaded.

"I'm too tired and sick to drive right now."

So I had to drive back. Saraj stayed behind, so we had no one who could speak fluent Farsi. I prayed that nothing out of the ordinary happened. Luckily, we returned home safely.

During the weeks before the wedding, we stayed very busy.

Mark left again for Pakistan so he could renew his Afghan entrance visa. So I had to make all the hash envelopes myself while he was away. I missed his company and so did Foxy.

Foxy was getting big and filling out. She grew to two feet high and weighed about twenty pounds. She had the features of a beautiful collie, with a soft and fluffy red and white coat. Her face had the features of a fox, especially the way her hair on her cheeks fluffed out. We took her everywhere with us. Carol was in love with her. Even though Carol had found the dog, I had always felt Foxy was mine because I fed her and took care of her.

One day when Carol and Foxy had taken the van into town, I was in the bed relaxing when I heard a knock on the door. I got up and answered it and to my surprise, one of the new occupants from across the hall introduced himself.

"How ya doing? My name is Dan, and I live in the apartment next door. Do you have any powered milk I can borrow?" he asked.

"Come on inside. My name is Robert."

Dan followed me into the kitchen, praising my apartment as we walked.

"You have fixed up your apartment real nice. How long have you lived in Kabul and what do you do here?" he asked.

I was a little paranoid and hesitant to answer his questions, but I answered them anyway.

"I've lived in Kabul for over a year, and I work at the university," I lied, as I looked through the cupboards.

I finally found a new can of powdered milk, so I opened it and filled his cup.

"Thanks very much. Do you want to come over to my apartment and meet the rest of the guys?"

I nodded and followed him to his apartment.

"Dan, what are you guys doing in Kabul?" I asked, as we walked inside to his living room.

"We are in the Peace Corps and for the next few weeks we'll be in school studying Farsi or Pashtu, depending on the area you work in," he explained.

Dan introduced me to his three roommates, Don, Fred, and Steve. They were all college graduates from all over the country. Don had been born in East Pakistan and was from Scottsdale, Arizona. His father was a big rich owner of a big international construction firm that built bridges all over the world. I would find out later that Don had a serious cocaine habit, which he had brought to Afghanistan from America. He had even brought his own stash of Bolivian cocaine with him.

Then there was Fred, who was from the state of Pennsylvania. He was tall and lanky, with long brown hair and reminded me of the actor Jimmy Stewart. He was a graduate of the University of Pennsylvania, where his father was on the board of regents and had a professorship. I would find out weeks later that he was also a head. He smoked pot and hash and snorted cocaine every once in awhile.

Dan graduated from Berkley and was from San Francisco. I would find out later that he was an LSD freak. He would drop a quarter or half a tab of some heavy acid, such as windowpane, and then go hiking in the woods of the Sierra Mountains.

Last but not least was Steve. He was from Indiana and very young. He was only seventeen and the genius of the group. He had graduated Harvard at sixteen. They said he had a photographic memory.

After they told me their background history, I told them mine.

"I'm from Michigan, and I work in the agriculture department at the University of Kabul," I lied, not willing to tell them my true reason for being in Afghanistan.

I still didn't trust them. I didn't trust anyone, for that matter. I had to be very discreet or I could end up in front of a firing squad or in a cold, dirty dungeon. Before they could question me further, I heard my apartment door open, so I excused myself from the group.

"I have to leave now," I told them. "I think my wife is back home. I will see you guys again."

"We have a few good games, like Risk, and if you ever want to play, you are more than welcome," said Dan. "Come back anytime."

I nodded in agreement and walked out of their apartment door.

Before I knew it, the wedding was upon us. But the day before the wedding, I got a big surprise.

As I was leaving one of my favorite hangouts, I bumped into a giant of a man. I looked up and I stared into his face and eyes. I took about four steps past him, then turned around and followed him into the ice cream parlor. He was standing in front of the soda fountain, figuring out what he wanted to order, when I patted him on the shoulder. When he turned to face me, I noticed that he still had the Van Dyke beard and mustache and looked exactly like he had the year before.

"Isn't your name Dan?" I asked him.

"Yeah, why?"

"Don't you remember me? I was the guy on the bus traveling from Istanbul to Germany," I reminded him. Suddenly, a big smile crossed his face. He grabbed my hand and began to shake it. "Now do you remember me, Dan?"

"I sure do." We shook hands.

"Come on over to my apartment and we'll talk over old times."

"Sure, why not?"

After ordering ice cream sundaes—which I paid for—we left the establishment and walked to my apartment a block away. Once there, he was amazed and couldn't believe his eyes.

"How long have you lived here, Robert?" he asked.

"Over a year," I replied.

I invited him into the living room and when Carol came in, I introduced her. Then I showed Dan the rest of my apartment and what we had done to it.

Foxy kept nuzzling his hand and rubbing against him, wanting to be petted. She was persistent, so Dan reached down and scratched her head as I showed him the view from the patio. Then we returned to the living room and sat down to talk.

Carol brought in ice-cold lemonade and her homemade apple pie. This was the life. We had the best of everything. I showed Dan the magic of our great stereo and how it flipped the cassette over automatically. Dan said he was impressed, but that's not what I was trying to do. I wasn't trying to impress anyone. I just wanted him to be comfortable, as if he were back in the good old U.S. of A. The difference was, you didn't have to worry about the police breaking down your door. They didn't do that here. Only if another country was involved. The more we talked, the more his attitude seemed to change. It went from being very friendly to acting very smug and uppity. He only stayed ten or fifteen minutes and then decided to leave.

"Come back and have dinner with us one night before you leave Kabul," I said. "I have an extra bedroom if you want to stay here for a few days. Carol won't mind."

Dan said goodbye and went on his way. Carol and I saw him a few days later and waved to him, but he seemed to ignore us. Carol even noticed it.

"Why does Dan have a bug up his ass?" she asked.

"Maybe he's tripping on acid or he's stoned on morphine, heroin, cocaine, or opium, or a combination of all five," I replied.

So we just went our own way. I still wondered why he had acted the way he had. He was a big help during that long bus ride to Germany. Now he seemed like a different person. Oh, well.

The day of the wedding was upon us and just a few hours away. Saraj stopped by after work in a rented taxi that was all decorated in plastic flowers and flashing Christmas lights. It looked terrible in my eyes, but it was a work of art to Saraj. For Afghanistan, these were first-class decorations. They just didn't have fresh flowers like other civilized countries had. This was the best he could do. I told Saraj that it looked good, so I wouldn't hurt his feelings. He was so nervous you'd have thought he was the one getting married. He wanted Carol and me to ride with him, but we would have to walk or rent a taxi to get back home. His taxi was to be used for the bride and groom.

"Saraj, we will follow you in my van," I told him. "Should I bring a gift or give them an envelope with some spending money?"

"Bob, they only want your company. You don't need to bring anything but yourselves," he replied.

But Carol and I decided to give them twenty American dollars. I put it in an envelope, between two Mickey Mouse postcards, similar to the ones I used to send hash. I was sure they would get a kick out of them. I showed Saraj the post cards and he smiled.

"They will like your gift," he said.

So off we went. We followed Saraj to the other side of the city, to old Kabul. The city was built high on a mountain. The mountain was full of small mud huts that reminded me of Fred Flintstone's village. We drove high up the mountain and stopped when we couldn't go any further. There were thousands of people milling around, dancing and singing to the small four-piece Afghan band that moved through the crowd as they played.

There were many barbecue spits covered with lamb and sheep turning slowly over the hot embers. Large tables were set up outside with many different types of foods and fruits. The whole village must have been invited. This was a night of celebration. This wedding had the atmosphere of the carnival to which we had gone. I noticed many people staring and pointing their fingers at us as we followed Saraj through the crowd. But I didn't think anything about it as we ran up a few hundred steps and into the house. It was a very big house. It was as full of people inside as outside.

Carol and I followed Saraj into a large room where the bride and groom were sitting. We were introduced to the young couple, but the woman had on a wedding chardari (or Berka, in Arabic), so we couldn't see her face. The long veil hid it. I just hoped the groom knew what she looked like.

I asked Carol for the envelope, and I handed it to the groom and thanked them for inviting us to their wedding. This was the first

Afghan wedding I had ever been to. It was quite different from American weddings. A few minutes later, the bride left the room.

The house was separated into two main rooms: one for the men and one for the women. The women were not allowed to visit the men's room and the men weren't allowed to visit the women's room. The bride and groom would meet again at their marriage ceremony.

"Carol must also go to the women's room," said Saraj. "She isn't supposed to sit with us. They let us get away with it because you are their guests and you are foreigners."

So they cut us some slack. But now some of the men in the room seemed to be uncomfortable with Carol present because she wasn't wearing a veil. You could see her face and body and they felt intimidated. So we respected their customs.

Carol left the room to visit and talk with the other women.

Soon after, the festivities started. The band that had been playing outside was now inside our room playing to the groom and his guests. There was a drummer playing a type of bass bongo drum and a Tiber, a four-stringed guitar type instrument, a flute, and a small pump organ, which could only be played with one hand because the other was used to pump its billows. The one who played the drum also played a tambourine at the same time. Thirty minutes after she had left, Carol returned to the room along with the bride.

Carol sat next to me and then whispered into my ear, "I tried to talk the bride into taking her veil off and to become liberated, but she told me if she did that, her husband-to-be would kill her. She would shame him and his family so much that he would have no recourse other than to kill her. Not only that, but the male is allowed up to four wives, if he can afford them. To the Afghan male, the female is only a material possession to be used as he sees fit."

Carol didn't like that and wouldn't keep quiet about it.

"Keep quiet, and don't be giving these women any ideas," I whispered. "I want to leave here alive."

I must have been a psychic because there seemed to be something brewing in the air. Many of the men were whispering to each other. I wondered what was going on. I looked at Saraj with questioning eyes.

"Some of the people here are getting upset that you were invited to the wedding," stated Saraj. "Some of these Afghans are racists and don't like Americans."

Saraj seemed to be nervous and anxious for us to leave. So we followed him out of the house and down the long flight of stairs, all the while being pushed and shoved by the crowd.

Just as we were getting into the van, some of the younger crowd members started pelting us with pieces of bread and fruit, so we got out of there as fast as we could. I didn't even bother turning the vehicle around. I just put it into reverse and started driving down the mountain backwards.

The crowd followed us and pelted the van with pieces of food, dirt, and rocks. Finally, we were far enough down the road that I could turn the van around without being harassed by a crazy mob. We had never really had this kind of trouble before and couldn't believe this was happening now. Most of the Afghans we had met at the party had become our friends. But a few incited the rest. I guess that happens in all races of nationality.

Saraj stopped by my apartment around 8:00 P.M. the following day.

"Bob, I apologize for last night," said Saraj sadly.

"What happened, Saraj? Why did they turn on us like that?" I asked him.

"There were some hateful and crazy Muslims who just don't like Americans," he explained.

That's all he would say about it, so we didn't discuss it any further. Saraj and I talked for another ten minutes before he departed. It was late, and Carol and I had to get up early in the morning to do some chores around the city.

We were getting to know the city and the people who worked in it—not only the sidewalk vendors but also the market and restaurant personnel. There was one restaurant in particular. It was an Italian restaurant that was run and owned by a friendly old Italian couple who had been in Kabul for over twenty-five years, since World War II. They had been good friends with Mussolini. His family had been one of the aristocratic families in Italy. He was a duke back then. They had to run for their lives or they would have ended up like Mussolini—murdered and hanging from a tree.

This old Italian couple had made their home away from home in Kabul. But they still had some friends in Italy, who sent them the best-made machines needed for the restaurant business. Even so, they made all their pasta and noodles by hand. Many of the Italian diplomats ate at their restaurant. It was a small, beautiful, intimate room designed for the young at heart. It was the perfect place for a romantic dinner with the woman you love. We ate there often.

Another restaurant that we frequented was the ice cream parlor;

many of the American diplomat's children frequented there also. I would buy one or two sundaes a day there. They had the best ice cream and sundaes in all of Afghanistan. They imported the toppings and ice cream from Beirut, Lebanon. It was as good as any in America, including Dairy Queen. They also had a great stereo system and played English and American rock music. We knew the owners and the workers of these establishments, even the supermarkets, where we shopped for our food. They all became our good friends.

One day while out shopping, I ran into my friend and his female Rhesus monkey. This time there was an addition to their family. The female monkey was carrying her offspring—a baby boy. I stopped and talked with the Afghan while I petted the adult monkey. She remembered me. I walked over to a sidewalk fruit vendor and bought a bunch of ripe bananas and handed them, one at a time, to her as her owner and I talked about the past few months.

The mother monkey peeled the banana and then fed her baby before feeding herself. It was a beautiful sight watching mother and son as they ate. The mother was very smart. She was a dancing monkey. That's how the Afghan made his money—by putting on small shows for the kids and adults and then he'd pass the hat.

He remembered that I had wanted a baby monkey and asked me if I wanted to buy his. This was a very hard decision for me. I wanted a monkey so badly, but I didn't know what Carol would say. I thought she might get angry with me if I brought it home. She might even be afraid of it, but I didn't think so. She loved all animals, just like me.

My Afghan friend gestured for me to hold the baby, so I gently grabbed it and pulled it away from its mother. The baby didn't know what to think. It looked into my eyes, and I looked into his. He was so cute. Just as I was deciding the baby's fate, the mother jumped onto my lap. She must have sensed that I was going to take her baby away from her. (Rhesus monkeys usually keep their young for five or six years before they go off and fend for themselves.) As she sat on my lap, she grabbed her baby back. She knew she was going to lose him.

I handed my Afghan friend about fifty dollars in American money, and he gave me the baby monkey. The mother looked deeply into my eyes as though she was telling me to take care of her baby. I gestured to her that I would love him and be his mother from now on. Then I hopped into my van and headed back to my apartment to show Carol my surprise. I also wanted to see how Foxy would react to our new family member.

Before I went up to the apartment, I stopped in the tailor shop and showed the owner my baby monkey.

"Will you make some clothes for him?" I asked the tailor.

He nodded in agreement, and then quickly took body measurements to make shirts, pants, shorts, and hats for him.

I then went upstairs to show the baby to Carol. I quietly opened the front door and tiptoed inside. As I walked into the bedroom, the baby held onto me like he had his mother, with his arms around my neck and his body resting on my chest.

"Carol, how do you like our new baby?" I asked.

She looked very surprised. Foxy was really excited and started licking the baby all over. She wanted to play with him. But Carol seemed distant.

"Where did you get that?" she asked.

"How do you like him, Carol? What should we name him?"

"The monkey's face looks just like Rex. He even has the same dimples in his cheeks. Name him Rex."

Rex was another person I had grown up with since childhood. He was another of my good friends. I was also sending him hash envelopes.

So that's how the baby monkey got his name. He and Foxy got along great. They played together all day long. Rex would even pick the fleas off Foxy and then eat them. When he had picked all of them off her back, Foxy would roll over and let him pick them off her stomach and chest. She loved it. They both did.

Every morning, as Carol made breakfast, I would take the animals into the living room and play a game of tag. First, I would place a board across the living room door so they couldn't escape. Then I would sit in a chair near the window, while Foxy would lie in wait in the middle of the floor and Rex would run from my lap to the other side of the room, usually to one of the shelves in the bookcase that was built into the wall. If Rex could run over to me without Foxy tackling and wrestling him to the floor, Rex would get one point. But if Foxy stopped Rex from reaching me, she got the point. The first one to ten points was the winner. We played this for an hour every day at least.

When I had Foxy do tricks for me, Rex would also show off. He would walk on his hands and do backward flips. He did them all by himself without me ever teaching him.

We took the animals everywhere with us. One place in particular was a block down the road to my friend's silk rug factory. His family was the last of many who had made carpets for the king during the last thousand years. All the other families had died. These designs had been handed down to his family from ancestor to ancestor since time began.

"Can I buy one of your rugs?" I asked him.

"These are only made for the king, to give as presents to diplomats of other countries," said the rug maker.

"How much money would it cost me if I could buy one?" I asked.

"It would cost you one-million dollars to buy one, if you were allowed," he replied.

So they were out of my price range. But I visited his rug factory so the kids could take a break from their long day's work and play with my animals. The owner didn't seem to mind. He invited me in every time I walked by.

Sometimes Carol would get jealous because I would spend more time with Rex and Foxy than with her. The monkey even slept with me every night. Carol became angry because I had the monkey in my bed and not her. But she didn't understand that Rex was a baby, and I was its surrogate mother.

Maybe I did love the animals more than her, but I still loved her. I even took them with us to Cargar Dam, along with the English family and the French girl, Janet, who lived in the apartment below. Keith's twin girls would play with Foxy and Rex at the lake while the women swam and I barbecued the hot dogs and hamburgers.

Sometimes the women would lie on the air mattresses to get suntans as they floated in the water. But this got them into trouble. The soldiers who were swimming nearby came over in their boat and ordered Carol and Keith's wife, Debby, out of the water. They were told that women were not allowed to swim—especially only wearing skimpy bathing suits. But the women ignored the soldier's orders. And when Carol tried again to get into the water, the soldiers returned and scolded us. So the girls stayed out of the water from that point on. But just for that day.

"Carol, if they don't like what you're wearing, what would happen if you had sunbathed in the nude?" I asked the women, jokingly of course.

Janet quickly stood up, pulled off her bikini top, and started to step out of her bottoms.

"Let's see what kind of reaction we will get from these soldiers now," said Janet.

Keith and I stood speechless. Then I suddenly snapped out of the trance I was in.

"Put your clothes back on or they're liable to throw us in jail if they see what you're doing. Janet. Even though Keith and I like the view, the Afghans might not have the same reaction," I told her.

"Hell, if you like that view, check this one out," said Carol, as she whipped off her top.

Boy, I was getting embarrassed. Any other time I would have been drooling and wetting my pants, but right at this moment, I was very nervous. Keith was still speechless. I quickly placed a towel over Carol's chest to hide her breasts from the soldier's view and scolded her.

"Quit screwing around or you're liable to get us shot," I snapped.

The women finally put their clothes back on. Luckily, we weren't hassled any more that day or any other time by the soldiers. The girls stayed close to shore after that and didn't go out in the middle of the reservoir. But that's how it went for most of the summer.

Soon fall would be upon us. It was near the end of August. The weather would stay hot during the day until December. Then winter would set in.

Mark finally returned to Kabul. I was happy to see him. He brought with him fifty bottles of morphine that he had bought in Pakistan, of which I bought twenty-five.

Now that he had returned, we had much work to do. We still had many hash envelopes to make, plus sandals and shoes to send.

Business was so good I was thinking about sending Carol and Janet to America with a couple of false-bottom suitcases full of hash. In fact, so much money was coming in that I had to open a savings account at the local bank. I didn't want to carry around too much cash, so I thought it would be safer at the bank. But I was still leery about trusting my money with a bank, so I questioned the banker about my fears.

"Sir, can I withdraw dollars if I cancel my account?" I asked.

"Yes. You can get dollars when you close your account," he replied.

So I handed over twelve thousand American dollars and was given my bankbook. I left the bank on a happy note and then headed for the post office. Not only was money coming in regularly, so were my letters.

Two of these letters were from Jim and a girl I knew from Michigan named Becky. I had gone to high school with her and had sex with her a few times, so I was anxious to see her. She wrote that she was on her way to Europe and then to Turkey with her friend, Pat. She wanted me to write to her at the Istanbul post office in a few weeks.

Jim wrote in his letter that he was coming to Kabul within a few months, during the fall break at the university. He wanted to have some rest and relaxation with Carol and me. So I wrote back to him, telling him to come as soon as he could and party with us and that I had an extra bedroom he could stay in. I also gave him my new address.

I also wrote to Becky and told her to come to Kabul and that she could live here on a dollar a day. I also asked her about her friend, Pat. I told her they were both welcome. I figured that when Becky and her girlfriend arrived, we would have a big orgy. That thought came to mind, anyway. I sent the letters as soon as I wrote them. I couldn't wait for my friends to visit. I had enough room at the apartment that they could all stay with me. But if need be, I would put them up at a nice hotel. Money wasn't a concern for me. I just wanted to see them.

I was also seeing Mr. Bareck more often. Each time I visited the post office, I would talk with him. He was building a house that he wanted to rent to diplomats for four thousand dollars per month. So he needed money to pay his construction crew. He was definitely a capitalist, even if he wouldn't admit it. I even began doing business with him.

In the beginning, I wasn't sure I could trust him, so I only sent one or two envelopes at a time to see if they would get through American customs. Sure enough, my friends received them. So I began sending more and more through Mr. Bareck. Now I had two post office officials sending hash envelopes and one customs man sending parcels. It couldn't have been going any better.

A few weeks after our introduction, Mr. Bareck invited Carol and me over to his house to meet his wife and son and we accepted. Shortly thereafter, we dressed up in our nicest clothes and visited them one evening. I even brought along a couple bottles of wine, just in case they wanted to party, and a Tyco matchbox racecar set as a gift for his three-year-old son. This would have cost Mr. Bareck a year's pay.

We arrived there about seven that evening. After knocking on the door, a female servant answered and let us through the house and into the living room where Mr. Bareck, his wife, and son were sitting. He had a very spacious and well-decorated home. It was two stories tall with about three thousand square feet on two hectares of land and made from brick, not mud. Mr. Bareck was quite wealthy in Afghan terms. His family was also related to the king, but on the side of the queen and the Daoud family.

Mrs. Bareck was very westernized. She was very beautiful, with long, straight, black hair. She had the face of a goddess, of Cleopatra. She was a very bright, intelligent, and classy woman. She was the same size as Carol, very petite, but very exotic and beautiful. She had gotten married at thirteen, had her first baby at fourteen, and still looked gorgeous. She didn't wear any veil or chardari. She did wear it, however, when she went out in public. If she didn't, the religious fanatics would stone her as she walked.

As we talked, I opened the bottle of wine and poured it into the wineglasses that Mrs. Bareck had set on the table.

"Mr. Bareck, do you like red wine?" I asked. "I bought it at the Kabul Hotel's wine vault. It's a 1928 Bordeaux burgundy and an excellent vintage."

I filled the glasses and handed them to my friends.

"Thank you, Bob," said Mr. Bareck.

"To Afghanistan and good friends," I said, as we toasted our glasses.

We made a few more toasts until the bottle of wine was nearly empty. Luckily, I had another bottle in the van so I went outside and retrieved it. When I returned, we quickly finished the first bottle and then opened the second. It was the same type of wine as the first, but a different year. This was a 1923 burgundy. By this time we were all quite drunk and having a good time. So we set our glasses down while the women went off to see the house and Mr. Bareck and I talked about sending hash.

"Bob, if I ever become president of the post department, we will send tons of hash and opium back to America," he said, with excitement in his voice.

"Mr. Bareck, I'll drink to that. We will make a fortune," I replied, as we toasted our glasses in the air.

As we talked, I handed Mr. Bareck the gift for his son. He called his three-year-old son, Ediat, over to us. This kid was big for his age. He was the size of a six-year-old, and very cute. I set up the racecar set and showed them how it worked. His kid loved it. The parents were very happy to see how much joy and excitement it brought to their son.

Carol and I stayed until two in the morning. Everyone was more or less passed out so we decided it was time to go home. We left that night as very close friends. In fact, Mr. Bareck made me his son's godfather.

When Carol and I arrived home, Foxy and Rex were anxiously awaiting our return. Rex jumped up on me and hugged me so tight that I thought we would fuse into one being. Foxy kept jumping up on me until I petted her and paid attention to her. These were my babies. They all slept in my bed that night, including Carol.

Near the end of October, we went to Cargar Dam for one last time. It had been a very hot day and we hadn't planned on going to the lake that day. But we changed our minds and decided to take the animals and relax at the lake. Even though we wanted company, everyone was away.

But when we arrived there, another family had taken our special picnic area. We had never used any other spot on the lake. This space had always been vacant, but not on this day. I wanted to turn around and go back home, but Carol wanted to try another spot. So I continued driving alongside the lake for more than a mile until we were away from everyone and near a wooded area. Actually, it was a forest.

I got out the barbecue and briquettes and quickly made a fire. Within ten minutes, I began making hot dogs and hamburgers for Carol and me while Foxy and Rex were playing tag. Rex would tag Foxy and then run until Foxy tackled and fell on top of him. Then, Rex would playfully bite Foxy's cheek until she let him go. Then they would begin all over again. They were fun to watch and very, very playful. When they tired of tag, Rex would climb a tree, jump down from a low branch onto Foxy's back, and ride her like a horse. Sometimes Foxy would buck like a horse and knock Rex off, but that didn't stop him. He would pick himself up and try to ride her again, if Foxy would let him, that is.

Carol was busy putting bug spray on her naked body. Sometimes she liked to sunbathe in the nude. She kept me aroused all the time. While the food cooked, I lay down next to her on one of the air mattresses, picked up the bottle of suntan lotion, and squirted it on her body. Then I rubbed it all over her back and her beautiful butt.

"Carol, flip over so I can rub the lotion on your front," I begged her.

She did as I asked. So I began rubbing the lotion over her

breasts and stomach and over her hairless, shaved mound. She started to get aroused and within five seconds, we were making love like two young honeymooners.

However, before we started, I had to take the food off the grill and feed the animals so they would stay busy while Carol and I made love. Our sexcapade lasted for hours until Foxy began making strange growling noises. I noticed something was making Foxy uneasy. Even Rex came over to my side for protection.

"Robert, what is it?" asked Carol, as I jumped up and quickly dressed.

"Carol, put your clothes on. It's getting late anyway."

But she refused. She wanted to continue our lovemaking. She finally agreed when I promised her that we would continue our sexcapade at the apartment.

We hadn't eaten yet, and I was hungry. And just as I started to reheat one of the hamburgers, I heard a loud roar. I also noticed some bushes ruffling ten yards away.

"Carol, start cleaning up and putting things back into the van so we can leave," I told her anxiously.

I looked for something to use as a weapon just in case this was a wild dog or some other kind of ferocious animal. Foxy was still growling and kicking up dirt with her rear paws as if she was getting ready for a fight. Rex was standing near Foxy, and I picked up a big stick for a weapon. As I bent down to pick up a box of kitchen utensils, out from the bushes came a spotted snow leopard. Foxy immediately tried to protect us by attacking the big cat.

I called Foxy to come to me, but she wouldn't obey my commands. She just held her ground. A few seconds later, Rex ran toward the cat, trying to turn its attention toward him and away from Foxy. He was trying to protect her. But Rex had gotten too close and the leopard reached out with her sharp claws and in one big powerful motion, hit Rex with such a force it threw him twenty feet through the air and into the bushes. Just as the cat was about to swing its claws at Foxy, I threw a rock and hit it right on top of its head, which sent it rolling into the lake. Then it ran back into the forest.

I ran over to Rex and saw that his body had been ripped apart. He was still alive, but just barely. He looked at me with his big, beautiful eyes, asking me to help him. Tears were streaming from my eyes, and I could barely see. I wrapped my shirt around his wounded body and tried to stop the bleeding but it was no use.

"Carol, you drive!" I cried, as I lifted Rex off the ground and ran to the van. I held onto my baby. He was so brave. We jumped into the van and raced back to Kabul.

"Hold on, Rex!" cried Carol.

Foxy kept licking Rex's face, not knowing what was about to happen. I was crying and praying out loud that Rex wouldn't die, praying that we would get to the vet's in time. But it was too late. He looked into my eyes one last time and that was it. He would breathe no more.

When I got to the apartment, I wrapped Rex into his blanket, the one he slept with, and placed him into a small, wooden antique box. I closed the lid, picked it up, and walked downstairs into the courtyard behind the apartment building. Then I asked Aslam to dig a small grave in the flowerbed.

"What are you burying, Bob?" asked Aslam.

"Aslam, it's my baby monkey, Rex. He was killed by a big leopard cat at Cargar Dam."

"I'm so sorry," he said sadly.

Aslam was saddened also. Even the kids came by to pay their respects. Not only Aslam's kids but also Keith's twin girls. Rex had given them many hours of pleasure. As I placed the last of the dirt over Rex's coffin, I silently said a small prayer and asked God to take care of my little buddy. Needless to say, I was very hurt and depressed for the next couple of weeks. Even Foxy could sense my depression. She, too, missed her little buddy badly. I cried my heart out, but Carol seemed happy that Rex was gone. She thought I would spend more time with her now that Rex wasn't around.

One morning, a few days after Rex's burial, I met my neighbor, Dan, in the third floor corridor of our apartment building.

"Robert, do you want to come to a party at the American Embassy to see and hear Senator Percy speak on the presidential nomination?" he asked.

"When is it?"

"It's only three days away."

"Dan, can Carol come along with me?"

"No, I'm sorry; it's only for Peace Corps and American Aid people."

"Then why am I allowed to go?" I asked him, confused by his answer.

"You can go in Don's place. He isn't going," he explained.

"Okay, Dan. Pick me up on your way and we can drive in my van," I said, as we shook hands and went our separate ways.

MEETING AFGHAN ELITE, THEN HIRED BY THE CIA

The last couple of times Carol and I visited the nightclub, my Afghan friends seemed to be very upset and uncomfortable around us. The conversations were always about Afghan politics. Rumors were running rampant. I listened very intently to their conversation.

It seemed the Russians were trying to buy their way into the Afghan government. The king had allowed them to expand their embassy, but they'd added too many people and most, they feared, were spies.

I had overheard the king's son say before that the Russians were trying to control his father and couldn't do it. The Russians threatened that if they couldn't control him then they would have to put their own man into office. It seemed that the Russians thought there was a geological gold mine in Afghanistan, but America and other industrialized nations didn't think so. The Russians wanted to reap the benefits from their geological riches and had built up a strong alliance within the hierarchy of the Afghan government. To find out if the rumors were true, I went to see my young friend, Baba. He was in the same spot on Chicken Street selling his wares.

"Baba, have you heard any of the rumors about the Russians?" I asked him.

He verified my suspicions. Many of the rumors I had heard at the nightclub seemed to be true. Just as we were talking, four Russians came out of the building directly in front of us. They jumped into a four-wheel-drive vehicle and drove away.

"There go four Russian agents. They say they work at the Russian embassy, but I know they are spies," he whispered.

"Thanks for the information, Baba," I replied, shaking his hand.

I gave him a few Afghanis for his information and went on my way.

Finding out that these rumors were true made me very nervous. So I decided to buy a large quantity of hash to hide in the van just in case Carol and I had to leave the country in a big hurry. At least I would have the van ready to smuggle hash out of the country. I thought I could also send Carol and Janet to America with a couple of false-bottom suitcases full of hashish. So the night before the party at the embassy, I decided to visit my hash connections. First, I went to Tiar's house, thinking we might have to go back up north to get the hash. As I entered through the courtyard, I noticed Tiar's wife looking out a window, so I spoke up.

"I need to buy some hash. Is Tiar home?" I asked her. She seemed to be very upset and nervous, and acted as though she hadn't heard me, so I tried again. "I need to buy some hash today. Is Tiar home?"

She said something to me, but I couldn't hear her. So I walked up and stood near the window, and that's when I saw Tiar sitting in his living room with six policemen. Just then, I realized what Tiar's wife had said. She told me to get away because of the police, so I high-tailed it out of there as calmly and quickly as I could. I didn't want to get busted.

A few minutes later, I hopped into my van and sped over to Moktar's place. Shortly thereafter, I was standing at his rooftop apartment, pounding on his door. However, someone I didn't recognize answered it.

"Is Moktar here?" I asked a big, burly man.

"Yes, come in."

As I walked into the dimly lit room, I noticed a big, black, dirty canvas tarp hanging from the ceiling to the floor, covering almost half of the room. I sat down with Moktar and his brother, Sabul, to talk about my visit.

"Bob, where is your monkey?" asked Moktar.

I tried to explain what had happened, but it was very difficult for me.

"He got ripped apart by a leopard cat at Cargar Dam. He died saving our lives. He died a hero. I'm sorry, I can't talk about it anymore," I told him sadly.

"That's all right, Bob," said Moktar, patting my shoulder.

Then my curiosity got to me concerning the black tarp.

"Moktar, what is that black curtain for? What's behind it?" I asked him, straining my neck as I tried to peer behind the curtain.

But I couldn't quite understand what he was telling me.

"Moktar, I don't understand. Show me," I pleaded.

"Okay, Bob, but stand ten feet away from the canvas," he told me, as he grabbed the curtain.

As soon as Moktar swung the curtain to one side, a big, black mass of hair came lunging at me with such force that it shook the whole house and nearly ripped the chain out of the wall. It was a huge Koochie dog, the size of a Shetland pony. It was a good four feet high, four feet long, and about two hundred pounds of vicious, deadly demon. It was an animal that he used in dogfights in the hopes of winning large sums of money from his competitors.

"Moktar, what the heck does that animal eat?" I asked him nervously.

"This is what it eats," he said, as he grabbed my upper leg with his bare hand.

"You can't feed me to him," I replied, frightened that he would.

Moktar sure had frightened me when he grabbed my leg. The Afghans thought it was hilarious.

"I don't feed him until after he fights, so he will stay vicious," he said.

"Moktar, will you please close the curtain, so the dog will calm down?" I asked.

I still felt rather frightened that they might feed me to their dog. Who would know if they did? Carol didn't know my dope connections. She didn't know that I had gone to see Moktar. So I wanted to get out of there as quickly as possible.

But then Moktar introduced me to his Iranian friend who had answered the door. He had traveled all the way from Tehran to buy hash and smuggle it across the border into Iran. If he were caught, they would shoot him. So to fool the Iranian customs, he made the hash into long, oblong-shaped beads and then placed them onto a string until it formed a necklace, so he could wear them as prayer beads around his neck or hold them in his hand. He had done it many times before and passed through customs without any problems.

While I watched them work, I asked Moktar if he could help me.

"Moktar, can you get me ten or fifteen kilos of hash pollen?" I asked. "I want to hide it in my van so I can smuggle it to Europe. Do you know anyone who can help me modify my van?"

"Yes, I might know someone who can help you modify your van. But I don't know what they will charge you," he replied.

Moktar and I continued to haggle over a price for the hash. We settled on a price of two-hundred dollars for the fifteen kilos.

"Bob, come back in a week's time, and I will have the hash. I will also take you to someone who can help you modify your van," he promised.

"That sounds great. Thanks, Moktar. I'll see you in a week." I then left for my apartment.

The next seven days I waited patiently. While I was waiting for the week to pass by, I went to the embassy party alone, while Dan, Fred, and Steve went with someone else, but we arrived at the same time. Everyone was searched for weapons before we were allowed on the embassy grounds. There were two long tables filled with every type of meat, fish, dessert, and fruit you could think of. There were nearly one hundred people, mostly Americans, to hear Senator Percy speak.

As Dan introduced me to his friends, I noticed that one man kept following me all over the embassy compound. Every time I looked over my shoulder to see if the person was following me, he was always nearby. I was getting paranoid, so I went and stood with Dan.

"Dan, who is that guy who keeps following me?" I asked him.

He replied, "Oh that's my boss, Mr. Beardon. He is the Peace Corps director." Then he called the man over and introduced me to him.

"Robert, let me introduce you to my boss. This is Mr. Beardon."

"I am glad to meet you, Robert."

"I am glad to meet you," I replied.

As we shook hands, he began asking me all kinds of questions, but I tried to ignore most of them.

"What do you do in Kabul?" asked Mr. Beardon.

"I work at the university."

"What department do you work in?" he asked inquisitively.

"I work in the agricultural department," I lied, as I tried to walk away from him.

"Do you know Mr. Carver? He works for the agricultural department," he asked.

"I might know him if I saw him. I'm very bad with names."

"Does Professor Johnson still work for the agricultural department?"

"Yes, I've seen him, and I think he is still working at the university," I lied.

"Say hello to him for me."

"How long have you been in Afghanistan, Mr. Beardon?" I asked him, but before he could answer, I continued talking, "I've always wanted to join the Peace Corps."

"Oh. Maybe I can help you in that endeavor," he told me. "Why don't you come to my office on Chicken Street...say on Tuesday morning at 10 A.M.? I'm not promising you anything, but I'll help you if I can. How long have you been living in Kabul?"

Just as I was about to answer him, one of the speakers of the party interrupted our conversation.

"Will everyone please take a seat? We are here to listen to a very prominent senator for the USA, so please give a warm welcome to Senator Percy."

Senator Percy came up to the podium and gave the typical political speech. He said a lot of nothing. He promised everything but said nothing. I wasn't impressed with his speech at all, but it seemed everyone else was. An hour later, the party broke up.

Before I drove back to the apartment, the guys wanted to go to the ice cream parlor and get an ice cream sundae. Fred, Dan, and Steve hitched a ride in my van, and we headed to the restaurant. When we arrived, the place was dead. Not one customer was there. It wasn't closed, so we went in. We noticed that there wasn't any ice cream in the freezer.

"Where is the ice cream?" I asked the clerk.

He replied sadly, "Due to the war in Beirut, Lebanon, I can't import the toppings, ice cream, or anything else from there."

We were bummed to say the least and quickly returned to the van, then drove back to the apartment building.

We decided to play the game Risk at their apartment. Dan got the game out and placed it in the middle of the living room floor.

"Hey, Don, do you want to play Risk?" yelled Dan toward Don's bedroom.

Soon, Don came out of his bedroom carrying a big bag of white powder and a small marble plate. Don sat with us on the floor and poured some of the white powder onto the plate. As I watched him smash and cut the white clumps into a fine powder, he began making long lines on the plate. He rolled up a dollar bill, inserted it into his right nostril, and then snorted the white powder up his nose. I just watched in disbelief. Once Don did a few of the lines, he passed the marble plate to Fred.

Fred grabbed the plate and rolled up bill, bent his face to the plate, and snorted some of the white powder up his nose. After passing the plate around the room, all four guys snorted some of the white powder. Then Dan passed the plate of narcotic to me.

"Don, what is it?" I asked.

"It's cocaine. Pure Bolivian cocaine," he replied enthusiastically.

"Thank you, but no thank you," I said, rejecting their offer.

They acted very surprised. So to ease their concerns, I explained my fear.

"I don't touch cocaine. I like something else—life. I get high on life," I said, not wanting them to know anything about my business or that I used drugs because I was still very paranoid and didn't trust them.

"But this is pure cocaine," said Dan. He couldn't believe I turned it down.

"You don't know what you are missing," said Don, disappointed.

"I don't mind, as long as you are only hurting yourselves and nobody else. But where did you get all that cocaine?"

"I brought it with me from America," he replied.

I surmised he must have had four or five ounces of the stuff.

"Don, I can buy pure Peruvian cocaine from the pharmacy for about three dollars a gram, and it's pure pharmaceutical cocaine. If you ever need any, let me know," I told him.

As we played the game, we started becoming closer friends and after being in their presence for a few hours, it seemed we had been friends all of our lives. I excused myself and ran over to my apartment to retrieve a piece of opiated hash and a small hash pipe. When I returned to their apartment, I pulled out the small piece of hash and began filling the bowl of my pipe.

"Do you guys mind if I smoke a bowl of hash?" I asked them.

"I thought you didn't get high?" asked Dan.

"I said I didn't get high on cocaine. Hash is another story. Here, try this." I passed the hash pipe around the room.

As they each inhaled the hash smoke, they each coughed their heads off. I just laughed as I watched them cough. They couldn't believe how strong the hash was. They wanted to buy some from me, so I returned to my apartment to retrieve some hash. I gave them about ten grams of my opiated hash. I refused any money for it. From that night on, we had become good friends. But I still had to be discreet and still didn't trust them completely. However, we began seeing each other more often.

Tuesday morning arrived, and I was at the Peace Corps office bright and early at exactly 10 A.M. Before I left the apartment, I had Carol braid my long hair, then hide it in the back of my shirt to make it look like I had short hair. I also wore a shorthaired blonde wig that Morgan had left behind and dressed up in a brand new handmade conservative suit and tie that gave me the look of a banker. Then I headed off to the Peace Corps office.

When I arrived, I was shown into the director's office. The clerk had mentioned that the director was waiting for me. I felt that maybe I would get lucky and be allowed to join the Peace Corps. As I entered the room, I noticed there was another person in the room sitting in a chair with his back to me. I couldn't tell if it was a man or woman. The director stood up and shook my hand.

"Take a seat," said the director.

"Thank you, Mr. Beardon," I replied nervously.

I sat in a chair facing his desk, but still not close enough to see who the other person was.

"You are interested in joining the Peace Corps, correct?" asked Mr. Beardon.

"Yes. I'm sure I could help the people of Afghanistan."

"Can you speak Pashtu fluently?" he asked, looking directly into my eyes.

"Not Pashtu, but Farsi. I only speak Farsi. I only know a few words in Pashtu."

"Say something in Farsi for me," he said, acting as if he had caught me in a lie.

"*Man pinja Afghani, bari shumo dodum, si Afghani shumo bari man biti.* That means, 'I will give you fifty-Afghani and you give me thirty-Afghani change,'" I told him proudly.

"Not bad. You speak Farsi very well. But if you are really serious about wanting to join the Peace Corps, you would have to return to Washington, D.C. and apply at the administration office. I can set up the appointment for you and make sure that your designated country is this one," he replied.

But that wasn't what I wanted to hear. "Can't I just apply here?" I asked. "Why go all the way back to America, when I'm already in the country of origin?"

"It doesn't work that way. You must follow procedure," he replied.

"Well, I don't want to return to America. If there is no other way, then I guess there's nothing more to say."

As I was about to stand up and leave, the person I didn't recognize beat me to the punch and stood up before me—a very well dressed man.

"There might be something you can do to help your government," said the quiet man.

"This is Mr. Helms, the ambassador to Iran," said Mr. Beardon. "He has some questions to ask you."

"Robert, we know that you visit the nightclub here and that you are good friends with many of the king's relatives. Is that correct?" asked Mr. Helms, a tone of seriousness in his voice.

"Yes, I'm good friends with some high Afghani officials. I go to the nightclub maybe once or twice a month when they are in town."

"We also know you are the only foreigner who is allowed to enter the nightclub," said Helms. "You could be useful to us if you could extract information from the conversations you hear from the king's relatives and then relay those conversations to us. This could help the USA immensely."

"How do you know I visited the disco? Have you been spying on me?" I asked him, with a little anger in my voice.

"We have our ways," said Beardon. "But it was Dan who told us about you. And...we have our own confidential sources. We could help each other. You can relay any information about Afghan politics, and we could get you Peace Corps identification to use at the American Aid compound. You can get free dental and medical attention, go to special outings, and watch the most recent movies that are sent from America. There are many benefits to helping us."

"What kind of information are you most concerned about?" I asked.

"We are interested in learning about any information concerning any communist insurgents, or any information concerning the king's health," Beardon replied.

"Also, anything you may think is important...just tell us the conversations, and we will do the analyzing," said Mr. Helms.

I wasn't into politics, so I didn't know anything about Mr. Helms. Only that he was supposedly the ambassador to Iran. I still didn't understand why the ambassador to Iran was interested in the politics of Afghanistan.

"Robert, I want you to contact Dan at his apartment to relay any messages you might have," said Beardon. "Then he will set up an appointment for you with me here at the office. If anyone asks you why you came here, tell them you filled out an application to join the Peace Corp."

"No problem," I retorted.

I shook both their hands, turned, and walked out of the room. I left still not really understanding the predicament I was in. I wondered just how much these people knew about me and if they had received the information from Dan. Well, I didn't worry about it. I didn't change my habits and went on as I had before. I acted as though nothing had changed. When I returned home, I went directly into my bedroom to relax. A few minutes later, Carol joined me.

"Carol, I was turned down for a job at the Peace Corps. I would have to return to America and apply for the job in Washington, D.C. It wasn't worth all the hassle. I'll just stay and live here without a visa."

Finally, the week had passed, and it was time to return to Moktar's place to pick up the hash and to see if he had found someone to help me modify my van. I drove to his apartment building, walked up to his rooftop shack, and then knocked on the door. Moktar answered it. The canvas tarp was still in place. The dog must have won its fight and was still alive, I thought to myself. Moktar invited me into his house. This time he was the only one at home.

"Moktar, did you get my hash for me?" I asked him.

But before Moktar answered me, he put some tobacco snuff between his mouth and gum. Thirty seconds later, he spit into a small Afghan spittoon.

"Yes, I have it. It is number one hashish," he said proudly. Moktar opened a large cardboard box and then the plastic bag that held the pollen. It was excellent, fresh pollen with a nice red tint. "It was picked just a few weeks ago."

"How many kilos is that?" I asked, as I looked into the plastic bag.

"Fifteen kilos—just what you asked for," he replied.

"Then here is the two-hundred dollars I promised you," I said, handing him the money. "Did you find someone to modify my van?"

"Yes, we can leave right now," he said, opening the front door. "Hide the hash under your blanket."

"No, it will look suspicious. I'll just carry it like it's an ordinary empty box. No one will even notice I'm carrying it."

"Okay, let's go," he said, throwing his automatic rifle over his shoulder.

"Do you have to bring your gun?"

"Yes. In case we run into bandits we will have some protection," he reassured me, patting his rifle as if it was a woman.

"Moktar, are you kidding? How far do we have to travel?" I asked, as we walked across the rooftop and down the stairs to the street below.

"Not too far, but it's better to be safe than sorry," he replied.

We hopped into my van and drove east, approximately thirteen miles outside the city limits, toward Jalalabad. We pulled into a big, garage-type building. A couple of Afghan men, freedom fighters, came over to the van and Moktar introduced me to them.

"My friend needs his van modified to hide fifteen kilos of hash," Moktar told them. "He wants to fabricate a false bottom someplace on the van."

For the next few hours, the men looked over the van, both inside and out. Every idea they came up with was one I didn't like. The fabrication would look like it was specially made—and it had to look natural, like it had come from the factory. If it didn't, customs would tear the van apart. They wouldn't hesitate to destroy it if they suspected illegal contraband. After two hours of listening to their ideas, Moktar and I were ready to return to Kabul.

"Thank you for helping me," I said to Moktar's friends. "I will think about your ideas, and if I decide to have my van modified, I will tell Moktar, and then we can set up a day and time to bring the van over to start the work."

"Well, goodbye and thanks. I'll keep in touch," said Moktar to his friends.

But the men wouldn't allow us to leave until they'd received some money for their time. They hadn't done a damn thing for two hours but talk about different ideas. Moktar pointed his rifle directly at the chest of one of the men and said something to them in Pashtu. But they still held their ground.

"Bob, start the van up and drive slowly away," whispered Moktar, with his index finger on the trigger of his rifle.

I didn't want to do that. I reached into my shoulder bag and took out two one-hundred Afghani bills.

"Moktar, give this to them. Give each of them one bill," I said, handing the money to Moktar.

He did as I asked. The men were now very happy and thankful and let us depart without any problems. So we drove back to Moktar's apartment building. I dropped him off outside the building, thanked him for the exciting evening, and then drove toward my place.

While driving back to the apartment, I noticed that my friend was back in town with his Rhesus monkey. The monkey was holding another baby monkey in her arms. I pulled over and stopped to say "hello."

He noticed me right away, as soon as he saw my van. We looked into each other's eyes and smiled. I quickly crossed the street and reached out and gave him an Afghan greeting, kissing both of his cheeks and placing my right hand over my heart to show warm, heart-felt feelings. He was truly a friend. He noticed that I didn't have Rex with me.

"Where is your monkey?" he asked.

I bowed my head and explained what had happened. He knew I had loved Rex more than life itself.

"I've been very depressed since I lost Rex," I said sadly. "Even my dog, Foxy, misses him. I've been hoping to see you. I want to replace Rex with another baby monkey."

The mother monkey seemed to know exactly what we were talking about because she tried to shy away and hide her baby, but her owner took it away from her and handed it to me. I really felt terrible that I was about to take her baby again. So I showed her that I really loved her baby. I pressed it against my chest, caressed him, and gave him sweet small kisses on his forehead. The mother looked at me with her big, sad eyes and grabbed her baby from my arms. She knew that I was about to take it away from her. The owner said something to the mother monkey and he tried to take the baby out of her hands, but she turned and shied away from him. She didn't want anyone taking this baby.

"I'm sorry," I said to him. "I can't take her baby away from her, not after seeing that."

But the owner went to her again. This time he was able to take the baby away from her. He handed it to me, so I reached into my money belt, took out the correct amount of money, and handed it to him. Then, I quickly walked away holding my new baby monkey close to my chest. The mother tried to follow, but the owner held tight to her leash. I felt very sad that she was losing her baby, but I was also feeling ecstatic with my new baby. Then it hit me—I won-dered how Carol was going to feel. Within a few minutes, I would find out.

When I walked into the apartment, Carol looked very surprised to see another monkey. But Foxy, on the other hand, was very ex-cited. She wanted to play with it immediately. Carol, however, reacted differently.

"Robert, you seem to like monkeys better than you like me," she snapped.

I thought to myself that she was probably right. I just ignored her and let the monkey get to know Foxy. They started playing immediately. I could tell right away that this monkey was just as intelligent as Rex had been. So I named him Rex Jr. Foxy got along great with our new family member. Carol, on the other hand, took a few weeks to get used to him.

During the next couple of weeks, I kept pretty busy. We were getting ready for Pat and Becky to arrive within a month or so, and Jim was supposed to come within a few weeks.

The apartment was looking better every day. We had all the amenities of home. But some days I became bored and looked for new ways to keep myself amused. So I started collecting lizards. I had made a big, screened cage to keep them in and then went across the street to the big mountain to search for them. I would carry a small one-foot-long stick, a small mirror, and a glass jar with a lid.

When I would see a small lizard run into its hole, I would kneel down in front of the hole and put the mirror up to it to see if the lizard was still there. If it was, I would poke the stick into the hole and chase the lizard into the glass jar, which I held in front of the hole. Then I would dump it into a larger jar and search for more. Once my hunt was finished, I would return to the apartment and dump my catch into the cage.

I even had the Afghan kids from the neighborhood help me catch them. But that was a mistake. They were coming to my apartment every day with lizards that they had caught. Some I bought and others I didn't want. In fact, they were coming over with so many lizards that I had to tell them to only bring a certain kind—ones with yellow and black stripes. These I only had a few. They were hard to catch and find and the only types I would buy from them.

After a week or so, my cage was full. I had decorated the cage as a forest with a small lake. The lizards seemed to like it. They soon started breeding. I tried to set up an exporting company to send the lizards to America, but due to American laws, I wasn't able to get an export license. Therefore, most of the lizards I had to turn loose and kept just a few as pets.

Foxy and Rex Jr. were really good friends. Rex Jr. had learned the same tricks as Rex. He also learned to play the same game of tag that Rex and Foxy had played in the living room. This is what we did while awaiting Jim's arrival. I forgot about modifying the van. I ended up stashing the fifteen kilos in a big cardboard box in our spare bedroom. I would use it to make envelopes and shoes. I wouldn't have to buy hash for a long time.

Near the end of November, Jim finally arrived. I heard a car door shut, so I went over to the living room window to see what the noise was and saw Saraj and Jim jump out of the taxi. Jim had gone to the post office and had Saraj escort him to my new apartment. Mark was over on this particular day making up some hash and hash envelopes. Tomorrow was Thanksgiving, and Carol was going to make a big dinner for us. Now Jim would also be included for Thanksgiving dinner.

When Jim entered my apartment, I gave him a big hug and handshake. We were very glad to see each other again. Saraj only stayed for a few minutes. He had to leave to catch the bus to his village. Before he did, I asked if he could return the following day for dinner.

"Saraj, can you come over tomorrow for Thanksgiving dinner?"

"I'm sorry Bob, but I can't make it," he replied.

"Well, take care...and I'll see you at the post office in a few days," I said, as I handed him ten hash envelopes to send for me.

I also gave Saraj five-thousand Afghani—well over a hundred American dollars. But it was well worth it. Once Saraj had departed, it was time to relax.

"It's time to celebrate!" I shouted.

Everyone went into my bedroom where Mark and I were making up the hash. We all sat around on the beds as I got out my morphine kit and a new bottle of morphine. I had bought extra syringes so we would have spares, just in case one of them broke. I handed one to Jim while he waited patiently for his fix. He had just traveled constantly for the last three days.

I handed out spoons to each one of us. I put two tabs in Carol's spoon, one in Jim's, two in Mark's, but he pleaded for two more, so I did as he asked and put another two tablets in his spoon and four half-grain tablets in my spoon. We each fixed our own, but I helped Jim inject his before I did mine. Within seconds, we all went from sitting on the beds to lying down, while the morphine rushed through our veins. For that thirty-second rush, there's not a feeling like it in the world. After a few minutes, one by one, we started coming back to life. Jim really liked the buzz.

"Boy, Robert, I forgot just how good this stuff was. I could get addicted to it very easy. In fact, let me clean my syringe and do another hit. I'm on vacation and want to get a good buzz," said Jim.

"Okay, just don't overdo it. I don't want you to o.d.," I told him.

"I won't. I know what I'm doing."

"I want to do another one, too," said Carol excitedly.

After I helped Jim and Carol fix again, Mark and I went back to making hash envelopes. A few minutes later, Jim and Carol returned to the living; both were floating on cloud nine. As Mark and I continued to work, Jim started raving about a new drug called hash oil. It was selling for five to ten times the price of hash. He said that people in America couldn't get enough of it.

As we talked, Rex Jr. jumped on Jim's lap and started playing with his long, thick beard. Jim still had his Jim Morrison-type beard and look. To be honest, he looked exactly like Jim Morrison. Everyone in the room began laughing as Rex Jr. picked at Jim's beard. When he became bored of that, he began doing back flips. He did four back flips in a row. Rex Jr. was so funny. Then he went over to Foxy and tried to ride her like a horse, but Foxy didn't want to play. She just sat down, while Rex Jr. tried to hold onto Foxy's hair. They sure played great together.

Jim began talking about hash oil again. He wanted me to start sending him hash oil instead of hash, and he wanted to smuggle some back to America when he returned.

"Jim, I know all about hash oil from the Brotherhood of Eternal Love," I said. "That's what they smuggle. They send five to seven girls per week by plane with plastic girdles filled with the stuff. These girdles were originally used for weight reducing and filled with air, then worn under their clothes. When they were patted down for weapons, the girdles felt just like flesh. Instead of filling them with air, they filled them with hash oil. You couldn't tell a difference once it was hidden under their clothing. But if I were you, Jim, I wouldn't take more than one hundred grams of oil, and then it would be easy to hide."

"That sounds good to me," he replied. "Wow, Rob, I can't get over your apartment. It's better than any house I lived in, in America."

Mark and I stopped our work just long enough to show Jim around the apartment. A few minutes later, we returned to the living room as the stereo played John Lennon songs, the colored lights flashed a rhythmic beat, and a nice fire burned in the living room fireplace. Soon after, Carol handed each one of us a big piece of her homemade banana cream pie. She had all the food ready to be cooked for the following day. We had gotten a twenty-pound turkey, and she was cooking it in our new electric oven. We thought Pat and

Becky might even arrive in time for Thanksgiving dinner. But they were in Turkey, and we hoped would soon be in Afghanistan.

As the animals played, the rest of us just kicked back and relaxed.

"Rob, I wish I could stay here forever," said Jim.

"Why not? Carol and me are gonna live here forever. That's why we've fixed up the apartment with all the comforts of home."

As we kicked back and relaxed by the fire, Rex Jr. suddenly ran across the room, jumped onto one of the empty chairs, and then jumped onto Foxy's back, as if she were a horse. Foxy started bucking him, trying to knock him off her back. It was really something to watch. It was a miniature bucking bronco and bareback rider. They were cute. Rex Jr. held on until Foxy was too tired and just collapsed on the floor. Then he went up to Foxy's face and began to pick and eat the fleas, or whatever, from Foxy's body.

We were so stoned, all we could do was watch the animals, listen to rock music, and kick back—that is, until it was time for bed. However, before we hit the sack, I got out my bottle of morphine. Everyone wanted a goodnight fix, even Jim. I was hesitant to give him anymore that night, but it had been a good four hours since his last fix so I agreed to let him do one more tablet. Mark and I each did three tabs, and Carol did two more. We had all done more than usual, but we were celebrating Jim's arrival and Thanksgiving.

Mark and Jim slept on air mattresses in the extra bedroom, while Carol and I went to our own room. Rex Jr. slept with me and Foxy slept with Carol. I went to sleep dreaming about Thanksgiving dinner.

Carol and I awoke early the next morning. She had a lot of cooking to do, and I had to visit the post office and the bank. I had to check the incoming mail to see if Becky had written me from Turkey and to pick up any other mail that I might have had. I also had to go to the bank to pick up any money that had come in. Then Jim and I would visit Tiar and have some hash oil made.

I thought about going to the Brotherhood's house to buy the oil from them. They made it themselves when they were in town, but it wasn't worth the chance. That house had been busted too many times before. Then I thought about going to Moktar's house, but I had never asked him to make hash oil and didn't know if he even knew how.

After doing my chores, I returned to the apartment. Jim and Mark were finally awake. I couldn't have arrived at a better time 'cause they wanted their morning fix. I had already fixed an hour before with Carol, but it was a day of celebration, so I decided to fix with them. When Carol came into the room and saw what we were doing, she also wanted another fix. What the hell, I thought, it was a holiday. It was the second consecutive Thanksgiving that I had celebrated in Kabul. As we fixed, Jim and I discussed our future.

"Jim, why don't we go to one of my hash connections to see about getting some hash oil made?"

"Sounds good, Rob."

We weren't going to eat Thanksgiving dinner until three or four that afternoon, so we had some time to waste.

"Mark, you can come with us if you want," I told him.

"No, I want to visit some friends at Ziggy's hotel. I'll be back before three to eat dinner. In fact, if you want to stop at Ziggy's after you see your Afghan friend I'll ride back to the apartment with you."

"Sure, no problem. As soon as we're finished with our business, I'll stop by there to pick you up."

"Rob, I have to be back in the States before Christmas," Jim remarked.

"Why? That's only three weeks away."

"I know. I have to be back before school starts. Martha and I decided to get married."

"Jim, you've got to be kidding?" I asked, not believing what I had heard.

"No, it's the truth."

"Well, it looks like my premonition came true. I told you before you left Kabul the last time that you would go back to school and marry Martha. But congratulations anyway," I said, shaking his hand.

Mark, Jim, and I jumped into the van and drove away. I dropped Mark off in front of Ziggy's, and Jim and I continued on our way.

We stopped at Moktar's place first. I parked the van on the side of the road, and then Jim and I walked up the dirt steps and through the narrow dimly lit hallways to the roof. I walked up to Moktar's door and knocked on it. A person I didn't recognize answered the door.

"Is Moktar at home?" I asked a giant of a man.

"No. Him and Sabul went to Kandahar to their home. Their mother was ill," he replied.

"Okay, we'll come back next week," I retorted.

We turned and walked back to the van. Next, we drove to Tiar's place. The last time I had been there, Tiar was being hassled by the

Afghan police. I just hoped it was safe to go there now.

We walked down the foul-smelling, urine-soaked, muddy alley, and after five minutes of dodging this minefield, we finally came upon Tiar's domain. We walked into the outside corridor of his mud-walled compound and saw Tiar's wife.

"Is Tiar at home?" I asked.

This time, she seemed happy to see me. She waved her hands, inviting us into her house. A few seconds later, Tiar emerged.

"Please, come into my house," he said.

We followed him up the stairs to his bedroom where we sat on the bedrolls that lay on the floor.

"Tiar, why did the policemen come to your house a few weeks ago?" I asked.

"They wanted baksheesh," he exclaimed. "They found out that I was selling hashish to tourists and wanted some of my profits. They do that from time to time, once or twice a year."

"I thought you were going to jail," I told him matter-of-factly.

"If I didn't pay them baksheesh they would have put me in jail. All they wanted was a little spending money. They only make thirty dollars a year. If I help them, then we become better friends."

"Tiar, I need to buy a kilo of hash oil. How much is it?"

"One kilo of hash oil is very expensive," he replied, playing with his beard. He was probably thinking that he could feed all of his kids for the next three years from the money he would make from this deal. "It will cost you three-hundred American dollars."

"What if I supply the hash?"

"No. I won't make any money. It is very hard and takes a long time to make the hash oil," he explained.

"Can we watch and see how the hash oil is made?" I begged.

"No, then you will start making it yourself, and I won't be able to make any money to feed my family. Please, let me make the hash oil for you. I really need the money."

"Okay, Tiar, when should we come back to pick up the hash oil?" I asked.

"Come back at this time tomorrow and it will be ready."

"I will give you half the money now and half tomorrow when it is finished," I said, handing him one-hundred and fifty dollars. "I will see you tomorrow about this same time."

The deal was settled, so Jim and I walked back to the van. We had to pick up Mark at Ziggy's and head back to the apartment for Thanksgiving dinner.

When we arrived at the apartment, it was almost two in the afternoon and Carol was still cooking the turkey. The whole apartment smelled of thyme, parsley, and sweet potatoes, all mixed together. It brought back memories of the home-cooked meals of past Thanksgiving dinners back in America.

I went into the kitchen and fondled Carol as she stood at the electric two-burner stove stirring the mashed potatoes. Carol loved it—it had been awhile since we'd had any foreplay, or for that matter, plain old sex. I had been too depressed after Rex died. Now I was paying too much attention to Rex Jr. But he was playing with Mark, Jim, and Foxy in the living room. So Carol and I had a few minutes to fool around. I had Carol's pants down below her knees and her blouse undone when Jim walked in. Carol quickly tried to hide behind me, so Jim turned and stepped into the hallway.

"Rob, can I get a glass of lemonade?" asked Jim, as Carol had redressed.

"Now you can come into the kitchen, Jim," I said.

"Sorry about that," he said apologetically.

"No problem, Jim. We were just trying to catch up," I replied, looking into Carol's eyes.

All of us went into the living room to relax and listen to music. Mark was playing with my pets. While we were just relaxing, I showed Jim the fifteen kilos of hash that I had bought from Moktar. His eyes nearly popped out of his head when I opened the lid of the box. He bent his head down, took a big whiff of the pollen, and damn near passed out from the smell. It was overwhelming. It smelled as if ten skunks had sprayed their foul scent all over the room at the same time. I grabbed a small handful of pollen and handed it to him. Then I quickly closed the lid and left the room.

We returned to the living room to smoke some of the hash pollen that I had just given to Jim. Soon after, Mark and I showed Jim how to play Caroms, the Afghan way, using the finger instead of a stick to shoot with. So while we waited for dinner, we played Caroms, listened to rock music, and smoked hash. It was really a day to remember. It couldn't get any better than this. And we were halfway around the world in a backward country with all the comforts of home.

We played Caroms until the animals became restless and Rex Jr. jumped onto the board game and knocked it over. That woke us out of our trance. When we came back down to earth, the turkey was done and it was time to eat our delicious Thanksgiving dinner. Carol set the kitchen table for four. When I noticed, I became upset.

"Carol, would you please set a little dish next to mine for Rex Jr.," I asked.

Carol didn't seem to like the monkey at the kitchen table. She gave me a dirty look and then set an extra plate next to mine. Carol had made the biggest dinner I had ever seen. She had made everything you could think of, including pumpkin and banana cream pies, turkey stuffing, mashed potatoes, sweet potatoes, biscuits, gravy, cream-style corn, coleslaw, cranberry sauce, peas, lemonade, and real cold non-pasteurized cow's milk. There were also two bottles of an old and rare red wine.

The table was beautifully decorated with flowers and candles. Carol had outdone herself. We couldn't believe how great this meal looked until we tasted it. It was exquisite.

Before we started the meal, Carol had me say grace. I thanked the Lord for the wonderful meal and especially for sending me this wonderful cook, amen. We ate like starved animals. We had our faces in our plates so the room was silent for twenty minutes. Even little Rex Jr. ate his food as he sucked on his bottle of milk. He ate nearly the same food as I did. Dinner was great. We all congratulated Carol on her wonderful meal. We toasted her as we held our glasses in the air.

"To the most beautiful and greatest chef in the world," I said with a wink.

We clinked our glasses together and drank our wine. After thirty minutes of gorging myself, my stomach was full.

I took Rex Jr. and went into the bedroom to rest after eating such a big meal. The others continued to eat. They ate for another hour before adjourning to the living room, and I did as well.

While we relaxed, Carol gave each of us a cup of gourmet coffee and a slice of pumpkin and banana cream pie as the colored lights flashed and the stereo played Carol King music. The room's hypnotic atmosphere seemed to put us into a trance. Once we had finished our dessert, we just talked and relaxed to the beat of the music. We were too bloated and stuffed with Thanksgiving dinner to move around. And before we knew it, it was time for bed.

All of us went into my bedroom for our midnight morphine fix. I took out a new bottle of morphine. This was the third bottle I had opened since Jim had come to Kabul to visit. I didn't mind, as long as I could afford it. And right now, business was good, so I could afford it. We were going through a bottle of morphine each day. We should have started slowing down and cutting back, but Jim still had two weeks to party before he departed for America. Mark, on the other hand, had to either return to Pakistan to renew his Afghan entrance visa or get an extension.

"Mark, do you plan on returning to Pakistan or are you going to try to get a three-or six-month extension?" I asked him.

"Well, I think I will go tomorrow and try to get an extension. If they refuse to give me one, then I'll have to return to Pakistan for a few weeks until I can get a new visa," he replied.

"Mark. Jim and I will give you a ride to the Interior Ministry tomorrow if you want," I told him.

"Sure, if you don't mind."

"When Jim and I go to Tiar's house to pick up the hash oil, we'll drop you off."

Everyone did their morphine and hit the sack. The next morning was déjà vu all over again. Everyone placed their spoons near me so I could put their morning wake-up tabs into them. I injected Jim before I injected myself. Once the rush was over, we were ready to start the day.

Carol was making coffee and breakfast for everybody. Mark wanted me to drop him off at the Ministry of Interior so he could get an extension visa. Jim and I had to pick up the hash oil later that afternoon.

While Carol was busy making breakfast, we went into the living room. I added wood to the fireplace and turned on the stereo. As we relaxed and talked over the chores that had to be done that day, Foxy and Rex Jr. decided to play tag. I was sitting in my usual chair, next to the window, holding Rex Jr. in my lap, when suddenly he jumped down and ran over to the other side of the living room.

He started climbing up on the bookcase and hung on to the top shelf sizing up the situation. He jumped from the bookcase to Jim's chair. In a flash, he jumped from the back of Jim's neck to his lap and then ran across the floor, teasing Foxy. Then he ran over to me and jumped onto my lap. Foxy came over to my chair, nuzzled her nose into my lap, and looked into my eyes, telling me that she wasn't ready for the game. But she backed up to the middle of the room and lay down, waiting for Rex Jr. to start the game again.

"Hey you guys, I didn't teach Rex Jr. this game. He must have learned it from Foxy," I told them.

We watched and waited for Rex Jr. to make his move. First, he faked to his right, then jumped down to the left and ran across the room to Jim's lap. Then he jumped from Jim's lap to his shoulders, up to the bookcase again, and hung from the top shelf by one hand as he looked over the playing field. Rex Jr. waited and waited as Foxy became restless and anxious for her little playmate to make his move. She began to make little growling noises. She would sit up, then lie down, sit up, and then lie down again. She wanted Rex Jr. to run across the room so she could try to tackle him.

If Rex Jr. made it to my chair without Foxy stopping him, he got a point. The first one up to five was the winner. Finally, Rex Jr. made his move. He jumped from the bookcase to Jim's lap, and then quickly jumped too close to Foxy and she caught him with her paws and lay on top of him. She got the point. Rex Jr. would give a love bite to Foxy's cheek and Foxy would let him up. They played exactly like Rex and Foxy had played before. They had taught themselves. They continued to play like that until we ate breakfast.

Carol outdid herself that morning. She made pancakes, French toast, and two pounds of Dutch bacon. We also had four different types of homemade syrups—strawberry, maple, sugar and water, and apple butter—plus fresh orange juice. I had bought Carol a new electric juicer, just like the ones the street vendors used. It had been a Christmas gift so she wouldn't have to squeeze the oranges by hand. This breakfast was magnificent. Even Jim and Mark complimented Carol for such an exquisite meal.

Mark and Jim had eaten as though they hadn't eaten in a week. I didn't eat that much because the morphine took my appetite away. I had one piece of French toast with one piece of bacon and a big glass of orange juice. Jim and Mark, on the other hand, must have eaten six or seven pancakes and the same amount of French toast. Between those two guys, they ate enough food to feed a family of eight. They stuffed themselves for an hour. Carol watched as they devoured their food and she loved it. Finally, she had someone to eat her food and to converse with at meals.

Once they finished their breakfast, we left the apartment to do our chores. Carol stayed behind to clean and cook. She was a great housewife. She kept bugging me that she wanted children, but I didn't want anything to do with kids. I liked monkeys and dogs. There were times when we would argue about this subject. This morning was one of them. So I wanted to get out of the apartment as quickly as possible. I didn't even give Jim and Mark a few minutes to relax after eating such a big breakfast. I hurried them to the van.

It was a beautiful morning. The sun was shining brightly and the air was clean and crisp. We were on our way to the Ministry of Interior and within five minutes had dropped Mark off in front of the building.

"Mark, meet us at the apartment," I said. "We're not sure how long we will be Tiar's house."

"No problem," he replied.

To look inconspicuous, Jim and I dressed up in the typical Afghan garb, including a light cotton blanket wrapped around the shoulders. We even put on turbans for the occasion. This was Jim's idea, to dress and look like an Afghan so we wouldn't call attention to ourselves. He was very paranoid. I didn't argue. It was better to be safe than sorry.

I brought one kilo of my hash pollen with us so Tiar could add opium to it. Then I could send my friends in America opiated hash for Christmas. I had sent some almost a year ago. But it was so expensive to make that I only sent it on special occasions. Christmas was just around the corner, and this would make a great gift for my friends.

I parked the van on the street near the alley leading to Tiar's house. I had the kilo of hash pollen hidden in my shoulder bag under my blanket. We walked past and through a small teashop and restaurant to get to the urine soaked, rat-infested alley that led to Tiar's house.

The smell from the raw, open sewage on this particular beautiful day was overbearing and repugnant. I nearly regurgitated my breakfast. Jim actually did, due to the putrid, foul smell. We held our blankets over our noses and mouths, trying to hold our breath while we dodged the streams of raw sewage. Our eyes and lungs burned as we breathed in this foul odor. Finally, after a ten-minute jog through a biological mine field, we made it to Tiar's house.

I knocked on the front door and waited for someone to invite us in. One of Tiar's younger boys opened the door and escorted us into the house and up the dirt stairs to Tiar's bedroom. Tiar entered the room with two of his Afghan friends. They were neighbors helping him make the hash oil.

"Tiar, is the hash oil finished yet?" I asked him.

"No, it still needs one or two more hours to cure," he replied.

Tiar asked one of his friends to bring the oil into the room. One of the men left the room to retrieve the hash oil. Within a minute, he returned carrying a large tin pan that was filled with a black, goo-like substance. The large pan was resting on top of a larger pan filled with ice. The pollen was mixed with a special chemical and heated for ten minutes or until it boiled and then quickly cooled. The chemical changed the molecular structure of the atoms and the oil thickened as it cooled. When the chemical was completely evaporated and the hash oil was cured, it was thick as molasses. But it still needed another two hours to cure, so I took the kilo of pollen from my shoulder bag and handed it to Tiar.

"Tiar, do you have any opium left?" I asked.

"I just came back from Badakhsan province and brought back some excellent opium," he said, showing me his potent opium. "It is very fresh.

"Who did you buy this pollen from?" He held up my bag of pollen and looked it over.

"This is the pollen we bought in Mazare Sarif," I lied. "I still have a few kilos left. This is the last of it."

I didn't want him to know about my other hash connection, Moktar. I didn't want to get Tiar angry or make him unhappy.

"How much opium do you want?" asked Tiar.

"How much do you want for three ounces and to mix it with my pollen, then press it into slabs?" I asked him.

"I will charge just for the opium and nothing for the pressing. I will mix the pollen and opium together, so the total for everything will cost four hundred and fifty dollars, and you still owe me one hundred and fifty dollars, plus three hundred dollars for the three ounces of opium," he said.

This was much too expensive for the opium, but I had no other place to go and had the money to spend, so I really didn't mind. And I was helping Tiar's family. So I agreed to Tiar's price and waited while he began to make the opiated hash. Jim and I sat back to watch Tiar perform his magic. We watched as Tiar held up a small balance scale and began to measure the three ounces of opium. He used small rocks as his weights. I never questioned him about the authenticity of his weights; I just took his word for it.

He set the three ounces of opium near the pan of boiling water. I reached down, grabbed the pungent opium, and held it up to the sunlight. Although it looked black, it was actually a deep violet in color. It was very bitter to the taste, and the texture was very gummy and sticky to the touch. Tiar prepared the pollen just as he had done many times before. The only difference was that he added the opium to the boiling water and then added the pollen to it. Then he mixed and kneaded the pollen as he had done many times before.

Tiar's wife brought in tea and cookies for us to munch on as we waited.

Within two hours, Tiar was finally finished pressing the pollen into the opiated hashish. Fifteen minutes later, the hash oil was also ready.

I reached into my money belt and pulled out a stack of American bills. I counted out four-hundred and fifty dollars and handed them to Tiar. He had a big smile on his face, reaching from ear to ear, as he took the money from my hands. He had made more money in those few hours than he could have made working in a government job for ten years.

Jim picked up the twenty slabs of black opiated hash, which were still warm to the touch, and placed them very carefully into a plastic bag. Tiar handed me a plastic quart container filled with one kilo of black, thick, molasses-type goo, called hash oil. I placed everything into my shoulder bag very carefully and then wrapped my blanket over my shoulders, hiding the bag.

We left Tiar's home and walked back through the alley to the van. Once we were inside the van, we felt safe. Then we headed to the post office to pick up my mail.

Saraj wasn't working, but I saw Mr. Bareck and introduced him to Jim.

"Jim, Mr. B and I are waiting for him to become president of the post office, then we'll become rich," I said enthusiastically.

"I sure hope so," replied Mr. Bareck.

I picked up my mail and letters from my friends. One of my friends had sent me two of the newly released rock and roll cassettes from America. We were anxious to play them on my magic stereo. So we left the post office and headed back to the apartment. But first, we wanted to stop by Ziggy's restaurant to drink a vanilla milkshake. As we drove down Chicken Street, we passed my little Afghan friend, Baba.

A few seconds later, we came to a stop in front of the restaurant, where there were many longhaired hippies and red-haired junkies hanging out. They were everywhere. We must have bumped into thirty of them as we walked up to the front door of the restaurant. Just as we were walking in, Mark was walking out. We grabbed him and pulled him back into the restaurant.

"Mark, sit and talk with us while we drink our milkshakes, then all three of us can ride back to the apartment together," I said.

He wasn't in any hurry, so he agreed.

"Rob, did you see your friend?" he asked.

"Yep, everything worked out perfectly."

As I looked around the room, I noticed two guys sitting at a table near the back of the room staring at me. As I got a better look, I was sure I had seen these guys before. Sure enough, these were two of the guys from the Brotherhood of Eternal Love. So I excused myself from Jim and Mark and walked over to their table. I sat down and introduced myself.

"Are you still selling cassette tapes?" I asked them.

"No, we don't have any more tapes to sell. The chick who was staying with us was selling them, but she returned to the States some time ago," said the guy with straight, long, blonde hair that stretched down to his waist.

"Are you guys still staying at the same house with your buddy, Claude, the European hash exporter?"

"We're still at the same house, but everyone who used to live there isn't there anymore," said the blonde-haired hippie.

"That's what we wanted to talk to you about," said the curly-haired Samoan. "We need to buy some pollen—lots of pollen."

"How much is lots?" I asked.

"About a thousand kilos," said the Samoan.

"What happened to your connections?"

"The guy you mentioned, Claude, went back to Europe due to poor health. He was our biggest supplier. He would buy forty or more tons at each harvest, then sell us a few tons for helping him press the pollen into kilo bricks. And the Afghan who had helped us before was shot about two months ago for smuggling narcotics. So to be on the safe side, we split to Pakistan. Now we're back and need to do this score before our visas expire. So we'll need the pollen within a month's time," said the Samoan.

"If you can help us out, or if you know someone who can, will you let us know?" asked the blonde-haired hippie.

"I'm sorry—I forgot to ask you your names."

"I'm John," said the blonde-haired hippie.

"And I'm Stoneman," said the Samoan.

"Stoneman?" I asked, not sure if I had heard him correctly.

"That's it," he replied, with a little snicker.

"I just wanted to make sure. What kind of price are you looking to pay?"

"We want the best pollen for the cheapest price. We don't want to pay more than ten dollars per kilo," said John.

"Well, I'll see what I can do. To get the pollen at that price, I would have to get it in the Balkh province and that's no easy trip. Meet me here in three days, at this time, and I'll give you my answer. I'm sure I can help you, but I'm not really sure of a price though."

I had nearly finished my milkshake by the time I left their table. When I returned to my table, Jim and Mark were ready to leave. They were waiting on me. In fact, they were giving me dirty looks all the way back to the apartment because I hadn't sat with them. I refused to play their little mind game. I didn't say a word until we reached the apartment. Dan and his roommates were just arriving home, too. We exchanged pleasantries and then went to our separate apartments.

As soon as I walked into the apartment my two babies, Foxy and Rex Jr., greeted me in the hallway. Rex Jr. climbed up my leg to my waist and hung onto me. Foxy came over and nuzzled me with her snout. This was real true love. Carol never greeted me like that. We all went into the living room and relaxed. I took out the two cassette tapes and gave them to Carol. She placed one into the stereo. It was a new group called Ziggy Stardust (David Bowie) and the Spiders from Mars.

As the music played, I started reading my letters. One of them was from Becky. She wrote that she and her friend were on their way to Kabul. They had just left Istanbul and would be here in another week or two.

It was only two weeks to Christmas. I wondered if they would be here to celebrate Christmas with us. Jim wouldn't. He had to leave in another week or so, maybe even sooner, although he hadn't mentioned it lately.

The second letter I read was from my mother. She wrote that she had sent me a box of Christmas gifts. I gave everyone a quick synopsis of the letters.

"We will soon be having more guests. Becky is bringing her girlfriend to Kabul. They can sleep with Mark and Jim in their bedroom," I said, with a wink.

"I won't be here," Jim replied. "I'll have to be leaving next week. I have to get back before Christmas because school starts a few days later."

"Well let's not talk about that. Let's look at this hash oil," I said, pulling the bag of opiated hash and the container of hash oil out of my shoulder bag.

I set the stuff down on the floor and started to make some hash joints using the opiated hash. Jim picked up the oil and started checking it out. Then he walked into the kitchen to retrieve a piece of aluminum foil and a straw so he could try out the hash oil to see how potent it was.

Jim came back with all the correct utensils and placed a small, pinhead size piece of oil on a six-inch-square piece of aluminum foil. He held the foil in one hand and with the other, placed one end of the straw into his mouth and the other end over the oil, while Mark put a small match flame to the bottom of the foil. The oil began to smoke, and Jim inhaled it through the straw. As soon as it went into his lungs, he started coughing his head off. He continued to cough for five minutes. He couldn't believe the potency of the hash oil. He was disoriented and dizzy just from one little toke.

Now it was Mark's turn. He waited as Jim held the match for him. Mark inhaled the smoke through the straw and started choking and coughing. He even passed out. When he awoke, he couldn't believe how high he was from just one toke. I was still busy making hash joints, so Carol tried the oil. Once she inhaled, she wished she hadn't. She coughed so hard that she ran to the bathroom and vomited. She had inhaled too much smoke too fast.

I let Jim and Mark smoke more of it before I even tried it. Finally, it was my turn. Mark lit and held the match as I held the straw and inhaled deeply. But before I could take it all in, I was coughing it out. This stuff exploded in my lungs. It seemed to expand my lungs to the max and then wham—you coughed your head off. That was enough for me. One toke knocked me for a loop. I decided I would stick to smoking the hash joints.

Mark and Jim continued to smoke the oil until they both passed out. They each had a total of four tokes and were totally out of it. I woke them both out of their dreamland and herded them to their bedroom.

Ten minutes after Carol and I had put the animals to bed, Mark and Jim got up and came into my room for their midnight morphine fix so they could return to their room to sleep. Finally, we were all snug in bed. It would be another bright and sunny day tomorrow, I thought to myself.

The next morning at breakfast, Mark beamed with confidence.

"Rob, I got a three-month extension visa so I could stay in Kabul and not have to go to Pakistan," exclaimed Mark.

I was happy for him, except there was a downside to that. He could purchase morphine in Pakistan much cheaper than in Afghanistan. But for the time being, I was feeding his habit and his stomach.

After breakfast, Jim, Mark, and I started making some more hash envelopes with the opiated hash. I wanted to get them out before Christmas. I wanted my friends in America to have a very Merry Christmas again this year.

Over the next few days, Jim and I went into town to buy gifts for the trip back to America. We bought a number of carpets and glims and a few other expensive gifts. This would make him look like a vacationing tourist. He should be able to slide through any customs without any problems. We loaded the van with gifts and headed for the apartment.

On the way, I remembered I had to stop at Ziggy's to meet the two hippies from the Brotherhood.

I parked my van near the restaurant, then Jim and I proceeded to walk through the dense jungle of junkies and hippies. There must have been one hundred freaks loitering around the grounds of the hotel and restaurant. The restaurant was packed, but we found our friends at the same table they were at a few days before. Looking into their eyes, I wondered if they had even left the table—or the room for that matter. They both looked sky-high. As Jim and I approached them, they finally came alive. They actually moved and waved their hands, then shouted, trying to be heard above the room noise, for us to sit down with them at their table.

The big Samoan pushed out two chairs for us to sit on. As we sat down, I introduced Jim to the two hippies from the Brotherhood and told them my name again. Then I got down to business.

"Well, John, are you guys still interested in the product that was discussed a few days ago? If so, I think I can help," I told him.

"Of course we are," he replied. "We need it done within a month. We have less than two months left on our visas, and it takes some time to set things in motion."

"We still have to turn the pollen into oil and that takes time," explained Stoneman. "So we need it by the end of January at the latest; the sooner the better."

"Well, I can get it at the price you wanted, ten dollars a kilo. But to get it that cheap, I'll have to go up north to Mazare Sarif to a few of the hash farms and deal through them. The only problem I have is that I want all the money up front."

"I don't know about that," replied John. "Why do you want all the money now? How do we know you won't rip us off?"

"I'm taking all the risk. The last time I bought pollen for some of your friends, Afghan soldiers nearly shot my friend and me to death. Then I had a rough time collecting the money that was due, and I'm not about to go through that again, ever. So it's my way or the high-way."

I was hoping they would turn me down. I really didn't want to take another trip up north, especially after all the near misses of getting busted. So I was more than a little surprised when they accepted my offer.

"You got yourself a deal," said John. "When do you want the money?"

"I'll meet you here three weeks from today to pick up the money. Once I get the ten grand, I will have the pollen here within five days. I will meet you here one week after you give me the money."

"Okay, we'll see you in three weeks, and if anything should go wrong before then, come either to Ziggy's or to the house and let us know what's going on," said a worried Stoneman.

We shook hands, and then Jim and I left the restaurant to return to the apartment.

That night, Carol and I wanted to take Jim to the nightclub at least one time before he left for America. Mark promised to watch the animals while we were gone, so Jim, Carol, and I dressed up in our best clothes—Jim and I in our best suit coats and ties, and Carol in her beautiful, dazzling, white lace handmade gown. She looked like a beautiful princess. We were dressed elegantly. We were ready to go to the king's ball. I wasn't sure if they would let Jim enter, but I didn't think they would mind. Within ten minutes, I would find out.

I parked the van in front of the disco. Jim followed Carol and me into the nightclub. As soon as we entered, we were stopped and taken aside. The doorman knew who Carol and I were, but he didn't know Jim and refused to let him inside.

"This man is an American rock star and a friend of mine," I told him. "He's traveling to America in a few days, and I want him to meet my Afghan friends and see what an Afghan disco looks like."

But I couldn't talk the doorman into letting Jim into the night-club. I even tried to bribe him with baksheesh, but all I did was insult him. I quickly apologized and thanked him for being my good friend.

"You and Carol are welcome," said the doorman. "You are good friends with the king's relatives, but no other American is welcome."

With that, we turned and left the nightclub. We went back to the apartment and had our own party. Once we had taken off our elegant garb and dressed into some comfortable ones, we each had our morphine fix. We had forgotten all about the hassle at the disco. A few hours later, we were all in dreamland.

The next few days seemed to go by very fast. Before we knew it, it was time for Jim to return to America. He had his clothes and gifts packed and his luggage all set to go. We just had one thing left to do—tape the small plastic baggie of hash oil to his body. I put the hundred grams of oil in four plastic baggies to make it less likely to leak. We then rolled it up and placed it into the crack of his butt, between the folds of the cheeks. It was well hidden. The only way he could possibly get busted was if they were to strip search him, which was very unlikely, unless he gave them a reason, like acting very nervous or suspicious.

We loaded all of his luggage, carpets, and gifts into the van and then ourselves. All of us went to see Jim off, including Mark. I wanted to be there just in case he got busted. Then I hoped I could bail him out. Once we had reached our destination, we each grabbed a piece of Jim's baggage and carried it into the airport.

As we waited while Jim stood in line to go through customs for baggage check, I noticed that the customs man who was searching Jim's luggage was the same one who had refused to let Carol enter Kabul with the electric tools she had brought from Denmark. I never liked this deformed, bald-headed geek. He never smiled and always disliked Americans.

Now Jim was about to be tested and searched thoroughly by him. But as long as he was interested in searching his luggage and gifts and not his person, then Jim didn't have anything to worry about. Well, the bald-headed Telly Savalis look-alike seemed disgusted and outraged that he didn't find any illegal contraband in Jim's luggage. As he motioned Jim through the door to the tarmac, Jim passed the last security checkpoint. Then he was up the stairs and in the plane, waiting to return to Detroit via Beirut, Paris, and New York.

I would know in less than a month whether or not he had made it. If he returned to America without any problems, he was to sell the oil and then come back with Martha and one of her girlfriends. Then we'd fix them up with the weight-reducing girdles, putting a couple of kilos of oil in each. Once that stuff was sold, we could send back six girls.

I wanted to work it similar to the way the Brotherhood had. At one time, they were sending almost twenty girls per plane. They were very well organized. It would take time, but we could do it, too. So we needed this to work. This would be the first of many trips toward our goal. I had the distribution network. Now I had to feed it.

CHAPTER 17
CHRISTMAS IN KABUL-1972

We were very quiet riding back from the airport. We acted as if the party was over because Jim had left. But as soon as we got back to the apartment, we each fixed our morphine and soon forgot about Jim.

A few hours later, I went to the post office and bank. I needed to do some of my daily chores.

When I visited the post office, I had many letters to pick up. One of these letters was from Becky, so I opened it up immediately. They were on their way to Kabul. When they arrived, they would stay at the Najib Hotel and leave a letter at the post office telling me they were in the city.

I placed the rest of my letters in my shoulder bag and then went to the incoming parcel department to pick up my Christmas gift box from my mother. Then I went to the bank and picked up some money transfers.

Before returning home, I decided to buy a small Christmas tree. I bought a small live tree that we could plant in the spring.

Carol was very surprised and happy to see the tree. She found the decorations that I had used the year before. The next day, we bought a few more ornaments and strings of flashing colored lights. Mark, Carol, and I spent the day decorating the tree. We even made icicles out of thin stripes of aluminum foil. Once the tree was decorated and our Christmas stockings hung, we were finally in the Christmas spirit.

With the warm fire in the fireplace and the stereo playing some soft Christmas music, the atmosphere in the room was magic. Add the hash and morphine high to it, and we were all in a hypnotic state.

We must have gone through twenty bottles or more of morphine when Jim was here. We were still doing over two bottles a day. I was doing nearly a bottle a day, so I decided to decrease my habit. I would do the same amount, just not as often.

Carol was doing five to ten tabs per day, and Mark was doing as much as I was. But business was doing great, and I hoped, soon to do better, if Jim got through. So money was coming in quite regularly. I didn't have to worry about anything as long as I had my hash and my morphine.

We were in a partying mood, so I suggested that we get dressed up and visit the nightclub. But Carol refused if Mark came along, so Mark volunteered to babysit the animals while Carol and I went. This would give me a chance to catch up on all the latest gossip about Kabul.

Carol and I, again, dressed up in our elegant clothes; Carol in her beautiful white gown and me in my bright orange corduroy suit. I wore that with my handmade embroidered boots. These were made with two hundred-year-old embroidered cloth. The front of each boot had a flower covering it. I called them my magic boots. Now we were ready to go. Ten minutes later, we were at the front door of the Afghan nightclub.

As we entered the disco, the same doorman who refused our entry the week before greeted us. This time he was all smiles and very cordial as we walked past him and up the stairs. We went directly to our regular table. Most of our Afghan friends were there already. It had been well over a month since we'd last seen them, so we were all glad to see each other.

As we said hello, I listened very intently as I tried to overhear what the king's son was saying to one of his cousins. He was talking about his father's eyesight—that he was going blind and needed an operation.

As the night wore on, I listened to the music and to the conversation. I listened more than I talked. I even broke up a very heated argument between the king's son and his cousin, the son of the king's brother-in-law. They were arguing over the monarchy. The king's son accused his cousin's father of trying to overthrow the government. Supposedly, his father had been the Prime Minister twenty years before but was fired by the king for being insubordinate. Since then, he had been trying to get control of the government.

My friends talked politics all night long, or should I say they argued politics. But I learned many important things that night. I learned that the Russians were trying to control Afghan politics. I would have a few things to tell the Peace Corps director. He would want to know about this information, I thought to myself. Heck, I had learned more about Afghan politics on this night than I ever had the last few times I had listened to the king's siblings and relatives.

I sat and listened to my friend's conversation as Carol danced up a storm. She was again teaching the other Afghan women traditional line dance steps. They loved it. By two in the morning, we were ready to go home. I was tired from listening and sitting, and Carol was pooped from dancing. We went home and made love that night.

Well, there were only nine more shopping days until Christmas. Carol and I were going into town to do some Christmas shopping the following morning. Mark would stay at the apartment to watch the animals and make up some hash envelopes.

That morning, I only gave Carol twenty dollars to buy me a Christmas gift. I wanted to see how thrifty she would be. I wanted to save the money and spend it on her. Today, we were just window-shopping anyway. Once I knew what I wanted to get Carol, I would return the following day without her and buy the gift.

As we were walking down the street, we noticed some commotion a few hundred yards ahead of us, but we couldn't tell what was happening. As we continued to walk in the same direction, more and more people were scattering and running away, screaming and yelling.

Then we finally saw what all the commotion was about. On the other side of the street, we saw a very large, dirty, and hairy male figure rumbling toward us. This man was awesome.

I was just too stunned to move, as if my feet were glued to the ground. I tried to run, but my feet wouldn't move, and this giant of a man was coming toward us.

Each step he took seemed to make the ground shake. In his right hand, he carried a large, four-foot-long club, which he pounded into the street with each step he took. He was at least seven and a half feet tall or taller and a good five hundred pounds of muscle and hair.

Even though it was winter, this thing didn't wear any shoes, a shirt, or pants and was completely covered in hair. He reminded me of the legend of Bigfoot or the Abominable Snowman. This male figure was incredibly huge. I had never seen anything like it, and I am still not convinced that is was human.

As he passed us, I looked directly into his huge, dark eyes. He seemed to look right through me. For some reason, he didn't seem human. Carol and I both shuddered as he walked past. A few seconds later, we scampered away and never looked back.

We decided to visit the post office, bank, and pharmacy, in that order. I picked up my letters. I usually received from one to twenty letters from friends in America. I had another letter from Becky. It seemed that their money was running low so they would be in Kabul sooner than expected. They were going to have money wired at the Bank of Kabul, so I expected them within the next few days.

After saying hello and goodbye to Mr. Bareck and Saraj, we headed to the bank. Carol waited in the van while I collected the money. Ten minutes later, we were at the Devil's pharmacy. I bought another ten bottles of morphine. I wanted to buy more, but I had purchased every bottle that he had. I hoped that he would have more before these ran out.

Once we reached the apartment, Carol took the van and decided to do some Christmas shopping. I went into the apartment to help Mark with the hash envelopes, but as I was walking up the stairs to the apartment, I saw Dan.

"Dan, I need to see the director in the next few days," I told him.

"I will relay the message," he replied, then went our separate ways.

Mark and I just played with the animals and relaxed as we waited for Carol to return home and make dinner. We didn't do too much work over the next few days. I bided my time doing my Christmas shopping for about ten people. I bought gifts for Mark, Mr. B, Saraj, and Aslam, my servant. I would also buy gifts for Becky and her friend, just in case they arrived before Christmas.

The day I went to see the Peace Corps director, I had another surprise. He seemed to be very interested in the information that I had obtained.

"Bob, I want you to obtain as much information as possible," said Beardon. "I want you to find out how many Russians are at the embassy, and if they are bribing any Afghan government officials?"

"I will do the best I can."

But it would be another month before I would visit the nightclub again. Too many things were happening to me. I was so busy with my business I had forgotten all about the nightclub.

After I left the Peace Corps office, I went to Saraj and Mr. Bareck. I invited them both to my apartment on Christmas Day to pick up their presents. I also picked up my letters from America. One was from Becky telling me they were in Kabul. I jumped into my van and headed to the Najib Hotel. As I walked into the main office, I noticed a tall girl wearing a wrap-around dress standing in front of me. When she turned to talk to a guy sitting at a table, I recognized the girl. It was Becky.

"Becky!" I yelled.

She turned and looked at me for a second, then we both hugged and kissed each other.

"Rob, you look great," she said.

"Becky, where is your girlfriend, Pat?"

"This is Pat," she said, pointing to a guy sitting at the table.

"Hell, I thought Pat was a female," I said, stunned by her answer.

"No, he's my boyfriend," she replied.

"How long do you plan on staying in Kabul?" I asked, looking into her red, tear-soaked eyes.

"Well, we are waiting for money from my parents so we can get back to Europe. We are nearly out of money, but we should hear something from my parents any day now. We wrote them from Istanbul over a week ago. I told them to wire the money to the Bank of Kabul. We have about ten dollars left," she said sadly.

"I'm surprised the Afghan consulate gave you a visa. They told me that I needed at least five hundred dollars in spending money to get a visa. Otherwise, they wouldn't have let me in their country for more than three days. They would have given me a transit visa, which allows you just enough time to travel through their country," I told her.

"I guess we were lucky then," she replied.

"Becky, you could do like me and just overstay your visa and pay a fine when you leave the country. That's what I did the first time I came here. But now I plan to stay in Afghanistan for the rest of my life. Why don't you guys come over to the house and see Mark and Carol?"

"Of course we can," she said.

Pat and Becky followed me to my van. They were impressed with my vehicle. Becky knew Mark and Carol, but Pat didn't know any of us.

When we arrived at the apartment, I surprised Mark and Carol when I introduced Pat and Becky. Carol immediately hugged Becky, and Mark and Pat shook hands. Everyone was quite happy. I had hoped that Becky was traveling with another female. I wanted to have an orgy. That was my fantasy. Now I was somewhat saddened that my fantasy wouldn't come true. But we were still happy to see them and quickly showed them my apartment.

"Becky, you are welcome to stay here," I exclaimed.

"Thanks, but we can't right now. We want to stay at the Najib Hotel. Once we receive our money, we want to return to Europe as quickly as possible," she replied.

They had been traveling for the last four months. They decided to come to Afghanistan to see me, but also because it was cheaper to live here. That was the biggest benefit.

"Well Becky, you are always welcome to stay if you change your mind. Mark can sleep in the living room and you and Pat can sleep in the spare bedroom," I told her.

Then Mark, Carol, and I walked into the kitchen. Once there I whispered, "Hey, you guys, don't let Pat and Becky know that we are addicted to morphine and don't let them know anything about my business. I don't want anything to get back to my friends in America. So the less they know the better. We have to be very discreet."

We walked back into the living room and saw Rex Jr. jump onto Pat's shoulders. Then he started picking the fleas or lice out of Pat's hair. He acted as if he had found not just one flea but the whole circus. We all started laughing watching Rex Jr. search through Pat's hair. Pat really didn't know what to do, but he didn't complain as Rex Jr. continued his grooming techniques. My animals reminded them of home.

Pat and Becky really liked our dog and monkey and were very impressed with the stereo and apartment.

"Rob, you are living better here than in America, plus you don't have to worry about getting busted for getting high," exclaimed Becky.

As we relaxed in the living room, I turned them on to some of my opiated hash and hash oil. Within ten minutes, they were as stoned as a marble statue. They both seemed to melt in their chairs. The Christmas tree was all lit up, the music was blasting, and the room put us in the holiday spirit.

"Robert, how long have you lived in this apartment?" asked Becky.

"Carol and I moved here almost a year ago. We were evicted from our last apartment for no reason, so we moved here."

As we were talking, Rex Jr. jumped down from Pat's shoulders onto Foxy's back. Foxy had just gotten up from lying on the floor and started bucking and spinning, trying anything and everything to get him off her back. It was hilarious. Rex Jr. was holding on for all he was worth. He held onto Foxy's hair on the back of her neck and rode her for at least ten seconds. I would have given him eighty points for his ride. We laughed so hard some of us were crying. My stomach ached from laughing so hard. It was great entertainment.

After partying all day long, I drove Pat and Becky back to their hotel. Before they stepped out of my van, we sat and talked.

"Becky, are you sure you don't want to stay at the apartment until your money comes?" I asked.

"No thank you, Robert. We don't want to inconvenience you and Carol. We'll be all right."

"Well, if you change your mind, you know where we live," I reminded her, as they hopped out of my van and walked toward their hotel.

Over the next few days, Carol and I showed Becky and her boyfriend the sights of Kabul. They learned the secrets of the city in a few days that took me years. They were enjoying themselves, and Carol and I were enjoying their company.

Becky and I had been very close friends in America. I was still trying to figure Pat out. I didn't really care for him too much, but I put up with him. He smelled quite bad at times. I never mentioned anything about it. I didn't want to make him upset. I was in the Christmas spirit. There wasn't anything that could make me angry or unhappy. We took them to the king's palace, the Kabul museum, and many other famous sights.

We also showed them all the hippie enclaves. One of the places they liked was Ziggy's, the hotel and restaurant of a thousand and one hippies. They stayed there while Carol and I went Christmas shopping. I spent over five hundred dollars on gifts that day just for Carol. But I only gave Carol twenty dollars to spend on her presents. She didn't need to buy much. I just wanted a pair of long johns. I wanted to give gifts, not receive them.

I also bought Saraj and Mr. Bareck gifts. I bought them each a nice wool scarf and leather gloves and added an American one hundred dollar bill in each glove. I got Mark three bottles of morphine and a few ounces of opiated hash. I also bought gifts for Becky and Pat—nothing special, just some Afghan trinkets and jewelry. There must have been over one hundred gifts under the tree, including the ones my mother had sent. Christmas in Kabul was very special to me.

Two days before Christmas, Becky and Pat stopped by my apartment with some bad news. I invited them into the living room where Becky began explaining their situation.

"Robert, I got bad news today. My parents refuse to send me any money. They said they warned me before I left not to expect any money or help from them. I guess I'm on my own," she said, with tears in her eyes.

"Pat, don't you have anyone who can wire you money?" I asked.

"No, everyone I know is poor."

"Robert, can you take us in?" pleaded Becky.

I didn't really have any other choice. I wasn't the type of person to withdraw my friendship. I was always willing to help anyone in need.

"All right, Becky. You can stay in the small bedroom. Mark uses that room, but I guess he will have to sleep in the living room."

I didn't know what I was going to tell Mark. He would learn soon enough that he would be sleeping in the living room. Pat and Becky were in turmoil. They didn't know what to do. They whined and cried all day long. They had been evicted from their hotel room, and the manager of the hotel kept their luggage until they paid their bill. After listening to them whine, I finally decided to help them with their money problems.

"Becky, do you have anyone in America who would sell hash for you?" I asked, looking into her red, tear-soaked eyes.

"I don't know. Pat, do you know anyone we could ask?" asked Becky. "My brother would probably help out."

"Pat, can't he wire you any money?" I asked.

"No, he's poor," he replied.

"How do you expect to get back to America?" I asked him.

"We never thought that far ahead. We thought we could work or panhandle," said Becky.

I couldn't believe what I was hearing. Becky must have eaten one too many LSD tabs in her earlier days. She just wasn't thinking very rationally. Becky was a very intelligent woman but just seemed to be a real airhead, especially when she was stoned—and she was stoned ninety-nine percent of the time. But I really liked her. She had a great personality.

"Becky, I guess I can help you guys if you want. But you'll need someone in America to help you out, too," I told her.

"Why, what will you do?" she asked.

"I'll send some hash to one or two of your friends so they can sell it and send you the money. That should get you more than enough money to live on and get you back to America. I'll pay for the hash and I'll pay the baksheesh to the customs man to send it. I usually charge half, but for you all I'll ask for is two pairs of Levi pants. I'll loan you one hundred dollars and you can pay that back when you get the money from the hash."

"Thank you, Rob," said Becky, as she hugged me and kissed my cheek, then started to cry.

"Don't cry, Becky. We got to help each other in this crazy world," I told her.

Just then, Mark came into the room and joined in the partying. Becky seemed to settle down and didn't seem as upset and nervous as before. My plan seemed to calm them, especially when I handed Becky two American fifty-dollar bills.

"What's this for?" asked Becky.

"That's to pay your hotel bill so you can retrieve your luggage and clothes and to live on until you get the money from America," I replied.

"What's going on, Rob?" asked Mark.

"Pat and Becky are going to stay with us for a while, so either they will sleep in the living room and you sleep in the bedroom or vice versa," I told him.

"Why don't I go to a hotel for now?" asked Mark.

"Can you afford it?"

"Not really. I was hoping I could get some money from you."

"I suppose I can help you out. We've got enough hash envelopes made up for the next couple of weeks, so here are a few dollars and when you need more, just ask." I handed him fifty dollars.

"Becky, how long do you plan on staying in Kabul?" asked Mark.

"We have a three-month visa, but we are just waiting for money so we can return to America," she replied.

"Mark, they are like a lot of people in this city," I said.

So Becky and Pat would stay in the small bedroom and Mark would stay at Ziggy's hotel. I would see him every day anyway. Two days from now was Christmas, and Becky and Carol started preparing for the dinner. We were like one big family. Kind of like a small hippie commune.

Before Mark left for the hotel, I wanted him to help me make some special hash envelopes for Pat. I didn't want to send my opiated hash—that stuff was too expensive to use. So I had to use nearly a pound of my pollen to make enough hash for his envelopes. I decided to make ten envelopes for them. Then I would give them to either Mr. Bareck or Saraj to send for me. I would even pay for the customs fee. I paid for everything. I even took the risk. They didn't have to do anything but wait for the money.

We partied until Christmas. Mark came over the day before and we showed Pat how to make hash from pollen. Pat and Becky watched with great interest and were quite intrigued with the process I used. Pat tried his hand at it but burned them when he tried to mix the hot pollen in his hands. But it was his own fault; he just wouldn't listen to me. He refused to rub ghee on them. I just laughed it off due to his inexperience.

We made twelve one hundred-gram slabs, then cut them to size to fit the post cards. I made six envelopes, which I'd give to Saraj on Christmas Day to send to America. Then I'd give Mr. Bareck four or five more. That should be more than enough money for Pat and Becky to return to the States.

Once we had completed that task, we continued to party.

While Pat and Becky were in the living room or when they rested in their bedroom, Mark, Carol, and I would go into my bedroom to fix and shoot up our morphine. Then we would go back and party with our guests. While we were gone, Rex Jr. kept them amused doing his tricks. He became a regular comedian. He looked so cute, especially in his tailor-made suits.

Foxy and Rex Jr. played tag every morning in the living room. In fact, they expected to play every morning and would start the game themselves. They were so funny to watch.

So the Christmas cheer was all around, and the Christmas spirit was everywhere. The guys from across the hall even came over for some eggnog and hash. Don came over with a bag of cocaine and passed lines of coke around the room. I was the only person who passed it up.

I had even bought gifts for the guys across the hall. Nothing too extravagant, though. I gave them each pieces of opiated hash and a handmade Afghan soapstone hash pipe. I bought Don a three-gram vial of pure pharmaceutical Peruvian flake cocaine that was made in Germany. I paid five dollars for it. I thought Don would get a kick out of it because he was such a cocaine freak. I handed them their gifts.

"Okay, you guys. Don't open them until Christmas morning," I told them.

They all thanked me for their gifts.

The gifts under the tree filled the living room. My mom had sent me all kinds of presents. It was unbelievable that this was my second consecutive Christmas in Kabul. I felt as though I was in a dream and if I awoke, all of this would be gone.

Christmas morning had finally arrived. Carol and I were the first to awaken. We did our morning wake-up fix and kissed each other a "Merry Christmas." Everyone else was still sleeping so we let them be while Carol started preparing the Christmas breakfast and I took a shower.

This was a wonderful, beautiful morning. I was very excited and couldn't wait to open the presents that my parents had sent to me. I had asked for board games such as Monopoly, Life, Yatzee, and others. The only games we played besides cards were Caroms and Risk, which Don had, so we needed some other type of entertainment.

After I showered, Carol braided my long hair. It was already three inches below my shoulders. Mark walked into my bedroom wanting his morning fix. He hadn't slept too well. His air mattress had deflated in the middle of the night and the fire in the fireplace had gone out. But he wouldn't get out of bed to light the fire or fix his mattress because the room was too cold. So he was a little bummed out in the morning. But he'd get over it. He was going back to his hotel later that day anyway.

Mark sat on the edge of my bed waiting as I filled his spoon with the evil narcotic. I decided to do another fix, too. I was celebrating Christmas. Carol also wanted another fix. So we all fixed together on Christmas morning in 1972 and then lay down to let the narcotic rush through our veins and bodies. Within seconds, it had warmed our insides. We weren't feeling any cold. In fact, we weren't feeling too much of anything. Within a few minutes, we were alive with flowing energy.

Carol went back to making breakfast and soon after Pat and Becky finally awakened.

Pat seemed to be in an ugly mood. Evidently, he nearly froze during the night, so he was pouting, grumpy, and complaining to Becky. I didn't say anything to him; it was Christmas. Nothing was going to make me angry on this holy day. So I wished everyone a "Merry Christmas."

By the time Pat and Becky had gotten dressed, Carol had breakfast made. It was another great meal consisting of pancakes, French toast, scrambled eggs, biscuits, melon, sausage, and fresh-squeezed orange juice. We all stared at Pat and Becky as they ate their food. They ate like starved animals that hadn't eaten in years. They made loud, outrageous burping and grunting noises as they ate. It was like watching pigs eating in a trough. They didn't even stop to breathe. They just kept shoveling the food into their mouths.

I watched in amazement as Pat vacuumed his food into his mouth. Carol, Mark, and I looked at each other as though we couldn't believe what we were seeing and hearing. Pat and Becky were so busy eating they didn't even notice us watching them. They were still eating thirty minutes after the rest of us had left the table. Once they had finished their meal, we all relaxed in the living room. The animals were wrestling, the tree was twinkling, and we were all in the Christmas spirit.

I started passing out the Christmas gifts. I had gifts for everyone but mostly for Carol. Ninety percent of the gifts were for her. I handed Pat, Becky, and Mark their gifts first. Then I gave Carol her gifts. She cleaned up for Christmas and got the motherload. I got her everything—lapis lazuli jewelry, bracelets made from pure gold and silver, handmade wool shawls and silk blouses, leather gloves, wool scarves, and cassette tapes. I also bought her electric kitchen utensils, such as an electric mixer and toaster. By the time Carol had finished opening her gifts, the living room was full of Christmas wrapping paper and cardboard boxes. She gave me a handmade leather cigarette case to carry my hash joints and a nice cigarette lighter. She hadn't gotten me any long johns, promising instead to keep me warm at night.

After opening all the gifts I had received from my parents, we decided to clean up the room to play some of the board games that I had received. We would have many games to play on cold and dreary days. I asked Pat and Becky to set up the Monopoly game as Carol, Mark, and I excused ourselves and headed for my bedroom. We wanted to do our morphine fix before we started playing the game. That would help us get in a relaxed mood.

Ten minutes later, we were playing Monopoly in Kabul, Afghanistan. I thought I was in a colorful, magical dreamland. We played the game for hours. We were still playing after we ate our Christmas dinner. Carol and Becky went all-out and made a feast. They cooked a twenty-five pound turkey with all the trimmings. This dinner was even better than Thanksgiving dinner.

As we were relaxing and digesting our meal, Saraj stopped by. I invited him into the living room and introduced him to everyone. Carol handed him a big piece of apple pie and a cup of hot tea. Saraj looked mesmerized as he stared at all the gifts under the Christmas tree. I could tell he was anxious to get his presents. I let him sweat and wait until he was near the tree looking for his presents, then I gave him his gifts before he had a nervous breakdown.

Last year on Christmas, Ron and I had gotten Saraj drunk and then took him bowling. This year was a little more conservative, a little more laid back. I handed Saraj his two gifts. He seemed a little unhappy with only two little packages, but he quickly opened the first one. It was a long, wool scarf. He really liked it. As he tried it on, throwing it around his neck, he quickly opened the second and last gift. They were black leather gloves with rabbit fur on the insides.

"Saraj, try your leather gloves on," I told him excitedly.

When he tried them on, he noticed something wasn't fitting right. "They don't fit. Something is in the gloves," he said.

He quickly took them off and shook the folded money from the insides. He thought it was just a scrap of paper, until he unfolded them. He had a big smile on his face. He stepped in front of me and hugged me, then kissed me on both cheeks. He was very, very happy and put the two-hundred dollars in his pocket.

"Saraj, that's for you and your family. It's a gift from me and Carol for your friendship and hospitality. Follow me into the bedroom," I said. As he did, I handed him the six envelopes I wanted sent for Pat and Becky and explained the predicament they were in. "Saraj, you are my only hope of helping them. They have nothing. I am doing this because they are my friends. I am using my own money and hash to help them, so you must send them for me. I will give you six for Pat and five for my friends in America."

"Bob, I need five-hundred Afghanis for each envelope," he said.

"That's a total of fifty-five-hundred Afghanis," I replied, reaching into my money belt and pulling out a thick stack of Afghan bills.

I counted out fifty-five-hundred Afghanis, which was about one-hundred American dollars. When I had first started sending the envelopes, it had only cost me less than five American dollars per envelope. Now the dollar had gone down to sixty-Afghanis from a high of over one hundred. As I handed the money to Saraj, there was a knock at my front door. It was Mr. Bareck. He had come over for his Christmas gifts, too.

"Saraj, don't say anything about the envelopes or the money in the gloves," I whispered.

"Okay, Bob," he replied, as he put the envelopes into his inside suit coat pocket.

We walked into the living room and greeted Mr. Bareck.

"Merry Christmas, Mr. Bareck," I said, hugging him and shaking his hand. "Please sit down."

"Your animals play quite well, Bob," remarked Mr. Bareck. "You'll have to bring them over to show my little boy."

"We'd be glad to. Maybe on New Year's Eve. I don't know yet. But one day we'll get together again and very soon," I told him.

"Here is some nice hot tea and homemade hot apple pie, Mr. B," said Carol, handing him the goodies.

"Mr. Bareck, we have some Christmas gifts for you," I said excitedly.

I looked under the tree and found his two gifts. I handed him both, telling him to open the smaller one first. That was the wool scarf. His was the same as Saraj's but a different color. He also tried it on. When he threw it around his neck, he noticed it was American made. Then he opened the second gift, which he really liked.

"Thank you, Bob. I have always wanted this type of leather glove, but I could never afford them," he said, as he shook my hand and hugged me. "And thank you, Carol."

"Mr. B, try the gloves on," I told him.

"That's all right. I know they will fit," he replied.

"I want to see how good they look on you. So please, try them on and make sure they fit," I said enthusiastically.

"All right, I'll try them on," he said, as he slid the right glove onto his hand. "Bob, they don't fit right. I think they're too small."

"Are you sure it's not paper or something inside the gloves?" I asked.

Mr. B put his fingers inside one of the gloves and pulled out a folded bill. It dropped onto his lap and he stared at it for a few seconds and then decided to look at it more closely. He picked it up and started unfolding it, at first slowly and then faster as he noticed it was American money. When he saw that it was an American one hundred-dollar bill, he quickly checked the other glove and pulled out the folded bill. He unfolded it, put the two bills together, and placed them in his front shirt pocket. He tried on the gloves once more. This time they fit perfectly. Mr. B really liked his Christmas gifts. Saraj was getting ready to leave, but Mr. Bareck stopped him.

"Saraj, wait a few minutes and I will leave with you," said Mr. B. So Saraj sat back down and drank his tea.

"Mr. B, please follow me into the bedroom," I said.

I wanted to give him five hash envelopes to send for me. A few minutes later, I handed him the envelopes and the same amount of money per envelope as I had given to Saraj. Then I explained Pat and Becky's predicament to him.

"Mr. B, I will probably have four or five more envelopes for you to send to Pat and Becky's friends," I told him. "I don't know when, but they need money to return to America. They are broke, that's why they're staying with us. I'm helping them as much as I can. I'm using my own money, and I'm not charging them a cent for helping them. I'm doing this out of friendship. And please, don't say a word to Saraj about the envelopes."

"Okay, Bob. I won't say a word to anyone. This will be our own little secret."

"Great. Let's get back to the living room and relax."

When we returned to the living room, Saraj was standing and ready to leave. He had all his gifts and wrapping paper in his hands. We hugged and kissed in the Afghan tradition of saying goodbye, then Saraj and Mr. B walked out of the apartment very happy. They really liked our Christmas holiday.

Everyone was exhausted and too stoned to move and ready for bed.

Mark wanted me to drive him to the hotel so he wouldn't have to walk or stay here. He wanted to sleep in a bed, not on a floor. So I quickly drove him to Ziggy's hotel and returned to my apartment just as fast.

When I returned, all the lights were turned down low and everyone was in bed. Carol was anxiously waiting for me. She had both the monkey and dog tied up so they couldn't interfere in our lovemaking. We didn't even need our electric heater to keep the room warm. We did that with our own body heat. We were like young newlyweds. It was wonderful, and Carol had kept her promise of keeping me warm.

Over the next few days, things were fairly quiet. Carol and I continued our groping and fondling. We were young lovers again.

Mark wasn't around. He had money in his pocket and morphine and hash to stay high on, so he was celebrating at his hotel room. Carol and I didn't mind. And Pat and Becky stayed in their bedroom most of the day, stoned. They came out only to eat, shit, and shower. That was all right by me. When I told them that I had sent six hash envelopes to Pat's brother, they never even thanked me for it. And Becky never helped Carol or me with any of our household chores, and she even stopped helping Carol cook the meals. Carol was getting pissed off.

"Carol, only make food for us. They can fix their own food."

I didn't think too much of Pat. He was a lazy slob and wouldn't do any work or help around the house. He would even complain to me about how cold it was in the morning. But instead of getting up and making a fire in the fireplace, he would wait until I made the fire. Once it was warm throughout the house, then he would get out of bed. He would only complain, but never help. He was staying in my house, eating my food, living for free like a king, and he complained constantly. So I decided to tell him face-to-face.

"Pat, if you are cold, you can get your lazy, fat ass up and make a damn fire in the fireplace. If not, then either shut up or get the hell out. You should be thankful, but instead you're resentful. I don't need that kind of aggravation."

"I'm sorry," whined Pat.

"I'll see if I can buy another electric heater, but you'll have to use it sparingly. It's very expensive to use," I told him with disdain.

Carol and I left to do some of our daily chores and during our shopping spree, we bought another small electric heater, one that Pat and Becky could use for their room.

The next day was New Year's Day and that night was New Year's Eve—Carol's night. I was taking her to the Italian restaurant for dinner. This was her special night on the town. So we each dressed in our finest outfits and went out to "party."

The Italian restaurant was packed, but we were good friends with the owners so we were seated immediately. Before we ordered anything to eat, we ordered some excellent red wine. Carol loved to drink good wine. She didn't drink alcohol that often, but when we went out to eat, we always ordered mixed drinks or wine. This Italian restaurant had some of the finest wines in the world. They had their wine sent directly from Italy for the last twenty-five years.

"Waiter, can we have your best red wine—not too dry and not too sweet. We'll leave it to your discretion," I told him.

The first bottle of red wine was a 1938 vintage.

"Sir, this is the same wine that Hitler and Mussolini drank when they dined at our restaurant in Rome," said the waiter.

"Thank you very much. This is our second consecutive New Year in Kabul," I told him.

"This is our twenty-fifth New Year in Kabul," he retorted.

"Make a toast with us," I asked the owner and waiter as Carol and I held our glasses in the air. "To good friends in a beautiful country," I shouted, as we toasted everyone in the vicinity.

Our restaurant friends went back to helping their customers while we ordered our dinner. Their food was exquisite. We had some mouth-watering lasagna, along with some excellent garlic bread. We ordered another bottle of red wine, and this time they came out with a 1933 vintage that was fruitier and a bit drier than the first bottle. Boy did my head start spinning after finishing the second bottle. When we had completely finished our meal and dessert, I wanted to leave, but Carol wanted to stay and order another bottle of wine and celebrate New Year's.

Everyone was waiting for the clock to strike midnight, which was only twenty minutes away. We ordered our third bottle of wine, which was the same kind as the first bottle but a different vintage. This was from 1934. All the tables had party hats and noisemakers to celebrate with, waiting to bring in the New Year. Then it was three, two, one, and everyone yelled, "Happy New Year!" Many of the patrons were Americans and Italians. While the song "Old Lang Zyne" played, Carol and I kissed and hugged, bringing in the New Year.

We were both very drunk. It was a wonder I was able to drive the van home without getting into an accident. I was completely blind drunk. We both were. We acted like giddy children. This was the start of a new year and the start for bigger and better things. I hoped for that, anyway.

The next morning, we both awoke with nasty hangovers. We didn't do much of anything for the next couple of days. We were still waiting to hear from Pat's brother about the hash envelopes, and I was anxious to hear from Jim. I hadn't received a letter from Jim yet, and I was beginning to worry.

Plus, I was getting ready to drive up north. Before I did, though, I wanted to visit the nightclub to see if I could learn any new information concerning the Russian embassy workers.

I also wanted to wish my Afghan friends a Happy New Year. Their New Year and Christmas were about to start. Within a few weeks, another Muslim holiday would begin, so there were a few things I needed and wanted to do before I left for Mazare Sarif. In fact, I had to meet my two friends from the Brotherhood in ten more days to pick up the money. Then I would know for sure if I was really going up north or not.

CHAPTER18

A TRIP FROM HELL

Over the next week or so, we hung around the house and played the board games that my parents had sent me for Christmas. There were still one or two games that we hadn't played yet. Nevertheless, we would get to them soon.

We visited the nightclub a few days before I left for Mazare Sarif. We dressed up in our best clothes, said goodnight to Pat and Becky, and then headed for the nightclub.

A few minutes later, we were there. One of our Afghan friends greeted us. We walked past the doorman without a word said and up the stairs to our regular table. As usual, most of the Afghan aristocracy was there. We said hello and Happy New Year to the king's son and all of his relatives and then sat down.

Carol and I ordered mixed drinks. This was the only Afghan nightspot that served liquor. Usually it was only allowed to the tourists, not Afghans. And tonight they had a live band that played Afghan-type rock music. It didn't sound too bad and even had a decent rhythm for dancing.

We talked about the latest fads in America.

"Bob, are American streets really lined in gold?" asked Mohammed, the king's third son.

Even though they were educated at European or English Colleges, they thought every American was a millionaire. They saw in the magazines that Americans lived in big houses, drove two or more cars, and had big swimming pools in their backyards. But I could tell they were just pulling my leg, joking around. For a change on this night, they were more concerned with my views on America than on Afghan politics. They did talk, once again however, about the king's dwindling eyesight. He would have to leave the country very soon to have eye surgery or he could go blind permanently. They seemed genuinely concerned for their leader. And Mohammed again was

406

worried that his uncle would take control of the Afghan government once his father was out of the country.

They also talked about the American government offering their government a twelve-million dollar loan, plus a bowl of rice and a loaf of bread for each person in Afghanistan. But the Russians countered the American offer and proposed a deal of twelve million in aid, plus two bowls of rice and two loaves of bread for each Afghan man, woman, and child.

But the most important difference in their proposals was that the Americans wanted the Afghan government to spend the twelve million dollars only with American approval and oversight. The Russians would let the Afghan government spend the twelve-million any way they wanted. Now the government was leaning toward Russia to help their country. If so, the Russians would have more control over the Afghan government than the Americans would.

There were no heated arguments on this particular night. The night went smoothly. We partied and danced all night. I learned many new things and would have some new political information for Mr. Beardon. But it would have to be after I returned from Mazare Sarif. Now it was time to go home and try to sleep.

The day before I was to leave for Mazare Sarif, I had to do my daily chores. First, I had to visit the pharmacy to purchase a few more bottles of morphine. Each bottle was costing more and more. Not only was the dollar being devalued practically every day, but also the Devil decided to raise his prices. Now he was charging an extra two dollars per bottle, which meant I was now paying nine dollars a bottle, but this was still very cheap compared to America's prices.

Next, I visited the bank, but there wasn't any money to pick up so I continued on my way to the post office. Once there, I went directly to the incoming mail tray and searched through hundreds of letters until I found two important ones. The first was addressed to Pat from his brother, and the second was addressed to me from Jim. I was anxious to hear what both had to say, so I left the post office and returned to my apartment. As soon as I entered, I gave Pat his letter and then read Jim's. It was both good and bad news. Jim would return to Kabul within a few months, as soon as his classes were finished. His college went by quarters, not semesters, so it wouldn't be that long of a wait. Also, he didn't get quite a hundred grams of oil. He lost some that stuck to the plastic bag. But it was close enough.

After I read Jim's letter, we listened to Pat as he read his brother's letter out loud. Pat's brother had received all six hash envelopes. He sold all the hash, which totaled five-hundred and eighty-six grams, at ten dollars per gram. He got nearly six-thousand dollars for it. Pat was ecstatic with joy as he read the letter. We were all ecstatic with joy listening to him read it. But our joy would soon turn to confusion when he read that his brother had decided to keep the money for himself so he could do his own smuggling trip to Bogota, Columbia, to score a few kilos of cocaine and smuggle it back to America. Then, after he had returned to America and sold the cocaine, he would send Pat the money. I couldn't believe what I was hearing.

"Pat, does your brother have any friends or connections in Columbia?" I asked him.

"No. He doesn't know anyone there. He's going on his own. He thinks it will be easy. He thinks he has it all figured out."

"Pat, if your brother doesn't know anyone over there, all they will do is take him out in the jungle and kill him, then take all his money. Those people in those countries are cutthroat murderers. They would think nothing about slitting your throat and stealing your money. Your brother is either crazy or stupid if he thinks he's gonna scam those people. They'll end up scamming him," I told him.

"He'll be all right," opined Pat.

"Pat, all they have to do is tell your brother to follow them, and they'll drive him into the jungle. No one will know where he is 'cause he wouldn't tell anyone that he was going out to buy cocaine. They'll take him out into the sticks, cut his head off with a machete, take his money, and nobody will ever hear from him again," I retorted, rather angry with his brother's antics.

"I hope not," he replied sadly.

"Believe me. Mark my words. If your brother goes through with his crazy idea, he's a dead man."

"Well, I can't do anything about it," said Pat. "I'm here and he has the money. What am I going to do now if he doesn't send us any money?"

"Do you have anyone else you can send hash to?" I asked him.

"Yeah, I wrote to a younger brother I know who would send me the money when he received and sold the hash."

"Well, I guess I don't have any other choice but to send a couple more envelopes for you. I will send two more hash envelopes for you, but when you get back to America, I want you to send me the money to pay me back for all the money I loaned you and Becky," I told him, without losing my cool.

"Okay. That is, if we ever get back to America," he said with sadness.

"Pat, I'll take the envelopes to the post office tomorrow. So write a letter to the person I'm sending them to so they'll be ready to check their mail. That ought to keep you going until and if your brother gets back from his trip and sends you the money to get back home," I said, while controlling my anger.

"I hope so. He's going to write me when he arrives in Columbia, so I'll know exactly when he'll get back to America and if all went well," he said.

"Why did your brother screw you like that?" I asked him.

"My brother has always had a fantasy that if he ever got the money he was going to do that trip. He thought about that for years."

"Even if it means throwing his brother into the street, starving and broke?" I asked.

"Yeah, that's how he is. My own brother is a snake."

"Then why did we send the envelopes to him, if you thought he was gonna screw you?"

Pat had no answer and shrugged his shoulders while looking at the floor.

Well, I sent more hash envelopes for Pat and Becky and waited for an answer. Within a few days, Pat received another letter from his brother. This time it was from Bogota, Columbia. I guess he had made it so far without any major problems. He also wrote that he had met some people who were going to help him in his endeavors and that he had sent two pairs of Levi's to me, but he couldn't find my size.

"Boy, Pat, I hope your brother knows what he's doing. You can't trust anyone over there unless they're your relatives or friends," I said matter-of-factly.

"Well, he'll write me again in a couple of days, after he scores."

Well my premonition came true 'cause his brother's passport and decomposed body was found forty miles away in the jungle nearly a week after reaching Bogotá. We didn't talk about his brother very much after that.

Ten minutes after hearing the demise of Pat's brother, I drove to Ziggy's to meet my two friends from the Brotherhood. I wanted to see if they still wanted to go through with their deal. I went to Ziggy's the day and time I had told them to meet me. Sure enough, they were sitting at their regular table waiting for me.

"Well, John, are we still on for the wedding?" I joked.

"I sure hope so. We've got the money you asked for, so let's go to our house and talk it over," he replied.

"Sure. I'll follow you in my van."

I followed them to the other side of town. It was the same house to which Morgan had invited me over two years before. I was still a little paranoid, but I didn't have anything on me to get busted for, so I followed them into the house.

"Come on in," said Stoneman.

"You guys have lived here a long time, haven't you?" I asked them.

"Yeah, off and on for the last four years," replied John.

"Where is Claude, the big-time dealer?" I asked.

"He's back in Europe," retorted Stoneman.

"Didn't he get you all the pollen before? I thought he bought tons at a time?" I asked them, wondering why they didn't just buy the stuff from their guy.

"He still does," replied John. "But he went back to Europe because he got a bad case of dysentery. He went back to one of his mansions in France."

"Well, let's get down to business. Did you get the money?" I asked.

"Yeah, here it is," said Stoneman, throwing a large paper sack full of stacks of American bills on the table in front of me.

"You don't mind if I count it, do you?" I asked, as I reached into the sack and pulled out a few stacks.

"Go ahead and count it. It's all there," said John.

The money was in stacks of one-thousand dollars. There were ten stacks. After I had counted the stacks of money, I placed it back into the paper sack and stuffed it into my shoulder bag.

"I will leave tomorrow morning, so I should be back within three days, two if I hurry. If I'm not back here by then, come to my apartment. But I shouldn't have any problems. I returned safely the last time I went for your friends."

"Good luck," said John, walking me out to the van.

"I'll see you in a couple of days," I replied and then drove away.

Now I was heading for Tiar's house and then back to my apartment. I would have to pick up Tiar in the morning, so I needed to tell him ahead of time. I walked very quickly through the sewage-infested alley to his abode. He answered the door, so I didn't go into his walled fortress.

"Hello, Bob," said Tiar.

"Tiar, we are leaving in the morning for Mazare Sarif, so be ready. I'll be here around ten or eleven in the morning. I'll see you then," I told him.

"I will be ready."

I turned and walked back to the van through that putrid, foul-smelling alley. Boy, that was an eye opener.

I didn't sleep too well that night. My anxiety attacks had me tossing and turning all night long thinking about the trip that lay ahead.

I had Carol pack Tiar and me some sandwiches and other munchies to eat on the way. I also had my morphine kit with me. I could never leave without it.

I was up before dawn, but I didn't leave until ten. I waited until Carol awoke so I could give her a fix. I also gave her enough morphine tablets so she wouldn't have to go without while I was away. She would have to fix by herself for the next two or three days. She'd handled it all right the last time I went off on a long excursion trip.

I ate a small breakfast of pancakes and orange juice and kissed Carol goodbye. Pat and Becky were still sleeping, so I didn't see them before I left. I was too busy getting the van clean and giving it an overall check up. I added wooden blocks under each rear end spring to take the added weight.

I didn't take any luggage. I would need all the room for the pollen. I would be buying five or ten or possibly twenty bags of pollen, depending on the weight of each bag. The last time, the pollen was in one hundred-kilo bags.

I only brought a small picnic basket of food and drink. Just enough stuff to feed two people for a couple of days. Other than that, the van was completely clean and empty. Tiar was waiting for me in front of the teashop. I parked my van there when I visited him. He also carried a small paper sack of kabob sandwiches and a thermos of hot tea. We put his things into the picnic basket.

A few minutes later, we were heading for Mazare Sarif. I just hoped we could make it without any blizzards, accidents, or mishaps. Traffic was very light. Other than a few buses and small commercial trucks, I saw more carts and camels on the road than automobiles. We went through the first two checkpoints without any problems, but after driving about four hours, the third checkpoint was backed up with traffic for almost half a mile.

After waiting for over two hours, we were finally able to move. There had been a bad accident between a bus carrying small children and a small Afghan truck. The bus had tipped over onto its side, and children were lying all around it.

"Tiar, should we stop to help?" I asked as the wind began to blow, throwing up sand, making it hard to see.

"No, it's better not to get involved."

So I continued to follow the other cars as the policeman and soldiers directed us to another road. I didn't see any detour signs, so I just followed the car in front of me. I thought the detour would end very shortly. The car in front of me turned toward a small village, but I continued to follow the main road.

"Tiar, should I stay on this road? When will this detour end?" I asked.

"Just stay on this road for now. The detour should end soon."

I continued to drive, looking for another main road or some road signs, something that would help me find the main road. After almost two hours of driving, I finally came to a cement-lined road. I was going to ask Tiar if I should take it, but he was taking a nap so I didn't wake him. I decided to take it. I figured I could always turn back if I didn't like it. I thought the road was going north, and that's all I cared about. At least I started out going north, but then the road weaved and zigzagged. There were no villages or checkpoints around. Then suddenly rain clouds appeared, the winds continued to blow and it was getting dark. I couldn't follow the sun, anymore. Now I wasn't sure which way I was traveling. Finally, Tiar woke up.

"Tiar, I think we're lost. I turned on the only good road that I saw, and I didn't see anyone to ask directions. It's been desolate since that last village four hours back."

"Well just stay on this road. We should come to a village pretty soon. Then we can ask them for directions if we need to," he said, with a lack of confidence.

"I hope we see someone pretty soon. It'll be my luck that we get caught in a blizzard and get stuck out here in nowhere land. Not only that, but it's getting awful cloudy and cold, and I still don't know which way we are heading. I think we are heading north, but I can't tell, can you?"

"Well, we'll be able to get our bearings tomorrow."

"But I was planning on arriving in Mazare Sarif by midnight tonight."

"Bob, pull over to the side of the road. I have to relieve myself."

"That's a good idea. I have to drain my pipe, too."

I quickly pulled the van over to the side of the road. We hadn't passed another car or seen one in many hours. I was actually starting to worry. I didn't have any idea where in the hell we were, and neither did Tiar.

I continued to drive and follow this long, lonesome, and winding road until we came upon a fallen tree completely blocking the road. I almost ran right into it and had to slam on my brakes with all my might just to stop in the nick of time without demolishing my van. I opened my door and got out to check out the debris lying across the road.

"Tiar, help me move this stuff off the road," I yelled.

But he still seemed to be half-asleep, moving very slowly. And just as he stepped out of the van and shut the door, we were suddenly surrounded by a band of bandits who had very mean-looking rifles and machine guns. They looked just like the bandits you'd see in the movies, except they wore turbans. They pointed their rifles toward our heads and bodies. I just stood frozen in my boots. Tiar tried to ask them what the hell was going on, but before he could utter more than three words, one of the bandits hit him in the face with the butt of his rifle. He knocked Tiar against the van, and as Tiar was falling to the ground, the same man kicked him in the side of the ribs.

"Stand up on your feet!" yelled the bandit.

Tiar staggered to his feet while his face began to swell. I just watched in amazement and utter disbelief. I began saying a silent prayer, waiting my turn to be beaten. Then suddenly, their leader came over and gave them instructions.

One of the bandits poked me in the chest with his rifle, directing me into the van. The side door slid open and Tiar and I were thrown into the back. I thought for sure they were going to kill us, take our money and the van, so I began to pray. I thought this was the end. Two of the bandits sat in back with us, and another drove.

Just as we started to leave, the other bandits jumped onto the van, mostly on the back bumper, and a couple held onto the sides. Then the two men guarding us blindfolded us.

After what seemed like hours, we finally reached their destination. They untied our blindfolds and we were taken by gunpoint to their village. They marched us into a small, dark, desolate, dirty mud hut. They wanted to tie us up but didn't have enough rope, so they just guarded us. We tried to ask the guards questions, but they refused to cooperate with us. One of the guards slapped Tiar across the face.

"Shut up!" yelled the guard, as Tiar spat the blood from his mouth to the dirt floor.

His face ballooned to twice its size. I was sure that they would find my money belt and then kill us. Many of the villagers were in another room talking amongst themselves. Tiar could understand a little of what they were talking about. He seemed to think we were in Nuristan. That was a lawless province. No wonder we hadn't seen any automobiles.

We both prayed, hoping to get out of there alive. We were in that room for what seemed to be an eternity. Finally, hours after we had arrived, one of the elders of the village came into the room. He asked Tiar a number of questions. Tiar answered without any hesitation.

While the elder was asking Tiar questions, another bandit entered the room carrying my picnic basket of food and my shoulder bag. He dumped the contents of my shoulder bag amongst the food and onto the floor. My morphine kit was still well hidden. It was inside a small pocket inside the shoulder bag.

The important thing was to keep them away from searching me. If they did, they would find the money. Once they found that, they would have no alternative but to kill us. It seemed the elder was telling Tiar just that.

"All I can find is food," said the elder.

One of his men began looking through the contents on the floor with his feet. Once he decided there was nothing of value, he picked up the mess and put it back in the picnic basket. Then he put it in a far corner of the room.

"Where were you going?" asked the elder.

"We were on our way to Mazare Sarif, but there was a detour and we ended up at the road block. We just got lost...honest," said Tiar meekly.

The more Tiar talked, the more the elder seemed to listen. After a few more minutes of questioning, he left the room. He was gone for quite a long time. We could hear him arguing with a number of his followers. But Tiar couldn't quite make out what they were arguing about. One thing was for sure, though, we waited in fear. I figured we were dead men. I didn't know what to do. And Tiar was looking bad. His face was very swollen and bruised. It was also getting very cold in the room.

"Tiar, ask them for some blankets. I'm freezing," I whispered. But Tiar refused my request. I guess he didn't want any more trouble, so I shouted to the people in the other room. "Please, can you give us some blankets? It's getting very cold in here."

To our surprise, one of the guards came in carrying a small charcoal stove full of red-hot coals and placed it in the middle of the small room. Within five minutes, the room was quite warm. That seemed to make things bearable anyway. But then our attention turned to the talk in the adjacent room. Many of the villagers were still arguing amongst themselves. One faction of the village wanted us dead. Now it was up to the rest of them to decide. Would they also vote for death? That's what they were arguing about.

As they continued to argue, one of the guards brought us a small pot of tea, two small teacups, and two small packets of opium. He placed the teapot on the floor in front of us, and then gave each of us a cup. But he gave Tiar both packets of opium. He must have brought the opium to help Tiar's pain—except Tiar refused to accept anything from him. But I hadn't had a fix all day long. Now it was past midnight, and I was feeling pretty sick. So I decided to ask Tiar for the opium.

"Tiar, if you're not going to use it, could I have the opium? But if you need it, keep it. If you don't want it, let me have it. I'm not feeling too good right now."

Tiar reached over and handed me the two small packets. The guard was watching us constantly, but he didn't try to stop us from communicating. I quickly opened the packets and tossed the small chunks of opium into my mouth. It tasted very, very bitter and I gagged on it a few times and then nearly threw up. Finally, with the help of the tea, I was able to get the opium down my throat.

I poured Tiar some tea also. But he still refused to drink it. I wondered why our kidnappers even bothered to offer us anything. Was this supposed to be our last meal, or were they being friendly? I was just too sick and tired to dwell on it. I just continued to pray, hoping to come out of here alive.

Within a few hours, it would be daylight. We hadn't slept all night. Some of the villagers were still arguing with the elder. Most of them had gone home to sleep and would have to wait until morning to decide our fate. They still hadn't found my money. As their argument proceeded, it seemed to get out of hand. In fact, they were shouting at one another.

Suddenly the elder stormed into the room shouting at Tiar. "You must give us money if you want to leave our village unharmed. You were judged to be trespassers."

I guess that's what the villagers were debating and arguing about all night. They were holding court.

All we had done was take a detour. Now we were fighting for our lives.

As the elder kept talking, more and more people kept coming into the room to see what was going on. One of the elder's sons was standing behind his father, eating some Afghan kabob, when all of a sudden, as his father was swinging his arms yelling at Tiar, he accidentally hit his son in the face, which made the son swallow his kabob. But it didn't go down correctly. Within a few seconds the boy was choking, gagging, and trying to cough. But nothing was happening. Everyone was in shock.

Nobody moved to help the boy. I stood up and tried to help but was knocked down by one of the guards. Then the elder tried to pound on his son's back to knock the food out of his throat but that didn't work. Then they held him high in the air by his ankles and started shaking and swinging him, while he was turned upside down. That still didn't help. Suddenly the boy began turning blue.

Now everyone was starting to panic. They stood the boy on his feet and tried again to knock the food out of him by pounding on the middle of his back with their fists. Nothing seemed to work. So I jumped up again and tried to help the boy. One of the guards tried to stop me, but I turned slightly when he reached out to grab me and I slipped past him. I quickly grabbed the boy in a reverse bear hug and clenched my hands together into his midsection. I shook him up and down once or twice, lifting him off the floor, but then the guard tried to tear me away from him. Just as I was about to lose hold, the guard pulled on me in such a way that my fists dug deep into the boy's sternum. Just then, the meat popped out of his throat onto the floor. The boy suddenly inhaled very loud and deeply. He was all right but still in shock and quite shaken. Seconds later, the guard threw me down to the dirt floor while the boy was quickly taken out of the room with the rest of the crowd.

Tiar and I were left guarded by one Afghan man. We waited nervously, wondering what was going to happen next. We were both frightened. We had been held hostage for over ten hours and were very sick, depressed, and tired. We just wanted to get out of that room and village. It must have been morning. I could here the birds singing and chirping. We still hadn't slept at all. And then, the elder came into the room.

"Please, come with me. Quickly," he said, pushing us towards the door.

Tiar and I looked at each other, wondering if this was the last time we would see each other alive. As we were being led out of the room, I grabbed my shoulder bag from the top of the picnic basket without anyone noticing and then threw it over my shoulder. We were being led out of the house to the back of the yard by gunpoint. I thought they were going to shoot us, so I started pleading with them.

"Please, I'll give you anything," I begged. "You can have my van. What do you want?"

"Be quiet," barked the elder. Then he began speaking to Tiar, but I couldn't understand what he was saying.

As we turned and walked behind a building, I noticed that the van was parked nearby. They started pushing us toward it. I thought they were going to line us up next it and then shoot and kill us. But to my surprise, instead of killing us, they opened the van's doors and pushed us into it. I was pushed into the driver's side.

"Hurry up. You must leave and never return. Please, you must hurry," pleaded the elder.

Just as I started the van and began to drive away, I looked into my rearview mirror and saw that many of the villagers were running toward us. Many of them stopped where the elder was standing and began firing their weapons at us. I could hear the bullets whiz by the van.

I floored the accelerator to the limit. I wanted to get out of there as fast as possible. I was afraid they would follow us in their vehicles. We weren't even sure if we were driving in the right direction.

We presumed we were heading west and in the right direction. All I knew for sure was that we were going in the opposite direction from the village. I didn't want to see those bandits ever again. I wanted to get far enough away and out of danger and then I could pull over to the side of the road and do my morphine. I wasn't even thinking of buying any hash pollen. I just wanted to return home to my warm apartment as quickly as possible.

After an hour or so, I slowed down. We were approaching the obstacle that had caused all our problems. I could see that the tree was still lying across the road, and two Afghan bandits were resting nearby, waiting to strike again. So instead of stopping, I picked up speed and drove the van around the tree. There was just enough room to pass on the side of the road where the bandits were sitting. Luckily, they didn't notice us until we were directly upon them. They scattered and jumped to get out of the way of my van. I actually had to swerve to miss them.

Within seconds, we were back on the road, driving west toward the main highway. By the time the bandits fired at us with their automatic weapons we were out of range. I just hoped they weren't following us.

After driving for more than two hours, we were certain that we were in the clear. We were relieved and could finally relax. Tiar was sleeping, but his head had swollen to twice its normal size. I didn't know how he could sleep with his face so badly bruised and swollen.

I continued to drive in the opposite direction of that evil village. After nearly four hours of driving, I saw the road on to which we should have turned. It was just a dirt road, but as you turned onto it, you could see the main highway heading north. So here, it was just one hundred feet off the road we were driving on. Just before I reached the main highway, I awakened Tiar.

"Tiar, do you want to drive all the way up to Mazare Sarif or do you know someone we can buy the pollen from that's closer to Kabul? I don't want to drive all that way after what happened."

"I don't really want to drive that far, either," he whispered, barely able to speak.

"Tiar, I would rather just go home empty-handed. I'm too tired and sick to drive that far. You don't look so good either."

"I think I know another place we can go. Drive toward Kabul and we'll go to Paghman. I know someone we might be able to buy that much pollen from, but we won't get as good a price, if we can get it at all."

Tiar spoke as though his jaw had been broken from that rifle blow. I turned and headed the van for Kabul. Within a few more hours, we would be near the city of Paghman. I wanted to stop and do my morphine, but we had no water. However, I still had my morphine. The villagers never bothered to look into my shoulder bag. But I would have to wait until I reached my apartment before I could make my fix. The little bit of opium I had eaten helped to relieve my withdrawal symptoms, but I was still very weak and nauseous. I tried not to think about it.

Finally, after a few more hours, we reached a fork in the road. Now I saw road signs. One was pointing to the left, toward Paghman, the other to the right, toward Kabul. Tiar pointed to turn left, so we headed toward Paghman. It was still daylight, so we had plenty of time before nightfall. Tiar and I hadn't said a word about our little adventure. We just wanted to forget about it, to pretend like it never happened. Except every time I looked at Tiar's face, it reminded me about it.

"Tiar, how much is it going to cost for the pollen?"

Tiar just shrugged his shoulders and shook his head, not saying anything. When we finally arrived in the small and old city of Paghman, Tiar directed me to a small house. We reached the place within a few minutes.

When I stopped, Tiar slid out of the van and walked to the house. Before he could knock on the door, two men came out and approached the vehicle. They were both armed to the teeth, each carrying an automatic carbine rifle, which they pointed directly at us. The taller one questioned us.

"What do you want? Why do you come here?" said the burly Afghan.

Tiar tried to speak but was having a very hard time with his swollen face.

These men were Tiar's friends, but with his injuries, they couldn't recognize him. So I spoke up instead. "This is Tiar. We came to buy some pollen if the price is right."

"What happened to Tiar?" asked the Afghan, walking up to the van.

"That's a long story, and we would rather not talk about it," I told him.

"So you want to buy some pollen? How much do you need?" asked the Afghan.

"That's what we're here for. I need one-thousand kilos. Do you have that much?"

"Yes, we can handle that and more. Follow us," said the Afghan.

"Come on, Tiar. We'll be back in Kabul very soon if nothing else happens," I said, tired as hell.

We walked into a small, one-room mud hut, similar to the one in which we had been held hostage, but this hut was full of hash pollen. In one corner of the room were all the stalks from the hash plants. Usually they mashed the whole plant soon after it's picked. But these plants had been dried and then the pollen beaten from them. They did it like that in Lebanon. This way, you get a much better grade of pollen, and most of this room was knee deep in it. It must have contained five tons. Usually the pollen was bagged, but this hadn't been bagged yet.

"How much do you want per kilo, for a thousand kilos?" I asked.

The two Afghan men talked amongst themselves and came up with a price of eight dollars per kilo. I tried to talk them down, but they wouldn't budge, and I was in no mood to argue. I didn't even bother to talk it over with Tiar. I just wanted to complete the deal and get back to Kabul as fast as possible. I wanted to be home in my nice warm bed and high on morphine.

"Well, let's start weighing it up so we can bag it and load it into the van. Do you have any bags or anything that I can put the pollen in?"

"No, I'm sorry we don't have any bags. Maybe we can find a big box," said the Afghan, leaving the room to hunt for something into which he could put a thousand kilos of pollen.

The other Afghan held up a balance scale and began weighing one kilo at a time. He laid a small four-foot-square piece of plastic on the dirt floor and after weighing each kilo, he dumped it onto the plastic. After he had about ten kilos weighed, his other friend came back into the room empty handed. He couldn't find anything to put the pollen into, so I decided to pile it into the van. Once I slid the side door open, we picked up the piece of plastic from the dirt floor and placed it on the floor of the van. Then we began to dump the weighed pollen onto it. And we also placed seven six-inch-wide boards along the length of the open door so the pollen wouldn't fall out when the side door was opened.

Within a short time, the van began filling up. But weighing one kilo at a time was taking too much time, so the other man decided to weigh the pollen with another scale. He used a bigger rock for his weight, which was a five-kilo weight instead of the one-kilo stone. With both of them weighing out the pollen, it only took a few hours to weigh out one thousand kilos. Each time they weighed out their amount, I made a mark on the dirt floor to keep track of the number of kilos weighed. This way we couldn't make a mistake on the weight. Before we were even half-finished, I had to shut the side door to keep the pollen from spilling over and onto the ground. Now we had to put the pollen in through the back door of the van.

By the time we were finished loading it in, it was over four feet deep. The pollen came up to the lid that covered the engine. There was practically no way to hide it. If we got stopped now, we would both be shot and executed or put into jail for the rest of our lives. All I could do was cover the one thousand kilos of pollen with a small piece of blue plastic. It didn't really hide it, but it kept it from blowing away and filling up the van with pollen dust.

I knew one thing for sure: I was glad that I had placed two wooden blocks, one on each side of the rear axle, so the van wouldn't sag. There was so much weight I just prayed that the van would pull it.

When we finished loading the van, I counted out eight-thousand American dollars and handed it to one of the Afghan men. They thanked us and wished us luck. Then Tiar and I headed back to Kabul with a vanload of hash pollen. The van reeked of a skunky smell, as if a thousand skunks had sprayed their scent at the same time. We had to keep the windows rolled up and closed or the pollen would fly all over.

We were within a few miles of the city when I noticed I was running very low on fuel. In fact, the gas tank was below empty. I didn't want to say anything to Tiar so he wouldn't get upset. I knew he wasn't feeling very well and needed medical attention. But the way our luck had been going, I figured we would run out of petrol before arriving to our homes. I was waiting for the van to spurt and sputter to a stop, but to my surprise, it continued to run.

We passed Cargar Dam, the police station, and the post office and finally arrived at Tiar's street. I parked in front of the teashop and counted out one thousand dollars, then handed the money to Tiar.

"Tiar, I'm sorry we didn't make as much money as I thought we would have. But I didn't know we would run into all this trouble. You take care of yourself, and I'll see you in a couple of days to see how you're doing," I said, placing my hand over his.

Tiar slowly left the van. When he shut the door, I made a U-turn and headed for the Brotherhood's house. I turned into their driveway and thanked God for returning me safely. I walked up to the house and knocked on the door. John greeted me.

"Come on in, Rob," he said. "How was your trip?"

"John, I'm too tired to talk about that tonight. I just want to unload my van so I can get back home and get a good night's sleep. You guys are gonna have to help me unload it. I'm too weak and sick to do it myself. You are going to need some bags or boxes to put the pollen into."

"What do you mean? Isn't it bagged already?" asked John.

"No. You'll see what I mean when you check the van," I replied, tired as hell.

We walked out to the van and tried to figure out what to do with the pollen. John went back into the house and came back out with two large garbage cans. He hopped into the van with one of the cans and started filling it with pollen. When the can was filled, Stoneman and I carried it into the house. After the second can was filled, we could open the side door and finish the clean up from outside the van.

By the time we had finished cleaning all the pollen out of the van, they had seven garbage cans full of hash pollen. They weren't very happy having to unload the van, but it couldn't be helped. I actually left angry. Anything I did for these guys was never good enough.

With all the trouble Tiar and I had just getting the pollen, they could have been a little more friendly and cordial. But this was business. I left there just as angry as I had the last time I had dealt with the people who lived at this house.

Just as I was a few hundred feet from my apartment, the van suddenly lost power and shut down. I was finally out of petrol. I coasted to the front of the apartment complex and parked the van.

When I reached my apartment, all was quiet and everyone was in bed, or so I thought. Carol greeted me when I walked in. She was surprised I had returned so soon. She hadn't expected my return for another two or three days.

"How come you're back so soon?" she asked.

"We ran into a few roadblocks and had to change our plans."

"Did something go wrong?"

"Well, let's just say it didn't go as planned and leave it at that, all right?"

I then walked into my bedroom to fix my morphine. I couldn't fix fast enough. Finally, the hot and tingling feeling rushed through my body. As I lay back to enjoy this incredible feeling, my troubles and pain seemed to disappear. I could handle reality once again. Carol waited patiently for her turn. Usually I fixed her first, but not this time. A few minutes later, I injected Carol with the drug. She enjoyed the rush as much as I did. Then Carol and I cuddled in bed together. I finally realized how close I had come to dying and slowly drifted off to sleep.

The next morning, Carol and I awoke to a loud argument between

Pat and Becky. Carol and I listened to them argue as we fixed our morning "do." Carol explained to me that Pat and Becky were completely broke and had no money whatsoever.

"Carol, don't tell me anything negative today. Only tell me positive things."

But she just sat silent. I didn't know whether she couldn't think of any positive things to say or whether she was just too stoned from her morning fix.

After a few days, I began to notice a change in Carol's personality. She seemed distant and in a world of her own. I just figured it was that time of month. I didn't say anything about it to her. I thought she would snap out of it, but that never happened. However, that was the least of my problems.

The Afghans were now celebrating another holiday. I wasn't sure which one. Ramadan had been over for months.

Pat and Becky still hadn't received any money or word from their friends in America. They were beginning to become one big headache. They finally had to ask me to loan them more money.

"Robert, can we borrow some money?" asked Becky.

"How much do you need?"

"Can we borrow a hundred dollars?" she asked.

"I guess I don't have any choice, do I?"

I reached into my money belt and pulled out a handful of American bills, then counted out five twenty-dollar bills.

"I hope you guys get the money that Pat's younger brother owes you. I'm still waiting for the Levi jeans that are owed to me. Pat, have you gotten a letter from your younger brother recently?"

"No, I haven't," he replied.

Two days later, I received the two pairs of Levi jeans from Pat's brother. They were exactly what I wanted, except they were four sizes too big. I had to have my tailor take them in so they would fit properly. Pat, though, still hadn't heard from him or received any money.

The following day, as Carol and I returned from shopping, we noticed the apartment was completely quiet and all the animals were tied up in our bedroom. Pat and Becky were nowhere around. We wondered what the heck was going on. Soon Carol and I realized that Pat and Becky weren't coming back. They didn't even have the decency to leave us a note or to even tell us to our faces that they were leaving. We noticed they had taken all of their belongings and luggage, just like Ron and Cindy had done. We thought maybe they had gone back to Europe or America. Within a few days, we had our answer, but we really didn't care. We were happy they were out of our hair.

About a week after Pat and Becky had snuck out of our apartment, without saying a word like, "Thanks for all the help and hospitality," Carol and I saw them coming out of a grocery store. Carol quickly went over to confront them.

"Becky, why didn't you guys tell us you were leaving? That was really a crude thing to do after all the help we gave you and Pat. We gave you a place to stay for two months. On top of that, Robert gave you hundreds of dollars to save your asses. He should have let you sleep in the street," said Carol angrily. You could almost see the steam coming out of her angry body.

"We just needed our space. We didn't want to get into a hassle or argument, so we decided it would be best just to leave and move into a hotel room," replied Becky.

Before leaving, they told us the name of the hotel at which they were staying. I also learned that they were using my connections to send hash to America.

One day while shopping, I saw Mr. Bareck leave their hotel room, so I confronted him about it. He admitted to me that they were paying him to send hash to America. I was very angry, more so at Pat and Becky than Mr. B. After all the help and money I had given them, they were treating me like some kind of chump.

"Mr. Bareck, don't send hash for them. You can take their money, but don't send the hash," I told him, with anger in my voice.

I just wasn't sure he would do as I had asked. With that, we went our separate ways.

While walking back to the van, I noticed that my Afghan friend and his monkey were back in town. I noticed that the big female monkey was carrying another baby. This one was a female. Within twenty minutes, I was driving home with a two-month-old female Rhesus monkey. I called her Chakila, which meant "beautiful girl" in Pashtu. Now I had a baby male and female Rhesus monkey. Carol, though, wasn't too enthusiastic about having another monkey in the house.

CHAPTER 19
KABUL: BUSTED AT THE AIRPORT

March was soon approaching. I had gotten a letter from Jim. He was getting ready to visit me again. This should be the deal that makes us rich if he brings the women with him. I figured we could smuggle at least four to five kilos of hash oil on each female.

I was getting very excited thinking about his visit. Jim was to bring his new wife and one of her girlfriends to Kabul. Then we would fill the plastic girdles with the oil, which they would wear under their clothing. Even if they were body searched and patted down, it would feel like their skin. There shouldn't be any problems at all.

The Brotherhood had been doing this for years and had never had anyone busted, so I was confident in this smuggling scam. Now all I had to do was wait for Jim and the girls to arrive.

I was worried about Carol. She was still in a weird mood. Ever since my return from the hash trip, Carol seemed to become more and more distant. She didn't seem like the happy-go-lucky girl she had always been. I couldn't figure out what was wrong with our relationship. It seemed stalled and strained but I just couldn't put my finger on it.

I soon forget about Carol's problems and thought about the days ahead. Plus, I had become ill since the trip. My eyes had turned yellow, which meant I probably had hepatitis. I had to stay in bed and rest, so I left the responsibility of the chores to Carol.

For the next week or two, Carol mailed the envelopes and did all the work around the house. She even refused to sleep with me, fearing she might catch whatever I had, so I couldn't blame her. Within ten days, I started getting my strength back. I felt alive and strong again, but our relationship was still strained. But I tried not to think about it.

People were coming and going from my apartment building.

The English couple on the second floor was leaving to drive back to England. They had their Land Rover van completely packed with all their belongings of furniture and kids. Keith had hidden over ten kilos of hash into the wooden frame of their bed.

"Rob, do you think we will have any trouble at customs?" asked Keith.

I saw the way he had everything packed. The bed was well hidden, with everything else lying on top of it, so I didn't think he would have any trouble. The customs officials wouldn't make him take all that stuff out. Even if they did, the hash was well hidden inside the wooden frame. With that, Carol and I said goodbye. They had been good neighbors for almost a year. We had enjoyed their company and told them so.

"Keith, we will never forget your family, and we will always think of you as our close and dear friends," I said. Then we waved goodbye and watched as the van slowly sped away, bobbing from side to side due to the excessive weight. I prayed that they would make it safely to England.

Now that the English couple was gone, and Pat and Becky no longer came by, I was anxious for some company. But soon Jim and the girls would arrive. In the meantime, I still had to visit the Peace Corps office and talk to the director about the information I had overheard at the nightclub. I wanted to tell him that to control Afghanistan, we must up the ante to buy off the Russians. Then we could have our intelligence surveillance from Turkey, Iran, Afghanistan, and Pakistan. That would give America a big advantage on intelligence issues with Russia.

I also wanted to tell the director about the king wanting to leave the country for Italy to have corrective eye surgery, but he needed assurances from his generals and cousin, Mohammed Daoud, that his country would be in safe hands while he was away. I would also tell Beardon that the king's son was worried his uncle might take over or overthrow the government if his father left the country. I would tell him how the king's brother-in-law and cousin was the secretary of defense more than twenty years before, then was fired when the king decided he was becoming too powerful.

Soon after, the king declared by law that no relatives could hold any government position. Ever since, Mohammed Daoud had been biding his time waiting to pounce at just the right moment. He really wanted to control the Afghan government and was power hungry. He was the one person America needed to worry about. He was also pro-Russian and anti-American.

I finally went to visit the director. He was sitting behind his desk. After telling him everything I had overheard, he seemed very, very interested.

"Robert, I want you to find out the exact date the king will leave the country," said Mr. Beardon, as he stood and began pacing back and forth.

"All I know is that he wanted to leave for Italy as soon as possible before his eyes and vision deteriorated too much. Then they wouldn't be able to correct his vision. I will do the best I can," I said, and then turned to leave his office.

"Remember, if you ever need the American government's help, don't hesitate to ask me, and I will do my best to help you. Either that, or go to the American Embassy and ask to talk to the consul general. He should be able to help you if you have any trouble in Afghanistan," he said, with an air of arrogance.

We shook hands, and I quietly left the building. As I walked back to the apartment, I noticed that the weather was finally changing. I could smell the sweet odor of Afghan bread baking in the cool, crisp spring weather. Compared to America, the industrial giant, there was absolutely no smog whatsoever in Kabul.

Spring was all around me, and with the Afghan holiday over, the disco would be reopening once again. I was anxious and excited to see and visit my rich aristocratic Afghan friends and learn the secrets of the Afghan government. That is, if they were in the country. I was anxious to listen and discuss the politics of Afghanistan. I hoped they would tell me the secrets Beardon was interested in hearing. I needed to find out the exact date when the king would leave the country.

I also was hoping they would tell me who the king wanted to help build his country—America, or Russia, or maybe even China. This was the type of intelligence I needed to learn and verify.

Now all I had to do was talk Carol into going with me for a night on the town. I still couldn't figure out why she was acting so aloof. She seemed like a different woman, not the one I had first asked to live with me in Kabul.

Carol agreed to go with me to the nightclub. Aslam, our Afghan servant, was left to babysit the animals. So a few days later, we went. As we entered the nightclub, I noticed that very few of my aristocratic and high ministry blue-bloods were sitting at their special table.

As Carol and I walked toward them, we were greeted with friendly, loud cheers. Many of the royalty stood up as we greeted them. They seemed very happy to see us. They were especially happy to see Carol. All the men at our table were falling all over each other to talk with her. Each one of these men probably had a stable of beautiful women in their harems but was utterly stupefied when they were around Carol.

We all sat around the table talking about the days past. As we talked, Carol and the Afghan women walked onto the dance floor so Carol could show them some American line dances. They loved it. Even some of the royalty got up and tried their best. They especially liked the line dances, but instead of dancing to American country music, they danced to the royal beat of Afghan music. I was surprised to see them keep a steady beat. The men drooled and fell over themselves as they watched Carol shake her tail feathers.

As the girls danced, the men continued their conversation. That night, I learned that the king would be leaving Kabul any day. The king's son was still very worried and concerned that his uncle would call his friends in the military and overthrow the government. His cousin tried to console him by telling him that the king had the loyalty of his generals, especially after handing out big pay raises to his commanding officers and the rest of his armed forces. The king believed his country would be in good hands while he was gone.

I had learned the Afghan government was interested in building a railroad and communication satellites for television and to spy on nearby enemy countries. But the king was also worried about ruffling the feathers of the Muslim Imams, or priests. He didn't want his country to grow too fast and too westernized. They didn't want to become another westernized Iran.

My friends also talked again about the offer the American government had given to their government: the one bowl of rice and one loaf of bread to every person in Afghanistan and the twelve-million dollar loan that had to be spent with the authorization and okay of the American government. On the other hand, the Russians had offered two bowls of rice and two loaves of bread to each and every person living in Afghanistan and also a gift of twelve million dollars to be spent any way the Afghan government saw fit. That was what it would take to get control of the Afghan government. This would be an update of the information I had given the Peace Corps director a week before.

This information should give America an edge or advantage in political negotiations with Afghanistan and maybe even Russia. America and Russia were always competing against each other on major projects built throughout Afghanistan. This information should also be useful in getting more control over the Afghan government. I was very pleased with myself that I was able to learn this information.

I needed to see Beardon and tell him the latest news. A few days later, I went to see him without getting an appointment from Dan. I thought this information was too important to wait. Luckily, he was in his office sitting behind his desk. I explained everything and every little detail I could remember. He was surprised I had learned so much information.

"Rob, your facts were right on the money. We are negotiating with the Afghan government as we speak. I'll relay this information to the right people in our government. We will be on high alert when the king leaves Kabul. If a coup does take place, this will be the perfect time. When the king is out of the country, that would be the best time for any group or person to overthrow the government," explained the director. We shook hands and I left the building.

The next few days seemed to go by slowly as I waited nervously for Jim to arrive. But today I needed to go to the small bank and deposit money into my savings account. The money was still coming in regularly, but there weren't as many people sending money as in months past. But every week I was receiving hundreds of dollars. Today I had about two-thousand dollars to put into the account.

I hopped into my van and drove to the bank. But as I did, I noticed that most of the stores were closed. The streets were very quiet and bare. I thought to myself, *Is this a holiday?* I didn't think so and continued on my merry way. But as I reached the bank, I found that it was closed. In fact, all the stores were closed. Nobody was on the streets at all. It seemed as if everyone had disappeared. I couldn't figure out what holiday it was. I was dazed and didn't know what was going on and there was nobody around to ask. So I decided to drive to the post office.

As I rounded a corner, I suddenly had to slam on my brakes. I stopped six inches from an Afghan soldier pointing a machine gun at me. As I stared in disbelief, I noticed there were many armed soldiers surrounding the main ministry buildings, such as the Treasury and Ministry of Interior. The soldiers even had the Kabul bank surrounded. I thought that maybe Henry Kissinger or President Nixon had arrived in Kabul.

The Afghan soldier ordered me to turn around and take another road. I made a U-turn and headed toward the post office. I wanted to ask Saraj or Mr. Bareck about the current situation. I didn't see any fighting, so I didn't think it was a coup. I still thought a high-ranking diplomat was visiting the city, so I continued to the post office. But that, too, was closed and surrounded by armed soldiers.

I decided to turn around and return to the apartment. I would ask my Peace Corps friends if they had any idea what was going on.

Ten minutes later, while walking up the stairs to the apartment, I saw Dan.

"Dan, do you know what all the soldiers are doing in the streets?"

"No, I don't have any idea. I haven't heard anything about that," he said, as we went in opposite directions.

I walked into my apartment and told Carol what I had encountered. It wasn't until three days later that I found out what had occurred. It seemed the king's son's premonitions had been right. Mohammed Daoud decided to overthrow the government.

As soon as the king boarded the plane to leave the country, Mohammed Daoud called his military hierarchy and started the coup in motion. One hour after the king had left the country, he was in control of the government. The coup was complete. Not one person had fired a shot from his weapon. It was a totally bloodless coup.

A few days later, I answered a loud knock at my apartment door. To my surprise, it was Jim. He had finally shown up. I was ecstatic. But he wasn't alone. John, another friend and roommate from America, was standing alongside of him. I was very happy and excited to see them and invited them into the apartment. However, I noticed the girls weren't with them. I also noticed that John was carrying a small wooden box.

As we hugged each other, I asked Jim an important question. "Jim, where are the girls? Are they at the hotel room?"

"No," he said, staring at the floor.

"So where are they?" I asked.

"I didn't bring them. I have something a whole lot better."

Right at that moment, I knew what the box was for.

I looked Jim straight in the eyes and questioned him. "Jim, don't tell me you want to smuggle the hash oil in that wooden box that John is holding, do you?"

"Exactly, he replied enthusiastically. "John's got it all figured out. He did it before from Columbia."

Then John interrupted our conversation.

"I shipped this box from Columbia to America filled with the best gold pot I ever smoked. I didn't have any problems at all," he said.

"Well, I know how the customs officials work here, and you will never get that box out of Afghanistan. You might have a chance if you carry it overland by bus. That's the only possible way to get it out of the country. Even then, it's still taking a big risk," I told him, trying to hold my cool.

"I'm going to carry it on the plane," John replied.

"It will never work. When they check your luggage at customs, the customs man will look at that wooden box and smash it on the ground. These people aren't stupid, John," I snapped.

At this point, I was getting upset. Jim hadn't done what we had planned.

"I know they're not stupid," John replied, trying to talk me into his stupid scam.

"How did you plan on hiding the hash oil? Not in a false bottom, I hope?" I asked him.

"Exactly," he replied. "We'll cut out small sections of the wood and then glue thin wood over it. We can put the hash oil in small plastic baggies and then fit them into the cut out sections."

"John, they won't even have to smash the box on the ground. All they'll have to do is press down with a sharp knife or even their finger and it will break right through the thin wood. You guys are crazy. You'll both end up in jail."

"No, we won't," replied John, trying to reassure me that his plan would work.

"Come on, Rob, help us do this," pleaded Jim.

"No way am I gonna waste my money and time on this stupid scam. If you guys end up in jail, I won't get you out. I will let you stay there and rot. So you will have to write your parents or friends for their help."

"That's all right. I know I can do it," John reassured me.

While he talked, I looked over the cheap wooden box. John called it a camera case, but I didn't see any camera.

"Where is the camera, John?" I asked.

"I don't have one."

"What if the customs officer asks you about your camera? What are you gonna tell them?"

He thought for a few seconds and replied, "I'll tell them I sold it."

"Then they'll ask you why you didn't give the box with the camera."

"Then I'll tell them I lost it," he said, becoming increasingly nervous trying to answer my questions.

"Why have a camera case when you don't have a camera?" I asked John. "These customs officials aren't stupid."

"But I know it will work, and I'm willing to take all the risk," he replied.

I still refused to help them. "If you guys end up in jail, I could never forgive myself."

After arguing about this for more than two hours, we agreed to forget about this crazy idea for now. It was time to get high. They had just gotten off the plane and were still wound up from such a long trip.

"Hey, Rob do you have any more of those white tablets?" asked Jim, grinning from ear to ear.

"Do you mean morphine?"

"Yeah," he replied, with a big smile on his face.

We walked into my bedroom and sat on the beds while I got out the morphine kit. Even though the stores and pharmacy were still closed, I still had quite a bit of morphine left and also a dozen or so new plastic syringes. As I began to fix the morphine, John interrupted me.

"Rob, do you mind if I smoke some hash?"

"John, there's a whole bunch over there," I replied, pointing to the big bowl of hash and hash joints Carol had rolled.

He picked up a hash joint and lit it. He took a deep drag and began coughing. He coughed so hard he had to lie down on the bed to catch his breath.

"Wow, this stuff is great," stated John, trying to sit up, but he was too dizzy and laid down again.

"What's wrong, John?" I asked, as he finally sat up.

"It was like someone hit me in the back of the head with a sledgehammer. Wow, this stuff is fantastic."

Just then, Carol walked into the apartment and into our bedroom. When she saw Jim, she stopped right in her tracks and looked very happy and surprised.

"You finally made it, hey, Jim?" she asked.

Jim just nodded his head as he began feeling the hot, tingling, fluid rush creep through his body. His face turned beet red. You could barely hear an audible "wow" out of his mouth.

Before I did my fix, Carol was waiting with her spoon and syringe. I put the morphine tabs into he into her spoon so she could mix it while I did my "do." As I injected myself, I introduced Carol to John. She remembered seeing him in Michigan at Jim's house. But right at that moment, Carol was only interested in her morphine. She wanted her fix and within a few minutes, she was in total ecstasy.

John declined the morphine. He, like Ron, didn't like needles. He was happy to smoke my excellent hashish.

Within thirty minutes, we were discussing business again. While we talked, Carol went into the kitchen to make dinner. Jim and John tried to talk me into going along with their crazy idea. By the time they were ready to return to their hotel room, I still refused to participate in their scam.

"Why don't you guys stay in my extra bedroom?" I asked them.

They declined. They wanted to stay at their nice warm hotel room at the Kabul Hotel, which was the second best hotel in Kabul. I couldn't blame them.

"Well, we better get back to our hotel," Jim told John.

"Why don't you come on over tomorrow morning? I want to show you guys the town."

The town was still bottled up and most of the stores were closed. I still hadn't seen Saraj or Mr. Bareck. I wondered if Mr. Bareck had gotten the promotion he had hoped for. I also wondered when things would get back to normal.

Within a couple of days, the stores had reopened, as did the bank, pharmacy, and post office. I needed to visit all of these places, especially wanting to see and talk with Saraj and Mr. Bareck. Another important stop was the Devil's pharmacy. I needed to refill my morphine stash.

Every day, Jim and John came over to the apartment and tried continuously to talk me into their crazy scam.

"Come on, Rob, help us with the box," pleaded Jim.

"I will, if you carry the box overland and buy a camera to put inside it. But don't take it out by air. That'll never work. I'm certain you'll get busted. They will smell it, feel it, and then smash it on the floor. Then they'll throw you guys in jail. No! I refuse to help you."

I also refused to spend any money to buy the hash oil. That would be a waste of five hundred dollars. I just didn't have that kind of money to throw away on a dumb scam that was sure to get them busted.

During the next week, Jim and John were relentless. They continued to badger and hound me to help them. They begged and pleaded with me to go along with their plan. And they promised to put up all the money. Finally, I couldn't take their onslaught any longer and agreed to help them with their crazy scam. I knew there would be no way this idea would work and was certain that they would end up in jail. I refused to take any responsibility for their actions, especially if they got busted. Jim decided he wasn't going to carry anything illegal. John would take all the risk. That was fine by me.

Jim and I drove to Tiar's house to buy the hash oil. Once again, we parked the van on the street and then had to walk down that dirty, foul smelling, urine-infested alleyway trying not to fall into the raw waste and sewage that flowed through it. Finally, we reached his house. I knocked on the door and Tiar answered it and invited us in. We followed Tiar into the same room he had always used to make the hash.

Tiar had been expecting us. I had explained to him almost two weeks before that I would be needing his expertise. He was very happy to see us, but he seemed more paranoid than usual.

"What's wrong, Tiar? You seem nervous. Is everything all right?" I asked.

"I must be very cautious now, Bob. The new president doesn't like foreigners. We aren't supposed to socialize with them, or we may get in trouble with the law. This new government is very bad for you and me. This president wants to kill all drug dealers," he said nervously.

"Tiar, I thought this president wanted to use drugs to disrupt the economy of the bordering countries?" I asked.

"This new president is very bad. He likes Russia and doesn't trust America. He wants to clean up the cities and throw out all foreigners, especially the longhaired hippies. He's a bad man. A very bad man," he replied.

When he told me this, I knew my days in Afghanistan were numbered. But I still had business to take care of.

"Tiar, we need one kilo of your number one hash oil," I told him.

"That is very expensive, Bob. It will take over ten kilos of the very best hash pollen to make one kilo of oil."

"That's fine. How much money is it going to cost?"

"I want five-hundred dollars," he replied.

"Can we watch you make it?" I asked him.

"No, it will take more than twenty-four hours before it's completely ready. Not only that, but if you see how it's done, then you will never come back to me. I wouldn't make any money and my family would starve," he said sadly.

"All right, we'll be back tomorrow about this time of day," I said, as I handed him two-hundred and fifty dollars. "I'll give you the other half when I pick up the oil," I told him.

I completely trusted Tiar. We said goodbye, and then Jim and I returned to the van and then headed back to the apartment. On the way, we discussed the situation about the new president of Afghanistan.

We returned to the apartment and partied. Jim invited us to his hotel room, but Carol didn't want to go, so I let her stay and babysit the animals while I went out with Jim and John. By the time I returned home, Carol was sleeping, and the animals were tied up outside and sitting on the porch in the cold night air. I was very angry with Carol for abusing my tiny baby monkeys. I brought the animals inside and sat them next to the warm fire. Then we all went to bed.

The next day, Jim and I returned to Tiar's house to pick up the hash oil. But we arrived too soon, and the oil wasn't completely cured. It was slowly curing over a pan of ice. While we waited, I had Tiar press a kilo of hashish. This was to be used for my envelopes. Now that the post office was open again, I needed to send some and very soon.

Within two hours, we were heading back to the apartment with the oil and the hash. Jim was very happy. Within a few days, he would be heading for America.

We finally reached the apartment. When I entered the bedroom, I noticed that Rex Jr. looked very sickly. The very next morning, he was dead. He died from pneumonia, which he'd caught when Carol put him and Chakila outside in the cold.

Chakila pulled through. But I was very hurt over Rex Jr.'s death. There was no reason for it. Carol knew better than to put those babies out in the cold. I figured she had done it on purpose. So for the next few days, I didn't speak to her. I was very upset at her stupidity. She didn't even seem remorseful and acted like she wanted both monkeys to die. I buried Rex Jr. in the backyard, next to Rex Sr.

Once the burial was finished, I returned to my apartment and waited for Jim and John to arrive. They finally stopped by around noon. So we started filling up baggies with hash oil. By the time we had finished, we had used the whole kilo of oil, plus another kilo of hash. Then we sandwiched the oil between two slabs of hash wrapped in plastic and placed them into the cutouts that we had made in the sides, top, and bottom of the wooden box. Then we glued the thin pieces of mahogany to it, covering the cutouts. With that done, the wooden box was completed, and Jim and John were ecstatic. They thought the box looked great. It might have, but I still knew their scam wasn't going to work. John was never going to get that box through airport security, especially through Afghan customs. But I didn't care anymore. John was taking all the risk. So I didn't say anything. I didn't want to hear them bellyache. Now all that was left for them to do was to make their reservations for their return trip to America.

I looked the box over and felt the wood with my hands. I could have pushed my thumbs right through the thin wood. I didn't say a word, though. I just kept my mouth shut. I knew we weren't going to make any money on this deal. In fact, we were gonna lose everything we had gained up to this point. This was our chance to make it big time, and Jim had failed me. I just figured it was John's ass and not mine.

Well, within two days, we would know if it was a go or no go. They were leaving Kabul for America in two days. Jim would take back souvenirs and nothing more. John was taking the risk. Over the next two days, we partied hearty. During this time, Mr. B stopped by.

"Come on in, Mr. Bareck. How are you?" I asked.

"I am very well, Bob. They have promoted me to the president of the Afghan post department. I'm the new postmaster general," he said, beaming with happiness.

Mr. B was related to the new president, Mohammed Daoud. I was very happy for him.

"Congratulations, Mr. Bareck. Now we'll send tons of hash back, won't we?" I asked eagerly.

He had told me many times before that if he ever became president of the post office that we would send many, many hundreds of kilos. I thought the time had come. But I would soon find out that wasn't the case.

"I don't know, Bob. They told me if I get caught sending any illegal contraband they would hang me or shoot me. I must be very careful," said Mr. Bareck.

I could see he was really worried about his life and family. I handed Mr. Bareck a few hash envelopes and money. Then I thanked him and after saying goodbye, I went to my bedroom and did a ten tablet "do."

The time had passed very quickly. My friends were heading back to America. I loaded Jim and John's luggage into the van, and then drove them to the airport. Jim went in first. Ten minutes later, John walked into the building. Soon after, I drove back to the apartment. I didn't even want to think about their trip, so I went home and did an extra dose of morphine—a heavy dose.

A few days later, when I checked the incoming mail tray at the post office, I found a letter addressed to me from Jim. It had just arrived. So I placed it into my shoulder bag and left the post office.

Once I had finished my chores, I returned to my apartment. Then I went into the living room and read Jim's letter; he had plenty to say. It seemed John never boarded the plane. Jim didn't know what had happened, but I had a pretty good idea. Jim had boarded the plane first, so he could watch as John boarded it. He waited and waited, but John never showed up—he never got on the plane.

Just as I began reading the second page of the letter, there was a knock on my front door. I answered it and saw two Afghan men standing there. Neither said a word. And then one handed me a folded-up piece of paper. They waited as I quickly unfolded it and read it. It was a note from John that these two guys had smuggled out of jail for him. He was sitting in a dark and dirty jail cell and wanted me to bail him out. He wanted me to give these two Afghans one-thousand dollars to pay his bail.

The letter went on to say how the customs man did exactly as I said he would. He looked at the wooden box and smiled a big, toothless smile. He asked John if it had hashish in it. John quickly denied the accusation. The customs man put it up to his nose, then felt it with his hands and threw it to the cement floor. The hashish and hash oil flew in every direction. Within nanoseconds, soldiers surrounded him with loaded machine guns pointed at every part of his anatomy. Then they handcuffed him and carted him off to the dungeon. After reading the letter, the Afghans asked me for the money.

"I don't know any, John," I told them. "I am not involved with this person, and I can't help him." I just shut the door and walked into my bedroom to do my morphine.

As I was telling Carol about the guys at the door, I noticed she was reading a letter.

"Carol, who is the letter from?"

"My mother," she said, trying to hide the letter behind her back.

"Let me read it and see what she has to say about the good old U.S. of A.," I said, as she handed me the letter.

I began reading it. My jaw suddenly dropped to the floor, and my eyes nearly popped out of my head. In the letter, Carol's mother was telling her not to stay with me if I beat her. I had never laid a hand on Carol or any other female in my life. I looked at Carol in disbelief.

"What the hell is going on?" I asked her, feeling very hurt and frustrated. "I never hit you. Why would your mother think that I hit and beat you?" I was becoming very angry and upset. "Would you explain to me what is going on?" I handed her the letter.

"I wrote my mother that you beat me because I want her to send me money so I can leave Kabul and return to Michigan. I knew you wanted to stay here forever and would never leave," she said.

"If you wanted to go back, why didn't you tell me? I would have sent you back. I got you here; I sure would have sent you back. But now I don't even want to look at you. In fact, I don't want to be in the same room with you. You can take your things and move into the other bedroom. If you don't like it, you can move out completely. You aren't the same person that I once knew."

I was really hurt. I adored Carol and would have never laid a hand on her. I only loved her and treated her like an angel or goddess. She made me out to be a monster, and I didn't appreciate it. I could no longer trust her. I didn't even want to look at her. I was disgusted, and I considered her dead in my eyes. She was nothing to me now.

I continued to do my daily chores, but I refused to use the van. I had put it in Carol's name, so I figured it was hers. She could sell it and get more than enough money to buy a ticket to return to America.

Within two weeks, Carol had taken Foxy and most of her belongings and moved out of the apartment. She moved into the same hotel at which Pat and Becky were staying. She returned to the apartment a few times, asking me to take her back. But I staunchly refused. I just couldn't trust her anymore. She had broken my heart, and it couldn't be mended. One time she came over and begged me to give her some morphine. She was pathetic. It was disgusting watching her make a fool of herself. Instead of prolonging her agony by giving her a fix, I decided to help her. I went into my stash and got a couple of bottles of a withdrawal medication. These were used for morphine withdrawal. I had been saving them for myself, and it was all I had. But I still felt sorry for her and respected her as a person, even though the love wasn't there anymore.

"Carol, read the directions and within a few days you'll have kicked your morphine habit without going through withdrawal symptoms." Then I handed her the pills and wished her the best.

She had already met some young American attorney. The only thing that bothered me was that she had taken my dog. And both my monkey and I missed Foxy. She was part of the family. Every time I thought about the dog, I quickly thought about something else. It always put me in a sad mood when I thought about Foxy and all the good times we'd had with the monkeys. Now it was only Chakila and I.

I needed transportation, so I bought a new bicycle that had been made in China. Chakila and I rode it all over the city. Once in awhile, I would see Carol driving the van. But within two weeks, I no longer saw her. She had left Kabul.

The money I was getting from America wasn't coming in as regularly as before, and the amounts were getting smaller and smaller. Some of my friends were writing in their letters that the number of envelopes I had sent were not getting through to their intended destination. But I knew if Saraj or Mr. B were sending them, they would definitely get through American customs. There was no doubt about it. But now for some reason my friends weren't getting all of them. I had to find out what the heck was going on.

Over the next few months, I stopped sending envelopes to over half of the people to whom I had been sending them. I had been sending envelopes to more than fifteen people. Now it was down to three or four of my closest and trusted friends. Plus, I was still sending one or two parcels of shoes each month. I thought that with Mr. Bareck as postmaster general, we would be sending tons of hash. Instead, he was afraid to send anything. He worried that if he were caught, they would execute him. Lately, he had become very paranoid, probably because Saraj had just gotten busted and was currently in jail.

This new Afghan president wanted to clean up his city, so he started a crackdown and kicked out many of the long-haired hippies. Anyone who had overstayed their visa was arrested, thrown in jail, and quickly deported if they could pay a huge fine. I had to be extremely careful.

When I visited the center of the city, I had to keep my hair tucked into my shirt or rolled up into a bun. But there was one thing that I did have—sanctuary at my apartment.

Mark stopped by my apartment and wanted my help to leave the country. He wanted to return to America.

"Rob, can you help me get back to America?" he asked.

"Sure, Mark. I'll help you. You're my dearest and best friend. What do you want from me?"

"I need to borrow some money to get me to Europe and a plane ticket to America."

"All right, Mark, but on one condition: If you travel overland, I'll give you the pair of boots that I was saving for myself, and you can take them with you. But you must only wear them when you cross the borders."

"Why is that?"

"Why? Because each boot has over eight hundred grams of hash in the soles. So you must only wear them for a few minutes at a time. You must be super careful and not wear them in any water or walk through any snow or puddles. Otherwise, they might fall apart. So you must be careful. All you have to do is sell half for me and you keep the rest." Then I handed him two-hundred American dollars.

"Thanks, Rob."

"That should be more than enough money to get you to Europe with enough left over to buy a student-fare plane ticket from Europe to New York. But if you don't have enough money for the plane ticket, you can always sell some of the hash. You get almost as much money per gram in Germany as you do in Michigan," I said, handing Mark the boots.

We hugged each other as we said goodbye.

"Rob, I'll send you a letter when I reach Europe."

"Mark, come back and visit me."

With that said, he walked out my apartment door heading for America.

I'm really gonna miss that guy, I thought to myself. Then I remembered I still had my friends across the hall. Dan and Don were still living there, while the other two guys moved out and rented apartments of their own. Don wanted to return to America because the Afghan government was giving him a hard time and he was nearly out of his Colombian cocaine. He wanted to go back so he could buy some more of that pure white evil narcotic to feed his addiction.

CHAPTER 20

FOREIGNERS KICKED OUT OF AFGHANISTAN

The month of May was just around the corner. Carol had left Afghanistan. Mark had gone. Jim had gone. Ron and Cindy had gone, and Saraj was still in jail. Mr. Bareck was my only connection and my only source for sending envelopes. But I still sent the wooden sandals without paying anything. I just told Mr. B that they were store-bought sandals and that we didn't have them in America. So far, he had believed me. I was only putting a small amount of hash in them, anyway, so they wouldn't be too heavy or overweight.

I was only receiving money now on the average on one wire per week, or maybe two, if I was lucky. My money was depleting fast, and the Devil was now charging me twenty dollars for each bottle of morphine. I was doing almost two bottles a day and that was just to stay normal. I wasn't getting that high from it anymore. My tolerance had really built up. I was using six tablets for each fix, six to seven times a day.

Just three years before, I had only been taking one tablet and getting much higher than now. My addiction was very bad. I was like a diabetic, injecting my insulin several times a day. Even the rush wasn't as strong as it once was. I would have to do ten or twelve tablets to get as high as I had before doing one tablet.

Not only was the morphine more expensive, but Mr. Bareck wanted twenty dollars more per envelope, and many that I had given him never made it to their destination. So I confronted him about it when he stopped by my apartment.

"Mr. Bareck, are you sending all the envelopes I give you?"

"Yes, Bob. I send them all."

"Are you sure, Mr. Bareck?" I looked him directly in the eyes.

"Yes."

"Mr. Bareck, if you are telling me the truth, swear to Allah that you are sending all of my envelopes."

"I'm sorry, Bob," he said, as he looked away.

"Damn it, Mr. B, I count on those envelopes for my money. That's why I haven't been getting much money from my friends. I wouldn't believe them when they wrote that they weren't getting all of the envelopes I had sent. I give you the money and you cheat me. I trusted you, Mr. Bareck. I thought you were my good friend, but I guess I was wrong."

"Bob, I am your good friend."

"Mr. Bareck, will you send all of the envelopes when I give them to you?"

"I promise, Bob," he said, his face turning red in embarrassment.

"I hope so." We shook hands, and then he left my apartment.

Two minutes after he left, there was a knock at my door. To my surprise, it was Becky. I hadn't seen her in almost three months. I thought she had gone a month ago. I invited her into my apartment. She was clearly upset about something. We went into the living room to talk. The moment we sat down, she started crying and mumbled something about Pat.

"Becky, what happened to Pat?" I asked her.

"Pat was arrested and thrown in jail today. The police and soldiers came into our hotel room and hauled him out by the scruff of the neck. They even kicked him and poked him in the back with their rifles when they thought he was moving too slow."

"You're lucky they didn't shoot him."

"Rob, I don't know what to do," she sobbed. "We don't have any money at all. The only thing I could think of was to ask you for help."

"Well let me see. You snuck out of my apartment and didn't have the decency to tell me or Carol. Plus, I haven't heard from you in over three months. You used my customs connection without asking me if it was all right, and now you come to me for help. Why should I help you, Becky, when you stabbed me in the back?" I asked, looking into her red, tear-soaked eyes.

"I'm sorry. I don't know where else to go."

"Becky, why don't you write to your parents and ask them for help?"

"I did, but they refused to help me," she sobbed.

"Your own parents won't help you, but you want me to help you. What happened? Did you stab your parents in the back, too? Did you use them like you used me?" Becky continued to cry. "Stop your crying and tell me what it will take to get Pat out of jail."

Becky finally stopped crying and whining when I showed interest in helping her. I could have had her do anything that I wanted. Since Carol had left, I hadn't had any sex, and Becky was a nympho. I could have used her as my slave, but I wasn't like that. At one time, I'd considered her one of my closest friends. We had gone to high school together. And because of that, I decided to help her.

"The policeman told me I needed one-thousand dollars to get Pat out of jail," she said.

"One-thousand dollars! I don't have that kind of money. My business has been slow lately—very slow. If I did help you out, what will you do when he gets out? You guys will still be broke."

"I have no idea what we'll do. I haven't thought that far ahead."

Becky was a very intelligent female, but right now, she was talking like an idiot.

"Becky, I thought Mr. Bareck sent hash envelopes for you. Didn't you make money from that?"

"Well we gave him money to send them but none of our friends received any of the envelopes. Either he never sent them and just kept the money or our friends are lying to us."

"Becky, I gave you a place to stay. I sent hash envelopes for you so you could get money to get home on. I gave you money to live on while you lived at my apartment waiting for money from America. Not only that, but you used the money I gave you to move into a hotel room and to send hash envelopes through my customs connection. And now you come to me broke—with no money—and Pat's in jail. That's your karma getting back at you."

"Please don't say that," she whined.

I sat back in my chair thinking about whether I should help her or show her the door. That's what I should have done. I shouldn't have let her into my apartment in the first place. But watching her cry, I felt sorry for her.

"All right, I'll help you, but on one condition. You will have to carry some hash oil on your body, overland. You keep half and sell my half. Pat can carry one baggie full and you can carry another baggie full. That should get you enough money to pay me back for helping Pat get out of jail bond to buy your plane fare to America. Plus, you should have enough left over to pay me back all the money I loaned you."

"I guess we can do that if you promise to help us."

"I will." With that said, a smile finally came across her beautiful face.

Becky finally stopped crying once I had promised to help her. She settled down and began to relax. Then I handed her a two-inch-round, three inch-long wooden dowel.

"Becky, go into the bathroom and see if it will fit in your vagina. It will give me an idea on the size so I can make the hash oil fit comfortably.

She took the dowel into the bathroom and returned to the living room a few minutes later. "Does it fit snug enough?"

"It fits all right. But you could even make it a few inches bigger and four or five inches longer. I didn't want to take it out once I put it up there." Then she pulled up her sari and pulled the dowel out of her vagina. As she set it down on her chair, her fingers played with her vagina while she flirted with me.

Becky was like a female bitch in heat. She acted as if she wanted to have sex with me. "Becky, are you trying to seduce me?"

"Well, I thought with Carol gone and you being alone, I figured you would want a good fuck," she said, as she walked over to me and sat in my lap.

This talk was exciting me and turning me on, and she knew it. I controlled myself and held my composure. As she started to unbuckle my pants, I grabbed her hand. The morphine kept me so high I never thought about sex or was interested in it. Before Becky had my pants completely down, I grabbed her hands and reluctantly stopped her. I didn't want it to go any further. Not today, anyway. I stood up and buckled my pants and unzipped my money belt. I pulled out a thick stack of one-hundred dollar bills.

Out of the corner of my eye, I noticed Becky was busy playing with herself. She was touching herself with her hands, and I thought she was going to strip and masturbate, so I began counting the money out loud. She stood alongside of me, rubbing her big breasts into my chest and rubbing her crotch against my leg as I counted out and handed her ten one hundred dollar bills. With one hand, she was rubbing my crotch, while she held onto the money with the other. Suddenly, she gave me a long French kiss and tried once again to seduce me, but I broke her hold.

"Becky, go get Pat out of jail," I said, as I walked her to the door. "Come back to the apartment with Pat, and I'll give you two or three hundred dollars more. By then, I'll have the hash oil bagged and ready for you."

She gave me another long French kiss at the door.

"Thank you for helping us," she cooed. Then she was gone.

After that little encounter with Becky, I had to go into the bedroom and fix another "do" of morphine. She had sparked my sparker.

Two days later, Pat and Becky stopped by. Now that Pat was out of jail and had a new visa, he didn't want to leave Kabul right away. He wanted to send some more hash envelopes and wait for his friends to send the money.

I couldn't believe my ears and told him so. "Pat, what makes you think those envelopes will make it when none of the other ones got through? If the envelopes are sent from here, they will not make it to their destination, so all you would be doing is giving your money away. You would be taking the money you borrowed from me and giving it right back to Mr. Bareck. You guys aren't making any sense. You're not thinking straight. The hash is clouding your minds. You should go back to America before you become completely broke, alone on the street, and with nobody to help you. Then what would you do?"

"I don't know," he said, looking at the floor.

I told him, "I will loan you enough money to travel overland by bus and enough hash oil to make it very profitable. If you keep the oil taped to your body and never take it off for anything until you are in America, you won't have any problems with customs. Just don't act nervous and be yourselves and you won't have a problem. Then I'll give you an address of a friend that you can give the oil to so he can sell it for me, unless you want to sell it. It doesn't matter to me as long as I get my money. Once it's sold, you should be able to pay me back the money I've loaned you."

I didn't want to do it, but I had no choice.

"I guess it's the right thing to do," declared Pat, after a few minutes of deep thought. "We only have five more days left on our visas, anyway."

Pat wasn't very happy about it, but he really didn't have any other choice. I went into my bedroom and got the two baggies of hash oil. One of them was completely taped up with red electrical tape to keep the smell down. That one was for Becky. It was much bigger than the one I had made for Pat.

When I had the oil made, I only paid for one kilo, but it was nearly twice that amount. Tiar had made nearly two kilos of hash oil and only charged me for one. I used the extra oil for this scam.

I handed one baggie to Pat and the other one to Becky. Becky looked at hers and laughed.

"It looks like a big red dildo. It'll be like having a cock up my pussy all day long. Let me try it out."

With that, she pulled up the front of her sari, showing me her exposed and bald womanhood. She took her baggie of hash oil in one hand and with the other, she opened up the lips of her vagina and pushed it up into her body. She swallowed it completely. Then, she let the front of her dress fall back down and licked off her fingers. Pat and I just stared at her in disbelief. As she looked at me, she smiled.

"Becky, I think you're arousing the men in this room," I opined.

"Boy, it feels good. So good...it makes me horny," she purred, as she massaged her vagina.

She had almost four-hundred grams of hash oil in her baggie. Pat's had about two-hundred and fifty grams.

"Pat, you can have Becky tape your baggie to the crack of your ass. Once it's taped, don't take it out, 'cause it may tear the baggies. Then it will leak and smell. Just be careful. Iran is the only country you have to worry about, so just act normal. Don't be nervous and you'll slide right through. The rest of the countries are a breeze. They don't even hassle you. I will give you three-hundred dollars for the trip back to Europe and for tickets to America." I then counted out the money and handed it to him. "By the way, Pat, how was the Kabul jail?"

"It was dark, dirty, smelly, and cold. You don't ever want to go there," he replied, saddened by the replay in his mind.

"That's not a place I want to visit any time soon," I said, wishing them good luck as we hugged and said goodbye. "Don't forget to write me. Write to me when you arrive in Turkey and again when you reach Europe, or just before you leave for America." And then I walked them down the three flights of stairs. "Take care." I waved them a heartfelt goodbye.

Well, that's the last I'll see of them, I thought to myself, as I returned to my apartment.

Everyone was gone, and I was alone once again. It was just me and my monkey.

Summer was just around the corner, and the air was clean and crisp. The smell of fresh frankincense filled the air.

I wasn't going to visit Cargar Dam this summer. It was too far to ride my bike. I didn't really care anymore. My kingdom was falling apart, and my money wasn't coming in much anymore, only one or two money transfers a month and that was it. Mr. Bareck was send-ing only half of the envelopes I was giving him. Saraj, as far as I knew, was still in jail, and Mr. B said they might execute him.

I started thinking very seriously about leaving Kabul and head-ing for another country. I never thought I would leave Afghanistan in my lifetime, but things weren't going very well. I needed a fresh start in another country, like Pakistan, India, or maybe even Nepal. The longer I thought about it the more I liked the idea. If I didn't leave soon, I wouldn't have the money to move. And I still had a houseful of furniture and appliances.

As I was in deep thought, there was a loud knock at the door. It was Don from across the hall. He was getting ready to return to America. He wanted me to get him some opium and hash to take back with him. I was a little surprised. I knew he got high, but I didn't think he would take a big risk like that. But being in the Peace Corps should get him right through customs without any trouble. I also talked him into taking a hundred grams of hash oil. He would take it to one of my friends in Michigan to sell for him. He also wanted me to get him two ounces of opium and one ounce of hash. I didn't tell him that I had everything right in my closet, but after talk-ing it over for an hour or so, I made a decision.

"Don, I will have all your product in two days," I told him.

He was paying me good money for the hash and opium, so I wanted him to think I had to go across town to buy it. Don was leav-ing for America in three days. *Heck, everyone is leaving Kabul,* I thought to myself. *All my friends are gone.* Again, I thought about leaving Kabul to try my luck in another country.

A day before Don left for the United States, he asked me if I knew of any shops where he could buy some gifts for his relatives. I knew of one—a small antique store where I had made a small down pay-ment on an antique rifle. It was a beautiful Winchester made in the late 1870s. Don and I decided to visit that store first, and within ten minutes, we were on our way. It was one of the classier, upper-class clientele-type stores.

As Don and I entered the store, my Afghan friend, who hap-pened to be the owner, greeted us with a big smile. He wasn't happy to see us; he was happy that we were going to spend money in his store. And within a few minutes, Don began to pick out many differ-ent items. One item in particular that he liked was an uncut ruby the size of a walnut. He drew me over to the glass counter to show me the gemstone.

"Rob, do you see that stone?" asked Don, as he pointed to it.

"Yeah, what about it?"

"That's an uncut ruby. I wonder how much money he wants for it."

"I don't know. How much is it worth? Don, do you know for sure if it's a real ruby? It sure doesn't look like any ruby I've ever seen."

"My brother is a jeweler, and I used to help him at his store. That's where I learned about semiprecious and precious stones…and this is a precious stone."

"Can I help you?" asked the store owner.

"I would like to see that stone," Don replied, pointing to the ruby. "What type of rock is that?"

"That is an uncut blood ruby. It is a very expensive stone," said the storeowner.

"How much money do you want for it?" Don asked him.

I noticed that the owner was looking at Don's wristwatch. I poked Don into the ribs to get his attention. I turned his attention to the owner, who was in a deep trance, and staring directly at Don's wristwatch. At that moment, I was thinking that Don should trade his watch for the stone. And to my surprise, as if Don had read my mind, he took the watch off of his wrist and handed it over to the storeowner to look at.

"I will trade you even up, the watch for the stone," said Don.

"Don, your watch is worth much more than that little stone," I said.

"That's all right. If he wants to trade, it will be a good deal for both of us," he replied.

The storeowner took the stone out of the glass case and handed it to Don and then shook hands with him. Now the deal was finished. Now it was my turn. I asked the owner to bring the rifle that I had in layaway so I could show it to Don. The owner climbed the ladder to take the rifle off the wall and dusted it as he handed it to me. I showed Don the rifle, but Don looked a little disgusted.

"Rob, you can't take that rifle out of the country. Can you?" asked Don.

"Sure you can. I mean, I'm pretty sure you can," I declared, but not being one-hundred percent certain.

Then I noticed a young couple who were sitting near us on bar stools listening to our conversation. The man was holding a beautiful, antique, silver-engraved double-barrel twelve-gauge shotgun. So

I asked him about it. "You can take that shotgun out of the country, can't you?"

"No," replied the man. "We went to the museum to get it stamped so we could take it out of the country legally, but they refused to stamp it."

"Why is that?" I asked him.

"Because Afghanistan has a weird law that won't allow foreign antique weapons to leave their country," said the shotgun owner. "We want our money returned, but the storeowner refuses to reimburse us. We paid over one-thousand dollars for this shotgun. Now he won't give us our refund. This gun is worth over twenty thousand dollars in the United States."

I confronted the store owner and demanded a refund. "I want my money back. If I can't take my rifle out of the country it does me no good."

"Yes, you can take it out of the country," replied the storeowner. "Just take it to the museum and let them stamp it. Then you can take it out of the country. I promise you, mister."

"That's the exact same words he used on us," remarked the shotgun owner.

"You promised them, too," I said to the owner, pointing to the couple. "And they didn't get their stamp."

But the owner didn't say a word and just turned away and walked to another part of the store.

"Rob, the American Embassy told us about this scam the day we arrived in Kabul," said Don. "They told us that the merchants sell the same guns over and over because foreigners can't take them out of the country legally. They have to be smuggled out of the country."

"Boy, this really makes me angry," I snapped.

"Hey, Rob, let's get going. I have all the gifts I need," said Don, wanting to get out of this argument with the storeowner.

When Don began to walk out of the store, I grabbed a small jewelry box in place of the twenty dollars I had given for the rifle as a down payment, and quickly walked out of the store with it under my arm. As I ran past Don on the sidewalk, I whispered to him to follow me. The owner saw me take the box and he began to give chase. He yelled for the police as he followed behind me. When Don finally caught up with me, I told him what I had done. He couldn't believe it.

"What did you do that for?" asked Don.

"I don't know," I replied, as we walked faster and faster.

"Man, they'll cut your hand off if they catch you," Don reminded me, dumbfounded.

Now there was a large crowd following us. A few minutes later, six blocks away from the store, the police started yelling at me to stop. After walking another block, I hid the box in a small sewer pipe along the side of the road. Then I turned and walked back toward the policeman and the crowd. The owner was telling the cop his side of the story, while I told him mine.

When the policeman asked me for my passport, I asked Don to give me his. He put up a little fuss but ended up handing it to me. As he gave me his passport, I noticed the word "Diplomat" written across the front cover. I wondered why Don would have a diplomatic passport, but at that moment, my predicament was more important. I handed the passport to the policeman. He seemed very surprised as he glanced through it, then handed it back to me and saluted. All he wanted was the box returned and nothing else would come of this incident.

I walked thirty feet to the sewer drain and grabbed the box. I handed it over to the storeowner and he seemed very satisfied. I wasn't, though. I was still out twenty dollars. But Don put it in perspective for me.

"Rob, just thank your lucky stars you were only out twenty dollars and not the thousand like that couple was schemed out of. What were you thinking when you took that box? They could have thrown your butt in jail, or for that matter, they could have executed you for stealing," said Don, shaking his head.

"I wasn't stealing. That storeowner owed me twenty dollars."

"Why did you want my passport?"

"I didn't have my passport on me," I lied.

I just didn't want to give that cop my passport in case he took me to jail. I thought Don's passport would have had "Peace Corps" written on it, and I figured that once the cop saw that, he wouldn't take me to jail. At the time, I didn't ask Don why the word "Diplomat" was stamped on the cover of his passport. I figured it was none of my business. But I would ask him when he came over to my apartment to pick up his drugs.

We finally made it back to the apartment building. Chakila was happy to see me. She had stayed alone all day long. She was my little girl. She usually went with me everywhere, but she hadn't been feeling very energetic so I left her with Aslam, my part-time servant.

The next day, Don stopped by to pick up his illegal contraband to carry back to America. I handed him two ounces of Badakhsan opium and two ounces of my opiated hash, which he placed inside his leather belt. Not only did it conceal the dope but it also held up his pants. Then we taped a baggie, which contained a hundred grams of hash oil, to the crack of his butt. It was well hidden between the cheeks of his buttocks. Once that task was completed, I wrote out an address and a telephone number of a friend of mine who would sell the hash oil for him. And then I asked him a few questions that had been on my mind.

"Don, why did you have the word *diplomat* on your passport?"

"Don't you know?"

"No. You're not CIA are you?"

"You guessed it. Aren't you?"

"Don, why do you think I'm with the CIA?"

"Everyone I know is either CIA or in some other intelligence organization. But everyone worked for our government."

"Well, I'm neither."

"But Rob, you did work for us for a while, didn't you?"

"You knew about that, Don?"

"Yeah. That's why I thought you were in the agency."

With that said, we shook hands and hugged. Then he grabbed his bag and headed out the front door. I watched from my window as Don left for the airport in a taxi. *Well, he'll be home in a few days,* I thought to myself, and I was alone once again.

Soon it would be fall, and winter was just around the corner. The new Afghan government was starting to clean up the city. The long-haired hippies were given seven days to leave the country or they would be thrown in jail. So I made sure to tuck my twenty-inch-long braid into my shirt, which made it look as though I had short hair.

This new Afghan president was a tyrant and a brutal, fearless dictator. He wanted to put fear into all foreigners and his own citizens. So I had to be very careful and discreet.

While I was at the apartment, I didn't have to worry. Aslam kept all government officials away from my door, but I still worried about getting thrown into jail. So I kept a very low profile.

Over the next few months, my kingdom began to crumble. Envelopes weren't getting through, and my money was coming in at a slow trickle. Just as I started thinking again about going to another country for a fresh start, Mr. Bareck stopped by for a few minutes and told me some startling news.

"Bob, Saraj has been executed for crimes against the state," he said, saddened by the loss of a good friend.

He seemed very worried and even had a premonition that he would be next. I tried to calm him down and assure him that that wouldn't happen.

"Mr. Bareck, you are the postmaster general of Afghanistan. You are important to the country." Then I gave him my hash envelopes and money and pleaded with him as he left the apartment. "Please send them all."

He promised he would, but I didn't really trust him anymore.

CHAPTER 21

BUSTED AND JAILED IN KABUL

One warm, beautiful November day in 1973, Chakila and I rode the bike toward the market.

As I approached the intersection, I noticed a policeman waving me over to the curb. I also noticed that this was the same policeman who had busted me a few years before. He flagged down a taxi and placed my bike in the trunk, then made me climb into it. We went to the same police station as before. This time, however, I was thrown into a dirty and cold cell, and they also took my monkey away from me.

I screamed and yelled, trying to stop them from taking my Chakila, but they were too strong. Then I began yelling Mr. Bareck's name.

"Bring Mr. Bareck to me. He is my good friend!" I yelled to my jailer.

But they didn't listen. They just shut and locked the barred door behind me. I was in a dark and dirty dungeon and didn't know if or when I would get out. Every second that went by seemed like an hour. But I was worried more about my baby monkey than myself. I hoped and prayed that somehow I would get out of this mess in one piece and alive.

After six hours of incarceration, but what seemed like days, I heard the key being inserted into the lock of the door. Once my eyes focused from being in the dark for so long, I could see two men standing in the doorway. I was swept up with joy as I saw that one of the men was Mr. Bareck.

Mr. Bareck said a few words to the guard, and the guard quickly left the room. I greeted Mr. Bareck with a smile and a handshake and then I thanked him. I explained my situation to him, but he already knew what had happened. I was in a bad situation. Mr. B figured he could get me out of jail for five-hundred dollars. So I reached into my money belt without hesitation and counted out five one-hundred-dollar bills and then handed them to him. He stuffed the bills into his pocket and left the room without saying another word.

I thought I would be out of jail within a matter of minutes, so I began to clean myself up. But the minutes turned into hours. And I was beginning to get sick. I needed my morphine, and I needed it badly. Just when I thought it was hopeless, the cell door opened. I thought Mr. Bareck had taken my money and left me here to rot, but I quickly found out that wasn't the case. My dear friend, Mr. Bareck, had returned to get me out of jail.

As we walked out of the cell, the captain stood in front of me and bellowed, "You must leave the country because I can't promise this won't happen again!"

I promised the captain that I would leave the country in the near future.

"But one day, Captain, I will return to Kabul and visit my Afghan friends," I told him matter-of-factly.

"Yes, but with a good visa," he replied.

"Where is my monkey and when can I pick her up?" I asked the captain.

"I'm sorry, but your monkey is dead."

I was in shock. I couldn't believe what I had just heard. When I tried to get more information concerning her death, two big, burly policemen forcefully escorted me to the front door.

As Mr. Bareck and I walked away from the jail, another big, burly policeman came over and explained to me how my monkey had died. As he began telling me the story, a crowd of policemen gathered around and surrounded us. He explained to me that most of these same policemen had gathered in a circle and watched Chakila show off and do her tricks. Everyone laughed and enjoyed her act except for one policeman, who had taunted and teased her until she bit him on his hand. He retaliated by smashing the butt of his rifle against her small little body. She went flying across the room. The blow from the rifle butt had crushed her skull.

I was very angry. I couldn't believe what I was hearing. I was in total shock and disbelief. I wanted to know which man had killed her. I wanted to see if he had the guts to do it to me, but nobody would take responsibility for their hideous behavior. I even tried to bribe the informant with money, but he still refused to show me who the coward was. I wanted to retaliate and bust his skull and to hell with the consequences. I would worry about that if and when it happened.

Just as Mr. Bareck began to leave, another policeman came over and handed my bike to me. I thanked Mr. Bareck for his help as he walked away and then rode my bike back to my apartment.

During my bike ride, I decided to leave the country. But first, I would ask the director of the Peace Corps if he could help me with my visa. He had told me that if I ever needed his help not to hesitate to visit him, so that's what I decided to do. The next morning, I did just that.

I walked into the Peace Corps office, past the secretary, and into the director's office. Someone I didn't recognize and had never seen before was sitting in the director's chair.

"Excuse me. Is the director here?" I asked him.

He seemed somewhat startled by my question. He seemed stunned and in shock.

"What? I am the director," he replied.

"When did you become the director?" I asked in disbelief.

"I've been the director of the Peace Corps in Afghanistan for almost four years."

"Then who was the man I had been talking to, and what about Mr. Helms?"

"I really don't know what you're talking about, Robert."

"Then how do you know my name? I never told you."

"My secretary must have mentioned it," he retorted, as perspiration began dripping from his forehead—something was making him very nervous.

"I don't know what the hell is happening here, but I came here to ask for help. I helped you guys when you needed it, and now you're playing head games." With that said, I quickly turned and walked out of the room slamming the door behind me.

As I walked out in disgust, I thought about asking the American Embassy for help. I figured it couldn't hurt. All they could say was either yes or no. So I hailed a taxi and headed for the American Embassy. When I finally reached the place, I was greeted at the front door by two nasty and burly marine guards. They immediately threw me up against the wall and proceeded to body search my person and my shoulder bag. They were very rude and nasty and conducted themselves in a very unprofessional manner. They searched for illegal contraband and weapons. After taking their abuse for nearly ten minutes, they finally let me proceed into the consulate office. I had never been treated so unfairly in all my life, especially by my own countrymen.

I explained my situation to the consulate general, about the intelligence I had gathered to help our country and government, but he didn't seem very interested. He said that they couldn't help me, that it was my responsibility to acquire the appropriate visas. Seconds later, I was escorted out the front door.

I finally gave up and returned to my apartment and then went directly to my closet to retrieve my morphine kit. I needed a fix desperately. I wanted this rush to grab hold of my problems and suck them into my body, and it did. The rush was so intense that I nodded out and didn't awake until morning.

That morning, I decided to try something different, to find help in all the wrong places, before I paid a fifteen-thousand-dollar fine or ended up in jail for overstaying my visa by three and a half years.

I wanted to talk with my friend, Moktar, the freedom fighter. I thought that he might have an idea or a way to smuggle my person out of the country. Then I could get an entrance visa into Pakistan and come back to Afghanistan with a legal three-month entrance visa. That would give me enough time to sell my possessions and furniture or send them to America.

It was the end of December when I visited Moktar's place. I knew him and his friends smuggled goods to and from Afghanistan, mostly opium, which was traded for weapons for the Afghan "mujahedeen," or freedom fighters. So I explained my situation to him.

"Can you help me, Moktar?"

As I surmised, he had a friend who traveled with a small caravan that smuggled goods across the borders.

"It will be a very hard trip because the mountains could be very treacherous this time of year," Moktar replied.

"Moktar, I have no other choice. It's that or jail or a fine so large I would end up in jail anyway because I wouldn't be able to pay it."

So it was decided that I would follow a small caravan through the Hindu Kush mountains. It would take about three days and two nights.

"My friend, I will have all the information within three days," he said.

I returned home and waited patiently for Moktar's arrival. Finally, word came down that I was to meet Moktar at his place in two days and be there by nine o'clock in the morning. All I needed was a warm coat and two-hundred dollars for the use of the guide. They would provide anything else that was needed.

Moktar and I were to drive by taxi to a small town at the base of the Hindu Kush Mountains in the Nuristan province. Once we had reached the city, we were to meet the caravan outside a small canteen.

That day had finally arrived, and I met Moktar at the designated time. We rode a taxi all the way to our destination and arrived just after noon. It was fairly warm for this winter's day, and there was very little snow on the ground.

The caravan was all set to travel, and the leader was in a hurry to leave. They wanted to be at a certain spot by a certain time so they could bed down the donkeys, which were packed with many different goods to trade for automatic weapons.

Things seemed to go wrong from the start. A couple of the smugglers didn't want me near them and didn't trust me. So Moktar began arguing with one of them, which lasted for nearly ten minutes, until Moktar settled it. Before I knew what was happening, Moktar sucker punched the guy and hit him with such force the guy flew fifteen feet into the air across the stable grounds. Moktar had knocked the guy out. The poor guy lay there for over five minutes. Nobody even bothered to check if he was alive. They just walked around him as if he wasn't there. Nearly ten minutes later, the guy began to move. Moktar came over to me to give me a few more pointers.

"Bob, stay close to my friend, Mamad," Moktar told me.

"Which one is that?" I asked, trying to figure out which guy was his friend.

Moktar pointed to the guy he had just knocked for a loop. I was to stay next to him until we reached Pakistan, which should take approximately two days. But the weather could change in a snap. One minute it could be nice and clear and the next minute a blizzard could erupt.

I said goodbye to Moktar and then the caravan began to move out and slowly climb the steep mountain pass. The first couple of hours seemed to go as planned, until one of the donkeys near the front of the caravan became irritable and stubborn and decided that it didn't want to go any farther so he just stopped and sat on his behind. All of the donkeys that followed behind did the same. Now it seemed all of the donkeys wanted to rest.

One of the smugglers tried desperately to move the front donkey. If they could get him to stand, then the other donkeys would follow. But the donkey was stubborn and refused to budge. So more of the smugglers joined in and tried to get the donkey's attention. They kicked it, hit it with their hands, and then whacked it across its back with a two-foot piece of two-by-four. When that didn't work, they punched the donkey in the mouth, the gut, the head, and any other place they thought might move the stubborn animal. But the animal seemed impervious to the pain—or was just too stupid to know any better.

Nearly ten minutes of torture, and the donkey still stood its ground. Then one of the smugglers got so frustrated he tried to light the donkey's tail on fire with a cigarette lighter. But one of the other smugglers thought it was a bad idea and kicked the lighter out of his hand. I decided to intercede to see if I could help. I picked up the two-by-four and placed it between the donkey's legs directly under its belly. Then I asked one of the smugglers to grab hold of the stick and lift straight up. When he grabbed it, we lifted the donkey nearly three feet into the air. Then we dropped the two-by-four to the ground. The donkey decided to land on its hind legs instead of its hind end. That was all it took—a little American ingenuity.

Now the smugglers were happy. They even patted me on the back and thanked me. They seemed to warm up to me a little bit after that. The caravan was back in action. We were once again slowly climbing up the high mountain. The longer we walked, the steeper it got. This pass was steeper than the others. We had to trek up and over the mountain, not around it.

In many places along the pass were very, very narrow ledges. A few times, I didn't think some of the donkeys would make it. One time some of the earth gave way right under one of the smuggler's feet and nearly caused his death. We were nearly four-thousand feet up and had about twelve-thousand more to go. The trail had become very narrow, and now we were in a falling rock area.

The smugglers were worried about rockslides. The trail had become so narrow that many of the donkeys were rubbing their packs and sides against the rocky mountain. They seemed to be tiptoeing across the narrow ledge. One donkey, however, did manage to fall off the cliff, down into the black hole of the ravine, five thousand feet below. If all of the donkeys had been tied together, they all would have taken the plunge into the deep, dark ravine. It had sucked many of God's creations into the abyss. But we continued on as if nothing had happened.

One hour later, we ran into another obstacle. The trail had become so narrow that the packs had to be taken off the donkeys and carried by hand to a point where the trail was a little wider. We ended up carrying the packs nearly one hundred yards before we could repack the donkeys.

I was beginning to tire and needed a fix, but I didn't dare. I didn't want them to see me shooting up. I had to be very discreet. And just to be on the safe side, along with my kit, I had also brought an extra bottle of morphine. I wasn't sure when or where I would fix, but I knew it would be sooner rather than later.

The sun began to fall and night would soon be upon us. We still had at least an hour or two of sunlight. And the weather seemed to change as we walked higher and higher up the mountain. As the sun set the cold came upon us. The weather had changed in a matter of minutes—the wind so fierce it nearly blew me off the ledge and into the dark abyss. I was a nervous wreck. I couldn't look down. I was afraid I would fall to my death if I looked into that black hole.

There was just enough light left to make camp. We walked for another ten minutes until we came to a small clearing, an area of about twenty-five feet. Thousands of years ago, smugglers had carved out this part of the mountain so they could have room to camp and rest their animals. I was told we would rest here until morning. Some of the men began to build a fire, but there wasn't a tree around us anywhere. They had packed one donkey with firewood, so I figured the tents and sleeping bags were also packed away.

I bided my time trying not to get in the way of my new friends. I didn't want to make anyone angry. I was under their control. I worried that if I made them angry they would throw me off the mountain into the black hole to my death. So I didn't want to make any waves. I just stayed away until they started a fire, and then walked over and sat near it. The smugglers paid absolutely no attention to me. They acted as if I wasn't there. But I didn't let it bother me. I just waited, wondering when they were going to put up the tents.

The sun was almost gone and the wind blew wildly, nearly blowing out the fire, and the temperature had dropped drastically. Night was now upon us, and the tents still had not been put up. All of the smugglers were sitting around the fire waiting to eat the stew that was warming over the fire.

As we waited for dinner, some of the men gave the donkeys oats and water. That was the first time that day that the animals had been fed and watered. By the time the animals had their packs removed, dinner was ready.

I was given a cup of hot tea and a small plastic bowl filled with hot stew, but no kitchen utensils. So I used my fingers as a fork and devoured the tasty food within minutes, which warmed my insides but the rest of my body was still cold. I had only brought what I had worn—my heavy leather coat and my light cotton blanket, which was worn over my coat. Plus, I had my long johns on under my Afghan clothes. I hadn't brought a sleeping bag or anything else because my guide was supposed to supply it. So I decided to get brave and speak up.

"When are you guys going to put up the tents so we can sleep?" I asked nobody in particular.

They looked at me as though I was crazy. They didn't know what I was talking about.

"We don't have any tents or sleeping bags," said Mamad. "We just sleep near the fire under our blankets."

Just as he was explaining the situation, the weather changed again. It had become even windier and much colder. It seemed the temperature had just dropped twenty degrees within ten seconds. So cold, in fact, that snowflakes began to trickle down onto the ground.

But the Afghans seemed oblivious to the weather. Hell, none of them even wore socks, only thick black rubber shoes. They each sat cross-legged two feet from the fire. None of them had sleeping bags or even heavy blankets. I was in shock. I just couldn't believe they could sit there and not feel the cold. *What are they,* I thought to myself, *Buddhist monks?*

It was about 10 P.M. and the temperature was dropping fast. It was about thirty degrees, but the wind had become much stronger and the snow began falling faster and faster, and within just a few minutes nearly half an inch of snow had accumulated on the ground. And within twenty minutes, the temperature had dropped another ten degrees. But the wind chill factor made the temperature around five above.

The fire was still raging, but it didn't keep me warm. I wanted to get right into it. The Afghans still seemed oblivious to our hazardous situation. The wind and snow was nearly putting the fire out. I was damn near frozen and sick, and getting sicker by the minute. I needed a fix and needed it now. But how would I cook my morphine? The snow and wind wouldn't allow it, unless I put the blanket over my head to keep the wind and snow out. But it was useless. I was too frozen to do anything and didn't want to take my hands out of my pockets.

Now the fire was nearly out but nobody moved to add wood to it to keep it going. They just sat as though they were in a trance—either that or they were already frozen and dead. I couldn't tell. A big gust of wind finally blew out the fire and the smugglers still didn't move.

"Fix the fire!" I yelled to the men in the dark.

"We will fix it tomorrow," said Mamad.

Even the donkeys were heehawing and making loud crying sounds. They were miserable, too. I had had enough and couldn't take it any longer. I was sick, frozen, wet, and miserable. And I didn't care about getting a visa anymore. I just wanted to be in my warm bed.

The snow was coming down so fast and thick I couldn't see a foot in front of me. It also began to drizzle, and the snow began to stick to my face and clothing. I begged the guide to take me back down the mountain. I pleaded with him and even tried to bribe him. But he refused. He had to stay with the caravan. He tried to talk me into staying there.

"Everything will soon blow over," said Mamad. "It will only last for an hour or so. It would be too dangerous to walk this narrow ledge in the dark night and hazardous weather."

I didn't believe him. I wanted to go back. I pleaded with him again to take me back to the city or even help me part of the way down the mountain. He still adamantly refused. I couldn't wait any longer and begged for help from the guys around the campfire. But they didn't answer me and I couldn't see them.

The snow was coming down so fast that it blinded me. So I decided to try it on my own, even though I had no flashlight—or anything else for that matter—to help me see my way. I didn't know if I would make it or not, but I was willing to die trying. There was an inch of snow on the ground already. And the wind was so fierce that it went right through me and the light rain had turned into rock-hard hail. It nearly cut the skin as it pelted my face. It felt as if a thousand small needles were piercing my face all at once.

I began my trek back down the mountain. My whole body went numb from the cold and from the shock of this misadventure. As the drizzly, wet snow came down, the wind blew it into my eyes and blinded me. I literally had to keep my eyes closed and walk down the mountain like a blind man. I had to keep my arm and body against the side of the mountain so I wouldn't fall off the narrow ledge into oblivion. I stayed so close to the mountainside I was stuck to it like a magnet on a refrigerator.

Even though I was freezing and worried about falling off the ledge into the black hole five-thousand feet below I continued forward, always thinking about my warm bed. But reality confronted me the longer I walked in this miserable weather.

An hour into my trek, my clothes were completely soaked through and the snow stuck to my body. I looked like the Abominable Snowman. I could honestly understand how someone could see an Abominable Snowman under these circumstances.

My fear had left my body and so did my feeling. The cold began to hurt. Each step I took was unbearable. I tried to walk very gingerly, but it still didn't help. My whole body was aching. Taking ten steps seemed like I had walked a mile. I had an extra twenty-five pounds of weight to carry due to all the snow sticking to my frozen clothes, and my flesh was becoming chaffed from rubbing against them. I wanted to be in my warm bed so badly that I began to pray to God to get me out of this hell.

The snow was so thick and coming down so fast I couldn't see, and the snow clouds covered any light from any stars that were out. I just knew I was in a blizzard, and if I didn't get down the mountain in a hurry, the vultures would have some good white meat to eat when I thawed out.

My body was becoming so numb and stiff that I wanted to stop to rest, and my feet were frozen and very sore. I must have walked for more than three hours. But I wasn't sure. I was so delirious I was oblivious to the world. I wondered why I was still alive. But I refused to give up and just pushed ahead. My body rubbed up against the rock hard mountain while my feet shuffled slowly down the steep mountain pass along the narrow ledge.

I prayed constantly just to get back safely. I didn't know how much longer I had to go to reach the base of the mountain, or even if I had passed that very narrow ledge yet. Actually, my mind was also numb and frozen. I wasn't thinking very clearly, if at all. It was as if I had been up for seventy-two hours. My mind and body were burnt out. I longed to be in my warm bed, feeling a warm morphine rush near a warm fire.

I continued forward and downward. I wondered if the Afghan smugglers from the caravan were still sitting around the campfire, freezing, or if they had started the fire again. If they hadn't and didn't find shelter, I was sure they would be frozen by morning.

I soon found myself worrying about my own life. I was still blinded by the snow, and the weight of it on my body had almost doubled. It was like carrying a hundred-pound backpack. My body and walking had become very stiff. I was so cold that I had completely forgotten about my morphine addiction.

Finally, I noticed light coming over the mountain. It was the sun. The snow was still coming down hard, but as I descended the mountain, it began to dissipate. Two hours after I saw the first light of day, and nearly wearing a hole in my leather coat from leaning up and rubbing against the mountainside, I was finally at the base of the mountain. I was at the same place where we had started our climb.

I walked to the nearest restaurant and tried to dry out. I sat next to the wood stove and tried to shake off the snow that had stuck to my body, but it wouldn't shake off. I had to break it off in chunks. Some pieces were over a half-inch thick. I was a walking snowman. My clothes were completely soaked, and I was soaked to the bones. It would take two hours for me to thaw out, so I decided to dry out while riding back to Kabul.

I wanted to get back to my apartment so badly that I rented a taxi to take me there. I wanted to get back as fast as I could. The taxi driver turned up the heat and also wrapped me in two thick blankets. That still didn't keep me warm. I shivered and sneezed all throughout the three-hour ride to Kabul.

Finally, we had reached my apartment complex. I paid the taxi driver with an American fifty-dollar bill and hopped out of his taxi. Then I flew up the three flights of stairs to my apartment, unlocked the door, and went directly to my bedroom where I turned on the electric heater and quickly peeled out of my wet clothes. I was drenched to the bones and completely soaked from my head to my toes. My feet felt as if I had frostbite.

I put on my robe and then reached into my shoulder bag and pulled out my bottle of morphine and my syringe. I put seven tabs into the spoon. I wanted to forget all my troubles and heat up my body from the inside out.

While cooking the morphine, I thought how lucky I had been to get through that horrendous experience alive. I thanked God for leading the way and lighting the path. Then I fixed my "do." The hot, tingly rush warmed and soothed my wounded body. My insides were on fire, so I lay back to relax. Finally, I began to thaw out.

Just as I began to close my eyes to get some rest, I heard someone knocking at my door. Then I heard Aslam's voice. He seemed quite agitated, so I let him into the apartment.

"Bob, the police have been to the apartment building looking for you," he said. "You have ten days to leave the country, or they will come back and arrest you."

Now I was beginning to worry—I really had to get out of the country. What was I to do?

"Thank you for telling me, Aslam. Tell them I left the country if they come back again." Then I handed him a one-hundred Afghani bill. It was payment for his trouble.

Aslam was a very good friend of mine. He treated me as a brother. After he left the apartment, I went back into the bedroom to lie down and think about what I needed to do.

So many questions were running through my mind. Should I sell my possessions, or should I start sending them to America? But why send them to America if I wasn't going to return there? And did I have enough money to pay the outlandish fine that the Afghan government would surely inflict on me, or would they throw me in prison anyway? I was thinking so hard that my head began to ache. Then I thought about Moktar again. Maybe he had another way or idea to get me out of the country other than going through the mountains.

I quickly dressed in dry, warm clothes and left my apartment. Then I boarded a taxi and headed to Moktar's house. Ten minutes later, I was there. Luckily, Moktar was at home. If I had waited one more day he'd have been in Kandahar visiting his mother.

Moktar was surprised to see me. He thought I would have been in Pakistan by now or nearly there. I explained my situation to him and he listened very intently. I told him how I had nearly frozen and fallen to my death, but Moktar couldn't understand why I'd had so much trouble. He blamed the weather for all the problems I'd had. However, he said he could help me again.

"Bob, I know another man who is leaving for Pakistan in two days," he said. "He smuggles goods across the border using his car. He has done this many times and pays the border guards to let him pass without any hassles."

"Moktar, how much money is this going to cost me this time?"

"The same amount as before: two-hundred American dollars."

"Will it work this time?"

"I would have suggested him before but he wasn't in town then. He never has any problems with the customs people."

"Well, I don't really have any other choice, unless you know someone that will give me an Afghan visa?" I was hoping he had a friend in this new government who could help me.

"I'm sorry, Bob. This government wants to kill me, if they ever catch me."

"Moktar, I must leave within the next few days."

"Bob, my friend is leaving for Pakistan in two days. You will have to hide in the trunk of his car. We will meet you at your apartment around ten o'clock in the morning."

"All right, I'll see you in two days, and I'll give you the money at the apartment."

I left Moktar's place and then headed for my apartment. The minute I returned, I went into my bedroom and fixed one more time before I nodded off to sleep.

The next day, Fred stopped by my apartment. He had heard that I was leaving the country and wanted to see if I wanted to sell my bike, stereo, and tapes. He didn't want my complete stereo system, only my tape player, the two small speakers, and the smaller box of cassette tapes. That box only held two-hundred tapes, but each tape had two or three different albums professionally dubbed on them. Fred gave me a fair price and walked away with everything he wanted.

I was sad to see my kingdom fall, but there was nothing I could do. If the police came back to my apartment, I could lose everything anyway, including my life.

The next day, while at the post office, I picked up two letters addressed to me. One was from my mother concerning my great-uncle, and that's what I called him—Uncle. He had died a few weeks earlier. I was very saddened by this bad news. I had really loved him. He had come from the old country to start a new family. All of his family and relatives also died in the holocaust caused by the Ottoman Empire. Now I knew I would eventually return to America, at least for a visit. I didn't want any more of my Armenian relatives dying without being there to pay my respects.

I had also received a letter from Becky. She wrote that she and Pat had become frightened and nervous at the Iranian border and threw all the hash oil away because the border guards gave them one chance to get rid of their dope or face jail time and possibly even execution. They were told that their blood pressure would be taken, and if it was higher than normal because of nervousness, the customs officials would have probable cause to search them. Then they would be taken into a little room and strip-searched. If any illegal contraband was found in their possession, they would have to suffer the consequences. So they decided to toss their illegal drugs into a trash can before they were searched.

I didn't believe what they had written in their letter. However, if you looked nervous and suspicious, you would get busted. That's the trick to smuggling.

So I wrote to them that they had ripped me off again. I was very angry. I had helped them so much and this was how they repaid me. They stabbed me in the back again. *What a jerk I was,* I thought to myself.

Now I had decided that I would send the rest of my belongings to America as soon as I came back from Pakistan. I was anxious to try my hand once again and sneak out of the country. I wasn't making any money sending hash. Either Mr. Bareck was screwing me or my friends were screwing me. But I figured they both were equally to blame. Well, I put all that out of my mind to concentrate on my new project.

The two days passed very quickly. Moktar and his friend were at my apartment at precisely ten that morning. As Moktar introduced me to his friend, Abdullah, I thought I had seen this man before but couldn't put my finger on it. I had a short conversation with him, and he told me some of his background.

"Actually, I am from Pashtunistan and don't need a visa to go to and from Pakistan or Afghanistan," said Abdullah. "I have hidden people in my trunk four times before and never had any trouble. This new government is very strict. It is trying to make the Pashtunistans pay a toll to cross into Afghanistan and also to leave. Our people are very angry with this new Afghan government. But don't worry, nothing will go wrong."

"Well, let's get going," I told him anxiously.

I paid Moktar with two one-hundred dollar bills. My money was slowly dwindling. If this didn't work, I didn't know what I would do.

As we left my apartment and walked down the three flights of stairs to the street below, Moktar talked about what had happened the night I decided to leave the caravan.

"As the men sat near the fire an avalanche swallowed them up. All of the animals and all but three of the men were killed. It was Allah's work," said Moktar.

I was in total shock—and very lucky to be alive.

A minute later, Moktar boarded the bus and I got into Abdullah's car—a beautiful and new fifty-thousand dollar Mercedes sedan. I would ride in the passenger seat until we reached Jalalabad, more than three hours away, then I would hide in the trunk.

An hour into the trip, I remembered where I had seen this guy. He was the one Carol hooked up with in Pakistan. She picked up the suitcases from him. I didn't say anything to him about it. I didn't want to create any more problems than necessary.

When we were just a few miles away from the Afghan-Pashtunistan border, Abdullah stopped his car and I stowed away in the trunk. It had a sunken area near the back seat. As I lay there, he covered me over with carpets and other goods. I had a very hard time breathing due to my bad sinuses and soon became claustrophobic. I wanted to get out of that trunk so badly I could taste it. I yelled a few times, "Stop the car" and "Let me out to breathe," but Abdullah either couldn't hear me or just ignored me. But a few minutes later, I heard his voice.

"Bob, be very quiet and still. We are coming up to the border checkpoint. We are twenty feet away."

I was sweating and very nervous. In fact, I thought I would piss my pants. And I was having a very hard time being still. Then I began to pray. Just then, I heard the border guards tell Abdullah to drive to the checkpoint and stop the car. Abdullah tried to argue with them, but they ignored his pleas and ordered him to follow them. I was beginning to get bad vibes. A minute later, Abdullah's car came to a sudden stop and then the guard ordered him to shut off the car's engine. Then Abdullah was asked many questions, but I couldn't make out what was being said. The two men argued back and forth for a few minutes, then the talking became louder and louder. Suddenly, something happened. It sounded like Abdullah was being pulled out of the car.

Then there was more yelling and screaming. I could make out pieces of the conversation. They were calling Abdullah a spy or traitor, something of that nature. Then I heard someone inside the car, searching it. My body began shaking uncontrollably. I even started pissing in my pants, and once I started, I couldn't hold it back. Then my breathing became very shallow and fast. I felt as if I was going to pass out. I heard the car doors shut. For a short second, I thought it was over—that is, until I heard the trunk door pop open. That's when I knew I was in big trouble.

I heard them searching the trunk. Soon after, I felt the butt of a rifle pounding me. They had discovered my frightened and shaking body. Within a few minutes, soldiers were pulling me out of the trunk with their weapons pointing directly at my head. They grabbed me very forcefully and threw me next to Abdullah. His face was full of blood. They yelled at us to kneel down on the ground. When Abdullah didn't move fast enough, one of the soldiers hit him in the back of the head with his rifle butt and Abdullah fell to the ground. I tried to speak to the soldier, but I was also hit with the butt of his rifle, which knocked me to the ground, too. All during this time, a crowd gathered around us. I kept yelling for someone to help us, but it fell on deaf ears. Nobody would respond.

Poor Abdullah, he was trying to speak but his face was so mangled and swollen his words were incomprehensible. The soldiers seemed very angry.

"You are spies and no one can help you," yelled a soldier.

The soldiers had their rifles pointed directly at our bodies and heads. I begged and pleaded with them as tears rolled down my eyes.

"Please, let us go," I whined. But they ignored me. So I shouted to them in anger, "I am an American and want to speak to my embassy!"

The soldiers just sneered and laughed at us. And at that moment, one of the rifles misfired. Abdullah's head exploded with blood and brain matter splattering everywhere, mostly all over the side of my face, and the bullet whizzed past my head and into Abdullah's car door. Abdullah slumped forward and lay on the ground shivering and wiggling in his own blood. Three quarters of his head and face had been blown off. I immediately began to regurgitate. I expected to be next. I did my best to plead my case. But again, they ignored me.

And then I screamed, "I'm not a spy! All I wanted was a visa!"

Just as one of the soldiers began to taunt me, another soldier kicked at the body lying on the ground and then knelt down and searched the deceased's pants pockets. As my antagonist sneered directly into my face and spit on me, his superior came out from his office and scolded him and the other men.

"You men carry the body away and clean up this mess," shouted the officer. "Then take the American into my office and interrogate him!"

I was relieved and praised the man. "Thank you for not letting them kill me. I'm an American."

The Afghan officer stopped in his tracks, turned, and slapped me hard across the face.

"Shut your mouth and speak when spoken to," he bellowed.

Then the soldiers proceeded to drag me into the customs office and then into a small, dirty room. *Here I am again,* I thought to myself, *back in jail.* I wondered if my luck would ever change from bad to good.

Within an hour, two soldiers came into the room and body searched me. They found and took my money belt and my morphine kit and then left. And then, two hours later, the soldiers returned. However, this time it was two different soldiers: one was the officer who had stopped the slaughter and the other, his superior. They started off being very nice to me and offered me cigarettes and tea. They asked if I wanted a doctor to check my wounds. I rejected the doctor but took the tea and cigarettes.

When I asked to see my ambassador, they became very angry. They wanted me to answer their questions but didn't want me to ask any. They interrogated me for about an hour before they left the room in disgust. They didn't get the answers they wanted. I knew, however, that they would interrogate me again. I worried that they would beat me or even kill me.

My anxiety grew by the minute. I didn't know what to expect. I just wanted to stay alive. But I was getting sicker by the minute. And my morphine kept calling me. My addiction began to gnaw at my insides and my head began pounding. I began to sweat profusely and couldn't shake it. But my interrogators returned, this time acting much tougher. Luckily for me, their questions took my mind off of my narcotic hunger—that is, until one of them threw my morphine kit on the table.

"American, are you a junkie or a spy?" asked the lower-ranking officer in his best broken English.

I didn't say a word, and that seemed to make them even madder. When I didn't answer their question, the man slapped me so hard I flew out of my chair onto the floor. When I picked myself up, I stared into their eyes and gave them an answer.

"I have stomach cancer, and I have to take daily injections for the pain," I lied, not knowing if they believed me, but I was desperate to try anything. "I want to speak with my ambassador!"

"We are the law here," boasted the higher-ranking officer.

I didn't know how to get through to these guys, so I started telling them names of my Afghan friends who worked in the Afghan government. I mentioned Mr. Bareck's name, Mr. Kazamie's name, and also the king's son's name. I mentioned anyone's name I could think of who worked or had worked in the Afghan government. That seemed to make a difference. They stopped talking to me and started talking amongst themselves. They left the room once again but left my morphine kit and money belt on the table in front of me. Five minutes later, one of the soldiers brought in my shoulder bag and then abruptly left the room.

I sat for more than five hours in the interrogating room waiting for my interrogators to return. And the money belt and morphine were still sitting in front of me. I dared not touch them in fear of retaliation from my accusers. I just sat nervously awaiting my fate. But then six armed soldiers burst into the room. One of them picked up my shoulder bag from the table and threw it at me.

"Pick up your things and follow me," snapped the officer who had saved me from being shot.

I quickly put on my money belt without checking its contents. And then I put the morphine kit into my bag and then threw the bag over my shoulder.

My face and head were still covered in Abdullah's blood. And I still had a terrible headache from being hit with the rifle butt. But that was of little consequence as the soldiers surrounded me and escorted me out of the building to an army truck.

They helped me up into the back of the truck, which was used to transport army personnel. I sat all the way toward the front while three soldiers sat next to me and three across from me, all the while pointing their rifles at me during the whole four-hour trip. We rode all the way to Kabul without saying a word, and then the truck pulled into the main prison and stopped.

I had returned to Kabul without my visa and with a very bad headache. I was very frightened and nervous not knowing what was going to happen. Then I was ordered out of the truck, and when I didn't move fast enough, one of the soldiers pushed me out and I fell to the ground. When I stood up, I was immediately grabbed by one of the soldiers as if I was going to escape. He held onto me until we entered the dark and dirty prison.

But we had to wait until one of the prison guards helped us and escorted us to one of the bleaker jail cells. We walked for five minutes down a long, narrow, dark, desolate, and stinking hallway. There were no bars or windows, and I couldn't see any other prisoners. As I shuffled along, I felt very sick to my stomach. Finally, the guard stopped in front of a door. Once he unlocked it, I was shoved into the dark room. It was a very old and dirty four-by-six-foot cell and smelled of death. Then the heavy door was shut and locked.

I was alone, but I still had my shoulder bag and money belt and my morphine. I lit a match and looked around my new digs. It contained a pitcher of water, a tin cup for drinking, a straw mat that was used for the bed and covered a large portion of the dirt floor, and a pail sitting in the far corner that was used for the toilet. That was it—no table, chair, or sink, and everything sat on the dirt floor, including me.

I didn't understand what was going on, and I didn't understand why my jailers let me keep my morphine. I expected them to burst into my cell any minute and beat me. I began thinking the worst. Then it finally hit me—I realized I was in big trouble.

As I became more aware of my situation, I became nervous and nauseated. I was very weak from not doing any morphine. I needed a fix, and I needed it badly. I had everything I needed to re-energize my body—my morphine kit, one bottle of morphine, and water. So I decided to get brave and fix my favorite narcotic. I figured all they could do was burst in and break my arms. But I decided to take a chance anyway.

My addiction was eating my insides out. I was worried more about my morphine habit than the fix I was in. I was shaking so badly, I was afraid I would shake the morphine out of the spoon. I didn't know if I could hold the spoon over the flame without spilling its contents all over the floor. But somehow, I managed.

Every second I cooked the morphine, I expected my captors to burst in, but it never happened. After injecting my "do," I lay back on the thin straw mat as the rush slowly flowed through my veins. I no longer felt my wet and bloody clothes, which stuck to my worn-out and wounded body. Within a few minutes, I became rejuvenated and re-energized.

But my anxiety grew even worse, not knowing what lay ahead. So I decided to cut back on my injections and do as little morphine each day as possible. I only had one bottle, and it had to last. I didn't know how long I was going to be in this dirty, germ-infested cell.

I also decided to hide the bottle of morphine before the guards decided to take it from me. I hid it in the safest place I knew—my rectum. I pushed the small glass bottle up as far as it would go. And once it was inside of me, I couldn't really feel it. It wasn't uncomfortable at all. Once that chore was accomplished, I tried to relax on the straw mat. Oh, how I wanted to be in my warm bed.

As I tried to get comfortable, I began to hear screams and moans from an inmate in one of the other cells. It sounded as if the guards were killing him. This lasted for more than ten minutes. I wondered when it would be my turn. I prayed I would get out of this terrible situation somehow. I waited for what seemed like days for someone to interrogate me. I had no sense of time, only by the number of injections I did.

The only light that came into my cell was from the flame of the match when I cooked my morphine. I only had a quarter of the bottle left. Once that was gone, I would be in deep trouble and probably end up dying in here from morphine withdrawal. I worried about that constantly.

The screams and moans continued day after day, and each day they became louder. I figured it was only a matter of time before they came to my cell. That day finally came.

I had just finished my bottle of morphine when the door to my cell burst open. Two very large mean-looking guards entered the room. They each grabbed me by an arm and carried me out of the cell. As my eyes focused to the dim light in the hallway, I asked them where they were taking me. But they didn't answer. For all I knew, they could be taking me to my execution.

A few minutes later, I had my answer when I was taken into a small office. They sat me in a chair and guarded me on either side. We waited quietly until a high-ranking Afghan military officer came into the room and sat behind the desk. I didn't know what rank he was, but by the way the guards respected him, I figured he was probably a general. He sat silently looking over some paperwork for more than ten minutes before he looked up and stared deep into my eyes.

I was very nervous, not knowing what to expect. When he began to speak, I couldn't understand him. He was speaking Pashtu and I could only understand a few words, so he decided to have one of the guards bring in an interpreter.

The interpreter introduced himself to me in English.

"This is a very serious matter," said the interpreter.

"I want to speak with my embassy," I demanded. But again I was refused.

"We are the law here," repeated the military official in Pashtu.

Those few words I *could* understand.

I was certain that I wouldn't be beaten as long as the interpreter was with me. And then, after the military official and interpreter conversed, the interpreter explained the situation to me.

"You are being charged with a very heinous crime of spying for a foreign government," he explained. "You are in a very serious predicament. You may be given life in prison or possibly even executed."

"I'm not a spy," I cried out. "I'm an American tourist! I just wanted to get an Afghan visa in Pakistan so I could come back into this country legally. I know I did a stupid thing, but I'm no spy. Can't I just pay a fine?"

The interpreter just shrugged his shoulders and shook his head, disgusted.

"You don't ask the questions, we do," said the military official through my interpreter.

All the questions directed to me by the military official were then asked by the interpreter, and then my answers were repeated to the official through my interpreter.

"I should be able to have my embassy defend me," I begged.

"We are the law here. The only people you will talk with are us," said the military official. His eyes seemed to look right through me.

"It's my right to be defended by my embassy," I pleaded with him.

But my pleas fell on deaf ears. My begging and pleading only made things worse.

"You have no rights here," said the military official. "This case is beyond my expertise. You will have to see my superior."

My interpreter and I waited another thirty minutes in the hallway before armed guards escorted us to a different building. We had to go outside and across the courtyard to a beautiful and exquisite marble building, which was built like a palace. This building was made from rare marble and stone, held up by giant marble pillars. It looked as though it had been built for a king.

As we walked into the lobby I began to tell the interpreter about my Afghan friends who worked for the Afghan government.

"Be silent! I will get the information from you if and when I need it," barked the interpreter.

I mumbled to myself, and he slapped me in the back of the head.

"Please don't hit me," I pleaded.

"Be quiet and follow me," he snapped, as we walked down a long hallway to a large office, where a man was sitting behind a big desk.

"What are we doing here?" I asked him.

"We have to see a judge," he replied. "Now be quiet, and only speak when spoken to."

I stood and waited while my interpreter walked up and spoke to the man behind the desk. I was not allowed to speak, only to listen. And after listening to the interpreter explain my situation to this judge, we again left the room and went to another. This time it was a large courtroom. And the same judge we had just spoken with was now sitting behind a big desk in a colorful, flowing robe.

The interpreter stood up and again explained my situation to him. After listening to the story, the judge began to ask me a few questions, through my interpreter, concerning my predicament. I tried to answer them, but I was so nervous and shaking so badly, I fainted and fell to the floor, hitting my head. And at that instant, I awakened. After a few minutes, I was able to stand, but only with the help of two armed guards. They stood on each side of me, with each man holding onto an arm. Now I was ready to answer the judge's questions, or should I say the interpreter's. The judge asked the interpreter a question in Farsi, and the interpreter repeated it to me in English.

"Where are you from?" the judge asked through the interpreter.

"America," I answered.

The judge stared at me with such hatred in his heart that his cold stare went right through me. I felt a cold shiver go through my body. If eyes could kill, I would be dead. Then the judge asked the interpreter another question and the interpreter, again, repeated it to me.

"Are you a spy for America?" asked my interpreter. I shook my head no. "Speak up!" he roared.

"No, I am not a spy. I am a tourist. At one time I wanted to spend the rest of my life in this country."

As the judge spoke to the interpreter, the interpreter spoke to me simultaneously. All the words seemed to be jumbled. I had a very hard time understanding what was being said, and all the questions were asked in this fashion.

"Tell the judge what happened and why you are here," said the interpreter. "Tell him how you got into this terrible situation and how you got involved with the traitor who was killed."

I was so nervous I had a hard time speaking. My voice stuttered and cracked, but somehow I managed to tell my story.

"I was arrested at the border. I was being taken out of the country in the trunk of a friend's car. My visa was long overdue, and I was trying to get a legitimate Afghan visa so I could come back legally."

"Where did you meet the driver?"

I didn't want to tell them the real story and possibly get Moktar into trouble, so I lied.

"I met the driver in a tea shop. He overheard a conversation I was having with another tourist, when he came over to my table and introduced himself."

"What did this man say to you?"

"He said he could help me by hiding me in the trunk of his car. He had taken four other people to Pakistan this way and never had trouble at customs."

"Why didn't you go to the ministry to update your visa?"

I explained to him that I thought I would have been thrown into jail if I had tried to leave through regular channels, adding, "My visa had been expired for more than three years. My Afghan friends told me I would have to pay many thousands of dollars in fines if I tried to leave legally."

"So you tried to leave illegally," he retorted.

"Yes. I paid that driver two hundred dollars, and he agreed to take me out of Afghanistan. That's it. I'm not a spy. At one time, I wanted to live in Kabul forever. I didn't want to get caught without having the proper visas, especially with the new government. So what happens? I end up in jail, anyway."

"What Afghan friends are you talking about?" he asked me.

I told him I had many friends who worked in the Afghan government. Just then, I thought I saw a twinkle in the judge's eyes. I mentioned the names of a few friends who worked in the hierarchy of the Afghan government. When I mentioned Mr. Bareck's name, he seemed to become interested. And then, to my surprise, he talked to me in perfect English.

"Mr. Bareck is your friend? Mr. Bareck of the post department?" asked the judge.

"Yes, he is my best friend. I am godfather to his son. Please find Mr. Bareck. He will verify my story and tell you I'm not a spy."

Then something strange happened. The judge spoke to my interpreter, and the next thing I knew the court was in recess. We were pushed out into the hallway to wait. Neither the interpreter nor I knew what was going on. The interpreter thought that the judge just needed to empty his bladder.

We waited and waited. Nearly two hours had passed, and we were still waiting. The two armed guards would not let me go anywhere. I had to sit patiently and be silent. I was still in very serious trouble. And I was beginning to feel the symptoms of withdrawal from my morphine addiction. It was time for another fix. But I was completely out.

If I had to stay another night in prison, I was going to be a very sick person. I tried not to think about it. I tried to put it out of my mind, but the morphine still called to me. It controlled my body and mind.

Finally, after a three-hour wait, I was escorted into the courtroom. Actually, the two burly armed guards were pushing me into it. They didn't like me too much.

To my surprise, when the judge entered the courtroom another person followed him. It was my good friend, Mr. Bareck. Mr. B and I acknowledged each other and then he went and stood in front of the judge's bench next to my interpreter. I was very happy to see my good friend. If anyone could help me, it was Mr. B. He had already saved me once from the police. Now I was hoping he could do it again.

As court came into session, Mr. Bareck and the judge began conversing.

I tried to get my interpreter's attention, but he refused to look in my direction. I didn't want to speak up and interrupt the judge, so I just kept quiet and waited. A few minutes later, the judge began to speak to the interpreter and then to me.

"Thanks to your good friend, Mr. Bareck, he has saved your life," said the judge. Just then, I thought I would be freed once court was adjourned. But my hopes were shattered with his next sentence. "You will not be executed."

I couldn't believe what the judge had just said. My stomach growled and became tied up in knots. My whole body began to cramp up and my head began to spin. I thought I was going to faint again. The guards seemed to sense my knees buckling and held me up. The way the judge was talking now, I thought I was going to be in jail for the rest of my life. He continued to lecture me, and after ten minutes, he was ready to give his decision. The guards held onto my arms very tightly, expecting me to erupt in anger. But everyone was surprised when the judge read the verdict. The sentence was unexpected.

"You will not be jailed, only fined," said the judge. "Even though the driver was shot and killed, the evidence showed that the death was accidental due to a soldier's rifle accidentally misfiring.

Although the crime of spying could not be totally verified, it is the finding of this court that you be fined fifteen-thousand dollars and given four days to leave the country, never to return. You may pay the fine on the day you depart our beautiful city. However, if you can't pay the fine then you will be incarcerated until you can." With that said, court was adjourned.

I also had to pay the interpreter almost one-hundred dollars for his work.

I would not have to go back to jail, but now I had to leave the country in four days. I was still very happy. I was also very lucky Mr. Bareck was my friend. Mr. Bareck walked over and shook my hand.

"Thank you very much, Mr. Bareck, for saving my life," I said. "Come over to my apartment later." Then we hugged just before I was led away by the guards.

Well, at least I was given four days to pay the fine, and I could pay it on the day I was leaving. But if I were still in the city after four days, then I would be thrown into jail. And if I didn't pay the fine, I would also be thrown in jail. But right now, all I was thinking about was getting back to the apartment and fixing my morphine.

The guards quickly escorted me out of the building and then literally pushed me out into the street, yelling, "And get out of our country!"

I ran down the street as fast as I could. But I tired quickly from exhaustion, so I rented a taxi to take me to my apartment. During my ride, I tried to figure out what I was going to do next. I had less than four days to get out of Afghanistan. My kingdom continued crumbling. It was coming down fast, and there was nothing I could do about it.

Five minutes later, I had entered my apartment and then went directly to my bedroom closet. I brought out a new bottle of morphine and a new syringe. I couldn't wait to feel that hot, tingly, euphoric narcotic rush flow through my body. I could finally relax and not worry about my problems, at least for a few minutes. I fixed ten tablets. And within ten minutes, I was doing another spoonful. I wanted to be totally numb and forget any and all problems I had. I wanted my head to be totally *tabula rosa.* I fell asleep thinking about my future.

I awoke early the next morning. I had only three days to evacuate my home and friends. But I had many chores to do before I could leave Kabul. The first was to visit the post office to pick up my mail and then to the bank to pick up any money I might have. Then I would visit the pharmacy and buy about ten bottles of morphine. I needed it for my trip, just in case I couldn't buy it in India. I didn't want to go through any more withdrawals. I also had to buy a plane ticket, because I didn't have enough time to do all my chores and then take overland transportation to another country. And last but not least, I needed to send many of my personal possessions to America.

But first, I had to sell my furniture and appliances. I would use that money to send my possessions to America. I had more than enough money to send them, but once I had paid my fine, I would have little money left over. So any money I made selling my possessions would be needed, for one, to pay a month's rent and my electric bill. Then I hoped to make a deal with my landlord. I would give him my electric water heater and the linoleum in exchange for the money I owed. That still left me with many things to do.

I left my apartment and hired a taxi to take me to the places I needed to go. After visiting the post office and bank, I stopped at the pharmacy to say goodbye to the Devil and buy my much-needed supply of morphine. I also bought an expensive cigar, which was sold in a plastic tube. I needed that tube to put the morphine tabs into. Then it would be shoved up my rectum to hide them from customs. I also stopped by the shoe store to buy a nice pair of handmade dress shoes to wear on the plane, with a few hundred grams of hash added to them, and then pick them up when they were finished.

When I had completed those few chores, I went to speak with the disco owner about buying some of my personal possessions. The disco was closed, but as I looked through the front window I saw the owner inside cleaning up. The front door wasn't locked, so I let myself in and walked up to him.

"Hello, my friend," I said. "I came to ask if you wanted to buy my stereo and cassette tapes…or any furniture or appliances."

"But why, Bob?" asked the disco owner.

"I am leaving Kabul in a few days, so I want to sell some of my things."

I could tell he was saddened by my news and told me he would stop by my apartment within the next few hours to talk about it.

Once I had spoken with him, I went to the Peace Corps office to look for Fred to tell him I was leaving Kabul for good and to say goodbye. But he wasn't there, so I left a note in his mailbox explaining my situation. Then I returned to the apartment to pack my clothes and package the stuff I wanted to send back to America. I also sent Aslam out to speak with the landlord concerning my offer. I had many things going on at once.

I was very busy for the next three days. I didn't have any time to relax. When I finished one chore, I had ten more to do. But, one by one, they were slowly disappearing.

I ended up selling the rest of my stereo equipment and over three hundred cassette tapes to the disco owner. He also bought the framed posters of Janis Joplin and Jimi Hendrix and my new refrigerator, but only gave me half of what I had paid for it. He wanted to buy my electric juicer, but I had already given it to my little friend, Baba. I wanted him to start his own business selling fruit juice. He was a good friend who I had watched grow up over the last three and a half years, and he had always helped me when I needed it.

I also made a deal with the landlord. I let him keep the electric hot water heater and linoleum for the last month's rent and electric bill.

When my garage sale was completed, I had Aslam take the possessions that I was sending to America to the Ariana Freight Company. I sent everything by boat. It was much cheaper than airfreight. I was allowed to send nearly everything except my beautiful two-foot-high hand-carved marble statue of Buddha. Customs determined it was a religious artifact, so I had to leave it behind at the apartment. What else could I do? I was running out of time. I had to leave quite a lot of stuff behind—five rooms full.

I gave Aslam my new silk robe and my beautiful knife collection of nearly two hundred knives.

When Mr. Bareck came over, I explained my situation. I showed him everything I was leaving behind and told him he could have it all or he could do whatever he wanted with it. I also mentioned that if Fred stopped by to let him take anything he wanted, including the big stash of hash and hash oil that I had left over. However, if he didn't want it, I told Mr. Bareck to sell it to the tourists.

I didn't care anymore. I was sick to my stomach. Everything I had worked for, for nearly four years I had to leave behind in Kabul. My business was finished. My kingdom had fallen.

Mr. Bareck and I said goodbye for the last time. That was the last time I would see him before I left Kabul.

I still had one important chore to do. I needed to buy a plane ticket. So I took a taxi to the only travel office in Kabul and ran into yet another dilemma. I couldn't fly to Pakistan. The Afghan and Pakistani governments were at odds over border squabbles. I could fly either to Tehran, Iran, or New Delhi, India. Those were my only choices, so I picked India. I had never been there before.

Once I had purchased my ticket, I headed for the shoe store. Thank goodness, my shoes were ready. I paid for my merchandise and told my Afghan friends there that I was leaving Kabul for India. They were sorry to be losing my business. I was sorry also, but it couldn't be helped. Now I could return to my apartment and relax with a few spoonfuls of morphine. The following day, I was flying out of Kabul.

Finally, my time was up. This was a day I thought would never come. These were my last few hours in Afghanistan. I fixed my last spoonful of morphine. I did the most I had ever done. I fixed twenty half-grain morphine tablets, one whole bottle in one fix. The rush was immaculate. This was the highest I had ever gotten from one fix.

Now I was ready to face my accusers. I had to go to the Interior Ministry to pay my fine so I could leave Afghanistan. I was actually looking forward to my trip to India.

I loaded my luggage into the taxi and headed to the ministry. None of my friends were around to say goodbye. I was completely alone.

A few minutes later, I arrived at my destination. While my taxi waited, I entered the ministry building. As I walked into the main office, all the people in the room noticed me. It was as if they were awaiting my arrival, betting to see if I would show up or not. I was very nervous as I walked up to the counter to pay my fine. I handed my passport to the clerk. He inspected it and asked for the money.

"Your fine is a total of fifteen-thousand dollars," he said.

"Is that all?" I asked, as I counted out the money and handed it to him.

"Pay me an extra thousand dollars or I will write the judge's verdict in your passport. I will have to write that you are a spy and not allowed in this country again," he said, trying to bribe me.

I thought that if I paid him he would arrest me for bribery, so I refused the extortion attempt. Actually, I didn't have the money to give him. I had made well over one-hundred-thousand dollars in a three-and-a-half-year period. Now I only had about four-hundred left, so I had to refuse the request.

The clerk just shrugged and wrote a full page of lies in my passport. I wasn't exactly sure what was written because it was in Farsi. But he did say he would write that I was a spy. I just wanted to get to the airport without causing any more trouble. The clerk handed my passport to me and then told me to leave. I couldn't get out of that office fast enough.

I boarded my taxi and headed for the airport. Twenty minutes later, I was standing in line waiting to have my luggage searched by one of the customs officials. I hoped and prayed that everything would go smoothly without any problems or hassles. I didn't want to end up in jail again, especially after paying such a hefty fine. And I didn't want to get some hard-ass customs official. Some of them were downright nasty.

I had brought many pieces of baggage with me. One was a large backpack filled with my clothes. The second was a large wooden handmade Afghan suitcase with a leather covering. It was the type that was used to smuggle hashish—but not this time. Instead, it contained all of my expensive and ancient antique treasures, which I had purchased during my three-year vacation in Kabul and from the king's estate auction, including a gold pocket watch that a Russian prince had given to the king. Plus, I had hundreds of old and rare gold and silver coins, some of which were over two-thousand years old. I was very worried about these beautiful treasures. I worried that they would be stolen.

Suddenly a customs man was questioning me, a familiar customs man. Carol and I had dealings with this customs official before. He was the man who had given her trouble over the tools she had brought from Denmark. And I had trouble with him when I sent a big load of carpets and other Afghan merchandise. Now I was confronting him again. I couldn't get away from this guy. He asked me to pick out my luggage from the pile behind the customs counter. This bald, deformed man was about to search my luggage. I pointed out the few pieces of luggage and pulled them out of the pile, then set them on the table in front of him. He checked my large handmade Afghan suitcase first. He thought he had found another smuggler. As he felt the top, bottom, and sides, he looked at me very suspiciously.

"Do you have hashish in this?" he asked me.

"I'm not crazy," I replied in Farsi, as I looked him straight into his eyes. The customs man continued to search and feel my suitcase until he was satisfied it didn't contain any illegal contraband. However, when he looked inside it and searched its contents, he found my hoard of rare and old gold and silver coins.

"Do you have a notarized stamp from the Ministry of Antiquities to take these coins out of the country?" he asked.

"No. I didn't know I needed to have one." I pleaded with him to let me keep them.

He just shook his head and confiscated them. He didn't ask me anything about my other antique valuables, which were just as valuable as the coins—he just ignored them. Being disappointed at not finding any illegal contraband after searching my suitcase and backpack, the customs man called an old blind man to check my luggage. The old man walked over very slowly and felt the pieces of luggage. Then he bent down and smelled them. He sniffed every inch of my suitcase and backpack. He assured the customs man that if there were any drugs in my luggage he would have found them. Soon after, the customs man ordered me to carry my luggage to the next line. I was glad to get away from that customs man.

Now I waited in line to be body searched before boarding the airplane. We were taken into a small room two at a time. I went in with another American, a woman in her sixties. She had worked as an executive for the Peace Corps in Washington, D.C. and was returning there via India. A female customs officer began searching her person, but the senior citizen became very irate. She exploded.

"Stop this insidious episode!" she screamed. "Why are you searching me?"

I tried to calm the old woman down.

"This is not personal," I told her. "They have a job to do just as you have a job to do."

That seemed to calm her down. She allowed the customs woman to finish her job. That made everyone happy, including the customs man who was about to search me. I was very nervous that he would find the hash hidden in my shoes or the morphine and syringe hidden in my pants. But instead, he just told us both to have a good flight. I was very relieved as I carried my luggage to the plane and then gave it to the ground personnel before we boarded.

Finally, I was on the plane waiting to fly to New Delhi, India. I was actually getting excited for the adventures that lay ahead. The plane headed down the runway and then up into the heavens.

CHAPTER 22

SURPRISE, SURPRISE

I arrived in India less than two hours after departing Kabul airport. It was a very short trip. Once on the ground, I picked up my luggage and went through customs without any trouble. They gave me a twenty-one-day visa and welcomed me into their country.

I walked out of the airport and hailed a taxi. The weather here was the exact opposite of Kabul—instead of cold and snow, it was ninety degrees with a clear blue sky. Just as I boarded the taxi, the woman I had calmed down while being body searched at Kabul airport asked to ride along to the hotel. I agreed.

But the ride turned into a challenge, as there were many bright and colorful parades blocking many of the roads. There were flowered floats decorated similar to the ones seen in the Pasadena Rose Bowl parade, except there was one basic difference—colorful and beautifully dressed elephants were pulling them, not cars, and the country's local and national politicians, along with India's famous celebrities, were riding the elephants, not the floats. We had arrived during India's Independence Day celebration. This was one of their major holidays. Millions of people lined the streets to watch the endless parade.

We watched the parade for a short time and then continued on our way to the hotel. When we arrived, the lady who was riding along asked to share a room with me. She stated that not only would I save money but that she was leaving for the United States the following morning. Her reasoning was sound, so I agreed. This wasn't a sexual rendezvous but more of a casual friendship. This was strictly a financial agreement to benefit two people living on a budget.

We each paid five American dollars to the hotel clerk and were then escorted to our room. There were two single beds and a big bathroom with a nice shower. I was beginning to feel the pains of addiction. I needed to fix my morphine. So as not to cause suspicion,

I excused myself and entered the bathroom, with shoulder bag in hand. Closing the door behind me, I quickly turned on the shower so my female roommate would think I was washing instead of shooting dope.

Once I had fixed my ration of four half-grain morphine tablets, I took a quick shower. While washing my body, I began thinking about my future that lay ahead. I wondered if I would start my drug business anew or leave India and try a different country. One thing that I'd noticed when entering India was their customs check for new arrivals. The customs officials didn't search any of my baggage. I could have smuggled at least fifty pounds of hash into India with no problem instead of the small amount that I had concealed on my body. I had also brought along approximately four hundred half-grain morphine tablets, just enough to last a few months until I was able to find a new source to supply my needs for my heavy addiction.

After I showered, I had my middle-aged female roommate braid my waist-length hair. When she noticed my long hair, she appeared to be frightened of me. I usually kept my hair tucked into the back of my shirt to look as if I had short hair. She thought I had worked at the American Embassy or that I had been a Peace Corps volunteer, not a drug smuggler. As the lady braided my hair, we discussed our future. Within a few minutes, once she had learned that I wasn't an employee of the U.S. government, she quit talking to me.

When it was time to sleep, we each slept in our own beds. As I reached up to shut off the light, the middle-aged lady wouldn't let me. She wanted to sleep with the light on. That's when I knew that she was frightened of me. I had to sleep through the night with my head under the covers to keep the light out of my eyes. However, when I awoke, she was gone. Thank God, I thought. Now I could look for a cheaper hotel in another part of the city.

First, I tried the old city of Delhi, but it was too congested, dirty, and overcrowded. This city was fifty times the size of Kabul. I didn't have any idea where the hippies and hot spots were, so I had the taxi driver take me back to the new city. He dropped me off in the nicer part of town. It was called Connaught Circle.

I found a rather nice hotel for a decent price but much more expensive than the hotels in Kabul—although cheap by New Delhi standards. It was called the York Hotel. It also had a nice little restaurant and bar that employed a decent rock and jazz band that played there seven nights a week.

After storing my luggage in my room, I went outside to check out the city. This was a very, very big city. I was anxious to find and speak with some longhaired hippies to find out where the hot spots were. I also wanted to find a new hash and morphine connection. I walked the streets of the city for hours without any luck.

Finally, after three hours, I spotted four junkies—by their red-dyed hair—sitting in a beautiful park. Two women and two men were sitting on the ground in a small circle. I slowly approached them, as they watched me in silence and eyed me suspiciously. I asked them if they knew where I could score some morphine.

They seemed to be a little leery and suspicious of me, until I broke the ice and showed them some of the morphine tablets I had brought from Afghanistan. Then one of the male junkies began to open up and showed me his powdered morphine, which was produced in India. He offered to trade me one gram of his powder for two of my tablets.

I wasn't sure about the trade, so I put a little tad of his white powder on the tip of my finger and tasted it to see if it was truly morphine. It tasted pharmaceutical, so I traded with him. However, the second the trade was completed, the junkie told me that the Indian morphine wasn't as strong as the German-made morphine.

When I wanted to renege on the trade, he refused my request. Then I asked the junkie if he knew where I could buy some good Kashmiri hash. But he didn't know. He told me to ask around in the old city of Delhi. He said that there were more hippies in that part of town because it was much cheaper to live. So I thanked the four junkies for the information and decided to try my luck in that part of the city.

I quickly hailed a taxi and set off for the old city of Delhi. Once there, I walked around the dirty city for a few hours but didn't have any luck and returned to the York Hotel. Then I went directly to the hotel's restaurant to eat lunch. I ordered two bowls of an American delicacy, "shark fin" soup. I topped it off with a bowl of fresh exotic fruits with a couple of scoops of homemade vanilla ice cream. This meal cost me a total of six rupees, which was equal to approximately sixty cents in American money.

After I had finished my meal, I relaxed to digest it and watched as the band was setting up some of their equipment. I walked over and introduced myself to the band members and then talked with the piano player for almost an hour. We got along fine. All the band members spoke proper English, better than I did, and had English surnames. I mentioned that I played guitar but didn't have it with me. They invited me to play the bass guitar if I ever wanted to sit in with them. They told me that they played seven nights a week at the restaurant. I promised them I would return when they were playing. Then I left for my hotel room.

I returned to my room to relax and smoke some of my Afghani hash, which I had brought with me from Kabul. I had only carried an ounce on my person. I didn't want to carry any more than that. With my luck, I would have gotten busted. But I needed to find a new hash source soon. Mine would be gone within a few days.

Just as I was getting ready for bed, I had fixed my morphine but the glass syringe slipped out of my grasp and broke on the tile floor. It was the only syringe I had. Within a few hours, I began to go through withdrawal. I needed to find a drugstore, but it was two o'clock in the morning and all the stores were closed. I would have to wait until morning before I could soothe my shakes.

I didn't sleep at all. I tried, but I just tossed and turned. So at first light, I went out to buy a syringe. Finally, at seven in the morning, a nearby drug store opened for business. As I entered the store, I bumped into another foreigner as we both tried to enter at the same time. After some small talk, I learned that the young man I had bumped into was a Thai national named Danny. He was also buying drug paraphernalia.

After I had purchased the necessary utensils, I invited Danny to my hotel room. As we walked, we talked. I explained to him about my addiction to morphine, while he told me of his addiction to speed.

Danny said that he was in India going to school because he had gotten kicked out of Thailand for smuggling gold using his father's fishing fleet of twelve large trawlers. He was twenty years old when they kicked him out of the country. He had been in India for the past few years waiting for the Thai government to authorize his return to his family.

Once we had entered my room, I began to fix my morphine. I offered to give Danny a tablet or two but he refused. He explained again that he was a speed freak. While I placed seven half-grain morphine tablets into the spoon and added the water, Danny and I conversed.

"Danny, do you know where I can buy some good Kashmiri hash?"

"Yeah, I think I know where I can get some good black hash.

But it's expensive."

"How much for an ounce?"

"Thirty U.S. dollars. But it's cheaper by the pound."

"Thirty dollars an ounce? Heck, I can buy nearly two kilos of hash in Kabul for that price. If I'd have known that I would have brought a few kilos of Affy hash with me," I said, holding a lit match under my spoon of narcotics.

"Rob, you could have sold that Afghani hash here for two hundred dollars a pound. Maybe three-hundred...if it's primo," said Danny eagerly.

"I thought hash would have been cheap in India. But I guess I was wrong. Oh well. It's just as well, I probably would have gotten busted at Kabul airport," I replied, as I placed a small cotton ball into the liquid drug of warm dreams and sucked it up through the needle and into my syringe.

I set the syringe to the side to cool down and reached into my pocket for a piece of Affy hash to show Danny and to smoke. As I grabbed a nice gram chunk, I also brought out the folded piece of paper that held the powdered morphine I'd received from the junkie. I would try that the next time I fixed. I wasn't even sure if that was morphine, but I would find out in another few hours.

After I loaded my hash pipe with the Affy hash, I handed it to Danny and then lit the bowl for him. He inhaled and quickly coughed up a big cloud of smoke. While he smoked the hash, I grabbed my syringe and injected its contents into my vein. I lay back on the bed, feeling the warm, tingling, euphoric rush overwhelm and overtake my body from the bottom of my feet to the top of my head. Within a few minutes, I was a new man, full of energy and ready to take on the world.

After Danny and I finished smoking the bowl of Affy hash, we decided to check out the city. Danny wanted to show me a few of the hot spots and take me to a place where I could buy some black Kashmiri hash that had been smuggled to New Delhi from the northern city of Srinagar, supposedly one of the most beautiful spots in the world.

I also had to keep my eyes and ears open for morphine. My tabs were slowly dwindling. I was doing nearly twenty a day. I would have to slow down or my tablets wouldn't last a month. I had to find a good morphine connection.

Danny and I hopped a taxi and headed for the old city to Danny's hotel. He knew a few hippies who might have some good hash for sale. When we arrived at his hotel, Danny wanted me to front him thirty U.S. dollars so he could buy me one ounce of hash. But I didn't want to front him the money. He wouldn't do it any other way. He was as paranoid of me as I was of him. So I went against my better judgment and handed him thirty dollars. I watched as he walked away and out of sight.

As I anxiously waited in the taxi, I was sure Danny was going to rip me off for my money and I would never see him again. After nearly fifteen minutes, I was about to tell the taxi driver to take me back to my hotel when Danny came running up to the taxi. He handed me a small paper bag that contained more than an ounce of black Kashmiri hash. I had never seen or smelled any like this before. It was made differently here than in Afghanistan.

In Kashmir, the potent plant's buds are rubbed between the hands and then the residue is scraped from their palms. This is done very early in the morning when the dew fills the buds. This Kashmiri hash was by far some of the best hash in the world. The smell was much more pungent than the hand-pressed Affy. I wanted to return to my hotel room as fast as possible so I could smoke some of this primo hash and see how it compared to my Affy.

Danny and I returned to my hotel room. I quickly filled the bowl of my hash pipe with many small tads of this black, sticky hash. I was so anxious I was shaking. But my shaking quickly faded as I inhaled this potent smoke. A total calm came over my being. It didn't knock me down like the Affy did, but it produced a colorful high. It was if I was tripping on a quarter tab of windowpane acid. It was an energetic high.

I passed the pipe to Danny and watched as he inhaled and then exhaled the hash smoke, but he didn't cough like he had with the Affy. Even so, I still wanted to purchase more of this Kashmiri hash.

"Danny, do you think I could buy a few more ounces of this hash?"

"I'll see what I can do," he said, as he set the hash pipe down and leaned back in the bed.

While Danny relaxed, I got out the powdered morphine that I had gotten from the junkie. I wanted to see if it was as potent as the tablets. I had learned that this was the only type of morphine in India, and it was hard to find. India's medical system was set up by the English and had fairly strict government controls. But there was still a black market. I just had to find it.

I soon learned that India wasn't at all like I thought it would be.

India was a very westernized country, not at all like Afghanistan. In Afghanistan the government controls very little—the people control their own destinies. In India, the government controls everything. There wouldn't be any hash or opium in India if it weren't for the Muslim citizens living in northern India. The two drugs are part of the Muslim diet. The opium is used for medicinal purposes and the hash is smoked in religious ceremonies. So the Indian government had a hard time stopping the use and cultivation of these plants.

The Muslim citizens are the ones who grow the illegal crops for export and their own consumption. These fields are near the Pakistani border and are guarded by Muslim extremists, government soldiers, and rebels. Once the drugs reached outside markets farther south, the price increased immensely.

The cost of one kilo of Kashmiri hash in Srinagar might cost a tourist fifty dollars. By the time that same kilo reached New Delhi, the price skyrocketed to three or four hundred—that is, if you could even find it.

I only had a few hundred dollars left to my name. I didn't even have enough money for a plane ticket to America. Soon I would have to decide to either return to the United States or stay in India and try to start another business. However, at this moment, I was only interested in getting high.

I had mixed the powdered morphine with boiling water and sucked it into my syringe. I was ready to shoot it into my vein. I only tried half of it because I didn't want to overdose. I was afraid it might be stronger than what I was used to. But as the narcotic surged through my body, I waited for the hot, tingly, explosive rush, but it never came. I barely felt a rush at all, so I fixed the rest of it. That, too, was a bust. The powdered morphine wasn't very potent. That whole gram of powder was equal to approximately two tablets of the German-made morphine. It wasn't even worth buying. I should have traveled to Pakistan where the German-made morphine was plentiful and cheap, but my funds were nearly depleted.

As Danny and I were smoking the black Kashmiri hash, we talked about our past. Danny was from an upper-class family who owned a fleet of fishing boats that were used for catching sharks. His family was originally from Penang, but their business was stationed in Thailand. One of Danny's uncles was an ambassador for Penang and some in his family were related to the king of Thailand.

Danny said that when he was kicked out of Thailand for smuggling gold and heroin, using his father's fishing fleet, he was sent to

New Delhi by his family to finish his schooling. He claimed to have smuggled illegal contraband to India for more than two years before he was finally caught by one of his relatives who worked for the Thai government.

But actually, the American government busted Danny. He explained that his fishing trawler had developed engine trouble and was taking on water when it was nearly capsized by a giant wave. Luckily, the U.S. Navy was doing war exercises nearby and rescued him and his crew from drowning. But before the boat sank, the crew members of the navy vessel found the floundering ship's illegal contraband.

Danny and his crewmembers were escorted and handed over to the Thai authorities, which turned out to be Danny's relatives. If Danny's father hadn't been rich or related to the king of Thailand, Danny would have been executed. But his father paid the Thai government officials almost a million dollars in bribes to get his son released. He was still charged with a crime, but not for smuggling heroin—that would have gotten him the death penalty. Instead, he was kicked out of the country and not allowed to return for five years.

Danny's father was still trying to get his sentence commuted or reversed so he would be allowed to return sooner. He had already been in India for nearly three years, and during the Pakistan-Indian war. He thought at the time that it would turn into World War III.

Danny and I were becoming close friends. He was like the younger brother I never had. We discussed many different subjects, especially about smuggling. Danny told me many stories about the American government smuggling opium and heroin from Thailand to Europe and the United States. He explained to me how the CIA had used the Italian Mafia during World War II as assassins and intelligence gatherers. He believed that the Mafia had been a part of the CIA ever since.

He saw in the northeastern fields of Thailand, American and Thai officials, including the U.S. military, loading up C-5 cargo aircraft with tons of illegal contraband, which included large sacks of opium and heroin. He believed that every time the CIA's budget was cut they would make up the loss by smuggling narcotics to be sold through its Mafia connections.

When I asked Danny how he knew all of this, he explained that he received his information from his uncle, the ambassador. Danny also believed that Charlie "Lucky" Luciano was the man who had helped the U.S. Navy and CIA contact the Italian Mafia. To reward Luciano for his help, he was rewarded with his release from prison and then allowed to return to the U.S. after he had been deported by using a phony passport and identification that was supplied to him by U.S. government officials of the CIA.

Danny also believed that high U.S. government officials were still smuggling illegal narcotics and contraband to this day. That was how they funded their covert operations, which weren't authorized by the U.S. Congress. Danny's uncle said that the CIA was a government in itself. No one was held accountable for its actions.

I remember when Tiar and I took a trip to Badakhsan, visiting some opium fields; we saw a big C-5 cargo plane being loaded with cargo. Tiar had told me that they were Americans smuggling opium. I thought they were just regular civilians, but now that I look back on it, they *were* probably CIA.

Danny and I talked for a few hours until it was time for dinner. Then we walked down to the hotel's restaurant to eat supper. The band had just begun to play as we were being seated at our table. Evidently, this was a very popular restaurant because the place was completely full of young adult customers. Every table was packed with at least four people per table. The restaurant held approximately two hundred well-dressed people, the majority being India's young and rich upper class. Not only did they all wear English-style clothing, but they also spoke English and spoke it well. I didn't have any trouble understanding them at all.

Danny and I ordered dinner as the band began to play. It was a small six-piece band, which included drums, piano, electric bass guitar, trumpet, trombone, and a mean saxophone, but they lacked a guitar player. One of the musicians played both the trumpet and the sax. They played mostly forties pop music. I was surprised when they played a few recent American hits. Being a musician, I listened intently to their music. I longed to jam with them, but I had sent my guitar back to the United States, so I didn't have any musical instruments with me.

As I bounced and swayed to the music's beat, our dinner finally arrived. I had an excellent meal of lobster, jumbo shrimp, shark fin soup, and a baked potato covered with melted cheese. I topped it off with a fruit salad ice cream sundae. This meal cost me a total of ten Indian rupees—that was one U.S. dollar.

Food and housing was very cheap in New Delhi—it was the drugs that were expensive. That is, if you could even find them. In

Kabul, nearly every teashop sold hash or opium. Drugs in Afghanistan were very easy to get and very cheap to purchase. But I was finding out that this just wasn't the case here in India, at least in New Delhi.

Danny and I finished our meal and sat back in our chairs to relax and think. The meal was excellent. The band was another matter. They couldn't hold a beat. One or two songs that they all seemed to like, they played fairly well. But on other songs, they couldn't keep a steady beat. The instruments didn't play together. The bass player seemed to be their problem. He just wasn't very good. Actually, he played very poorly.

I looked around the room and watched the actions of the other customers. They swayed their heads and bounced to the beat, but nobody was dancing. They just sat in their seats waiting for the band to play a lively tune. However, nothing seemed to energize the band…or the audience.

After nearly thirty minutes of non-stop music, the band finally took a short break. I walked over to the piano player and talked with him about his band. I soon learned that his name was Jerry. He was the leader of the group and was also a professional piano teacher. The other members were also teachers of their respective instruments, except the bass player. He had just purchased it and wasn't used to playing it. That was the excuse that was used for being off the beat.

I invited some of the band members up to my hotel room to smoke some of my Affy hashish. Two of them joined Danny and me. The band didn't have a long break. So as soon as I entered my room, I began filling the bowl of my hash pipe. I let the band members, Jerry and Louis, smoke the first bowl. I wanted them to get high enough to feel their music from their insides out.

After my new friends learned that I was also a musician, I was invited to play the bass guitar and join them on stage. But if I was going to play the bass guitar with them, I wanted them to feel the beat of the music. So I made them smoke an extra bowl of Affy hash. As we smoked, we talked. But within a few minutes, Jerry and Louis had to get back to the restaurant to join their band members on stage. I told them I would be down in a little while to jam with them.

Danny and I continued to smoke both types of hash. I also fixed another seven tabs of my morphine. Once I re-energized myself with the potent narcotic, I began to show Danny how I pressed the hash to send in post cards. I began to roll the thick, black clump of Kashmiri hash into a thin slab, using a drinking glass. I set the clump of hash on the wooden table and began to roll the glass over it.

Within a few seconds, the clump began to get thinner and thinner until the glass shattered into the palm of my right hand. I screamed, not in pain and agony, but in shock. I slowly pulled out a large piece of broken glass, which was embedded more than a half-inch into my palm. Just as I pulled out the last remnants of broken glass, blood squirted everywhere. A thin three-foot-long stream had splattered on the freshly painted walls and carpeted floor. I had cut an artery. Before I could slow down the flow of blood, I had lost over an ounce of it. I immediately wrapped a towel around my injured hand to slow the bleeding.

Danny and I ran out of the room into the dark night looking for a doctor to suture my bleeding wound. A passerby pointed to a doctor's office just down the street, so Danny and I ran as fast as we could in that direction. When we found the place, we ran up three flights of stairs and into the office, only to be told that they couldn't help me. They were baby doctors. They referred me to another doctor a block away.

Now we ran back down the three flights of stairs and out in the dark night looking for another doctor to help me before I bled to death. My towel, which had been white, was now a dark red and dripping blood onto the street. We were back out on Connaught Circle wondering what to do next.

"Robert, let's take a taxi to the hospital before you bleed to death," Danny said excitedly.

"There must a doctor nearby who can stitch my hand back together," I whined.

I began walking faster and faster looking for the next doctor's office. Danny quickly followed. Within a few minutes and after climbing two flights of stairs, I was standing in another doctor's office begging for help. But again, I was told they couldn't help me. I just couldn't believe that a doctor, any kind of doctor, couldn't stitch my wound. But I didn't stay around to argue the point.

I finally gave up and took Danny's advice, hiring a taxi to take me to the hospital. My hand was still bleeding profusely and within a few minutes had soaked the floor of the taxi in blood. I was beginning to feel weak from the lack of it. Fifteen minutes later, we arrived at the hospital. I jumped out of the taxi and ran into the hospital expecting to get help immediately, but instead I was told to take a seat. I refused. I wanted a doctor now. But the clerk at the desk had a job to do. He would not let me see the doctor until he had the information he needed. Even if I was near death, he would not let me see a doctor until his job was done.

After ten minutes of answering the clerk's questions, I was finally allowed to see the doctor. By the time I was escorted into the emergency room, I was very weak and faint from the lack of blood. The young Indian doctor cleaned the wound and then started to stitch it without giving me any anesthetic.

"Doc, aren't you going to give me anything to numb the pain?" I asked, as he pushed the dull needle through the skin of my wound. "STOP! That hurts!"

"Oh, that doesn't hurt. Stop whining," exclaimed the doctor, laughing as he pushed the needle through the skin again.

"Please stop, Doc," I whined.

"I only have one more stitch to do and then we will be through."

But I continued to scream in pain each time the doctor pushed the dull needle into my skin. When he made the next stitch, I thought it was the last, but I was wrong. He lied and continued to give me four additional stitches. I was given a total of seven stitches in my right palm without any anesthetic. When the doctor had finished, I couldn't leave the hospital fast enough.

I paid the bill and then Danny and I rode the taxi back to the hotel. We went directly to my room and took the works out of my bag. Danny waited patiently while I fixed my painkiller. When I was finished, we went to the restaurant to listen to our new friends' band. I was hoping to sit in with them, but my right hand was completely wrapped in white gauze and bandages.

I listened to their music until the band had their first break. That's when Jerry asked me to play the bass guitar and jam with his band. I tried to make excuses about my injured hand but Jerry and the other band members wouldn't take "no" for an answer. So I decided to play a few songs with them. I only knew a few licks on the bass, but I had the beat.

I became the leader of the band. I started each song, and then the other instruments followed. I played simple songs with a good, heavy beat. Soon the crowd began to liven up. They began to sway and move their bodies to the beat of my funky bass guitar. I had never seen any of the restaurant's customer's dance to the band's music until now. One by one, they began rising from their seats to dance. Soon the tables were empty, as everyone was dancing on the dance floor. We played the first song for more than ten minutes. And when we finished the crowd gave us a standing ovation and yelled for more. So we obliged them.

I started another song with a heavy, funky beat, and once again, the other instruments followed. I would start a rhythm and then the other band members would play along. Then each instrument would play a solo. I had the band playing together and tight.

We had the whole room buzzing and rocking from our music. This was the very first time that I saw people get out of their seats and dance, western-style, like in the United States. The lively crowd loved our music, and they swiveled and swayed to the heavy beat.

When the band tried to take a short break, the crowd refused to let us off the stage. They yelled, hooted, and hollered for the band to play on, so we obliged the rocking crowd. We played another four songs before the crowd allowed us a short break. And I needed one. My injured hand was aching and swollen. I returned the bass guitar to the original bass player. He felt left out, especially after the other band members had chastised and belittled him. They wanted me to continue playing the bass. But I refused, using the injured hand as my excuse so the original bass player could play.

Danny and I returned to my hotel room to smoke some hash, but I also needed to fix my morphine again to take away the aching pain in my injured hand.

My morphine stash was slowly depleting, along with my money. I needed to start my business soon so I could survive and continue living in India. So I decided to start looking for a way to smuggle hash from India to the United States. I didn't have the customs connections that I'd had in Afghanistan, so I had to find a shoemaker or some other means of transporting the hash out of India and to America.

After a long day and night, Danny returned to his residence while I fell asleep thinking about the days that lay ahead.

The next morning, I hopped a taxi to begin looking for the right merchandise in which to hide the drugs without it being detected. I asked the taxi driver if he had any friends who could help me with my endeavors. He said he did, and then he drove me to a wood-maker's shop where he explained to the owner what I needed. The wood-maker started showing me different wooden statues and other objects that could hide hash. He showed me a wooden glass with a stainless steel liner that only went halfway to the bottom and worked similar to a false bottom. When the liner was taken out, you could see there was a two-inch difference between the steel liner and the bottom of the wooden glass, which was used to hide the hash. However, I didn't like any of the man's ideas. I was very fussy. I didn't want to end up in an Indian jail. After all the hell I had gone through in Kabul, I didn't want to go through the same thing in India, especially when I had neither friends in the government nor the money to bribe my way out of jail.

I had the taxi driver take me to another shop that might be able to help me. But the shop's owner seemed to be a scam artist. He told me that I wouldn't have to smuggle the hash—he would send it to me. And to do that all I would have to give him was the money for postage and he paid for everything else. When I asked to see the type of hash that he would send for me he couldn't come up with any, so I became very suspicious. I told him he was a con man. He became irate at my suggestion and quickly pulled out a small address book and showed me many different names of people and their addresses that he said he had sent hash to. I still didn't believe him. When I told him I would think it over, he asked me to write my name and address in his book. I refused. I didn't trust this guy at all. He could have been a narc for all I knew. So I quickly left his place of business and then paid the taxi man for his services, as I no longer trusted him either.

I decided to walk around the town alone. I wanted to check out some shoe stores and speak with the store owners to see if I could talk one of them into making hash sandals.

While walking around the old city of Delhi, I walked through a beautiful park. It seemed to be the place to be. Many different things were going on. I saw yoga masters showing off their skills to the onlookers. There were musicians, magicians, jugglers, and even some gymnasts. There were also public speakers who were allowed to talk about anything they wanted.

I noticed a large crowd to my right and walked over to see what all the commotion was about. I pushed my way up to the front only to see a yoga master lying on a bed of sharpened nails, while another man using a sledgehammer broke cement blocks on the yoga's chest. Five feet to the right of that yoga was another old Hindu who supposedly had been sitting in a trance for over two years. He was sitting in the yoga position, with his legs crossed, staring at a brick wall. Two Australians I was standing next to explained that the yoga master was "building up his power" to transcend his body through the brick wall.

One of the longhaired Australians showed me a freshly repaired wall within ten feet of the old yoga master. He explained that another yoga master had tried the same stunt a few months before but didn't make it, or so they said. It seemed that as the yoga master was transcending his body through the brick wall, he was interfered with by a crazy crowd member. As the yoga master's body was nearly halfway through the wall, he suddenly awakened from his trance and his body went from the spirit world back to the physical world. At that moment, the brick wall cut his body in two.

And now another yoga master from the same sect was trying his skills and that's why he had been in his trance for over two years, sitting through storms, monsoons and any other obstacle that came his way. The Australian stopped talking when the yoga master's assistant began telling the crowd that within a week the yoga master would try his luck and transcend his body through the brick wall. I had heard enough, and so had the two Australians.

After introducing myself, the two Australians and I became friends. We walked around the park together and stopped to watch the magicians and jugglers. While we walked, the Australians told me their stories. They were on vacation and had just traveled to India from Thailand. They bragged about that country and all the beautiful women that were there to please the man.

The more they talked about Thailand and its gorgeous women, the more I liked it. Danny never told me anything like that. He never mentioned anything about the Thai women. The Australians, however, told me everything about Thailand. They also told me about their country and how they would work in the oil fields in northern Australia for six months or so, save their money, then buy a student-fare plane ticket for Thailand for less than one-hundred dollars. Then they would travel throughout Asia and Indonesia until their money ran out. When their pockets were empty, they would return to northern Australia and start work again.

The Australians were so enthusiastic about Thailand that they talked me into traveling with them to Bangkok. But first, they had to travel to Bombay to sell their thirty-five-millimeter camera equipment, where they thought they could get a much higher price for it than in Delhi.

As the two Australians and I walked through the park, heading toward my hotel room, we bumped into Danny. We all left the park together and talked about Thailand and the beautiful women. I was very eager to visit the country, but my money was nearly depleted. I had less than four-hundred dollars, but the Australians promised to show me how to send pot from Thailand without getting busted. I was all for that. Danny wished he could go with us because he really missed his family.

We finally reached my hotel. I invited Danny and my two new friends up to my room to smoke some good hash. They all accepted. As we smoked, we talked about the trip to Thailand. It was decided that the two Australians would leave New Delhi the following morning and head for Bombay. As soon as they sold their camera outfit, they would wire me with the news and tell me when I could expect them.

I didn't want to travel with my extra luggage, so I asked Danny if he wanted my backpack of clothes. He was more than happy to take them off my hands. They were mostly clothes made in Afghanistan, my collection of almost four years.

After smoking a few bowls of hash, we went to the hotel's restaurant to eat dinner. After having a great dinner, we said goodbye. I would see Danny in the morning and I would hear from the Australians within three days once they arrived in Bombay.

While alone in my hotel room, I decided to call my mother in America. I had a telephone right next to my bed, which was unheard of in Afghanistan.

My mother was very happy to hear from me. However, she was unhappy to hear that I was traveling to Thailand instead of returning to America. I was torn between two worlds. I missed my family immensely. But on the other hand, I didn't want anything to do with that country.

The U.S. government was full of hypocrites. These politicians only cared about two things: what was good for their particular party and what was good for their bank account, not what was good for their constituents. They used the excuse that drugs kill and therefore should be banned. The politicians felt anyone who used them should be branded as a criminal and thrown in jail. Yet tobacco and alcohol killed a thousand times the amount of people, and they were legal.... Why? Because these companies bribed the politicians with huge amounts of cash to keep it that way. But that was all right. Their day would come. These criminal politicians would rather put a pot smoker in jail than a violent offender. I didn't understand their reasoning or the logic behind their madness. I guess I never will.

Anyway, I explained the situation to my mother and told her that I would keep in touch. I promised to call her every few days. When I finished my conversation, I needed to fix my morphine. I figured I only had a couple of hundred tablets left, just enough for two or three weeks, if that. But after counting them, I soon learned I had more than expected—a few hundred more, which meant I had over six hundred tablets. That was my lucky day.

But I wasn't having much luck in the hash smuggling business or with finding more morphine. India had too many government controls and regulations, at least in the pharmaceutical area. The only drugs I had been able to find were the hash that Danny had gotten for me and the poor quality morphine that I had traded for. That was it.

I hoped I could start something in Thailand with the help of my Australian friends. I had talked with them about my adventures in Afghanistan so they were well aware of my business.

However, two days after they had departed for Bombay, I ran into a slight problem. I needed to cash some U.S. dollars for some Indian rupees. But I didn't want to go to the banks because they levied a tax to exchange foreign currency into rupees. And the moneychangers were giving a better rate, but this was illegal in India, at least for tourists. I had been warned that a foreigner could go to jail if he was caught changing money illegally. But a moneychanger would give an extra five rupees per dollar. So it was well worth the risk, but I would have to be very discreet.

After approaching a few different moneychangers and arguing over the rate, greed got the best of me and I went with the guy who gave me the most money for my buck. American dollars were better than gold in India.

As the moneychanger and I walked to his office, he talked about having to be very discreet.

"We could both land in jail if we're caught changing money," opined the moneychanger.

"I don't want that," I replied nervously.

As we entered an office building, we walked into a dimly lit staircase.

"How much money do you wish to change?" asked the moneychanger.

"I want to change two-hundred American dollars into Indian rupees." And then I pulled out the money from my hidden money belt.

"Before I hand you my money, I want to see the rupees."

The moneychanger began counting out the correct amount of rupees. But as we were about to exchange the money, a man dressed in a dark suit came down the stairs from the floor above and yelled at us.

"Police, police!" said the stranger.

I turned to see what the man was yelling about and as I did, the moneychanger grabbed my wad of dollars out of my hand and shoved his rolled up wad of rupees into mine.

"Get out of here," said the moneychanger, as he bolted out the rear door of the building.

As I turned to leave by the front door, the man who had run down the stairs yelling "police!" came over to me and asked me for my passport. He told me he was the police and had been watching the transaction. As we walked outside into a parking lot, he put his arm around my shoulder and lectured me on the evils of money-changers. He gave me back my passport and drifted away into a crowd of onlookers. When he was out of sight, I unrolled the bills and began to count the rupees. I noticed there was only one large bill and the rest were one-rupee bills. That's when I knew I had been scammed.

The moneychanger had ripped me off. He had given me twenty dollars worth of Indian rupees for two-hundred U.S. dollars. *Boy, was I a sucker,* I thought to myself. Then I turned and ran back to the office building, through the back door and out into the alley. I ran down one end and then the other, looking for the moneychanger. Now I realized two scammers had set me up, the moneychanger and his buddy who acted like the cop.

All I could do now was to return to my hotel room and change money with a legal moneychanger. After explaining my story to this moneychanger, I even offered him a reward if he could find the guys who ripped me off. But in reality, I knew I would never see them again.

A few days after the incident, I returned to the scene of the crime, hoping to come face-to-face with my scam artists, but it wasn't to be. I never saw them again. I put that experience behind me. I should have known better.

I finally received the wire from the two Australians, but it was bad news. They couldn't sell their camera outfit or go to Thailand. They were going to stay in Bombay, then fly directly to Australia from there.

Now I didn't know what I was going to do. I was in a very bad predicament, one in which I hadn't been in years. I decided to fix some morphine. That always seemed to settle my nerves and help me think. But I knew that just prolonged my agony.

My narcotic rush was interrupted by a knock on my hotel room door. It was Danny. I was happy to see him. I told him about my change of plans.

I didn't want to travel to Thailand alone. Not having any connections made things difficult in any country.

Danny and I decided to go out to eat and then look for a shoe store that made shoes by hand. Every shoe store I had visited only sold mass-produced shoes. I wasn't having any good luck at all in India.

As Danny and I were leaving the hotel lobby, the police barged through the lobby door and grabbed Danny as if he was a wanted gangster. They surrounded us, with their automatic weapons pointing at our bodies, and ordered us to turn over our passports. Then the police handcuffed Danny but didn't touch me. We couldn't have escaped if we'd wanted to. There must have been over thirty police in the hotel lobby. I didn't know what the hell was going on. But I was very paranoid, having hash and morphine on my person and especially after what had transpired in Afghanistan.

Once the police had checked our passports, they immediately handed mine back to me and then marched Danny outside into a tiny car. I was in shock. I wondered what I had gotten myself into. I was lucky that the police didn't search me or I would be in jail.

Once my nerves had settled down, I returned to my hotel room and took out my morphine kit. I needed to fix my morphine so I could stop worrying about my problems. But even the morphine hadn't resolved my situation. I had to make a decision and soon. My money was disappearing fast, and there was no way to replace it. If I had brought my guitar, I could have performed for money. But nothing was going my way.

As I lay back to enjoy the rush, my thoughts were on the United States. I didn't have much choice but to return to my family in America. I had to decide which mode of travel to use. Would I fly? Would I take a boat? I couldn't go overland because I couldn't get a visa to go through Afghanistan. I sure didn't have enough money to fly back. So I had to think about my transportation to the United States, if that was the place I decided to travel. But I just couldn't make up my mind.

I hated my country's government and all that it stood for. So I had the hotel clerk check a few different cruise lines for the cheapest ticket price to Italy or Europe. But the cheapest ticket price was beyond my means. I couldn't afford the fare. So after beating my head against the wall for five or six hours over my predicament, I made the decision to return to the United States, but only if my mother would buy my plane ticket because I didn't have the funds to buy it.

I put my call through to my parents' house. My mother answered. She was happy to hear from me and to hear that her prayer had been answered. I was coming back home. She would wire the ticket within the next couple of days. I asked her to buy a cheap, student-fare, one-way, non-stop plane ticket.

I wasn't too anxious to return to America, but I figured I would return for just a few months, until I could save enough money to travel again. Then I would return to Afghanistan to see my Afghan friends once again.

And now that I was leaving India, I decided to buy some gifts for the family and a few friends. I visited a few stores just around the corner from my hotel. I bought many different exquisite items, everything from Hindu art books to brass and ivory statues. I even bought a beautiful, handmade, hand-painted carving set for my mother.

Many of my newly purchased gifts were mostly antique ivory statues. I became so fascinated with Hindu artwork that I spent nearly all of my money at one store.

I was leaving for the United States within a few days anyway, and I could make more money once I arrived home. I could sell the hash from my shoes, which I had specially made in Kabul and had been wearing for the last few weeks, and I could also sell many of the items that I had sent from Afghanistan.

When I returned to my hotel, I noticed that Danny was sitting in the lobby waiting for me.

"Danny, what the hell are you doing here? I thought you were in jail?" I asked.

"No. The police made a mistake. They were looking for me to relay a message to my uncle. I can return to Thailand. The government is allowing me to return as long as I don't get into anymore trouble."

"Congratulations. When are you leaving?" I asked.

"Soon I hope. Just as soon as I get my ticket."

"By the way, I'm returning to the United States."

"Wow, this is a day of celebration," said Danny, excited.

We walked up to my room to smoke some hash to celebrate. Just as we entered and shut the door, the phone rang. It was the hotel clerk telling me that my plane ticket had arrived and to pick it up at the front desk. I hung up the phone, excused myself from the room, then bolted out the door and ran down the hall to the front desk. I retrieved the airline ticket that my mother had wired. It was for Air India with stops in Lebanon, Germany, France, England, and then to New York. It sure wasn't a non-stop fare or a one-way ticket. It was a round trip ticket from New Delhi to New York, departing Delhi airport in two days at two in the afternoon. I figured that it must have been cheaper to buy an economy round-trip fare than a one-way fare. But I was more than happy with it.

I immediately ran back to my room and showed Danny my ticket. He celebrated by smoking hash, and I celebrated by injecting eight half-grain tabs of morphine. Then it hit me. I realized that I would be returning to the United States with a very bad drug habit. I had enough morphine to last me at least a month or more, that is, if I cut my daily habit in half. But right at this moment, it was time for a celebration.

I would be returning to the United States in two days, and Danny would be returning to Thailand in three. We exchanged addresses and agreed to keep in touch. Danny offered to send me heroin from Bangkok, Thailand, and I agreed to send him money. We decided to start our own drug business. It sounded promising and that made me want to return to my family even more, even though four years before I had promised never to set foot in that country again. I had to tell myself over and over again that I would be there just a short while, until I had saved enough money to return to Asia. I really intended on returning to Afghanistan. Even though they had kicked me out of their country, I was willing to try my luck and visit there again.

Danny and I spent the rest of the day together. We talked about the future and planned to see each other again very soon. We shook hands and hugged, then said goodbye. Danny promised to write to me as soon as he got a place to stay and a telephone number. I waved goodbye as he disappeared into the darkness. That was the last time I would see Danny.

A few minutes later, I telephoned my mother and told her that I had received the ticket. As soon as I hung up the phone, I fixed my morphine and then went to bed, thinking about tomorrow.

The next morning I awoke bright and early. After I had done my "do," I packed my luggage and then walked to the hotel's reception desk and paid my hotel bill. Then I went to the restaurant and ate breakfast. While I sat back digesting my meal, I decided to spend my last day shopping for gifts. And that's what I did. I could spend the rest of my money and not worry about any repercussions. I had made sure that I wouldn't have to pay an airport tax or any other un-expected tax to leave the country. So I felt at ease when I returned to the same gift shop that I had visited the day before.

Once I entered the store, all I wanted to do was to buy gifts and spend money. I shopped till I dropped and only had a few dollars left when I remembered that I had put a twenty-dollar down payment on a beautiful handmade Indian carpet the day before at this very store. So when the salesman reminded me about my carpet in layaway, I explained to him that I had no money left and would appreciate it if he would return my twenty dollars, but he refused. The store had a no-refund policy, just like the shop in Kabul. I was between a rock and a hard place.

I argued with the salesman until I was blue in the face. But he wouldn't budge. If I wanted to buy the carpet, they would hold it for me for one year. If the carpet wasn't claimed in that time, they would repossess it and resell it. So I had no choice. I had to leave the carpet in layaway. I hoped I would pay off the bill and pick it up within a year.

By the time I had finished my shopping, I had spent nearly all of my money and had just enough left over to pay for the taxi ride to the airport, and that was it. I was cutting it very close. I thought I would have learned from my Moroccan trip, but I guess I didn't. My pockets were empty, so I gathered my gifts and returned to my hotel room.

The following afternoon, I would be leaving for the United States. It had been nearly four years since I had last visited the coun-try. I had my luggage packed and ready to go. But I was loaded down with gifts—too many gifts.

I would have to carry three big suitcases full of gifts and clothes plus two carry-on bags. They contained breakable items and my very delicate carving set. I wanted to carry that with me so it wouldn't be damaged in the cargo hold. I also carried all of my ex-pensive jewelry, pocket watches, and other valuable objects of art.

I would fix my morphine just before I checked out of my hotel room. I didn't want to take the chance and carry my syringe with me. I wanted to get to America without ending up in jail. But when I thought about it, it made absolutely no sense, due to the fact I was smuggling hashish and morphine on my body.

I had lost fifty pounds of body weight over a four-year period. I weighed only one hundred and twenty pounds. My hand was infected and swollen and still wrapped in bandages. My long, braided hair was badly snarled and unkempt because it hadn't been braided in nearly a week.

My last night in India went by very slowly. Even though I had fixed a large dose of that evil narcotic, I tossed and turned all through the night. I didn't get one minute of sleep thinking about my trip to America.

When I awoke early the next morning, I still had a few important things to do. The first was to do my morphine. When that chore was out of the way, I took ten morphine tablets out of the cigar tube and set them aside on my bedside table. Then I shoved the tube and its contents up my rectum. Now I had to hide the rest of the dope that I wanted to smuggle to America. I rolled my black Kashmiri hash into a long cylinder shape, placed it into two plastic baggies, and taped it to the crack of my ass and then taped my Affy hash near my private parts. Customs would have to strip search me to find it. I wasn't worried about the morphine because that was completely hidden from sight. I would also be wearing my hash shoes onto the plane. I was certain that with all my gifts I wouldn't be searched at all.

To look like an ordinary tourist, I dressed respectably for the long plane ride to America. I still had a few hours to kill, so I lay down on my bed to relax.

Finally, the time had come. It was time to depart for the airport. But I needed one last fix. I quickly laid the ten half-grain morphine tablets that I had set aside for this occasion into my spoonful of water and boiled it until the tablets liquefied. Then, after placing a small cotton filter into the liquid narcotic, I sucked it up through the filter and into my syringe. I let it cool down for a minute or two and then injected the liquid dreams into my vein. The rush was more powerful than ever. The hot, tingly rush raced through and overwhelmed my body, knocking me back onto the bed. I lay spellbound as the evil narcotic raced through my veins and turned my pale, white body beet red for just a few seconds before the rush subsided.

After a few more minutes of rest, I was once again endowed with new life. I felt like a new and confident person. I arose from the bed, threw my dope kit into the garbage can, and straightened up my clothes. Now I was ready to leave for the airport.

I telephoned the clerk to have my bags picked up and carried to the taxi. It would take an hour to reach New Delhi Airport.

Ten minutes after I had done my last morphine fix in India, I was on my way to the airport. I arrived with only an hour before my flight departed for New York. Once I had paid the taxi fare, my pockets were empty. I didn't have a penny to my name and was completely broke. But I was certain I wouldn't need any money for my trip. I figured I would have plenty once I arrived in my homeland.

However, things never went easy for me. I struggled with five pieces of luggage but managed to carry them up to the checkout counter. I was in quite a happy mood as I set my three suitcases onto the scales to be tagged for shipping.

As the airline's attendant checked my ticket, he mentioned that I would be the only passenger on the plane until we reached Beirut, Lebanon.

I couldn't believe that I would be the only passenger for the twelve-hour plane ride. But that was all right by me. I would have the plane all to myself. I just hoped it was a jet and not propeller-driven. As long as it got me to my destination, I didn't really care. I was too excited about the trip to worry about the type of plane in which I would be flying.

Before the airline's attendant handed me my confirmation slip and seat number, he asked for something I wasn't expecting.

"Sir, your luggage is forty pounds overweight, which will cost you a total of fifty-six dollars."

"You've got to be kidding," I whined. "My luggage is full of gifts that I purchased here to give to my family, whom I haven't seen in nearly four years. I spent all my money on the gifts. I don't have any money left to pay for the extra weight. Isn't there something that you can do?"

"I'm sorry, sir. I can't put your baggage onto the plane until the fifty-six-dollar fee is paid."

I couldn't believe what I was hearing. Either I would have to pay the outrageous fee or leave all of my family's gifts behind. At least he wasn't asking me for money for a tax—that I couldn't pay either. At least I could still board the plane. I would just have to leave the extra baggage.

"Please, sir," I pleaded. "Couldn't I pay the fifty-six dollars at a later date? All that extra weight is gifts for my family that I purchased here. Believe me, if I had the money I would gladly pay you. But I promise, if you can let me slide this time, I will pay the fee when I return to the United States."

"You say you bought all of these gifts in India?" asked the attendant.

"Yes. They're all gifts for my family. That's why I don't have any money left. I left it here in your country. That's why I'm carrying so much luggage. If it wasn't for all of these gifts, I would have only carried my two carry-on bags."

"Well, I guess just this once, I'll let you get away without paying the extra weight. Now, you'll have to have your carry-on luggage searched." He handed me my ticket and directed me to the baggage search area.

"Thank you, mister. You have a beautiful country. I hope I can visit here again one day," I said, as he walked away and left me standing in front of a long table.

I was the only one waiting to have my carry-on baggage checked. Besides me, there were only three other people in the room, and those were the three customs officials waiting to check my luggage. I placed my two bags onto the table in front of them.

For some odd reason they seemed suspicious of me, and for good reason. This was the day of the terrorist. President Nixon and other leaders of the free world began a war against terrorism to which nobody was immune. I wasn't worried though. I didn't have any illegal contraband or bombs in my carry-on luggage. My illegal contraband was on my person, taped to my body.

After nearly having a heart attack over the extra weight problem, I was quite certain that I wouldn't have any other problems. But that was before the customs man pulled out a rolled-up shirt from the bottom of the first bag he checked. When he unrolled the shirt and saw the butcher knives and forks from the carving set that I had purchased, the customs man thought I was a terrorist. He thought I was going to highjack the aircraft using the butcher knife as my weapons.

"Explain yourself," snapped the customs man. "Why are you carrying these knives onto the plane? You were going to highjack the plane, weren't you?"

"No, sir, I'm not a terrorist. If you look into my other bag, you'll see that the knives and forks that you are holding in your hands are to a handmade carving set that I purchased here in your country. It is a gift for my mother. I carried the utensils with me so they wouldn't get damaged in flight. I swear to you, I'm not a terrorist. I just want to go home and see my parents."

When they checked my other bag, they knew then that I had

been telling them the truth.

"We'll keep your bags with the pilot until you reach your destination," said the customs man. "Then he'll return your bags to you. Is that understood?"

"Yes. That's fine with me."

"Good, then that's settled," replied the customs man. "Now if you'll just follow me I'll tell you what you have to do next." I followed him to a small changing room. "Before we let you on the plane, you have to be body searched."

"Why? I told you I'm not a terrorist."

I knew that my time was near. I thought that if this guy made me strip, he would find my illegal contraband and throw me into an Indian jail. I was certain that I would never make my flight.

"Please raise your arms up over your head and spread your legs apart so I can frisk you," demanded the customs man, as his hands began feeling all areas of my body.

"I don't know why you have to do this," I whined.

The customs man searched over every inch of my body while I was still fully clothed. When he reached up and felt my crotch and buttocks area, his hand bumped the cylindrical lump taped to the crack of my ass. He became excited when he felt this area and began hitting the hard object again and again, trying to figure out what it was.

"What is this?" he asked, hitting the hash with his hand.

"What do you think it is? Let me take off my pants and you can see for yourself. It's my asshole. If you like it so much, let me show it to you so you can see it up close." Then I began to unbutton my pants.

I remembered when a young customs man at Metro airport in Michigan searched me as I was about to board a flight to Germany and found my hash pipe. Then he began frisking me with much more enthusiasm, wanting to find the drugs to go with it. But he came up empty-handed. When he became angry, he ordered me into the bathroom. That's when I became irate and embarrassed him in front of his female peers when I shouted, "Sure, let's go into the bathroom and you can search my asshole!" He was so offended by my outrageous outburst that in order to keep me quiet, he allowed me to board the plane. I used the same tactics on this Indian customs man and it worked. He was so embarrassed by my words and actions that he ordered me to button my pants and board the plane. I don't know how I did it, but I kept my cool and was able to flee the country with my drugs intact.

Finally, an hour after arriving at New Delhi airport, I was climbing the stairs to board the 747 jet aircraft. When I entered the huge airplane, I was flabbergasted at the size of it and was greeted by four young and beautiful female Indian stewardesses. They allowed me to sit anywhere I wanted. I was the only passenger on the twelve-hour flight to Beirut. I couldn't believe it.

Once the plane had departed the airport, I was allowed to walk up to the second level. I was treated like a king for the long journey to Lebanon. I was able to stretch out over four large chairs and sleep for nearly the whole trip. I was even shown a movie after my first-class dinner.

My royal treatment stopped after we landed in Beirut. The plane completely filled up with passengers. A civil war had broken out and everyone but the warmongers were leaving.

A beautiful blonde-haired, middle-aged German woman sat next to me while I sat in an aisle seat. We introduced ourselves and began a long conversation. Her name was Elsa. She was very outgoing and talkative during our plane ride to Europe. She mentioned to me that she was a tour leader to nearly one hundred tourists.

While having a nice conversation with her, she suddenly began staring at me. I wondered what I had done wrong. I tried not to notice, but her eyes burned a hole right through me. I ignored her and figured that maybe she was in a trance. That is, until she began asking me questions.

"I know I've seen you before.... Give me a minute, and I'll remember where," said Elsa.

"I never saw you before until today.... I would remember a beautiful woman like you," I told her.

"Did you ever act in any plays or in the theater?" she asked.

"No. I lived in Afghanistan for the last four years. Maybe you saw me in Kabul."

"No. I never traveled to Afghanistan," she replied.

"Then maybe you saw me traveling through Europe or Germany."

Just then, I saw her eyes light up. She suddenly remembered where she had seen me. "Were you ever in a movie?"

I thought for a second and replied, "No, not that I know of."

But then it dawned on me. I had been in a movie—the one that the Austrian professor had filmed.

"Are you sure you were never in a film?" asked Elsa.

"Was it a documentary film on Afghanistan made by an Austrian professor?"

"Yes, that's where I saw you," she said, with excitement. "You were the one playing your guitar and smoking a chillum of hash."

"You're right. I was in that film...although I've never seen it."

"I knew I had seen you before. You should see the movie. You were the star. Can I have your autograph?"

What a small world this is, I thought to myself. I had forgotten all about being in that film. It was no big deal to me. This woman acted like I was some big movie star. So I signed my name on her paper napkin as she told her friends about me.

Just then, another person came up to me and asked a few questions. "Rob, do you remember me?" asked a big, longhaired hippie.

"No. Who are you?" I asked, as I looked him over while he kneeled in the aisle of the jetliner.

"I'm Gunther. I partied with you at Najib Hotel a few years ago."

"Oh yeah, now I remember. How are you doing, Gunther? What were you doing in Beirut?"

"I was in Baalbek, checking over this year's hash crop. Then the civil war began getting out of hand. Now I'm going back to Amsterdam to pick up some money, then I'm heading for India."

"Well, I'm returning to the United States to see my family and to save enough money so I can return to Asia."

"I thought you were never going to leave Kabul," Gunther reminded me.

"I didn't want to, but I had no choice. I was lucky to leave that country alive."

"Rob, if you give me your address in the United States, I'll write to you as soon as I get to India. Maybe we can set up a business. I'll send hash to you and you send me LSD and money," said Gunther.

"That sounds good to me. I don't know how long I'll be in America.... But I'm sure I'll be there for a few months, anyway." So we exchanged addresses.

"Rob, there's a guy I want you to meet," said Gunther. "He's the biggest hash dealer in Europe. That's why I was in Lebanon. My friend wants to buy the complete Baalbek hash crop. He's offered millions for this year's harvest. He wants to purchase more than one-hundred tons of Lebanese hash. I think this is someone you might want to know."

"Sounds good, Gunther; introduce me to him. If he's as big as you say, maybe I can get him to ship half of his load to my country. I could unload it overnight." With that said, we walked up to first class.

Gunther introduced me to Rolf, a businessman from Amsterdam at least ten or fifteen years my senior, and I explained my business to him. Rolf and I hit it off immediately. We talked and drank champagne for hours. I promised him that I could sell every kilo of hash he could get into America. He said he was putting together a plan for next year's Lebanese hash crop. He had made agreements with the hash syndicate to have more than one-hundred tons shipped from Lebanon to Europe.

My new hash connection said that he would have to find a way to ship the illegal contraband to the United States without losing the load. But that wouldn't happen for another year. He and Gunther promised to keep me informed of their progress.

After hours of conversation, I went back to my seat and fell asleep until the plane arrived in Frankfurt. That's when I said goodbye to Gunther and Rolf, along with most of the other passengers. The plane left Frankfurt and headed for Paris for a short stopover and then onto London before gassing up and heading for New York.

Nothing exciting happened for the rest of the trip. After nearly thirty hours of flying, I had finally arrived at Kennedy airport. Except I was so excited about being in the United States that I forgot to pick up my carry-on bags that had been sitting with the pilot in the cockpit. When I departed the aircraft, I headed directly for the baggage claim area.

I grabbed my three suitcases and waited in line for my customs search. I was so exited at being back in America that I had forgotten all about my illegal contraband. It must have showed in my face because I wasn't hassled at all at customs. They did question me about my injured hand and sent me to a special room. I thought it was another body search, but it was only to receive a pamphlet about different diseases. That was it. I was allowed to leave the customs area with my luggage without incident. I was elated. I had gotten into the United States with all of my drugs. Now I had to make my way for my connected flight to Detroit Metro Airport.

I quickly telephoned my mother and told her I was on my way home.

She would meet me at the airport with many of our relatives. I couldn't wait to see them, especially my Armenian grandparents. I had been to their homeland where their families had been massacred

and wanted to tell them about it. I hated the United States government, but I loved my family and relatives.

513

EPILOGUE

When I returned to my hometown, my nightmare truly began. Gangsters and dopers surrounded my life. And my morphine habit was out of control. However, I made the best of it and continued where I had left off, but on an even larger scale. Instead of dealing pounds, I was now about to deal in tons.

My friend in Europe kept me informed of the progress he was making putting together a hash run to America, and he wanted me to distribute it all—one hundred tons. I agreed. But that was just the beginning of what lay ahead, which continued non-stop until I left again in 1976 for the country that had kicked me out—the country that I loved, Afghanistan. And my adventures—or nightmares—began anew. But you will have to read *The Age of Aquarius II* to find out what happened next.

www.ingramcontent.com/pod-product-compliance
Lightning Source LLC
Chambersburg PA
CBHW051549100726
47898CB00001B/29